Under The Gun

Lori L. Lake

Quest Books
a Division of
RENAISSANCE ALLIANCE PUBLISHING, INC.
Nederland, Texas

ISBN 1-930928-44-0

First Printing 2002

9 8 7 6 5 4 3 2 1

Cover design by Mary D. Brooks

Published by:

Renaissance Alliance Publishing, Inc.
PMB 238, 8691 9th Avenue
Port Arthur, Texas 77642-8025

Find us on the World Wide Web at
http://www.rapbooks.biz

Printed in the United States of America

"Dez Reilly and Jaylynn Savage from *Gun Shy* are back! Engaging storyteller Lori L. Lake has introduced two original lesbian characters, both police officers in St. Paul, Minnesota. Jay and Dez are tough, smart, complex women—and the antithesis of the standard "U-haul" joke. Read how their relationship evolves."

"Once again, Lori L. Lake has written a novel that draws us willingly and eagerly into the lives of her *Gun Shy* characters, Dez and Jaylynn. I found myself moved for them and by them throughout the reading of the second story of the series. *Under the Gun* is a wonderful book, full of love and promise, that I could not put down."

"I am thrilled to see a writer like Lake take the risk, leave formula and genre restrictions behind, and be willing to put in the hard work necessary to put forth a truly creative product. Lake continues to grow and mature in her craft and is poised to guide the characters she has sent out into the world through the grappling necessary for their own maturity. Get introduced to Reilly and Savage now so that you can appreciate their personal and professional struggles as Lake develops them throughout the coming sequels."

Musical Lyric Permissions

Acknowledgments

Thanks and praise to my publisher and friend, Cathy LeNoir, and to my patient editors, Barb "Captain Doc" Coles and her partner, my Division Director Linda Daniel. As far as I'm concerned, they're my publishing Trinity.

Warm thanks to my "First Editor," Day Petersen, for all the advice and encouragement. For beta reading,: Carrie Carr, Janet Catran, Nann Dunne, Lois Hart, Karen "Kas" King, Sue O'Brien, Svítla Ritschlova, Alix Stokes, Jan Trumbo, and Beverly Zawacki. For proofing and galley reviewing: Betty Crandall, Nann Dunne, Kim Miller, and my judicious buddy Norma.

Synchronicity has given me a dear friend who lives halfway around the world. MaryD, you're *fair dinkum* and a friend for life. Thank you for personally snapping the cop picture on the front of the book (in daylight, no less) and then turning it into the piece of art you created. I don't think that Australian constable knew what he was getting into!

Much appreciation to the fine artists who continue to share their art with me: L.J. Maas, Encarnación, and Mary D. Brooks. I am also very grateful for the help of promotions wiz, Joyce McNeil, a Gutter Buddy for life.

Mille grazie to Sabina Schippa for patient help with the Italian translations, and to Lindsey Bullard for frightening photos, descriptions, and treatments for hyphemic injuries.

To Kristen Schuldt for "Dez's Song" and for the other lyrics you allowed me to use in the story. Your talent and creativity are boundless, and your music lifts my heart. I hope people will go to www.HydraulicWoman.com and buy your CD.

To all the Fans and Bards in the Xenaverse: you continue to amaze me. The energy and encouragement you share is like electricity in my veins. Thanks especially to the women of Carrie's Crossing for continual support and good humor, with many blessings to Sam and to Anne, the Archangel, who's always got my back.

Best love to Angela Reese, my talented "Websister" who created and maintains my website. Love and appreciation to all my sisters and their families, as well as to those who have helped me with my writing: Peg Thompson, Jean Stewart, Kristen Schuldt, Pruferblue, Marianne K. Martin, M.J. Lowe, Denise Karamafrooz, Karin Kallmaker, Mary-Ann Howard, Susan Thurston Hamerski, Jeanne Foguth, Ronald L. Donaghe, and Carrie Carr.

As always, Diane is last on the list, but first in my heart. Thanks for being my Sugar Mama.

Lori L. Lake
August, 2002

This one is dedicated to Barb Coles,
who believed in me from the beginning.

Chapter
One

Officer Dez Reilly squinted into the late afternoon sun as she cruised University Avenue in the warm squad car. Despite the dark sunglasses she wore, the sun hit the hood of the white car just so, and the glare irritated her eyes. She turned on Lexington, heading north through the heart of the St. Paul neighborhood she'd come to know so well in all the years she had lived and worked there. She was relieved that with the change of direction, the flickering October sunlight no longer bothered her eyes. As she relaxed her face into its usual passive expression, she moved her jaw from side to side and realized that her cheek muscles ached. She frowned for a moment, then bit back a smile, which made her face feel even more sore. Smiling. Her jaw was actually achy from smiling.

She glanced toward the passenger seat at the source of her facial fatigue. Rookie Officer Jaylynn Savage, five-and-a-half feet of blonde-headed, hazel-eyed energy, sat two feet away, her eyes bright with a natural cheer that drew Dez to her like bees to honey.

"Dez," Jaylynn said as she pointed out toward the Como Lake parking lot. "Check out the Pavilion. Looks like they have a band there tonight. Wouldn't that be a blast?" She turned her head and gazed at her partner, her face open and warm.

Though Dez knew the rookie couldn't actually see her eyes through the reflective mirrors of her sunglasses, she still felt as though Jaylynn could look in anyway, and a quick shot of adrenaline, which she tried to ignore, raced through her bloodstream. She leaned forward and peered out the windshield at the parking lot filling up with cars. A silver bus with *Baby Bee's Blues Band* scripted on the side was being unloaded. Two men carried two guitar cases each, and behind them, three more figures wrestled with large speakers. As the squad car passed slowly, Dez caught sight of a metal trailer—a refreshment stand—down at the end of the parking lot, past a circular fountain that spewed water four to six feet into the air. The stand looked like it was being set up to sell snacks and soda pop.

"It's just like you, Jay, to think that's such a great deal," Dez said. "All these people here are gonna sneak in beer, get drunk, and cause trouble in about—" she glanced at her wrist watch, "six hours. And we'll still be on duty."

Jaylynn shook her head, still grinning. "Whatever would you do if we had a totally boring night with no calls at all? You should be *happy* that the Baby Bee's Blues Band is in town. Maybe something interesting will happen."

They passed the Pavilion, which sat next to Como Lake. The tall white columns around the front glared brilliantly in the slanting sun. The back three sides of the building were open with more columns holding up the dark green roof. On the inside of the fourth wall, a stage was positioned with plenty of room for a full orchestra. Many times Jaylynn and her friends had walked over to the Pavilion from her house, which was only half a mile around the lake. They'd seen local bands, high school orchestras, and dancing extravaganzas. The Pavilion was a wonderful venue for listening to music and watching bands play.

They motored past the end of the long parking lot and went up the hill and around the corner toward the golf course. Jaylynn smiled mischievously and reached over to put her hand on Dez's knee. She gave it a squeeze causing Dez to jump.

"Hey!" the bigger woman said.

"Hey, yourself." She stretched her arm out and smoothed a lock of dark hair off Dez's forehead. "I wish you wouldn't wear those sunglasses. I like to see your eyes."

"Unlike that band, these baby blues are sensitive."

Jaylynn's hand traveled down the side of her partner's face and came to rest, palm side down, on Dez's right shoulder. She massaged the muscular arm, feeling the powerful deltoids, and then slid her palm down to the biceps and triceps. She sighed. "Just about when you take off the Miss Macho Cop glasses, it gets dark and then I can't see your eyes anymore anyway. Guess I'll have to settle for the occasional blush to tell me how you're feeling."

"I do not blush," was the low answer.

"Yeah, right." In answer to that, the veteran cop's face began to glow pink, and Jaylynn laughed out loud. "You are way too cute when you blush."

Dez glanced over her left shoulder, hit the gas, and flipped a U-turn at the top of the incline.

Jaylynn grinned. "You're going to go back and check the permits at the Pavilion."

"Yup."

She sat back in her seat and smiled to herself. It wasn't that Dez was predictable. But she was thorough. Jaylynn could count on that. After riding with Dez as her FTO—Field Training Officer—for most of the last ten months, the rookie had come to understand her taciturn partner: what she said, what she didn't say, and why she clammed up on occasion. And after spending every single night together at Jaylynn's house for the past five weeks, she also thought she knew why Dez was growing edgier. Jaylynn glanced over at her partner and nodded to herself. They had been together close to 24 hours a day every day. Even though the big cop wouldn't admit it, Jaylynn wondered if maybe she needed a break.

They rolled up to the driveway for the Pavilion, and Dez swung into the lot, pulling alongside the refreshment stand. Behind the small aluminum-shrouded stand stood a swarthy bald man. He wore a white canvas apron over blue pants and a white t-shirt. Bending down, he picked up a box from the back of a panel station wagon and slammed the door shut. He puffed on a cigarette, and as he moved closer, Jaylynn saw he carried a packing carton labeled Peanut M&M's. When he caught sight of the cruiser, he stopped and stared at the two women emerging from the car. Spitting his cigarette out, he ground it into the grass with the heel of a worn-down brown leather work boot, then set the box on a tall green garbage can under the awning of his stand. Running his hand over a stubble of day old beard, he nervously asked, "What seems to be the problem, officers?"

Dez kept silent as Jaylynn stepped forward. "Good evening," the rookie said. "We're just doing rounds and thought we'd stop, check things out, and make sure everything is squared away. Do you have a permit you can show us?"

"Oh, sure. Yeah, I do." He went around the side of the stand, up three rickety metal stairs, and ducked through an undersized aluminum screen door. The service window on the side of the stand was quite high. Dez could see over it and into the interior of the snack shack, but as usual, Jaylynn's height was a problem. The eight-inch-wide Formica counter, which folded out when the window was open, hit her a little above chin level. She glanced up at her partner, benignly jealous of the fact that the other cop was over six feet tall in her patrol boots. Height had advantages.

The man came out the screen door and moved heavily down the stairs. He handed a piece of paper to Jaylynn, all the while staring respectfully up at Dez, his nearly black eyes anxious. The rookie looked the permit over quickly and handed it back.

"Looks fine," she said. "We're hoping there won't be any trouble. Are you manning this by yourself tonight?"

He nodded. "*Every* night this week I have been. Monday and Tuesday was some really good music. There's been a different band playing every evening, and I have a permit to sell snacks here for the whole run."

"You got a phone?"

"Yeah." He looked at her, his face puzzled. "I have a cell phone in the car."

"You may want to keep it nearby and call if there are any problems."

He peered down at Jaylynn, concern on his face. "What kind of problems could there be? Didn't have any on Monday or Tuesday." He looked past them out at the tidy parking lot.

Jaylynn shrugged and smiled. "You never know. I hope things go smoothly, but sometimes it's best to be prepared for the worst. You know, a mean drunk, some rowdy kids, whatever. We're on duty until midnight, so call 911 if necessary and Dispatch will send us or another car out if you need anyone."

His hand came up and stroked the whiskers on his chin. "Okay, thanks. I think I'll run out of supplies long before the concert is over. I didn't realize tonight was such a big deal. They say a lot of people will show up."

With a nod, Jaylynn said, "Guess you'll have a good take tonight, and tomorrow you can bring even more stock, huh?"

The man nodded.

"See you," the rookie said, then she turned and strode back to the cruiser. The two women got in, and Dez started the engine, but she didn't drive off right away.

Jaylynn said, "You think there's something odd, too, huh?"

"Gut feeling. I have a hunch that it's nothing big though."

"Me, too."

"Did you get his—"

Jaylynn was already typing into the cruiser's computer. "Yup. Stephen D. Tivoli." She waited a moment, fingers tapping on the computer, until the information came up. "Tivoli, Stephen Dimitrius. Two convictions, both for theft. He did nine months in Faribault four years back. No recent arrests." Her fingers flew over the keyboard, and she closed out the record.

Dez nodded and hit the gas. *Nervous ex-con. Wants to stay on the right side of the law.* That made sense to her. Out of the corner of her eye she sneaked a look at Jaylynn who was busily writing in her black notebook. When the rookie looked up after tucking the notebook away in her breast pocket, Dez quickly averted her eyes to the road.

Since the weekend after Labor Day, when the two women had consummated their relationship, they had been through an intense and incredible month. After half a year of missed signals, misunderstandings, and plain old anguish, the veteran cop had finally given in and admitted her feelings for the younger woman. There were so many reasons she should not have expressed those feelings. For one thing, Jaylynn was a new officer, not scheduled to complete her year's probation until the end of December, and as her FTO, Dez was technically the rookie's supervisor while they were on duty. That was a troublesome issue for the tall cop. It was important to her that Jaylynn's probation period not be marked by any accusations of unfairness or favoritism. The fact that they were both women was also problematic. Dez had thought she was well in the closet...at least she had believed that until Jaylynn explained otherwise. She felt herself begin to blush when she considered the fact that some of her fellow officers even had a betting pool going about whether she was gay or not. She was afraid that when they discovered she and the rookie were an item—which she felt could happen at any moment—some of them would have a field day.

Dez knew full well that more-than-friend relationships between partners were dangerous. They probably shouldn't be on duty together. She knew logically that it could compromise objectivity and was, therefore, against the rules. She had been meaning to go talk to Lt. Malcolm, to explain everything, but he had been on vacation the two weeks after Labor Day, and with one thing or another, she had not gathered up her courage to go "out" herself to her commanding officer. Actually, she had no idea how to even broach the subject with him. With a sickening feeling of dread in the pit of her stomach, she admitted to herself that she did need to talk to him before someone untrustworthy found out and reported them, which could cause an awful lot of trouble. The whole idea worried her to no end.

But the thing that concerned her most had nothing at all to do with the St. Paul Police Department. It had to do with the 135-pound bundle of energy sitting beside her, currently humming tunelessly as she gazed out the windshield into the rapidly darkening evening. In the weeks since Dez first spent the night in Jay-lynn's arms, neither of them had specifically used the word "love." They'd both alluded to it, but neither had actually said those three little words beginning with "I" and ending with "you." Dez wanted desperately to do so, but again and again, her courage failed her. She had always thought herself to be strong and brave—perhaps even bold—but every time she started to say those three special words, her heart came up into her throat and pre-vented any conversation at all.

She wanted to kick herself every time it happened.

So she tried to enjoy each day as completely as possible, knowing in her heart that Jaylynn could get tired of her and maybe move on to someone else. The thought of that made her even more sick to her stomach than the thought of talking to the lieu-tenant did. She couldn't go back to how she was before—before Jaylynn, before the rookie had eased the grief of her previous work partner's death, before the rookie had dragged her up out of a hole so deep she hadn't even known there was an escape.

She couldn't bear to think about any of it anymore, and in an effort to lighten her mood, she reached over and turned on the radio. The song playing was the theme from the "Titanic" movie, the beautiful voice plaintively mourning her lost love. She hit the button with her thumb and snapped off the radio.

"Hey," Jaylynn said. "That's 'My Heart Will Go On.' It's a terrific song."

"True."

"So why did you turn it off?"

Dez debated: lie or tell the truth? She opted for the latter. "It's too sad. I just—I don't want to hear anything sad right now."

Jaylynn nodded. She turned to the side in her seat, her left shoulder against the seat back and her left knee pulled up so she could face Dez. "Anything you want to talk about?"

Dez shook her head. She took off her sunglasses and rubbed the bridge of her nose. Tucking the glasses in her breast pocket, she scanned the street and sidewalks, acutely aware of the inquisi-tive hazel eyes upon her. She let herself cast a glance over to Jay-lynn, only to find her partner looking at her with concern on her face. She looked away.

"We've been together nonstop for over four weeks now, Dez. Do you need a break?"

Dez's head whipped around in surprise, and the women's eyes met. Again, just as it had happened the very first time they met each other and many times since, an electrical current ran between the two, and if she hadn't been driving, Dez would have reached out to touch Jaylynn. She felt the butterflies lift her stomach out of the pit of dread it had been sitting in for the last half-hour. "Nope. I don't need a break. Do you?"

Jaylynn smiled and reached over to touch Dez's cheek with the back of her knuckles. "No, not really, but Sara is off work all day tomorrow, and I want to spend some time with her. I have hardly seen her—or Tim—for ages."

Dez nodded. She knew that they had been spending so much time together at her own apartment or locked up in Jaylynn's room that the rookie hadn't seen her two housemates for days on end. "We should have them over for dinner sometime."

Jaylynn chuckled. "Where? Your apartment has two rooms, both rather small, I might add." She poked a finger into Dez's ribs and giggled when the taller woman flinched and gave her a mock-stern look.

"It's three rooms."

"Like the bathroom would count?"

Dez ignored that. "We'll just go downstairs and take over Luella's part of the duplex. She won't mind."

"I told Sara I would go to the movies with her tomorrow at noon. Want to come?"

Hesitating, the veteran cop looked across the dim car and found a pair of shiny, smiling eyes gazing her way. "Nah," she said. "There's some things I really ought to do for Luella. She hasn't complained yet, but I haven't spent any time with her either, and I'd like to." She sighed quietly and thought about the lonely day ahead. Maybe she could play her guitar, watch a video, walk around Como Lake. But the thought of sitting home alone— without Jaylynn—actually made a spot behind her rib cage hurt. *Geez,* she thought, *I am in way too deep here. How embarrassing.*

Jaylynn reached across the computer gear and over the night light between them and took Dez's hand from the steering wheel. She laced her fingers with her partner's. "We do get to meet up later then, right?"

Dez's breath caught and she fought the urge to smile like a silly fool. "Sure," she said calmly. "Your place or mine?"

"I really don't care. It doesn't matter—" Just then, the dispatcher's voice crackled over the radio, and they were off to a call.

****

Dez lay on her back in Jaylynn's bed, one forearm on the sleeping woman's thigh, the other over her own eyes. She had lain that way for what seemed like hours as the woman next to her took slow, even breaths.

Turning on her side, away from Jaylynn, Dez opened her eyes and saw a shaft of moonlight shining in through a crack in the blinds covering the casement window. She wondered how many nights this would happen. Was she ever going to start sleeping "normally"? She wasn't sure how much time had passed, but it had been at least an hour. Insomnia was something she was accustomed to—had even come to expect—at home anyway. But here...what was she to do? She gritted her teeth, enduring a sudden wave of desperation, and her heartbeat kicked up so that she could feel her pulse throughout her body. She thought back to when she and Jaylynn started spending the nights together. She figured there had been about a week of comfort and solace. Actually, maybe less than that. Now that she thought about it, maybe it had only been a few days. Then—boom!—the insomnia was back, as were the nightmares whenever she did manage to fall asleep. She could never quite remember the content of the dreams, but she knew full well they were awful. That was probably exactly why she didn't remember them. Already she had awakened Jaylynn two times in the last week because of bad dreams, and it worried her that she might have to admit to the rookie that she had apparently developed a nightmare syndrome that only small children are known to display.

She groaned and turned over, trying to get comfortable, but she knew sleep was not in her near future. *Either I can lie here awake, bored to death, or—if I finally do fall asleep—I can have embarrassing dreams that might wake her up. Isn't there a third alternative?*

She sat up, extricating herself from the covers without letting any cold air in on the sleeping rookie, then eased herself down to the foot of the bed. She found her jeans on the couch next to the bed and stepped into them, letting her t-shirt hang loose. Pulling her watch out of her pants pocket, she pressed the Indiglo button and noted that it was 3:39 a.m. *Geez. I've got to get up in five or six hours. I'm gonna be tired.*

She sat down near the bed on the orange sofa, elbows on her knees, and gazed over at Jaylynn. The young woman lay on her left side, facing out. Usually Dez liked to curl up behind her, put one arm around the solid middle, and breathe in the scent from that short, white-blonde hair. They fit together well. Naturally. As though someone had designed the arcs and curves of their bodies to mesh just so. Dez examined the relaxed face, admiring the long blonde eyelashes, the unlined forehead, and the slight smile on Jaylynn's lips. She looked like she was having a pleasant dream. Dez shook her head. Her partner slept like a rock, waking after seven or eight hours of sleep with plenty of energy. She envied Jaylynn.

Barefoot, she slipped out of Jaylynn's room and into the darkened hallway. She turned toward the stairwell and crept down, being careful not to make any more noise than the creaking old steps made necessary. She headed into the living room and turned on a lamp, then went to the bookshelf and hunted around until she came up with a sci-fi paperback. Settling into the overstuffed couch, she put her bare feet up on the coffee table and began reading.

Two chapters into the book, she felt fatigue wash over her, but she'd been fooled too many times. If she returned to Jaylynn's room, got undressed, and crawled into bed, she knew she would snap awake, fully alert, and this whole cycle would start over. Instead, she tucked her legs under her, leaned a shoulder into the arm of the couch and continued to read. Soon the words in the novel began to run together and the book slipped into her lap. She let her head drop onto the arm of the brown sofa, and sleep overtook her.

The dream began, as it often did:

Her chest hurt, and she could hardly breathe. Flashing lights—neon red and blue and white—swirled around her. Each time her eyes readjusted, she made out a narrow walkway with a chain-link fence on one side and a black hulk of a building on the other side. But then the lights would flare bright again, blinding her. She moved slowly down the cracked walkway, trying not to trip. When she looked down, she was alarmed to see her hands covered in blood. She reached into her holster, feeling for her gun, but it wasn't there. The abrupt movement hurt her chest, and for a moment she couldn't breathe for the pain. When she was finally able to draw a breath, she smelled something sour and metallic, something that brought tears to her eyes. For a moment, she thought she might vomit, but she forced the feeling down. I have to go on, *she thought.* I have to take care of this, once and for all.

With effort, she stepped forward, closer to the flashing lights. Now every time they flashed and shone on her, she felt a warmth bathe her, and suddenly she was sweating and unable to breathe at all. Taking two strong steps down the concrete walk, she burst into an open area. Without warning, she fell to her knees. As she did so, she saw the crumpled blue-clad body before her.

"Dez, help me," he croaked out. He lifted his blond head, blue eyes imploring. Kneeling above him, she reached out to

touch him, but instead of warm skin, his hands felt cold, like damp bread dough. She shifted back into a squatting position. Her knees stung and ached, and when she looked down, her blue pants were ripped to shreds and the skin below was a mass of rawness, warm blood running freely down her shins. She brought her hand up, her fingers brushing her abdomen until they were stopped by something shiny and hard protruding from her breastbone. With trembling fingers she groped at a metal rod so firmly embedded that she could not pull it out. Her blue eyes met those of the man below her and she shook her head and heard her own hoarse whisper, "No, Ryan. Not you."

He nodded. "Yes! Let me, Dez. Let me help you. Please..." *The blue eyes, illuminated briefly in the flashing lights, pleaded, and the thought crossed her mind that she owed him this, owed him something.*

She didn't resist when he reached up, grabbed the metal bar and pulled.

The lights flashed, blinding her again, and the pain ripped through her heart, searing like a white-hot branding iron.

She screamed.

The hand at her chest continued to pull, mercilessly, at the metal shaft, and it hurt so much that her breath came in short sharp wheezes. She screamed again.

Sinking...sinking...flashing lights receding...darkness all around. She fought it, twisting and struggling. Now when she opened her mouth to scream, nothing came out. A brackish taste of bile rose up in her throat and choked her. "No, no, no! Ryan, no!"

"Dez! Dez! Wake up!"

She awoke on her knees, her arms crossed over her chest, with her face pressed into firm cloth that smelled musty. Her cheeks were wet with tears, and she was chilled with sweat.

Warm hands patted her shoulder, and she lifted her head to find herself kneeling on the couch cushion, hunched over the arm of the brown sofa. For a long moment, she didn't know where she was or what was wrong, but then the face of Jaylynn's roommate, Sara, came into focus from the other side of the couch, the dark brown eyes worried and inquiring. "Are you okay?"

Dez shifted and turned away from the brown-haired woman, kicking her legs out from under her until she felt the soft yarn of the shag carpet under her bare feet and the firm cushion of the couch beneath her butt. Her heart beat hard and loud, the blood still rushing to her ears. Face in hands, she took a deep breath and forced back the tears that were threatening to come.

Sara came around the side of the couch and sat next to Dez. She patted the other woman on the thigh. "Bad dream, huh?"

Dez shivered and nodded.

"You get 'em often?"

Slowly, Dez nodded. As she sat, taking long breaths, her heart rate gradually returned to normal.

"Do you remember what happened in it?"

With the smallest shake of the head, Dez whispered, "No...no, I don't think so." She racked her brain to remember the events or flow of what surely had to have been a nightmare, but none of it floated up into consciousness. "Was I talking in my sleep?"

Sara chuckled, a low throaty laugh that sounded like the purr of a zoo leopard. "If you call screaming in middle C *talking*, then yes, you were talking in your sleep."

Dez felt the blood in her face drain away, and she shivered with cold. "You're kidding me, right?"

Sara rose and walked over to the upright piano, her tan flannel pajamas baggy on her. She flipped open the cover and softly tapped a high C. She waited a moment, letting the sound ring, then touched a key two notes lower. "Nope, I was wrong. It was a B-flat, not a C."

"Are you teasing me or what?"

Sara closed the cover and turned, leaning back against the polished wood. She crossed her arms over her chest and shook her head, all the while giving a pleasant smile. "I'm a music major, and I've got pretty good relative pitch. So, hey, I was off a little bit. You screamed twice before I could get down here. And when I tried to wake you, you kept saying, 'No. No, Ryan.'"

Oh shit. Must have been a really bad dream. "I can't remember any of that, but if you say so." She looked down at her hands, then yawned. "Don't tell Jaylynn, okay?"

Sara strode over and sat on the sofa again, this time tucking herself into the corner on the opposite end with her bare feet under her, the tan pajama pants stretched tight over her knees. "Why?"

Dez was at a loss for words. Why *didn't* she want her lover to know? The answer seemed simple enough: she was embarrassed. It felt like a major weakness to have bad dreams, somehow childish and vulnerable, like a little kid whining for her mama. But Sara didn't need to know that—and neither did Jaylynn. "I'm sorry I woke you, Sara."

"You didn't wake me at all. Startle me, yes, but wake me?

No way. I've got my own nightmares to deal with."

Dez frowned and looked toward Sara out of the corner of her eye. Her blue eyes met the deep brown eyes of Jaylynn's best friend, and she found the other woman smiling ever so slightly. "What do you mean?"

Sara took a deep breath and sighed. "I used to sleep like a baby, like a log, like the dead, like there was no tomorrow. You name the cliché, and I slept that way. And then last year happened."

Dez nodded slowly. She had never talked much to the brown-eyed woman about the night she had first met her—and Jaylynn—a year earlier when the big cop was on Third Watch and two men intent on rape and robbery had broken into this very house. Dez had been foolhardy, but timely, when she entered the house without backup. She crawled in through the same downstairs dining room window by which the assailants had entered, crept upstairs, and burst in upon the scene. She subdued the two men and got her arm broken in the process. But she had prevented the assault and collared two serial rapists who had since been convicted of 18 robberies and six rapes. Sara had watched the entire ordeal from a position half under one of the beds, her hands, feet, and mouth bound by duct tape.

Dez remembered that night as a turning point in her life, for that was when she first laid eyes on the blonde spitfire who was asleep right now in what used to be Sara's room. After the attack, Sara had not wanted to sleep in there anymore, and she had exchanged rooms with Jaylynn.

Dez cleared her throat. "Will you feel better when Bill comes home? It's only a few weeks, right?"

Sara nodded. "I think I'll feel better, but I don't know how long it will be until I get back to *normal*, if you know what I mean."

"Did counseling help?"

"Yeah, it's helping a lot. I'm still going two or three times a month."

Dez was surprised. It was bad enough when she had to go see the department shrink half a dozen times after Ryan died. Then she herself had taken a bullet in her protective vest, and Jaylynn had shot their assailant. The lieutenant forced each of them to go see Dr. Raina Goldman again, and Jaylynn was still seeing Goldman for counseling. It occurred to Dez that the last year or so had been hell on her. Still, she hated counseling—all that digging around in her psychological processes. She preferred to keep her private life and thoughts just that: private. "You couldn't pay me to do that two or three times a month, Sara."

The younger woman grinned and shook her head. "If you were in enough pain, you would."

Dez shrugged, thinking to herself that she would never be in so much pain that she'd attend counseling of her own volition. She didn't share those thoughts with Sara, saying instead, "Well, I'd better go hit the hay before Jay wakes up and finds me missing. She's the lucky one, sleeps like a log all the time."

Sara gave the tall woman a funny look. "Jay has her moments, too, though not since you came along."

"What do you mean?"

Sara started to say something, then hesitated. Dez waited, biting back her curiosity. The brown-eyed woman looked away. "Let's just say that everyone has their own personal terrors, and we all have nightmares every once in a while."

"Not Jaylynn. Lucky little cuss gets her forty winks and most of mine, too."

Sara nodded, still smiling quizzically. "Good night, Dez. Hope you get at least a few good hours of shut-eye."

"You, too."

****

Dez awakened, curled up around Jaylynn, and fully aware that she had not had enough sleep. She tried to close her eyes and slip back into unconsciousness, but despite the peach-colored blinds covering the two casement windows, the bright sun streamed through cracks. For a couple of minutes she examined the three Monet prints hanging on the wall across the room, but soon enough she grew tired of the fuzzy flowers and muted brush. She raised her head and peered over her slumbering partner's shoulder to see the bedside clock. *7:50. Too damn early.* She couldn't prevent the sigh that escaped her, and at that, the body next to her shivered and turned over.

"Geez, Dez. First you toss and turn all night long. Then you throw the blankets off every chance you get. And now, after what—two total hours of sleep?—you wake up ready to go run ten miles." She let out a big yawn and stretched her arms above her head. Casting tired eyes upon Dez, in a grumpy voice she said, "It's like sleeping with a gymnast. Next thing you know, we'll have to hang rings above the bed."

Dez smiled through her fatigue and reached over to wrap her arms around Jaylynn's solid midsection. She kicked her feet out from under the covers and felt cooler air where her feet protruded past the mattress and off the end of the bed. Warm arms stroked her back as she nuzzled her face into the soft cotton t-shirt Jaylynn wore. In a muffled voice, she said, "I don't know how you could complain about being cold. It's like an oven in here."

Jaylynn smoothed the dark hair off Dez's forehead and planted a kiss there. "*You*, honey, are the oven. Me and the rest of this room are perfectly comfortable."

Dez closed her eyes and relaxed into the smaller woman, a little smile twitching at her lips. Jaylynn was funny when she woke up in the morning, usually cranky for a few minutes, then wonderfully warm and sensual. She stroked the soft skin on Jaylynn's thigh and felt her shiver, then tense up the muscle. Dez prodded at the quadriceps and said, "Not bad for such a little slip of a thing."

Jaylynn pushed Dez away and tossed the covers aside. Pointing at her legs, she said, "Whaddya mean? Look at those muscles."

"Yeah, you got muscles all right." The bigger woman poked at the tight midsection, reducing Jaylynn to shrieks.

"Stop, stop! Stop or I'll—"

"You'll what?" Dez teased.

Jaylynn twisted away and off the bed, landing on her feet. She dove right back onto the bed, landing on Dez with an *oomph* sound and knocking the taller woman onto her back. Arms encircled the rookie as she nuzzled into the pale white neck below her. "I'll give you a hickey every other officer on the squad will ask about—that's what I'll do!"

Dez laughed out loud. "Go ahead. I'll just wear a turtleneck."

Poised above her, Jaylynn grinned, looking down into the striking blue eyes. "It's Indian Summer and supposed to be 75 today. You'll roast your butt off, and I'll be laughing the whole shift."

"Is that right?" Dez challenged. She brought a callused hand up to the face peering down at her and cupped the pinkened cheek, then let her hand slip around the back of the blonde head to pull it down to rest in the hollow under her chin. She closed her eyes and enfolded the toasty figure in her arms, noticing how she and Jaylynn adjusted slightly and settled into the curves and contours of one another's bodies until they fit together like entwined vines. Warm and drowsy and relaxed, a soft sigh escaped. It occurred to her that now would be a good time to tell Jaylynn that she loved her, that she wanted to spend the rest of her life waking up together like this. And she almost did it, too, but then, before she could form the words, a vision began to take shape in her mind, a vision of darkness and blood and flashing lights. In the bloody scene, the comforting body she held so tightly was wrested away from her, pulled screaming from her arms. Jaylynn shouted for her but kept whirling away, receding as though she were falling down a pit into a fiery furnace. Dez stiffened and gasped, unable to breathe for a moment.

"Dez? What's the matter?"

Dez opened her eyes, confused, and found concerned hazel green eyes inches from her own.

"Uh, nothing. Let's get up."

The rookie shifted back, still studying the blue eyes before her as Dez moved away. The tall woman swung her legs over the side of the bed and sat for a moment with a hand on either side of her hips, clutching the edge of the bed.

Jaylynn scooted over, grabbed hold of a broad shoulder, and brought herself up on her knees to lean into the bigger woman and peer over her left shoulder. Dez was frowning. Jaylynn hesitated, bit her tongue, and held back what she really wanted to say. Instead, she asked, "What are you going to do today?"

Dez paused a moment, then took a deep breath. "Go home, I guess. There's some things I'd like to do for Luella. I should get out the mower and mulch up that yard full of leaves."

"Okay." Jaylynn detached herself from the broad back and slid a leg past the seated woman, using Dez's shoulder to hoist herself up off the bed and to stand on the edge of the cinnamon brown oval rug. "You want to shower first or me?"

"You go ahead," Dez said. She picked up her jeans from the arm of the sofa and stood to slip them on. "Think I'll just head home and do my chores, then shower there."

Jaylynn stood, uncertainly, as Dez slipped on her tennis shoes and picked up a few items from around the room, then turned, finally, to face her. The rookie didn't know what was wrong, but she decided not to press it. If there was one thing she had discovered about Dez, it was that she revealed things in her own sweet time—and not a moment earlier. She looked up into troubled blue eyes, then impulsively took two steps forward, wrapped her arms around Dez's waist, and buried her face in the light blue t-shirt. She felt arms enfold her tightly, and the message she felt—intuited, really—from the body before her was that whatever was troubling Dez wasn't about her.

She tipped her head back and looked up at the tired face. "See you at work, sweetie."

Dez leaned down and placed a soft kiss on the forehead

below. She paused for a moment, as though considering what to say, then thinking the better of it. "Yeah—and just for the record, I'm no sweetie."

Jaylynn broke out in a grin. "Hmmm. Just for the record, you *are*, but I won't tell if you don't."

Dez rolled her eyes and swatted Jaylynn lightly on the butt, then stepped away and turned to open the door. With one backward glance, she pulled the door shut and disappeared, leaving the rookie to stare after her and wonder. She reminded herself that her partner was moody and a very private person. Other people would have used the terms cranky and secretive, but Jaylynn had seen sides of the tall woman to which others were not privy. She wanted to think that perhaps Dez was just overtired, but no, that wasn't it. There was something more troubling her.

She turned toward the rumpled bed and straightened up the sheet and blanket trailing on the floor. Jaylynn heard the rumble outside of Dez's big Ford F-150, and she stepped to the window, pulled up a slat to the blinds, and watched the cranberry red truck back out from the gravel parking strip behind the house and drive away. It was probably better to have some time apart, giving them both a chance to take care of mundane details. She looked around the large room they spent so much time in. The couch was heaped with unfolded clean clothes as well as her backpack, a duffel bag with dirty clothes from work, and other odds and ends. Her closet door was open, and the small, walk-in room was stacked with bags and cartons and disorganized shoeboxes. There were shoes in jumbles all over the floor, and several items had fallen off the hangers onto them. Next to the closet door sat a huge bookshelf overflowing with books. With a little bit of rearranging and sorting, she could get rid of some of the books and put the rest in order, and she figured that would only take about fifteen minutes.

Her desk, at the other end of the room next to the door, was another matter. In the last three weeks she had put bills, papers, and magazines there, and now there was so much junk in sight that she couldn't work at the desk or on her computer if she had wanted to.

She let out a big breath of air and grabbed a pair of shorts off the pile of clothes on the couch. Slipping on the shorts, she looked at the bedside clock. She had a little over three hours before she and Sara were planning to leave for a noon movie. To make roll call on time, she needed to eat, tidy up her room, and get her uniform and lunch—and vacuum. Vacuuming was a must, she decided, upon seeing a dust bunny peeking out from under her desk chair. Like a whirlwind, she began working.

****

Dez dragged the lawn mower into the garage behind the house where she rented. The neat, two-story stucco house was divided into the main floor apartment where her landlady, Luella Williams, lived, and a small apartment up under the eaves, which Dez had rented from Luella since she left college nearly a decade earlier and joined the St. Paul Police Force. She brushed dirt and grass off the knees of her jeans, then locked the garage and came up the four cement stairs to the walkway that led to the back of the duplex. Surveying the lawn, she thought it looked fine, though she wanted to take the weed whacker to some spots along the back fence one last time before winter hit.

Despite the stiff October breeze, she was overly warm and perspiring. She wiped her forehead on the sleeve of her t-shirt and went to the back door. Peeping out the back window was the cheery face of her landlady and friend. With dismay, Dez noted that the window was covered with splotches and badly needed a washing. Then the door pushed open and Luella was gesturing her inside.

Dez and Luella were about as opposite as two women could be. Luella stood a head shorter, and her dark mahogany skin was a total contrast to the stark white of her tenant's face and arms. The tall woman's hair was as black as her landlady's was silver, and where Dez was long and lean, Luella was soft and full-bodied. They had a mutual respect and caring for one another, and in the absence of Dez's mother, Luella had served well as confidante, nurturer, and friend. She and Luella had worked out an arrangement perfect for both of them. Dez kept up the house, yard, and lawn, fixed anything mechanical that she could, and helped with heavy spring cleaning. In return, the older woman did her tenant's wash and ironed her uniforms, tried to get the tall woman to eat "normal" people's food, and generally enjoyed her young friend's company, despite their age difference.

Now the older woman wore a bemused smile along with a purple and pink flowered housedress and clunky white Nike tennis shoes. She pulled the sweating woman through the door. "Good Lord, Dez. You wouldn't get so overwrought if you'd mow the lawn like a normal person. There's no need to run behind the mower!"

Dez grinned. They'd had this conversation a million times. "Why waste time? It's self-propelled, so why not put it on high and let 'er rip?"

"You're all in a lather—like a horse. Go take a shower and

get back down here lickety-split. I have some roast chicken for
you—and don't worry, I baked the potatoes, even though *I* really
wanted homemade French fries."

Dez strode over to the closet next to the door to Luella's
apartment. She opened it and rummaged around on the top shelf
until she came up with a bottle of Windex. "You have some paper
towels?"

"Sure. Why?" She stepped past the tall woman and disappeared into the hallway leading to her kitchen while Dez waited
near the closet door.

When Luella returned with half a roll of Viva paper towels,
Dez opened the back door, sprayed down the window inside and
outside, set the Windex on the floor, and wiped the glass clean.
"There. That's been buggin' me." She shut the door and looked
out to see a thin, weak sun trying to fight through a huge bank of
fluffy white clouds.

"Thanks for doing that. Here, give me those, and you scoot
up to your place for a well-deserved bath. Thirty minutes, missy,
and lunch will be on the table." The silver-haired woman tucked
the paper towels under one arm and swatted Dez on the behind as
she turned to go. Luella shook her head and smiled. Work ethic
wasn't something Desiree Reilly lacked, that was for sure. *I
haven't seen the crazy fool for days, and now when she comes
home, she spends the first three hours racing around the yard,
clearing sticks, planting new shrubs by the front door, raking
leaves and pine cones, and mowing. Makes me tired just to watch.*

Bending over with some difficulty, Luella snagged the bottle
of window cleaner and took it over to the closet to stow it on the
top shelf, which she could just barely reach. She wasn't sure why
they were keeping window cleaner there or the variety of other
cans and bottles of cleaning supplies. *Oh well.* She had everything she needed under the sink in her own kitchen, so if Dez
wanted to store extra stuff there, she didn't care. Besides, it wasn't
like she could even *see* the top shelf.

She shut the closet door and stood for a moment admiring the
creamy yellow color of the back entryway. Dez and Jaylynn had
painted it for her during the summer, and she was still glad they'd
done it. Until it was finished, she hadn't realized how awful the
previous drab light gray color had been. She liked bright colors
and sunlight, something of which her quiet tenant was well aware.
With a smile on her face, she meandered back into her kitchen to
take in the aroma of the baking chicken and to peel carrots to go
with the meal.

****

Dez twisted her long hair into a knot on top of her head and sank down into the tub. She turned on the whirlpool jets and closed her eyes, feeling bone-weary through and through. Some of it was lack of sleep, she realized, but that didn't explain the anxiety and worries that kept creeping into her thoughts. From Labor Day onward, up until just a few days ago, she had thought she was sleeping a little better. *What is the problem now? I'm happy. My job is going well. I'm crazy about Jaylynn. So why this—and why now?*

Bending her knees, she slipped lower into the tub until her face and the top of her head were just a couple inches above the water line. She took deep breaths and tried to think happy thoughts.

She'd chased gun-toting criminals, even been shot by one. Over the last decade, she'd watched three men die in different gunfights, including her best friend and work partner, Ryan Michaelson. Every year, she found at least one dead body in the course of her job. Fires, shootings, beatings, car crashes, stabbings, explosions—you name it, she'd seen it. It wasn't that she liked violence. Most of the time it made her feel slightly sick to her stomach. But she was *used* to it. It was commonplace for her to see the results of the worst behavior people could perform and sometimes more than once in a shift. For over nine years she had weathered every brutal and destructive thing she had encountered. Now she found herself wondering if there was only so much a human being could see and experience before it became too much, and it overflowed, like a cesspool.

She thought then about the fact that she was lucky she didn't live and work in a big city like Chicago or L.A. or New York. St. Paul was tame by those standards. But there was a lot of ugliness and pain, not to mention stupidity and meanness out on those streets. And yet, when she considered working her shift, which was scheduled to begin in less than three hours, she was not averse to putting on her uniform and getting in the car. Every time she heard a siren or saw an emergency vehicle racing to the scene, she got a lump in her throat—sometimes she even felt tears in her eyes. Her job still held meaning. It still mattered a great deal to her.

So why the unease? She hated to admit it, but maybe it was PMS. Then again, it wasn't exactly the right time for that to strike. Maybe it was just the fatigue.

But *why* couldn't she sleep? It's not like she wasn't wearing

herself out. *Okay, what if it's personal—all about my relationships?* Correction: relationship, singular, since—unless she
counted Luella—she didn't seem to have many. Well, she had
friends on the force. Crystal, Cowboy, Oster. But that wasn't the
same as really close friends and family. She was getting to know
Jaylynn's roommates, Sara and Tim, plus Tim's lover, Kevin. But
the truth was she'd never had a lover stick by her for more than a
couple months, and she didn't have a relationship worth counting
with either her mother or her brother. She wasn't even sure why
Jaylynn was so smitten with her. *So maybe that's it. I'm insecure.
Geez, yet another embarrassing thing to worry about.*

She turned the jets off and let the water settle around her. It
was still quite warm, but not nearly as hot as it had been when
she'd gotten in ten minutes earlier. She sat for a few moments
longer, stretching out her arms, rolling her head to ease the tension in her neck, then pulled the plug and listened to the glugging
sound as the water drained. When it reached waist level, the cool
air on her back made her shiver. She put a hand on either side of
the tub and rose, reached for a maroon towel, and dried herself off
from top to bottom, stepping out onto the mat, then drying off her
still-damp feet. She got out a hairdryer and spent a few minutes
running it on low over the damp spots in her long hair, then
worked the dark mane into a tight French braid.

She didn't know what to do about her insecurity. Maybe she
needed to give herself a chance to adjust. Time to trust. There
was no reason *not* to trust Jaylynn. Something in her head
screamed: *Relax! Enjoy your partner!* Unfortunately, something
else inside her was screaming dire warnings. Now was the time
she wished she had a mother she could talk to.

She put away the dryer, tossed her towel in the hamper, and
strode, nude, across the living room to the side of the room where
clean clothes waited on her queen-sized bed. She dressed in black
jeans, a purple Vikings t-shirt, and a pair of black tennis shoes.
Maybe I should talk to Luella about these feelings, these worries.
She put on her watch and looked at it, calculating in her head as
she headed down the stairs to dinner. If she spent an hour with
Luella, she'd still have time to try to nap before shift started.

Chapter
Two

It was full dark and breezy, the air thick and warm. Even Jaylynn, dressed in her full uniform and bulletproof vest, was warm as they stood on the sidewalk on University Avenue. She leaned on a parking meter next to Dez as the taller woman spoke to an angry man in a shabby blue polyester suit. He kept puffing on a cigarette, pointing with his other hand at his electronics store that had a sign on it: *Huge Sale! Truckloads of Bargains.* Jaylynn looked in the store and didn't see anything remotely approaching truckloads. *Maybe he means wheelbarrow loads,* she thought, then bit back a smile. The shopkeeper was complaining bitterly that vandals spray-painted swear words on his back windows in the alley behind his store.

The big cop sighed. "Do you want to make a report?"

"What I *want* is for you people to do your jobs! This is the second time in two years that somebody has done this shit to my store. I'm tired of it. I pay good money—lots of taxes—and what do I get? Nothing!" His angry eyes scanned the shop, passed over the cops, and watched the passing traffic. He didn't look either of them in the eye, except when he paused to take a drag from his cigarette.

Jaylynn gazed up at Dez, saw dark circles under her eyes, and thought about how tired the tall woman looked. She also noted that Dez didn't rise to the bait even though the shopkeeper kept hissing complaints in his venomous voice.

"Do you want to make a report?" Dez repeated.

Shaking his head in disgust, he dropped the cigarette and ground it into the sidewalk with his ancient wing-tipped heel. "What the hell good would it do!" He tossed his hands up in the air and turned to go back into his store.

Dez pressed her lips together, then shook her head. With a weary sigh she returned to the squad car, followed by Jaylynn. They both got in, with Jaylynn driving. She started up the car, but before she pulled away from the curb, she reached over and touched Dez's warm forearm with the flat of her hand. "You feeling all right?"

"I'm just tired."

"Tired or not, you sure are warm. You got a fever?"

"Nah. I'm fine."

Jaylynn put her hands on the steering wheel, shifted into drive, and hit the gas. She was already wearing her long sleeved blue uniform shirts with a turtleneck underneath. Not Dez. She figured it would have to snow before her partner started wearing long sleeves.

She cruised University all the way to Lexington, then went north along the darkened streets, slowing to visually check out the convenience store on Front Street. All was quiet, so she drove on until she came to the Como Park Pavilion. It was after eleven p.m., and the parking lot contained only two cars and the tan panel station wagon. The light was still on in the concession stand.

"Wonder how our good friend Tivoli is," Dez said. "Swing in and see, why don't you?"

Jaylynn steered around the giant fountain and over toward the refreshment stand. When the car lights hit the shiny aluminum, a head popped up over the ledge where customers were usually served. The rookie wheeled the car to the left until it was parallel to the stand. Dez rolled down her window.

"Hey, Tivoli."

"Evening, officers. Everything okay?"

"We were just going to ask you the same thing."

"Yes," he said. "Just shutting down for the night."

Dez nodded. "See ya, then."

He waved and disappeared from the window. Jaylynn motored around the parking lot while Dez, from her passenger seat, scanned the area and checked parked cars from the distance.

"Which band was it tonight?" the rookie said.

"Dunno."

"Saturday, I know, is *Hydraulic Woman*. If we weren't on duty, I'd definitely be going to see her band."

"Never heard of 'em."

"They're a really good local band. Sara bought the CD recently, and I've heard it a few times. You'd probably like it."

"That the one with the girl with the husky blues voice?"

"Yeah, she sings 'Late At Night' and that one called 'Bring It On.' I can't stop listening to it."

Dez nodded. "I've heard it around your house. Didn't know who she was."

Jaylynn reached the lot exit and put on her turn signal to turn right. "Maybe we'll have to stop by here and check things out tomorrow, for about half an hour, 'kay?" She gave Dez a bright, hopeful smile.

"Sure."

All was quiet for another few minutes, but just before shift ended, they were dispatched to a late call—an assault in progress—at a bar on Dale Street near Larpenteur. The Hole In The Wall was just that, in addition to being dirty, dank, and drafty. Before they got there, the patrons with cars had split leaving only a couple of old geezers who lived in the neighborhood and the three men who'd been fighting, all of whom were too drunk to be coherent.

Jaylynn took charge of the scene while Dez watched. Technically, the rookie was still in training, and as her FTO, Dez was supposed to stand back and let her handle calls like this. Usually the tall officer was impatient, but tonight she felt so tired that she didn't mind standing aside and watching as Jaylynn rounded up statements, talked to the bartender, and briefed the paramedics who came to take the bleeding drunks to the hospital, then probably to Detox.

The rookie finished up, and Dez followed her out to the car. The ambulance was a speck in the distance when another cop car pulled up behind them, lights flashing. The doors opened and Officers Alvarez and Neilsen emerged.

Both men were of similar build: six-two or six-three, broad-shouldered, slim-hipped. The similarities ended there. Arturo Alvarez was dark-complected; Dwayne Neilsen was blond with a rugged face and dirty blond hair. Alvarez, a fifteen year veteran, had spent exactly the same amount of time serving as Neilsen's FTO as Dez had with Jaylynn, and Dez didn't envy him the task. She considered Alvarez excellent backup, but not his rookie partner. Neilsen, who had been in the Academy with Jaylynn, was immature, hotheaded, and far too prone to pull his weapon. Rather than inspiring confidence at their calls, he tended to cause anger and dissension, or, as Dez put it, he just plain pissed people off.

The two men ambled over. Alvarez smoothed back jet-black hair and jammed his police cap on. Dez had always liked the handsome Latino, and she had learned a lot about writing FTO reports from him. "Hey, Reilly," he said. "Guess we missed all the fun."

She shook her head slowly. "All the fun was over when Savage and I got here."

"Well, that's lucky," Neilsen said, as he sneered toward Jaylynn. "Wouldn't want the little princess to dirty up her hands."

Dez's eyes narrowed, but she didn't say anything. Alvarez looked at her and rolled his eyes. "Been a good night, Reilly." He looked at his watch. "Twelve minutes and we all get home safe. And that's all that counts. 'Night, you two. C'mon, Neilsen," he said impatiently. He nodded Jaylynn's way, then turned on his heel.

Dez opened the door to their squad car. In the distance she heard Alvarez saying, "For cripesake, Neilsen. Why you gotta be such an ass all the time?" That made her feel better. At least Alvarez was trying to do his job to civilize the kid. She wondered how he could stand it night in and night out. Last winter when she'd caught Neilsen behind the station threatening to rough up Jaylynn, she had mentally axed him from the roster of effective and capable cops. She didn't think she would ever trust him to watch her back. No way.

Jaylynn started the car and let out a little growl. Dez looked over to see her partner was fuming. "Don't let that loser get to you, Jay. He's a punk."

"I just wish, for once, that he'd let up. You'd think he'd have enough riff-raff out on the street to focus on, instead of his fellow officers."

"Guys like that—they're throwbacks to the Stone Age. Probably watched *Dirty Harry* a few too many times as a kid."

Jaylynn laughed out loud. She shifted into gear and did a U-turn in the middle of the street. "Thought I'd meander back towards the precinct. You comin' over tonight?"

"Um hmm."

"We leaving right after we sign out or—"

"Nah, let's work out."

"Thought you were wiped."

"Yeah I am, but I need to lift a little. It's been three days."

"I can just finally say that I'm not sore, Dez."

"Perfect, then." She smiled toward her partner. "We'll get you aching again in short order."

****

Dez lay in that half-awake, half-asleep state where the mind wanders through green hills and floats on blue water in a comforting, hazy sort of way even while some logical little voice marvels that it is still awake. She lay curled up next to a lightly wheezing Jaylynn, feeling the silken softness of the young woman against her bare body. Her legs were leaden and fatigued from the hard weight workout, and she felt like a giant lump of putty. She slipped deeper into a dream where she stood at the prow of a heavy wooden boat, wind in her hair, with a far-off sound of gulls making a high-pitched squealing noise.

She jerked awake when the body next to her sat up abruptly.

"Dez? Do you *hear* that? There's something in here with us."

Dez yawned, reached up a long arm, and ran her hand down Jaylynn's smooth bare back. "Lay back down. You just had a bad dream. Relax and go back to sleep."

"No! I'm *not* dreaming. Listen...do you hear that?"

Dez paused and let her ears strain. Outside she heard a rumble from a distant car engine, but that faded leaving only silence. "Jay, there's nothing." She found herself feeling grumpy. She had actually been sleeping, for the first time in what seemed like days, and now Jaylynn had ruined it. "Lay down. Shh, it's all right."

"YOU HEAR THAT?" Jaylynn hissed.

"That's just the house settling. It's—"

"NO! There it is again!"

Dez heard a ticker-ticker-ticker sound, then the sound of crumpling plastic. She was out of bed in an instant and to the light switch by the door. She flicked it on and stepped back frowning. Hanging from the doorknob was a plastic sack from the Target store. Empty now, it had earlier contained a t-shirt, socks, and a CD Jaylynn had bought. The tall woman bent and peered closely.

Jaylynn huddled under the sheet in the bed. "What is it, Dez? Do you see something?"

"Hmm...well, you better get up and come look at this."

"No. What is it? Just tell me."

"Well...I think you should come look."

She slipped out of bed and sidled over next to Dez. "Oh my God! What the hell is that?"

Dez picked up a t-shirt that lay over the back of the computer chair and advanced toward the bag. "That, my dear, is a bat."

"Oh, ick! What are you going to—Dez!" She backed up as the tall woman whipped the shirt against the bag, wrapping it around the bag and hastily spinning it in her hands.

"I'll take it out and let it go in the backyard."

Jaylynn nodded. "Oh, *that'll* be fun."

Dez gave her an odd look. "What do you mean?"

"Kevin and Tim are downstairs watching videos, and you—well, Dez, in case you haven't noticed, you're buck naked." She started laughing.

Dez glared at her, then jumped as the plastic bag rattled and the shirt shifted in her hands. They both froze when they heard a thin, high-pitched squeal, and Jaylynn backed up toward the bed.

Dez raised an eyebrow and tilted her head a little. "You gonna chicken out on me now?"

"Who me? Never!" Jaylynn said in an exaggerated fashion.

With a toss of her head, Dez said, "Well, then, you wanna slip my sweats on?" Torn between amusement and fear, Jaylynn hovered at the edge of the bed. "C'mon Jay!"

"Certainly, Miss Lady Godiva. You can just let your hair hang down over your lovely breasts." She grabbed up some blue sweatpants that had been lying on the couch.

"Oh please! Toss something—a towel, whatever—over me, and I'll take a shirt to put on once I let this thing go." She lifted each leg in turn so that her partner could slip the sweats on. "Hurry up. The bat is getting restless." With a sly tone in her voice, she said, "Or maybe you'd like me to set it down to get dressed?"

"No, no, no! Just...just...here, I'll give you the sheet." In haste, Jaylynn pulled the top sheet off the bed and quickly wrapped Dez up in it. "Go. Do your duty to God and your country. Free at last. Let Count Chocula free!"

Dez rolled her eyes and held back a laugh. Jaylynn opened the door and her partner hustled down the stairs, through the living room, and to the kitchen's back door, which she opened with difficulty, juggling the twitching bundle in her hands. As soon as she got the door and screen open, she pitched the entire handful right out the door and quickly slammed it shut, unable to suppress a shudder. She wasn't any fonder of bats than Jaylynn, but she wasn't going to give that little bit of information away. She headed out of the kitchen, glad that was over with.

Jaylynn had been right. Tim and Kevin sat on the couch, and a video was running, but neither of them was watching. Kevin had his arm around the red-haired man who was leaning quite comfortably on the blond man's shoulder. Neither of them had stirred when Dez first moved past nor when she returned and mounted the stairs. She figured she could have roller-skated by, and the two of them wouldn't have wakened.

Halfway up the stairs she heard excited whispers and realized that Sara and Jaylynn were talking. She pulled the sheet around her waist and shoulders, feeling overly warm but grateful not to have to enter nude. Jaylynn was wrapped up in her emerald colored terry cloth robe. The brown-haired woman sat next to Jaylynn on the couch, wearing tan and white pinstriped flannel pajama bottoms and top. They both burst into cackles when Dez came into the room.

She stopped. "What?"

Sara pointed at her legs. "Your sweats are on inside out."

The tall woman looked down and could see the pockets hanging down. She fingered a tag on the waistband. "Backwards, too. You can blame that on your best friend there." She pointed at Jaylynn.

"Who *me?*"

"*You* dressed me," Dez said, a mocking tone in her voice.

"*Moi?*"

Dez shook her head, then moved over to the bed. With her back to the two women, she unwrapped herself from the sheet, shook it out, then tucked it in at the foot of the bed. Without looking back at the two giggling women, she slipped under the sheet and pulled it up over her bare upper torso. Under the covers, she slipped the sweat bottoms off and wormed a hand out from under the sheet to drop them next to the bed. She turned on her side to see Sara grinning at her from the couch and waving her hand over her head.

"Uh, Dez, what are you doing?"

The tall woman glanced back and forth between the two grinning fools in front of her. She had no idea what Sara meant, so she opted for the safest response to any question—another question. "What does it look like?"

"You and Jay are going to *sleep* in here?"

Dez wanted to say, *No, Jaylynn will probably sleep and lucky me will be awake the rest of the night, so don't worry, I'll be keeping watch.* Instead, she replied, "Yeah. Why?"

"I think maybe we ought to all go to a hotel or something."

Dez frowned. "And that would accomplish what?"

In an excited voice Jaylynn said, "Don't they travel in packs, or droves, or swarms? You know what I mean?"

"Jay, it was one little bat. It probably flew in the door and got trapped in here."

"But what if there are more waiting 'til we turn the lights out to attack?"

Dez let her eyes scan the room. "I doubt it. You see any other little fiends swooping around?"

Sara tucked her feet under her and angled herself back in the corner of the couch, her arms crossed over her chest. "I think I still want to vote for the hotel. They have room service and everything."

Dez turned on her side. "Now there's something we all really need at two a.m. Listen, you two have bats in your belfries. You want to stay at a hotel the rest of your lives?"

"Easy for you to say," Sara said. "Tim and Kevin are downstairs, so they've got each other—"

"Fat lot of protection they've been," Dez grumbled.

"And you two have each other," Sara went on. "I'm stuck in my little room all alone, a ready victim for any dive-bombing vampire bat."

Dez sighed. "You look perfectly comfortable there on that couch, which, I seem to remember, is your couch anyway, so why don't you just stay in here?"

The two women turned to one another, and Jaylynn held a hand out which Sara slapped. "See?" Jaylynn said. "Told ya so."

"Yeah, yeah," Sara answered. "You're always right about her."

Dez had the distinct feeling that she had been conned, but really, she didn't care if Sara stayed in their room. She just hoped daylight came soon because if she didn't miss her guess, she wouldn't be sleeping much anyway.

****

Jaylynn found herself waking every hour or so for the rest of the night remembering wisps of bad dreams where aliens with shiny teeth, dripping blood, and decayed flesh chased her. To battle the scary dreams, she did what she had been doing ever since her psychologist aunt taught it to her when she was a kid: she conjured up a hero, a broad-shouldered, fierce, resourceful protector dressed in black leather. Her hero rode a lightning fast silver motorcycle, and under her helmet she had long beautiful black hair. She carried so many space guns and knives and martial arts weapons that Jaylynn had no fear of the monsters.

Through her teen years and into her twenties, Jaylynn had mastered her nightmares with this fantasy woman, but it still came as a huge surprise the year before, on a sweltering August night, when a real-life hero in the form of Dez Reilly burst into this very room and saved the day. Two serial rapists had broken in and duct taped Sara, intent on raping her, when Jaylynn arrived home and walked in on them. She was very grateful that neighbors heard their screams and called the police. Jaylynn still remembered how Dez had burst into the room, subdued the attackers, and gotten her arm broken in the process.

She could easily recall her sense of wonder at seeing Dez in action. She remembered the entire episode, almost in slow motion, as though Dez were some sort of superhuman dynamo. The awe she felt later—and still felt at times—was that this hero, this childhood construct, came to life just when she needed her that one night, and even stranger, had stayed on in her life. How could she explain how mind-boggling it was? She hadn't even mentioned it to Dez yet, fearing that somehow, the tall cop would think she was a little bit wacky.

She turned over and snuggled up to the warm form next to her. No one had ever made her feel as safe, as cared for, as Dez did. Her mind, her gut, her intuition—all told her this was a forever thing. Soon she would find a way to share the depth of her feelings with Dez, but for now, she was happy to just revel in the comfort of having her near. She curled up as close as she could get and drifted off to sleep.

Chapter
Three

"Sure gets dark sooner now." Jaylynn was driving the squad car again. She glanced over at her partner who still wore her reflective sunglasses despite the fact that the sun had dipped below the horizon and the day was quickly moving from dusk to dark. "You want to stop for something to eat?"

"Nah. I'm not that hungry." Dez took off her sunglasses and tucked them in her pocket, then rubbed her eyes. The rookie knew Dez hated riding shotgun. The passenger side of the car was far too cramped for her liking, but Jaylynn needed the driving experience, and besides, for this part of the field training, Dez really was just along for the ride. They rode in silence for quite some time. Soon, the last of the daylight disappeared, and streetlights started popping on all over.

Over the next hour, Jaylynn completed a circuit of their sector, and all was quiet. She peered at her watch in the dim light of the car. "What do you say we take a quick break and head over to the Pavilion to check out the band? I think *Hydraulic Woman* went on at seven, so they should be jamming for a while."

"Sure."

No sooner had Jaylynn headed down Lexington Avenue than Dispatch came on with the report of a shooting near Como Lake.

"So much for listening to the band," the rookie sighed.

Dez pressed her shoulder mic and spoke to Dispatch as Jaylynn hit the lights and siren. The big cop opened up the glove compartment and grabbed a scene kit. "Two down, Jay. Sounds like the parking lot by the fountain."

"Oh, crap. That's near the Pavilion. I hope nobody opened fire on the crowd." She maneuvered the car around the bend and hit the brakes with force when she saw a woman scuttle across the road pushing a baby stroller. Swerving, she hit the gas, then rode the brake as she turned into the parking lot, tires squealing. She passed the fountain, screeched to a stop, and got out of the car in a hurry. In the background, the sound of acoustic guitars, drums, and a bass wafted across the lot, followed by a soulful voice singing, *Oh when the cold days come, babe, I'll keep you safe and warm, in the windy rainy thunder nights you'll never hear the storm...*

A trio of young boys, all Asian, let their bikes drop to the ground and came running toward them. The tallest kid, dressed in a leather jacket and jeans, skidded to a halt a few feet from them. "It's bad," he said. Shivering, he turned and pointed across the parking lot toward the aluminum concession stand. "They look seriously dead."

Dez strode quickly in the direction indicated by the boy, followed by Jaylynn and the kids. The undersized door that led up into the snack stand was open to the inside, but the screen on the outside was shut. Because of Dez's height, before she was a dozen feet away she could see the body lying facedown on the floor. Even through the screen, she could tell the back of Steven Tivoli's head was blown away, much of it spattered low on the far wall of the concession stand.

The tall cop stopped and turned around, holding up a hand. "Hold it, everyone. You, too, Savage." She didn't respond when Jaylynn gave her a puzzled look. Instead she kept one hand in the air, her five fingers spread. She handed over to Jaylynn the package she held. "Here, take the kit, Savage, and set up a perimeter of police tape. You boys, stay right here by me. Nobody moves." She hit her shoulder mic to make a preliminary report to Dispatch and to ask for backup for crowd control, a supervisor, the crime lab techs, and investigators.

When she signed off, she watched as Jaylynn finished stringing the yellow tape using nearby trees, lampposts, and garbage cans to make a sizable perimeter around the area. She turned to the three boys standing off to the side. The music was still playing, but some of the spectators two hundred yards away at the Pavilion were starting to wander toward them, curious about the police car lights.

Dez realized time was short and that any minute, all hell would break loose. "Okay, boys, now tell me the truth." She looked the tallest one in the eye. "Did any of you go in there?"

They all shook their heads.

She pointed at the tall boy. "What's your name?" Catching Jaylynn's eye, she nodded when the rookie got out her notebook and started to write.

"S-Sai," he stuttered. "I—I'm Sai Vang."

"Sai, how did you know he was dead if you didn't go in?"

"We could see!" Gesturing and pointing with his right hand, he moved toward the front of the stand.

Dez frowned. She wondered how they could see in when all of them were shorter than Jaylynn.

Sai closed his eyes, stepped up to the tall service window, hooked an arm over the counter, and pulled himself up. He dropped back to the ground. "You see? The man, he didn't answer. So I looked. Then they both looked." The boys all nodded, their faces solemn and scared. "There's, like, brains blown up all over the place in there."

Alarmed, Jaylynn looked up from what she was writing. Dez cast her a warning look and shook her head slightly, but she could see that the rookie wasn't going to hang back. "Kids, Officer Savage here needs to take down all your names and addresses. Do any of you have your student ID's?" When they shook their heads, she went on. "You may be important witnesses. I want each of you to go over to your bicycles and get on them and stay put. Please don't talk to each other." She gave a toss of her head and the three boys scrambled to get to their bikes. She hoped to keep the rookie busy writing until backup and the crime scene team arrived. Already she could hear the whine of sirens in the distance. There was no reason any more people needed to see the gruesome scene. As she looked around, she could see curious people from the Pavilion had made their way to the police line. A man called out asking what was happening. She ignored him, instead motioning to the people to back up. "Police business. Everybody stay back."

Off to the side, Jaylynn finished taking down the boys' information, and Dez watched as each of the kids dragged their bikes under the POLICE SCENE—DO NOT CROSS tape. Over at the Pavilion, one song ended, and there was the sound of applause. A bass line started up in four-four time, then a rhythm guitar strummed a chord. Dez remembered this song from the CD. She wondered if she would still like it the next time she heard it, given the circumstances now. She tried to put the melody of it out of her mind so that she wouldn't associate it with the grisly murder scene behind her.

Jaylynn stepped to the side, craning her neck, while the boys stood outside the perimeter watching her, but Dez managed to screen the doorway with her body so that the rookie couldn't see in. Jaylynn seemed to give up reluctantly. She moved aside, toward the rear of the snack shack, and Dez felt a sense of relief. But a sudden gasp from Jaylynn brought the tall cop to attention.

"Oh my God! What is *this?*" The rookie stood looking down at something in the shadows to the rear of the stand.

The tall boy, Sai, called out, "Oh yeah. We thought you saw that. She's dead, too."

Jaylynn moved too quickly. Before Dez could react, the younger woman dropped her notebook and fell to her knees. She pulled her flashlight off her belt and shined it on the body lying on the cement. She knelt there, frozen in place, making choking sounds.

Dez's blood ran cold. "Aw, shit." She hurried to her partner's side, grabbed her arm, and pulled her to her feet. The flashlight bumped against the bigger woman's stomach, slipped from Jaylynn's grasp, and fell to the ground. Dez picked it up, snapped it off, and handed it to the rookie. "Hold it together, Jay," she whispered. Out loud, she said, "First rule: don't touch a damn thing. Second rule: don't touch a damn thing. Our job here is to secure the perimeter. Let's keep things together."

"I will. I will. But Dez, she's a kid—just a young kid."

Dez nodded. "Okay. I know. And so are these boys. Go concentrate on them. We'll talk later...go keep them separated so when the detectives show up, they get good statements."

Like a trouper, Jaylynn turned and moved back toward the boys to keep them company. Dez took her flashlight off her belt and sauntered over to the body in the shadows. Five seconds of light told her everything she needed to know. White female, thin, approximately 100 pounds, dark hair, Levi skirt and jacket, shot in the back and at close range in the back of the head. A smudged trail of blood led from the foot of the metal stairs, and Dez could see that this little person had likely tried to escape. She had been shot in the back, then had crawled and dragged herself fifteen feet to her present location where someone had caught up with her and pulled the trigger one last time into the back of her head.

She snapped off the flash and returned it to her belt. Police cars approaching from opposite directions converged on the parking lot. The three-ring circus was all set to begin now.

****

Much later, Dez lay next to Jaylynn, one arm held protectively around the crying woman. Moonlight shone in through the slats of the blinds they had not remembered to close at two a.m. when they stripped off their clothes and fell into bed. Jaylynn had

huddled there, cold and shaking, for some time before the sobs
came, and now after several minutes, the smaller woman's tears
were slowing.

They lay on their sides, face to face, with Jaylynn's hands in
fists below her chin. Dez's right arm was over the slim waist, and
her warm legs transmitted heat to the chilled woman before her.

"Why, Dez? Who would kill such a young girl? It's not
right—not fair."

"No, it's not." The bigger woman reached a hand up and
wiped a tear away from Jaylynn's cheek. She felt helpless to comfort her lover, and in the face of such pain and grief, an uneasiness
stole over her. It was all she could do not to get up and run from
the room. But Jaylynn needed her, so she was not going to let her
down. She forced her own apprehension away, pulled the smaller
woman nearer, and slipped her other arm under the trembling
waist to encircle her.

Jaylynn snuggled in closer, pressing her face into the warmth
of the tall woman's shoulder. "Lucky I go see my counselor
tomorrow. I'm sorry to be such a mess."

"You're not a mess."

Jaylynn leaned back a little and searched out the blue eyes
before her in the silvery moonlight. "Yeah, right. You're the one
who told me cops don't cry."

Dez shook her head. "You *know* what I meant—at least now
you do. You don't cry *there*, at the scene. You cry later, if you
have to, when no citizens are around."

Jaylynn pulled away and reached behind her to the nightstand
for a tissue. She blew her nose and took another tissue to wipe her
tears. "Maybe it wouldn't be so bad if I hadn't known the guy."

"Jay, a couple brief conversations with him doesn't constitute
knowing him."

"But he was a *person*, somebody who was pleasant to us, who
was just...just like...you know, a regular guy."

"That regular guy was probably into something more than
you realize. Those two victims were executed. It wasn't a random
attack. It sure seems like someone went there to kill Tivoli."

"And that little girl must have stumbled upon it. Who would
want to kill the two of them? It doesn't make any sense."

Dez figured it would make sense soon enough, but she kept
her thoughts to herself. Experience from a couple dozen previous
homicides as well as two decades of discussions about murders
had led her to believe there were really only four types of killings:
those revolving around greedy money schemes, hate crimes,
domestic cases, or the protection of secrets. Everything else—and

those were small in number—was pretty much accidental or random maliciousness. She thought the media's focus on thrill killing and bizarre serial murderers was itself nearly criminal because
the vast majority of murders were committed by drunken or
drugged fools who got out of control with family or friends and
went too far with a gun or a knife or a fist. That didn't make it
any easier to solve the crimes, given the huge capacity of human
beings for denial and subterfuge.

"It was a pretty tough scene for your first homicide, Jay."

"Do you remember yours?"

Dez nodded slowly. "I saw my first homicide when I was
twelve."

"Whoa! Twelve? How'd you manage that?" She pulled herself up on her elbow and peered down into her partner's face.

Dez rolled onto her back as she kicked a leg out from under
the covers. "I was riding shotgun with my dad on a real slow Sunday afternoon. Somebody reported a possible heart attack in their
neighbor's backyard."

She recalled that they had beaten the ambulance to the scene.
In her mind's eye, she got out of the cruiser and followed her
father, the autumn air crisp and punctuated by the falling of leaves
from the maples that lined the avenue. A wide-eyed, plump
woman in a pale blue apron came out the front screen door and
without a word, gestured toward the back of the house. Dez
remembered staring at the woman's face for a moment and realizing something was out of place.

She turned away and hurried to catch up with her father as he
moved, almost at a trot, past some tall, neatly clipped hedges and
around the side of the house. A man lay on his back next to a
heavy-duty white plastic birdbath that held no water. He was clad
in brown oxfords, jeans, and a red plaid flannel shirt. Even from
the distance, Dez could see that his eyes were open, staring
straight up. Her father went down on one knee, next to the body,
his back to her. He stood up. "He's dead. He's been stabbed.
You don't need to see this, Desiree. Go get in the car."

Dez was already looking. There was blood all over the front
of the man, but it hadn't been so noticeable since the flannel shirt
was mostly red.

"Desiree Reilly. Do you hear me? Get back to the car and
hurry up. Now!"

He followed her back along the path to the front of the house,
and she knew he needed to radio in right away. As they came
around the corner past the hedges, they found the aproned woman
sitting at the very top of the cement stairs, shaking her sandy

blonde head back and forth. She looked dazed. Dez squinted to
see her face better, and now she could see what was out of place.
The side of her face was red and puffy, as though she had been
struck.

"Go on to the car, Dez," her father commanded. She did as
he said, but as she opened the door to the cruiser, she heard him
say, "Ma'am, do you know what happened out back?"

The women nodded and burst into tears. She reached into
her apron pocket and pulled out a wood-handled kitchen knife,
then dropped it on the stairs below her.

From the car, even with the window down, Dez couldn't hear
all of what was said, but she put two and two together. It made
her feel sad, but even more than that, it made her curious. Why
had the young woman stabbed the man with a kitchen knife?

Now it was nearly eighteen years later, and Dez had a much
better understanding.

"Jay, it was no heart attack. The wife stabbed her husband
after he slugged her, and he staggered out to the backyard and
died."

"Wasn't that a horrible thing to see—I mean at 12 years old?"

Dez considered that. "I don't remember being traumatized
by it or anything. It was something my dad and I talked about—
quite a bit, in fact. Her name was Delia Tyesen. I think his was
Dennis. She didn't mean to kill him. She said she was making pot
roast, trimming the fat off the meat, when he came up behind and
hauled off and smacked her upside the head. She was four months
pregnant, their house was in foreclosure, and she ended up miscar-
rying and then getting convicted of manslaughter. It was the first
case I ever followed closely. I went to the initial hearing with my
dad—they didn't have a trial. She pled no contest."

Jaylynn shivered. She pulled the covers up over her shoulders
and got comfortable on her back with her head high on the pillow.
Dez turned on her side, facing Jaylynn, and put an arm around
her. She tucked her head against the smaller woman's shoulder
and was rewarded with an arm encircling her neck.

In a quiet voice, Dez said, "That was sort of the beginning of
my interest in the law. I wanted to do what my dad did. Make
people get along. Solve crimes. Enforce the rules. I sat there in
the car that day, and every officer at the scene came over and
talked to me. Some of them were worried I'd be upset, but some
of them just wanted to show off for their buddy's kid. I liked talking to them. I liked the camaraderie."

"What ever happened to her—the woman?"

"Don't know. She went to prison for a short while, but I don't know after that."

Jaylynn lay there, holding Dez, and wondered how she would have felt coming upon a murder at age twelve. She thought back...age twelve...sixth grade. She was still climbing on the monkey bars, playing tetherball, and reading Nancy Drew mysteries. Her best friend was crazy about Barbie, and Jaylynn's favorite TV show was *Highway to Heaven*. Her mother had just remarried after her father's death three years earlier. She sighed. "Nope. I don't think I'd have wanted to be in your shoes that day, Dez."

The dark woman grinned. "Size nine when I was twelve."

"Wha—oh, you goofball."

"Shhhh. It's practically three in the morning. Aren't you tired?"

"Yes. I want to sleep until noon."

Dez hoped that would happen. She didn't count on it though.

Chapter
Four

Dez parked her truck and headed into the station. All was quiet, which was out of the ordinary. Usually there were officers strolling the halls or hanging around outside smoking. She checked her watch and realized that she was earlier than her normal arrival time and decided that explained it. She'd have plenty of time to dress leisurely, maybe even organize her locker.

She sauntered down the hall, past the communication center, past the watch commander's office, and to the stairs that led down to the briefing room, also called the roll call room. Past it lay stairs down to the department gym, outfitted with fairly new weight equipment that Dez and Jaylynn regularly used. Beyond the first set of stairs lay another smaller flight of steps that led down to the men's and women's locker rooms which were also connected to the gym.

The tall cop shouldered her way through the swinging door and into the locker room. She opened her locker and set to work sorting and sifting through her gear. She took advantage of the unused benches all around her and laid out her clean uniforms, weapons, three sets of cuffs, an older vest and the new one she wore now, two flashlights, two half-filled boxes of bullets, a pack of batteries, two ASR's—aerosol subject restraint cans—also known as "mace," and various other odds and ends. On the top shelf in the back she found a red hand gripper and pulled it out, looking at it with no fondness. Fourteen months earlier, a rapist wielding a baseball bat had attacked her. He broke the radius bone in her left forearm, and she'd worn a cast for several weeks. She gave the gripper a few squeezes, happy to see that her hand felt as strong as ever. In fact, she had forgotten all about the grip exercises she had done every day for the first months after the cast came off. .

She tossed the gripper into a bag with a few other items she was planning to take home, then arranged things on the two shelves, rehung her clothes, dumped bullets from one box into another, and disposed of the extra cardboard container. Once she felt her gear was properly organized, she undressed and donned her police uniform, carefully hanging her street clothes in the locker.

Buttoning her light blue shirt, she looked up over the big blue lockers and around the gray room, surprised that Jaylynn hadn't yet arrived. When she left the house on Como Boulevard earlier, Sara and Jay had been finishing up dishes, and the rookie had said she'd be right behind her. *Ha. Jaylynn is never early.* She looked at her watch to see that it was a good thirty-five minutes until roll call. She gave her another twenty minutes.

They had been coming to work in separate vehicles, she in her Ford truck and the rookie in her little gray Camry. Without any conversation about it at all, they had just adapted to that practice. There was an unspoken understanding that they should downplay their personal relationship at work. No need for others to find out and make a big deal about it.

She heard a sound and stopped for a moment to listen, then realized it was only the pipes in the bathroom. The locker room was large and square with a main aisle running down the middle from the entrance to the far wall. The bathroom was back near the entrance door. On either side of the aisle were four sets of oversized royal blue lockers, the only color in the otherwise gun-metal gray room. Rickety backless wooden benches, embedded into the concrete, sat in front of the lockers. From what Dez remembered, her high school locker room was better appointed than this tacky room, which was brightened by multiple rows of dazzling fluorescent lights. Every time she entered she had the desire to put on her sunglasses. Since the lockers were located in the basement level, there were no windows whatsoever, so apparently the highly skilled police interior decorators thought they would make up for it by blinding everyone. That thought brought a brief smile to her face.

Dez smacked her locker door shut and sat on the wooden bench to check and adjust everything on her duty belt. Nothing was fitting right—neither one of her belts, not her pants or shirts, and most of all, not her TriFlex protective vest. She unbuttoned her shirt and ripped at the Velcro straps of the vest until she got them where she wanted them. She had lost twenty-six pounds over the last summer in order to compete in a bodybuilding show in August, and it seemed that in the weeks since then, she had put all of that weight back on—and more. Of course, who wouldn't while hanging around a whole household of junk food junkies? French toast and syrup for breakfast, hot hoagie sandwiches before noon, and pizza with the crew there at the house at 1:30. She patted her stomach. *I'm stuffed! I shouldn't eat another mouthful of anything for the whole shift.*

She got her gun and holster situated comfortably on her dominant, right side, then made sure the pouch for the ASR can was exactly where she could get to it, behind her gun, but not too close. There were "keepers" in between which held both her belts together and served as spacers between pouches. Her trouser belt went through the belt loops of her pants, so the duty belt required keepers to space her equipment to keep it all from sliding around or shifting as she moved. She wanted her gun, cuffs, baton, and ASR within easy reach close to her sides. The latex glove pouch, flashlight, radio holder, and double magazine holder were also necessary, and she had them spaced on the belt around the back and on her weak side.

She buttoned her cuffs and snapped the lock on her locker, then headed upstairs to put in a call to Investigations. She wanted information about the homicides from the night before. She had a hunch that it was a case both she and Jaylynn would be following.

She strode down the long hall, by the main entrance, and past the lieutenant's office. The duty sergeant looked up. "Hey, Reilly," he called out after her.

The tall cop stopped abruptly and turned around. "Hi, Belton."

"Busy night last night." She nodded. Belton straightened some papers on his desk. "Who caught the Tivoli murders from last Saturday night?"

She crossed her arms over her chest. "Your personal favorites, Tsorro and Parkins."

Belton rolled his eyes and sighed, then grinned up at her, his teeth sparkling in his thin, dark face. "You'd think those two would have retired by now. They've been here longer than me— and I'm a fixture."

She smiled.

Dinosaurs. Tsorro and Parkins were two of the oldest, most sexist, and least innovative investigators she had ever met. They knew their stuff, and they closed a lot of cases, but they had also been on duty the night Ryan had died. Just remembering them— and that night—made her shudder. Had they always been such a pain to talk to? Or was it just since her partner's death? She wasn't sure. All she knew was that she didn't relish the thought of spending any time with them at all. Belton, on the other hand, she had always liked. He'd worked the desk for as long as she could remember, and he could be counted on to use good judgment about the parade of cops who passed by him each day.

"You can stay as long as you like, Belton." She started to turn away.

"Reilly, wait. Lieutenant wants to see you."

She paused. "Oh? Why?"

Belton grinned again, and Dez thought he looked positively mischievous. "He knows how much you enjoy special assignments."

She gazed at him, steel in her blue eyes. "I hate special assignments."

"You know that. And I know that. You'll have to work harder to let *him* know that." He squelched a laugh, his sable forehead gleaming in the fluorescent light. "You can go on in now. He's expecting you."

She stepped around Belton's desk and tapped on the frame of the door, which was ajar, then pushed it open and poked her head in. Lt. Malcolm looked up. "Hey, Reilly. Come in and have a seat. No need to shut the door."

The lieutenant, a balding Scandinavian in his mid-forties, set aside the papers on his desk. His cuffs were rolled up to mid-forearm. He rolled each of them up another turn, then turned his gray eyes on the glowering woman.

With a sigh, she sat in the ancient solid wood visitor's chair, shifting twice and banging her right elbow on the clunky armrest.

"I think you know this already, but you're doing a great job with the rookies, and especially with Savage. She is shaping up to be a fine officer. I reviewed her documentation from last night's homicides and everything is in order."

"Yes, sir."

"I've got an assignment for you and Savage. Como Middle School is running their DARE program—Drug Awareness Resistance Education."

She knew what the acronym stood for, and she already didn't like the sound of the assignment.

"In the course of providing DARE services, the assigned officers, Hartwick and Sorenson, have learned that there is no self-defense course being taught for the girls at the school. Apparently, the school is not fully staffed, and the teachers for the Phys Ed program are filling in from other disciplines." He leaned back in his tattered leather chair and pulled at his mustache. "I know it's short notice, but I want you and Savage to spend a little time over there—maybe an hour or two twice a week—teaching self-defense until sometime after the Thanksgiving holiday."

"When?"

"Starting next Tuesday. Will you do it?"

"Of course, sir."

He smiled and leaned back in his chair. "Did I mention how pleased I am with the work you are doing—both as an FTO and as an officer on the street? I put in a request for a commendation for you, Reilly, for all the extra work you have done over the last year. Keep up the good work. And by the way, you might want to think seriously about taking the sergeant's exam. It's coming up, you know. I'd be happy to give you pointers and steer you toward what you need to study.

She nodded. "Thank you, sir."

"Now back to the self-defense issues. It would work best if you could cycle through the sixth and seventh grades and be done sometime after Thanksgiving and well before Christmas. I'll leave it up to you to design a course in concert with the school administrators. You can file a report later with me so that I know what you designed. Maybe we can use it to assist other schools in the future. And I think you should do this in the early afternoon, then join the shift on time. Your shift sergeant will make sure to adjust your hours or give you O.T. pay, all right?"

"Yes, sir. Is that all?"

"Isn't that enough?" He smiled at her, his face lighting up.

It occurred to her that she should probably discuss the situation with Jaylynn—but after a split second of thought, she rose instead. "How soon do you want that report, Lieutenant?"

"Just give me verbal prelim info by the end of next week, okay? You and Savage can write up the rest later, once you have a plan in place. Might take you a while to settle into something that works, so just get it to me in the next few weeks. Have a good—and safe—shift, Reilly."

She thanked him and left his office, allowing herself to fume once she reached the hallway. *Sixth graders! What?—twelve-year-olds? A bunch of rude brats to deal with.* She took a deep breath. She'd let Jaylynn handle this. She had a hunch the rookie would have some good ideas for this new project.

She looked at her watch, debating whether to call over to the main station. She now had only twelve minutes until roll call so she headed down to the locker room to get some water. When she made it to the briefing room, she was still seething.

****

Jaylynn rushed into the precinct, by the communication center, past the watch commander's office, and to the stairs. She clattered down the flight of steps that led to the men's and women's locker rooms and hustled into the gray room, keeping her eye open for Dez. The tall woman was nowhere to be found, so she quickly changed and checked her watch to see that she had seven minutes until roll call.

When she entered the briefing room, she found a surly-looking Dez sitting toward the back, a bottle of water gripped in her right fist. The rest of the personnel for the two sectors milled around, half of them seated and the others standing, and the main topic seemed to be the previous night's murders. She stopped and listened for a minute, but when they began discussing the crime scene, she shuddered and squeezed her way past a heavy-set officer to settle into a chair next to Dez. She looked over at her partner to see the closed face and restless eyes. "Hey. What's up?" she asked softly.

"I'll tell ya after roll call," the big cop said, her voice low.

Just then the sergeant called everyone to order and for the next ten minutes, Jaylynn listened closely, all the while aware that Dez was out of sorts about something. The rookie was constantly curious about the mercurial cop. One minute they were laughing and relaxed; the next, Dez had retreated behind tall walls. Jaylynn had already gotten to the point where she realized that nothing she said or did had much to do with her moody partner's reactions to things, and the only thing she could do was wait to see what was going on behind those steely blue eyes.

Walking out to the squad car, Jaylynn waited patiently and watched the six-foot-tall cop out of the corner of her eye. It wasn't until she was in the cruiser, belted in, and backing the vehicle out that her passenger spoke up. "The lieutenant is assigning us additional duties."

"Oh?" She fell in line behind another departing squad car and turned out onto Dale Street.

"We have to go teach self-defense at Como Middle School."

"Really? That's great! When?"

"Geez! I should've known you would think it was a good idea."

The big cop sounded so petulant that Jaylynn laughed out loud. "Of course. It will be fun. We get to teach kids, and that'll be great. Boys and girls?"

"I think just girls. Head downtown."

Jaylynn frowned and glanced over, puzzlement on her face, but she turned the car and headed down a side street back toward University Avenue. "Where downtown?"

"Main station. We need to drop by and see Tsorro and Parkins, the two homicide cops for the Tivoli killings."

Jaylynn nodded. This would be her first opportunity to talk with detectives about a homicide she knew something about. Though she was sorry for the victims, she looked forward to the chance to learn more about investigating this kind of case. It was important to her that the killer—or killers—be brought to justice. She could still see the small heap that was once a young girl, and it made her skin crawl.

When they arrived at the main station house, the Second Watch officers were straggling out after the end of their shift. Third Watch was well underway, but there were plenty of cops hanging out in the squad room and near the commanders' offices. When they turned the corner, a six-and-a-half-foot-tall male officer suddenly loomed up in front of them. He leaned against the wall in the hallway near the break room. Still dressed in his work uniform, his shirt was unbuttoned partly, revealing a bleached white t-shirt underneath. The white-blond hair on his head was ultra-short and practically standing on end as though he had been running his hands through it. He held a pair of gold colored wire-rimmed glasses in his left hand and rubbed his eyes with his right, which explained why Jaylynn could take him by surprise. In two quick steps she was at his side, poking him in the middle and startling him. "Cowboy!"

"You little runt!" The big man put his glasses on in haste, then reached out and picked her up by the scruff of her jacket and let her dangle.

"You big oaf," the rookie said, but she was laughing too hard to make it sound serious.

He set her down and gave her a pat on the head, which caused her to aim a small fist at his midsection.

Dez crossed her arms and stood off to the side. "Cowboy, we haven't got all day."

He grinned at her and swaggered over, his stride a little bit bowlegged. "And hello to you, too, Ms. Desiree Reilly." He grabbed her around the middle and squeezed, picking her up off her feet.

"Hey! Save that physical stuff for Jaylynn."

He eased up and set her back on the tiled floor, but he still kept his arms around her. He was one of the few people on the planet whom Dez would allow into her personal space, and one of even fewer from whom she would accept a bear hug like that. Her partner, Ryan, and Cowboy had been best friends. When Ryan was shot and killed in the line of duty, it cemented an already strong bond between Dez and her work partner's best buddy. For the rest of her days, she would consider him more than her brother in blue. He was a friend for life.

"You don't want to be picked up," he teased, "because you don't want anyone to know how much weight you've packed on."

"Ha. Look at yourself, ape man."

They had both gained weight after competing in the body-building competition in August. Cowboy made an excellent "Pairs" partner, and they had walked off with the first place trophy as well as individual trophies for their weight classes. They agreed that the dieting to cut weight was outrageously painful, and since then, they both vowed never to compete in bodybuilding again.

Jaylynn cleared her throat and made a show of looking at her watch. "I don't mean to break up this little love fest, but we've got work to do."

Blushing, Dez pushed Cowboy away.

He laughed and put his fists up. "Let's see your dukes, Dez, honey. Let's see if I can still whip your butt."

"Yeah, right, Cowboy. Doesn't hitting women go against your Wild West code of honor?"

"For you, I'd make an exception." Smiling, he dropped his hands to his sides, and Jaylynn thought he was one of the most handsome men she had ever seen. His broad shoulders, lean hips, white teeth, and the sparkling blue eyes...reminded her of someone she knew. She gazed up at Dez, then turned back to Cowboy.

"Hey, Culpepper. Big party at my house for Sara's fiancé's return from the Army."

"Oh yeah?"

"Yeah. Come over Saturday night, okay? Should be a lot of fun. Luella's coming, and we'll be there. Drop by any time after seven."

"That'd be fun—but I'm on duty."

"If you can get away—even for a while—stop by."

"Okay. I might just do that."

They stood smiling at one another until Dez interrupted. "Let's go, Jay." She turned to the big blond man. "See ya around, Cowboy."

He nodded. "Yup. Take it easy, Dez."

****

As Dez had expected, Tsorro and Parkins had been a real education for Jaylynn. At first, they had discussed the Tivoli crime scene dispassionately, as though each victim were nameless, faceless, just a number—numbers 16 and 17, to be exact. She could tell Jaylynn was struggling not to take the two men to task, and with a pointed look, she shut down the younger woman's impulse to mouth off to them.

Tsorro didn't look like a cop at all. He resembled a cross between the singer Tom Jones and any conventional movie star hit man. With his wavy black hair greased back and gold rings and necklaces in abundance, he could also have been a cheap lounge act in Las Vegas. His black oxfords were well-shined and his gray suit pressed, but he was tie-less with his top two shirt buttons open and revealing tufts of thick black chest hair tangled up in gold chains. He and Parkins were near the same height—about five-foot-nine. Tsorro had an irritating way of clicking his tongue against his teeth while shifting his shoulders around in his jacket, then reaching down to shoot his cuffs. Later, she knew Jaylynn would be surprised to hear that Tsorro was a year short of 60. He didn't appear to be even 50 yet.

Parkins didn't look like a cop either. He reminded Dez of the driver on her junior high bus route. Beefy and balding, he'd obviously eaten his share of doughnuts in his street cop days. Despite the fact that he wore well-pressed suits similar to his partner's, they never appeared to fit him quite right, and every move he made served only to make him more uncomfortable. His eyes were as pale as Tsorro's were dark, his skin almost as white as Dez's. He looked like an average cranky middle-aged man, so much so that if it weren't for the extra bulge under his left arm, most people wouldn't peg him for a cop. Unlike Tsorro, he could blend into a crowd with little difficulty. In high schools, kids thought he was a visiting administrator. At athletic events, he looked like an unhappy, pot-bellied fan. Out on the street he was perceived to be a struggling businessman having a very bad day.

They were long ago dubbed Zorro and Tonto, but Tsorro was no Lone Ranger. In actuality, it was Parkins who had the smarts and was the eyes and ears of the partnership. While Tsorro yukked it up, threatened, or strong-armed witnesses and suspects, Parkins watched and made the observations that often cracked cases. During their long careers, they'd both worked with other partners, but over the last decade, it had been together that they had encountered the most success, despite the fact that both of them were sexist, homophobic, and almost completely computer illiterate. It bothered Dez more that the brass didn't require them to take some computer courses so they could do better investigative work than it did that she was just as likely to be referred to as "that young thing" or "the little lady." Never mind that she stood four inches taller than either of them in her duty boots and could probably crush them barehanded.

They seemed like throwbacks to an earlier time, a time when all cops were male, belonging to a "brotherhood" truly made up of men only. In this modern day and age, they had adjusted to many aspects of the new world of police work, but Zorro and Tonto were also allowed to operate as though they existed in a time warp back to the Fifties. While their cool and disconnected attitude toward the victims always bothered her, their dedication to catching killers made up for it, and for that she respected them.

When Tsorro learned that the Tivoli case was the first homicide Jaylynn was involved with, he patiently explained to her the steps they were taking to conduct witness interviews. He had his arm around her, called her "honeybun" and an Italian endearment, and spoke as though she were a teenager on a career day visit to the station. Dez couldn't hear most of what was being said, but she had to bite back a smile because she could see the color flaming in her partner's face. She had a pretty good idea what the topic of conversation would be once they returned to their cruiser.

Parkins leafed through a folder of autopsy photos. "Reilly, this one's pretty ugly. That little girl, according to the medical examiner's prelim report, wasn't but a slip of a thing—maybe fourteen. Also PG."

Across the room, Jaylynn turned away from the fawning Tsorro to listen. "Pregnant?"

Parkins nodded. "Seems pretty sick to me. We know Tivoli was thirty-six. He's an old greaser ex-con, and there he is sticking it to a tiny little White girl not even out of junior high."

Jaylynn and the lounge lizard moved the few steps to close the gap between the four of them. The rookie was obviously biting her tongue, and Dez found herself feeling a little sorry for her.

Tsorro said, "Too bad he's dead. Would've liked to nail the *malfattore* for statutory rape." He rolled his shoulders and shot his cuffs, then reached up with his right hand to finger the gold chains around his neck.

Jaylynn's face was returning from hot pink to its normal peachy color. "Any indication of who did this? Gang-related? Drugs? Robbery motive?"

Both detectives shook their heads. Parkins leaned back against the desk, his hefty behind crinkling the sheaf of loose papers spread all over it. "No money missing—not from the till and not from the victim's pockets. Well, the little girl didn't have any ID and no money other than change. Still, I don't think she was robbed. We'll get some more info from the ME once he gets the tox screens back. It'll be a few days before we get the complete autopsy report. But we do know for a fact that the tests show neither of the victims had shot a gun lately, so it's not like he killed the girl or vice versa."

Tsorro said, "We don't have a clue yet why someone would murder the two of them—unless it was some sort of thrill kill. We've been getting a few of those here in the Twin Cities lately."

Dez nodded. "Maybe when you ID the girl?"

"We're on that," Parkins said. He looked at his watch. "We've got some canvassing to do. There's a good 180 witnesses to interview—that we know of—so far. Got several dozen car license numbers to track. Thanks for getting on that so quickly last night." He nodded to both of them, then sighed. "It's gonna be a shitload of work." He stood up from the desk, causing two pieces of paper to flutter to the ground. He ignored them. "Come by or call anytime you like. Savage, I remember my first murder case. Learned a lot from it. You will, too."

Tsorro nodded and smiled, his white dentures gleaming in the fluorescent light. "See you lovely ladies another time." Both men headed over to the coat rack and grabbed London Fog overcoats. Dez and Jaylynn exited the room and headed out to their squad car.

Jaylynn waited until the car doors were closed before exclaiming, "Dinosaurs! That Tsorro is *worse* than a dinosaur. He's pond scum!"

Dez laughed out loud as she put on her seatbelt. "My sentiments exactly."

"Where does he get off?" She started the car, put it in gear, and peeled out of the parking lot. "Reminded me of cops back in the days of *Peter Gunn* or *Perry Mason*. Why, they're practically caricatures of cops, Dez!"

"They do close a lot of cases."

"I'd positively *hate* dealing with them if I were a witness or a victim of a crime."

"Yeah. Well, they're not so bad, but let's hope you never have to. If you want to stay abreast of their investigation, you're gonna have to put up with them."

Jaylynn just shook her head and drove on in silence.

****

At one p.m. the following Tuesday, Dez and Jaylynn showed up at Como Middle School, reported to the office, and were escorted to the gym by a talkative young receptionist who didn't look old enough to have even graduated from high school. They had left their duty belts locked in the car along with their weapons. She wondered how long it would take for the kids to ask them where their guns were. Usually every child's first questions were: "Can I see your gun?" and "Hey, how many people have you shot?"

Dez didn't listen to the young receptionist's chatter as they passed down narrow hallways lined with scratched and dented lockers. The school was old—maybe built in the Sixties—and it had definitely seen better days. It smelled just like all schools seemed to smell—like chalk and erasers, paint and dust. Lots of dust. Her nose twitched and she was reminded of her allergies.

They entered the gym, a large and drafty cavern with a discolored wood floor. The ceiling was high with metal rafters criss-crossing it. Dez revised her estimate and guessed the school to have been built in the Fifties. Rickety wooden bleachers that could probably seat five hundred sat on either side of the basketball court. Set up in the middle of the floor were four gigantic blue wrestling mats in a large square with about sixty girls sitting cross legged all around the perimeter.

A man in navy blue Adidas sweatpants stood in the middle of them. His tennis shoes were brand new and shiny white, but his blue sweats and plain tan t-shirt were old and worn.

The office receptionist made a final comment to Jaylynn, then turned and departed, leaving the two of them facing the man under the scrutiny of five dozen seventh graders.

"Good morning, Officers. I'm Paul Hawley. Health and Phys Ed teacher." He moved across the mat, stepped between two girls, and walked toward them. Jaylynn shifted a manila envelope from her right to left hand as he reached out to shake each of their hands. "I also coach girls' softball. It's great to have you. The girls have been looking forward to this."

He took his whistle and lanyard from around his neck and handed it to Dez.

Jaylynn asked, "So what's your plan, Coach Hawley?"

"They're all yours. See those double doors?" He pointed to the end of the gym. "I'm going to leave them open, and my office is just inside, first door on the right. I'm leaving 'em open just in case you need me." He gave the young girls a knowing look. "Listen to what the officers have to say, or there'll be laps for anyone who causes trouble." He turned back to them with a bright smile. "You've got," he glanced at his watch, "43 minutes, then I'll be back."

He turned and trotted toward the double doors, propped them open, then disappeared.

The two women looked at one another, trying to disguise their surprise. Dez handed the lanyard to Jaylynn who put it around her neck, then blew one short report, which was probably unnecessary since all the girls were staring at them, waiting patiently. The rookie unbuttoned her breast pocket and pulled out a pack of blank stickers. "Listen up, kids, my name is Jaylynn Savage, and this is Dez Reilly. You can call us Dez and Jaylynn. There's a lot of you and only two of us, so everybody take a tag and put your first name on it." She took six thick felt markers out of her jacket pocket and handed them around. "Hustle up, girls. You've got sixty seconds to get all set with the name tag on your shirt."

The two officers slipped out of their jackets and laid them on the bleachers to the side of the gym along with Jaylynn's manila folder, then began walking around the ring of seated girls. Dez crossed her arms as she took stock of the group: 58 girls of all shapes and sizes. They wore various colored shorts and athletic shoes, but each wore the same type of plain white t-shirt. About a quarter were Asian, a quarter Black, maybe six were Hispanic, and the rest White, which pretty much reflected the makeup of the Como neighborhood. All of them were eyeing her, openly curious.

Jaylynn waited until they got their name stickers on, then clapped her hands together and walked into the center of the mats. "All right, everyone, on your feet. Everybody off the mats and on the gym floor in a big ring." The girls rose and backed up into a large circle. "Let's do a little running in place, get some blood flowing."

Some of the girls rolled their eyes, but they all went through the motions of jogging in place with Jaylynn hollering encouragement. After a minute she blew her whistle. "All right, good." She glanced around the circle and pointed at two girls. "You, Ramona, and you, Tess, come stand by me. The rest of you sit back down at the edge of the mats. Do a little stretching of your arms and legs while you're down there watching."

She gestured to the two girls left standing. Ramona, a tall, thin White girl with glasses, looked scared. In contrast, Tess was a compact Asian kid who looked a lot more confident.

"Come here, both of you, and face one another. Either one of you ever been pushed or hit before?"

Both girls nodded.

"What did you do?"

The girls looked at each other. Ramona said, "I ran away."

"Me, too," Tess said. "Except when it was my brother. Him, I pushed back."

Jaylynn smiled. "Good answer." She looked around at the group on the floor. "One of the first rules of self-defense is to run away any time you can—that, and make a lot of noise—but we'll get to that shortly. Now what should you do if you *can't* run away?"

A voice from the crowd piped up, "I thought that was why you guys are here—to teach us."

Jaylynn nodded. "That's right. So let's talk about balance first." She turned to the taller girl. "Ramona, shove Tess—not a killer shove, but just a solid shove, right here at the chest." She gestured at her own chest, right below her collarbones.

Tentatively Ramona reached out with one hand and gave the smaller girl a timid push. Tess didn't even have to step back.

"No, a little more—wait." She beckoned toward the tall cop. "Dez, come over and push me to show them what I mean."

Dez stepped over the girls sitting around the mat and strode up to Jaylynn. Without stopping, she reached out with two hands and gave the rookie a firm shove, causing Jaylynn to step back but not to lose her balance.

Jaylynn turned toward her volunteers. "See what I mean, Ramona?"

The girl nodded. She gave Tess a hard push that thrust the smaller girl backwards and onto the mat. Tess popped back up, her face red. "I wasn't ready for that!" she protested.

Jaylynn nodded. "That's right. Being ready is really important." She looked up at Dez. "Push me again, Dez." The big cop complied. "See how she can push me pretty hard, but it doesn't knock me over? That's because I'm balanced for the impact."

She showed the two girls how to take a wider stance, bending their knees slightly. The next time Ramona shoved the Asian girl, Tess didn't fall.

"Good," Jaylynn said. "Now Tess, you push her. Ramona! If you stand there like that..."

Tess's shove knocked Ramona flat on her butt, and the girls around the circle laughed.

"See," Jaylynn said, "if you're just standing there, unprepared, your attacker will always get the advantage over you. Try that again. One foot slightly in front, a wider stance...yes, that's it, Ramona." The tall girl stumbled a little bit when Tess smacked her on the chest, but she stayed on her feet, recovering well.

"Just standing around, knees locked, is a weak position. Balanced, with knees slightly bent, is a much better stance to come from." She gestured at the two girls. "I've embarrassed you two enough, and you can sit down. You, Elizabeth—and how about you, Lakeisha, come on up."

Two girls, evenly matched for size, stood. Lakeisha was a solid-looking Black girl with lots of cornrows in her hair. Elizabeth was long-legged and pale skinned with her blonde hair tied back in a ponytail. They grinned at one another, sheepish and awkward.

"Dez, show them a grab."

The big cop reached out a hand and grabbed at Jaylynn's left arm. The smaller cop twisted her arm and pulled away without difficulty.

"With a ready stance, you will be able to withstand a push and the same thing goes for a grab. If I am just standing here, knees locked, see how easy it is for someone bigger than me to get control of me?"

Dez reached out again, and this time when she grabbed Jaylynn's left arm, the smaller woman was jerked off balance. The tall cop grinned and for a brief moment her partner gave her a dirty look. Dez suppressed the grin and assumed her mask of indifference.

Jaylynn looked back at the girls sitting around the circle. "Balance is everything. If you lose your balance and end up on the ground, you can't run. You can't hit back. You're at a big disadvantage. Okay, show us, Elizabeth. Go ahead and grab Lakeisha's arm."

The girls went through the drill, both of them assuming strong stances.

"Don't worry about the actual releases from holds. We'll get to them later. For now, all we're going to concentrate on is making sure you get used to adopting a powerful stance whether you are being pushed or pulled. All of you, on your feet. Pair off, and I want you to each practice some controlled pushing and grabbing."

Dez and Jaylynn moved through the pairs of girls, giving encouragement and making sure the shoving didn't get too out of hand.

After a few minutes, Jaylynn blew a short blast on the whistle. "Okay, you've been taken by surprise, you assumed a strong stance to deal with a push or grab. What do you do next?"

In an unsure voice, Tess said, "Run?"

Jaylynn inclined her head slightly. "Yes, if you can, you are going to run, but along with your stance, there's another piece we want you to do." She looked around at all the expectant faces. "You want to shout out. Everyone take a deep breath." She put her fists at her abdomen. "Now, shout out 'No!'"

Half the group bellowed loudly, while the other half let out shy peeps.

"Girls, you can all do better than that. Someone has just entered your space, invaded your safety zone. You've been grabbed or pushed, and you're on alert now. As you go on alert, I want your automatic response to be to let your attacker know, very clearly, that you're setting a boundary. Most of you would rather die than make a scene, but that's what might scare off an attacker or bring help to you. You want the attacker to know that you won't stand for being manhandled."

She waved Dez toward her, and the tall cop advanced, a wicked grin on her face. The big cop grabbed the front of the smaller woman's shirt and moved her backwards. Jaylynn went into her power stance, shrugged the big hands off, and almost simultaneously shouted, "No!" with her voice coming out in a loud bark.

"It needs to come from your diaphragm, girls. Everybody face me and feel your abdomens. Okay, all together now, say 'No!'" The sound rang out in the gym, much louder than before. She looked around at the students. "That's better. Now couldn't you feel the tenseness in your middle when you shouted?" Most of the girls nodded. "Good, very good. Now then, let's pair up again and practice your stance and the shout."

Jaylynn was happy to see that all the girls took the drill seriously. Some of them were shy and needed coaxing and coaching, but all of them seemed to be trying. After a couple minutes she blew her whistle again. "Okay, everybody back to the mats, and go ahead and sit back down." While surveying her audience, she pointed at Dez who stood next to her, touching her on the shoulder. "Now what do we do if we get grabbed and we can't run?"

Someone in the audience said, "Deck 'em!"

Jaylynn turned toward the speaker. "But what if the person is way bigger and way stronger?"

A well-muscled, brown-haired girl said, "Sock 'em in the stomach, knock the wind out of them, and then run."

"Oh, I see," Jaylynn nodded as though this made total sense. She turned to Dez with an impish look on her face. "Go ahead, Dez." Under her breath she said, "And be ready."

Dez grabbed at her partner, catching hold of her forearm and jerking her forward. Jaylynn wound up and slammed a fist into Dez's middle. Nothing happened, except a quiet grunt from the taller cop. With both hands, Dez yanked the smaller woman toward her and lifted her off the ground onto her right shoulder. Jaylynn let her body go slack, and Dez set her down.

The brown-haired girl frowned. "You pulled the punch," she said in a scornful voice.

Jaylynn, still catching her breath, shook her head. "Oh, no. I didn't. Stand up, uh, Amber."

The brown-haired girl stood, unconvinced by the small cop's comments. She stood half a head taller than Jaylynn, but a good four inches shorter than Dez.

Jaylynn waved her over and gestured toward her partner. "Go ahead. Punch away."

Dez scrutinized the advancing brown-haired girl. With broad shoulders and lean muscles, she looked like an athlete, maybe a budding basketball player. The girl met her eyes, almost as if she was asking permission. Dez stood up tall and pointed at her own midsection with both her index fingers. "Fire away."

Amber pounced forward and delivered a powerful blow. Her fist made contact with the tall woman's abdomen and bounced back. The girl looked at her hand, surprised. She was even more surprised when her arm was grabbed, twisted behind her back, and she found herself facedown on the mat with a solid knee in her back. Almost as quickly as she hit the floor, she was released, and by the time she rolled over and got to her feet, she was looking up at the looming policewoman with respect.

Jaylynn said, "Self-defense is just that: defense. We're not going to focus on you attacking your assailant. We want to teach you how to defend yourself and get away with the least amount of harm done to you as possible. There's a lot to learn, but with practice, you can all learn ways to protect yourself." She glanced at her watch. "We're running out of time for today, but we'll be back twice a week to work on self-defense skills. We'll teach you how to get away if somebody grabs you. We'll teach you what to do if someone does strike you. You're all going to learn where to hit an attacker to disable him so you can get away. You'll all get to practice a lot." She stepped off the blue mat and strode over to the bleachers and picked up the manila envelope. "Next time, Dez and I are going to talk about the common characteristics and behavior of attackers and ways to be aware of possible bad situations before they happen." She pulled out a sheaf of papers, split it into two bunches, and sent one stack to the right and one to the left of the circle. "Everybody take this information and read it.

Come back on Thursday prepared to talk about it with us. It's not boring. It could save your life." She looked around the group. "Any questions?"

Tess spoke up. "Why can't we do this every day?"

Jaylynn smiled. "Twice a week until a couple weeks before Christmas. Dez and I have a job to do, too, you know."

Another girl named Yolanda spoke up. "Have either of you ever shot anybody?"

Dez shook her head. "We're here to teach you self-defense, kids, not talk about that sort of thing."

"That's right," Jaylynn said. "Okay, off to the locker room you go. We'll let Mr. Hawley know how you all did. See you Thursday."

Chapter
Five

Dez awakened. The light shining in Jaylynn's bedroom was bright, and she shut her eyes against the glare. With one arm she patted next to her. No Jaylynn. Now that was unusual. The rookie didn't usually wake up before her. She rolled to the outside of the bed and snagged her watch off the nightstand. 10:14. Unbelievable. She had slept over seven hours.

She rose and showered, and when she emerged from the bathroom, she smelled something good, like cinnamon, which made her stomach grumble and growl. The tall woman dressed quickly in jeans, tennis shoes, and a blue and white flannel shirt, then headed downstairs.

She moved through the living room and strode toward the kitchen, slowing when she heard Sara's voice.

"Oh yeah. Right there! Right there! Yes, yes! You've got it now."

Jaylynn murmured something Dez couldn't quite hear, then said, "Hold real still...good...good...this is great!"

Dez frowned. She slowly pushed open the swinging door to the kitchen and surveyed the scene before her. "What in the *hell* are you two doing?"

Jaylynn straightened up abruptly and turned to face her. Dressed in jeans, tennies, and a sweatshirt, she brandished a long skinny knife. Sara sat next to the kitchen table in one of the rickety chairs, one forearm on the table, holding a metal bar out in both fists.

With a big grin, Jaylynn moved next to Dez, put an arm around her waist, and pressed her face into the tall woman's chest. She pulled away a little, and with her other hand, held up a black-handled knife. "This is so cool. Sara ordered this knife from the

Home Shopping Network. It's supposed to cut through anything, even metal."

Sara held out the metal dowel. "Look! It's working. We've got it going."

Dez nodded, holding back a laugh. "I see." She pressed her lips together to keep the smile back and gave Jaylynn a one-armed hug. "So you two are down here sawing metal rods in half instead of getting things ready for Bill's party?"

Jaylynn gazed up at her. "Why do I get the distinct feeling that you're not impressed with our handiwork with the Aikuchi All-Purpose Utility Knife?" She picked up a heavy-duty cardboard sleeve that read *CAUTION: EXTREMELY SHARP* on the side and turned it over. The print on the other side was too small for Dez to read from the distance. "Now this, Dez, was a real buy. Listen up. It says it is guaranteed to stay sharp for ten years, cut through anything but diamonds, and assist its owner in kitchen, shed, stable, or garage. A *fine* acquisition for our household, if you ask me."

Dez reached an arm out, palm up, and Sara placed the piece of metal in her hand. She extricated herself from Jaylynn and turned the bar over and examined it. Though it was a good fifteen inches long, it was perhaps only three-eighths of an inch thick. In the middle were two faint markings, then one deeper slice where the two women had obviously sawed successfully. She hefted it in her hand, feeling its cool solidness, then paused for a moment as a scrap of memory, a tiny snippet of a dream, clicked in her mind—then disappeared. The grin she was holding back evaporated, and she felt her hands go cold. Pushing down the burgeoning feeling of panic, she quickly handed the rod back to Sara before her hands started to shake. In a gruff voice she said, "Do you realize that knife could slip? One of you could get hurt."

Jaylynn hit her with a soft jab to the upper arm. "Quit being a worrywart. We were very careful."

Dez frowned. "What are you going to do with it when you cut it in half—and what's it from anyway?"

Sara set it on the table and shrugged. "We just wanted to test it out on something. I found this lying in the garage. There are some others in there, so I didn't think anyone would miss it. I have no idea what it is. Do you?"

Dez shook her head, trying not to notice that Jaylynn was studying her intently. She took a deep breath and turned to the shorter woman. "When do you want Luella over to help?"

The hazel green eyes softened and stopped their examination. "Anytime. Anytime is fine. Is Vanita coming too?"

"No, she's got something going today—but she'll be at the party."

Sara nodded. "Good. That'll be a kick."

Jaylynn asked, "Maybe Luella would like to come over for lunch?"

Sara took the sheath from Jaylynn. "Yeah, we can certainly make lunch for her. We don't want to wear her out or take advantage of her."

"Are you kidding?" Dez asked. "She's probably standing at the back door even as we speak with her purse over her arm waiting for me."

Jaylynn laughed and handed the knife over to Sara.

The tall woman lowered herself into one of the other rickety vinyl covered chairs and leaned her flannel-clad arms on the table. "Before I go get her, can I have a snack? What smells good?"

"That'd be Jay's world-famous cinnamon sugar toast." In a conspiratorial voice, Sara added, "Heavy emphasis on the sugar ingredient."

"Hey!" Jaylynn said as she opened a bag of bread. "You certainly weren't complaining earlier when I served you up the tasty delicacies I so carefully created."

"Yeah, yeah, yeah." The brown-eyed woman gazed at her best friend with affection. "I don't have the high standards that Dez does. I don't mind scarfing down lots of sweet glucose, but if I recall correctly, *she's* not big on straight sugar."

"I'll make an exception this morning. Lay it on me, Jay."

The rookie popped two pieces of bread in the toaster and leaned back against the counter, her arms crossed over her tan and green flannel shirt. "Let's get the timeline down here. Bill will arrive at the military airport tonight—sometime—and you'll get him and bring him back as soon as you can. Then you guys will spend the following 24 hours—pretty much all of Friday—in bed—"

"Jay!" Sara said. She glanced over at Dez and blushed.

The toast popped up and Jaylynn turned her back on the two at the table to butter it at the counter. Over her shoulder, she said, "It's not like Dez wouldn't understand, hon. If we'd been apart for eighteen months, believe me, we'd be spending *at least* 24 hours in bed."

"Well, *hon*," Sara said, "he and I will be spending as much time as possible together—alone—through tomorrow. But Saturday night we'll fill the house with whoever wants to show up to welcome him home."

"Provided, of course," Dez said in a dry voice, "that the two of you have emerged from cocooning."

Sara looked back and forth between the two of them and slowly shook her head. "What is it with you two? Sex, sex, sex—that's all you have on your minds these days."

Jaylynn turned and presented Dez with a plate containing two slices of warm toast covered completely with a thick layer of melting butter and cinnamon sugar. "That's not the only thing on our minds. We think about food, too. Besides, cocooning is *not* all about sex." She stood over the two women, one hand on each shoulder and smiled.

Dez picked up a slice of toast and sunk her teeth into it. Sara was right. Sugar was, truly, the main ingredient. It was sweeter than Dez preferred, but still good nonetheless. Munching away, she glanced up into the hazel eyes above her and felt herself immediately bathed in warmth and light. Her stomach fluttered—and she realized it wasn't from hunger. *So this is love. How totally utterly completely*—her mind blanked for a moment as it searched for the right word—*frightening.* How would she live without this, without Jaylynn, if something were ever to happen to her? The toast stuck in her throat and she swallowed with difficulty.

Jaylynn dropped her hands from the two women's shoulders and moved to the fridge, asking, "You want some milk or orange juice, Dez? Something to wash down the dry toast?"

"Just a shot of milk—but you don't have to wait on me, Jay."

"I know that. But I'm up." She opened the fridge door. "And I like to wait on you." She placed a short glass of milk on the table, catching Sara rolling her eyes. "Oh, yeah, sure. You go ahead and laugh now, my friend, but I'll have the last laugh tomorrow when you're down here whipping up snacks to fortify Billy Boy!"

Sara rose. "We'll see about that. Seems to me that you two clowns laze about in bed most of the day yourselves, and with all the party prep, I don't think you'll have a lot of time to make fun of me."

"I'll work on it though," Jaylynn said.

Dez rose, too, and started to clear the plate and glass, but Sara snapped them up first. "Don't worry about these. You go get Luella, and Jay and I will start pulling things together here."

"After I get her," Dez asked, "what do you want *me* to do?"

Sara said, "We've got quite the shopping list. If you and Jay don't mind, I'll work on the lasagna while you two go off to the grocery store for more tasty vittles."

"Fine with me," Jaylynn said, looking up at Dez to find her nodding, too. "I'm going down into the dungeon to get how many pounds of burger?"

Sara closed one eye, squinted, and looked up toward the ceiling. "Hmmm...three huge pans of lasagna...let's do...four pounds—no, five pounds. All those big, tough Army types will want lots of protein."

Jaylynn cut past Dez and looked back at her from the fridge, then gestured with a quick jerk of the head. Dez ambled around the corner to the basement door and followed the rookie down the poorly lit stairs. As they reached the bottom, she asked, "Need some protection in the scary basement, Little Lady?"

"No. Just wanted one last passionate hug and kiss before the house is overrun for the day." Jaylynn wrapped her arms around the taller woman and pressed her face into the warm flannel. Dez cradled her, snug against her midsection, feeling a string of emotions: tenderness, protectiveness, helplessness, love. When her partner tipped her head back, Dez brought up her right palm and touched the soft cheek gently. She leaned down, closed her eyes, and met soft lips—lips she thought she would now know under any circumstances, anytime, anywhere. The hold around her middle tightened as the kiss deepened, and when they came up for air, Jaylynn whispered, "I love the way you kiss me. You are by far the best at it of anyone I've ever known."

Dez grinned sheepishly, repeating something the rookie had said to her before they had made love for the first time. "And that would be what—a cast of thousands?"

Even in the dim light, she could see Jaylynn start to blush. "I can't believe I said that."

"I thought it was a pretty cute way of asking, actually."

"You did? How come you didn't ask me how many other relationships *I'd* had?" She let her hands slide from Dez's waist to the slim hips and pulled her snug against her.

"Figured I'd get around to it sooner or later."

"Well? Is it sooner or later now?"

Dez raised an eyebrow. "You can tell me now if you like—or not. Your choice."

Jaylynn paused for a moment, then said, "Third time's a charm. That's how I look at it."

Dez nodded, then leaned down and nuzzled into Jaylynn's neck. Dez thought she smelled wonderful, like sugar and spice and everything nice—actually, like cinnamon toast. She smiled to herself as she tucked the blonde head under her chin. From her vantage point, she surveyed the basement. The ceiling was low, only about a foot above her head. It was dark and cramped, but tidy, with mismatched wall-to-wall shelving on two long walls and the furnace and water heater taking up a whole quarter of the room. For such a small area, there was a lot of stuff stacked around. "I didn't realize this was so small. You'd think it would be as big as the whole house."

Jaylynn looked over her shoulder. "Yeah, it's small, but it works for us. It didn't take on a drop of water during that last big storm, so it's a really sound basement."

Dez reluctantly loosened her hold on the rookie and stood waiting at the foot of the stairs. The freezer was around the side of the stairs beyond boxes stacked four deep, which Jaylynn had to sidle past. She opened the lid of the chest freezer and a faint light shone up.

"Geez!" Dez said. "That thing is huge."

"We joke that you could easily put a body or two in there and still have room for the ice cream and frozen foods."

"How did they even get it down here?"

Jaylynn cradled five packages in her left arm as she pressed the lid shut. "I have no idea. You'd think they would have had to build the house around this monstrosity. The doorway and stairs are wide enough for it, so they must have stood it on end and bounced it down."

Dez turned and looked up the stairs, gauging the dimensions. She thought Jaylynn was right, though the steep steps must have been a bear to navigate.

Jaylynn brushed past her and took two steps up, then turned around, a grin on her face. "This is one of the few times I can be taller than you."

"But too far away." The tall woman took one stair up, which put her only a couple inches below the rookie, but able to pull her close and encircle her with strong arms.

"Hey! This hamburger is cold." Jaylynn held the five pounds along her forearms and pressed up against her chest.

In a hoarse whisper, Dez said, "I'll warm you up," then kissed her again.

"Ex-cuuuuse me," a voice said from the top of the stairs. "If I'd known it would take you two lovebirds half an hour to bring up the freezer goods, I'd have asked you to clean the basement, too."

Dez choked back a laugh and smacked Jaylynn lightly on the butt. "Up we go."

Jaylynn spun around and mounted the stairs, shaking her head and complaining to Sara about the complete and total lack of privacy. Dez followed, still feeling the race of her pulse as well as the Jaylynn-generated heat against the cool of the basement. It occurred to her that everything that had happened with the younger woman in the last several weeks was enough to make her head spin.

She told the two roommates that she'd be back shortly with Luella, then headed over in her truck, still feeling the effects of holding her favorite blonde woman. They had not been apart, not even for one night, for the last seven-plus weeks. As far as she was concerned, things could stay exactly that way forever. In fact, sometimes she felt like she had known Jaylynn forever. She had never in her whole life felt so close or so comfortable with any-one—not even her mother, brother, or father. Sometimes she felt a connection that seemed ages old and that went soul deep. She couldn't quite explain it, not to herself, and certainly not to Jay-lynn. *She said she loved kissing me. But she hasn't come right out and said she loves me. Of course, neither have I, and I proba-bly should. I want to.*

She wished she could say the words, had rehearsed them in her head in a number of situations, but so far, it didn't seem the opportunity had presented itself. It bothered her that she felt this sense of alarm and apprehension. *I can't imagine being without her—correction: I actually* can *imagine being without her, and I never want it to happen. How did I ever survive before she came along?*

It was a puzzle to her, and one that was troubling. It was just as well that she arrived at the duplex to get her landlady just then, because it was clear she was making herself awfully nervous.

****

"I can't wait for Bill to see you and Dez together," Sara said. Chewing on the eraser end of a pencil, she leaned over a list lying on the table in the nook corner of the kitchen. She named off ingredients while Jaylynn scurried around pulling spices and noo-dles and cans of sauce out of various cupboards.

"I can't wait to see you and Bill together, either. I know you've been waiting and waiting. And really, Sara, I don't know how you've done it. Eighteen months. I'd just die without Dez for eighteen months."

The brown-eyed woman laughed. "You would not. You were perfectly self-sufficient without her, just as you are now with her. You'd get by just fine." She picked up a container of oregano. "Is this enough for a triple batch?"

Jaylynn stood next to her, shoulder to shoulder, as they both examined the contents of the plastic container. "I think so. But that's the nice thing about spices. If you have enough just to give the flavor, it works out. We'll throw other stuff in, maybe chili powder or something. It's kind of fun when every batch ends up tasting a little different."

"We got any basil leaves?"

"Tons. Don't fret." She scooted around the other side of the table and sat in one of the wobbly orange and red vinyl chairs. "Wow, eighteen months is a terribly long time. It's going to be bad enough that I have to go off to driver training in Michigan for four days. I'll miss her a lot."

"But homecomings are so much fun."

"Yeah—but lots more fun when they're after four days. Eighteen months would be a real killer!" Sara nodded at her thoughtfully. "Are you worried, Sara? Do you feel you've changed much—and has he?"

The brown-eyed woman slid into the chair nearest to her and across from Jaylynn. She put her elbow on the table and chin in one hand. "Yes and no. Bad things have happened to both of us. I was nearly raped, and he got beat up in that German tavern last year. Maybe it's easier for guys though. It wasn't like anyone was trying to rape him."

Jaylynn nodded. "Sad to say, guys are a lot more used to fighting and violence. It's really a shame. None of us should have to feel that terror or anger or fear. It really sucks."

"Sucks, huh? What a way with words you have."

"Thanks. I done learnt it all in college." Jaylynn grinned.

"So you would worry if you and Dez were apart for a long period?"

Jaylynn's face took on a thoughtful look as she considered the question. "I'd just be so damn lonely for her. I read some stuff in my psych class that talked about how, when you love someone, you share more than just good feelings. You also share all kinds of pheromones and hormones and chemicals, and you get used to that. You get used to a certain level of daily interaction, and you get so accustomed to the hormonal exchange that when the other person goes away, you can't help but feel homesick for them, physically *and* emotionally. You get something along the lines of the DT's—it's almost like drying out from drugs or alcohol. Isn't that something? Scientists are only just beginning to understand some of it."

"No wonder battered wives stay with the batterer."

"Could be a piece of it."

They gazed out the nook window at the sunny October day. The fall had been so mild that there were still birds to be seen in the black walnut in the middle of the yard and in the maple trees along the side yard.

The brown-eyed woman said, "I am afraid—a little bit any-way. What if he comes home, after having traveled all of Europe, seeing the Mona Lisa and the Louvre and the Sistine Chapel and Stonehenge and all those famous places, and I'm no longer enough for him?"

Jaylynn nodded. "I don't think that will happen. I *hope* it won't happen, but I can understand why you'd feel that way."

"Don't get me wrong. I am more excited than worried, that's for sure. But every once in a while a little kernel of doubt inches its way in."

"You both have a lot in common, and he left crazy about you, Sara." This caused her friend to smile a little. "He was more than crazy. I've never seen an Army man cry—"

"And you weren't supposed to notice! Don't you *ever* mention it to him," Sara said, admonishing her.

Jaylynn put her thumb and forefinger up to the side of her mouth and drew them across her lips, then pretended to toss something over her shoulder. "My lips are sealed. I'll never tell. But I have to say, that was one of the sweetest things I've ever seen...almost sweet enough for me to consider liking a guy."

In mock horror, Sara said, "No way! I can see it now, he comes home and *you* try to steal *my* boyfriend!"

They both burst into laughter, and simultaneously said, "Bloody unlikely!"

Clump, clump, clump. They heard steps on the back porch, and Sara leaned back to look out the window behind her. The door opened, and in came Tim and Kevin, faces ruddy from bik-ing.

The brown-haired woman stood, crossed her arms, and tapped her foot on the floor. "About time you two showed up. We've been slaving away!"

Tim gave her a long look starting at her feet and slowly travel-ing up her shapely figure. In his best drag queen voice, he said, "Well, hey, honey, a fella's got to get a little exercise at times." He ran his hand through his red hair as Kevin nudged him out of the way to shut the back door.

The handsome blond-haired man rolled his eyes. "Don't give him a moment's notice. We got halfway around Como Lake and ended up freezing our butts off on a bench watching the Canada geese packing up to fly south for the winter."

Tim pinched Kevin on the butt and made him jump. "Shhhh, boyfriend. Don't tell these ungrateful girls *all* our little secrets." Turning to Sara and Jaylynn, he said, "We'll just go get out of these terribly unattractive biking shorts and be down directly. The supreme chef and his unerringly tasteful lover will be right back to dazzle you with our *fabulous* concoctions." He swished over to the swinging door, smacked it open, and disappeared.

Both women burst into laughter.

Kevin rolled his eyes again. "He's been like this all morning—in fact, he's been insufferable ever since last week when he found out he got into chef school."

Jaylynn composed herself and said, "We'll put him in charge of something like the salad. That'll keep him busy chopping and shredding and dicing and arranging and crying over onions."

"Fine with me. All right. I'll be back in a few minutes." He turned, then stopped. "Say, where's Tall, Dark and Deadly?"

Jaylynn's face split with a grin. "She went to pick up Luella."

"Luella's coming over? Yes!" He made a pumping motion with his arm. "That's just great." He headed out of the kitchen, leaving the swinging door whapping back and forth behind him.

Sara looked at Jaylynn. "Why do these guys like Luella so much?"

Jaylynn shrugged. "I don't know. Well, actually, *everybody* loves Luella. Maybe gay guys are the only ones who are confident enough to gush about it. Maybe it's because she's so accepting. She truly sees the good in everyone, even thoroughly rotten people. And she has such a way of bringing out the best in the people she knows."

Sara stepped over and put an arm across her friend's shoulders. "Just like you, Jay. That's an accurate description of you."

Jaylynn blushed. "Oh, get outta here."

"It's true. As usual, I'm right." Sara smiled at her blushing friend. "Now, let's open the tomato paste and sauté some tomatoes. We've got a lot of work ahead of us."

****

Dez pulled up in front of the neat, two-story stucco house, not bothering to go around back. Sure enough, she saw the curtains in the front porch open, and a silver head peeked through for just an instant. Dez counted to five before the door opened, and Luella emerged, turned and locked the door, and came down the walk carrying a hefty-sized black leather handbag with a bright smile on her face.

Luella Williams was 75 years young, going on 16, but at the most, she looked 60. An elegant Black woman, she had silver hair swept up on either side of her head and held in place with fine silver combs. She and her sister Vanita were all that was left of their generation, but Vanita had a thriving brood of children, grandchildren, and great-grandchildren. Ever since Luella's husband and two sons had died in a tragic house fire in the Sixties, she had taken her nieces and nephews under her wing as well as a lot of other misfits and odd ducks. Dez thought that she herself was one of the latter.

Dez got out of the truck and met Luella at the passenger door. The deep, mahogany-colored eyes sought her out. "So, Desiree, what's shakin'?"

"Not much." She gave the older woman her arm and helped her up into the Ford truck.

"I swear," Luella said, as she settled into the seat, "this truck keeps growing taller every time I'm not looking."

Dez grabbed the retractable seatbelt, and handed it to the silver-haired woman, then slammed the door and went around to get in the driver's side. She put it in drive and started off down Como Boulevard.

Luella reached across the cab and patted Dez on the arm. "Please tell me I haven't missed anything good."

"Nope. Not unless you count using some sort of all-purpose utility knife to saw metal in half."

"Hmm. Doesn't sound particularly appetizing...no, not at all. Whose idea was that?"

"You should just ask. Okay?" With a devilish look in her eye, Dez zipped around the block and headed back to the other house. "Why don't you see if they'll let you make the metal rod dessert? Just ask about that, okay?"

Luella gave her a strange look, then turned her eyes back to the road.

****

It was a madhouse in the kitchen. Luella was camped out at the kitchen table between Tim and Kevin, all three shelling walnuts and talking in excited tones. Every few words were punctuated with a solid *thwack* as Kevin cracked the walnuts on a cutting board. Tim and Luella picked out the meats and dropped them into a bowl. Periodically Luella collected up the shards of shells and tossed them into a brown paper bag on the floor.

Jaylynn and Sara stood next to the stove arguing about whether to lace the pot of lasagna sauce with chili powder. The rookie was in favor of jazzing it up, while Sara was concerned that it would be too strong.

Dez stood off to the side, a cookbook on the counter in front of her. She was searching for a good recipe for walnut cake. Out of the corner of her eye, she watched the group and listened to the squabbles and conversations.

She knew she wasn't in a dream, but sometimes things felt a little unreal. She wondered how she got so lucky to be associated with these people. They were a bit unusual; and yet, they seemed completely normal, too. They appeared to accept her and like her just fine, exactly as she was, and it had been that way immediately upon meeting all of them. That puzzled her. She had built the relationship with Luella over time, revealing a little bit of herself every so often until now the older woman knew her better than anyone on the planet, perhaps even Jaylynn. The trust to do that had taken a great deal of time, a number of years. Luella had never been pushy, though. As a matter of fact, she was so warm and patient that Dez had always felt comfortable with the slow pace of their friendship.

Jaylynn was a whole other story. She was like a whirlwind of movement and emotions, yet she was also gentle and serene. Whip-smart and at the same time, still a little naïve. Passionate, self-assured, curious, and funny. Dez had never met anyone like her before.

Paradox. That's the word that came to Dez's mind to describe her young partner. How could she have developed so much personality at such a young age? Jaylynn turned 25 in August, and in some ways, Dez thought the blonde bundle of energy was older and wiser than she, at the ripe old age of nearly 30. No matter how she thought about it, the tall woman couldn't quite get her mind around her own good fortune. How had she been so lucky to have the laughing woman like her so much—maybe even love her?

Over the din of the voices, the stove fan, and the kitchen radio, which was currently playing Sara MacLachlan's song, "Your Love is Better Than Ice Cream," Dez heard Luella holler, "Hey Jaylynn! We're done with these nuts now. You want us to start in on the steel rod dessert?"

Both Sara and Jaylynn paused in their good-natured bickering and simultaneously asked, "What?"

Luella's white teeth flashed, and she looked positively mischievous. Tim and Kevin, sitting on either side of her, glanced over at the girls and back to the older woman. Tim said, "Never heard of such a thing. What are the ingredients?"

Luella gazed at the two roommates, pausing for a couple seconds. "Well? You going to enlighten us?"

Jaylynn turned around and squinted at Dez, obviously suppressing a grin. "*You* must be carrying tales again, Miss Big Mouth Cop."

Dez held her hands out to either side of her, palms up. "Just thought you might like to share your cutlery technique with Tim, especially now that he's in chef training."

"Look," Tim said in a dry voice, "if you're going to make Ginsu knife jokes, you can forget about it. I'm partial to Wusthof Cutlery."

Jaylynn spun around to meet the brown-haired woman's amused eyes. Sara said, "Obviously we're going to be mocked, Jay. We should just ignore them."

Kevin waved a hand. "Wait a minute! I never did any mocking. What is this special dessert?"

So Sara and Jaylynn got out the Aikuchi All-Purpose Utility Knife and explained all of its fine features as Dez checked the cupboards for brown sugar. She opened the doors to all four cupboards and left them open, fumbling around inside until she found a bag containing no more than two tablespoons of dried up brown crystals. She tossed the bag toward the kitchen garbage and added brown sugar to her ever-expanding grocery list. She was glad she had thought to case the cupboards ahead of time, and even so, she was still not sure whether she would end up having to make two trips to the store as they discovered more items they needed.

She wondered how Tim, Kevin, Sara, and Jaylynn could live together without killing one another. Their kitchen cupboards were in a shambles, and since none of them were over five feet eight inches tall, they obviously never used the top shelves, which were stuffed full of mismatched Tupperware pieces, old pie tins, and a multitude of plastic butter tubs. Pretty much everything on the top shelves seemed to have been pitched up there just before the door was quickly closed. She moved some items, rearranged the cereal, and nested all of the plastic-ware together. If she lived here, the kitchen alone would drive her crazy. The thought struck her that she practically *did* live there. She hadn't slept in her own bed at the apartment more than once or twice in the last couple weeks. Her tiny three-room place was now serving as nothing more than a glorified closet to which she went only when she had to get clean clothes or Luella needed help with something.

She and Jaylynn had not discussed being apart nights since a couple weeks earlier when the tall cop decided to go home after Third Watch. Jaylynn was supposed to get up very early for a one-day Saturday writing class she was taking. Dez told her she should be rested and insisted on sleeping at her own place so that they wouldn't stay up all night talking and making love. So the tall woman had gone home, turned on all the lights in her tiny apartment, and sat on the couch. Picking up her acoustic guitar, she played a few chords, lost interest, and set the golden colored instrument back on the stand. She couldn't help it. She felt restless and inexplicably lonely.

She lasted all of twenty minutes. Just when she was ready to give up and go get in the truck to drive over and confess her weakness, the phone rang, and it was Jaylynn telling her she missed her too much and to please come over right away. Pride intact, she threw some clean clothes in a duffel bag and arrived, breathless, at the house on the boulevard in less than ten minutes.

Since then, it had been a given that they would spend nights sleeping together, even if they didn't ride together that day or if their schedules were off in some way. Jaylynn gave her keys to both doors, and that was that.

But now, in a few hours, Bill would arrive, and there would then be six twenty-somethings living in the three-story house. Kevin and Tim were comfortable in the sizable third level attic. Dez and Jaylynn were managing just fine in Sara's old room. But Bill and Sara were going to be quite cramped in the remaining bedroom on the second floor. No one had addressed this issue, and Dez wondered how to go about bringing it up. Maybe she should talk to Jaylynn about moving into her apartment above Luella's place—but then again, that was awfully small, too. Maybe they should get their own place. *But then I'd have to leave Luella. I don't want to do that.*

It was a quandary.

Dez had never lived with anyone, not since leaving her childhood home, that is. Even in college she had her own dorm room all to herself. Only once had she ever considered moving in with someone, but she had been young and innocent at the time, fresh out of the Police Academy. She hadn't been careful with her heart and had fallen in love with someone who turned out to be a user. The woman, another cop, had trifled with her, seduced her, played mind games, then had thrown Dez away once the younger woman grew attached. It had been tremendously painful, and Dez had sworn never ever to get involved with a fellow officer again. She hadn't counted on Jaylynn though.

So lost in thought was she that it took a moment before she realized the din of conversation had ceased. The stove fan still hummed and the radio played a Sheryl Crow song. She glanced back over her shoulder to find five pairs of eyes staring her way. "What?"

Jaylynn moved away from the stove and put an arm around Dez's waist. "You don't have to do that—"

"But it sure looks ship-shape," Tim hollered across the kitchen.

Dez let her eyes focus on the four open cupboards. She hadn't intended to rearrange things so entirely, but it seemed that she had. And now there was open space in nearly a third of the lower shelves. The kitchen garbage can was overflowing with boxes and bags that contained little or nothing. "I-I...well, I hope you don't mind."

"No," Jay said, admiring the shelves. "They look much better. Thanks. I think we're ready to go for more groceries now. We've certainly got room for them!" She looked at her watch. "Only got a few hours 'til we have to go in to work, so we better get a move on." Turning, she announced, "Any last requests? Speak now or forever hold your peace."

"Nilla wafers," Tim said.

Sara looked around the big woman's arm at the list. "Did you write down teriyaki sauce and brown rice?"

Dez perused the list and nodded when she found them.

Jaylynn peered over at Luella who was sharing a quiet conversation with Kevin. "Luella, you want any special delicacies?"

"Nope. I could use something now to wet my whistle though."

Sara opened the fridge door. "Lemonade, orange juice, canned ice tea, milk—both two percent and skim—Coke, Diet Coke, 7-Up, Gatorade, or Hawaiian Fruit Punch?"

The silver-haired woman paused. "I do believe that the punch would suit me fine."

"If that's it, then we're gone," Jaylynn said.

Dez picked up the grocery list and tucked it in the pocket of her plaid shirt along with the pen. She felt a warm pressure on her hand and looked down to find Jaylynn's hand in hers, pulling her toward the swinging door. Glancing back over her shoulder she found Luella's eyes on her, amusement spreading across the smiling face. With one last backward glance, she shrugged, then let herself be drawn out of the kitchen, through the living room, and out the front door.

Chapter
Six

Dez felt more lighthearted than usual as she dressed in the locker room at the precinct. *Nothing like a little sleep to perk me up.* And she'd had a great time shopping with Jaylynn and getting things ready for the party with Sara, Luella, and the boys. She thought that the homecoming celebration for Bill on Saturday was going to be fun, even if she wasn't much for parties. As long as Jaylynn was there, Dez knew she would enjoy herself.

She grabbed her water bottle and headed up to roll call. No one else was in the briefing room, so she dialed the main precinct from the house phone and asked for Tsorro or Parkins. When told they were out on a call, she declined to leave a message. She was curious about the Tivoli investigation, but not enough to bother them with a message.

She heard someone coming down the hall. When she turned and sat, a figure rounded the corner and entered the room.

"Yo! Dez, baby. What's hap'nin'?"

Few officers could get away with calling her "baby," but she made many exceptions for Crystal Lopez. The Latina woman had eighteen years of experience and had worked with Dez since she joined the force nearly ten years earlier. Crystal had never let the younger cop down and had been an especially loyal friend in the months after Ryan had been shot and killed in the line of duty. She was shorter and much stockier than Dez, but very nearly as wide-shouldered. Her short-cropped hair was jet-black without a speck of gray in it, despite the fact that her fortieth birthday was coming up after the New Year. The tall cop liked to tease Crystal sometimes about "robbing the cradle" because her girlfriend, Shayna, was closer in age to Dez. She also liked to taunt her every once in a while about always being late. And Shayna was even worse. The two of them couldn't ever get anywhere on time. Dez had given up on them ever arriving at the appointed time set and usually lied about start times, moving them up at least half an hour.

"Nothing's happening, Crystal. What are you doing here so early?"

"FTO feedback to the sergeant." As she moved toward Dez, she ticked off names on her fingers. "I've had Oster, Mahoney, Pike, Neilsen, Grainger, and that new transfer from Houston. Oh, and also Jaylynn." She sighed. "Seven oral reports to give."

"You've *had* all of them, huh?"

Crystal smacked the big cop in the upper arm, hard, then sat in a chair next to her. "You know what I mean, *chica*. Supervisors are always looking for information on the probationers, and I've ridden with a variety. I still can't believe that asshole, Neilsen, is probably gonna make it. I had a talk with Alvarez, but he says you can't kick someone off the force for being an ass. Alvarez says Neilsen's patrol work is proficient."

Dez shook her head and closed her eyes. Dwayne Neilsen, the rookie jerk from Jaylynn's Academy class, had been nothing by rude to both of them. Sexist, racist, and homophobic—he was a throwback to the old days. If she didn't know better, she would have thought he had joined the force in the Fifties. She knew cops who had thirty and forty years in who were more open-minded than that twenty-two-year-old bigot. He was one of her least favorite people on the force, especially because of the disrespectful way he treated Jaylynn. She changed the subject. "How's Shayna?"

"Real good." She stretched out her short legs, crossing them at the ankle. "They just made her manager at the store. She's got more bookwork and does the staff schedules now. She doesn't like worrying about whether everyone's going to show up or not, but she got a two dollar an hour raise, so that's a little bit of incentive."

The noise level increased out in the hall, and officers began to trickle into the roll call room. Braswell, one of the old dinosaurs who Neilsen made look halfway decent, wandered in carrying a giant slab of fudge. Calvin Braswell had a prodigious potbelly hanging out over his duty belt. He looked like he hadn't washed his sandy-colored hair for a couple days, and his 70's "porkchop" sideburns puffed out far enough to indicate to her that it was time for a serious trim. Another officer walked up to him and said, "Jesus, Cal, like you need that big ol' piece of fudge!"

Braswell grinned and wolfed down a huge bite. "You're just

jealous." He gave a little salute toward the two women, then found a seat a few chairs ahead of them.

Crystal and Dez exchanged a smile. Braswell was an okay guy, but nobody ever wanted to ride with him. He was lazy, preferring to sit in a café or coffee shop and wait to be dispatched to a scene. He couldn't run a block—with or without fudge—and all he wanted to talk about was football. But he wasn't nearly as boring as some of the other old-timers. Trenton, Steussel, and Franklin were all dull and bland. On the other hand, Reed, a gray-haired Black man who had over thirty years in was full of stories about things that had happened in the past. He even remembered the old days when Dez's father was still alive and arresting bad guys. So *all* the old-timers weren't too bad. And all of them were vastly better than some of the younger guys like Barstow, who thought he was God's gift to women, or Neilsen who Dez felt was God's punishment to all of them.

Another day with this happy little family of wackos. Dez bit back a smile. These sisters and brothers in blue *were* like family sometimes. They gossiped and worried about each other, backed each other up, and carried on feuds just like any family. Some didn't get along, but some of them were people you'd want to know for life. Like Crystal. And Cowboy. Like Ryan had been.

A feeling of sadness washed over her. It was the same emotion she always felt when she thought of Ryan. Thirty-eight was too young to die. She thought about his wife, Julie, and the two kids, Jeremy and Jill. She hadn't seen them for a while. That was still hard. The grief threatened to well up and spill over whenever she was in their presence. But maybe after Sara and Bill's party, she would call Julie and ask to take the kids somewhere. And she ought to start thinking about holiday presents for them...but later. She put it out of her mind in haste.

An energetic, blonde-headed dynamo whisked into the room, and Dez's gaze was drawn to her, soaking in the intensity of her presence. All of the veteran cop's past griefs had been made bearable because of this smiling being. It was a wonder that everyone in the room didn't sense the energy that so often passed back and forth between the two of them. She felt the heat rise up her neck to her ears, and she grabbed up her water bottle from the floor and drank from it, hoping that no one noticed her red face. Jaylynn flounced over and sat next to Crystal, two seats away from Dez, which was just as well. If she had sat beside the tall cop, Dez might not have been able to recover her balance as quickly as she did. And it was a good thing that she regained her emotional equilibrium because the duty sergeant stalked into the room to update them about the latest crimes and stolen cars to watch out for. In short order, he sent them out to their cars to begin the shift.

****

The air was cold outside, and Jaylynn was glad to be riding for once in a squad car with a decent heater. Once the sun had gone down four hours earlier, the air took on quite a chill. Like the last few nights, it had been a quiet shift, and she had stayed warm for all of it. Dez was driving to allow her the chance to finish off a hamburger, and now she felt slightly over-full as she looked out on the deserted streets of the Frogtown area.

She couldn't believe how time was flying. Already it was marching on toward the end of October. Any day now, the sunny weather could change from the balmy 40's and 50's to below freezing. As usual, she was not looking forward to it. For the past six years, every winter she wondered why she hadn't yet moved to a warmer state.

The rookie drained the last of a bottle of warm Pepsi and stuck the plastic container in a paper bag under her feet. "You know what, Dez?" The dark-haired cop glanced her way, arching an eyebrow in answer. "We sure aren't eating very well lately. I swear I've gained five pounds."

Shaking her head, Dez growled, "Tell me about it."

"We need to spend a little more time in the gym, I think."

"We need to spend a little less time at the pig trough, Jay."

The rookie laughed out loud. "I always liked your plan of eating five or six times a day—but I suppose you didn't intend for pizza and fried chicken and Taco Bell burritos to be on the list."

"Nope."

"What are we going to do about this?"

"You mean before we're as big as that poor woman in *What's Eating Gilbert Grape*?"

"Yeah. Way before that."

Before Dez could answer, Dispatch came over the radio to report a fire.

"That's right down the street there! Look, Dez! You can see the smoke. We should have noticed."

Dez was already wheeling to the right as Jaylynn responded to Dispatch. Dez didn't even bother to turn the siren on, though she did flip on the lights. They pulled up in front of a two-story stucco house, and in seconds they were both out of the car and up on the lawn, flashlights out. Dez ran up the cement stairway and beat on the front door. She called out, "Police!" but no one came.

She tried the front door. It was locked and the metal knob was hot. She pulled her hand back with a yelp, then turned and ran down the stairs. "Circle the place, Jay. Look to see if anyone's home. Watch for open doors and windows." She started to back away, pointing as she moved. "If you see anything unusual— footprints in the flower beds, tools, gas cans, bomb parts, whatever—take note. Don't touch anything. I'll meet you around back and compare notes."

Dez took off to the right at a fast clip, using her flashlight to survey the house and surroundings. Jaylynn trotted to the left, sweeping her heavy-duty light across the porch. Beyond the porch railing she could see in the front window, and something in the background glowed a dull red. She moved to the side of the house checking out the windows in the upper and lower story, examining the flowerbed alongside the house. Of the three double casement windows along the top story, only the middle one, near the front of the house, was open. She could see wisps of smoke coming out of the window and floating upwards. The air smelled acrid, like burning plastic.

Otherwise, nothing looked out of the ordinary. She ran to the back of the house and met Dez, just as the bigger woman climbed up the back stairs and tried the rear door. She beat on it with her flashlight. It, too, was locked, though not hot like the front knob. She stood on her toes and looked through a tiny window in the upper part of the door. "Dammit! I can see flames coming toward the kitchen now, too." She turned and hurtled down the wooden stairs. "You see anything?"

Jaylynn shook her head. "Just one open window, upper west side.

Dez touched her shoulder mic. "Two-Five Boston to Dispatch. Where is the fire department?"

A tinny voice came back. "On their way, Two-Five Boston. ETA less than five minutes."

"Right," Dez snarled to Jaylynn. "If they're on the way, why don't we hear them?"

Jaylynn grabbed her partner's forearm. "Listen...do you hear that?" She pivoted and walked toward the west side of the house, her head cocked to the side. Dez followed. "There! You hear it? A whimpering sound."

Just as she said that, very clearly they both heard a high-pitched wail. "It's hot, Mommy! It's hot! I want Mommy! Mommy, where are you?"

They spotlighted the side of the house with a criss-cross of lights from their two flashlights as they both moved toward the front of the house.

"Hey!" Dez shouted. "Hey, kid!" Under her breath she said, "I hope to hell that's not coming from *this* house."

"Oh my God, Dez, it is." For a brief moment, the beam of the rookie's flashlight captured a shock of light-colored hair in the open window in the second story, then the little head disappeared.

Both cops backed up in the yard and shone their lights up at the window. Dez touched her shoulder mic. "Two-Five Boston to Dispatch. We have a small child in the upper story of the house. Confirmed visual. We request immediate assistance."

The dispatcher sounded irritated when he informed them again that the Fire Department was on the way.

Jaylynn was pacing with anxiety. "We can't go in, can we?"

"Even if we break the door down, I don't think there's a way to get upstairs. I'm afraid we have to wait."

The blond head was back at the window, and now he was wailing. "Mommy! It's hot. Help me!" Jaylynn thought he looked to be three or so. He put his hands on the windowsill and pulled himself up, leaning forward.

In unison, both Dez and Jaylynn screamed, "No!" and rushed below the window.

The boy was startled and dropped back six inches until his feet must have hit the ground. They could just barely see the top of his little shoulders and head as he squinted into their lights. "Get me down," he commanded.

Dez shone her flash onto her own face. "Hey, kid. Look at me. I'm gonna help you. Look behind you." The little boy turned, and Dez asked, "Can you see any fire?"

He looked back, nodding. "It's berry wed in here." He coughed as a puff of smoke billowed out.

"Oh, shit," Jaylynn whispered.

"Catch me," the little boy said. He pulled himself up onto the windowsill again.

"No!" they screamed, and he dropped back, shaking and con-fused.

Jaylynn muttered, "What if he does jump?"

Dez shook her head. "I can't guarantee I could catch him. He could fall in toward the house and bounce off. Even if he just kicked the house or bumped it, we might not be able to get him." She took a deep breath. "So that's not a good idea."

Jaylynn craned her neck, stepping back three strides as she did so. "What's your name, honey?" She listened closely, but his answer wasn't clear. She thought he said "Bicker." She glanced at Dez, a frown on her face. "Oh. Victor, he means." She raised her voice. "Victor, the Fire Department is coming any minute."

He let out a scream. "It's hot! I want my mommy!"

Dez raised her hands in the air, sweeping the light back and forth. "Wait, Victor. Wait." She looked at the rookie. "I really don't want him to jump fifteen or twenty feet—if we missed..." She shook her head.

By now a small crowd of neighbors appeared in the yard.

"You've got to get him down," shrieked a woman in curlers, housecoat, and slippers. She held her hands to her mouth, looking for all the world like she was going to be sick. "Oh, God— he's just a little boy."

"Yes, ma'am," Jaylynn said. She faced the five women standing behind her. "Can any of you get a ladder from your house or garage?"

They looked at one another, shrugging and shaking their heads as if ashamed. One woman said, "We have a ladder but it's only about five feet. That won't do it. I'll go get a thick blanket." She turned and scurried off.

"A blanket won't be enough," Jaylynn said, her face worried.

Dez said, "No. The firefighters have those special ones—not the same as someone's old afghan."

Jaylynn turned away and looked up at the little boy crying in the window. She saw Dez gauging the height and looking at her. "What?"

Dez grimaced, like she was gritting her teeth. "If I could just get up high enough..." A surprised look came over her face. "Wait!" She turned and ran toward the street, jumped in the squad car, and gunned it up on the lawn right next to the house. She parked so close that there wasn't more than three inches between the stucco of the house and the passenger door.

Victor leaned out the window, one little leg over the sill.

Dez got out of the car. "Wait, Victor! We're coming up to get you." She stepped up onto the hood in one smooth motion, then sprang on top of the car's roof. Jaylynn stood for a moment, her mouth open, then followed in her footsteps, scrambling and inwardly cursing the fact that her legs were so short. Dez reached up toward the window, but she was a good five feet short of the boy.

"Shit! I can't reach. But I can boost you up high enough, Jay, and steady you. You get an arm hooked over the sill, then get a hold of him and hand him down." Jaylynn put her hand flat against the rough stucco and raised a foot into Dez's interlaced hands. Suddenly she was flying upward, her head zooming above the window level. She got her arms over the sill, pulled herself up, and was shocked at what she saw. No wonder Victor wanted out so badly. The far wall of his small bedroom was burning, flames licking toward the ceiling. The room was thick with smoke. Over the crinkling sound of the fire, she finally heard the tiny whine of a siren.

Below her Dez shouted instructions to the bystanders while holding steady pressure on her feet and legs. The rookie angled her left arm and shoulder over the sill and reached to the side to grab the boy by his flannel pajama top, hoping it would hold. Victor already had one bare leg over the sill. As his little behind cleared the windowsill, he choked back a sob and gave a little wave into the room. "Bye bye, Cee Cee."

Puzzled, Jaylynn hefted the boy out and away from the window, letting him dangle for an instant until he was taken by someone below. *Cee Cee?* The pressure on her legs and feet shifted, and she was, for a moment, supporting most of her own weight by hanging on to the sill, but then Dez shouted something. She could see over the sill into the room, and through a break in the smoke, white slats swam into her vision. Dez shouted again, but she swung her other arm onto the windowsill, and with difficulty pulled herself up. Below, she could very clearly hear her partner screaming at her to get down. Instead, she let herself go headfirst into the smoking room.

Coughing and panting for breath, she got on her hands and knees and crawled. *It's only maybe four feet, and over to the left of the window...should be here...* Her head hit something solid. She reached up and felt the slats of the crib. The smoke cleared for a brief second, and in the light of the raging fire, she could see the tiny form. She stood, choking as the smoke engulfed her. Coughing, she snatched up the small bundle, then threw herself toward the light of the open window. The carpet around her feet burst into flames and the room was very nearly engulfed. *Air. Air. It's so close...* Black dots swam in front of her eyes as she got her left leg over the windowsill. And then Dez was there, up in the air, one arm over the sill and her eyes wide and face frantic. Wordlessly, she grabbed the rookie by the front of her leather jacket.

"Wait—the baby."

"The hell with the baby," the big cop growled, but she took the limp bundle in her free hand and passed it down to the women who had boosted her up.

Jaylynn was now more out of the window than in. She couldn't quit coughing. "Hurry," she gasped. "The wall is on fire."

"Follow me down." Dez's head disappeared, and Jaylynn was alone. Now the sirens were blaring and she saw flashing lights coming toward them. She looked out, in a sort of daze. Later, it occurred to her that if her right pant leg hadn't caught fire, she might have enjoyed the view for a few seconds longer. Instead, she let out a shriek, grabbed the sill and kicked her other leg out the window. She dangled for a mere second before strong hands guided her down. She landed, off balance, on the right front fender. Dez jumped off the car a split second after Jaylynn, then tackled the rookie and rolled her on the ground until the flames on the cuff of her pant leg went out. They lay tangled on the ground, coughing and panting until Dez pulled her feet away and got up. She bent over, wheezing, and patted Jaylynn's shoulder. "You okay?" Her voice shook. She repeated the question over the increasing roar of the fire.

The rookie nodded, and Dez straightened up and moved away, gesturing at the bystanders, who by now numbered several dozen. "Get away from the house," she hollered. "Everybody back on the street."

Jaylynn lay on her side, still choking and gasping for air, fighting back the urge to vomit up the hamburger she had recently eaten.

Seconds later, when she opened her eyes, she found she had a perfect view of several pairs of paramedics' and fire fighters' boots as they approached her. A little blond-haired boy squatted down beside her head and touched her cheek. "You is real dirty." He stood up and brushed his hands together as though he was finished with her, then turned and watched the medics. She marveled at how calm the little boy was.

One of the paramedics, who had heard the boy's comment, snickered as he went down on his knees next to her, an oxygen mask in his hand. He looked at her nametag. "Well, Savage. You can wash up later. This ought to help. Take a big gulp of some clean air."

The mask slipped over her nose and mouth, and he was indeed right. The cool air soothed her ragged throat and almost instantly she felt better. Later, she would be surprised to find that their entire rescue operation had taken less than three minutes. When she thought back, it seemed to have lasted much more time, almost as if it were in slow motion.

In fact, all around her everything moved as if in slow motion. She saw two squad cars parked at an angle up on the curb. Red and white and orange neon lights flashed, and police officers held back a large crowd that lined the sidewalk and edges of the lawn.

Exasperated, she thought, *Where were all of those people when we needed them earlier?* Another fire engine approached, followed by two more cop cars. One set of fire fighters had a hose up in the front of the house, and another crew pulled a second hose past her around to the back. As they passed, one of them paused to shout, "Whoever parked this—get it the hell outta here."

Jaylynn rolled onto her back, oblivious to the fact that the paramedics had a blood pressure cuff on her. She sucked in more good air, then tensed her stomach muscles and raised her head. Dez leaned against the front fender of their squad car, which, Jaylynn now noticed, was sporting a very dented roof and hood. The tall woman was bent half over, her hands on her knees. Something was wrong. Jaylynn wanted to go to her, but when she made a move to get up, the paramedics restrained her.

"It's off to the hospital for you, Savage. Your lungs need to be checked."

She shook her head, tried to speak, but the mask prevented it.

Dez straightened up, strode over, and pulled a paramedic aside. They spoke for just a moment, then she spun around and approached the rookie. "Jay, you're gonna be all right. They have to take you in though...it's policy. I'll stay here, update the detectives, and meet you at the hospital in about half an hour." She ran her hand over her dark hair as she stared into Jaylynn's eyes. Then, abruptly, she turned and walked over to the squad car, got in, and backed it away from the house.

****

Jaylynn wanted to go back on duty after she was given a clean bill of health at the hospital, but the sergeant on duty arrived and insisted she go home on sick leave for the rest of the night. Once she knew that the choice was not up to her, she let herself relax and found that she was worn out. It was just as well that she go home.

The nurse who came in to discharge her couldn't tell her anything about the baby from the fire. She wondered if Cee Cee had been dead when she picked her up. The tiny bundle hadn't made any movement.

She found Dez in the waiting room, pacing nervously. "Hey. Want to run me home?"

The tall cop nodded. Wordlessly, she turned and headed out the automatic doors of the ER and the rookie followed her, hastening to catch up.

They got in the car, and Dez backed up in a lurch. She

shifted gears, hit the gas, and navigated out of the parking lot.

"Dez?" The veteran cop gave her a quick glance and looked away. Jaylynn frowned. "What's the matter?"

Her partner shook her head. "Not now. I've got to finish out the shift."

"What? What do you mean?"

"We'll talk later."

"So you *are* coming by after shift?"

She turned onto Como Boulevard. "Yeah."

No further words passed between them until Dez pulled up in front of the house.

Jaylynn got out and leaned back into the open door of the squad car. "So I'll see you in a couple hours?"

Dez nodded and looked away. The rookie slammed the door shut and turned to walk up to her front door. Puzzled and feeling unsettled, she unlocked the door and pushed it open, then glanced back. The white cop car still sat out front. She couldn't see in the dark windows, but as she stepped up and into the house, the squad car rolled forward and accelerated down the street. She didn't know why she had a bad feeling, but Dez surely hadn't been herself. *Oh well, it must be stress. We certainly had enough of that tonight.*

Nobody was home. She went toward the kitchen, shrugging off her jacket, which she hung on the hook near the back door. She opened the refrigerator door and got a glass of milk, then opened the cupboard and picked up a plastic Winnie the Pooh plate and took a big hunk of banana bread off the counter to set on it, and then headed up the stairs. Her left shoulder ached as though she had pulled some muscle—probably while hanging from the windowsill.

In her room, she set the glass and the plate on her bedside table, flicked on the light, and went into the bathroom. She would have laughed, looking in the mirror, if she hadn't been so tired. The little boy at the scene had been right. She was *very* dirty. Her white-blonde hair was streaked with black soot. Her face was smudged. The dirt and ash smeared all over her uniform made her look like she had just rolled in someone's outdoor fireplace. The side of her right pant leg was charred from hem to mid-calf. *So much for those slacks. Forty bucks totally trashed.*

Standing in the bathroom, she disrobed, letting all her clothes drop to the floor behind the door. She turned on the water and ran it 'til it was good and steamy, then stepped under the shower.

She let the water splash over her for a couple of minutes, then soaped up, relishing the feeling of cleanliness and the lemony smell of the soap. Another wave of fatigue washed over her as she shut off the water and stepped out of the tub.   She dried off, brushed her teeth, and opened the door to the darkened hallway. Arms crossed over her naked chest, she paused to listen.   After a few seconds, she was sure that the house was still empty, so she hurried across the hall to her room, shut the door, and slipped into her warmest flannel pajamas.   She sat on the edge of the bed and picked up the glass of milk and took a gulp.   It tasted funny because of the leftover toothpaste flavor, but she drank it and ate the banana bread anyway.   She was still hungry when she finished it, but she was too tired to go downstairs for anything more.

She lay down on her bed and pulled the covers over her.   Her heartbeat picked up, and she felt a shudder.   She shivered again, but the bed was starting to feel warmer. *I am so tired. Shift isn't even over, and I'm exhausted.*   Once she closed her eyes and started to drift, she could see the closed-in little bedroom, the crib on one side, the twin bed on the other.   Sound in her head was muffled and everything swirled around her. She fought to see, but the room was full of smoke and the walls were covered with fire. Surrounded by fire, she started to choke.   In the far distance, someone was screaming her name. She looked around, but all she could see was flames. And then the floor gave out beneath her, and she fell into the abyss.

Jaylynn gasped, and her eyes popped open, her heart beating staccato.   Without warning, it hit her that she could have been killed. If the floor had collapsed while she was standing on it, she'd have fallen down into an inferno of flames. She trembled. Despite all the images of fire, her whole body felt cold. She shuddered again, then sat up and grabbed the blanket at the foot of the bed to make another layer.

Why did I do that? What was I thinking? But she realized she *hadn't* been thinking. It had just happened, with no fore-thought. If there was a baby there, she couldn't just abandon the child. Her instinct was to act, to try to get to the child.

She wondered if that was a bad instinct—or not. Somehow, in the darkness of her bedroom and with all the thoughts now run-ning through her mind, it seemed like it had been a very stupid impulse. But then again, she believed Dez would have done the same thing. Neither one of them could have lived with themselves if they could have grabbed the child to safety and instead had let her die.

Rolling over on her side, she curled into a ball and felt the warmth from the thick blankets begin to soothe her. She felt like she might cry, but she didn't. Before she knew it, she was asleep.

****

Dez finished out the shift, stopping to make a full report to the sergeant on duty and to Lt. Malcolm. She knew that the way she phrased things would go a long ways toward making Jaylynn seem brave and judicious—or stupid and foolhardy. A part of her wanted to emphasize the latter, because as far as she was concerned, what the rookie had just done *was* stupid. Reckless. Dangerous. But she was purposefully neutral, stating only the facts and downplaying how rash and careless she thought Jaylynn had been. Several cops as well as both the lieutenants on duty congratulated her on their quick thinking. So far, nobody had made a big deal about the dented-in squad car, but she thought they might be called on the carpet about that later.

She left as quickly as she could, not even pausing to change clothes, and strode out to the parking lot, passing Jaylynn's Camry on the way to her truck. They'd have to come get the Camry in the morning. She climbed into her truck and sat for a moment, not sure what to do. Even though she felt numb, she was also sure that any minute Mount Vesuvius was going to come blasting up and out of her. She didn't want that to happen in the parking lot, so she started up the Ford and got out of there.

She knew she was going to Jaylynn's, but first, she wanted to go home to her apartment, sit for a bit, think about things. A part of her wanted to grab the rookie by the neck and choke her. A cold wave passed through her body, and she felt shaky through and through. She had just barely gotten Jaylynn out of there—just barely. After she dropped the rookie to the ground and rolled her to put the fire out, she had stood up and seen the flash of light and fire roar past the windows on the main floor. A matter of seconds more and the upper floor would have caved in, taking someone precious down with it. Dez shuddered, her breath coming fast. She pulled up in front of Luella's house, cut the lights, and turned off the ignition. *I need to talk. I need to talk to Luella.* She pressed the Indiglo on her watch to see that it was 12:38. But a dim light glowed from the back of the main floor, so she knew the older woman was still up and about, probably watching TV.

She went around to the back entrance, unlocked the outer door, and trudged up the stairs to her back door. She had time to take off her jacket, uniform shirt, vest, and bra before she heard the thump-thump-thump of her landlady banging a broom handle on the ceiling below. She shook her head. As usual, Luella seemed to have her radar running. Dez didn't know how the old woman did it, but she always seemed to know when something was up. She stomped twice on the floor with the heel of her boot, and the thumping stopped.

She knelt and untied her duty boots, kicked them off, and slipped out of her uniform pants and underwear. All of her dirty clothes went directly into the hamper. She got out clean briefs, a pair of jeans, socks, and tennis shoes and put them on, then opened the drawer to her bureau, pulled out a gray sweatshirt, and slipped it over her broad bare shoulders. In the bathroom she checked her face and long hair. She was nowhere near as dirty as Jaylynn had been, but she pushed up her sweatshirt sleeves and washed her hands, arms, face, and neck, then shook out her French braids and let her hair hang loose. Running a brush through it, she could see that it was kinked up and hopeless but she didn't care. She took one more minute to brush her hair, then grabbed a coat, wallet, and keys and descended the stairs.

When she tapped on the door, it was already open, and Luella called out from the dining room. "Get in here. I've got ham and fried potatoes going."

Dez smiled fondly and rolled her eyes. If she ate all the goodies that Luella presented to her, she'd weigh three hundred pounds in no time. But tonight she wasn't going to turn down hot food. She hadn't eaten anything since their dinner break hours earlier, and her stomach had been growling for over an hour.

She moved down the hall and through the kitchen, glancing down at the steaming food in a large black frying pan on the stove. The silver-haired woman set some silverware on the table and turned to meet her at the dining room doorway. She ran a soft, warm hand down Dez's arm from shoulder to forearm. Then, she squinched up her face and sniffed. "You smell like barbecue, Dez." She sniffed again. "Really *bad* barbecue. What *is* that?"

"Fire up on Thomas Avenue tonight."

"Ah, that explains it. Heard something about it on the news. Sit down, sit down." She ushered the tall woman over to the dining room table and shuffled back over to the stove where Dez could still see her as she dished up a plate of food. "Milk? Water? Glass of wine?"

"Milk would be great."

In moments she had in front of her a steaming plate of flavorful ham and succulent fried potatoes that were crunchy on the outside and moist on the inside. Dez lit into all of it like she hadn't eaten in ages while Luella sat across from her drinking a cup of tea and munching on store-bought shortbread cookies.

"They didn't say your names on the ten o'clock news, but Channel 4 did a quick story about the house fire. So you're the one who pulled two children out of a burning house? Seems like that's kind of a replay of what happened a few years ago."

"No, I didn't pull the kids out. Jaylynn did." The time Dez had gone into a burning house, the fire had been contained in the front of the building, and she had merely busted in the back door, awakened the parents, and helped drag three sleepy kids out of the back bedroom. It was nothing like tonight's fire, which was close to out of control by the time the fire department arrived.

She forked up the last of the potatoes, chewed, and swallowed them with difficulty. Usually she didn't scarf her food down so fast, but she could tell an attack of nerves was about to hit her. Pushing the plate away, she drank down the last of the milk, aware that Luella was studying her.

"You don't seem very happy about it, Dez."

"Nope. I'm not." She sat still, finally acknowledging the fatigue that had been threatening for an hour.

Luella finished a cookie, then picked up the package, closed the top and set it to the side. "Well? Why not?"

"It was a crazy thing for her to do." She took a minute to describe the scene and what had happened. "I only intended for her to get that kid down. Didn't even know about the baby. Little three-year-old was hanging out the window, trying to escape the heat. Next thing I know, she's disappeared through the window into fire and smoke going after a baby that was probably already dead from smoke inhalation. You would've had a heart attack."

"But it all turned out fine. Jaylynn is okay, and the baby is, too. That's what they said on the news."

Dez crossed her arms and glared. "She was seconds away from the floor falling in, Lu. It was stupid and damn dangerous!" She smacked a fist on the table and the china jumped and jiggled. "I just wanna kill her."

Luella chuckled. She stood and picked up the empty glass, stacked it on the plate with the fork and knife. With her other hand she stroked her tenant's hair. "But it all turned out okay. I repeat: everything's fine."

Dez bowed her head, accepting the gentle touch. "It just makes me feel so—so—"

"Helpless?"

Dez crossed her arms in front of her and scowled. "Mostly just angry."

"That's your fear talking. You have to focus on the fact that everything is all right, and she's fine. She *is* fine, right?"

"She had to make a little trip to the hospital to get checked for smoke inhalation, but yeah, she's okay."

"Well, honey, you just have to chalk it up to experience."

"I'll tell you what. Nothing like this is gonna happen again. I'll be watching her like a hawk."

Luella bit back a grin and picked up the plate and glass. "You do that." She carried the dishes and silverware in to the sink and turned on the tap. Dez rose and followed her into the kitchen.

"Thanks for the midnight snack, Luella. I feel a little better."

The older woman turned the water off and wiped her hands on a kitchen towel. She came over to Dez and took one of her hands. "What are you going to do now? You *are* going to go check on her, aren't you?"

The tall woman frowned. She met Luella's eyes, still scowling, but she nodded.

"Good. She'll probably appreciate that. Go on."

"I'll do the dishes up."

"No, I got nothing better to do, and it's not like I'm tired." She looked at her wristwatch. "There's still twenty minutes left of that alien conspiracy radio show, so I'll turn it on in here."

Dez looked at her landlady to see if she was serious. "You're still listening to that?"

"Oh yeah. I work a crossword or two and listen in. There are just scads of goofball people who call in. It's a laugh a minute." She reached up and tugged on the tall woman's hair. Dez bent and her landlady planted a dry kiss on her cheek. "Go be with her. And you're not allowed to kill her, all right?"

The tall cop let out a snort. "Yeah. Right."

"I'll see you at the party tomorrow."

"Oh, geez. I forgot all about that."

"Well, don't forget all about showering. Your hair smells like it's been slow roasted in a fire pit."

****

Dez pulled up to the front of the house on Como Boulevard. She shut off the engine. The downstairs lights were on, so someone was up, though she had a hunch it might not be Jaylynn. She expected the rookie to have crashed as soon as she got home—but then again, she could be wrong. Tim's banged up red Corolla was parked in front of her truck, so he was home. She didn't know about Sara.

She sat in the truck, her heart racing. After closing her eyes, she did some deep breathing in an effort to still her uncooperative heart. Instead, she felt like she was going to start crying. She couldn't confront Jaylynn feeling like this. For a moment she contemplated going back to her own apartment, but she couldn't make herself do it without checking first on the rookie.

So she got out of the truck and made her way up the walk, her legs shakier than she expected. *Dammit! Cut that out. Luella's right. Everything's fine.* As she drew closer to the house, she could see a blue flicker of light through the slats of the front window blinds. Someone was up watching TV. She didn't have her key with her so she tapped on the front door. No response. She tapped a little louder, then heard the hollow thump-thump of footsteps. The curtain was drawn aside, then the door flew open. The slender, red-haired man standing before her gave her a big grin. "Dez. Hey, how are you?" Tim stood in stocking feet and wore baggy sweat bottoms and a white long-sleeved jersey with a brown streak across the chest. He held the door wide as she passed, then quickly shut it to keep the cold out.

"Good. You?"

"Fine. Just fine. Kevin and I are in the kitchen making homemade dark chocolate truffles."

"That's a relief." She pointed to the streak on his shirt. "That looks pretty poopy—if you get my meaning.

He looked down as he turned the lock for the door, then giggled. "It'll wash. You want to come in the kitchen and have one? They are *really* luscious."

"Nah. Not hungry."

He grinned up at her. "So where's Jay?"

Dez paused. In tennis shoes, she towered six inches over him. She didn't know why he looked so short tonight. "I was hoping she was here."

He threw his hands up in the air in a mock gesture of ignorance. "She could be for all I know. We've only been home an hour or so. Check out her *boudoir.*" He leered at her and gave her a wink, which she ignored, instead heading for the stairs and taking them two at a time. At the top of the stairs, she found Jaylynn's door closed. She turned the knob and poked her head into the dim room. Once her eyes grew adjusted to the darkness, she could make out a motionless lump on the far side of the queen-sized bed and Jaylynn's blonde head poking out of the blankets.

She eased into the room and shut the door behind her. She slipped out of her jacket and pulled her sweatshirt over her head, then shed her shoes, jeans, and socks. Tiptoeing, she lifted the blankets and crawled into bed, trying hard not to let any cold air in. She maneuvered onto her side, facing Jaylynn. In the moonlight shining through the partly open blinds, she could make out the top half of the rookie's slumbering face. It was no longer covered with soot and didn't seem to have a single mark on it. She shuddered, thinking again about how close her partner had come to disaster at the fire earlier. It was hard to stop thinking about that and how there was nothing she could have done to stop it. She wanted to reach out and touch the younger woman, but she was afraid she would wake her.

"Why are you staring at me?"

Startled, Dez took in a quick gasp of air.

Hazel eyes popped open and looked at her with amusement. "You some kind of spy now, or what?"

"I-I didn't want to wake you."

"As if the furnace of heat you're emitting wouldn't have been noticeable?" Jaylynn wormed her way over and pulled Dez close. "Oooh, warm bare skin. *That* is nice." She nuzzled into Dez's neck and wrapped herself around her. With a sigh, she said, "It's not the same sleeping here without you."

Dez rolled onto her back, pulling the smaller woman on top of her. Her racing heart stilled a little. *She's safe. It's okay. Nothing bad is going to happen.* She felt the flannel under her hands and stroked skin through the warm material. Jaylynn molded into her, and the big woman worked at relaxing.

"That was pretty scary tonight, Dez."

"Tell me about it," was Dez's low reply.

"Next time, we'll have to move faster."

"Next time you're staying in the car." Jaylynn laughed out loud. "Don't laugh. I mean it."

"Yeah, right." She burrowed her nose into Dez's hair. "I do hope this little reminder of the fire isn't a permanent fixture."

"Huh?" Dez looked at her quizzically.

"Your hair smells like burnt wood."

The big woman opened her arms wide. "Geez! Everybody's a critic."

Jaylynn planted a lingering kiss on her lips. "It's okay," she whispered. "It's kind of sexy...like making love near a fire pit at the beach."

"Only no sand."

Chapter
Seven

Dez awoke the next morning and crept out of bed, leaving the rookie crashed. She dressed in shorts, running shoes, and a sweatshirt. She went downstairs for a bite to eat, then retrieved the newspaper from the porch only to find that the Thomas Street fire had made the front page of the Saturday morning paper. There was even a small photo of Jaylynn, obviously cut out from her Academy graduation picture. Their quick thinking was credited with saving the boy and his three-month-old sister, both of whom had been left sleeping in the house alone while the mother ran to the grocery store. Dez suspected the mother would be doing some real fancy explaining—perhaps even some time in the workhouse.

Taking Jaylynn's car keys, she jogged the two miles to the station, using the time in the cool autumn air to think about the events of the last twenty-four hours. She realized she was still freaked by what had happened. When Jaylynn had gone up and over the windowsill, she had leapt up, trying to catch the rookie's foot before the smaller woman disappeared into the house. She just barely missed, falling back and landing heavily on the squad car. Maybe she missed grabbing the rookie, but she sure hadn't failed to notice how she had landed and crunched in the roof of the cruiser, that was for sure. Thank God so many neighbors had shown up by then. When she yelled for help, some of them actually did.

It had felt like minutes before she was helped up to the window ledge. Even now, jogging down Dale Street, she still felt the same wash of relief as she had the night before when she visualized how the rookie came stumbling toward the window. She couldn't quite remember feeling that level of desperation—at least, not since Ryan had died. And then, a bit later, when the upstairs floor caved in... She shuddered. Try as she might, she couldn't get the images out of her mind. Fire, crashing timbers, smoke, the squeal of sirens. She had a hard time believing she had slept at all last night.

She reached the parking lot and, breathing hard, stopped next to the gray Camry. Despite the chilly air, she was sweating. She took a couple minutes to stretch out the backs of her legs, then managed to jackknife herself into Jaylynn's small car.

The rest of the day passed in a blur of preparations, of meeting Bill, and of keeping a close eye on the cheerful, laughing woman. Dez ran errands, picked up more odds and ends at the grocery store, and delivered Vanita and Luella to the party. Each time she left the rookie, she found herself replaying the fire scene over and over in her head. After a while, she became grumpy from the constant reminder. It didn't help that she was hungry, either.

Things calmed down for her once the party was in full swing. She watched the antics with amusement from the corner where she leaned, a plate of lasagna in hand. She was on her third piece, though this one was smaller than the previous two. The tall cop skipped the lemon-butter green beans, the garlic French bread, all of the *hors d'ouevres*, the desserts, and the salad upon which Tim had worked so long, and she cut right to the steamy, fragrant, chili-pepper flavored lasagna. She chewed slowly as she leaned up against the wall in the living room near the door that led to the kitchen.

The light of her life was currently bent over with two hands on a large multi-dotted plastic mat, her cute tush in the air, and surrounded by Sara and four big hulky Army men in various ridiculous poses. Dez took a bite and listened to Jaylynn laugh as she watched her try to shove Bill aside and get her foot on a large red dot on the plastic mat.

They had tried to get her to join in the game of *Twister*, but Dez refused. It was much more fun to watch. In fact, it was even more fun to keep an eye on everyone else who was watching: Luella, her sister Vanita, Tim and Kevin, Shayna and Crystal, two other Army buddies, various young women who had come along with Bill's friends, and Bill's younger brother, Jimmy, who kept trying to hit on Jaylynn. Dez wondered when Jimmy would catch a clue. She hoped she wouldn't have to be the one to let him know that Jaylynn was very unavailable.

Sara let out a shriek and slipped to the floor on her side, laughing so maniacally that it was infectious. Luella and Vanita sat on the couch in ringside seats and laughed so hard that tears ran down Luella's cheeks. Dez caught Crystal's eye and they grinned at one another. The dark-eyed cop got up from the piano bench where her partner, Shayna, sat. She sidled through the crowd hovering behind the couch and came to stand by Dez. "Pretty good party."

Dez set the plate down on the corner of the table and wiped her mouth with a napkin. "Great food, too."

"Yeah, I noticed you pretty much polished off an entire pan all by yourself, *chica*."

Dez smiled. "Not quite." But she *had* hacked off two more pieces, wrapped them in foil, and hid them in the back of the refrigerator. She figured they would make a great midnight snack—and breakfast, too.

Crystal ran her hands through her short black hair and shook her head. "You know, I always have fun at these get-togethers with you guys, but this one really takes the cake. Look at 'em— playing a kid's game like crazy ass fools."

Dez agreed. She wouldn't be caught dead joining that game, not because it wasn't fun but because she didn't even know the Army buddies, and she'd only just met Bill. She figured it would take a lot more than the half glass of wine she'd had to loosen her up that much. "Notice there's no cops playing. I guess Army guys have lower standards."

A puzzled look came over the Latina's face as she looked into Dez's eyes. "What about Jaylynn?"

A slow blush crept up Dez's neck to her face. She didn't answer. It hit her that she didn't really consider Jaylynn a cop. Sidekick, yes. Helper on the shift, yes. Partner? Only as a lover—and one hundred percent in that capacity. But as a professional partner, the tall woman had to admit that the answer was no. As Crystal turned away to watch the ruckus on the *Twister* mat, Dez reasoned with herself silently. Just last summer she and the rookie had walked into a convenience store and been shot at by a robber. Dez took a bullet in the vest, and with excellent reflexes, Jaylynn had shot and killed the man. The rookie followed every rule, responding appropriately in every way. It had been ruled a clean shoot. Even after all that, after all the calls they had been through, after last night's fire, after all the work discussions and training, Dez was astonished to realize she did not want the young woman to be a police officer, and didn't, in actuality, consider her a cop.

Unsettled, she picked up several plates and moved through the swinging door into the kitchen. It smelled like chili pepper and cinnamon, and someone had left a gallon of milk out on the table. She screwed on the green plastic cap and returned the container to the refrigerator, all the while wondering what this new observation meant.

She set the dishes in the sink, then turned around and leaned back against the counter with her arms crossed over her blue and white flannel shirt. She thought long and hard about her relationship with Jaylynn, but before she could get too far, something interrupted her train of thought. It took a moment to sink in that something in the timber of the party din had changed. It was still loud, but no longer joyous. She took a breath and listened, then strode across the floor and smacked the door open. Several people were shouting at once as they clustered around the couch. Before Dez could take a step, Sara separated from the crowd and headed toward the tall cop. At the same time, one of the Army men, a handsome black guy she thought was named Mike, peeled off in the opposite direction, ripped the front door open, and disappeared into the night, letting a blast of cold air into the house.

As Sara pushed past, Dez grabbed her arm. "What's going on?"

Sara slipped out of her grasp. "Gotta call 911! She's having some sort of attack."

"Who? What—" A vision of Luella came to her mind, and Dez took two long strides to the crowd of people. "Make room!" She jostled everyone aside as though she were on duty out on the street and responsible for separating bystanders. "Back up and let her breathe."

As people stepped back, Mike burst back into the house carrying an oversized duffel. "I've got the jump kit," he said in a loud voice.

Dez got a good look at the ladies on the couch. Luella was holding her sister. Usually the two of them looked a great deal alike, but not right now. Vanita's eyes were closed, her mahogany colored face was gray-brown, and her head lolled to the side. She had vomited down the front of her dress, and she didn't seem to be breathing.

"Get her on the floor," Mike commanded. He unzipped the duffel and grabbed something out that was wrapped in plastic. He ripped it open, dropping some latex gloves out which he pulled on until they were snapped tight. Meanwhile, as though they had practiced the move over and over, Bill and his buddies lifted the limp woman and placed her gently on the carpet near the piano. Jaylynn was on the floor in an instant, her hands on either side to steady the elderly woman's head. Dez couldn't hear what she was saying, but it was clear she was talking to Vanita, even though the old woman was unconscious.

Dez pushed her way past the crowd and went down on her knees at Vanita's shins next to Mike who was pressing two fingers against Vanita's neck with his ear near her mouth. "What happened?"

He shrugged, looked past her. "Dave, Smitty, I need CPR here. Now! She's not breathing." He ripped open a plastic container, dropped a device out of it, and adjusted it over Vanita's mouth.

"Let me do that," Dez said.

He turned his head to look at her, his brown eyes piercing. "I mean no disrespect, but back off. Let my guys in."

Dave and Smitty squeezed past her and she rolled back onto her heels, then up to her feet. She was surprised at how shaky she felt. *Go into cop mode. Come on—get a hold of yourself.* But she couldn't do that. The lasagna felt like a giant lump in her stomach, and for one passing moment, she thought she might be sick. She glanced around helplessly, but there was nothing she could do.

Except go to Luella.

Her landlady huddled on the couch, one hand clutching a cloth handkerchief, eyes wide with fear. Dez pushed past two women—Dave's or Smitty's girlfriends she thought—and swung long legs over the back of the couch to slide down next to Luella. She didn't speak, just took two cold hands into her own and rubbed them.

Luella shook. Dez put an arm around her, alarmed that the silver-haired woman might have a heart attack from the stress. "Shhh...it's okay, Luella."

Sara settled in next to Luella on the other side where Vanita had been sitting. "I got through to 911. Help is on the way now."

Looking past the old woman, Dez met Sara's eyes and could see the fear in them. She turned her attention back to Luella and patted her again. "It's gonna be all right, Lu," she said as much for Sara as for her landlady.

The three of them watched and waited as Bill's friends worked on Luella's older sister, the rhythm of the CPR commands almost musical in cadence. Mike rummaged in his jump kit and removed a stethoscope and a blood pressure cuff, which he applied to her upper arm. Dez watched his movements carefully, hoping that he knew what he was doing.

"Where is the ambulance?" Luella asked, a hint of anger creeping into her voice.

Dez checked her watch. "It's only been a couple minutes. Don't worry—any time now...they'll be here." She looked over at

Jaylynn who still knelt at Vanita's head, and the rookie met her gaze with a worried expression. At that moment two things happened. The sound of a high-pitched siren whined into the room, and Vanita raised a hand into the air as if she were waving. Dave and Smitty stopped chest compressions.

Jaylynn caught hold of the fluttering hand and said, "It's okay, Van. Hold on. You're going to be all right. We're taking you to the hospital in a minute."

Mike pulled the CPR mask off Vanita's face and bent down close to her mouth. "She's breathing on her own!" In an excited voice he said, "Hold on, sweetie. Keep on breathing. Yeah, beautiful—that's the way!" He patted her leg, then smoothed the flowered dress down and left his hand on the motionless thigh.

At that moment, Tim clattered down the stairs with a thick wool blanket and helped to cover Vanita with it.

In minutes, two paramedics were in the house, taking vital statistics information from Mike and checking on the gray-haired woman. Before Dez could get Luella up from the sofa, the uniformed men had her sister packed on a gurney, hooked up to an I.V., and on the way out the front door. Dez rose, helped Luella to her feet, and called to Jaylynn for help. The younger woman was there in an instant, kicking aside the sheet of plastic from the *Twister* game aside.

Dez had one arm around the trembling silver-haired woman as she directed Tim and Kevin to lock up the house behind them. "Jay, let's take Luella in your car."

The rookie nodded and went to the hall closet to start handing coats around. Some of the women said they would stay behind and tidy up the house, and Jaylynn assented, quickly explaining that someone would call with news shortly.

As they made their way out the front door, Tim said, "I thought Bill's unit were all munitions experts."

"Not Mike," Sara said. "He's a medic."

At the bottom of the steps, Luella piped up with "And thank God for that."

****

It was a long night in the ER but it took little time to learn that Vanita had had a heart attack. They implanted a pacemaker, and toward morning, they moved her from the operating room to Intensive Care where she was unconscious, partly due to the trauma, and partly due to the medications they had given her. Only two visitors were allowed in at a time, so Dez and Jaylynn took turns going into the room with Luella who sat in the one comfortable chair by Vanita's bedside, her own face nearly as gray as her sister's. With one hand she held onto her sister's forearm, stroking it lightly. It was one of the only exposed places on the old woman's body not covered with bandages or inserted with tubes.

Dez leaned cross-armed against the wall at the foot of the bed watching Luella. Her legs were tired and her feet sore as she had stood for most of the last nine hours, first outside the ER, then in two different waiting rooms. There was no second chair in the hospital room, but she wouldn't have sat anyway. She preferred pacing or leaning.

She wondered how Vanita could get any quality of rest. The machinery monitoring her made so many clicking and beeping and whooshing noises that she knew she would never even be able to shut her eyes. Luella, on the other hand, was struggling with fatigue. Dez stepped in front of her friend and squatted down before her. "Luella, I think you need to go home and get some sleep... Come back in a few hours."

She shook her head emphatically.

"You're exhausted."

"Doesn't matter. I can't do that."

"Sure you can."

Luella rose with great effort and Dez popped up to a standing position. She patted her tall tenant on the stomach until she backed up to the wall.

Dez frowned. "What?" She put both of her big hands lightly on Luella's shoulders.

The silver-haired woman leaned into her young friend, her arms encircling the big woman's waist and her tired head resting against the solid breastbone.

Dez drew her close and in a choked voice whispered, "You're shrinking, old woman."

Luella leaned away and gave Dez the first smile she'd seen in nine hours. "It's from the major stress you put me through all of the time."

"I'll try to do something about that."

In a quiet voice, Luella said, "Listen, I don't want Vanita to hear this." She hesitated, taking a deep breath as she craned her neck up at her protective friend. "If she were to die, I couldn't live with myself, knowing she passed on alone. I *need* to be here, Dez, even if I am exhausted."

"You could go lie down on the couch in the waiting room."

She shook her head. "Not good enough. I need to be *here*. If she wakes up, she'll need me, need some assurance. You're the one who should go home and get some sleep. You work today?"

Dez shook her head.

"Good. I'd feel bad if you had to work on no sleep."

"What about her grandkids? When are you going to call them?"

"What time is it?"

"Twenty to seven."

Luella nodded and stood thinking. Dez patted her on the back as she looked around the small room full of monitors and devices, hoses and tubes, flashing lights and beeping alarms. The silver haired woman pondered a moment longer, then sighed. "I hate to ask this of you, but I don't want to leave the room. Will you call Ardella? She can get a hold of her mother and brother and sisters. Once they get here—as long as the doctor says Vanita is doing all right—I'll go home and get a little sleep. How's that sound?"

Dez nodded. "Deal."

Luella let loose of her and shuffled back to the chair.

"Are you warm enough?" Dez, herself, was roasting in the heat of the room, but she knew that older people didn't have the same circulation she did.

"I'm okay. My feet never seem warm enough, but really, I'm fine."

"Okay. I'm sending Jay in, and I'll go call Ardella. I'll try to get her to leave the wild great-grandkids home."

"Tanishia's old enough to babysit her little brothers. Specifically tell Ardella to leave the boys behind. I'm not even sure they are allowed on this floor."

"All right."

"And don't scare her, Dez."

"Of course not."

"You need to give her some details, but downplay it all. Make it sound sort of run-of-the-mill—not life-threatening."

Dez rolled her eyes. "Yeah, yeah. I think I can do that, Luella."

"I'm relying on you." She smiled in her regular mischievous way, and Dez couldn't help but smile back.

She left the room and headed to the waiting room. Jaylynn sat yawning near Kevin and Tim who were watching the morning news on a TV set with muted sound. Sara was snuggled in a ball on the vinyl two-person couch, Bill's arms around her, and both of them were asleep. When Jaylynn caught sight of her outside the doorway, she jumped to her feet. "Everything okay?"

"So far."

With a toss of her head, she gestured to Jaylynn, who bounded up and to her side. Taking the tall woman's hand, she gazed at her with tired eyes.

"I'm calling Vanita's granddaughter now, and once that whole clan descends, Luella has agreed to go home and rest for a while. Will you go hang with her for a few minutes 'til I call?"

"Sure."

It was still another hour before they left the hospital, got Luella settled, then slipped into bed upstairs in Dez's apartment. The big cop fell into a dreamless sleep, then awakened less than an hour later. She lay in bed holding Jaylynn who slumbered so deeply that even Dez disentangling from her didn't cause her to stir. The tall woman pulled the covers up and smoothed them over the still figure, then turned over onto her side and looked out toward light shining through the small window in the bathroom.

She felt terrible for Luella. *What would happen if Vanita did die? Neither one of them is going to last forever. They are both in their seventies.* But somehow, both Luella and Vanita seemed timeless to her—sturdy, jaunty, resilient. *She can't die...can she?* Vanita was the last of Luella's generation, and if she died—or even became incapacitated mentally—Luella would be alone. Sure, she'd have the nieces and nephews and all their kids, but that wasn't the same as having someone there who'd fought and loved and shared every problem or secret from an early age onward.

And Dez knew what that was like, the loneliness of it. She hadn't spoken to her own brother for so long, she didn't even remember when last it was. Soon, it would be another Thanksgiving, another Christmas, another new year without her brother, without her mother. She knew what it was like to be isolated from others, and frankly, she thought it sucked. Rolling over on her back, she fidgeted, shifted once, then again. Without Luella and her family, she would have had an awful lot of solitary holidays. *Maybe this Christmas will be different.* She still had not talked to her brother for ages, but since last summer when she had been shot, her mother had been in contact more frequently. Her mother was also apparently living with one of Dez's former supervisors, Xavier Aloysius MacArthur, "Mac" to his friends and fellow officers. Mac had been one of the best watch commanders the St. Paul Police Department had ever produced. He had also been her father's very best friend, and her former mentor. Another person she had "lost" once she became an adult and struck out on her own.

She turned over again. *What a mess my life has been. But it's been better since Jaylynn came into it.*

She rolled onto her side and moved close to the slumbering woman. Jaylynn let out a sigh and nestled her backside into the bigger woman. Dez slipped an arm around the small waist. She hoped this would last forever...but could it? In all her life she had never felt such a combination of happiness and vulnerability. She was convinced that it wouldn't be long before Jaylynn would get to know more about her and push her away. How could she prepare for that? She didn't know the answer to the question, but at the moment, it didn't seem all that important. She closed her eyes and slept.

****

For the next twenty-four hours, it was touch and go for Vanita, but as Luella said, her big sister was "a strong-willed old cuss." Dez and Jaylynn spent quite a bit of time at the hospital Sunday and Monday, and neither one of them really wanted to work their shift on Tuesday afternoon, but they had no choice. They had both traded Tuesday and Wednesday so they could have Saturday and Sunday off for the party, and neither wanted to let down the officers who had switched with them. Besides, they were scheduled for another self-defense session with the Como Middle School kids on Tuesday. Fortunately, by the time Vanita was moved from Intensive Care on Monday, everyone knew she would be all right. The old woman was already complaining about the bland food and tasteless coffee, and Luella was making plans to care for her sister at home once Vanita was released. With a sense of relief, the two cops were able to turn their attention back to their jobs.

Wednesday rolled around, and it was Halloween, which was always a busy night. The two women rode in the squad car, both scanning the busy streets as the late afternoon sun slipped lower and lower. Everywhere they looked, children in colorful costumes scurried about. Most of them were accompanied by their parents. Once it got dark, the older kids would start to come out, and all the real action would begin.

Jaylynn's stomach grumbled loud enough for Dez to hear it over the crackle of the radio. "You're not hungry already." The veteran cop said it as a statement and looked at her watch. It had been over three hours since they'd last stopped for lunch. She knew her partner would be hungry.

"How 'bout a nice deli sandwich, Dez? Maybe even two—

one for now and one for the road for later."

"Yeah, fine by me. Should've said something three miles and fifteen minutes ago when we passed *The Cutting Board*."

"Didn't occur to me 'til now."

Dez reversed course and meandered through a residential section they hadn't patrolled yet. It had been a slow week all around. Oddly enough, the highlight had been working with the girls at the school the day before, and as far as Dez was concerned, it was a big pain. Literally. She was still sporting a big and painful bruise on the left side of her abdomen where that Amber kid had socked her. She shifted in her seat and ran her left hand over the spot. It hadn't hurt at the time, but she sure could feel it now.

"Dez, next week I leave for pursuit training. I had forty hours of good solid pursuit training, not to mention the bookwork about it, at the Academy. Why am I going to Pursuit 101 again?"

"It's not the same. You'll be simulating computer pursuits as well as doing driving courses."

"Like I said, we did that at the Academy."

"It'll be more than just car chases. You'll also learn more about roadblocks, stop sticks, different intervention tactics."

The rookie eyed her partner for a moment. "Dez, what's wrong?"

The big cop turned to look at Jaylynn. "Nothing. Whaddya mean?"

"You keep rubbing your stomach and wincing like you're in pain."

The tall cop looked out her side window. She felt the blush rising up her neck. Some days she wished the rookie wasn't so damn observant.

"Dez! You're embarrassed. What's the matter?" She reached an arm out to the top of Dez's shoulder, kneading the muscle there. "Wait a minute...you're not sore from that punch you took a week or so ago...oh, that's it, isn't it?"

"You can just drop it, Jay."

The rookie let out a cackle. "She nailed you a good one, didn't she? Miss Abs of Steel actually took a good shot—and from a sixth grader."

Dez stared daggers at her, then turned back to the road. "She's lucky as hell that I didn't bust her ribs when I flipped her to the floor."

Now Jaylynn was laughing to herself. Between giggles, she said, "I didn't realize she would pack such a good punch."

"Maybe it wouldn't have been so bad if she hadn't thumped me in exactly the same place where another bony little fist had just been. Now I have quite the bruise. Hurts more now than it did then."

"Poor baby. I'll take good care of you tonight." She reached over and poked Dez in the right side. "I'll only tickle you on the sides—not in your middle."

Dez gave her a warning glance. "You touch my abs and you'll live to regret it."

Jaylynn went off into peals of laughter, and even Dez had to fight back a smile. She hated to admit it but this was one little squirt who totally had her number. She could be as tough, as threatening, as mean in tone and mood as she could muster up, and Jaylynn had a way of just worming her way around it and right up next to her heart—literally and figuratively. Nobody else had ever done that, not her mother, not her brother. Even Ryan had known to give her lots of space when she radiated this kind of surliness. Not so with Jaylynn. And she'd be damned if she could explain how the grinning jokester did it.

She let out a sigh and glanced to her right. The rookie had stopped chuckling and leaned against the passenger door, her face relaxed with a slight smile.

They pulled up to *The Cutting Board*, Dez's favorite place for deli sandwiches, barbecue, fried chicken, and pulled pork sandwiches. She put the car into park and was reaching for the key in the ignition when Dispatch came over the radio to send them to a call, an assault in progress.

Jaylynn gave her a tortured look, then responded. "Two-Five Boston, responding. ETA three minutes."

Dez hit the lights and siren and threw the car into gear. She pulled away from the curb with a squeal of tires. "Geez. We should've called in our break quicker."

"We're a little short tonight, though. It's just as well."

"The address, Jay, isn't it for that frat house up by Hamline U?"

"I'm not sure...want me to check with Dispatch?"

"Nah. I'm pretty sure it is." She navigated around vehicles on Rice Street and passed the State Capitol. Traffic was picking up now that it was half past four. She hated drivers on four lane streets. Instead of everyone pulling to the right when they heard and saw an emergency vehicle, the left lane usually inched left and the right lane inched right, forcing her to barrel down the middle in the right lane. She never knew whether some idiot on the left was suddenly going to decide to slide over to the right curb. There'd been plenty enough fender benders in department cars in situations like that, though she had been lucky not to have it happen—yet. She'd come close though.

She turned on University and headed for the cross street, turned there, and sped down the avenue, arriving at the front of the rambling two-story house in less than the three minutes Jaylynn had estimated. Dez left the lights running, hoping that would discourage any early trick-or-treaters from visiting the house. They were both out of the car, up the walk, and on the porch in seconds.

"It's all yours," Dez said.

Jaylynn beat on the door. "Open up. Police."

The door was thrown wide, but the person who opened it disappeared, calling out in a high voice, "Come in and help me!"

Jaylynn grabbed the screen door handle and pulled it open. Both cops peered into the darkened front room. A slim woman knelt next to a figure lying on the floor in front of a brick fireplace. To their left, on a sofa along the front wall, a beefy-looking man with long blond hair sat, panting, his eyes wide with fear. His lip was split, half his face blotchy and red, and there was blood coming from a cut above his eye.

The kneeling woman looked back over her shoulder. "Help him!"

They entered the house. Dez moved toward the young man on the couch. The rookie strode swiftly to the young woman who was holding a terry-cloth towel to the back of the man's head. His eyes were closed and he muttered something she couldn't understand.

Jaylynn hit her shoulder mic and requested paramedics.

The woman shook her head and scowled up at the young officer. "Forget that. I already called 911. I can't get this bleeding to stop. Help me."

"You're doing a good job, ma'am. Just hold the compress steady." She went down on one knee on the other side of the man, slipping on a pair of latex gloves. "It looks like more blood than it is. Just keep pressure on it. Help is on the way. You can hear the sirens coming. What's your name?"

"Violet Adams."

Jaylynn took a pad of paper and a pen out of her pocket. All three people looked like college students, perhaps even underclassmen. The dark-haired man on the floor shuddered. His eyelids fluttered open, and he groaned. His tan polo shirt was stained with blood, and there were dark, sticky patches on the brick of the fireplace.

Jaylynn rose and grabbed an afghan from a chair to the right of the fireplace and spread it over the shaking man. Inspecting the slim woman, she noticed a streak of blood on her cheek. She wasn't sure if it was blood from the man on the floor or if Violet was injured.

"Are you hurt?"

Pleading brown eyes rose to meet hers. "No, I'm fine. It's just Larry I'm worried about."

"Can you tell me what happened here?"

"I came downstairs. These two idiots were fighting, rolling around on the floor. I couldn't get them to stop. When they heard me yelling into the phone, screaming for the police, they broke it off. But Larry here couldn't leave well enough alone. He took one last shot at Daniel, and Daniel pushed him away...next thing I knew there was blood all over."

Jaylynn made notes on her pad. Behind her, she could hear Dez speaking to the man on the couch.

"I—I didn't mean—he was *hitting* me. I pushed him away and he just...just tripped backwards. If he's dead, it's my fault." His voice broke.

The doorbell rang, and Dez went to look out the screen. Jaylynn heard her say, "Sorry kids. Emergency here. Move on to the next house."

The paramedics chose that moment to arrive, pushing into the front room with their orange bags and bulky coats. Jaylynn rose to give them access to the man, then backed away to stand near Dez. Daniel stayed on the couch, his head in his hands. He looked up at them and held his shaking hands out. "You can cuff me," he said.

The veteran cop slipped her notebook into her shirt pocket. "That won't be necessary. First, I'd like the paramedics to take a look at you. You may need to go to the hospital, too."

****

Later, back in the squad car, Jaylynn could only shake her head. "Those young men have been in that frat house together for almost two years. I can't get over how brutal they were to each other."

"And all over a woman."

"I got the impression Violet had broken up with Larry quite some time ago. You'd think he'd be a better sport even though one of his good friends was now dating her. She seemed like a nice enough person."

"People aren't logical, Jay."

"I'll say!"

"And who knows what's going on with Larry. He could be certifiably insane. We don't know."

Jaylynn could only shake her head and sigh. "Can we grab a bite to eat, partner? I am about to faint from hunger."

"That's just where I was headed."

"I'm going to start packing snacks for when stuff like this happens. I can't take it being hungry at a crime scene."

Dez was surprised that the rookie would even think of food when they got a call. She rarely did. "It's not like I'd want to eat anything at a scene like that."

"No, but I need to do a better job of having regular food. My blood sugar must be at about zero right now. It's not good for me to feel light-headed."

Dez turned back onto the street where *The Cutting Board* was located. "And all this time I thought the lightheadedness was due to riding with me."

Jaylynn grinned at her as they parked. "That, too. But that's an entirely *different* type of hunger."

The big cop rolled her eyes and got out of the car, glad that the evening disguised the fact that she was, again, blushing.

****

Dez and Jaylynn walked down a long hallway, passing nurses and physicians, most of whom were dressed in pale blue or green scrubs. They were making their way toward the Cardiac Care Unit.

In a grouchy voice, Dez asked, "How come this place is like a maze? They ought to hand out maps when you arrive."

Jaylynn wanted to reach out and take the tall woman's hand, but she knew Dez would be too self-conscious. Instead she moved closer and jostled her as they walked. "Actually, they do have maps up front. I think we can find our way though." She bumped the bigger woman again.

"You having trouble with your balance?"

Jaylynn grinned up at her and leaned into her again. "Not really. Just wanted to touch you."

Dez gave her the eye, even though she knew it didn't work very well on the rookie. Just then they reached Vanita's room.

"Hey, Van," Jaylynn called out.

The gray-haired woman was alone in the room and watching a T.V. soap program, complete with dire-sounding orchestral music in the background. She summoned them in. "Can you believe this crap? Veronica's making the moves on Dirk, and she knows full well that she's three months pregnant by Robert."

Jaylynn moved over to the bed and gave her a gentle hug while Dez hung back. "I sure hope that hussy Veronica isn't causing your blood pressure to rise."

"Oh, no, of course not. Have a seat. Go ahead. I finally got them to bring some chairs in—just in time for me to be leaving."

"Today?" Jaylynn asked.

"No such luck—but tomorrow is likely, least that's what they say."

The two women sat, and Dez listened as Jaylynn and Vanita gabbed back and forth about the T.V. program. Dez studied the older woman. Vanita's color had returned, and she didn't look nearly so haggard as she had even a day earlier. Other than an I.V. attached to the top of her hand, Vanita seemed back to normal.

At a break in the conversation, Dez asked about Luella.

"She's taking me home tomorrow."

"Hey, that's great," Jaylynn said. "Your place or hers?"

"I think mine, for the time being."

Dez asked, "Do you two need a lift then?"

"My granddaughter, Ardella, is coming with her mini-van, so we should be fine. Thanks for asking. Hopefully she'll leave all the little ones behind. When Micah and Marcus were here yesterday, they crawled under the bed and unplugged everything. Thank the Lord that I wasn't on some sort of life support! Three-year-olds are just too much."

Jaylynn rose and patted Vanita on the arm. "We'll do grocery runs for you then. You'll let us know if—when—you need things, right?"

"Oh yes. Thanks so much, Jay, honey. And when I'm feeling better, we need to have a big party and invite all those young folks back. I still can't get over the fact that those sweet young men gave me mouth-to-mouth, and I wasn't even awake to enjoy it."

Jaylynn cracked up. Through her laughter, she said, "I hate to break the bad news, Van, but they used a plastic mask to do the CPR."

Vanita shrugged. "Still...you know, it was really something what they did."

Dez stood and Vanita craned her neck up to look at her. "All right then, you two've got better things to do than hanging with a recuperating old lady. Go on now. Do some dancing or something fun. Life's short. You should enjoy yourselves as much as you can. Won't be long and you'll be old and decrepit like me." She smiled and shook her head. "Go live it up, girls."

She gave them each a goodbye hug and returned to her T.V.

program.

Retracing their steps out to the parking lot, Jaylynn said, "You know what? She's right. We *should* go dancing."

"Yeah? Why's that?"

They reached the truck and Jaylynn crawled up into it. "Life *is* short. Anything can happen. We ought to do some fun things, in honor of Vanita. We haven't been out for a long time. Let's grab Crystal and Shayna and go have some fun after shift on Saturday night."

Dez started up the truck and backed out. She didn't mind dancing, but she hated the crowds. And the smoke and noise. But Jaylynn enjoyed it, so she agreed.

****

Dez gazed around the nightclub, wrinkling up her nose at the smell of cigarettes. She stood with her arm across the shoulders of the shorter, blonde-haired woman who was currently gazing up at her with a smirk on her face.

"Dez," Jaylynn asked, "are we *ever* going to dance?"

"I've been waiting for a decent song, Jay." As she spoke, one song ended and the next began. The DJ had been playing fast dance songs, one right after another, and occasionally he threw in a slower tune. They moved out onto the dance floor, warming up to an old Blondie song, "Call Me." And then he spun a quiet one, "Angel" by Sarah McLachlan.

Dez smiled. She leaned in and said, "*This* is the kind of song I was waiting for." Jaylynn moved close to her, and they gracefully fell into step with one another. While other couples tended to shift back and forth from one foot to the other, the two cops quickly glided into an intricate pattern.

In her partner's ear, Dez said, "I'm only letting you lead because you seem to be enjoying it so much."

Jaylynn tipped her head back and looked up into twinkling blue eyes. "Can't take a little direction, huh?"

"I can always take a little—not much—but a little. Be careful though, I could dip ya any time now."

"Ha!" Jaylynn let out a guffaw. She snuggled closer and continued giggling. After a moment she looked up again. "You really are a good dancer, Miss Fred Astaire. How'd you learn?"

Even in the dim light Jaylynn could see Dez blush. The taller woman said, "Well, Miss Ginger Rogers, I cursed my mother for it, but she made me take dance lessons in eighth and ninth grade."

"Why, Desiree, you went to *charm* school?"

In a grumbling voice, Dez answered, "Something like that. I hated it. Had to learn to waltz, foxtrot, swing, square dance, polka—like I was ever gonna use any of it!"

"What a wise mother you had. She must have known the day would arrive where those skills would come in handy dancing in a nice lesbian bar. You're quite impressive, you know."

"You're not so bad yourself," Dez said grudgingly. "How'd *you* learn?"

"I loved dancing and took a few classes in high school and college." The last strains of Sarah McLachlan trailed off, and the DJ faded in a Gloria Estefan song with a medium beat. "Hmm," Jaylynn said as they changed the tempo of their movements, "did you ever learn the mambo?"

"What?"

"You know something like...like the cha-cha?"

Dez grinned. "Yeah. Why?"

"Think you can still do it?"

"Who's leading?" the big woman said mock seriously.

Now it was Jaylynn's turn to laugh. "We could both lead—but hey, really, that won't work. Go ahead, you lead."

"No," Dez said, with a sigh. "You probably remember the moves better than me."

"Okay, and I'll try not to step on your size 10's."

Dez scowled at her, then couldn't help but smile. "Yeah, all right. Let's do it."

The smaller woman expected there to be some knee knocking—or at least awkwardness—so she was thoroughly surprised when they slipped into the syncopated rhythm without hesitation or problems. She found herself grinning, then bubbling over with jubilation. Who would have ever thought that dancing with the tight-lipped tall woman could be so much fun? Who on the force would even *believe* it? She eyed her companion, loving how she moved with an effortless fluidity, her long limbs coordinated and graceful. It made Jaylynn want to wrap her arms around Dez in a tight embrace and just squeeze.

The song ended and the head-banging beat from a hard rock song took its place. With just the slightest of glances, they simultaneously turned and headed off the dance floor with Jaylynn holding Dez's hand tightly. They stood in the throng at the bar counter, waiting to order a drink, and the rookie said, "That was a blast—totally exciting." She looked up at her partner, eyes shining, and said, "Ever notice how the *best* words all start with E? Exciting, elation, exhilaration. What *great* words!"

"Yeah? What about errors? Evil?" She frowned. "And

embarrassment...or wait a minute, how 'bout executions?"

"Oh, Dez," Jaylynn said, a quirky grin passing over her lips. "What about electricity?" She moved closer. "How about elegance?" She reached her hand out and caught the bigger woman about the waist, pulling her until the two women were pressed together at the hips. She arched her back and leaned her upper body away, smiling up at the blue eyes above her. "What about energy...or emotion?" Jaylynn reached up and cupped the bigger woman's face in her hands, confident that the strong arms wrapped around her would not let go. "Entertainment. Enthusiasm. Or hey—how about enjoyment?"

Dez leaned down and in a husky voice said, "Erotic embrace. Two for the price of one."

"Now you're in the spirit." She thought a moment as she gazed up into intense dark blue eyes. "How about enraptured? Or even better, enthralled?"

"What about everlasting?" The low whisper came from lips right at her ear. A shiver ran through the shorter woman, and suddenly her heart pounded and her legs went weak. She tucked her head under Dez's chin and let her arms slip down around the broad back, then to her waist. She could hear the thundering heartbeat under her ear, which caused her to feel even weaker and more breathless.

Crystal's voice fluttered in. "You two gonna stand there all night?"

Jaylynn lifted her head but didn't let go of Dez. She angled her face to the side until she caught sight of the laughing Latina. Crystal reached over and socked Dez in the arm lightly. "Hey, *chica*," she belted out over the loud music. "If I'd known you could dance *my* kind of dance, I would've had you to one of our family parties a long time ago."

Over the music, Dez said, "I've never seen you do the cha-cha."

"Not here, but with *mi familia* it's a different story."

In a loud voice, Dez said, "I can't imagine *su familia* enjoying the sight of you and me dancing."

Crystal frowned. "Well, guess you got me there. But there are a lot of men in my family who'd kill to dance with you."

Dez tightened her grip on Jaylynn in front of her. Looking down her shoulder at her friend she said, "My dance card is now full." This caused Crystal to go off into gales of laughter.

Shayna came up bchind Crystal, shaking her head. From behind, she wrapped her brown arms around her partner's middle and rested her chin on her shorter partner's shoulder. "Is she bothering you two lovebirds?"

Dez pursed her lips to keep from smiling, but before she could say anything, Jaylynn piped up and said, "I think I'd pay money to see the two of you dancing at one of Crystal's family soirees. In fact, I'd pay to see the two of you dance *now.*" She grinned up at Dez, then shared a conspiratorial look with Shayna.

Both Jaylynn and Shayna let go of their partners. Hands on hips, the two women looked back and forth between Dez and Crystal, who were both blushing and looking everywhere but at each other. The two instigators burst into hysterical laughter and fell all over each other, gasping for air as they cackled out of control.

Dez and Crystal exchanged sympathetic looks with one another, then Crystal jerked a thumb toward the dance floor. "You 'n' me, kid," she hollered over the dance track. Without a look back, the two tough cops stomped out to the floor and into the squirming mass of bodies, leaving Shayna and Jaylynn startled.

Shayna draped an arm over Jaylynn's shoulder and said, "Oooh, guess we hit a nerve on our girls."

Jaylynn smiled up at her. "Doesn't take much. You could only imagine what it would be like playing *Truth or Dare* with either of them!"

They both laughed, then Shayna said, "Let's go rescue them from each other. I can see the top of Dez's head, and they don't seem to be moving much, so they're probably standing out there plotting against us." She ushered Jaylynn out to the floor, where they found the two women shifting back and forth from foot to foot as they stood close enough to hear one another. Jaylynn was fairly certain that they had to be discussing work, a thought that was verified when she heard Crystal say something about misdemeanor arrests. She sighed. Just once she'd like to forget about police work for a while.

****

Outside the Club Metro Bar, as his FTO watched, Rookie Officer Dwayne Neilsen handcuffed a drunken young man and supported him as he half-dragged, half-pushed him toward the squad car. "Come on!" the officer muttered. "It's bad enough that you're drunk as a skunk, but for chrissake! You pissed in someone else's car. Jesus, what an idiot you are. It's off to Detox for you, asshole."

Neilsen put a big hand on the top of the man's head to guide him down and into the squad car, then lifted the drunk's leg and shoved him into the rear seat. He slammed the door and turned to his FTO, Officer Alvarez. "Art, I gotta take a piss myself. I'll be right back."

Alvarez nodded and opened the driver's door as Neilsen strode quickly toward the club. The young cop took the stairs down two at a time and slipped through the open door as another man opened it to leave. The bar ran the length of the far wall, across from the entrance. The left half of the room contained tables and chairs while the right section was a dance floor, currently full of writhing bodies moving to the thump of the canned music.

Neilsen wasn't familiar with the layout of the bar—and, in fact, had never been in it—so he stood in the dimly lit room, letting his eyes adjust as he scanned for a restroom sign. To his right, he saw two men kissing passionately. His head whipped around, and he inspected the groups of people: men with men, women with women. *Geez, this is a goddamn gay bar. Great. Hope it's safe to pee here with this bunch of perverts!* His eyes skimmed along the crowd in front of the bar, then he did a double take, back to a figure a head taller than the gang surrounding her. A familiar woman stood facing the entrance, her lips turned up in a happy, smug half-smile that Neilsen had never seen before. *Reilly!* he thought. *Dez Reilly. For chrissake, I knew it. I just knew it!*

Dez Reilly's arms were locked around a smaller, laughing figure topped with short white-blonde hair. The shorter person leaned away, but the dark-haired woman tightened her grip, leaning down and whispering something that caused the two to suddenly stand still. Then the blonde wrapped her arms around the tall woman's middle and pressed the side of her cheek against Dez's chest.

Holy shit! Neilsen grinned with delight. *It's Savage. For chrissake, it's Savage! This is going to be sweet. Sweet revenge.*

The tall woman's head came up, and Neilsen could swear she caught sight of him. He stepped to the side, behind two men who had just entered the club, and breathed a sigh of relief when the dark-haired cop's eyes swept past him. He skulked over to the side, ducking behind happy patrons and angling toward the men's room, but not before catching sight of Crystal Lopez, another cop who just so happened to have some woman Neilsen had never seen hanging over her shoulder.

Got 'em dead to rights, he thought gleefully. *I'll teach those bitches a lesson this time.*

Chapter
Eight

Dez sat at a stop sign on Hoyt Street in an unmarked car with the radar gun aimed out the window at the traffic traveling on Dale. It was cold out, but only her hands felt it. The car's heater, even on low, was doing an admirable job keeping her warm on this early November Wednesday night.

Jaylynn had departed Monday morning for Pursuit Training, and with her out of town, Dez had been assigned to a speed sting with Reed and Barstow. Right now, her job was to shoot the radar, then radio data about the speeder ahead. The other two units, which were posted five or six blocks ahead, took turns pulling over the surprised offender. When she got tired of the radar role, she'd switch with one of the guys. The speed limit on Dale Street was only 35. So far, in two hours, they'd nailed six cars in excess of 45 and three in excess of 55. One fool had been careening along at 62. He'd also been legally drunk, so Barstow had been gone for a while to book him at the station. She and Reed carried on.

With Jaylynn off at pursuit training for the past two days, Dez was starting to get crabby. She was glad the rookie would be returning Thursday. Only one more day to get through without her. The day before, the tall cop had confided in Luella that she was now ruined. Once upon a time, she had been thoroughly self-sufficient. Now after a couple of months of spending nights with the rookie, she didn't seem to know what to do with herself when Jaylynn wasn't with her. What had she done before Jaylynn entered her life? She couldn't quite recall. And to be honest, she was disconcerted to realize how much she had come to rely upon the pleasure of the younger woman's company.

She zapped a late model Chrysler...47 mph. She radioed

ahead to Reed, then returned to her musings, waiting for Reed to call and say he was ready for the next speeder. Jaylynn had called late the night before to report that the first day at Michigan International Speedway had gone well. She bubbled over with excitement about how much fun she was having driving like a maniac. She had also been happy because two of her classmates from the Academy, who had gone to work for other agencies, had also been there. She was having the chance to get caught up with her buddies' lives. Obviously, Dez thought the rookie wasn't missing her work partner as much as Dez was missing her.

Today and tomorrow, Jaylynn would be at a different site to learn the elements of more aggressive pursuits. In addition to the art of roadblocks and the use of stop sticks, which punctured tires, she'd be introduced to pursuit intervention techniques—PIT training—which was basically having contact or ramming another vehicle to conclude a pursuit. Dez hoped her young partner wouldn't take as much delight in that as she had enjoyed speeding around the racetrack. Intentional collisions or even light contact were considered deadly force and not allowed by the department unless the suspect had committed a violent crime against persons or if somebody's life was in immediate danger. Still, all officers had to learn the techniques, because no one ever knew when they would be necessary. The tall cop had last attended that training the year before—for the seventh time in her career. She was glad she had fast reflexes because the cars could easily go out of control, even at low speeds. But she had to admit, spinning and skidding on the safe, flat surface was a lot of fun.

The radio crackled, and Reed reported that he was done with the Chrysler, so she turned her attention to the oncoming traffic. A small car, which looked like a Neon, sped toward her. She hit the trigger on the radar gun and radioed the results right away. "Here's a good one, Reed. 53 mph. Yellow Neon." She recited the license number and waited for his response. Glancing at her watch, she realized it was going to be a long night. She gave a sigh. *This would be a lot more fun with Jaylynn.* Just one more day, and she'd see her again.

****

Dez arrived at the precinct early on Thursday and in a good mood. Jaylynn and the rest of the crew would be returning this afternoon from their long drive. She hoped they'd come rolling in before shift started, but she knew she couldn't count on it. They had a six hour drive ahead of them.

Full of happy expectation, she climbed the stairs, camped out in the roll call room, and sat on alert, awaiting the first sign of the caravan's return.   She was disappointed when the sergeant released them all to their cars and there was no sign of Jaylynn. She went out to her assigned cruiser and left to patrol her sector.

Many times during the course of the shift she was tempted to call in to Dispatch to ask about the travelers, but she knew they'd have to call her precinct to get information, and she could do that herself.   She didn't want to draw attention to herself, so she just did her job.   The first few hours of the afternoon and evening were quiet, almost boring.   Around nine p.m., things started to pick up with a noise complaint and then a backup at a repeat domestic dispute.   Sorenson answered the initial domestic call, but nobody liked to go into those kinds of inflammatory scenes without a second officer nearby, so she joined him as quickly as she could get there.   It was a standard call—drunk man shows up at ex-girlfriend's house to slap her around and terrorize her.

The tall cop watched from the doorway as Sorenson handled it.   Unlike Jaylynn, Sorenson tried to give the intruder every opportunity to get out of the mess.   If there was any evidence of assault, Jaylynn just cuffed the abuser immediately and almost always hauled the person in.   Sorenson was patient, but the man was scathing and insulting, so the other cop finally arrested him. As he dragged the man out to his squad car, Dez asked the woman if she would be pressing charges.

"You bet, Officer!"   She pushed her long blonde hair away from her face and pointed at her bleeding lip defiantly.   "That's the last time he's *ever* gonna do this to me.   Next time, I'll have a gun waiting for him."

Dez winced.   "You know, you'd do better to spend the money on a peephole for your front door."

"What?"

"He came to the door—you opened it."

"Oh, so this is my fault?"   Now she focused her anger on the tall cop, her pretty blue eyes sparkling with rage.

"No, ma'am.   Not at all.   He made the choice to assault you. He's in the wrong.   But look," she pointed at the front door and the wall next to it, "you can't tell who's out there without opening the door, right?"

"Um, no."

"That's the problem.   If you have a peephole, you can see when it's him and just call 911.   We'd come and haul him away, and that's that.   Saves you a lot of money, too.   Guns aren't cheap, you know.   And it would also prevent a criminal charge of manslaughter or murder. You rent here?"

The woman nodded as she reached for a tissue and dabbed at her cut lip.

"Here," Dez pulled a card out of her pocket. "Call me there at the station and leave your landlord's name and phone number on the voicemail. I'll call him or her and see if I can get them to install something in the front door. Maybe if you purchase it—and they're pretty cheap—the landlord will put it in. Okay?"

The woman looked surprised. She nodded. "Thank you. Thanks for your understanding."

"No problem. Now lock up good." She turned and with a wave of her hand, went out the door and headed to her car. She was constantly amazed at how little foresight some people had. This was a repeat performance by the assaultive ex-boyfriend. *You'd think the ex-girlfriend would catch a clue and do something to avoid the scene.* She hoped that the woman would leave her the landlord's information. She didn't mind calling and trying to help, but so many times people didn't listen.

The rest of the evening dragged by, and finally, she arrived back at the station, turned the car in, signed out, and went down to her locker. There was a note taped to the blue door. "Call me before you leave" was all it said. Jaylynn hadn't signed it, but she knew the rookie's scribble.

With a light heart, she changed clothes and went upstairs to use a phone. "Hey! You're back."

Jaylynn's warm voice came over the line. "I am."

"You sound tired."

"I am."

"Is that all you can say—'I am'?"

"No. Mostly I just wanted to check and see if you'd still want to come over—"

"Sure," Dez interrupted.

"—but there's a catch."

Dez waited, puzzled.

"Do you mind sleeping against the wall?"

"What?"

"I sort of hurt my left shoulder a little bit, and...well, I—I guess I need to sleep on the outside so I don't bump it."

Dez's blood ran cold. "You're hurt?"

"Um, well, sort of."

"Badly?"

"Well—not exactly."

"What do you mean, 'Not exactly'? What happened?"

Jaylynn hesitated. "Come over, okay? It's easier to explain

in person."

Dez didn't bother to say anything further. She hung up the phone and took off toward the parking lot. She didn't stop for pleasantries in the doorway when she ran into some officers who said hello to her. She leapt into her truck and zoomed down Dale Avenue, glad that there was no speed sting there tonight.

She passed the string of darkened homes, everyone hunkered down for the night and likely sleeping. Then she got to Jaylynn's house, from which light spilled out of every window, both upstairs and down. A chill wind blew from the north, cutting through her leather jacket, making her shiver as she walked toward the brightly lit two-story house.

Before she could even knock, the rookie opened the door and let her in, and they stood for just a moment, both uncertain. Dez glanced at the navy blue, heavy-duty sling Jaylynn wore on her left arm. She looked across the room to see that Sara and Bill were sitting next to one another on the couch, eating a bowl of popcorn, and watching a video.

"Dez," Sara called out. "We just started this. It's *Pitch Black*. Want to join us?"

Without taking her eyes off Jaylynn's face, Dez said, "Not right now. Maybe later." She gave a jerk of her head and gestured to the stairs.

With a miserable look on her face, Jaylynn turned and mounted the steps. Dez followed her up to the peach-colored bedroom, where she found Jaylynn's bags and gear strewn haphazardly across the bed and couch. The room was much more disorganized than usual, and the smaller woman leaned down slowly to pick up a suitcase and slide it aside. Dez stepped in the room and shut the door behind her. She leaned back against the door and crossed her arms.

"Sorry," the rookie said. "I haven't even unpacked." She stood in the middle of the room and looked back apologetically. Dez wanted to go to her, wrap her in her arms, but first she wanted to know the extent of Jaylynn's injury.

"What happened?" It came out in a flat voice, almost accusatory.

"I broke—or kinda like cracked—my collarbone." Jaylynn sighed, then moved her black duffel with her good hand off the couch and onto the floor. She clambered onto the soft orange sofa and squeezed back in the corner, her feet up under her as she cradled her left arm.

In silence, Dez remained leaning against the door, her heart beating fast.

Tired hazel eyes looked over at her. "It was totally an accident on the last run of the day. All I was supposed to do was accelerate to catch up with the other vehicle and use my left front quarter panel to tap its right rear and send him out of control. Guy named Davison was driving the tank—it's like a tank, you know, since they're the vehicle that is supposed to go out of control."

Dez nodded. She remembered exactly what it was like from the last training she had attended.

"The car I was in was pretty much like a regular squad car, though it did have a nice roll bar and some extra internal reinforcement, which, as it turns out, was lucky. Anyway, I was cruising along, drawing close to him, going about 45, when suddenly I heard a pop and my car—well, it kind of like dipped, and I skidded. I was fishtailing and losing control, so I hit the brakes. I spun out."

"And?"

"I ran off the flat area onto the side of the course."

"What the hell caused it? You blew a tire?"

Jaylynn nodded. "Somebody left a string of stop sticks real close to the side of the course, and I hit one. They told me that when my tire punctured, they saw a poof of dirt go up, then I started skidding."

"Weren't you in your protective gear?"

"Oh yeah! Of course. Helmet, vest, and everything"

"But the steering wheel hit you hard—or what?"

"No." Jaylynn shook her head and looked away. "It was the tree."

"What? You hit a tree?"

"Dez! You make it sound like I'm a rotten driver or something! The instructor said I did an admirable job steering out of the spin and bringing the car to a stop."

"You slammed into a tree?"

"No...not exactly. Actually it was just the one big branch that came in through the driver's side window."

"Oh, I see. So you didn't hit the tree—it hit you?"

"Something like that. But don't worry, I had already passed the driving class before the final runs, so I don't have to go again for two years."

"Like I give a shit whether you pass pursuit training?" It came out in a shout, and Dez straightened up and pushed away from the door she was leaning on. "You're hurt, Jay! You could have been killed."

"Nuh uh! No way! It was just...just an accident. Kind of a

freak thing. Davison joked that it would have been better to have the branch smack me in the head instead of the chest since I had that great helmet on."

"For cripesake! The guy must be an idiot! Who the hell do they have running training these days!" She clenched her fists against her hips as she worked hard to contain her fury.

Jaylynn turned red and looked like she might cry. "Why are you so angry, Dez? Stuff like this happens. One cop from Faribault actually rolled one of the cars. He didn't get hurt though."

Dez shook her head. She closed her eyes and took a deep breath, then made herself relax her fists. Opening her eyes, she stepped into the middle of the bedroom, square in the center of the braided carpet. Her hands were cold, and when she looked down at them, she was surprised to see that she wasn't outwardly shaking. Inside, her heart was pounding and she suddenly found she could hardly breathe. The images in her head frightened her: blood and darkness, bright lights, and screaming sirens.

There was no way to communicate the feelings of terror—not without sounding like a three-year-old. She looked at the worried hazel eyes peering up at her from the couch, eyes in a face that looked afraid and hurt. Taking a deep breath, she moved over to the couch, put one knee on a cushion and lowered herself onto it, her other long leg still planted on the floor next to the sofa. In a gentle voice, she said, "Let me see. Are you in a cast or splint?"

Jaylynn shook her head. "No. I'm just dinged up a little so I have to use this support." With her right hand she unbuttoned her blouse and shifted the heavy canvas sling to the side. She flinched as she moved her arm and the sling. Closing her eyes, she took a deep, ragged breath. "Hurts like hell."

Dez nodded.

Jaylynn pulled her blouse open. Peering down, she missed the horrified expression on Dez's face and didn't look up until the other woman sank down beside her on the couch.

"Jesus, Jay...that looks terrible."

All around the collarbone, the skin was blue and purple with bruising, and a jagged two-inch gash was held together by three butterfly bandaids. It was swollen and puffy.

Jaylynn shook her head slowly, and Dez had to restrain herself from taking the smaller woman into her arms. She sighed. "I don't even know how to touch you without hurting you."

With that, Jaylynn teared up. "I know...I know, and it's all my fault." A tear rolled down her cheek. Dez reached over and wiped it away. "I can't even button up my shirt by myself," she said, her voice cracking.

The tall woman scooted over right next to her. "Oh, Jay...it's not really your fault." She started with the lowest button and worked her way up, careful not to touch anything but the cotton material and the little white buttons. "Looks like you're going to be wearing shirts like this for a couple of weeks."

The rookie nodded in agreement. She sniffed. "I can't put my arms over my head. It hurts to turn my head quickly. I can't even blow my own nose very well." She shifted her arm back in front of her, looking forlorn and pained.

"Bet you don't do all that well with your Aikuchi knife for a while either."

Jaylynn smiled through her tears. "I just want you to hold me."

Dez shrugged. "Okay." She shifted back against the sofa cushion and put both feet flat on the floor and her arms up along the back of the couch. "Arrange me how you want me—just so I don't hurt you."

The rookie stood and went to Dez's left side and sat next to her. She brought her legs up on the couch off to the left side and leaned into the bigger woman's chest, cradling her sore left arm carefully. Once the smaller woman got settled, Dez brought her left arm around her shoulders. "Is that okay?"

"Yeah, I'm fine." She snuggled in close, the side of her face pressed against the flannel of the bigger woman's shirt.

They sat quietly for a moment until Dez suddenly sighed.

"What was that for?"

"I suppose I'm stuck doing that damn DARE class by myself again."

"Ohhh...never thought of that." She grinned. "Those kids like you. You'll do fine." She began to giggle. "It's kind of funny, you know. They listen to me, but they're transfixed by you. You'll have a captive audience."

"Yeah, right," she grumbled. In an irritated voice, she asked, "How long before this will heal? And how long will you be off work?"

"Two to three weeks. My own doctor will be able to tell more when the swelling goes down. I stopped to see Lt. Malcolm, and he said I'm on desk duty starting tomorrow night."

"That'll be fun," Dez said, the sarcasm in her voice evident.

"I'm sure there's something I can do to help."

"Yeah, coffee patrol, sorting, filing, phone messages, and the like. It'll be very stimulating." She chuckled and shook her head, then after a moment, felt a cold chill pass over her. She wanted to speak her mind, tell Jaylynn that she didn't think the younger woman was cut out to be a cop. Ninety-nine percent of the time, she thought the rookie handled things just fine, but her small, slender stature was a distinct disadvantage. It was too easy for her to get hurt. *Am I just being sexist,* she wondered? *Or size-ist?* Half of the women on the force were Jaylynn's size, maybe only slightly bigger or taller. The rookie had smarts, that was for sure, and she had determination, but still, Dez couldn't help but feel constant apprehension, especially when they rode separately. More than ever, she decided that it was important that the two of them continue as partners, otherwise, who could she trust? There were few officers she had total faith in—and even then, errors and mistakes could happen. She couldn't stand to see anything more happen to this miraculous person who was now drowsing against her chest.

Chapter
Nine

Jaylynn looked down at the last two reports on the desk. Once she filed them away, she was caught up with all the tasks she had been assigned. The only thing good about being on desk duty was that she didn't have to carry every single item on her duty belt—just her weapon and cuffs. The difference in weight was amazing. She filed the second to the last report and thought about how it was going to be a very long night. Dez had been so right. After three days, the rookie had to admit that light duty was no fun. She ran out of computer updating to do after the last shift. With only one good hand, she couldn't do a variety of tasks, and now that she had organized, sorted, filed, tidied, and cleaned up everything within sight, there wasn't anything further to do, except wait to answer the phone, which, tonight, was just not ringing. Sunday nights were usually a crashing bore. Nearly two more hours to kill.

She let out a sigh just as Lt. Malcolm came into the room.

"Hey, Savage. You've got things looking pretty good around here."

She smiled at her superior. "Thank you, sir." She liked him a lot. He was always respectful, always calm, even when other officers were in serious trouble or had done something stupid beyond compare. So far, she had received only praise and constructive criticism from him, never any sort of reproval, despite the fact that in her less than a year with the department, she had been involved in a shooting, several physical tussles with suspects on the beat, a fire, and now a training accident. This was the first time she'd had to be taken off patrol though.

The gray-eyed man hitched up his trousers and swung a thigh up onto the edge of the desk, sitting comfortably half on and half off. "How long before you get released for duty?"

Jaylynn opened and closed her left hand, flexing the forearm muscles. She still couldn't move her arm away from her torso without pain. "Couple weeks, Lieutenant."

He nodded. "That's what I thought. I can't keep you busy, Savage. Unless you have an objection, I am going to reassign you to Lt. Finn over at the main station."

"Oh?" She was surprised. "What will I do there?"

"It's a *lot* busier, for one thing. Besides doing some phone detail, Finn can assign you to something, maybe an active case or two, maybe some follow-up on citizen complaints. I'm not sure what she'll want you to do, but I guarantee it'll be a lot more interesting than this." He gestured out at the empty room.

"I haven't minded, Lieutenant, really."

He smiled. "I know. But you'll start minding pretty quick when there's absolutely nothing to work on at all." He laughed and said, "I couldn't even assign you to paint the lockers. I just had Cameron do that when he broke his foot." He stood. "I'll get you back over here once you're healed up, okay?"

"Okay."

"You're to report to Lieutenant Denise Finn tomorrow at two. Your hours are going to change for the next couple weeks— two to eleven, Monday through Friday. You ever meet Finn?"

"No, sir."

"She's a good leader. You'll like her. Just follow her instructions and you'll get along great with her."

"Okay, thanks. Sorry about this, Lieutenant. I know this leaves you short."

"We'll get by. Reilly and Patterson both said they'd pick up a couple extra shifts, and I can move people around. We'll be all right through the end of the month." He stepped away, then turned back. "You want some coffee or something, Savage?"

"No, thank you." She gestured at a thermos on the desk. "I'm drinking tea right now."

He gave a curt nod and strode out into the quiet hall. She watched him leave, wondering how old he was. He reminded her a little of her stepfather—the light colored eyes, the calmness, the gentle disposition. But he was no softie. She had seen him upset, stern, eyes flashing, and being very direct with his officers. He was not someone she would want to disappoint either. Somehow, he had a way of making her want to do her very best, and she liked that about him. She respected the three sergeants who rotated on and off her shift, but she didn't feel that they cared quite as much about her well-being or her professional progress.

The phone rang, and as she picked it up, she looked at her watch. Nearly ten-thirty. She hoped this call would keep her busy for a long time.

****

Lieutenant Denise Finn was a solidly compact brunette who wore her dark blue pant suit and jacket well. Her shoulder length hair was swept off her forehead and held back by metal combs. She wore a rock of a wedding ring on her left hand. Jaylynn had already been clued in that Lt. Finn was married to a police captain who worked at the Minneapolis Police Department, and that one of her four children was a rookie on the Duluth force north of the Cities. Finn didn't look old enough to have an adult son. Jaylynn guessed the attractive woman's age to be less than 45, but she figured she was wrong.

The brunette crossed the room with quick steps and stuck her hand out. "Savage. Good to meet you. I've heard good things about you from Culpepper."

It took a brief second before Jaylynn realized the lieutenant meant Cowboy. As she released the strong, warm hand, she said, "Yes, ma'am. He's a great guy and an excellent cop."

Finn nodded. "That's what he says about you. Lt. Malcolm also speaks highly of you." She turned, making a gesture for Jaylynn to follow her, saying over her shoulder, "I don't know how you feel about investigations, but we've got too many things going on right now and not enough clerical help. I've got three detectives out with that dratted flu bug, and we've got two priority murder cases, both of them somewhat political. The heat is on."

She led Jaylynn into a cubbyhole of an office and pointed at the visitor's chair on the other side of the desk. The rookie sat, carefully arranging her sling so the arm of the chair didn't press against her. She looked around. The room was perhaps eight-by-ten and completely dwarfed by the metal desk and two battered file cabinets. On the only wall with open space, three framed items hung: a diploma from the University of Minnesota, an advanced P.O.S.T. certification from the Peace Officer's Standards and Training school, and a photo of Finn reaching out to shake the hand of a familiar looking woman wearing a blocky reddish-orange colored dress.

Before Jaylynn could figure out who the other woman in the photo was, the lieutenant smiled wickedly and said, "How do you like working with sexist, egotistical, and overly-cologned men?"

The rookie sensed a presence behind her and a deep voice she recognized said, "Now is that any way to refer to two of your best detectives?"

Dark-haired Tsorro sidled past Jaylynn's chair and moved into the room to stand next to the filing cabinet. Parkins slid by, too, saying, "Besides, boss, it's not *me* wearing all that smelly stuff."

Finn smiled up at them, then turned back to Jaylynn. "I hear you've met Tsorro and Parkins and that you've been interested in this case they caught—the Tivoli case. We've got a lot of clerical work and phoning to do. That's what I want to assign you to. You will work under the direction of these two. Basically, you're going to be communications central for them."

Jaylynn was having trouble holding back the grin that was bubbling up. She'd expected to sit out in the reception area or file police reports. Instead, it sounded like she was being given the opportunity to be junior investigator.

"Don't get too excited, though, Savage. You won't be doing any field investigation."

"Ah, Lieutenant," Tsorro said, "the little lady might want to come along on a few calls. You know, just to get the lay of the land."

Finn nodded. "That's fine. You guys make that decision. But Savage," she turned her attention back to the rookie, looking very serious, "you're a total greenhorn at this. I can't have you do anything, *not make one move*, without clearing it with the detectives or me. If you get a lead or even the smallest scrap of information, you bring it up immediately, okay?"

"Sure. No problem, Lieutenant."

"All right. The first thing you have to do—which I guarantee you will take most of the day—is get up-to-speed on what's happened since the night of October 13th. There's the initial reports—yours included." She smiled, her dark eyes looking warm and kind. "Look at the coroner's autopsy reports on both vics and the folders of photos. They're pretty graphic, so I hope you have a strong stomach."

Jaylynn nodded. "I remember the scene quite clearly, Lieutenant."

"We've got some preliminary tox screens, but DNA hasn't come in yet." She turned her head up toward the detectives. "And we've got—what, guys?—over a hundred statements?"

Parkins nodded. "I think we're at 129 now."

"And about that many more to go," Tsorro grumbled. "Damn amazing how people make themselves scarce after something like this happens."

Finn gave a curt nod. "It'll take you all day to read the

reports. But once you're current with what's gone on, you can start helping us track down the other witnesses. Hope you've got a tough ear because you're going to be on the phone a lot."

Jaylynn smiled at her temporary supervisor, then looked up at Tsorro and Parkins. The Italian man hunched his shoulders and took a deep breath. He looked tan, his hair well-oiled, and his suit impeccable. Parkins sighed and looked around, as though he expected the ceiling to fall in at any moment.

"Let's get some answers on this one, people."

The two men squeezed by Jaylynn's chair. She waited to rise until they had passed, but before she could get up, the lieutenant held a hand up. "One more thing." She glanced out into the hall, then turned back to the rookie. "I was serious that my guys are a bit sexist. They don't direct it at a person, but they do seem a little small-minded at times. If they—Tsorro in particular—should say anything that offends you, I want you in my office immediately. I can rein him in any time."

She must have seen some confusion on Jaylynn's face because she went on. "Don't get me wrong, Savage. They're good cops and they really are gentlemen, but in the old school sense. You'll get the full respect befitting a *lady,* but some women officers have felt their competence is questioned, perhaps even denigrated."

"I've got to admit, that's nothing new to me."

Finn chuckled. "Don't sit out there stewing. If you need to blow off steam about anything they say, come in. I need to know what's going on, if you're unhappy, running into roadblocks, having difficulties with any aspect of the job, whether it's minor or major. Question their assumptions. Ask for clarifications. Be a pain in their hides all you want." Now she was grinning. "They need a little of that."

"You can count on it."

"You'll learn a lot, Officer. They really know their stuff. Make 'em share it." She winked. "Also, if you like, this is plain-clothes division. You can wear your uniform, but you can also dress business casual if you'd rather."

"I'll stick with the uniform, Lieutenant. I think it would be better than wearing civvies which might give other officers the wrong idea."

Finn paused a moment, then nodded. "Okay. I see your point." She rose then, and Jaylynn did, too, following her out to the floor where she was assigned a desk right across from Tsorro's so that his phone could be slid over for her use. After some initial instructions and encouragement from Zorro and Tonto, she scooted up to the big desk and gazed at the stack of paperwork in front of her.

From across the room, Parkins asked, "Want a little advice?"

She looked over, raising her eyebrows.

"Start at the beginning and work forward." He put a tooth-pick between his lips as he strode toward the desk and came to stand next to it. Putting a sizable thigh on the edge of her desk, he lowered himself and half-sat there, arms crossed, as he worked the toothpick with one side of his mouth and talked through the other side. "Re-read your own initial report, then look over the crime scene lab work. Examine the photos first, then the scene description and sketches, our reports, then the autopsy report. And finally, you've got a multitude of witness statements to review. The lieutenant was right. This'll take you the better part of the day." He patted the desk twice. "It'll keep you going into tomorrow I bet. Meantime, me and Zorro are off to track some of these reluctant witnesses at their workplaces. We'll check back in toward the end of the day, 'kay?"

She smiled. "Thanks. I'm going to do exactly what you said."

"I tried to stack things up in a linear progression—might've got it off on a few items, so watch for that."

"Okay, Parkins. I appreciate it."

He rose with a sigh. "May as well call me Tonto. Everyone else does." He shook his head wearily and walked back over to his desk, opened a drawer, and pulled out some keys. "Ready to roll?" Parkins asked his partner.

With a nod, Tsorro adjusted his suit, buttoned the jacket, and strolled past. "Later, doll," he called over his shoulder as he shot his cuffs.

Jaylynn snickered. She looked over her left shoulder to see the lieutenant staring out inquisitively from her small office. The rookie raised her eyebrows and shrugged. Finn nodded once, then looked back down at her paperwork, and Jaylynn opened the first folder of reports.

****

Hours passed, punctuated by a quick sandwich and an occasional call. Parkins had forwarded his phone to Tsorro's line one, which Jaylynn understood she would soon be answering. Line two calls were transferred internally from other desks or departments and were unlikely to be about this investigation, so she was to concentrate on line one. She figured she may as well start taking messages right away, since it would save the detectives time.

Eventually a Tivoli witness returned a previous call and stated he was ready to meet with the investigators. She put him on hold, and went to the lieutenant's office and stood in the doorway to ask what she should do.

"They're out in the field now, but they've got cell phones." Finn reached down and opened a drawer, pulled out a sheet of paper, and held it out for Jaylynn. The rookie entered the office and accepted the sheet. "This is a list of every detective's cell and pager. You'll get an occasional misdirected call, too, so if it sounds like something important, relay it out. When in doubt, just come ask me."

Jaylynn thanked her and went back to the desk. She called Parkins, gave him the name and address for the witness, and was told that they could be to that location in twenty minutes. She rang off, picked up the other phone, and got back to the man on hold to explain. When she hung up, she picked up a legal pad and started a four column log: Caller's Name, Address, Phone Number, Notes.

She went back to the crime scene reports. The photos had been harrowing—and sad. Although the medical exam had fixed the man's physiological age at as much as a decade older, Tivoli had only been age 36. The medical examiner's report indicated that he already had the beginning of hardening of the arteries as well as lungs damaged by heavy smoking. Still, he probably had many years before him. She knew he didn't deserve to have his life end in such a brutal way.

Even worse was the girl's murder. Jaylynn gave an involuntary shudder when she thought of the terror the young teenager had known in those last few seconds of her life. The evidence and the ME's report verified that Tivoli had been shot in the right side of the parietal region of his brain. He had been kneeling in the trailer at the time. The girl, in contrast, had been shot in the back as she opened the screen door to the snack stand. They knew this because she had been spattered with blood not her own, and she left a smeared footprint near the victim. She must have also been in the snack shack at the time of the shooting, but had somehow managed to get up and to the door. Once hit by the .38 caliber bullet, she tumbled down the stairs, out onto the parking lot cement, and somehow got onto her hands and knees. Exactly fourteen feet, three inches, from the foot of the metal stairs, she had dragged herself, over into the shadows behind the stand. Her life ended there with a gunshot to very nearly the same spot in the back of her head, parietal lobe, right side.

Jaylynn came up for air and focused her bleary eyes up at the

ceiling. *A right-handed killer. That rules out about twelve percent of the U.S. population.* She arched her back, which made for
an unpleasant pull on the muscles in her shoulder, and shifted in
her chair, then looked around the homicide squad room. After
years of watching *NYPD Blue* and *Homicide: Life on the Street,*
she wouldn't have been surprised to find herself in a cramped,
dingy, dirty hole of an office. Instead, the large windows let in
light. Clean walls were painted beige, the carpeting was relatively
new, and the place actually looked downright cheery. But it was
cramped. There were desks angled into every nook and cranny, on
either side of the windows, next to the pipes that ran along one
wall, and pushed right up against the large support pillars
throughout the room. She sat at one of four desks placed end to
end up the middle of the room. It was tight, but workable. At the
moment, two other detectives were in the room working studi-
ously at computers, compiling reports, she assumed. She was surprised at how quiet it was.

   She went back to the pile of reports before her and began
examining pages and pages of copies of fingerprint lift cards. She
discovered that the investigators had had a stroke of good luck.
Someone they assumed to be the shooter had left partial prints on
the inner and outer frame of the metal doorway, part of which was
made all the more vivid by the fact that one finger had pressed
against a speckle of blood. Most of the palm print was smeared as
though the assailant had grabbed the frame and pulled himself
through in a hurry. It was a big palm print, presumably a man's.
Jaylynn paged through the sheets of fingerprint information and
the results received from the FBI's AFIS—the Automated Fingerprint Identification System. The submissions had gone to the
AFIS computers less than 24 hours after the murders, and the
results had been returned electronically one day later. Tivoli was
a positive match. Seven other prints from inside the stand, including the bloody ones, were unknown. The prints for the Jane Doe
were unknown. It was unlikely that AFIS would have had her
prints on file. Jaylynn remembered learning that the Feds had
about thirty-five million prints, but unless this teenage girl had
been arrested for something major and fingerprinted, she wouldn't
show up in their records.

   She was disappointed to see that the prints from the doorjamb
were not identified. The preponderance of prints lifted from the
scene came from Tivoli and the girl. There were also prints from
the three young boys on the shelf that stuck out from the snack
shack. She found the cards for Sai Vang, his cousin Xiong Vang,
and the other boy, Pao Lee. Many other prints were taken from

that shelf, but she speculated that the killer's weren't there. None of them matched the doorframe prints, and she thought it unlikely that he—or possibly she—had ever touched the shelf. The murderer had entered intent on killing. He probably never approached the window.

Jaylynn looked at her watch. 6:20 already. She had been sitting in the same place for the better part of the last two hours. Her left shoulder throbbed, and she felt a deep ache somewhere in the vicinity of her collarbone. The skin there also itched, but she resisted the temptation to scratch, knowing that it would only cause problems, maybe even make it bleed. All her shoulder and neck muscles ached, so she stood and tried to stretch and move without causing any pain. While occupied with the reports, she had been able to ignore it. Now it was time to take some ibuprofen and move around a little. She strode down the hallway and filled up a cup at the water cooler.

She had just swallowed the pills and thrown away the paper cup when her pager went off. Looking at the display, she saw a familiar number and smiled. Holding her slinged arm close to her, she cut through a group of cops blocking her way in the hallway. From Tsorro's phone she dialed the number. "What's up?"

The reception was clear. "I get dinner break at 6:30. Want me to meet you there at the station?"

"Sure. Where are you now?"

"Turning into the lot."

Jaylynn smiled. "No wonder this sounds so clear. Meet you in the lunch room?"

"Yup."

The connection broke. She put the phone back on the cradle, and went to the lieutenant's office. "Do you mind if I take a dinner break, ma'am?"

A tired looking pair of brown eyes met hers. "I hate being called ma'am, Savage. Boss, Lieutenant, even sir—but ma'am?"

With a sheepish look on her face, Jaylynn said, "No problem, Boss."

The lieutenant looked at her watch. "Good God. It's already half past six." She stood, grabbing the dark blue jacket off the back of her chair. "Go take dinner break. In fact, use your own judgment whenever you need your breaks. I have to leave by seven, but first I need to check in with the Captain. Lt. Graul will be here shortly. You'll report to him for the rest of your shift." She came around the desk. "You meet him before?"

Jaylynn shook her head.

"Quiet guy. He'll answer any questions you have. Won't take

your head off if you ask something obvious. Come on. I'll walk with you toward the lunch room—that's where you're going, right?"

Jaylynn nodded.

The lieutenant pulled her suit jacket on and adjusted the sleeves. "What do you think so far? Of the Tivoli case, I mean." They turned and walked out into the squad room and toward the hall.

"Well, it seems to me that if we could figure out the Jane Doe's identity, we might have something to go on." She hesitated, and when the lieutenant didn't comment, she went on uncertainly. "But then again, Tivoli is an ex-con. I haven't read far enough to get into the interviews and investigation of his old associates, but I assume Tsorro and Parkins are hunting up that angle."

"Oh yeah. As you read on, you'll see that's being looked into. Got any hunches on motive?"

"Hard to say what the motive is. They were executed. Could be drug-related, gambling, old debts, something personal?"

The lieutenant nodded. "We're thinking it wasn't a professional job—they wouldn't have left fingerprints."

"I didn't think of that. Believe me, the whole case has got me very curious."

They reached the lunchroom door, and the lieutenant paused. "That's perhaps one of the most important qualities of a good investigator: curiosity. Talk about the case out loud to Tsorro and Parkins. Ask questions. Perhaps some odd angle or a small fact will jiggle loose, and it will give us something to go on. Fresh eyes are always an advantage."

Before Jaylynn had a chance to say anything, a six-foot-tall, dark-haired woman ambled up.

"Dez!" the lieutenant said.

"Hey, Denise, how's tricks?"

"Good. Real good. You know Savage here, right?"

Dez nodded solemnly. "Been her FTO—at least until she went and had a close encounter of the tree kind."

Finn smiled. "I meant to ask you more about your injury, Savage, but I've been so consumed with paperwork today. I'll get it out of you tomorrow. Gotta run now." She reached over and patted Jaylynn's upper arm with the flat of her hand. "Keep studying, and I'll see you tomorrow." She turned and hustled off, and Jaylynn preceded Dez into the empty lunchroom.

The smaller woman glanced over her shoulder. "How do you know the lieutenant?"

"She was on patrol over in our sector when I first joined. We know each other pretty well. She and Ryan rode together sometimes. Then she made sergeant and got reassigned across town."

"She seems to know her stuff, and she's quite pleasant."

"Yeah. Denise has always been able to handle people well. That's probably how she has moved ahead like she has." She pulled a chair out and lowered herself into it.

The room was small and claustrophobic and contained only two tables and eight chairs total. The counter sported the smallest and deepest sink Jaylynn had ever seen, and the tiny bit of counter top was completely covered with an ancient fake-wood-colored microwave with silver trim. Next to all of that sat a huge Frigidaire. Somebody must have just tidied up, though, because the counter was clean, the sink empty of any dishes or food, and when Jaylynn opened the refrigerator door, things inside looked orderly. She rooted around to find her own lunch bag and took it over to the table. "What? No lunch for you?"

"Not hungry yet."

"How's the overtime shift going?"

"Quiet. Nothing much going on besides a little petty vandalism over at the junior high. What'd they give you to work on?"

Jaylynn's eyes brightened and she set her sandwich down on the lumpy paper bag. She swallowed quickly. "They're letting me work on the Tivoli murder! And Dez, it's really interesting—all the evidence and what they've done to try to track this killer down."

Dez nodded. "That'll be a real education. I hope you can help. And even if you don't, I sure as hell want them to find the bastard who did that."

Jaylynn took another bite and with her mouth full, said, "No kidding."

Dez reached over and picked up a napkin, stretched a long arm out to blot mayonnaise from the corner of the smaller woman's mouth, then handed her the napkin.

Jaylynn took it, and they brushed hands. She looked up into shiny blue eyes, feeling her heart skip a beat. She chewed vigorously and swallowed. In a soft voice, barely audible, she said, "You are so sweet, Dez."

The tall woman rolled her eyes. "How many times I gotta tell you? I'm not sweet."

"You can say that all you want, but I'll believe what I know to be true."

"Yeah, right. Let's stick to business here, all right?" She bit back a smile and settled back into her chair, legs stretched out under the table, her hands clasped and forearms on the dark brown Formica surface. "How's your shoulder feeling?"

"Oh, *that's* really business! For your information, it still hurts—not like hell—but it definitely hurts. Looks like you'll be riding alone for quite a while."

"That's what I figured. You still want me to come get you after work?"

"Absolutely. Or would you rather I walked home?" She grinned mischievously and took another bite.

"That's not what I meant. If you get off at eleven, the soonest I can get up here would be around 12:15. I thought maybe you might want to go home earlier."

"Nope. I don't mind hanging out until you come."

"What if I get a late call?"

Jaylynn looked into her paper sack. "I've got two more sandwiches in here and a candy machine down the hall. What more could a woman want?" She put her right hand on the blue-sleeved forearm on the table. "I swear, if they'd let me, I'd take all these reports with me and read until I fell asleep. It's just fascinating, Dez."

"That's just what we need—a foot tall stack of police reports in our already cramped quarters."

"Oh, no. It's way more than a foot tall. I'll bet it's going on *two* feet tall. And they still have piles of witnesses to interrogate."

"They *question* witnesses. Only suspects get interrogated."

"Whatever." She frowned. "Quit smirking at me. I'll get the lingo down."

Dez grinned and shook her head. "Yeah, that's my girl. I just bet you will."

****

The week passed swiftly for Jaylynn as she became familiar with all of the facts of the Tivoli case. The full tox screens came back—negative for both victims. Nothing unusual. She served well as Reception Central: scheduling interviews, taking information by phone, and relaying data to Tsorro and Parkins. She printed out motor vehicle records, requested credit bureau histories, and systematically checked every jurisdiction in the Midwest for missing teenagers fitting the description of the Jane Doe. She traced information about Tivoli's co-conspirators and cellmates, and the detectives followed up everything local.

Finally, one day, as she sat sorting the mounds of paper and writing lists and charts to try to keep track of everything, she got so frustrated that she stomped into Lt. Finn's office and requested a few minutes of her time.

"Sure, Savage. What's up?" She motioned the rookie toward her visitor's chair across the desk.

"It's like this, Boss. I am wasting hours of time here arranging and rearranging all this paper and trying to help Tsorro and Parkins stay organized. Why in the world doesn't the department use databases?"

The lieutenant looked at her, surprised. "We do." Now it was Jaylynn's turn to look startled. Finn went on. "But Tsorro and Parkins can't be persuaded to make a giant leap into the 21st Century. You can't even imagine what I had to go through to get them to start carrying cell phones. For the longest time, they preferred getting paged and then stopping somewhere to call." She let out a sigh. "We have C.I.T. to help them—" When she saw Jaylynn didn't understand, she said, "Criminal Intelligence Technicians, people who create the databases, follow the paper trails, sort the tips and records. But, oh no. The guys won't even think of it. They'd rather carry around a thousand scraps of paper." She rolled her eyes and leaned back in her chair.

Jaylynn sat for a moment. "Hmm...is there anything to stop me from creating a database, Boss—for my own organizational use, I mean?"

The lieutenant shook her head. "Go ahead. And if you can sell them on the idea, I will personally put in for a commendation for you." She shook her head slowly. "But you don't have a chance with them. I'm surprised they even watch TV."

Jaylynn laughed. She stood and moved toward the door. "Okay, Boss. I am going to monkey with a database."

"Wait a minute." Finn opened a drawer and pulled out a department directory and wrote a number down on a post-it note. "Call this woman. She's our best C.I. Tech, and she can give you an already created format to use."

"That would be great." The rookie accepted the slip of yellow paper. "I thought I'd have to start from scratch."

"Oh, no. We have used a good system for a few years. It'll keep track of all sorts of stuff—names, addresses, dates of birth, interview dates, general facts, tips, conviction records, driver's license numbers, et cetera. It's really a great program, and you'll be able to get that awful stack of paper off the desk once you load the data. It'll help you keep track of what's missing from the interviews, too, and whenever you want, you can print out cross-referenced info from other databases like arrests, convicted felons, even property records. Instead of giving the detectives little slips of handwritten paper, you can print out what you need."

"All right," she said enthusiastically. "Thanks for the help."

"I don't know how much help it'll be, Savage." With a twinkle in her eye, she said, "The dinosaurs you're working with might take exception to it. Come see me if they give you a bad time."

Jaylynn returned to the desk and put the call through to the woman the lieutenant referred her to, and by the next day she was loading the data every chance she had. Despite her sore arm and slow typing, inside a week, the program was up and running. Once she had everything loaded that she could input, she pulled two printouts: one of witnesses interviewed and the other of witnesses left to interview. Instead of the sheaf of dog-eared sheets of legal paper, she handed a total of 7 sheets to Parkins saying, "Here you go. This will be easier to read." She purposely did not mention the word "database."

He looked at the labeled printouts, then at her. "Must've taken a while to type all this up."

She smiled. "It's all on the computer now, so you let me know anytime when you want a new list. I'll keep *retyping* it every single day."

"Good work, Savage. Thanks." He wandered off down the hall, and Jaylynn didn't think he looked upset at all. In fact, each day when she presented him with an updated version, he seemed quite pleased. After three days, Tsorro confronted her and demanded his own copy.

After nine days on the unit, she felt she had the entire investigation organized for anyone who came after her.

And every day, the ache in her collarbone abated a little bit more until one morning she woke up, and it didn't hurt to lift her arm until she got it up to chin level.

She scooted up in bed, her back against the headboard. "Look at this, Dez!" She lifted her elbow up, dropped it to her side, and lifted it up again.

Her sleepy companion nodded, her eyelids at half-mast, then turned over and fell back asleep.

Jaylynn was jubilant. She took off the sling she had been struggling with every night and tossed it aside hoping she never had to use it again. She got out of bed and put on slippers and her warm emerald green terrycloth robe. As she wandered downstairs to the kitchen, she stretched and moved her stiff arm with glee, then got to work pulling together the ingredients for pancakes. Today, she felt like making them with some sort of fruit, but she couldn't find anything in the fridge except some Red Delicious apples that seemed a little too soft. She debated going to the store, but then decided cinnamon would have to do. She whipped

Under The Gun 133

up the batter without fruit and poured three circlets into a frying pan.

She poured maple syrup into another pan to heat, then got out eggs to scramble. For a moment, she almost took out extra eggs to make some for Dez, but then decided it would be better to wait until the tall woman made an appearance—which might not be for a while. Cracking eggs into a small Teflon fry pan and using a fork to whip and scramble them, she thought about how things had been going.

She was worried about Dez. She had almost seemed depressed lately. She tossed and turned half the night, and usually didn't settle down until dawn or later. The last couple of weeks Jaylynn had been rising hours before her taciturn partner. She looked at the kitchen clock. It was just before eleven a.m., and she knew she had fallen asleep around two, awakening only once just before seven when Dez began talking in her sleep and thrashing around. Jaylynn was surprised at how poorly the big cop was sleeping. She didn't seem to have any recollection of it when she was awakened—or at least she didn't acknowledge that she'd had a bad dream or anything like that.

Worst of all, at this rate, their schedules were going to be so different that she didn't think they'd get to spend much time together. It was bad enough that she was working Monday through Friday, two o'clock until eleven, while Dez worked three to midnight Wednesday through Sunday one week and Thursday through Sunday the next. She was also putting in a lot of overtime on patrol to cover the shortage of officers. The waking hours that overlapped were not many—at least not enough for Jaylynn.

She put a piece of bread in the toaster and picked up a fork to scramble the eggs again. She liked them nice and dry, with lots of salt and pepper. When the toast popped up, she flipped it onto a plate and scraped the cooked eggs on top of it, then added the three pancakes on the side. She poured the warm syrup into a small pitcher and got herself a glass of milk.

Chewing on a piece of cinnamon-flavored pancake, she sat at the breakfast table looking out the window into the backyard. *Looks like snow.* The clouds in the sky were thick, and everything in her view appeared just a little bit gray and dull. There was a stiff north wind. She could tell because all the branches on the trees were swaying to the right as if they were over-stretching.

Someone clunked down the stairs, and she hoped it might be Dez, but then she realized Dez rarely clunked when she went anywhere. Sure enough, it was Kevin. He entered the kitchen barefoot, his blond hair tousled, wearing a royal blue pajama top with white sleeves and blue bottoms to match.

Yawning, he said, "Hey, Jay. What smells good?"

"Pancakes. Want some? I made a gallon of batter."

He yawned again. "Yeah. Thanks."

Jaylynn looked at him fondly. She could see why Tim was nuts about him. The guy even looked great in the morning with his hair standing on end. His eyes were nearly as blue as Dez's, and he had long, graceful eyelashes, making his eyes wide and dreamy. His white-blond hair was cut short, and he allowed about an inch of sideburns. High cheekbones, broad shoulders, and a narrow waist made him a beautiful man to look at. Jaylynn had known men this handsome before who were vain, self-centered, or cruel. Not Kevin. He had a kind heart. She would bet money that his mother had loved him to pieces. He spoke highly of his parents, and so did Tim. They'd obviously raised him well.

The batter in the pan sizzled as he poured it in. "How's your shoulder doing?" He slid into the chair across from her, appearing more awake than when he'd first walked in.

"It's lots better. See?" She raised her arm up, feeling the tightness in her front deltoid and pectoral muscles. "It's not back to normal yet, but it's healing." She loosened her robe and pulled the collar of her t-shirt down to reveal the reddened scar from the gash on her collarbone. "That doesn't hurt at all anymore."

He inclined his head. "Amazing how fast the body can heal." Holding out his hand, he pointed to a scar in his palm near the base of his little finger. "I was cutting potatoes on a utility board in a kitchen once and whacked this all the way to the bone. Missed the tendon. Just hurt like hell. I couldn't close my fist for weeks. And then all of a sudden, out of the blue, it didn't hurt anymore and never hurt since. It seems like forever...and then it's over." He rose and flipped his pancakes, then returned to the table.

"I think it might take me a while to get the flexibility back. The doctor said I'd have to do a couple sessions of physical therapy to learn some exercises to do. I see somebody for that on Monday. You want me to whip you up some eggs?"

"Nah. Pancakes will be enough. Where's Tall, Dark, and Dangerous?"

"Do you ever call her by her name?"

He grinned. "I just like to tease you. What a contrast you two make. Short and tall. Light and dark. Rowdy and quiet."

"Hey, I'm not rowdy. I'll have you know I go hours each day sitting in one place concentrating."

He shook his head and smiled at her. "Face it, Jay. You're an extrovert—and big time, at that. And she's an introvert. It's a nice balance...like Tim and me. I let him make all the noise and do all the talking. She does the same thing with you."

"What's the appeal for you then, speaking from the introvert's point-of-view, that is."

"The show, of course. Extroverts are very entertaining. And fortunately, you need us introverts or else you wouldn't have an audience. They're matches made in heaven." He got up and flipped four pancakes onto a plate, then opened the refrigerator and took out the butter, which he sliced off in cold chunks and set to melting on the hot cakes. Carrying the plate over to the table, he said, "Speaking of extroverts and introverts, Bill and Sara have been real good sports lately, but how long do you think they'll stay, beings that they're cramped up in that little room?"

Jaylynn nodded. "I've thought of that, too. I should give them back my room—that is, if Sara could stomach it after what happened last summer. I have thought of asking Dez if we could move over to her place, but whew! Her place is smaller than small—more like miniature. I'd probably drive her crazy. It's really only big enough for one."

"I know Tim doesn't want to move." Kevin poured the syrup out so fast that some splashed onto the handle of his fork. He got up and dropped it in the sink, then opened the silverware drawer and got a clean one. Returning to the table, he said, "I don't want anyone to have to move. I like all of you." He cut into a pancake and guided a large wedge into his mouth. "Mmmm...I so love good pancakes."

Jaylynn rose and went to the sink to rinse her plate and put it in the dishwasher. She picked up the bowl containing the batter, intending to put it in the fridge, but Kevin spoke up. Though his mouth was full, she understood him to say, "Leave that, will you? Tim will want some, too." He finished chewing and swallowed. "Leave it all. I'll clean up. We're going to work on some kind of double baked cake creation he has to make for class. Ever seen anyone so compulsive? He tries out the recipe here before they do it at school."

"I don't blame him for not wanting to screw up."

Kevin made a face and shook his head. "He's not gonna screw up. It's a class on experimenting with food. The whole goal is to make sure you have problems so that you can try oddball things. I tell you, he's just compulsive."

"Who's compulsive?" The red-haired man rounded the corner, dressed in Nikes, sweat bottoms, and a white t-shirt.

Kevin smirked. "The valet at the restaurant."

"That weasel?" Tim said. "He's too dumb to be compulsive."

Jaylynn winked at Kevin and headed out of the kitchen. She tickled Tim on the way by, then scooted out the swinging door before he could recover. Heading upstairs to take a shower, she decided she had never been quite as happy ever before as she felt lately. It was a good feeling to have.

****

Jaylynn sat at the desk in the crowded squad room, happy not to be wearing the sling anymore. She flexed her hand and moved her forearm and shoulder gingerly whenever she thought of it. By Monday, when she was to see the physical therapist, she hoped to have increased the flexibility even more.

It was nearly five p.m., so there was a lull in the squad room due to change of shift. Only one of the secretaries was left for the moment. Tsorro and Parkins had been out following up leads on two old cases as well as talking to various witnesses for the Tivoli murder. Jaylynn shook her head. They were getting nowhere— and not even fast. Nobody had noticed anything out of the ordinary. A few people had heard what they thought was a car backfiring during the band performance, but that didn't help any since they already had a solid time of death for the two victims.

She went over the case in her head. At approximately 7:42 p.m. on that Saturday night, someone had confronted Tivoli in the snack stand. He—she thought of the assailant as male—forced Tivoli onto his knees, facing the south side of the trailer. The murderer was almost certainly right-handed. He shot the bald man in the head, and in the process got some blood on his hands and probably also on his clothes. The physical evidence indicated that he then turned and fired toward the screen door. The bullet hit the girl in the back, and she fell to the ground at the foot of the metal stairs that led up into the stand. The killer slammed through the screen door, grabbing the metal doorframe on the way out. He left fingerprints and a partial palm print along with a smear of Tivoli's blood. He followed the girl, who was crawling on the cement, trying to get away, and put a bullet into the back of her head. After that, he left, but no one knew how. Nobody saw anything, and he disappeared off the face of the earth. The three Hmong boys had come upon the murders moments later. She and Dez arrived on the scene two minutes after the 911 call and secured the scene.

What were they missing? Better yet, *who* were they missing? Someone had to have seen something. Who was the girl? Jaylynn knew that the Jane Doe had been hanging around the snack stand for a couple days because witnesses reported seeing her. The investigation of Tivoli's apartment had turned up a travel bag of size two clothes that contained some cheap jewelry and teen magazines as well as her fingerprints. The girl had been with him, not an innocent bystander who just happened to come by at the wrong time. The thought occurred to the rookie that without more information, more evidence, they might not ever solve this crime. *I can't let that happen. That girl, that man—they deserve to have their killer brought to justice.* She closed her eyes only to have the scene swim up in her memory. *The girl was such a little slip of a thing...* she opened her eyes and exhaled quickly, shuddering, then looked out toward the light shining in the window. *Whoever did this must be punished...*

"Hey, sweetie pie."

Jaylynn wheeled around in her chair to find Tsorro, trailed by Parkins, heading her way. Tsorro had never once called her by her name, but he had graced her with every sickeningly sweet endearment she had ever heard.

"DNA results are in, sweet *tesoro.*" Tsorro sounded excited.

Parkins held a folder up in the air as he moved past his partner and into Lt. Finn's office.

Tsorro's dark eyes sparkled. "Wanna take a run down to the ME's office with us and find out what the hell it all means?"

She was up on her feet in a shot. "Sure." She looked at her watch. "But don't they close? It's after five."

"Nah—doesn't matter to The Corpse. He's there until late every day, even Sundays."

Parkins came out of Finn's office. "We're clear to go. C'mon, Jaylynn."

She hustled over to the coat rack, her forehead furrowed as she wondered who "The Corpse" was. She'd never been to the medical examiner's office and didn't know who worked there or even where it was located.

Parkins headed off down the hall, but Tsorro stopped to hold her heavy, down jacket for her and help her get her sore arm in. He patted her on the back once he slipped the coat over her shoulders and said, "Parkins has no manners."

Jaylynn didn't know what to say to that. She pulled her gloves from her pocket as she turned to face the dark-haired man. "Thanks for the help. Won't be long before my shoulder is totally back to normal."

"That's good to hear."

She followed Tsorro out of the squad room door, watching

from behind as he adjusted the collar of his long coat. They stopped at the door, and he buttoned his coat, all the while gazing out the glass door. An unmarked blue sedan pulled up. "That's our ride, doll. Let's go."

It was cold outside, and the chilled air immediately got to her. She was glad to be wearing her warmest winter coat and gloves, but her legs, even in wool duty pants, felt the frigid air immediately.

During the short trip over to the medical examiner's office, she took the opportunity to ask a few questions. She found out that "The Corpse" was the nickname for Leland Corsican, the autopsy specialist the detectives liked the most. He had worked with the two investigators for the better part of three decades. Rather than rely on in-house police expertise, they almost always turned to him for a more precise scientific interpretation of DNA or autopsy reports. She asked for the report that Parkins had in the front seat next to him, and from her spot in the back seat, she pored over the paperwork.

She had spent time in Police Academy learning about DNA. It didn't come easy to her. Vague remembrance of chemistry and biology classes in high school didn't help much, and she found the concepts difficult to remember—too many acronyms and oddly spelled words. She couldn't even remember now what the D and N stood for, though she knew the A was for acid, and that DNA were microscopic strands, like a zipper, that revealed hereditary characteristics in every human being. She had learned that with even an almost microscopic sample of blood or tissue, a person's DNA "fingerprint" could be determined.

She looked at the charts of smudgy marks attached to the complicated report. One chart was labeled with Tivoli's name, a second with "Fetus Doe 01-02A," and the third with "Jane Doe 01-02." She frowned. Arraying them in front of her as best she could, she compared them to one another. Before she could say anything further, Parkins wheeled into the lot and slammed on the brakes.

"Let's go find out what The Corpse has to say, honeybun," Tsorro said. He was out of the car and opening her back door before she could get the report put back in order and into the folder. He waited while she organized the paperwork, then she got out and followed them into the building.

When they arrived in the lab, she saw that Leland Corsican's nickname was rather appropriate. He appeared to be in his late sixties and was a gaunt, cadaverous looking fellow wearing a blue dress shirt and a wrinkled white lab coat. His coloring was nothing less than gray—gray with dark circles under his eyes. His rheumy blue eyes watered, and she watched as he pulled a folded handkerchief out of the voluminous lab coat pocket and dabbed his eyes, then returned the hanky to his pocket. He stood to the side of the room, facing them, from behind a free-standing counter, which was covered with test tubes and beakers. There were metal tables in the center of the room, but none of them contained a body.

When "The Corpse" heard them enter, he looked up, startled. "Gentlemen," he nodded toward her, "and ma'am. I do not believe I have had the pleasure..."

Tsorro made introductions and Jaylynn smiled and said, "Nice to meet you, sir."

He made no move to shake her hand, instead plunging his hands into his pockets and stepping around the counter to follow them. They walked from the lab, down the hall, and around the corner to a large window-less office. A desk, table, and four visitor's chairs sat in the middle of the room, and all around, on every stretch of wall were bookcases, file cabinets, and shelves stacked and packed full of books, papers, notebooks, and folders. Next to the desk on a wide table sat a printer, a fax machine, and some other device that Jaylynn assumed was a small copy machine. The desk was piled at least six inches high with papers that formed an upside-down U around the sides and back of the ME's desk. One open space perhaps two feet square gave Corsican enough room to write, but otherwise, there were no clear surfaces in the room.

He gestured to them to have seats, then went around the desk and sat in an executive-type tall black chair. Jaylynn sat in a chair near an overburdened bookshelf literally stacked to the ceiling. She looked up, and she could swear that the books and papers on the shelves swayed ever so slightly. It made her nervous.

Corsican reached a hand out over the desk, looking at Jaylynn. She froze, then realized he wanted the folder she held in her hand. Taking it from her, he opened the manila folder and spent less than a minute perusing the reports. "Hmm. This one's simple." He closed the folder and handed it back to her, then turned to the men. Pulling his handkerchief out, he dabbed at his eyes, then stuffed the hanky back in his pocket. "I know you fellows figured on this being a happy little family—father, mother, and unborn baby. But I got bad news for you. The DNA shows otherwise, though they are all related."

Jaylynn watched the detectives out of the corner of her eye as her excitement rose. *Ah, that's why the DNA smudge patterns looked funny to me. They're similar! And they're similar because they share some of the same genes.*

Tsorro had a puzzled expression on his face, but his partner was nodding. Parkins said, "So Tivoli is related to the girl, but he did not father the fetus?"

"Exactly." The gaunt man sat back in the chair and crossed his arms over his chest.

"Well, I'll be damned," the Italian said. "What is he then? The girl's father? Uncle? Grandpa?"

Corsican said, "Looks like they did enough calculations to verify a 99% probability that Mr. Tivoli was Jane Doe's birth father."

Tsorro shook his head. "Well, shit. So the kid sees her papa shot in the head, then gets chased down herself." He looked over at Parkins and sighed. "At least we have a new lead. All we need to do now is find out about the kid."

Parkins was shaking his head slowly. "I gotta bad feeling here, Zorro. We never turned up a single scrap of evidence pointing to Tivoli having a child. No kid ever visited him in prison."

"Kinda reminds me of that one case a couple of years ago," Parkins said.

The three men began to discuss an old case they had resolved with the help of DNA. Jaylynn stopped listening to the men's conversation as her mind spun through investigative possibilities. *Canvass every public school in St. Paul? Go through Tivoli's bank records and see if he ever paid child support to the girl's mother? Check with the county child support enforcement people?* Her thoughts were halted when the three men rose. She stood, glancing up at the teetering stack of books and documents on the shelves over her head, then eased her way back.

"Nice to meet you, Mr. Corsican—"

He interrupted her by raising a hand and shaking his head from side-to-side. "No need for formalities here. I'll call you Savage—you can call me Corpse like the rest of them do."

"Okay, sure. Thanks." She started to move as though she would reach for his hand, but Parkins hip checked her. She frowned and shifted past the chair, dodged the bookcase, and squeezed out the door in front of the two detectives.

"See you guys around," the ME said.

"Yeah," Tsorro said. "We owe you. Again."

"No problem. You guys pay your debts."

They strode silently to the front door, and Parkins grabbed the bar and pushed, sliding the heavy metal door open for Jaylynn to exit. He followed her and Tsorro brought up the rear. When they got to the car, Parkins opened the back door for her and said,

"Savage, I apologize for pushing you out the door in there. I figured you didn't know the unwritten rule at the ME's office."

She had not yet gotten into the sedan and stood, one leg in the car and one leg out. "What do you mean?"

"*Never* shake hands with those guys." He must have been able to see that she did not understand. "The Corpse just walked out of the lab. Who knows what he's been touching? Dead people, blood and guts, bacteria, germs. You just never shake their hand."

"Oh. I see." She sat back onto the car seat and pulled her other leg in. It occurred to her that there were a lot of rules—written and unwritten—that she had no clue about in the world of homicide investigation.

****

Dez sat on the couch in her apartment, Shawn Colvin's latest CD playing in the background. She had just finished cleaning the bathroom, and now her apartment was spotless. She looked at her watch. Six-thirty p.m. Picking up the phone, she dialed the phone number and extension for Jaylynn. Instead of a female voice, however, someone else picked up and informed her that the rookie was out on a call.

"What do you mean 'out on a call'? She's on desk duty."

There was a pause and Dez could hear a crinkling of papers, and then the male voice said, "I don't know where they went, but she and the detectives are on a call. That's all I know."

"Okay, thanks." Dez hung up the phone feeling a vague sense of unease.

She rose and went into the bathroom to look out the window there. She had a good view of the street in front of the duplex. Right now, the streetlights blazed and it was almost full dark, though she couldn't see any moonlight at all. She hunched down and looked up at as much of the sky as she could see. She didn't think the moon would be visible at all tonight. Earlier in the day, heavy clouds had moved in, and the forecast was for snow. As she watched, an oversized kid on a bike wheeled past on the sidewalk, and a fluttering around him caught her eye. Staring over at the streetlight, she saw the flecks clearly. *Snow. The first snow of the season.*

The tall woman stood and ran her hands through her long, dark hair. If Jaylynn was with Zorro and Tonto, she was probably just fine. She just hoped that they hadn't cracked the case and gone off to collar the bad guy, the rookie in tow. The thought of that made her shudder. *Parkins wouldn't be that stupid...would he?*

Staring at the angry face in the mirror, she grabbed a brush and raked it through her hair, then reached up and worked the thick mane into a French braid. She stared down at the scale on the floor near the big Jacuzzi tub. She couldn't resist and stepped up on it. She let out a sigh. 186. She was 28 pounds heavier than when she had competed in the bodybuilding competition earlier in the summer. She was carrying a minimum of ten pounds she didn't want. No wonder all her clothes were tight.

When she stepped off the scale, disconsolate and disgusted, she looked at her watch again. Six-forty. *What am I going to do for the next four-and-a-half hours until Jaylynn comes home safe?*

Moving out of the bathroom, she returned to the couch and picked up the mystery she was reading. Maybe she could kill time with a good book.

Chapter
Ten

Jaylynn reached out and touched the blue sleeve of her morose partner. They sat in the break room at the main precinct at Dez's dinner break. "What are we going to do about Thanksgiving?"

Dez turned and looked at Jaylynn with a frown on her face, and the rookie almost laughed because the look on Dez's face said it all: *Thanksgiving? What do you mean, Thanksgiving?*

Before Dez could respond, Jaylynn rolled her eyes. "You know, Thanksgiving? The fourth Thursday in November when family and friends come together to celebrate their love for God, country, and each other?"

Dez gave her a level gaze. "I'm perfectly aware of the tradition of Thanksgiving." She looked at her watch. She had twenty minutes before she needed to be back in the car and on patrol. "What's your point?"

"Listen, Miss Anti-Holiday, Turkey Day is coming up in three days. What are we going to do?"

Dez shrugged. She didn't much care about the holiday. Most years she either worked or hung out helping Luella host her rag tag family. She hadn't given it any thought this year.

"Dez! We've got four invitations. Do you plan on attending all four and eating until we die of surfeit?"

"Where do you come up with this stuff? What the hell is surfeit?"

Jaylynn jabbed her in the ribs, but she couldn't get any pressure due to the thick protective vest her partner wore. "This is no fair. You deserve a good poke in the ribs for that."

In a low voice, the big cop said, "Guess you'll have to wait until we're in private—and unclothed." Dez watched a flush of pink creep up into the rookie's face, and she found herself grinning in response.

"Listen, you can avoid the question all you want, but we have to make a decision—unless you want to go to two and me to the other two."

"What? I don't want to do that. I'm not interested in *any* of them."

"Have you got a clue who's invited us?" Dez frowned. "You haven't paid the slightest bit of attention lately, have you?"

"Luella. Luella and Vanita invited us."

"That was a no-brainer!"

Dez searched her memory. *Nope, nothing coming up.* With a guilty look on her face, she mugged a funny face and shrugged again.

"You can remember every single car on the Hot List, but you can't think who might invite us to Thanksgiving?"

"I'm pretty sure it wasn't my mother."

"Good thinking." Jaylynn ticked off the names on her fingers. "Luella and Vanita. Kevin and Tim. Julie and the kids. Crystal and Shayna."

"What? Julie asked us to Thanksgiving?" She hadn't heard from Ryan's widow for several weeks.

"Dez! She called last weekend. I left a note on the table."

The big cop shook her head. "Never saw it."

"It's still sitting there, right on the kitchen table along with several other notes." She rolled her eyes and shook her head. "So what should we do?"

"Run away to Duluth?"

"Dez!"

"Okay, then, *drive* to Duluth?"

Jaylynn gave her a withering look. "Will you be serious?"

Dez sighed. It was so much easier if she just worked, but even so, they still had time before shift started this coming Thursday to make an appearance somewhere. "Do you have a preference?"

"Don't tell the guys, but I don't have any desire to get all dressed up for their Gay Soiree. They are having a formal luncheon, and Tim is doing all the food. He's been cooking and baking and doing origami with napkins all week. All those fussy gay guys will be there. I could do without all that pressure." Dez made a snorting sound. She was in total agreement with the rookie. Jaylynn went on. "Crystal and Shayna are hosting friends and various parts of both of their families, and I could do without all that Latino versus African energy and everyone arguing about everything."

Dez smiled and gave a little nod. Crystal's family was a very opinionated bunch, and Shayna's crew wasn't far behind. They all *liked* to argue—and with great volume, too. It always sounded like fighting to Dez, though she had to admit that there was also genuine affection between various members of each clan. Still, she had no desire to try to eat at a table where everyone shouted at once. She looked to the side at the serious look on her partner's face. When Jaylynn was thinking hard, she got a frown on her face and a little furrow of wrinkles just above her eyebrows. She looked so cute that Dez longed to reach over and take her into her arms, but of course, that was not an option, especially not when she could hear voices out in the hall and footfalls on the stairwell.

Hazel eyes met hers thoughtfully, and Jaylynn took a deep breath. "So it's down to Julie or Luella, and if you want to know the truth, I vote for Luella. Even if Vanita's little squirt grandkids come, it'll still be a more peaceful day."

Dez arched an eyebrow. "Luella, huh? My choice, too. We haven't seen Vanita for a while, and I'd like to."

"Okay, then. It's settled. You call everyone and—"

"Oh, no. I hate doing that."

"Well, I had to field all the calls, why can't you call 'em all back?"

"I hate social engagements."

"It's not so bad. Come on, admit it."

Dez refused to admit anything. She crossed her arms and looked away. She thought that having obligations to other people was often a big pain. Expectations—another "E" word that she didn't like. She never knew what to say at parties, so she was glad they weren't going to Tim and Kevin's event or to Crystal and Shayna's. She wouldn't mind seeing Julie and the kids, but some of Ryan's family might be there, and it was just too hard still. She didn't want to think about him; didn't want to deal with the feelings his memory brought up. She was relieved that a group of officers entered the break room then. She half-listened to the good-natured bantering for a few minutes, responding to a few comments they directed her way. Looking toward Jaylynn, she knew they would have to resolve this issue soon. She changed the subject. "You told me the P.T. appointment went great, but did they say when you go back to work?"

Jaylynn nodded with enthusiasm. "The therapist is going to work with me two more times, and then it looks like I am all set for next Wednesday." Dez accepted the information without comment. "I'll miss Tsorro and Parkins."

"You will, huh?" Dez held back a smile. "You've enjoyed being coddled and called 'Dollhead' and all?"

"He's never called me 'Dollhead'! But he does use a lot of goofy endearments and Italian words that I don't even know the meaning of. He doesn't mean anything by it. I've grown to like working with Tsorro, and you know what? Parkins is really something. He looks like this cloddy, chubby duffer, but he's not. He's very astute. Doesn't miss much at all."

"Hmm. If you say so."

"What? You don't believe me?"

The tall cop shrugged. "I know they close a lot of cases."

"Now you know why. They do a good job. They may be comical looking, but they're effective."

Dez checked her watch, then stood and scooted her chair back. "I better get back out there."

Jaylynn looked at her own watch and stayed seated. "I've got a few minutes left. See you shortly after midnight?"

"Yup."

"Just think, starting tomorrow, I can drive myself to and from work."

Dez reached an arm out and patted the rookie on the shoulder, then gave her a wink. "Later." She strode across the room and out the door, never looking back.

Jaylynn's eyes followed her until the tall cop turned the corner and disappeared. *I can't believe how lucky I am. I just can't believe it.*

****

Thanksgiving morning dawned cold and clear, with a silvery layer of frost on the yards all around the house on Como Lake. Jaylynn looked out the window into the early morning quiet. She had slept well, but Dez had been restless, so she decided to let her sleep. Creeping out of bed, she slipped into some insulated warmup pants, a heavy sweatshirt, and running shoes. She headed downstairs for some orange juice, then slipped out the back door and walked around to the front of the house, across the street, and down the slope that led to the paved paths around the lake.

The air was so chilled that she could see her breath. She stepped onto the path, grateful that it was clear of ice. It hadn't snowed much so far after all, but it wouldn't be too long before ice and snowdrifts prevented her from running outside. That was one of the things she disliked about Minnesota. Even when the jogging path was clear, sometimes it was just too cold to run outdoors. And a workout just wasn't quite the same on a treadmill in a health club.

Shivering, she moved into a light jog, pumping her arms and letting her body loosen. Halfway around the lake, at about the three-quarter mile mark, she felt warm and her muscles moved effortlessly. She slipped into a faster, steady rhythm, legs stretching out and flying over the smooth concrete. By the time she had run for twenty minutes, her mind and body were in sync, and she no longer even noticed her surroundings. She strode smoothly, at about a nine-minute mile pace, and her thoughts turned to her reticent partner. She was still worried about her. She couldn't shake the feeling that something was wrong, but she also couldn't figure out a single way to subtly broach the subject without seeming to pry or poke around in Dez's private thoughts. She was sure the other woman would not appreciate that.

She moved to the side of the path to pass a woman pulling a red wagon. Two tired-looking girls, very well bundled in pink coats and swathed in bright-colored scarves and winter hats, sat motionless. Jaylynn moved past them, her warm breath emerging from her mouth in white gusts.

I don't think I have ever been happier in my entire life while feeling more on edge. Something doesn't feel quite right. For the remaining laps around the lake, she puzzled over that, but she was unable to explain her uneasiness.

When she returned to the house, she found Dez sitting in the kitchen, elbows on the rickety table, with a cup of hot tea in front of her. The kitchen felt like a hothouse compared to the brisk air outside, and it felt good. She broke out into a sweat before she even got the door shut.

"Hey, sweetie," Jaylynn said to the big woman as she went to stand next to her. She leaned into her and put her arm across her shoulders. Stooping down, she placed a soft kiss on the pale forehead. "How'd you sleep?"

Dez shrugged. Her arm came up and wrapped around the smaller woman's waist and she leaned her head into the warm body next to her. "You're up early."

"Yeah, I needed to run."

"Should've got me up."

Jaylynn pulled away and went to the cupboard for a bowl. "Seemed like you needed your sleep." Dez didn't respond. When Jaylynn looked down, the big woman was staring out the window. "You want some cereal?"

"No, thanks. Tea's good for now."

She gathered up the bowl, silverware, Rice Crispies, milk, and a banana and sat across from Dez. She set to work slicing up the fruit to put in her cereal. "What have you got planned for this morning?"

"Not much." The tall woman glanced at her wristwatch. "It's nine a.m. We go over to Vanita's in three hours."

Jaylynn nodded. "I probably should do a load of laundry—"

"Already in. I put in a dark load a bit ago."

Jaylynn smiled and reached across the table to grasp a warm hand. "Thanks for doing that. You're spoiling me."

"Nah...you were already spoiled rotten."

The warm affection in the big woman's voice was a relief to Jaylynn. She looked up into the tired eyes and puffy face and without thinking said, "Should I be worried about you, Dez? You seem so exhausted lately."

Like a shade being pulled down over a window, the other woman's open look changed and she released Jaylynn's hand and looked away, out the frosty pane to the backyard. "I'm fine."

Jaylynn busied herself with her cereal. She knew now that something was wrong, but she decided there was no use pressing it. "Are you sure Luella didn't want us to bring *something* over?"

Piercing blue eyes turned back to her. "She won't let us bring anything—you should know that. Thanksgiving is one of her favorite holidays. So she'll have whatever she needs."

"Okay, just checking." She shoveled in another big mouthful of crispy cereal and banana slices.

"Maybe I should go back to my place and pick up a few things."

Jaylynn nodded. "I've got some chores to do around here that'll keep me busy. I am really thankful that we get a late start today at four."

Dez rose and carried her tea mug to the sink. "Yeah, that works out well." She turned and headed out of the kitchen, and Jaylynn could hear the creaking of the steps as she went upstairs. She finished her cereal and cleaned up after herself, wondering when Tim and Kevin would descend upon the kitchen. Their Thanksgiving party didn't start until three p.m., so they could afford to sleep in. She crammed the milk carton into the bulging refrigerator and put her dishes in the sink, then headed upstairs where she found Dez lying on her side on the bed, fast asleep. She picked up an afghan and spread it over the tall woman, grabbed up her journal and a pen, and crept out of the room, leaving her partner to sleep.

Chapter
Eleven

On her last night in homicide, it was with some reluctance that Jaylynn bid farewell to Tsorro and Parkins when they went off duty at six. Her collarbone was healed, and the physical therapist had given her a clean bill of health. She was cleared to return to patrol the next day. She felt real regret about not being instrumental in solving the Tivoli murders, and she told the two detectives that.

"Don't worry about it, hon," Tsorro said. "We'll keep working on it, and when we track down the bastard who did this, you'll be the first to know."

She shook hands with both of the detectives.

Parkins patted her on the shoulder. "Thanks for your help, Savage. You really sped things up. I bet you saved us *days*— maybe weeks—of paperwork."

She smiled. "That's good to know. I just wish I could be here when you crack the case."

Lt. Finn came out of her office just then. Some days she was gone for the day by five or so, but tonight she had stayed late. She joined the three of them. "Savage, thanks for the good work you've done. You can come do desk duty here any time you're injured."

The two men chuckled as Jaylynn shook her head. "I think I've had enough injuries to last a few years, thank you very much." She flashed a bright smile. "But I've learned a lot working here temporarily. I appreciate everything the three of you have done for me."

The lieutenant shook her hand and gave her a wave, and the rookie watched her follow the detectives out of the squad room.

The rest of the evening passed slowly. She made several calls to follow up on small details with witnesses, and she put the database in order. She was well aware that after she left, the guys wouldn't update it again, so she reformatted the whole document, leaving lots of space between the 188 people listed. She printed out two clean copies, one for each detective. She knew they would keep notes all over this final copy, and maybe it would help them after all.

When eleven p.m. rolled around, she tidied everything up, returned all files to Parkins' desk, and said goodbye to Lt. Graul and some of the other cops who happened to be in the squad room. Without fanfare, she strolled down the long hallway to the door, which led to the parking lot.

It was bitingly cold, with a stiff north wind whipping at her. She hustled to her Camry and wrenched the door open with difficulty. As she squeezed in, the blowing wind nearly shut the lightweight door on her leg. She sat shivering for a moment, then looked at her watch. Only about an hour and Dez would be off duty. Jaylynn looked forward to it. In the last few days, her chest and shoulder had finally started to feel more like normal. She longed to make some popcorn and cuddle up on the coach with her partner, and now she wouldn't have to worry about feeling kinked up or twisting wrong. The last couple of nights she had slept more comfortably, too. It made a huge amount of difference in her energy level.

She started her car and sat, waiting for the motor to run for a minute and heat up. A peppy pop rock song was just ending on the radio. She closed her eyes and inhaled, thinking of snuggling up close to Dez, running her hands over soft skin, kneading lean muscle, kissing her neck, her mouth, her—she opened her eyes and took another deep breath. Suddenly it was warmer in the car than she expected. *Whew! I think I've missed making love.* Throwing the car into gear, she backed out of the lot and headed toward home.

Sometimes she didn't understand things at all. Sara had asked her recently what exactly it was about Dez that drew her to the tall woman. She was at a loss to explain. She just had a craving to be with her, to talk with her, to touch her, to be touched. Nobody had ever made her feel so cared for or nurtured. She liked how the big cop made her feel.

A new song came on the radio, one that Jaylynn didn't like, so she pressed the CD button and the *Hydraulic Woman* disk clicked on, right in the middle of a song.

Come on baby bring it on
Half a mile down the road
You'll see me waiting for you
How do I discreetly say
I'm dyin' baby,
I adore you...

She smiled and turned onto University Avenue. *Yes, this singer's got it right on! It's really something to adore someone.* She headed down the dark street, passed the State Capitol, all lit up with spotlights, then wheeled by all the closed-up office buildings and stores.

She turned the song up and drove along, humming and tapping her foot to the music. She didn't understand Dez, and she didn't always understand herself. What she did know was that she wanted to make a life with Desiree Reilly. She hoped and prayed that her partner felt the same way, and for a moment she allowed herself to imagine a taste of the anguish she might feel if things didn't work out. She got a lump in her throat and felt tears spring to her eyes. She pushed back the feelings and reasoned with herself that it was unlikely. She was pretty sure of Dez's love for her—even if the other woman hadn't yet shared it in precise words. She shared it every day in the way she touched the rookie, the way she listened to her.

That's it. Tonight I'm talking to her.

She steered the car down Dale Street and over toward Como Lake. When she pulled up to the house, she was surprised to find it dark. She knew Tim and Kevin were working at the restaurant. Bill and Sara must have also gone out somewhere. She parked and ran from her car to the front door, entered the house, and was relieved to find that someone had left the heat on. Lately, their fuel bills had been high, so half the time it was less than sixty degrees in the old house when she arrived home. She hated that. It took a good hour to warm up ten more degrees, and her electric blanket had stopped working weeks earlier. She kept meaning to get a new one, but hadn't gotten around to it. After checking the thermostat and cranking it up another five degrees, she went to the kitchen and foraged for a snack, coming up with milk and some Oreo cookies.

She went up to her room, flipped on the radio next to her bed, and changed from her uniform into flannel pajama bottoms and top, socks, and slippers. Rummaging around her desk, she pulled out a pad of paper and a pen, then sat on the couch to munch on cookies and write a letter to her Aunt Lynn.

An hour passed quickly, and it was nearing midnight. She couldn't keep her eyes open any longer and leaned her head against the back of the couch. The pad slipped from her lap along with the pen, and she drifted into a warm, blissful place.

It felt like hours had passed, but it must have only been a few minutes when Jaylynn felt something. A tremor of alarm coursed through her, and she stirred. She didn't want to open her eyes, didn't want to awaken at all, but she did, her heart beating wildly.

In the dim light of the doorway stood six feet of tension topped off by a face more pale than usual. The big cop held her black duty boots in one hand with her other hand clenched tightly into a fist.

Jaylynn jerked to attention. "Dez! What's the matter?"

The dark-haired woman, still dressed in her blue uniform, radiated fury. Through gritted teeth she said, "I probably shouldn't be here."

"Why? Why not?"

"Because I am so goddamn angry I want to kill somebody." The boots in her right hand hit the floor hard, and she kicked them, one at a time, across the room. They each came to a stop against the wall near the foot of the bed. She stepped into the room, shut the door, and paced five steps forward, five steps back, like a tiger in a cage.

Jaylynn watched as the tall cop put her hands to the sides of her head and literally pulled her hair until it came loose from the neat French braid. The rookie debated rising from the couch and going to Dez, but instead, she waited, watching the taut figure in front of her.

After a few moments, Dez came to a stop and stood looking across the room toward the younger woman.

Jaylynn frowned. *My God, she* is *furious.* "What in the world...Dez tell me."

Shaking, the big woman spat the words out. "Lt. Malcolm called me into his office after shift was over. He...he...dammit!"

She looked at Jaylynn, misery etched on her pale white face. Still Jaylynn waited, her heart beating fast.

Dez shook her head and let out a big sigh. "We aren't allowed to ride together anymore. Some fuckhead reported us, Jay." All the air seemed to go out of her, and she took two big steps over to the unmade bed and sank down onto the edge with her head in her hands.

Jaylynn stayed on the couch, stunned. *Reported us? Reported us for what?* "I don't understand, Dez. What—"

"For cripesake, Jay! Somebody told the brass that we're lovers."

"Oh." She sat back on the couch, letting it sink in. "Did he say who?"

"Hell, no! They never tell you shit like that." She stood again and paced back and forth.

"I see." Jaylynn nodded absently. Somebody ratted them out. She wondered who, but it could have been a number of people. It could also have been something innocent that led the lieutenant to put things together. Who could tell?

"Are either of us facing any sort of discipline?"

"No," Dez said in a scathing voice. "He was pissed as hell, though, that I hadn't informed him. Said I shouldn't have stayed your FTO and that it puts him in a hell of a position now that he has some performance problems with another rookie." She passed her hand through her hair again, which was looking quite bedraggled. "Dammit! I should have told him. I knew it."

Jaylynn wondered what the source of Dez's desperation was. Was she ashamed? Caught off guard and embarrassed? She hoped it wasn't either of those. "You know, it's not the end of the world."

Dez gave her a withering look and turned away. She put her right forearm up against the wall and leaned her head on it. Even from ten feet away, Jaylynn could see that her partner was shaking, so she rose from the couch and moved over behind the tall cop. She put her arms around the trembling waist, realizing that Dez still wore her protective vest. Pressing herself against long legs, she laid the side of her head on the broad back. Even through the vest she could hear the beat of her heart, fast and loud. Dez did not respond, but her heart rate slowed perceptibly.

Jaylynn pulled the big cop away from the wall and turned her around.

"I should go," Dez said. Her eyes filled with tears, and she turned her head to the side, toward the door, so that Jaylynn wouldn't see.

Jaylynn didn't say anything. She reached up and undid the top button of the blue uniform top, then the second button, then the third. She unbuckled the belt, untucked the shirt, and finished unbuttoning it. Reaching up, she tugged the shirt down off the broad shoulders and let it drop on the floor behind them. She ripped away the Velcro straps and loosened the vest.

Dez shrugged out of it and let it fall on top of the shirt behind her. She unsnapped and unzipped her pants and let them fall so she could step out of them. Still quivering, she stood uncertainly in briefs, t-shirt, and socks until the rookie took her arm and led her over to the bed. Jaylynn all but pushed her onto the bed and crawled in with her only to find the big cop stiff and unyielding. She turned on her side, away from the rookie.

Jaylynn went up on her knees and leaned over as Dez curled into a near fetal position. With her arms on either side of her, she said, "Dez. Talk to me. C'mon Dez."

"There's nothing more to say."

Jaylynn sat back. She reached a hand out and stroked Dez's left shoulder. "Gosh, you are unusually cold." The pallid skin was chilly to the touch, and even in the dim lamplight, she could see goosebumps on the tall woman's back. She pulled the sheet and blankets up from the foot of the bed and covered them both with them, then arranged the pillows next to Dez. She curled her body around the bigger woman, her right arm under the dark head and her left around her shoulders.

They lay like that for several minutes until Jaylynn felt warmth emanating from her partner. She pressed her lips to the warm neck next to her and leaned her cheek against the side of the wan face. A big hand moved up and took hold of the fingers on her left hand.

In a whisper, Jaylynn said, "It's going to be all right, Dez. Really."

The tall cop didn't respond.

****

Morning found the two women wrapped in one another's arms, Dez's head against the smaller woman's chest. She could hear Jaylynn's heart beat, feel the slow, steady pull of her breath. She didn't move for fear that she would awaken her.

Dez had not slept well—as usual. She awoke remembering wisps of dreams, but before she could nail them down, they were gone. Then the events of the previous evening came rushing back to her: the lieutenant's patient, hurt face; her own feelings of panic and dismay; throwing her gear and gun into her locker and stomping out of the precinct; the surreal drive over to this house. She hardly remembered how she got from the truck, through the cold wind, and into the house. She was suddenly standing, boot-less, at the top of the stairs in the doorway to Jaylynn's room, and she felt exactly like a volcano must feel moments before it erupted. She had wanted to throw things out the window—maybe bust in a few walls.

How had Jaylynn been so calm and reasonable? *She didn't seem particularly shocked about the new revelation—just con-*

cerned about my feelings. Dez winced and closed her eyes tight. *For cripesake, I was a total jerk. I would never forgive me if I were her.*

She opened her eyes and stared across the room at Jaylynn's messy desk. The entire room looked like a tornado had whirled through. Her own castoff uniform across the way on the floor didn't help matters.

Jaylynn let out a little whimper, and Dez looked up with a start to find a pair of hazel eyes gazing at her.

"'Morning, Jay."

"Hard to believe it could already be morning what with being kept up all night with you tossing and turning," she said in a grouchy voice. "It was the longest night of my life."

Dez scooted up and rolled onto her back next to Jaylynn, then situated the pillow under her head. "Hmm, I thought the longest night of your life was in the ER when I got shot."

Jaylynn let out a snort. "No, that was the most *stressful* night of my life. There's a difference."

"I see."

Jaylynn turned on her side, facing the tall woman, and snuggled up next to her. She put her arm across her partner's ribs, and Dez put her hand on top of it. She rubbed the soft forearm with the side of her thumb, feeling the silky skin. The rookie's breathing evened out, and Dez could tell she had fallen back to sleep.

She lay there thinking about all the things she liked about their life together. She liked the sheer comfort of it, the decadence of reveling in warmth and tranquility. She liked the way this sunny woman could turn her day from dark to bright, all with just a few words. She liked to touch her, to hold her, to make love with her. She liked it all far too much.

Her stomach tightened up, and she felt a wave of tension come over her body. *What will I do if she leaves? What if something happens to her?*

When the lieutenant talked with her the night before, she had been thrown into a state of panic. Who would he send the rookie out with? There were few officers she trusted with such a precious charge. She wondered how she could influence his decisions or the decisions of the shift sergeant. And how long would it be before the gossip about their relationship got around? She wasn't sure about any of this at all, and the uncertainty made her feel crazy with alarm.

"Dez?" The sleepy breath blew softly on the skin of her shoulder.

"Yeah?"

"Why are you clenching your muscles like that? It's like sleeping with someone in rigor mortis."

"Oh—well, that sure makes me sound appealing."

The smaller woman sighed. "You are *very* appealing. Just stop with the convulsions."

Dez let out a quiet chuckle. Obviously last night's scene hadn't turned Jaylynn against her. Still, she figured she had better apologize. Later, though. Much later. For now, she had one very tired blonde on her hands.

Chapter
Twelve

Dez drove in silence, her eyes systematically scanning the streets of the University "Frogtown" neighborhood. Three days had passed since Neilsen had ratted out her relationship with Jaylynn to Lt. Malcolm. She wouldn't even have known *who* had reported them if it weren't for the fact that Neilsen had gone around the precinct bragging about it. She was surprised that Jaylynn hadn't been called on the carpet, but the lieutenant didn't confront her. He had just ordered the duty sergeant to reassign them.

Now here she was, bored, angry, stuck in a one-man car, and wishing she could get Neilsen alone in a dark alley.

She found she despised riding alone. It was bad enough during the weeks when Jaylynn's collarbone had been injured, but at least she had something to look forward to after the rookie healed up. But now they would never be paired again. Neilsen had made sure of that. *What an asshole. I hope he fails probation!*

She cruised down University Avenue, slowing to eyeball anyone walking on the sidewalk. So far, she had seen no "Ladies of the Night." Of course, it was only about twelve degrees out. Not a good night for mini-skirts and fishnet stockings—although she was constantly surprised at the fortitude of the women who braved the bad weather to make a few bucks off the willing johns who cruised the area.

She came to a stop at a red light on Snelling and University, and the car idled while she thought about the situation. What had she done after Ryan died and before Jaylynn entered her life? She didn't have much memory of the time other than the feeling of a heavy weight pressing, non-stop, on her chest. Unfortunately, in the last few days, the feeling had returned, though not to such a painful degree. Every night at roll call she held her breath, hoping Jaylynn would be assigned to a cop with integrity, one who would watch her back. So far the duty sergeant had succeeded in assigning Jaylynn to Pilcher, when Pilcher's regular partner, Stevens, was off for the day, and to Crystal Lopez. Pilcher was okay, but Dez breathed a sigh of relief when the rookie was assigned to ride with Crystal. She knew Crystal would never let anything bad happen. She'd been friends with Crystal since she'd joined the force almost ten years ago, and Dez relied on her buddy. That didn't stop her from worrying. She had programmed her radio to scan several extra channels so she could listen to Dispatch for both of the sectors. She paid careful attention to the calls that the rookie's squad was sent out on.

Tonight was quiet. Too quiet to help the time pass. She pulled over into the Big K parking lot near Hamline and University, angling her car toward the main street so that she could make a fast departure if Dispatch called. She clicked on the sidelight and picked up a sheaf of papers and a clipboard to start completing reports.

After thirty minutes, she was bored with the paperwork. She was grateful not to be riding a desk. She didn't much care for filling out forms and trying to figure out how to explain things in the fewest words possible. That was one of the reasons she had never taken the sergeant's exam. Every step up the ladder seemed to decrease street action and increase the amount of time spent poring over statements and records. She liked being on her feet, moving around. Sometimes she got into a flow where time just sped by, and her shift was over before she knew it. Some days, though, like today, nothing she did could hasten the slow hours.

She looked at her watch. Crystal and Jaylynn were scheduled for meal break at nine. Some nights they had been able to meet at a restaurant on the border of the two sectors—not that she needed to eat. After all the Thanksgiving treats she had packed away the week before, she felt she shouldn't eat again for about a month. But she was hungry now, so she pulled out her cell phone and dialed the rookie's pager, then started counting. She knew if it took longer than about fifteen seconds, they were likely on a call, but the rookie returned the page right away.

The tall cop's spirits rose when the cheery voice came loud and clear over the line. "Is it as dead over in your sector as it is in ours, Dez?"

"Yup."

"Want to go hang out for break?"

"Yup." In the background she could hear Crystal's voice,

though Dez couldn't understand what she said.

"Same bat place, same bat channel?"

"Yup."

"'Kay. ETA six minutes."

They both hung up simultaneously. Dez turned on the ignition key and the engine roared to life. Her ETA, without speeding, would be at least six minutes. She was glad there was so little traffic out. It didn't matter if she exceeded the speed limit.

Only seconds apart, they arrived at Danny Boy's, a quiet Irish pub that served excellent hamburgers and sandwiches. There were two sections of the bar. One side sported open tables surrounded by huge TV's tuned in to local sports events. Little food was served in that section, but the beer ran like water from the taps. A brick wall separated tonight's crowd of football fans from the other, darker side where there were wooden booths, cloth napkins, and menus on the tables. They were greeted warmly by the waitress who had been around long enough to know that they might get a call in the middle of dinner, but could be counted on to come back for their boxes of food, not to mention pay for it.

Crystal slid into one side of the booth, right in the center, leaving the other two cops to squeeze in next to one another on the other side—not that they minded. Dez liked the feeling of Jaylynn's blue clad leg pressed up against her thigh. She found herself smiling, for no reason, and she pushed down the happy feeling and tried not to look so lovestruck.

Crystal gazed across at her and shook her head. "You, *chica*, got it bad."

Dez raised an eyebrow and let her face take on a passive expression. "I sure have no idea what you mean."

She felt a warm hand slide over her leg and stop at her knee to give a squeeze. *Boom!* Her knee came up reflexively and smacked against the underside of the table. "Ouch! Geez, Jay. Thanks for giving her fodder for her sick twisted mind."

"You're welcome."

The waitress arrived with three glasses of water and a recitation of the evening's specials. They all ordered sandwiches, which were quick and portable. Crystal ordered a diet Coke.

The tall cop shook her head. "How can you drink that stuff, Crys? It's like battery acid."

"Yeah, but no calories. I need to keep the weight down. Gotta run that two mile thing again here in a couple weeks, and the less I'm packin' the better." Jaylynn nodded. Crystal pointed her finger at the rookie. "Don't you be nodding. You never have trouble with the qualifying run." She turned her gaze toward

Dez. "But you'll be a bit slower, I see."

"What?" The tall cop squinted in the dim light at her pal.

"You know what I mean. Must be the honeymoon. You're packing the poundage, too."

Dez's face burned. If she could have gotten up and walked out, she might have, but she was parked on the inside of the booth. Besides, though she knew Crystal was teasing, her first response was to go across the table and choke the ever-living life out of her friend. She restrained herself.

"Hey, earth to Desiree." Crystal snapped her fingers up in the air. Dez stared daggers at her causing the Latina to raise both hands in the air, palms facing them. "Sorry. Sorry. Didn't know you were so sensitive. Just thought maybe you could give *me* a little moral support."

The tall cop glanced to the side to find hazel green eyes peering up at her, puzzlement showing. "Dez, is it just me, or is she calling you fat?" A smiled twitched at the sides of Jaylynn's mouth, an infectious look that made Dez relax. Jaylynn grinned and said, "Well, Officer Lopez, obviously you've never seen my honey naked."

"Oh, geez, Jay!" Dez rolled her eyes, but she was gratified to see, even in the dim light, that the black-haired cop was blushing.

The rookie went on. "Just sticking up for my loved one." She picked up her menu and returned it to the holder at the end of the table. "Enough of this poor body image discussion. Let's talk about other things."

The rest of the conversation was much less embarrassing to Dez, and she was glad she had ordered a turkey sandwich instead of the cheeseburger she had originally planned to have. The sandwich came piled high on wheat bread and was much better for her than the burger would have been.

After they finished their food, talk turned to station politics. They debated about who would pass probation and speculated about the new group from the Academy. The latest crew, which had signed on mid-year, had one woman, and Jaylynn's class had only had two. Nobody understood why so few women were joining up. They knew the classes were small because unemployment was low. Despite vigorous recruiting, not many young people were applying. They were short on patrol and in the investigation squads—with more retirements on the horizon. Several promotions had occurred, and Dez and Crystal agreed that they didn't respect a couple of the officers promoted.

Jaylynn scooped out a last bite of coleslaw. With her mouth partly full, she said, "A lot of people are slated for retirement. I heard two of the lieutenants talking about it when I was on desk duty. They said something about having ten percent salary savings because of vacancies."

Crystal wiped her mouth on the napkin, then folded it and set it on the table. "You'd think they'd use some of that cash to replace a couple of those caca cruisers. I'm sick of the heat going out in 223. It's a piece of junk."

Dez nodded.

Jaylynn said, "They've got the whole budget based on line items, though. You can't take money from one line item because it's dedicated for that purpose only. I think they have to get special permission from the City Council. So instead, they try to run quite a bit of overtime, not just to cover the job, but also to use up the money."

"Where'd you get that idea?" Her partner looked at her out of the corner of her eye, and Jaylynn gazed back.

"Heard a lot of things when I was at the main stationhouse."

Crystal sighed. "Somebody ought to take a stick to the City Council then. What's the point of a budget if it isn't flexible?"

Dez checked her watch, then reached for her wallet. "Speaking of funds, my turn to leave the tip." Everybody ponied up cash for the meal, and the three of them wormed their way out of the booth.

Jaylynn reached her hand over and placed it flat on Dez's stomach. "She's not so fat, Crystal. It's just the vest."

The Latina rolled her eyes and muttered, "Yeah, sure. Otherwise we'd be able to see her six-pack right through her shirt, right?"

Dez turned and stalked out. She'd taken all the flak she could stomach. Her long legs carried her out to the car, and she unlocked it and got in. As she drove past the front of the pub, Jaylynn gave her a little wave, so she saluted, then hit the gas.

She didn't know why Crystal's comments irritated her so much, but they did. She headed back to the north end of her sector to patrol the dark streets by herself, knowing she had two-plus more hours left alone.

Chapter
Thirteen

Dez didn't think it had been a good night at all. *Why does Friday night have to bring out so many drunks?* She sighed. There had been a slight warming trend, and the late afternoon and early evening were uncommonly balmy. Only now, after dark, had the cold set in. Despite the dropping temperatures, even at seven p.m. the loonies were out, and everyone seemed to be grumbling about the sudden onset of the cold. Homeless people, drunks, vandals—seemed everyone was fighting or yelling and disturbing the peace. Dez had already been to a nightclub on Selby Avenue twice because the residences around it reported fights in the alley. The Sharks and the Jets scattered when she drove her car down the alleyway. She wondered how many more times she'd have to go back before someone got knifed or knocked unconscious.

It didn't help that she was exhausted. She hadn't had more than three consecutive hours of sleep for nearly a week. Didn't matter how late she stayed up. Even when she should have been tired, she wasn't. Lying next to the slumbering Jaylynn used to be thrilling, but had lately grown old when she couldn't get enough rest to be anything but crabby the next day.

Seeing another unit with flashing lights in front of the Tora Tora Bar on University, Dez turned onto a side street and parked along the curb near the vacant lot on the corner. She had heard the call a while ago, but she'd been busy at the nightclub and hadn't paid attention to who had been dispatched. It was still early in the evening, but the sun had set long ago, and it was dark. She got out of the car and realized it wasn't balmy any more. She found she was actually shivering from the cold breeze. Zipping up her jacket, she made a mental note that it was time to break out the winter coat for cold nights such as this.

She stood on the corner, with the street on her left, and looked ahead down the sidewalk. The bar was on the right, and its door led right out on to the sidewalk. Ahead of her, in front of that doorway, Arturo Alvarez stood, his back to her, his hands behind him, as he spoke to three teenage youths on bicycles that seemed too small for the kids' large frames.

To her left, Alvarez's Crown Victoria cruiser was parked on the street, up close to the curb. Dwayne Neilsen lounged against the right quarter panel of the squad car, his feet crossed at the ankles and hands pressed together at his chest as though he were praying. As she drew nearer, she saw him break into a wide smile and tip his head first to one side, then the other.

She looked at him, knowing that the hatred shone in her eyes, but not wanting to give him the satisfaction of knowing how much he had hurt her. She knew that if she were given the opportunity, she'd deck him, and she was sorry that wasn't a possibility.

His eyes darted toward the bar where Alvarez stood under the dim streetlight, speaking earnestly to the boys. Neilsen uncoiled himself and slithered toward her, his gait smooth, his face mocking. "Where's your little gal pal, Dez honey?" he hissed.

She slowed to a halt, her hands in fists. In a soft voice, she said, "You're making—no, you have *made*—a big mistake."

He stopped four feet from her, grinning and giggling softly. "Uh huh, right. Seems like you're the one suffering."

The tall cop eyed the rookie officer. They stood nearly eye-to-eye with Dez being only perhaps an inch shorter, though he probably outweighed her by thirty pounds. She maintained eye contact, letting the hate she felt surge through her. Crossing her arms, she began counting silently, all the while staring him in the eye. By the time she got to six, he was laughing nervously. "Big, tough Reilly. You think you're so great—"

"Little weasely Neilsen. How does it make you feel that most of the precinct is wondering why, why, why were you at a gay bar? Everybody knows about me, but they simply had *no* idea about you."

If it hadn't been so dark out, Dez was sure she would have clearly been able to see Neilsen's face blanch.

"Bullshit!" His voice rasped, but she noticed that he kept it down. He glanced back over his shoulder to see Alvarez still busy with the boys, then stepped closer to Dez. He pointed his index finger at her jacket and punctuated his next sentence by nearly touching her with every syllable. "You. Lying. Bitch!"

She grinned and nodded. "I'm *so* sad that you don't believe me—a reliable FTO who's done everything to give you a fair shake. Why don't you ask around, you poor sweet thing? I am sure some of the old timers will have *many* choice words for ya."

Now he got in her face, stabbing his finger viciously, nearly poking her in the eye. "I should've filed a complaint against you before!"

She leaned away from him, letting her hands drop to her sides and casually taking a stronger stance, feet apart with one foot slightly ahead of the other. "You mean back when you were going around beating up on small women who weigh about a hundred pounds less than you?"

"That's right," he snarled, little bits of spit flying from his lips.

She backed up and to the side, off the sidewalk and into the gravel of the parking lot. "You know what? You're disgusting. Totally revolting. A poor excuse for a human being."

He started to turn away, making a motion with his hands like he was shooing her off. She laughed out loud and said, "Once a weasel, always a weasel."

Over his shoulder he said, "Fuck you."

In a mocking tone, she sneered, "I didn't know you were that kind of fella."

With a snarl of rage, he whirled around and rushed her, his big hands forceful against the front of her bulletproof vest. She couldn't help but grin, and her laughter further enraged him. He shoved her again, and she let herself be driven back two steps. As he gathered his hands to push her a third time, she stepped to the side, then moved in close, bringing her knee up squarely into his groin.

Instead of slowing him down, it infuriated him. With a bellow, he took a wild swing at her, which she ducked under. She tried to step around him, but he got hold of her gun belt, which pulled her off balance so that she stumbled.

From a distance she heard Alvarez shouting. "Hey! Cut it out!"

She spun, slipping out of Neilsen's grasp, and with unerring accuracy mashed her right fist into his face. Instant blood. By then Alvarez was there shouting, "Stop it! Stop it!" and pulling his partner away.

Dez shook her hand out, relaxing and tensing her fingers. She figured she was going to have bruises on her knuckles, but as far as she was concerned, it was well worth it. *Only one punch, but hey! It was something, wasn't it?*

****

Dez had no idea about any problems until the end of her shift. She signed out and headed for the locker room only to have Sgt. Belton buttonhole her to tell her the lieutenant wanted to see her.

She reversed course and went back up the stairs to Lt. Malcolm's office. When she tapped on the doorframe, he was standing with his back to her. "Lieutenant, you wanted to see me?"

He turned to face her, his face livid. She hadn't seen him upset like this in quite some time, perhaps not since last summer when she had gone alone without backup into a now familiar house near Como Lake where an assault was in progress. He hadn't been this upset when he had found out about her relationship with Jaylynn—disappointed, yes—but he hadn't been angry. Now his voice was curt, and she knew something was up. "Reilly. Come with me. Got something to show you."

He came around the desk and pushed past. Puzzled, she followed him as he led her out into one of the workrooms down the hall from the roll call area. He picked up a remote control and pointed it at the TV set over in the corner, then popped a video into an attached VCR. Dez stood in the middle of the room next to piles of newspapers, file folders, and video cassettes marked with dates, times, and places. She waited as the fuzz on the screen turned into a recognizable picture. The lieutenant fast forwarded through a commercial, then hit the play button. He pressed the button to increase volume, and Dez heard one of the local TV newscasters. She recognized the woman but didn't know her name.

"Citizens often wonder and worry about police brutality, and occasionally, we newscasters can't help but wonder ourselves, especially when faced with the evidence that officers on the St. Paul Police Force can't even get along with *each other.*"

The camera cut to a hazy and dark scene, but it was instantly identifiable to Dez. Two figures stood about thirty feet from a remote camera, which was likely perched beneath the rafters at the Tora Tora Bar on University. The broken glass in the gravel of the vacant lot glittered in the moonlight, giving the picture a shimmery fluidity. Dez watched with a sinking feeling as Neilsen shook his finger in her face, pushed her once, twice, and tried a third time. Her knee moved quickly, cat-like, though his body obscured the camera angle, but it was very clear then that he took a swing at her. She frowned. *He looks pathetic. Terrible form for such a big guy.* She looked almost balletic as she stepped around him—until he grabbed her belt, and then she was obviously off balance.

Alvarez's back appeared on camera, large at first, then reducing in size, as he rushed toward them. One more step and he would partially obscure her jab...but no. There it was, clear as day on video. Neilsen's head snapped back and he stumbled. Dez saw how she had brought her hand up, shaking it, but the grin on her face, even from thirty feet, was unmistakable. It was the same grin she currently sported and attempted to suppress.

Lt. Malcolm snapped the video off and hit rewind, then shut off the set. Tossing the remote on the table, he crossed his arms. In a voice filled with fury, he asked, "You want to tell me what the hell that was all about, Reilly?"

Lt. Malcolm rarely swore, and the fact that he just had made Dez's blood run cold. "What do you want to know, sir?"

"I want to know what that was all about."

"Sir, I'd rather not say." He glared at her. She met his gaze, then shrugged a little. "You might say I could have avoided it, Lieutenant, and that I'm at fault."

"It's pretty clear to me that he pushed you first and that you didn't respond—at first. But the fact that you struck him..." He put his hands on his hips and looked down at the floor, his bald head glistening.

"Yes, sir," she said in a resigned voice. "You do what you have to do, 'cause you can bet that I'll understand."

"What is the problem with him and you?" When she didn't answer, he looked down, ran his hand over his bald head. "Reilly...Reilly. Geez, what am I gonna do with you?" He stared at her. "You're one of my best officers. You've got nearly a decade with the force. You've got so many talents, so much opportunity for advancement. One day you could be a lieutenant—or captain. Hell, you could be Chief for all I know! But lately...oh boy. Lately you've made some dumb choices." She looked down at the floor and waited. He scratched the top of his head and sighed. "I'll let you know tomorrow—or later in the week—I have to talk to Commander Paar and wait to see what the political fallout is."

"Yes sir."

"You know what really ticks me off?" She waited, not meeting his eyes. "I just put in a request for a commendation for you, and you can be pretty certain it's going to wind up back on my desk with a great big red denial on it." He let out a big sigh and slowly shook his head. "Go home, Reilly. And please, I beg you, stay out of trouble." With a wisp of a smile on his face, he turned and headed for the door. Almost as an afterthought, he threw a final comment over his shoulder: "Remind me never to get in the way of your fist. I hear Neilsen's got a deviated septum."

She was glad he wasn't looking because she wasn't able to force back a grim smile of satisfaction.

****

The day following the altercation with Neilsen, the tall cop was in good spirits as she drove her squad car toward her special assignment. For the first three hours of her shift, she had been on regular patrol, but now she was headed downtown to join other officers who were working crowd control at a Saturday evening convention center event.

She'd already been quietly joshed by some of her fellow patrol officers about the previous day's events. She was still surprised to learn how many of them despised Neilsen. She hid her amazement as officer after officer indicated support and faulted the hot-headed rookie for accosting her and for turning her and Jaylynn in to the brass. A couple of them said they had known about her personal relationship with Jaylynn for a while, and *they* would never have squawked to the bosses. She hadn't expected that at all from so many of her peers. Not one person was negative, though a couple of cops were silent on the topic. The ones who did speak up didn't seem to mind about her choice of lovers as much as they were incensed that the young upstart had ratted her out to the commanders.

She thought about that for a little while, remembering how many years she had carefully guarded her personal life. *Did I need to do that?* She didn't know. What she did know was that there was quite a double standard for men and women. If she and Jaylynn had been male, she could bet they'd be ostracized. In her opinion, that was unconscionable. She knew there was no reason that a gay officer couldn't and wouldn't be just as good a cop as a straight guy—or a lesbian. *I sure hope that changes some day. We desperately need more cops, and I don't care if they're gay or straight, men or women, younger or older. We just need more good cops.*

She turned her thoughts to the "special assignment" ahead of her. Even though crowd control details were ordinarily boring and tedious, she looked forward to this one because Jaylynn was already there, working at the River Centre for the entire shift. The International Food Fair ran from noon to midnight, and if years past were any indication, it promised to be a madhouse right up to the end. There were extra officers on duty inside, and she, Jaylynn, and two others would work the Kellogg Boulevard traffic posts. She didn't think she had any worries about the rookie's safety tonight. She figured the worst of her worries would be that Jaylynn would complain of the cold. It was down to twenty-eight degrees and dropping when they left home, and snow was in the forecast.

She pulled up to the River Centre parking ramp, which was directly across from the convention center, and parked the cruiser in a No Parking zone behind another cop car. After updating Dispatch, she emerged from comfortable warmth into crisp, damp air. *Yup, snow is on the way.* She grabbed her patrol jacket out of the back seat and shrugged it on. With her t-shirt, protective vest, and blue uniform shirt, she knew she would be plenty warm so long as she kept moving. She locked up, then stood for a moment appraising the activity on the street. In the waning light, she could see people of all shapes, sizes, and colors scurrying across the wide boulevard, dodging cars, and slowing down traffic. Someone in a big white Dodge Ram honked his horn at two women in colorful African headdresses and bulky coats. They dragged two small children each by the hand, and another two young boys stumbled along behind them. As quickly as they disappeared into the center, ten more people emerged and wandered off the curb, over to the center island, and then across the other double lane to her side of the street.

She shook her head and rolled her eyes. *Someone is going to get hit here. Why don't people cross at the lights—or even better, take the skywalk? How hard could that be? What idiots!*

She scanned the street and located her fellow officers, Cheryl Pilcher to the east at the intersection of the boulevard and Seventh Street, Jaylynn in front of the entrance, and Crystal Lopez to the west. *Well, whaddya know—an all-woman detail tonight. Now that's unusual.*

She stood on the curb at the crosswalk and waited for a string of cars on her side of the street, then strolled across to the twenty-foot wide center island. She waited again, and when the road was clear, she strode straight toward Jaylynn.

The rookie watched as the tall cop ambled her way, and she couldn't keep the smile off her face. She was so glad to see Dez that if they hadn't been in public and on duty, she would have hugged her.

"Keepin' warm, Jay?"

"So far, so good. How's your night?"

"Really quiet. Nothing happening in sector two."

Jaylynn nodded. "That's because everyone in the city is here." She sniffed the air. "Get a load of that smell! Every time someone opens the doors, I want to storm the place."

"Take a break and go in. You could buy whatever you want, you know."

"Ha. There's over two hundred booths. I'd be in there snarfing down the food for so long that I'd get reprimanded. No, it's just as well that we stay out here and do our jobs, so don't tempt me. We've had a couple of scuffles so far." Dez raised an eyebrow. "You'd think that multi-cultural events would bring out the best in everyone. You know, peace, love, and international understanding."

Dez crossed her arms. "What happened?"

"We have two groups of kids who seem to be at war, and there've been two minor run-ins so far." The tall woman waited for more. "Four Asian youths came out about an hour ago followed by a pack of White kids, and they were exchanging words. I radioed to Crys and went over and yelled at 'em. The Asians took off, and the ones who were left gave me a little lip. For a minute there I thought I was going to have to pull out the baton, but finally I told them to beat it or I'd call their parents."

"And they did?" An amused look came over Dez's face.

"They were all of about thirteen years old, so yes, they took off in opposite directions before Crystal even got here."

"Okay. What else?"

"Same scenario, only these kids were older—maybe seventeen or eighteen—and they were a lot more worked up. The officers inside herded them out and told them to split, but they stood out here and taunted one another until I put a stop to it."

"Huh. They ran when they got a look at you and your spanking baton?" She bit back a smile, and Jaylynn gave her a mock glare.

"Yes, that is exactly what they did, Miss Know-It-All. And hey! Have I smacked anyone lately? Huh?" She gave Dez a smug look.

"Yeah, yeah, not you, too. Geez, I've been taking enough crap from our other fellow officers. You can just lay off."

Jaylynn flashed a bright smile. "All right, but I just wish I could have seen it."

"You should watch more TV."

The rookie laughed. "That is definitely one show that I need to make sure I get on tape. Anyway, back to these gangs. Gentry and Kelvin, inside, say there is an awful lot of tension between the teens in there. Nobody's flashing gang colors or anything, but still, they're watching closely."

"That's good. We've got plenty of backup out on patrol

tonight, so if anything goes down, we're well covered. Now if we could just make sure that nobody gets run over by a car, we'll have a good shift." She turned to survey the area. "How about you get your whistle and baton, and stand right in the middle over there." She pointed to a spot mid-point between the two crosswalks at either end of the block. "When people exit and start toward you intending to jaywalk, direct them to the crosswalks. I'll go down by the corner there and stop traffic as needed."

"Sounds like a plan."

"Yeah, we'll make sure there's no *Jay* walking tonight." She smiled broadly, her white teeth flashing in the diminishing light.

"Very funny." She reached over and smacked Dez on the upper arm with the flat of her hand.

****

The last of the light in the sky had long ago faded away, but with the streetlamps and the warm glow emitted by the convention center itself, the street and sidewalks were well-lit. Even the sky-walk that ran from the second floor of the convention center over the street and to the parking ramp spilled light out and illuminated the boulevard. Jaylynn stood for a moment and studied the square metal walkway stretched over the street above. The light inside gleamed dull gold through the thick plate glass windows. Bright red lettering on the outside of the skywalk spelled out *River Centre*, and the gold light reflected glossy orange rays off that lettering. Jaylynn looked around and thought everything appeared a little shiny and surreal. She tipped her head back and looked up at the sky, which was dark with no moon evident anywhere. She hated to admit it, but it smelled like snow. The air was heavy, and the cloud cover was so thick that she just knew snow would fall before morning. *I just hope it waits until after midnight when my shift is over.*

She pulled her coat sleeve up and pushed her glove down to look at her watch. 10:40. More people were straggling out of the River Centre than were entering, and the volume of new visitors had decreased in the last half-hour or so. She shivered. Despite wearing fancy super-intensity thermal long underwear under her slacks, she was still cold. It didn't help that she was in a patrol jacket that only came down to her waist, leaving her legs and rear end less protected from the elements.

She did a three-hundred-sixty-degree turn and scanned the area. For the moment, nobody was coming or going, and for several more minutes, all was silent. At the west end of the street,

Pilcher still stood, but Jaylynn could see her leaning against a lamppost, watching the few cars going by. To the east Crystal and Dez stood on the sidewalk talking. The rookie took a moment to readjust her belt. The only advantage to having gained a few pounds was that she had another inch or so at her waist for all the gear she had to carry. That was one of the things she liked the least about the job. It had taken her a while to get used to where her gear was and to decide what arrangement on the belt made the most sense for her. She liked to cross-draw her baton, and she was right handed, so the baton went on her left hip, and her Glock went on her right hip. Right in front of the gun, she kept her ASR, often called Mace, which she had not yet ever had to use. She liked to keep her handcuffs right behind her gun, with only a keeper in between to make sure that her holster stayed firmly in place. Along her back were her flashlight and radio holder. Lastly, in front of the baton and against her left hipbone was her double magazine holder, mounted upright.

Some cops liked to have their baton and their ASR on the left side and their gun on the right side, but the rookie's personal theory was that it was unlikely that she would use more than one weapon at a time. She also recognized that she was limited severely by space issues. *Good old Cal Braswell sure doesn't have to deal with that!* She reached behind her gun onto her hip, and there was the clasp for her cuffs. She flipped it up and snapped the cuffs into her hand. She felt most comfortable doing tactical handcuffing with her strong hand, and she doubted that she would ever cuff someone while holding her gun so it was perfect to keep those two items to the right.

She looked around her. Two women came out the River Centre door, hustled quickly to the crosswalk, and hurried across the street. Crystal and Dez didn't pay any attention to them at all. The women disappeared into the parking ramp, and Jaylynn focused back on her gear. She pulled her flashlight off the left side of her belt and flicked it on. She used it so rarely, mostly on traffic stops at night and that was it. She kept it on her weak side because she wanted to be able to keep her gun hand free at all times on traffic stops. She was pleased with her familiarity with her equipment. She had everything set so that she could get out of the car and turn on her portable radio, then grab her light in one motion. It had become a habit, and she realized with satisfaction that the tools of the job were there, right where she expected, whenever she reached for them. Still, she disliked the amount of awkward gear arrayed around her waist.

Looking at her watch again, she began to pace. Ten steps

east, turn, ten steps back. Occasionally a small group left the River Centre, laughing, carrying food in paper bags and Styrofoam containers, but nobody was crossing the street to enter the Food Fair. The party was definitely winding down.

Just when she was starting to think that perhaps they should call in and suggest knocking off for the night, she saw movement above her in the glass skywalk and stopped to stare. From her right and traveling across toward the ramp, three small men sprinted, followed by four bigger figures. The chasers caught up with the smaller guys in the middle of the skywalk, and all but two of the seven were suddenly in a pile. Jaylynn touched the button on her shoulder mic to call in the fight in progress, which also alerted her fellow officers. As she sprinted across the street, she listened to Dispatch's acknowledgment and the instructions for backup. Both Crystal's and Dez's voices came through the shoulder mic, and the rookie knew her buddies were right behind her.

She picked up her pace as she crossed over the center island. In the glowing light from the catwalk, she could see a scramble of arms and legs, fists, and falling bodies. The back of a dark-haired man slammed against the glass, and he slipped down. When she reached the other side of the street, she hit her shoulder mic and informed Dispatch that there were seven subjects fighting.

Pilcher's voice scratched over the radio indicating that she was moving into backup position, but the rookie couldn't see her yet. Without waiting for the others to catch up, Jaylynn dashed toward the parking ramp's flight of stairs up to the skyway. She hit the first of six stairs that led to heavy metal doors. Beyond them were thirty or more stairs up to the skywalk which extended off to the right. Behind her she heard the rat-tat-tat of footfalls, and Dez called out, "Right behind ya." She wrenched open the metal door and tore up the steps two at a time, hugging the wall on her right. Above, she heard shouting, grunting, and swearing, then a scream of pain.

Jaylynn reached the top three stairs, squatted down, and leaned out over the top step to look around the corner. She heard Crystal and Dez come through the door and hit the stairs below her but she focused on the same melee she had originally seen from below. She scanned the area for weapons but didn't see any knives, guns, or sticks. One of the White kids looked knocked out or dead. He lay motionless on his side along the far window. She wasn't sure, but there seemed to be blood on the floor near him.

She glanced behind when Dez and Crystal, breathing hard, caught up with her. Gentry and Kelvin were not yet in sight, but she knew they were on the way. Staying low, she went up the last three stairs with backup behind her. "Police, break it up!"

One of the small Asians, on the floor on his stomach, was squirming wildly while being pummeled from behind by a bigger White boy wearing jeans, a bulky jacket, and a backwards red baseball cap. The red-capped kid's head shot up. He rolled away and got up to run the opposite direction, as did two of the other White kids. The remaining young men, on the floor and bleeding, stayed down.

Crystal shouted, "I've got 'em! You two, go!"

Pilcher made it to the top of the stairs as Jaylynn and Dez took off after the three runners, leaving Crystal to call in.

If the kids made it to the underground garage, Jaylynn figured they had a good chance of getting away through the parking exits, and once out on the street, they had a lot of options for escape. But just then, two of the three young men split to the right, toward glass doors leading into the convention center. *Bad decision*, thought the rookie. Out of the corner of her eye, she saw the two runners skid to a halt when Kelvin and Gentry came through the doors and apprehended them. She fumbled for her ASR. Because she slowed slightly, Dez passed her. With a good grip on the ASR can, she watched as the one remaining suspect hit the horizontal metal handle on the stairwell door ahead. As quick as he was through, Dez was behind him, with the rookie on her heels.

Dez leapt down the stairs two and three at a time. At the bottom of the first flight, Jaylynn leaned over the handrail and pointed her aerosol can down to the flight of stairs below. When she saw the red-capped man's face, she shouted, "Dez! I'm gonna spray him!"

The canister in her hand made a "shhhkeeee" sound as she nailed the man in the face—and then he was through the trajectory of Mace and down to the next landing. Two beats passed, Dez still in pursuit, before they heard a gasp and then a wail. "Owww...get this shit off me!" She heard the sound of stumbling as she continued down the stairs, holding her breath. Dez was on him. With a jerk, she grabbed his coat collar and knocked him to the floor where he knelt gasping and coughing. After cuffing his hands behind his back, she opened the door on the landing and coughed a few times herself as Jaylynn descended the stairs. "Geez, Jay, thanks for the warning. I hate that stuff."

Even though Jaylynn was trying not to breathe any more than she had to, it still felt like pins and needles in her throat. "Yeah, me, too."

The kneeling man choked out, "Me three."

Dez stayed in the stairwell doorway and coughed several

times as the rookie took hold of the young man's arm. She said,
"Get up, champ, and let's get you out of here." He rose, his eyes
watering uncontrollably. He made choking and wheezing sounds
as he let her half-drag him into the underground parking area
where she proceeded to read him his rights.

Dez clicked her shoulder mic and called in, then gestured
toward the well-lit elevator area. "I think we'll stay out of the
stairwell and ride back up."

"Good idea. And this bozo here needs to have his eyes and
face washed up."

The red-capped man said, "You got that right. Shit, I need a
Kleenex."

In a weary voice, Dez said, "Yeah, yeah, we all do."

It wasn't until they got the suspect outside that Jaylynn saw
what she had predicted all night. Big fluffy flakes of snow were
falling.

Chapter
Fourteen

Jaylynn sat, her arms crossed over her chest, as Crystal recounted all the ways she'd like to help her wreak revenge on rookie officer Dwayne Neilsen. It was the end of another night working Third Watch without Dez, and the young officer was already tired of spending yet another shift paired with someone other than her partner. Being apart gave her an ache in her chest, behind her breastbone. It faded when she wasn't thinking of Dez, but when she did conjure up the lovely blue eyes, the ache returned. She knew there would be many nights in the future when she wouldn't even see the veteran cop at meal breaks because the sergeant would now always assign them to different sectors. Tonight she and Crystal were on the East Side, several miles away from Frogtown, where Dez was assigned.

The first five hours of Third Watch had been quiet: two possible breaking and enterings reported, a barking dog complaint, and a drunk and disorderly at the QT Tavern. It was full dark now, with a light breeze in the air. Last night's snow had already melted, leaving everything looking bleak and washed out. Jaylynn was happy to feel exactly comfortable temperature-wise, not too hot, not too cold, just right. But now that it was December—any time soon it could start snowing non-stop and turn bitter cold.

Dispatch came over the radio to summon them to a domestic dispute on Forest Street. Crystal gunned the car up Mounds View Boulevard to Kellogg, and turned on Forest, and pulled up to a dilapidated, brown, two-story house on the corner. As she got out of the car, Jaylynn could hear high-pitched shrieking and a lower, deeper voice shouting. The windows weren't even open, and she could hear thuds and scuffling. "Great," she said. "Sounds like a real dandy."

"What is *wrong* with people?" Crystal asked, as she shook her head.

They moved swiftly up a walk bordered by bunches of patchy grass. Three not-quite-life-size Fiberglas deer—a buck, a doe, and a spotted fawn—grazed in the dirt to the left of the stairs and below the front room window. The deer looked out of place in the shabby yard. Jaylynn followed Crystal up five cement steps to the concrete porch. She leaned on the black wrought iron railing that ran up the left side of the stairs and attached to the side of the house.

"Open up!" Crystal shouted as she beat on the front door. "It's the police."

All sound in the house ceased abruptly, and Jaylynn heard a shuffle of footsteps. The lock turned and the door swung inward, revealing the face of a frightened child, about seven years old. With dark, solemn eyes, he looked up at the officers. He wore a ragged yellow Pokémon t-shirt and blue sweat bottoms that were much too tight.

"St. Paul Police," Crystal said. "Can we see the adults who are here?"

The boy stepped back and opened the door wide to admit the two women. They walked into a tidy living room. The ancient gold carpeting still bore the signs of a recent vacuuming, and as they moved into the room their duty boots left footprints in the deep nap. Two shabby couches, a standing pole lamp, and a recliner were the only furniture in the room. The sole illumination in the front room came from the light shining in from the street lamp outside.

Just then a door ahead of them on the opposite wall opened up, and a woman emerged who appeared to be Jaylynn's age. She pulled the door shut behind her and stood leaning against it. Holding her left arm crossed over her chest, her opposite hand covered her mouth and chin. Perilously thin, with bags under her eyes, she displayed the same dark eyes as the young boy standing by the front door. She had obviously been crying but had tried to dab away the tears. As Jaylynn stood looking at the woman's impassive face, she saw water collect in the corners of her eyes and seep out onto her cheekbones.

"Ma'am," Crystal said, "we received a report of a dispute. Is everything all right?"

The woman mumbled through her hand, and Jaylynn thought she said, "Yes, Officer. No trouble."

Jaylynn watched the woman closely. It was clear something wasn't quite right, but she wasn't sure what.

Crystal asked, "What's your name, ma'am?"

Jaylynn thought the woman said Cindy Sterling. She stepped closer to the woman and said, "Ms. Sterling, please hold your hands out in front of you so I can see them." She saw the look of fright in the brown eyes, but the woman did as she was told. Her right hand came away covered with a generous amount of blood. Her bottom lip was split in at least three places, and Jaylynn wondered if some of her teeth had been knocked out because of all the blood in her mouth. In the dim light, her teeth looked black and white, like something out of a Bela Lugosi movie.

"Who did this to you?" barked Crystal.

The little boy, still holding the front door handle, piped up and said, "Bucky hits mommy all the time."

"Shut up, Vinny!" the woman hissed.

The little boy ran to the stairwell leading up to the second floor and hid on the other side, his scared, white face peeking out between the spindles of the railing.

"All right, lady," Crystal said. "That's enough. Where is this Bucky?"

Defiantly, Ms. Sterling turned the handle of the door behind her, stepped aside, and let the door swing slowly open. A short hallway, about six feet long, led back into another dimly lit room. From where they stood, Jaylynn could see a large figure lying on a couch against the opposite wall, the only light the flickering blue emitted from a TV somewhere else in the room.

"Sir," Crystal said loudly, "please get up and come out here. Now."

The man didn't move.

Jaylynn and Crystal looked at one another. They waited a moment. Jaylynn thought perhaps the man was asleep—or dead—but then she saw one large arm lift and scratch his chest. She saw no weapons anywhere, and she could see both his hands, so she moved down the tight hallway, Crystal at her back. "You're under arrest, sir, for domestic assault. Get up. You're going downtown."

"Screw you." The man's voice was deep and soft. Crystal paused in the hallway, one hand on her ASR, the other hand on her gun, as Jaylynn moved into the center of the room. Bucky continued to look past her at the TV set where *WWF Smackdown* participants were tossing one another around in the ring. He lay motionless, wearing black Levi pants, square-toed brown leather boots, and a dirty white t-shirt that didn't completely cover his mound of a beer belly. He had three days growth of beard on his face and chin, and he looked like he hadn't bathed for a few days either.

"Listen, Bucky, don't make me do this the hard way." The rookie glanced over her shoulder at Crystal, who just shrugged and seemed to be encouraging Jaylynn.

The man tore his eyes away from the television and looked at her. "*You* are going to do what the hard way? Take *me* in? Ha!" He crossed his hands over his chest, chuckling quietly to himself.

Crystal moved into the room, standing next to Jaylynn. "We can call for backup, Mister, and you're just going to get a charge for resisting arrest. Be a good sport and get up off your ass."

The man rolled his eyes, showed them a two second display of his middle finger, then turned his attention back to the television.

Jaylynn saw the remote control on the floor. As Crystal pressed her shoulder mic to report to Dispatch, the rookie bent and darted out a hand. She grabbed the remote and pointed it at the huge TV set. She pushed the off button, and the set went black.

"Hey, you little fucker!" roared the man. He was up off the couch much faster than Jaylynn ever expected. He moved so suddenly that he knocked Crystal backwards onto the floor, then lunged for the rookie. Jaylynn twisted away, turned, and blasted through the little hallway, knowing Crystal would follow and back her up. She headed toward the front door. As she emerged onto the blocky, cement porch, Bucky caught her in one ham-sized hand by the collar of her leather jacket, stopping her in her tracks.

Jaylynn drove her elbow back into the big man's stomach and tried to pull away. He grunted but held fast.

"You bitch...I'll show you..."

"Crystal!" She could smell the alcohol on his breath as he loomed over her. She swung wildly with her right arm, but succeeded only in smashing the remote control against the porch railing. Twisting to her left, which caused her head to be forced below his arms, she leaned back against the wrought iron railing and grabbed her baton in her right hand. With one smooth swing, she struck out at his left knee connecting to make a solid *thwack* noise. He snarled, a wild beastly roar, and slammed her against the railing, mashing her ribs and reinjuring the muscles around her tender collarbone. She dropped the baton, but he didn't let go of her.

"Freeze, buddy," shouted Crystal. She stood behind him in the doorway, both hands cradling her weapon. "Hands behind your head, asshole, or I swear to God I'll shoot you!"

For a split second, the big man stood very still, one arm wrapped around Jaylynn's waist, his other hand clutching the collar of her jacket. Her left side was pressed into his mammoth middle, and she could feel him breathing. She let her body go slack, hoping he would let go. For a freak second, she thought his hold was loosening, then he spun, swinging her around in front of him as he backed down the stairs.

In a high-pitched squeal, he said, "Go ahead. Shoot me! But you'll have to go through this little bitch first." He laughed maniacally and continued to back down the cracked cement walkway, holding her well off the ground.

Her legs dangling, and one arm free, she took every opportunity to kick backwards and to strike him with her right arm. Her left arm was pinned in front of her, and she wasn't able to pull away, and his arm was over her gun, so she couldn't draw. She squirmed and kicked, feeling the hard edge of her heel nailing him in the shins and knees a number of times, but it didn't slow him in the slightest.

Wide-eyed, Crystal followed them down the stairs, her Glock trained on the man. She lifted a hand to her shoulder mic, called the code, and quickly reported the situation. Clicking the mic off, she said, "Put her down. Now. You're in enough trouble already. Let. Her. Go!"

Jaylynn could feel the man's hold slipping, and his breath was coming in labored gasps. He let her slip down several inches, but she was still pinned tightly across the middle, her protective vest shifting upwards slightly. He hiked her higher up in the air so that her gunbelt dug in to her back and hip. The rookie realized her gun had to be poking him, too, and she thought, *Oh, please God, don't let him get my gun. Please!* She formed a fist and brought her elbow back into his stomach, but to no avail. He made an *oomph* sound, but it didn't stop him. Now he was to the curb, still backing up. He sidled backwards between the police car and an old red Camaro, which were parked about three feet apart.

Jaylynn saw her chance. She pulled her feet up, put one on the back bumper of the Camaro and the other on the front of the police car, and used her legs to push off and slightly to the left. This threw Bucky off balance, and because Jaylynn's feet were placed at different levels, it threw her off, too. They fell against the Camaro, the side of her head striking the back windshield. The rookie twisted and kicked. The big man lost his hold, and she rolled off the rusted red vehicle.

Crystal was on them in an instant, but not before he had a chance to pull back his foot and nail Jaylynn solidly in the chin with his square-toed boot. The last things she remembered as the world went blank were a flash of pain in her jaw, the taste of metal

in her mouth, and an antlered Fiberglas deer gazing her way as
though surprised to see her.

****

Cruising University near Rice Street, Dez heard the first call
and Crystal's clipped tense words to Dispatch. Holding down the
panic, she flipped on lights and siren and did a U turn right in
front of oncoming traffic. She didn't care that the other cars had
the right-of-way. She hit the gas and drove up University, turned
on Jackson, and careened around the corner onto 7th Street. She
weaved and swerved as cars attempted to get out of her way, once
even going up on the curb.

Another loud, clear voice came over the radio instructing
backup units to head to the Forest Street address, and shortly
after, another series of messages came over between Dispatch and
Crystal. They used the cryptic 10-codes, but it was very clear to
Dez that an officer was down and needed medical attention in a
hurry. If she could hear Crystal's voice, who else could it be other
than Jaylynn?

The cold, hard knot in Dez's stomach twisted into a frozen
ball. She forgot how to breathe. She was conscious of the whine
in her ears, the flashing lights, the grainy black and white and
gray of the world she passed by, but her mind held no thoughts.
Driving purely by instinct, she was impelled forward by a liquid-
cold fear surrounded by a deadly calm.

She made the right turn onto Mounds Boulevard going forty,
slowed enough to negotiate the red light on Kellogg, and sped
toward Forest. She heard the tires scream when she made the
right turn but she was intent only on reaching the house. She
caught sight of the police car and saw figures in a yard on the
right. A limp figure lay sprawled on the sidewalk ahead, between
a large laughing man and Crystal, who stood, feet apart, left hand
cradling her right, with her gun trained on him. Dez's squad car
rolled easily up onto the sidewalk. Ripping the door open, she
was out as though ejected and moving smoothly with the speed
and velocity of a Mack truck.

In the six running strides to the man, Dez saw the small
woman's face, covered in blood and unmoving. *She's dead! Jaylynn is dead!* Dez let out a shriek, a sound of desperate fury and
loss, and all about her the world suddenly became muted. The
colors washed out. Sound muffled. Her vision narrowed until all
she saw was a dirty white t-shirt.

Like a lineman tackling the quarterback, she lowered her

head and plowed into the beer belly, driving the big man several steps back into the street. He brought a large fist up and mashed it into her brow, but that was the last blow he got in. She kneed him in the groin, and when he doubled over, hit him with an uppercut. She laced her hands together and brought them to the side like a batter, then smashed them into the side of his head. He made a choking sound and tried to back away. She hit him in the stomach, again and again.

"You killed him," she sobbed. "I should've killed you when I had the chance. You murderer, you killed him, you scum, you...you..."

She nailed him with a roundhouse to the side of the jaw. The big man fell to his knees, and she brought her bloodied fist back. Her entire world reduced to a gray whirling tunnel that led from her fist to his face. A gash opened up in his brow, spurting blood that looked black in the moonlight. She drew her fist back again, unconscious of the damage she was doing to her own hand, and suddenly she was off balance, being pulled away. In her ear a familiar male voice shouted.

"Cut it out, Reilly! Calm down. Calm down, for chrissake!"

With a shriek of frustration she tried to extricate herself, but two sets of arms held her.

"Let me go! Let go of me! He killed Ryan. He deserves to *die*." The last word came out a rasping shout, and she found herself panting, wheezing. She was filled through and through with a feeling of horror and rage. "Goddammit, let me go!" she screamed. She kicked out, flailing with hands and feet, twisting, and shouting.

Gritting her teeth, she closed her eyes and continued to struggle. In her mind's eye she saw the blond hair, the blue eyes—the vision from a hundred terrifying dreams—and she redoubled her efforts to free herself.

She was on her back, heavy weights on her chest, arms and legs. A sharp rock dug into her right hip. The whine of a siren split her eardrums, then quavered down to nothing. She heard slamming doors, shouts, and the murmur of urgent voices. She opened her eyes, gulping air as best she could, and the world changed from the gray swirling confusion it had been to solid black and blue—the solid, dark hues of blue uniforms. Gasping for breath, she came to her senses, a feeling of dread coursing through her. "Oh, shit. Braswell, get the hell off me."

Nobody moved.

She gazed up at the fat cop, Braswell, with his porkchop sideburns. His red, sweating face looked at her with concern. He straddled her thighs and pressed down on her collarbones while two other cops, Tilden and Oster, knelt on her arms and pressed her shoulders into the dirt. She thought for a moment that she might vomit, but she forced the feeling back. "Let me up," she said in a quiet and reasonable voice.

Braswell asked, "You ain't gonna go nutso on us now, are you, Reilly?"

She took a deep breath. "No."

Mitch Oster was the first to loosen his grip. He shifted from his knees back to a squat, peering at her with worry in his eyes. Tilden let go and stood up to brush off his pants legs. Braswell rose with effort, hitching up his pants over his prodigious belly.

In a hoarse whisper, Oster asked, "Dez, what in the hell are you *doing* over here?"

She sat up, feeling queasy once again. It all came back to her in a jumbled flood of sounds and images: the roar of a gun going off loud in her ear; short blond hair; the sound of laughter; her own legs running; the pool of blood under a still body. *But no. Wait.* Something was wrong. It was all out of order, confused. The mishmash of scenes wasn't right. There were two scenes, two separate events, both equally terrifying.

"Jay!" she whispered, and she was on her feet, ready to move again, but not before the three cops could grab her once more.

Braswell grunted, "Hold your horses, Reilly!"

She stood motionless, her knees weak, with the three cops grasping her, their hands and arms firm against her. She had the feeling that if it weren't for their touch, she wouldn't be able to support herself. Across the street, three EMT's clustered around a figure seated on the ground. Turning her head, she saw on the grass to her left, about forty feet away, another EMT kneeling next to the huge man in the dirty t-shirt.

She stepped forward. One short step. Then another. The three cops fell into stride with her, Oster and Braswell on either side with Tilden bringing up the rear. She crossed the street, stepping around neighborhood onlookers who backed away in fear, and came to stand a few feet from the knot of people surrounding Jaylynn. A dark head popped up to see who was towering above, and Dez met Crystal's anxious eyes.

"Dez." Crystal slowly rose.

Now Dez could see the rookie's battered face, blood on her left cheek and chin. The young woman was not dead, after all, but she didn't seem to be fully conscious, despite the fact that her eyes were open.

Crystal reached over to put a hand on Dez's forearm.

"Dez—"

In a whisper, Dez said, "You were supposed to watch her back, keep her safe—"

"Dez, there was nothing I could do. She was—"

"I *trusted* you."

An EMT rose just then and gestured the two cops out of the way as he went to the ambulance for the stretcher.

The tall cop turned away and put her face in her hands. *Oh my God. What have I done? What in the hell do I do now?*

****

It was seven a.m. and Dez sat, dressed in street clothes, in the Commander's office. Her department issue gun was in its holster on the floor next to her right foot. She'd already been read the riot act by Lt. Malcolm hours before, and now she waited for Commander Paar to show up on his day off and finish the reaming. With her left hand, she held her right fist, rubbing the knuckles gently. She couldn't close her hand, and her index and middle two fingers were swollen and bruised. She knew she needed to ice them, but she hadn't had the time or opportunity.

Compounding the fact that she left her sector the previous night and beat up an alleged attacker, she had also chosen to ignore Dispatch's order that she return to her sector. Instead, she had driven the squad car to the hospital. Not until she received word near eleven p.m. that Jaylynn was going to be all right did she return to the car, call in, and ask if she should go back on patrol. By then, Lt. Malcolm had left orders for her to return to the precinct.

She had listened to his diatribe calmly. In fact, she barely took it in at all. She felt curiously disconnected, as though someone else, some sort of puppet, was moving her through the proper motions, saying "Yes, sir," nodding, shifting in her chair. Meanwhile, part of her hovered a few inches above and behind her, observing dispassionately. She supposed she was in some sort of shock. She had to admit that she certainly felt numb enough. It wasn't that she didn't care about all that had happened; she just didn't have the energy or strength to *feel* any caring. Dez chalked that up to lack of sleep.

Only when he said the words "medical leave" did she snap into some semblance of attention. "What?"

"I'm sending you to the psychiatrist, Reilly."

She looked at him in disbelief, not quite able to comprehend what she had just heard.

After Lt. Malcolm dismissed her, telling her she was on paid suspension pending psychiatric evaluation, she changed clothes mechanically, as though in a trance. She went out to her truck and drove to the hospital where she was promptly informed that only family could be admitted. She had to flash her badge before the overly cautious nurse reluctantly allowed her in.

The nurse back on the unit explained that Jaylynn would be spending the night for observation because of a concussion. She ushered Dez into the hospital room, saying that the young woman had a badly bruised jawbone, numerous facial cuts and bruises, and a broken wrist. "We've given her something to calm her, so she may not awaken. She needs her rest, now, so don't stay too long." The nurse pulled the door shut, and Dez stood several feet from the still figure on the bed.

Jaylynn's head was turned away from the bedside light, but even from where Dez stood, she could see how puffy and bruised the pale face was. Something bubbled up from deep inside, and Dez was at a loss for a moment to determine what it was. It made the back of her knees weak and took her breath away, leaving her heart fluttering and her temples pounding. She had to force back the feeling that she was going to be sick. Staggering slightly, she stumbled over to the bedside chair, sat, and put her head between her knees. After a few breaths, the world stopped spinning, and she lifted her head tentatively.

Jaylynn slept on, her face relaxed, her breathing regular. She didn't wake for the next three hours, and Dez sat quietly next to the bed, not thinking, unable to sleep, feeling little or nothing. At 6:30 she left in order to meet Captain Paar at seven a.m., and now she sat brooding outside his office, wondering what would become of her.

Chapter Fifteen

Jaylynn awakened to a crashing headache that seemed to encompass the entire left side of her head all the way to her jaw. *Throbbing. My head is literally throbbing. Gawd! I've had one hell of a dream!* She didn't recall exactly what had happened, but what she did remember involved struggle and fighting and pain. She winced as she opened her eyes, taking a moment to get adjusted to the bright light. She frowned. Her bedroom walls were now white. *Wait a minute! I painted them peach colored...why are they...*

She sat up, looked around, and immediately hit upon the amazing realization that she was in a hospital room. To her left was a metal rail with a call device hooked to it. She lifted her left hand, then did a double take—her arm was in a shiny white cast that ran halfway up her forearm. Rotating her wrist a little, it hit her that her hand was throbbing in concert with her head. She reached across her body with her good hand and pressed the red button, and when it stayed red, she lay back in the bed, feeling a rush of fatigue.

Only a minute passed before a slender black man in blue scrubs appeared. "You're awake. Good." He stepped up to the bed railing and pressed a button on the side so that the bed inclined up. "Jaylynn, my name's Everett, and I'm one of the nurse's assistants. How would you like a little something to drink?"

"Okay." She let him straighten out her covers and arrange pillows. "Why am I here? Besides the fact that there is something obviously wrong with my hand, I mean."

"I'll let the doctor come talk to you in a bit, Officer."

With that word—Officer—everything abruptly came back to

her...the big man, the fight, trying to get away. She had this fuzzy recollection of Dez standing above her, looking down, her face angry and fearful. Must have been a dream. Dez couldn't have been there. She did remember the doctor in the ER. She had been very soothing, very warm, reminding Jaylynn of her own mother. After that, she couldn't summon up any memory. "What time is it?"

The slim man looked at his wristwatch. "Ten after seven. Would you like some tea or coffee?"

She nodded. "Coffee would be great."

"Okay. What else?"

"I'm hungry. I'll take whatever you can get me."

He grinned. "That's what we like to hear. Appetite is a good thing, but I can't get you anything solid until the doctor does her rounds."

"Oh." Her stomach was clenching painfully. "How long will that be?"

"Shouldn't be too long. She comes on duty today at half past seven."

****

"Reilly, you realize you're in big trouble." The captain made it a statement, not a question. She nodded, watching him warily from across his desk. Lt. Malcolm sat in the chair to her right. "You have the right to have a union rep here, you know."

She nodded.

"Sure you don't want to call for one?'

"Are you disciplining me?"

He glared at her. "Not at this point, I'm not."

"All right then, I don't need a rep now."

"You're awful goddamn calm for someone who I understand went fuckin' nuts last night."

There was no reasonable response to that, so Dez kept her mouth shut. She looked down at her hands, rubbing the knuckles of her right hand.

The captain picked up a folder and leafed through it. "You left your sector—which I might have done, too, under the circumstances. Then you beat the crap out of the suspect." He looked up at her over his glasses. "I might have done that, too. But you ignored communication from Dispatch, failed to return to your assignment, just did what you pleased without even calling in to let the duty sergeant or anyone know." He slapped the folder down on the desk. "It's not enough that you're personally involved with the officer who got hurt last night—Savage—you also had to go postal? What the hell is wrong with you, Reilly? And what's the deal with your hand?"

He rose from his chair and came around the other side of the desk. Smoothing out his gray slacks, he crossed his arms, leaning back against the desk as he looked down at the top of her head. "Hold your hand out—no, dammit! Your right hand."

She sighed and held her hand out, palm up.

He smiled a grim smirk and shook his head. "Turn it over." He surveyed her hand, pointed at her knuckles. "You're going to the doctor today to get that checked. That's an order. And then you're going to the psychiatrist. You haven't been yourself for months, Reilly. We should have made you keep going." He stood, his arms still crossed over his white starched shirt. "Lt. Malcolm here thought you'd pull through on your own. It's obvious to me you haven't." He paused. "Have you got anything to say for yourself?"

She looked up at him, trying to hide her misery. Very slowly, she shook her head from side to side.

"Nothing at all, huh? Fine," he said in an angry voice. "Get an appointment for an x-ray today." He glanced over at the lieutenant. "You'll need to file work comp papers, so Malcolm, get in touch with H R. And Reilly, I want verification that you saw the doctor for that hand by the end of the day tomorrow. As for the psych eval, we'll let you know when it is. Go home. Your lieutenant will be calling later in the day with instructions for you. For now, you're on medical leave."

She reached down next to her chair and picked up her holster, extracting the department issued gun, which she laid on his desk. From her back pocket she removed her leather ID folder which contained her badge, but before she could set it next to the gun, he interrupted her. "Oh no. You're not suspended. Yet. You keep all that. Put it in a safe place. I'm giving you four weeks to get your act together. *Then* I'll decide whether we need to take further action. Lt. Malcolm has great faith in you. You go get your head straight, then we'll talk more."

She rose, her legs a good deal shakier than she expected them to be. He uncrossed his arms and turned away, so without another word, she left his office and drove herself to the Urgent Care Clinic where she sat for two hours before finding out that the bone in her right middle finger was cracked. They gave her a splint and told her to ice it—exactly what she would have done anyway.

****

Jaylynn was sitting up in the hospital bed, leaning back against two pillows, with the tall, rolling tray in front of her. Upon it were two cartons of juice—apple and grape—and a Styrofoam plate with one piece of dry toast cut in half. She'd been waiting for food for almost three hours and wasn't too thrilled when all they had brought was toast and juice. She would have preferred cereal and yogurt and bacon and pancakes and—the list in her head seemed endless. Instead, she was stuck with a miserable piece of cold bread and juice. *What kind of hospital is this, anyway?*

She held a plastic fork in the fingers of her casted left hand and, with her good hand, was trying to peel away the plastic from a tiny container that had a picture of a bunch of grapes on the front. So intent was she that she didn't notice the tall, dark-haired figure in the doorway.

Dez crossed her arms and leaned against the doorframe to watch the rookie. She saw that a hank of blonde hair had fallen into Jaylynn's eyes, which the younger woman impatiently brushed back. She set the plastic knife down and leaned forward, trying to open the jam, so focused, so occupied with her task—so like Jaylynn. Dez thought about how the rookie threw herself into everything, into life in general, with a passion and an energy she herself seemed to lack. *And to think that the big loser on Forest Street could have deprived the world of that.* To have this woman's love, her caring, just her attention was frightening and overwhelming to the tall cop.

Click: a huge fist striking the sunny, blonde woman. Click: the small figure crumpling, falling. Click: Jaylynn on the ground, blood all over her face. Click—Dez didn't want to see anymore of the images and forced them out of her mind. Taking a deep ragged breath, she realized that the weak feeling behind her knees and the shakiness of the last several hours was fear, pure and simple. Endangered. Exposed. Now there were two "E" words that explained her feelings. She was terrified, and there wasn't anyone on the planet, least of all Jaylynn, to whom she wanted to admit that. It made Dez shudder, and that small movement caught the rookie's eye.

"Dez! Where have you been?" She held a hand out, gesturing her to come close, and Dez automatically allowed herself to be reeled in. Next thing she knew, she was seated on the edge of the bed, facing the rookie, and wrapped in a tight hug, tight enough to disguise how shaky she felt.

Jaylynn leaned back and examined her. "You look like hell! I swear, I'm the beat up one who's been in the hospital all night, but you look like *you* should be the one here in the bed!"

"Oh, Jay..." She made a huffing noise and looked away.

"Have you slept at all?" Without waiting for an answer, Jay-lynn picked up the jam packet and put it in Dez's palm. "Can you get a fingernail under that? I can't get this stupid little teeny thing open."

Dez reached over and picked up the plastic knife and plunged it right through the plastic top a little more viciously than she'd meant to. Jam oozed out the sides onto her palm.

Jaylynn grabbed it out of her hand. "Geez, Dez! *I* could have done *that!*" She dumped the remaining jam onto the cold toast, scraped some out with the plastic knife and spread it around, then reached for the tall woman's hand and rolled her eyes. "You gonna go around with jam on you like that?" She bent her blonde head, and sporting a mischievous look, licked away the sticky grape stuff from Dez's thumb and palm. "There. Better, huh? You get any on your other hand?"

She reached for Dez's right fingers, but her touch caused Dez to gulp and draw it back.

"Hey, what'd you do there?" She gently examined the splinted finger. "Ouch, that looks painful—it looks awful. Is it broken?" With a puzzled frown on her face, she looked up into the troubled blue eyes. "What happened?"

"Buckminster—a.k.a. Bucky—Reginald happened."

Jaylynn looked at her blankly. "Buckmin—whoa! You didn't go over this morning and beat up that asshole Bucky from the call last night?"

"No, I didn't beat up Bucky today. I answered your backup call."

Jaylynn frowned, and Dez could almost see the wheels spinning behind the hazel green eyes. "You were there?"

"Too late. I was there too late. You were already down. I thought he'd killed you."

"So you helped Crystal subdue him?"

"I nailed the bastard," she said, feeling a tiny sense of satisfaction, even though she also felt regret she wasn't going to admit.

"Dez, you weren't working our sector. You—you left your post?" The dark head nodded slowly, and in response, Jaylynn's jaw dropped. "Ow! God, it hurts to open my mouth. How the hell am I supposed to eat?"

"Your jawbone is badly bruised."

Jaylynn reached up and lightly touched the side of her face. "I know. My whole head is just pounding. But that will go away. What I want to know is what happened last night? Didn't you get in trouble with the lieutenant?"

"Yes. And with Captain Paar."

"Oh no." Jaylynn looked positively horrified. "You *are* in deep doo-doo then. Start at the beginning. Tell me everything. I want a blow-by-blow account—no pun intended."

Dez shook her head. She closed her eyes and took a deep breath. "I can't—not now. I really don't want to talk about it."

"But Dez, wait. I—"

The tall cop held up a hand and scooted back down the bed slightly. "Stop. Listen to me. It doesn't matter what happened or why. What matters is that you're safe. And once you get outta here, you can put in your resignation. This kind of thing—"

"What?" Jaylynn's forehead crinkled and her face took on a perplexed look.

Dez leaned in close. In a low voice she said, "You don't have to put up with this shit. They'll probably make a settlement with you for your injuries. You can use the money to go to law school or something."

"What? Are you crazy? I'm less than a month away from passing probation. Why would I quit now?"

"Jay, it's dangerous for a small person like you. You're too— too—"

"I'm not small! I'm five and a half feet tall!"

"You're barely five-foot-five—unless you have shoes on."

"I'm just as big as about half the women on the force, Dez!"

Dez exhaled forcefully, then stood up, crossing her arms. She paced toward the wall, then came back four steps and glanced over at Jaylynn who held the mangled jam container in one hand as though she had forgotten all about it. "Jay, honey, you're not listening to me."

"I'm listening quite well, Desiree, and I *don't* like what I'm hearing."

"Look. This is your chance to get out before you get hurt. That's what I'm saying. You're a good cop, but you're little...and...and...you know...you're at a disadvantage." She wheeled on her heel and paced toward the wall again.

"Little? Shrimpy? You're calling me delicate?" In an ominous voice she asked, "Or do you mean spineless?"

Dez turned again, putting her right hand up to her forehead. "No! That's not what I'm saying. I just mean that you're no match for some huge monster of a guy like he was—"

"What! Who the hell do you think you are, telling me I'm too frail, like, like some sort of *puny* little baby doll?" She smacked the jam container down on the rolling table and heaved out a deep breath from a very angry mouth.

"No, no, that's not what I meant..."

The rookie's face was flushing red, and Dez could see it coming. She raised a hand as though to ward it off, but it was too late. With fury in her voice, Jaylynn said, "How dare you call me a wimp?"

"I didn't say wimp—"

"That's what you *mean!* I'll have you know you couldn't have dealt with this guy yourself. He *was* big—big as a mountain. And we got sort of ambushed by him, but believe me, nothing like that's ever going to happen again."

Dez bent forward, holding one fist up in front of her. In a tight, clipped voice, she said, "You're right. It won't happen again, Jay, if you just resign. If you want to stay in law enforcement, there's plenty of civilian jobs at the station that—"

A growling noise came from the younger woman, startling the tall cop. Jaylynn crossed her arms and glowered. "I am *not* resigning. Never. I can't believe you'd even suggest it. So, I got into a beat-down. It happens. I'm fine now. I'll heal up in just a day or so. Dammit! You listen, Dez. Crystal and I should have called for backup sooner. There's not a person on the force who could have dealt with that giant idiot."

"You're wrong, Jay."

"What do you mean—*wrong?* I am not wrong. He was mammoth. *You* couldn't have handled him."

"I more than handled him," Dez said sharply, and the words came pouring out, like a leak in a roof that she couldn't stop. "I beat the *hell* out of him. He's in intensive care right now, and it'll take his broken ribs, bruised kidneys, busted cheekbone, and mashed-in nose a hell of a lot longer to heal than your injuries will ever need!"

Jaylynn sat back against her pillows, speechless, and Dez felt her fierce pride deflate and shrink, replaced with shame. The cold knot in the pit of her stomach expanded, like water freezing in a glass jar, threatening any minute to crack and explode. She struggled for words. How could she tell her partner that if they went on like this—Jaylynn out on the street, unprotected, away from her—she would quite simply have a nervous breakdown from the fear and stress of it? She couldn't explain that. Nobody would ever understand. "Jay! Jay, honey, listen. Last year, you offered to quit the force if it meant that we could be together. This isn't all that different."

"What do you mean?" The rookie's voice was soft. "Are you saying that we can't be together anymore if I don't quit?"

Dez looked down at her hands, trying unsuccessfully to flex the right one.

"I can't believe you would say that," Jaylynn said, amazement in her voice. Neither spoke for several seconds, then the rookie's face gradually went from pink to pale. After a moment, she said, "You can't control me, Dez Reilly. It's *my* life, *my* job, *my* choice to decide what I do. Get out! You need to go away and leave me alone. I don't want to see you again until you can accept that I'm a cop, just like you."

Dez stared at her, shock on her face. Jaylynn pushed the rolling table a few inches away and looked toward the gray light coming through the hospital window. The tall woman backed up, and now her legs were really shaking. She wanted to say *you don't mean that, Jay...please, take it back...don't send me away.* But it seemed that her voice would not work. Jaylynn did not turn her head, would not meet her eyes. Tears sprang to the tall woman's eyes, but before a single drop could fall, Dez spun on her heel and sped from the room.

She hustled down the long hallway, found the stairs, and ran down four flights, bursting out into the lobby area. She didn't even see Crystal and Shayna striding across the open lounge area, and she never heard them when they called out her name.

****

It had been so long since she had spent any time at her apartment that it took Dez a while to find all the things she needed. She wasn't thinking very clearly. Any minute she was sure she would shatter into a couple thousand pieces on the floor, but somehow she held it together to get herself ready. She grabbed her comfortable old St. Patrick's Day sweatshirt off the hook on the back of the door in the bathroom, but she was disappointed when she realized her favorite jeans were over at Jaylynn's house along with at least a third of her wardrobe. She would have to make do without those things. She packed quickly, stuffing clothes, clean towels, and various toiletry items in the big bag. She had already called to make arrangements for her stay, and she knew she wouldn't be back for several days or a week, so she moved around the apartment, mentally checking things off. She picked out CD's to listen to in the truck. On the way out of the main room to the kitchen, she stopped to grab two paperback books that had sat so long on top of her desk that she could see a few flecks of fine dust.

She stacked her things on the landing outside her door and sat at the kitchen table. Taking a sheet of paper from the pad she kept there, she wrote a note to Luella, then got up and rooted around in the junk drawer until she found some masking tape. She ripped off a three-inch strip and stuck it to the note, then dashed downstairs to tape it to her landlady's door. She strode back up the stairs, locked her door, and picked everything up from the landing. With each step she took, as she descended the stairs, her grief threatened to spill over. She pushed it back, biting her bottom lip so hard that it began to bleed.

Unlocking the truck with the remote, she balanced her bag on her upraised knee and opened the door to the Xtra cab. She tossed in a heavy jacket, a pair of snow boots, and a large duffel bag, then slammed the door with more force than was necessary. She climbed up into the driver's seat and paused. She had CD's, but she realized she hadn't brought any other music. For a moment she considered going back up to the apartment for her guitar, but then she changed her mind. Luella could come home any time. Someone else could drop by. She felt too precarious, too vulnerable. She pulled the door shut and started up the engine. She'd probably be back soon enough for her psych evaluation, and she could get it then if she wanted it. For now she was traveling light.

She backed out of the parking spot and pulled onto the road and in short order was on the highway heading north.

So it's over and done with. That's it. Tears filled her eyes, and she wiped them impatiently on the sleeve of her shirt, but they wouldn't stop. *Well, what's new? Nothing good has ever lasted for me.*

****

It was afternoon before Jaylynn was released. By then she had told everyone who entered her room that she was starving, but the nurses and aides kept telling her she would be released any moment so they weren't ordering any meals. When Sara came to get her, Jaylynn talked her into stopping at the first fast food place they drove by, which was the drive-thru at Burger King. The hungry rookie began eating the French fries right away in the car, but she wasn't sure she could chew the hamburger. As she carefully ate the soft, greasy fries, all the rest of the way home she explained to her friend what had happened the night before.

"Geez!" Sara said. "You should have called me at the video store. I would have come over last night, you know."

"Sara, I didn't even wake up until this morning."

"Oh. Well, did you call your parents?"

Jaylynn frowned and shook her head. "I'm afraid they'll have a cow like Dez did."

"What do you mean?" The brown-eyed woman slowed the car at a light and idled, taking a moment to look at her friend. Jaylynn's face was pale, and her uniform rumpled and blood stained.

Jaylynn closed her eyes and shook her head. "Sara, she just pissed me off to beat the band. She showed up this morning and started telling me I have to quit the force—that I'm too small and weak for the job. Damn, she made me mad!"

Sara turned on Como Avenue, and took a second to look across the car at her roommate. "I wouldn't say that you're weak, Jay—you've got a lot of muscle packed on your frame—but you *have* gotten hurt a number of times now."

"Well, so what! It happens to everybody now and then!" She tried to cross her arms and winced when her wrist flared in pain, so she set her hands in her lap.

Sara pulled up to the front of their house and turned the car off. "Dez cares a lot about you. Remember how you felt when she was shot in the vest? Imagine how scared and upset you were then, and that's probably how she feels."

"Yeah, I know, but did I tell *her* she had to quit being a cop? No! I never even thought of that." With an indignant exhalation, she hauled herself up out of the car. They walked up to the house, Jaylynn holding the Burger King bag and her holstered gun awkwardly in her good hand. "I'm not supposed to have my gun at home, you know."

Sara nodded as she jingled the house keys looking for the right one.

"Dammit! That's a stupid rule. Only twenty-nine days until I pass probation and then I can keep it at home all I want."

"Maybe I can run you down to the station later on so you can drop it off."

Jaylynn sighed and nodded. Her hand and head were both throbbing in two-part harmony, and it wasn't pleasant.

Sara unlocked the front door, and they both went in and headed for the kitchen. Jaylynn shrugged out of her leather jacket with difficulty, her cast getting hung up on the coat sleeve. "For cripesake, now I know what a pain that cast was for Dez. Geez!"

"You want a cup of tea?" the brown-haired woman asked.

"Yeah, sure." She threw herself wearily into a chair at the kitchen table and opened up the bag to dig out the hamburger. "Will you give me a knife?"

Sara turned from her tea making and set a silver table knife before Jaylynn, which the rookie used to cut the hamburger into tiny slices.

"How long are you in that cast for?"

Wincing, and with one small piece of the burger in her mouth, Jaylynn said, "Ten days. Then I'll get a removable splint."

"You're off work for a while then?"

Jaylynn looked surprised. "No, just for today and tomorrow. Then I get light duty again. Lt. Malcolm came by to see me this morning. He said that Tsorro and Parkins would be pleased to get help again on the Tivoli case." She set the hamburger down on the greasy yellow wrapper and wiped her mouth with a paper napkin. "To be honest, I would really like to work on that case some more. If we could just catch a break..."

Sara leaned back against the counter, waiting for the teapot to boil. "You know, Jay, Dez is right about one thing. Your talents are wasted on patrol. You should be an investigator."

"Fat chance of that. I've only got a year of experience."

The teapot started to whistle. Sara turned to pull it off the burner. "But you're good at that, and you'd enjoy it a lot more. Admit it."

Jaylynn took another piece of the sandwich and chewed it grimly, refusing to comment.

****

Dez pulled into a pot-holed gravel lot outside a solid-looking log cabin. Gray smoke billowed from the stone chimney, giving the cabin a homey look. There were traces of the last snowfall clumped here and there around the house, but much of it had melted away, leaving patches of gray and brown and pale green. The deciduous trees were bare, but the little tan cabin was surrounded by a stand of evergreens, which afforded the brightest color in evidence. Dez parked and got out. Shivering, she opened the rear door and reached in the Xtra cab for her heavy jacket.

Before she could start toward the cabin, the front door burst open, and a barrel chested man in jeans and a red plaid shirt appeared on the threshold. He wore tan leather slip-on scuffs on his feet and sported a full gray beard. When she was little, Dez had always thought Dewey Cantrell looked just like Paul Bunyan. She had told him that when she first met him, at the age of eight, and ever after, he teased her about it whenever he saw her.

His deep voice rang across the parking lot. "You got a blue ox in that there pickup, Desiree?"

She smiled and shook her head, shouldered her gear, and headed toward him. "How ya doing, Dewey?"

"As well as can be expected." He took her duffel from her and patted her on the shoulder. "Get in here and get warm, you little urchin." He chuckled as he ushered her into his home, taking her jacket and hanging it on a hook next to the front door. "Sit there by the fire and get ready for some of the best hot cocoa you've ever had."

She did as he said, choosing the rocking chair furthest from the blazing fireplace. There had to be a 75-degree difference between the temperature inside and outside, and already she found herself feeling too warm. Unbuttoning the top button of her rugby shirt and pushing up the sleeves, she let herself relax for a moment, her breath wheezing out of her. She listened to the big man as he whistled tunelessly behind her.

The log cabin was the same as she remembered it—one large room with a galley kitchen on the north side and a small bedroom and bathroom through doors on either side of the fireplace. It was a double-sided fireplace, too, which served to heat both rooms. Through the flames she could just barely make out the fire screen on the other side and the outline of the bed beyond it. The hearth truly was the center of this home.

The main room was furnished with a leather recliner, a well-worn couch and matching loveseat, and the rocking chair she currently sat in. Behind her, newspapers were heaped upon an oversized dining table with eight chairs around. The framed pictures on the walls were of pastoral scenes, ducks, and forests. Two wooden bookshelves, packed full, sat against the wall to her right, and she noted a hardcover copy of Michael Crichton's *Timeline* and a paperback by Robert Harris. *Now there's something I can do when I finish my other paperbacks and get bored. I haven't read a book for quite a while.*

Dewey came toward her carrying two steaming mugs. He put one down on the end table near her rocker, then went to the couch and set his on the heavily ringed coffee table in front of it, sat on the couch, then put his feet up on the scarred surface next to the mug. When he saw her examining the table, he said, "What's the use of furniture like this if you can't abuse it a little bit, right?"

"I'd say that thing has taken some major abuse." He laughed, his solid middle shaking. She thought he looked happy. Once upon a time, he'd ridden with her father on a regular beat, and the day Michael Reilly died, Dewey had been with him. She still remembered how kind he'd been to her during the funeral and before and after all of that terrible time. He'd retired from the department three years earlier after twenty years of service to the citizens of St. Paul and bought the log cabin and a string of ramshackle cottages, which he had been working to clean up and remodel. He rented them out during the busy season, mostly to hunters and fishermen, and during the cold weather, he closed up for the season, winterized the cottages, and hunkered down for the winter himself.

"I was surprised you wanted to take a vacation now, Dez."

She picked up the mug and took a sip, expecting the cocoa to be rich and fragrant. Instead, it was thin and flat.

Noting the look on her face, he said, "Uh oh, I think I forgot something." He launched himself up off the couch and across the room, where he opened a drawer and pulled out two spoons. He handed her one and stuck the other in his own cup, stirring slowly. She did the same, and her second taste of the steaming chocolate was not a disappointment.

"I'm not on vacation, Dewey. I'm on leave."

He frowned and nodded slowly. "Medical leave or you-got-yourself-into-a-heap-of-trouble leave?"

Her eyes narrowed, and she crossed her arms. "Maybe both."

"Hmm." He let out a big sigh and shook his head. "What'd you get yourself into, kiddo?"

She debated at how much to tell him, opting for the spare truth. "Excessive force. I beat up a suspect."

He looked at her quizzically. "Reilly. That isn't your style."

She gave him a level stare. "He knocked out my partner— bruised her jaw, broke her wrist, and tossed her around like a cat in a gunnysack. So I conked him good." She hesitated. "And I didn't stop when he was down either."

He put his mug on the coffee table and winced. "Oh, I see. Lots of witnesses?"

She shrugged. "Could be. It was dark, but it also happened in the middle of a residential street."

He ran his hand through his beard, tugging on it for a moment as he thought. "Who'll rule on this?"

"First I see a shrink, then Commander Paar will decide."

"You'll get a fair shake then. And if the guy assaulted a police officer, the whole thing may get shoved right under the rug. He got priors?"

"Lots—mostly drugs and assault."

"Ahh—I'd quit worrying if I were you."

"Yeah, well, we'll see. In the meantime, thanks for letting me stay here."

"Oh sure. No problem. I've got that great cabin for you— you'll remember G—but not until tomorrow. Guy in it now is leaving in the morning. But you can stay in that other little crib—

you know, cabin D—the one with the baseboard heat."

She knew exactly which one he was talking about. It was little more than ten-by-ten with a small, full-size bed, a side table, and a tiny bathroom with a shower the size of a phone booth. But the one large window looked out through the trees upon Lake Superior, and two summers earlier when she had stopped to see the place, out that very window she had seen a buck, doe, and fawn silhouetted in the waning evening light.

"I could just stay in that one, Dewey. Then you can rent the bigger cottage out."

"Nah. I don't have any prospective renters coming now. You take G. It's a good spot. No phone service in any of the cabins though—maybe next spring."

"I don't care. I have a pager and my cell phone. I talked to my lieutenant before I left. If the department decides to have a hearing or wants me for anything, they know how to page me."

"Okay, that works out well then."

She reached into her back pocket and pulled out her checkbook, but before she could open it, he said, "You can just put that away, young woman. I don't need your money."

"Hey, Mr. Bunyan. I didn't come up here expecting a free ride."

"Look, I owe your dad a lot and wish he was still alive so I could pay it back. He always watched my ass, especially when I was a young rookie who didn't know his head from a hole in the ground. This is the least I could do."

"I don't know how long I'll be here, though." She felt uncomfortable about this, but tried hard not to show it. For the first time, she realized that a part of her was tempted to move up here and leave everything behind.

"Fine by me. You can stay as long as you like, Dez. I could use a hand around here as I winterize things. If you wouldn't mind giving me a couple hours a day, I'd be very grateful."

She nodded. She'd give him more than a couple hours. She had a lot of empty hours ahead of her before any administrative hearings. And there was always the psych eval—that is, if she *went* to the shrink appointment. Maybe she'd just tell them to shove it. But she wasn't yet sure. She needed time to think.

They spent a little more time talking, with Dewey mostly reminiscing about the old days when her dad was still alive. Dez listened with half an ear, responding appropriately when it was called for, but the other half of her focused on keeping back a rising feeling she couldn't quite define. The longer she sat in the warmth of the cabin, the more exhausted she felt, but her mind was clicking along, seventy miles a minute. She wanted to stay and half listen to Dewey for the rest of the night, but before long, he rose and took a keyring from the rack of keys next to the door.

"You know where D sits, so go make yourself comfortable. If there's anything you need, come on by. I'm up all hours of the night, so if a light is on, feel free to knock."

She pocketed the keyring. "Thanks, Dewey. I really appreciate your hospitality."

"Think nothing of it."

Heading back out into the cold, she shivered and plunged her hands deeper into her coat pockets. *I should have borrowed some of his books. Oh well. I'm tired tonight. Maybe tomorrow.*

Chapter
Sixteen

Jaylynn sat on the couch in her room. She looked around at the rumpled bed, the messy desk, and the stack of clean laundry at the other end of the sofa. The place was entirely too disorganized, but her wrist hurt so much that she just wanted to sit and not do a thing to straighten things out. Her stomach was so upset that it was doing flip-flops. She thought it was the combination of greasy fast food and the pain pill—medication, which had obviously not yet taken affect. With every beat of her heart, her jaw and wrist pounded with pain.

She had changed, with difficulty, out of her blue uniform and into sweat bottoms and one of Dez's baggy sweatshirts, and she sat with a pair of white athletic socks in her lap, attempting to summon up enough energy to put them on. She crossed her left ankle onto her right knee and began to work the sock over her foot. With a sour look on her face, she thought, *I guess breaking my collarbone was a real stroke of good fortune—otherwise, how would I have ever learned how to dress myself one-handed?* Putting a sock on her right foot was a little bit harder because of the odd angle, but she managed, then slumped back on the couch, feet on the floor.

God, I am tired. She didn't want to go to sleep, though. It was two in the afternoon and she still had a long day ahead of her. She would prefer going to sleep at midnight, close to her regular schedule, so that she got up on time in the morning. She knew the day after tomorrow she'd be back on the two to ten-thirty p.m. shift, and it wouldn't look too good if she were to drowse through her assignments.

She wondered where Dez was, whether she had gone home to sleep. Glancing over at her bedside clock, she debated whether she should call or not. *She was so upset when she stomped out this morning. I shouldn't have been so bitchy to her, but geez! She just made me so mad.* She took one deep breath, then another, then let out a long sigh. *Even though she infuriates me, I still think I need to call and apologize.* She debated, finally deciding to wait a few hours, just in case Dez was sleeping. *In the meantime, what should I do to make myself useful and keep from falling to sleep?* She rose and shuffled over to the walk-in closet and found a pair of slippers to put on, then went down the stairs to the living room. She picked up the TV guide and found that the movie *Romancing the Stone* had just begun a few minutes earlier, so she picked up the remote control and settled in on the couch, an afghan wrapped around her legs.

****

Sara came downstairs a little before six p.m. to find Jaylynn curled up, asleep on the couch, while a rerun of *Any Day Now* played. She paused behind the sofa and looked down at the blonde head, debating whether to wake her or not. Instead, she went around to the other side of the couch and picked up the remote control to click off the TV. Jaylynn slept on, her face peaceful and unlined. Sara tiptoed out of the darkened room and into the kitchen, letting the swinging door shut quietly behind her.

Today was the first day since the big doings at Thanksgiving that the kitchen seemed back to normal. Tim and Kevin had made a monumental mess of it over the holiday and nobody had really cleaned up very well since then. The guys had run one load of dishes, and since then, Sara had loaded up two more dishwasher loads full, wiped the counters down, and thrown out quite a lot of junk from the refrigerator. *Men. Gay or straight, they're such slobs.*

She took a plastic Tupperware container out of the fridge and poured the contents into a saucepan, then set it to heating on the stove. She turned the oven on to pre-heat, then got out salad makings and began putting a salad together. As soon as the smell of beef stew began to permeate the kitchen, she got a pan ready for a loaf of bread-from-a-tube. She was just opening the oven door to slide the dough in when the kitchen door swung open, and Jaylynn dragged in wrapped in the afghan. Sara grinned. A broken wrist would never stop Jaylynn if she smelled food.

She shut the oven door and turned to watch her friend hobble over to the rickety table and sit down. "You sleep for a while?"

"I guess. What time is it?"

"Quarter after six." The brown-eyed woman went over to Jaylynn and put her hand on her forehead. "You look over-warm. Feels like you might have a bit of a fever." She brushed the white-blonde hair back and examined the tired looking face.

Jaylynn sighed. "I hate taking pain pills. They just screw me all up. I'm cutting the dose in half each time I take it from now on. Maybe by the day after tomorrow I'll feel halfway normal."

"You want a little supper?"

She nodded. "Sure. That'd be nice. What smells so good?"

"Beef stew, salad, bread. It'll be a few minutes though."

"Okay," she said as she rose, leaving the afghan over the back of the orange chair. "I think I'll give Dez a buzz."

Sara watched her move slowly across the kitchen floor and through the swinging doors. In less than a minute she was back with the cordless phone.

"No answer at Dez's. Wonder where she is now?"

"Work?"

"No, it's Sunday. We're both off." She set the phone on the table and eased into a chair. "God, I'm tired. I hate this."

Sara leaned back against the counter and crossed her arms over her chest. "I'd be sore, too. Seems like you just got out of a sling, and here you are in a cast again."

"I could go a lot more years now without any injuries, thank you very much. The only thing good is that I can go back to work on that case with Zorro and Tonto." Sara moved over to the table and sat. She put her chin in her hands. Jaylynn looked at her a moment, then said, "Where's Bill tonight?"

"He's been gone all weekend for Watch Duty. Should be home now about nine."

"Oh. What have you been doing all day?"

"Nothing. Just reading. Laundry. Taking it easy."

"It's Sunday—why aren't you working at the video store?"

"Another guy wanted the hours so I let him have 'em. I'm quitting that crummy job as soon as Bill and I figure out what we're going to do."

A look of alarm passed over Jaylynn's face. "What do you mean—you're still getting married, aren't you?"

"Of course. This spring. I just mean that we aren't sure if we want to stay here or move into an apartment or go buy a house or what."

"Oh. That's a relief. You had me worried for a minute." She frowned. "I feel sort of bad. You two should have your old room back—"

"No! I do not want that, Jay. Thank you anyway." The

buzzer on the stove went off, and she rose abruptly and opened the oven door to check on the bread. It was done, so she pulled it out and set it on some hot pads on the counter. "Should I just dish you up?"

"That would be good. I suppose I should be grateful that this stupid broken wrist is my left hand. I am *so* right-handed. I don't know what I would do if I couldn't use my right hand." Sara set a small bowl of stew in front of her, a plate of salad, and a plate with a hot slice of bread on it. Jaylynn closed her eyes and inhaled. "This smells really good. Thanks for making it."

"There's plenty, Jay. I didn't know how much you'd be up to eating, so I started with a conservative amount." She settled in across from her friend and opened a bottle of French dressing. "Want some?" Jaylynn nodded and accepted the bottle from her. "Were you going to take some pain pills?"

"Oh yeah." She moved to get up, but Sara rose and waved her back into her seat.

"Where are they? I'll go get 'em for you."

"You don't mind?"

"Nope." She started across the kitchen.

"They're on my bedside table."

While Sara was gone, Jaylynn picked up the phone and dialed Dez's apartment again. No answer. On impulse, she called Van ita's house and briefly talked to Luella who had no idea where Dez was. When Sara returned to the room, Jaylynn was filling in Luella about her latest accident. Sara set the small brown plastic container on the table, and the rookie juggled the phone trying to get it open. Sara took it from her, twisted the cap off and handed it back. By then, Jaylynn was saying goodbye. She clicked it off and set the phone to the side of the table.

Sara met her gaze. "Find Dez?"

"No. Luella doesn't know where she is either. Where the heck could she be?"

"Shopping...at the movies...visiting other friends...sleeping with the phone turned off...driving around..."

Jaylynn sighed. "Guess I'll wait until around midnight and try again. She ought to be home by then."

"Good idea. You want to watch a video with me until then?"

"All right. What've you got checked out?"

"You name it, I've got it—drama, comedy, suspense, even an oldie."

"What's the oldie?"

"*North by Northwest*."

"Hey, that's a good one. Let's watch that."

Sara scooped out the last bite of her stew and noticed that Jaylynn's bowl was empty. "You want some more?"

"No, but I could use some butter for this bread."

Sara rose and went to the fridge. "Butter or margarine?"

"Butter, of course."

"We've got three kinds of tub-o-butter going here.   Just thought I'd offer."

"Let Kevin eat that crap. I'll take butter any day."

****

The tall police officer's chest hurt, and her breath came in short gasps.   Flashing lights—neon red and blue and white— swirled all around her in the darkest night she had ever experi- enced. She looked up but there was no moon, no light from street lamps. Only the neon swirls cast light, but they made her sick to her stomach. She smelled something dank and sour, like poison gas, and it stung her eyes. Scalding hot tears ran down her face. She reached up to wipe them away and was shocked to see, in the flashing lights, that there was blood all over her hands.

She almost cried out, but then looked around in fear. Who is after me? What is happening?

Wiping her bloody hands on her pants, she moved down an uneven walkway, squinting into the flashing lights that kept blind- ing her. Her chest hurt, her eyes burned, but she forced herself on, closer to the glare of the multi-colored lights.

No. No no no...I won't...I can't....

A voice in her head whispered, "You must, coward.   You must."

No, I won't—I can't! I can't!

With a howl, she turned to run, but the ground tilted. She fell to her knees, then slid backwards down the cracked walkway. Frantically she scrambled upwards, grabbing at anything, trying desperately to get purchase on some solid land. Her bloody hands grabbed at crevices in the walkway, but the cement pulled away each time, and she continued to slide closer to the neon lights. Frozen ground, like a sheet of ice, chilled and numbed her. As she slid and struggled, she grew colder until she could hardly move, then she had no control of her body at all. Only then did she stop her downhill slide. She closed her eyes and rolled over to her side, breaths coming fast.

Don't look...don't look. It will go away if you don't look.

A voice in her head whispered, "You must, coward. For once, you must."

Oh God, please... *She opened her eyes saw the crumpled blue-clad body face down before her, but she couldn't see who it was. Grabbing one shoulder, she started to roll the body over...until she saw those dead blue eyes. She let out a scream...*

No! No, Ryan, no! *Sinking...sinking...flashing lights receding...darkness all around. She screamed again.*

Dez awoke. She lay from corner to corner on a surprisingly comfortable mattress, but the air was bitter cold. The covers were all on the floor. She sat up, moved back and against the bed's headboard, and grabbed at the sheet and blankets, still remembering the images in the dream. *It's a nightmare—just a nightmare.* But no, she understood that it was real. It had really happened. He was dead. Her best friend was dead. She couldn't quite believe it. Tears sprang to her eyes. She reached up to blot them away and found her face already covered with water.

Huddled against the wooden headboard in the dark cottage, knees to her chest and swathed in a blanket, she let the tears come. Little mewling sounds mingled with sobs as she cried. She banged her forehead against the top of her knee until it began to throb too much to continue, then scooted down, curled up on her side, and shook with cold and fear and mourning until finally, sometime later, she fell into restless sleep punctuated with more bad dreams.

****

Dez woke the next morning and lay motionless in the small bed. She remembered her dream about Ryan, and even worse, she remembered another one in which a towering man with flaming red eyes beat her to the ground, then punched and kicked Jaylynn until the young officer fell dead in the street. It seemed that every time she had awakened, frightened and heart beating wildly, she had gone back to sleep only to dream a similar horrible nightmare.

Tears filled her eyes. She ached for the comfort of Jaylynn beside her, holding her, consoling her. The anguish was so intense that she couldn't move, and a pain in her chest swelled and grew until she thought she would burst from the sheer intensity of it. She didn't remember feeling this misery ever before, not even when her father had died...but then again, she hardly remembered the death of her father. It was a dry fact, not something with memories attached. She couldn't even call up clear memories of the house they were living in at the time.

She looked around the cabin, which was blazing bright with the early morning sun shining in through the bay window on the east side of the cabin. The sun hurt her eyes, so she closed them and curled up into a ball, her long t-shirt soft against her arms.

Her eyes popped open, and she let a burst of anger fuel her. *Stubborn, pigheaded woman! Jaylynn doesn't know what's good for her. Geez, I hate choices. And it's even worse when someone else needs to make a choice and the one they make is stupid!* Dez was certain that if Jaylynn continued on the police force, something terrible would happen—and no one would be there to protect her. *Oh God. What if something awful happens?*

She sat up, resisting the urge to pull her hair out as her emotions swept back and forth between anger and desolation. Before she could begin to make any sense of her feelings, she was startled out of them by an insistent, shrill beeping. She sprang from the bed, and grabbed her duffel bag, rooted around in it, found the small black device and pushed the button. The number the pager displayed was familiar. She knew why Lt. Malcolm was calling. The department had either scheduled her psychiatric evaluation or else a hearing with internal affairs.

With a heavy heart, she turned the pager off and threw it back in the bag, then found her cell phone and punched in the numbers.

****

Jaylynn rose at ten the next day. She had tried calling Dez up until two a.m., but no answer. No response at ten a.m. either. Now she was starting to get worried. Maybe Dez was so mad at her that she wasn't answering the phone...but no, that wasn't how Dez reacted. *Maybe something is wrong, like she's sick or something.* Jaylynn was struck with fear. *What if something awful has happened? What if she's been in an accident?*

She kept calling until early afternoon, then decided to just get in the car and drive over to the duplex. But when she got there, the curtains on the main floor were closed, and the upstairs looked dark. Shivering, she strode around to the back door and rang both bells. Nobody answered. She went back down the back porch stairs, through the yard, and to the stairs that led down to the garage. By going up on her toes, she could see in the garage window, and it was empty. No truck, no Dez.

Where the hell are you, Dez?

She retraced her steps and hurried through the cold air back to her car. With her casted left arm cradled against her chest, she drove to Vanita's house. Although she had a pleasant visit with Luella and her sister, neither of them had heard from Dez other than a cryptic note left taped to Luella's back door.

Jaylynn went back to her house an hour later and ate some lunch, then fell asleep in front of the TV until Sara and Bill awakened her to ask if she wanted take-out Chinese.

Chapter
Seventeen

Tuesday morning, the first thing that surprised Dez when she arrived at the therapist's office in downtown St. Paul was that it wasn't an office at all, but an old converted warehouse containing an enormous art gallery in the spacious entrance, a printing company in the west wing, and in the east wing, a small publishing company called Jumping Bean Press. Scanning the directory, she could see that the second and third floors were inhabited by doctors, lawyers, and small businesses, while the remaining nine stories housed an apartment collective. Dr. Montague was listed on the third floor, east wing.

Forgoing the elevator, the tall woman took the stairs two at a time, all the while seething with resentment. *I do not want to be here. I can't believe they can make me do this.* She shook her head slowly from side to side, and as she reached the top of the last flight of stairs, she let out a forceful breath. Opening the door, she walked down a dusty hallway toward 305, which she found was at the very end of the east wing. Each door along the way was painted a different color—red, orange, green, then yellow, and she found the one she was looking for was a deep rich royal blue. *It figures*, she thought. *Shrinks always want everything to be restful blue and comforting hues so they can lull you into admissions or revealing things that are none of their damn business.* With great reluctance, she reached for the doorknob.

She entered a small waiting room with three chairs on either side facing one another. There was room for nothing else, other than one small table in the corner where an oversized lamp perched, shedding golden light. Ivory-colored walls were adorned with 12x15" framed glossy photos of the North Shore. None of the twelve frames matched, some being plain light wood, some ornate plastic, others fancy, engraved metal. She glanced at her watch. 9:56. She was on time.

Before she could make a move to be seated, a door opened, and a woman stood before her, coffee mug in hand. Sunlight shone from a window behind the woman's head, so Dez could not get a good look at her. All she could see was a plump, wild-haired person wearing red stretch pants, a white top, and white Nike tennis shoes. She glanced at her watch again—still 9:56. *Just my luck she's going to start early.* She let out a sigh.

"You must be Desiree Reilly."

Dez nodded grimly and stood waiting, her hands clenching and unclenching.

"I'm Marie Montague. Come on in." She stepped back to allow Dez entrance, and then Dez could see that the wild hair was actually very curly and silver-gray. Rather than being a young woman in her 30's, like Dr. Goldman, Dez guessed her to be closer to 60.

The second thing to surprise Dez was that the office she trudged into was much larger than she expected. She estimated it to be thirty feet square. It was divided into quadrants. One quadrant was filled with toys and dolls and games, haphazardly stacked on two benches and spilling out of two toy boxes. Next to it was an area containing a kitchenette complete with microwave, sink, and cupboards. An over-sized, wooden-framed window from which bright sunlight spilled was above a dinette type of table where packages of crackers and cookies were stacked. There were pots of flowers on the windowsill and on plant stands in every corner of the room.

Two doors, neither of which was painted, were off to the left, but both were closed, so Dez didn't know where they led.

The other half of the office was separated from the kitchen and play area by two large round posts that served as structural support for the building. Chairs formed a circle in the nearer part of the third quadrant, and there was a large wooden table pushed up against the far wall, dozens of photographs strewn across it. Above the table, hanging on the wall, were five framed 8 x10" photographs. Unlike the ones in the waiting room, these were black and white. The center photo showed a slender, young woman with curly black hair. She wore Army fatigues and a billed Army cap, which Dez assumed to be olive green. The shot was a full body profile with a lush background of foliage behind the figure. The woman's pant legs were rolled up to mid-calf, and she stood in a couple inches of water, deep enough that you couldn't see her feet. Laughing, she looked back over her shoulder toward the photographer, one hand raised as though to wave. Dez didn't get a chance to inspect the other four photos. The therapist gestured toward two chairs facing one another.

There was a coffee table in between on which sat a variety of objects, but Dez did not take time to survey them, instead stealing suspicious glances at the other woman, who was now saying, "Would you like a cup of coffee?" She raised her white mug, which sported a comic of Minnie Mouse in a hot pink dress.

Dez shook her head. "Never drink the stuff."

"Okay. Well then, have a seat."

Dez folded her long frame down into a soft brown chair that sat low to the ground. She expected to be cramped, but found instead that it was comfortable. Taking a deep breath, she crossed her arms tightly and settled in for what she figured to be a long hour.

The therapist bent and carefully placed her steaming, full mug on the coffee table. She picked up a clipboard that was leaning against the chair and sat, squirming a little to get comfortable. She adjusted the clipboard on her lap, giving Dez time to study her. In police fashion, the description "Caucasian, 5'4", 145 pounds, gray hair, brown eyes, no scars" flashed through the policewoman's head. Someone with whom she had little in common. Someone from a whole different world than the one in which she—and her police cohorts—existed. She decided the silver haired woman looked a lot like the young woman in the Army photo, perhaps enough to be the Army girl's mother. Strong jaw, high cheekbones, lightly tanned complexion, unruly hair. She had probably been a pretty woman in her day, and now she was what Dez would call an appealingly handsome older woman.

The eyes that rose to meet Dez's were warm and dark brown, almost black, signifying that she might be descended from a Greek or Italian family. A slight smile on her lips, Marie Montague let a breath out and didn't break her gaze. Dez watched her warily, waiting. Her heart began to beat faster, and she felt like she was being scanned, emptied of her secrets. But no, that couldn't happen. This woman couldn't get in any further than Dez allowed, of that she was sure.

A long pause went by and finally the older woman asked, "Desiree, why are you here today?"

"It's Dez, Doctor Montague. Call me Dez."

The doctor inclined her head once, her eyes never leaving Dez's, as though she were waiting for more.

Impatiently, Dez said, "I'm here because I *have* to be here. You should know it's required."

The doctor nodded slowly, her hands motionless on the clip-board in her lap. "I see." She paused for a long moment, looking toward the sunny window across the room. "Why don't you call me Marie, then, and I'll call you Dez."

The black-haired woman nodded. *Great. That's settled.* She glanced down at her watch to see it read 10:01. *One down, 59 to go.*

"So you're here because you *have* to be, not because you want to be."

Dez nodded again.

"If you don't want to be here, why are you here then?"

The tall cop frowned. "It's required. If I don't show up three times a week until you release me, I get deep-sixed by the depart-ment." She uncrossed her arms and let her fists drop into her lap.

"You're saying they would throw you away?"

"Pretty much."

"Why do you think that is?"

Dez looked down at her hands. She could see one of the veins throbbing on top of her right hand, which was still sore and bruised. She turned that hand over and looked at her palm, then made a fist. "They think I'm out of control, that I've lost it." She moved her fingers, including the one that was supposed to have a hairline crack, and she found it didn't hurt much.

"Have you?"

"Have I what?"

"Lost it. Gone out of control?"

Dez shook her head and looked toward the window. In the distance she could see part of the Capitol dome and a flash of gold from the Quadriga sculpture above the columned marble entrance-way. In sixth grade she had mounted the stairs and climbed up to the portico where the Quadriga was displayed. She had always liked the gilded statue of Prosperity with the two women walking on either side of the four horses pulling the chariot. She thought it was the head of one of the golden horses that was shining so brightly. Turning her head back toward the curly-haired woman, she asked, "Don't you want to know about my childhood? My family? About my schooling? I thought all you psych people started out with a history from birth to now that takes about six hours."

Marie surprised her by laughing out loud. Her teeth were white, and Dez could see that there was a small chip in the right front incisor.

"No, I prefer not to start with the past because it's the here and now that is apparently causing you a problem. Perhaps if you

could tell me, from your point of view, what possessed your lieutenant and Dr. Goldman to refer you to me, then we could move
through all of this swiftly and get you on your way."

Dez crossed her arms again. "Don't you have a report, some
sort of explanation from Goldman or my supervisor?"

"Yes, I do. But that's from *their* point of view. I want to hear
what you think."

Dez had no desire to relive the experience at the house on
Forest, when she felt the terror ripple through her, when she lost
her cool. People always talked about "seeing red" when doing
drastic and violent things, but red was not the color she had seen.
Gray and silver and crystal clear pictures of the location—that is
what she had observed—in mostly black and white splendor.
Click: Jaylynn on the ground covered in blood. Click: the man
laughing gleefully after having wounded the rookie. Click: the
look of surprise and pain on the fat man's face as she struck him
and he fell to his knees on the ground.

Dez was certain she could have killed the man. She'd *wanted*
to kill him. But the department couldn't have known her feelings,
and she hadn't killed him after all. Broke his nose and cheekbone,
bruised his kidneys, fractured seven ribs, but she hadn't killed
him. She never even unholstered her gun. She felt a grim satisfaction about that.

"Dez?"

Snapping to alertness, Dez's eyes narrowed as she focused in
on the doctor.

"Dez, you know you're free to go."

Confused, Dez looked at Marie long and hard. "What do you
mean?"

"I'm not holding you here. You can go anytime you wish."

Dez leaned forward. With more hope in her voice than she
intended to reveal, the tall woman asked, "You'll give a report to
my lieutenant that I cooperated?"

A faint wisp of a smile crossed the older woman's face.
"Actually, I can't give any sort of report to him. You haven't told
me anything."

Dez glared at the other woman. *Why is she jerking me
around?* She didn't bother to disguise raising her wristwatch to
look at the time, which showed 10:07. A gust of air escaped from
her lips, and she sank further down into the chair.

Marie took a loud slurp of coffee and set the Minnie Mouse
mug back on the table. "It's important to me that you understand
that I'm not holding you here. You can go anytime you wish."

"I'll lose my job then." It came out in a hoarse whisper, and for the first time Dez felt a feeling of hopelessness surface.

"What could be so serious that you would be fired?"

The rage bubbled up, and through gritted teeth, Dez said, "Didn't you read the goddamn report? What the hell kind of doctor are you anyway?"

The third thing to surprise Dez was the therapist's response. She laughed. And it wasn't a snicker or a sneer. Marie Montague burst forth with a deep, loud, belly laugh, genuinely amused, reminding her of Jaylynn and sending a stab of pain into her heart and tears to her eyes. She looked down at the coffee table and, through the tears swimming in her eyes, saw a jumble of objects. *Get a hold of yourself!* The thought occurred to her that she could get up and march right on out, leave all of this behind. She imagined herself doing it: rising, grabbing the brass handle, flinging the door wide, stomping out into the hallway, and kicking each and every one of those multicolored doors on the way to the stairwell. *Who gives a shit about the job? I don't care. I don't want to care anymore...*

Before she could say or do anything, though, the psychiatrist said, "Dez Reilly, it's clear that you don't want to talk to me about you—at least not right at this moment. So how about I tell you a little bit about me?"

Dez sat still for a moment, then nodded. Her vision was clearing, with the threat of tears and her momentary panic subsiding. Without thinking, she leaned forward and from the coffee table picked up a carving of two wooden bears. She didn't know what kind of wood it was, but she liked the toasty dark brown animal. She cradled it in both hands and then turned it over. Between the bear's front paws, she protected a bear cub, whose smaller head peeked out from the underside of the larger bear. The eyes and ears on both bears were small and the mouth and nostrils were carefully indented, showing that the woodworker had paid attention to detail. Holding the carving in her left hand, she rubbed the smooth surface of the mama bear's coat with the side of her left thumb, feeling an odd comfort from the burnished surface. Recovered, she looked up into the warm brown eyes, and felt a twinge of guilt that she would not—could not—give this doctor what she seemed to want and need in order to do her job.

"I'm sixty-one years old, Dez. I came of age in the late fifties and early sixties after growing up in a healthy and well-to-do family, most of whom still live in and around Mankato. I come from a long line of farmers, all the way back to seventeenth century olive growers in the Mediterranean. In southern Minnesota, my family raised cattle, corn, soybeans, and wheat. I didn't have much to do with it, being a girl, but my four older brothers worked the farm.

"I wasn't satisfied hanging around small town Minnesota. I wanted to see the world. I was also interested in healing the body, so I went to college in Minneapolis for a year, then joined the Army where I could take college classes and train simultaneously to be a nurse and field medic. I was a good student, but I had a lot of fun, too. Went to many, many dances. Dated a few very sweet men. Enjoyed the whole free, liberating experience of the early sixties."

She shifted the clipboard in her lap, turning it one-quarter, and letting her forearms rest on it, then went on. "Six months before I graduated from nursing school, a U.S. destroyer was bombed off the coast of North Vietnam, and our troops retaliated. The war started to escalate, and tensions at home and in Vietnam went through the roof. Once I got out of school, I spent the next couple years working in a hospital state-side, but I really wanted to help more with the war effort. By the time Ho Chi Minh became a household name, I was on an Army transport to a port city called Da Nang, which had a huge military base. I was twenty-six years old. Young. Idealistic. Hopeful that I could make a difference and help save the lives of the wounded."

She picked up the Minnie Mouse cup and took a sip, then took the clipboard from her lap and set it next to her chair. Curling her feet to the side and under her, the doctor leaned on the arm of her chair. She took a deep breath. "No matter how many times I've told this story, I still can't quite believe how young and naïve I was. It's like I was a whole different person, just a sliver of who I have since turned out to be."

Pausing, she stared off toward the window, lost in thought. After a moment, she shrugged, shook her head as though to rouse herself and then went on. "I lasted nearly a year, which, I have since then learned, was a tough stint for all medical support personnel. I didn't know that at the time. They rotated doctors in and out fairly frequently every few months, but the nurses and medics—well, we stayed, and we pretty much ran the operation and kept everything going smoothly. Daily, sometimes hourly, the wounded were airlifted and delivered to us for medical treatment. Burned, shot, and fragged young men who were bloodied, bruised, with body parts ripped off. We triaged. We operated. We sutured and amputated and did the best we could to ease all the pain and agony these young guys were feeling. More died than we could save. We worked feverishly, like we were superhuman. Twelve hours on, twelve hours off. At first I cried myself to sleep after each shift. I had nightmares. I couldn't eat. I lost twenty pounds in two months. I cried and cried and cried, but we were all in it together, and sometimes my best buddies—Mark and Sandy and Deb and DeShawn—cried with me. It was hard, but we all managed, and it got better as I got used to the utter carnage. Sandy and I were extra close and told each other the daily prayers we said for one another. We all talked about how much we wanted the war to end, and we dreamed about the parties we'd have once we got back to the States."

Dez didn't look at Marie straight on. She watched the psychiatrist out of the corner of her eye, alternating her gaze between the wooden bears in her hands and the sunny window. She wondered why the doctor was telling her all this. Doctor Goldman had never told her much of anything about herself. She looked at her watch. 10:32. She would listen to Marie for 28 more minutes, and then she could escape. If the good doctor wanted to take a trip down memory lane, then it was fine with her.

"On a rainy morning in November, 1968, the day after Richard Nixon was elected President—incidentally, on the campaign platform of winning and ending the Vietnam war—ha ha—the Vietcong bombed the medical facility we all worked at. Direct hit on the hospital. I was standing in O.R., a scalpel in one hand, helping Sandy debride a burn wound in a G.I.'s leg, when we heard a horrible, high-pitched whistling sound. I looked up at Sandy. I still remember how she rolled her eyes and said, 'If that makes the power go off, I'll be pissed.' And then poof! The whole place exploded in flying dirt and fire and medical equipment. The G.I. on the table was screaming, and everywhere around me was chaos and noise and these horrible ripping, crushing sounds. The walls folded in like playing cards. The roof caved in. I looked down at my hand, and I was still holding the scalpel, but Sandy was no longer standing in front of me. She was on the floor on the other side of the gurney. I stepped around and called her name. She lay there in a puddle of blood, cut in half by a jagged sheet of metal. I looked around me, and as far as I could tell, the G.I. and I were the only ones left standing—actually, *I* was standing, he was lying on the operating table and screaming bloody murder. But then he shut up. Everything grew quiet. A numbness descended upon me."

Marie picked up her coffee mug and took a sip. "Ish. This needs some serious warming." She rose and strode to the kitchen area and poured coffee from a Mr. Coffee glass pot.

Dez held the wooden carving in her hands, squeezing it so tightly that her fingers hurt. Her heart beat a fast staccato, and she found herself worrying that she wouldn't be able to breathe.

While Marie's back was to her, she gulped in three deep breaths, steeling herself for the rest of the story. She didn't want to hear the rest...but at the same time, she was morbidly fascinated, like a teenager reading her first Stephen King horror novel.

The psychiatrist made her way back to her chair. "You're probably wondering why I'm telling you this, aren't you, Dez?" Dez shook her head and shrugged, not trusting her voice. "There is a point, and I'll get to it. Let me finish up the last little part, and then I know you'll understand." She took a big swig of the hot coffee and sputtered, "That's much hotter!" Minnie went back on the coffee table, and Marie went on.

"All the Army medical personnel—Sandy, Mark, DeShawn, Deb, and sixteen others, as well as 33 of the 46 patients died. It took 24 hours before the Army was able to airlift survivors out. I did my own triage. Saved who I could. Was very calm and orderly and efficient. I didn't even realize that I had lacerations all down the front of me until they came later and made me stop working on the wounded. Army medics who I don't even remember treated me and bandaged me up. They sent me briefly to a hospital in Hawaii. I wasn't happy to be taken from Da Nang. I wanted to help, to do something, to keep moving. But in a curious way, I also didn't care anymore. Forty hours after the bombing, in a tiny hospital bed hardly big enough for me, I slept for the first time, and I woke up screaming. For days on end, I never slept for more than an hour or two at a time and then would wake after having bloody, horrendously frightening dreams. It was worse than the LSD trip gone bad that some of my patients have described. I really don't remember what happened next. My sense of time passing was all out of sync, but I was found in the middle of the night walking half-naked down a dirt road six miles away from the military installation. I don't know how I got there, or where I was going. I had no will to care anymore. I was completely numb.

"It was 1968, a few weeks before Christmas. I didn't care. My family called, told me they loved me and asked me to hang in there. I didn't care. My father flew 2,700 miles to accompany me home. I didn't care. Some part of me had died. I went home to the farm in a deep depression, almost like a fog. A few weeks after the holidays, my favorite uncle—Uncle Fritz—died in a tractor rollover out in the fields. I went to the funeral. I have no real memory of it. I didn't cry. I didn't really seem able to feel at all.

"One of the GI's I saved that day in 1968 sent me a Christmas card—in fact, he still sends me one every year. In it he wrote, 'It was a terrible tragedy, and if not for you, I'd be dead, too.' When

I read that, something happened, and I was overcome with a kind of hopelessness that I never ever want to feel again. I took to my bed and slept and slept and slept. I never wanted to wake up again. In the middle of January, my father and mother took me to Minneapolis to the Veteran's Hospital. The VA people knew a little bit about what was wrong—not as much as they do now—but they were already dealing with soldiers in my predicament."

Marie picked up her coffee cup and drank from it for a moment. She set the mug on her knee, holding it there with a steady hand. "I stayed there in treatment for sixteen weeks, and when I came out, I knew that I would change the focus of my career from healing bodies to healing minds." She set the mug down on the table and leaned forward, her elbows on her knees. Her eyes drilled into the tall woman's, and Dez felt herself shiver. "You know why, Dez?"

She paused, and Dez loosened her grip on the bears. She didn't answer the therapist, instead swallowing and holding her breath.

"I'll tell you why. Because what I learned there in that god-forsaken jungle hole is that the human heart can only take so much horror, so much loss, and then it collapses and falls into itself, becoming numb in order to protect itself from further pain. Your mind will do everything in its power to help anesthetize you from the enormity of that much pain. And once it starts protecting you that way, it won't stop without assistance. Your mind is a marvelous thing, but once it takes a hit like that, it doesn't know how to reverse the protection process—not by itself." She paused. "Do you understand?"

Dez stared at the older woman, unable to breathe.

"Officer Reilly, you and I have something in common." The curly-haired woman gazed intently at Dez. "Ahhh. You don't believe me, hmmm? Do you remember that old saying, 'It's better to have loved and lost than never to have loved at all'?"

Dez nodded slowly, unable to tear her eyes away from the doctor.

"Here's what we have in common. You and I both know that saying's *not* true. Under the circumstances of your life—and mine—to have loved and lost is about the worst thing that ever happened, wouldn't you agree?"

Dez couldn't take it any more. She rose from the chair and stumbled to the window across the room, still holding the carving of the bears cradled against her chest in her right hand. With her left hand, she reached up, to the top of the window frame, and rested her hand there to steady herself. She gasped air in and out, closing her eyes until her heart rate slowed down to something closer to normal.

I'm not like her, she thought. *I'm not at all...not like her...she's—she's—normal. She's normal, and I...am...a...wreck.* The bright sun shone in, bathing her face in warmth, but she didn't feel it. She opened her eyes slightly, squinting into the glare, which made her eyelids itch with warmth. Letting her left hand drop from the top of the window frame, she rubbed it across her forehead and down over her eyes, which she was surprised to find were wet.

All was quiet behind her, and she didn't want to turn around. Her eyes slowly adjusted to the bright sunlight, and after a few moments, she heard Marie clear her throat, and then the older woman said, "Dez, you don't have to turn around, but I want you to consider a list I'm about to read to you, then answer one simple question. I'll give you the list, then the question. Here's the list: nightmares, flashbacks when you are awake, intrusive memories, numbed emotions, insomnia, bottled up rage, irritation, feelings of helplessness, and the inability to respond to others in social situations in the way you used to or the way you want to." She shuffled some papers. "Okay? Now here's the question: are you experiencing any of the above?"

Dez looked out at the capitol building several blocks away. The golden figure of Prosperity stood flanked by the women next to the golden horses. The sun shimmered so brightly that the golden display reminded her of the locket her father had given her on her ninth birthday. The contrast of all that gold against the white marble of the capitol was striking. Far off in the distance, she saw tiny figures walking up the marble stairs. She took a deep breath. "Yes."

Dez heard the click of the coffee mug on the table. "Yes to which ones?"

The pale woman hugged the wooden carving to her midsection, and with her arms held tightly across her middle, she turned to face Marie, who still sat calmly across the room in the low-slung chair. "All. I experience *all* of those things. Every day. All day. Every night, most nights."

Marie nodded. "I see." She looked down and wrote something on the clipboard in her lap.

Dez stood there awkwardly, not knowing what to say and appalled at her admission. If she could have taken it back, she would have, but it was now too late.

Marie set down her clipboard and pen. "Dez, you don't have to feel that way anymore. There's a way out, and I can help you.

Will you come back on Thursday?"

For a moment Dez was confused. *Thursday? Come back?* Then she turned her wrist, glanced at her Timex, and was astounded to see that it was 11:08. She ran a big hand through her hair, brushing back the long tresses. "Okay."

"How about the same time—ten a.m.?"

Dez nodded.

Marie reached over to the coffee table and opened a wooden box. She took something out and rose. "Can you do something for me now?" Dez shrugged, feeling like a grade-schooler struck dumb in the principal's office. "Promise me that if you get upset later in the day or anytime before Thursday, you'll either call me—or you can call or see somebody you care about and trust. Can you do that?"

"Yeah."

"Here's a card with my number on it. The answering service will refer you to me day or night." Dez took the card and tucked it in her back pocket.

"All right then," the doctor said. "I'll see you the day after tomorrow." Marie moved toward the door, and opened it wide. "Take extra good care of yourself, Dez. Try to get as much rest as you can."

Dez passed through the waiting room and out the blue door into the hall. Confusion, doubt, fear—she was a mass of conflicting feelings. It wasn't until she reached the door on the first floor that she realized she was still holding the wood carving. She stopped, one hand on the metal bar of the door, and hesitated, thinking she should retrace her steps and return the carving, but suddenly her knees felt weak. She tightened her grasp on the door and took a deep breath, feeling almost like she could faint. In a moment the sensation passed, and she pushed out into the fresh November air. *I'll bring the bears back on Thursday. She can wait until then.*

Chapter
Eighteen

Jaylynn reported to the main station, Investigations Division, at precisely two p.m. In a perfect world, she would have liked to arrive early, but she stopped at the precinct on the way in, and chatting with a variety of people had slowed her down. It was worth it, though, because she had managed to get a little information out of Sergeant Belton. In their conversation, he mentioned that Third Watch was terribly short-handed with her on light duty and Dez on leave. She confided that she hadn't talked to Dez since the altercation where she got injured, and he looked surprised, then said that she had left town for a short while. That was all that she could get out of him without prying, but it was enough.

Now she stood in the middle of the division, holding her lunch in a brown paper bag, and trying to get her bearings. Someone new was sitting in the desk next to Parkins' that she had used before. Right now, several more plainclothes officers sat working at desks than she had been used to seeing there previously. But there had been a drive-by shooting the week before, and an eight-year-old boy had been shot and killed. She suspected that a few of these detectives were working on that case. She moved across the room, keeping her sling tight against her middle, and tapped on Lt. Finn's door.

"Savage. Good to have you back. C'mon in and have a chair."

Jaylynn sat, feeling a little sheepish.

"The guys are saying you'd do anything to work with them again—even get clonked in a beat-down."

"No, Lieutenant, it's not—"

Finn waved at her. "I'm just kidding. Take it as a compliment, okay? Working as well as you did with Zorro and Tonto is a real feat. They are happy you're back, though nobody wishes an injury on a fellow officer."

Jaylynn nodded, her face flushing.

"We're pretty tight here right now, what with the Kenolly murder. You're going to have to share desk space with Tsorro and Parkins, but they're out in the field so much that it won't be too bad. I'll call Tech and have them bring a computer up." She opened her desk drawer and pulled something out. "I saved your database to disk. Will you get it up and running again?" She handed it across the desk, and Jaylynn accepted the black diskette.

"Sure, Boss. No problem."

"Good. The guys have run into a dead end with Tivoli, and now we have this new murder, which they are working on part-time. It's time to go back over everything on Tivoli again, re-interview, and refigure every angle. How long will you be on light duty?"

Jaylynn shrugged. "Could be two weeks, or worst case scenario, as much as six weeks. I won't know for sure until I have a follow-up appointment with the doctor next week."

Finn inclined her head slowly. "Okay, well, maybe that's enough time to make a dent in this case again."

It took over an hour, but finally Jaylynn was set up at Tsorro's desk and reviewing her database. As she'd expected, nobody had done anything on it after she left. Pausing for a moment to consider, she opened Tsorro's desk drawers, and in the top side drawer, she discovered the old list, dated from her last day. She pulled it out, along with a sheaf of notes and pieces of scratch paper. She went over to Parkin's desk and did the same thing, finding a similar pile of papers. She set to work deciphering the notes on each page of paper and gradually updating the database.

She was hard at it when the two detectives slipped into the squad room and crept up behind her. So intent was she at the task that it wasn't until she smelled Tsorro's cologne that she knew they were standing behind her. She spun around in the chair.

The dark-haired man grinned, flashing his even teeth. "Nice sling, Savage. With the white trim, it's very fashionable. Much more feminine than that last one."

Parkins rolled his eyes. "It's the same one, you schmuck. Such powers of observation you have. Geez. How do I work with you?"

Tsorro ignored him. "How ya doing, little lady? Sorry to hear you got hurt."

Jaylynn didn't know how he could get by with such sexist

endearments, but somehow, she didn't take any of it to heart. "I'm hanging in there. Thanks." She gestured toward the paperwork strewn across the desk. "Sorry I had to commandeer your desk."

"Oh no, think nothing of it."

Parkins shifted a toothpick from one side of his mouth to the other. "Don't worry about it, Savage. He never does any work at the desk anyway."

Tsorro ignored him. "You need anything, *dolcezza*? A soda? Something from the vending machine? We're off duty pretty quick here."

"No, thanks. Brought my own lunch tonight."

"Okay, then. Tomorrow we hit the Tivoli case hard again."

She nodded. "I'm working a little slow, but I'll get your master database updated. I rifled through your desks to find your notes. Hope you don't mind."

Tsorro put his hands behind his back and smiled at her. "No problem at all. Glad to have you back on board—even if only for a while."

They bid her farewell and she returned to the computer. After another two hours, she was bleary-eyed and her arm throbbed. She rose from the desk and meandered back into the break room. She sat alone at one of the tables, eating a ham and cheese sandwich. The pulse in her hand surged a steady beat. She wished she could go home and elevate it, but it was only half past seven, and she still had three hours to go. She sat, feeling the fatigue through and through, when out of the corner of her eye she saw a tall, dark-haired figure flit past the doorway. She was up in an instant and across the room. She skidded out into the hall, the name "Dez" on her lips—only to find that it wasn't the tall cop after all, but another officer several inches shorter.

She returned to the break room and slid wearily into her seat. Now the fatigue washed over her anew, and she felt even more tired than she had before.

Oh, Dez. Where are you? She willed her partner to call her, leave her a message, send her a note—anything. Tears sprang to her eyes, and she pushed them back. *Cops don't cry...at least not at work. I am not crying here. But dammit, where are you, Dez?* Underneath the feeling of grief, a current of anger ran through her. She pushed all the feelings down and finished the last bite of her sandwich, then rose and put away the cookie, carrots, and celery. She would eat them later. For now, she would go concentrate on the database.

****

Wednesday afternoon found Jaylynn back at the Investigations computer, polishing up the work she had done on the database. She printed a scratch copy, corrected a few mistakes, then printed out two corrected copies, one for Tsorro and one for Parkins.

The phone at Parkins' desk rang, and she picked up.

"Hey, cutie pie," a deep male voice said.

"Tsorro?"

"The very same. Parkins and I are coming to get you. ETA two minutes."

"You are? Why?"

"Just talked to the lieutenant, and she approved us taking you on some interviews with us."

A shadow loomed over her, and she looked up to find Lt. Finn standing above her. Jaylynn said, "Speaking of the boss—hold on a moment." She met Finn's eyes.

"That Parkins?"

Jaylynn gave a little shake of her head. "Tsorro."

Finn nodded. "I've okay'd you going out in the field to observe. Tell him you'll be out in a minute."

Jaylynn spoke into the phone. "See you out front," then without waiting for a response, she hung up. The rookie rose and looked up at the lieutenant.

"Here are the rules, Savage. You may observe. You may not question any witnesses. You may—you *should*—take notes, if you can, given your bad hand and all."

"No problem, Boss." She reached down to the desk and picked up a small spiral notebook.

"Just get a feel for what the detectives are doing, and after each interview, let them know if you noticed anything in particular. Go get your coat and head out."

Jaylynn rushed over to the coat rack and slipped her down coat from a hook, then hustled back to the desk and grabbed her cell phone, which she put in the deep pocket. "This is great, Boss. I am really happy to get to observe. Thanks."

"No problem."

The rookie got her good arm in one sleeve, then did a weird gyration to try to swing the coat up over her other arm, all the while juggling the notebook. The cell phone and house keys in her pocket jingled around.

"Here, let me give you a hand." Lt. Finn adjusted the jacket. "You want it zipped?"

"If you wouldn't mind?"

Finn bent and joined the zipper then pulled it up. "This must be a giant pain."

"It is, believe me."

"See you when they go off duty." She smiled, her eyes bright and warm. "Don't let 'em stop for too many doughnut breaks."

Jaylynn started off toward the doorway and was two steps into the hall before she remembered her database. She backtracked to the desk and picked up three printouts. She folded one in quarters and tucked it into her notebook, then turned to go. The lieutenant was already in her office and didn't seem to notice. When the rookie hustled out to the front, she found the detectives waiting. Tsorro leapt out of the front seat and held the door open for her.

"I can sit in back."

"Don't be silly. Get in. I'll hop in back."

She handed him a copy of the database, which was now 17 pages long, got in the front seat, and set a copy down next to Parkins. As soon as the dark cop was in the back, Parkins floored it.

"So what's the plan?" she asked.

Parkins drove with his left arm on the driver's door and his right loosely gripping the steering wheel. His light blue suit sleeve stuck out from his overcoat, and he looked rumpled but at home in the car. Jaylynn could imagine him having once been a street cop.

. Tsorro spoke up from the back seat. "We start at the very beginning, honey. Back to the beginning. First stop, the company that rented the snack shack to Tivoli. Then we talk to the private security cop who was around each night. Then we interview the first witnesses again—you know, those kids."

Jaylynn was relieved that they were doing this today and not yesterday when she had been so tired. She had gotten a good night's sleep. This helped considerably because they proceeded to spend the next three hours getting in and out of the car, standing around talking to people, and drinking the very bad coffee various witnesses offered.

They reached the Lee household shortly after four p.m. and entered a small apartment. Pao Lee, one of the three boys from the original scene, ushered them into the living room and brought in three wooden straight-back chairs from another room. He remembered her and said a special hello to her, then sat on a couch protected by a forest green slipcover. Next to him on either side sat an older woman and man who Jaylynn soon found out were Pao's grandparents. His mother and father were at work.

The boy, who Jaylynn knew was age eleven, said something in the Hmong language to his grandparents. They answered, and Pao turned to Jaylynn and asked if they could offer refreshments.

Parkins said, "Please tell your grandparents we are very grateful, but that will not be necessary."

Pao translated, and his grandmother nodded. She had dark hair, streaked with gray. Her skin was light brown and much lighter than her husband's. He appeared older, with unruly white hair and many wrinkles around his eyes and mouth. The old woman pointed toward the rookie and said something to Pao.

The boy turned to Jaylynn and said, "My grandmother is curious how you hurt yourself. She asks if you are comfortable because you look like you are in pain."

Jaylynn, was, in fact, in pain. Her wrist and hand were aching, but she had been ignoring it. Now that it had been mentioned, the throbbing seemed twice as bad. Looking the woman in the eye, she nodded. "Yes, it hurts a little. I was injured trying to arrest a suspect, but I am okay."

As the translation was made, the woman said, "Aha. O.K." She gave a little half-smile and a nod, then turned her attention to Parkins as he asked, "Pao, could you please tell us again everything that happened that night when the man and the girl were shot?"

Jaylynn opened her notebook and steadied it on her lap. She made notes as Pao retold the story. There was nothing new that she could ascertain. As she watched the young boy, it occurred to her that he seemed very well-adjusted. The way he described the murders showed that he was appalled and that the event had upset him, but he spoke in a matter-of-fact manner. He also asked whether they had found out who had done the killing and was disappointed when they told him, "Not yet."

They were finished in fifteen minutes. When they rose to go, Pao's grandparents stood. Jaylynn was surprised to find that she towered over the old lady by a good four inches. The grandmother was taller than her husband. On impulse, the rookie reached out a hand, and each of the adults shook it, grave expressions on their faces.

"Thank you," Jaylynn said.

"My grandparents say that you are welcome, and we all wish to know when you find the killer."

Tsorro nodded. "We have your phone number, and we will let you know as soon as we can. Thank you, Pao."

When they reached the car and got settled, both men sighed. "Nothing new," Parkins said.

Tsorro shook his head slowly. "It's too much to expect that anything would turn up, but you never know. On to the Vang place. Maybe those Orientals will give us a lead."

Jaylynn glanced toward Parkins to find him glancing her way. They both rolled their eyes simultaneously and looked away.

Sai Vang and his cousin Xiong Vang lived in the same apartment complex just two blocks away from the Lee household. Before Jaylynn had a chance to even feel any warmth from the heater, they were getting out again. Xiong told much the same story as Pao had. They had each remembered small details in slightly different order, but their stories were essentially the same as they had been the night of the murders.

By five p.m., they were trudging through snow across the parking lot to Sai Vang's family's apartment. Great big fluffy flakes fell all around, obscuring Jaylynn's vision for more than about ten feet ahead. She was glad to go up some stairs and under the cover of an outdoor walkway.

They were introduced by Sai to his mother, Blia Her, to his younger brother, Tong, and to a little sister named Sue who appeared to be only about four-years-old. Jaylynn had learned early on that in the Hmong culture, the mother kept her maiden name, and all the children took the father's last name. When Tsorro called her Mrs. Vang, Jaylynn elbowed him and reminded him of that fact.

"Oh, sorry, Mrs. Her. My mistake."

She was very gracious and spoke perfect English. Though almost exactly Jaylynn's height, she was totally the opposite in looks and build. Where Jaylynn was fair and solid, Mrs. Her was dark-eyed, dark-haired, and very thin with almost no apparent muscle. If the rookie had been asked how old the woman was, she would have said fourteen or fifteen, but a glance at the database printout showed that she was 28, older than Jaylynn.

They sat in a living room cramped with furniture. There was a couch, a smaller divan, two rocking chairs, a shabby olive green recliner, and a rolling hassock upon which Sue was lying and using her feet to move slowly around the room. The way her head bobbed about made Jaylynn think she looked like a small turtle. Jaylynn sat in an ornate rocking chair next to a boxy old-fashioned console television, which was on, but with the sound off. Tong, who looked to be about nine, sat with art supplies in front of the TV, off to her left.

The detectives perched on the edge of a divan across from Mrs. Her and Sai, both of whom sat on the couch. A dark-haired, leggy youth who was on the verge of leaving boyhood, Sai wore baggy jeans and a t-shirt. He didn't seem to know what to do with his legs, and Jaylynn watched him as he scooted back onto the couch and squirmed around before finally crossing his legs to sit Indian style. His mother gave him a frown, and he sighed and slipped his shoes off, then recrossed his legs.

Parkins began to ask questions, and Sai answered. Jaylynn made notes. It soon became apparent that there was nothing new in Sai's recollection either. As the interview wound down, she stopped taking notes, half-listening as her gaze wandered around the room. Over the couch was an elaborate wall hanging. Colorful tigers and birds, deer, and other animals were embroidered on a rich royal blue background. Through the archway into the next room she saw a wood table with six chairs around it. On the walls of that room hung a gallery of 8 x 10 inch photographs of the three children. The room was dim enough that it was hard for Jaylynn to see the pictures very well.

A *Scooby Doo* cartoon played on the TV. Tong lay on his stomach, facing the set, with an array of crayons, felt markers, and colored pencils spread out in front of him. He drew intently in an over-sized artist's sketchbook, his nose three inches from the page. The half of the page Jaylynn could see contained some trees, a path, a tank-like car, and a dark figure with a gun. Drops of blood dripped from the muzzle of one of the weapons.

Tsorro and Parkins were wrapping things up. Jaylynn leaned forward in the rocking chair, ready to rise. Sai got up off the couch and came toward her, asking what she did to her hand. She explained that she had been hurt arresting someone and then asked if the boys wanted to sign her cast.

"Sure," said Sai.

"Your brother is quite the artist. Think he'd let us use one of his markers?"

Tong rolled over and sat up. With a very serious look on his face, he offered two pens, one black and one green. He kept a red one for himself. Sai signed his name with a flourish and helped Sue draw squiggles that no one would recognize as an S, a U, or an E. Tong knelt next to her, and in block letters wrote his name on the topside of her cast.

She looked down at his artwork again. "You are drawing a very complicated picture there, Tong."

Tong's dark eyes met hers, but he didn't say anything.

Sai squatted and surveyed the half-finished drawing. "Hey Tong, is that the flight out of the mountains?" When Tong did not answer, he turned to Jaylynn. "Did you know our grandfather was a hero? When mama was little, littler than Sue, she had to run a hundred miles through the forest."

Mrs. Her interrupted. "I didn't run, Sai. My father carried me through most of it."

Sai went on. "Soldiers were chasing them, and they shot anyone they could find. My grandfather saved thirty people's lives."

The detectives rose, and Mrs. Her stood as Jaylynn did. She moved toward her children. "My father created a diversion so that the rest of us could escape. He was shot and killed by the Viet Cong."

Jaylynn nodded. "So your family is from the mountains of Laos?"

"Yes. When the war was over, my people were hunted down and killed. My brothers and sisters and I were lucky. We lost our father, but my mother and other adults got us to safety in Thailand. The United States government allowed us to come here when I was five."

Twenty-three years later, Jaylynn could see the woman was still bothered by the death of her father, though she spoke in a calm, factual voice. Having lost her own father, Jaylynn's sympathies rose to the surface, but she could think of nothing appropriate to say.

"We honor my grandfather," Sai said proudly, "and I am named after him."

"I am named after my father, too," Jaylynn said. Sai smiled at her as she moved to take her coat off the chair.

Tsorro cleared his voice. "We'd best be going."

As Jaylynn lifted her brown coat, she said, "Nice to meet you, Mrs. Her. You've got very nice children."

The woman smiled. "Thank you, Officer. I'll tell my husband you said so." Sai reached over and helped the rookie into her coat and she thanked him.

They said goodbye to Mrs. Her and the children, and headed to the car through swirls of snow. Jaylynn wished she had a hat. The snowflakes were big and moist, and as fast as they hit her hair, they seemed to melt. Her whole head was chilled and damp by the time they reached the car. She wasted no time getting in.

Parkins started the engine. Shivering, Jaylynn said, "Well, that was a shame."

"Yeah," grumbled Tsorro. "Those kids were the first on the scene and they didn't see a damn thing."

"That's not what I meant. I'm talking about the family having to flee their homeland."

Tsorro said, "Practically everybody's family had to do that, Savage. My grandparents fled Mussolini during World War II."

"Really? I didn't know that."

"But we came here and *worked*. None of my family got put up in government housing and given refugee money and a bunch of welfare."

In a soft voice, Parkins said, "Different time—different climate, Tony. And your people weren't systematically hunted down and killed like the Hmong people were. It's different."

"Maybe. Maybe not."

Parkins shuffled the database printout in his hands. "Besides, it says here Mr. Vang works at the Ford plant and Mrs. Her is a—"

"Office worker," Jaylynn said.

"Yeah, that's right." Parkins nodded. "That family looks like they are working plenty hard." Tsorro didn't respond.

They arrived back at the station and Jaylynn got out. The detectives drove off to return the car, and the rookie plodded up the stairs through the gathering snow into the warm station. By the time she reached the coat rack, she was yawning from fatigue, lack of food, and the muggy warmth in the squad room.

After checking in with Lt. Finn and giving her a brief update, she went to the break room and got her brown bag out of the refrigerator. She sat at the table and ate, not really tasting any of the tuna sandwich. As long as she was busy, she was fine, but it was quiet times like these when she found she missed Dez the most. She had continued to call the apartment periodically, but no one ever answered and the cell phone was not in service.

She finished her sandwich and some carrots, and put the remaining items back in the bag and into the refrigerator for later. She still had a long night ahead of her.

Chapter
Nineteen

The curly-haired psychiatrist pushed a lock of hair out of her eyes. She hummed an old John Denver tune as she moved around her office watering plants. She'd already had her morning cup of coffee—multiple cups, in fact—and seen an eight a.m. client. Now she was ready for her ten o'clock challenge, but she had a twenty-minute break until then.

She opened a door near the kitchen area and leaned in to set the watering pitcher on the back of the toilet tank in the small bathroom, then pulled that door closed and opened the one next to it to enter her office. Her sanctuary from her patients was a pleasant haven. One wall of the large, square room contained six 4-drawer file cabinets next to a tall table with a fax machine on it. The west wall was floor to ceiling bookcases spilling over with many volumes: medical books, novels, self-help/how-to books, and diagnostic manuals. The remaining two adjoining walls had a built-in corner desk with work surfaces that stretched twelve feet along the walls each way. Built-in drawers underneath and cabinets overhead gave her plenty of space for storage. Her computer fit nicely at the point where the two desk surfaces met in the corner. She had paid a pretty penny to outfit the office, but it was worth it to her. She had plenty of room to organize, to sort, to research, and to work.

In the middle of the room was a long table, three feet wide and about six feet long. On it were papers and research cards for the topic of her current investigation about a new therapy, EMDR, which was short for Eye Movement Desensitization and Reprocessing. She hoped the treatment would be a useful tool to help patients who were dealing with the after-effects of trauma and extreme stress.

She sat at her desk and went over the notes she'd made after Monday's session with Desiree Reilly, then looked over the reports from the police department and from her colleague, Dr. Raina Goldman. In a sidenote on a Post-it attached to her official report, Raina had written: "Uncooperative, headstrong, unresponsive, and damn hard to deal with. You'll be lucky to pry any information at all out of this client."

Making a tsk-tsk noise, the therapist muttered, "Raina, Raina, what you don't know..." Marie liked Raina, but the younger psychologist wasn't always very patient, and some clients—particularly cops and firemen—needed a certain amount of coaxing. Reilly was probably no exception.

Marie had attempted to mentor the younger doctor, but Goldman was just as headstrong as she claimed Officer Reilly to be. Marie smiled. *Ah, youth*, she thought. *To be that young again...*

She wondered how old Reilly was. The tall woman seemed weary and worldly wise—and yet, her face was unlined. By her demeanor, she would seem to be in her early 40's, but her appearance put her in late 20's. Marie flipped through her reports until she found Goldman's biographical notes.

Desiree Reilly, born 12-16-71
Single (?)
Father, deceased police officer, heart attack 1985, at age 42
Mother, living, ophthalmologist, age 54
One younger sibling, Patrick
Grandparents, deceased
Numerous aunts and uncles
Estranged

Marie frowned. *Estranged from the aunts and uncles? Or from the whole family? And why the question mark next to "Single"?* Goldman's notes were less than clear. She would have to touch base with her colleague and verify this information. The one thing that seemed clear was that her new patient would soon celebrate her thirtieth birthday. *Twenty-nine years old now...hmmm.*

She reorganized the loose paperwork, evened up the edges, and inserted the top under a two-hole punch, then tacked the reports in a folder that she labeled with the officer's name. She grabbed a sheaf of blank paper on which to write notes and tacked it to the other side of the file. She had no doubt that before she and Dez Reilly completed their appointments, she would have written a great many pages of notes.

She checked her watch and discovered she still had ten minutes before her patient was due. Setting the case file aside, she
rose and left her office. In the kitchen area, she rinsed out her latest favorite coffee conveyor, the Minnie Mouse mug, which was a
gift following her granddaughter's recent visit to Disneyland. The
creak of the front door signaled her client's arrival, so she poured
herself a mug of hot black coffee and took it to the coffee table.
Next to that low table was a basket full of Barbie dolls in various
stages of undress. Little shoes and jackets and dresses were piled
underneath a jumbled assortment of long, multicolored limbs and
impossibly ratty hair. She sighed. Why children liked Barbie
dolls was beyond her. Just about every morning she attempted to
bring some semblance of order to the collection.

It was early, but she opened the door to the waiting room to
find her patient seated stiffly in a blue chair. Once again she
noted the fatigue and misery that enveloped the tall woman.
"Hey, Dez. You're early."

"Yup."

"Want to come in and help me with something?"

The lanky policewoman rose, cradling something in her left
hand. "Depends on what it is."

Marie smiled. "It's nothing too terribly onerous. Come on
in."

As Dez reached the doorway, she held her hand out with the
wooden carving resting in it. "I—uh—well, I accidentally made
off with this on Tuesday. Sorry about that."

Marie smiled again. "Not to worry. I knew you'd bring it in
today."

Dez stopped and took an almost imperceptible step back.
"How'd you know I'd come back?"

Marie had to fight to hold back a chuckle. "Dez, every report
I read said you are an honest person. I knew you'd bring back the
carving."

"I could have mailed it."

"Too much trouble. You're here before it'd ever have come in
the mail." She ushered her patient in. "Have a seat, and let's see
if we can get this stuff organized."

Dez looked at her blankly, but folded herself down into the
same chair she'd sat in two days earlier. Marie set the bear carving on the coffee table and slid it and all the knick-knacks to the
far left. She picked up the basket of Barbie paraphernalia and
dumped it onto the right side of the table. The woman across
from her cocked her head to the side and frowned. Marie picked
up the Rainbow Princess Barbie and rooted around until she

found a pink tulle dress and a pair of matching slippers. She glanced up at Dez. "Well? You going to help or just watch me?"

"I know you must do some child psychiatry, but," Dez shook her head slowly from side to side, "you're not going to make me play with dolls, are you?"

Marie let out a peal of laughter. "No, no, no, no. Just help me get these damn things dressed. I have little girls to see all afternoon, and I feel it's best if the dolls at least *start out* clothed. In matters of sexual and physical abuse, when the kids play with the dolls they usually undress them, and it tells me a lot about what they're coping with. But most of them don't ever get the clothes back on them. There are plenty of fancy getups here. Just grab anything that sort of matches and put it on."

Despite her still sore finger, Dez proved adept at threading the stiff plastic limbs into their little outfits and getting them snapped up, something that Marie had trouble with. She was starting to worry that she might need reading glasses. The snaps never seemed to line up for her. Dez, however, was easily dressing two dolls to every one Marie worked on.

"How many of these things do you have?" Dez asked, gesturing at the heap of dolls.

"Oh, maybe twenty. But sometimes I let a child take one, and they do break occasionally. I have a whole drawer full of new ones that replace these as I dump 'em or give 'em away."

Dez nodded. They worked quietly for a couple more minutes until Marie picked up the last doll. The black haired woman tossed a Skipper doll on the table, after dressing her in pink and white striped pants, a hot pink blouse, and pink shoes. "Doctor, you can talk me into dressing these ridiculous creatures, but I will not brush that rat's nest of hair."

Marie looked up in surprise, expecting a sly smirk on the other woman's face, but instead, Dez looked dour and serious. The tall woman leaned back in her chair, crossed her arms, and said, "I never liked Barbie dolls. I pretty much hated them. My mother was so disappointed." She paused. "Pretty much everybody is disappointed in me."

Marie tried once more to snap the top of a tiny fur coat, then gave up. She set the final doll on the table, along with the stack of others, and looked at the woman across from her. "Is there a list of everyone who is disappointed in you?"

Dez shrugged. "I could make one."

"Are you disappointed in yourself?"

Looking down at the floor, Dez nodded.

"Tell me why."

With vehemence, the younger woman said, "Because I have to be here. Because I'm not able to work. Because my whole life has fallen into shit."

Marie nodded. "Tell me more." She wondered what had happened in the intervening 48 hours since she had last seen Dez. Something had changed.

But the well had run dry, and though the tall woman did talk some more, she didn't say anything of great consequence. For just a moment, Marie had seen a little crack in the façade, but just as quickly, it closed up. Still, it was a start. Maybe today would not be a break-through day, but soon. *Patience, that's what I need. All will be revealed if I just wait.*

****

Dez rolled over and stared up at the ceiling. She had a splitting headache, and everything was bleary. *Now I know why I so rarely drink.* She sat up slowly, on the edge of the bed, and waited until the pounding lessened, then rose and crept toward the bathroom.

One look at herself in the mirror was enough to make her happy she wasn't going anywhere for the day.

She didn't think she was ready for a pelting shower, and she didn't have any aspirin, so she ran some cool water, scooped it up in her hands, and immersed her face in the clear water over and over. It didn't help. Leaning over the sink, she let the water drip from her face as she reached for a towel to dry herself off. She looked in the mirror. If anything, she looked worse, paler than before. Her eyes were bloodshot, and her skin looked transparent. She could see blue veins under the surface.

For cripesake, why did I go and do that? Sometimes, I'm a total idiot. She stumbled out of the bathroom and back to bed. She lowered herself cautiously, then thought that perhaps she should go get some water to flush her system out, but she was suddenly woozy and fatigued.

She had stopped the night before at the tavern half a mile up the highway, and after eating a hamburger and drinking a beer, she'd ordered another Michelob. And another. She stayed and watched basketball and boxing on the sports channel. She sat in the back of the bar by herself, her feet up on the bench on the other side of the booth. Nobody bothered her. The waitress stopped by every twenty minutes or so to refresh her drink, and almost three hours later, when she rose to go, she had wobbly legs and a $27.95 bill to pay.

She made her way out to the truck, but realized she was too drunk to drive. She wasn't too drunk to walk, though. She took her gun and holster, locked up the Ford, and set off down the road to Dewey's cabins. The cold cleared her head a little, but all that beer made her feel mournful. She thought of Jaylynn, of Luella, of Ryan. She thought of her family, remembering the handsome face of her father, and found herself crying. When a car came around the bend toward her on the road, she could hardly see through the blur of tears. As the car passed, she wiped them away with the sleeve of her Levi jacket and kept walking.

By the time she reached the cabin, her face was freezing cold from tears and falling snow. Though it was only nine p.m., she struggled out of her clothes and got into bed, wearing only a t-shirt, and spent the night dreaming troubling nightmares that she could not banish by sheer dint of will or by any other means.

Now, in the light of day, she realized that when she slept—or any time her conscious thought wandered—she had a little movie going in her mind, some sort of timeless, tireless projector that was running soundless, wordless movies. Images, clear scenes, flashed on her mind's screen, with a sequence of events that ran in slow motion. She could hear her own breath, but nothing else. She couldn't taste or smell, only see. And what she saw terrified her.

She didn't think any amount of alcohol would obliterate the visions, and actually, last night they had seemed worse—bloodier, more confusing, with strange scenes eddying totally out of control around her. *Nope, no more beer for me.*

After a while, she fell back to sleep again, and when she woke up three hours later, her head wasn't pounding nearly as badly. She took a warm shower and made some tea. Sitting at the breakfast table, she looked out the window toward the trees behind Dewey's spread. A chattering chipmunk ran up the trunk of a giant oak, then along a branch. *Isn't he a lively fellow? How come he's not hibernating?* He made a little hop from one branch to another and disappeared on the other side of the tree. In the night, about four inches of snow had fallen, and the blanket of white stretched as far as she could see out the window. She rose and looked around the corner into the living room. She had quite a bit of wood, but it wouldn't hurt to split some more. She looked at her watch. Eleven a.m. She'd give herself a little more time, time for her head to stop beating like a snare drum. In a few hours, before dark, she would go out to Dewey's woodshed and chop up a storm.

Chapter
Twenty

It had been five days since Jaylynn had last seen Dez, and she was sick with worry about her. It was all she could do to keep from crying every time she thought of her. She felt entirely out of sorts, both physically and emotionally. Tonight she tried to take her mind off it by cleaning and organizing her room. She had her stereo cranked up and was humming along to Melissa Etheridge's new song. Despite the fact that it was peppy, it wasn't helping much.

The heap of clothes on the couch belonged mostly to Dez. She pulled her own sweats and two t-shirts out of the pile, leaving a pair of jeans, two long-sleeved shirts, three t-shirts, and a sweatshirt, which she began folding and stacking at the far end of the couch. She picked up the a navy blue Police sweatshirt last and pressed her face to it. It smelled like Dez, sort of woodsy and sweet.

Tears sprang to her eyes. *Why don't you call and tell me where you are? Why? You can't think I meant what I said at the hospital?* A sick feeling rolled over her. She sat on the couch, still holding the sweatshirt, and let the tears come. She had tried paging the tall cop to no avail. Every time she dialed the cell phone number, the carrier's recording came on to say that the phone was out of service. Dez didn't answer the phone at the apartment either.

The Melissa song ended, and she heard some strings, then a rhythmic bass beat began. The mournful song that started up next didn't ease her worries. It was like a message from Dez directly to her, and she didn't like the sound of it. The song went on until the chorus. She wadded up the sweatshirt in her lap and threw it across the room. It hit the wall and slid down. "Damn you, Dez!

Why are you doing this? To punish me?" She reached over and turned the radio off, and as she did, a figure appeared in her doorway, startling her. "Sara! Geez! You snuck up on me."

The brown-haired woman gave her a funny look. "Your music was loud. It's not like I meant to scare you. Jay?"

Jaylynn looked away. "What?"

"What's the matter?" This brought on a fresh spate of tears. Sara came into the room and sat on the couch next to her friend. "Are you okay?"

"Yes, I'm fine."

"You don't seem fine."

In an angry voice, Jaylynn said, "It's like every sappy song that comes on the radio makes me cry. I can't stop wondering and worrying about Dez, and I don't know what to do."

Sara scooted over until she was sitting thigh to thigh with Jaylynn. She patted the smaller woman's leg. "There isn't anything you *can* do until she chooses to resurface."

"But *why*? Why is she doing this?"

Sara shrugged. "Who can tell? I think you have to wait until she's ready to talk to you." She looked at Jaylynn out of the corner of her eye. "Little Miss Patience—waiting is no fun, is it?"

"No! I want to smack her. The minute I see her, I'm going to walk right up and sock her in the stomach."

Sara giggled. "I'm sure that will incapacitate her immediately, and then she will spill her guts right away to tell you what's been happening."

"You know what I mean!"

"Not really, but I'll take your word for it."

Jaylynn leaned into her friend and put her head on Sara's shoulder. They sat there for a few moments until they heard footsteps coming up the stairs. Tim and Kevin appeared in the doorway, holding hands.

"Hi, guys," Sara said.

"Well, you girlie girls." Tim tipped his head to the side slightly and frowned. "Jaylynn? What's wrong?" he asked in a worried voice. He let go of Kevin's hand and strode right up to the couch, squatted down, and looked at her with concern. Kevin crossed his arms and leaned against the doorframe.

"It's nothing. I'm just missing Dez."

"Where the hell is she?" the red-haired man spat out. "Do you mean to tell me she still hasn't called you?"

Jaylynn shook her head, her eyes red-rimmed and her face a mask of misery.

Tim stood up. He pounded his right fist into the palm of his

left hand. "I'll take care of her. Kevin and I will track her down
and teach her a lesson. We ought to go beat the crap out of her for
this."

Sara burst out laughing. "Oh, please...you and what gay
army? She'd beat the hell out of both of you. One-handed. Blind-
folded. Lying down."

Tim ignored Sara. "She seemed so devoted to you, Jay.
Where'd she go?"

"I don't know," the rookie said. "No one seems to know at
the station either. I mean, I know she's in trouble for everything
that happened at the beat-down, but none of the brass seem very
concerned. I don't understand why she's on leave or why she
doesn't call me."

Sara asked, "Well, you did sort of tell her off at the hospital,
didn't you?"

A fresh wave of tears came over her, and Jaylynn fought for
control. She didn't quite remember exactly what she had said to
the tall cop—she didn't *want* to think of it.

Tim shook his head. "I still think we ought to go have a word
with her."

Sara said, "We wish you could, but no one knows where she
is, Tim."

Jaylynn listened to her friends discussing possible ways of
locating the tall cop. She knew they were just concerned for her,
but really, there was nothing anyone could do to help her. She just
had to wait. It didn't seem fair—and it wasn't, as far as she was
concerned—but that's the way it was. "Thanks for the generous
offer of murder and mayhem, guys—"

"Hey," Kevin said from the doorway, "*I* never offered any violence."

"I stand corrected," Jaylynn said. "Tim, thanks for your
offer, and thanks to you, Kevin, and Sara, for the moral support,
but I just have to deal with this on my own."

Tim put his hands out, palms up. "I still think someone
ought to teach her a lesson."

Sara giggled again. "Tim, you remind me of the Lion in *The
Wizard of Oz*."

Everyone but Tim laughed.

"You know, I am pretty sure that was a slam," he said.

"Oh, no," Sara said with mock seriousness, "I would never
slam either you *or* the Lion, since you both have such pretty hair."
He narrowed his eyes and advanced toward her. "Officer Savage,
help! A homicidal maniac is after me!" Shrieking with laughter,
the two women rose and grabbed at Tim, dragging him down to

the floor in front of the couch.

Tim twisted and struggled, but Jaylynn held up her casted arm. "Careful, Little Big Man, you don't want to hurt my wrist, do you?"

In a strangled voice, Tim said, "Kevin, help."

"Not a chance," a voice from the doorway said. "You got yourself into this mess, and you can get yourself out."

Pinned to the floor, the red-haired man gasped, "You two are evil! You're...you're she-demons from hell." This only provoked Jaylynn and Sara, and they tickled him mercilessly. "This is what I get for—ugh—sticking up for my friends."

"No," Sara said. "This is what you get for being bossy and uppity."

They wrestled with him for a few more moments and then finally let him up. With his dignity badly bruised, he left the room, swearing revenge, which everyone knew would probably come in the form of some sort of fattening cake or pie.

The two women sat on the floor, catching their breath while leaning back against the couch. Sara poked Jaylynn in the leg. "You want to go out for something to eat and to a late movie?"

"What about Bill?"

"He's beat. He wants to watch a little TV and hit the hay early, so it's just you 'n' me, kid. What do ya say?"

Jaylynn nodded. "I'd like that. Thanks." She sprang to her feet and reached down with her good hand to pull Sara to hers. "Give me a few minutes, and I'll be ready."

Sara left the room, and Jaylynn lowered herself to the edge of the couch. *I'm really lucky to have such good friends. I don't know what I would do without them.* She got up and went to the other side of the room, picked up the Police sweatshirt, and folded it carefully. She set it on the stack at the end of the sofa and went into the walk-in closet to find a pair of warm, high-top boots.

Chapter
Twenty-One

Dez sat on a weight bench and alternately lifted dumbbells, first with her left hand, then right, until she had done eight heavy repetitions on each arm. She set the weights on the floor and stood so she could move around, stretching her biceps and triceps as she paced. Her t-shirt felt bunched up, so she tucked it back into her shorts, glad that she didn't feel as blocky and heavy as she had a couple weeks earlier.

She looked around the workout center. At nine a.m. there were only two women walking on treadmills and a retired gentleman doing lat pull-downs on the other side of the gym. Quiet. Just how she liked it.

She looked at the clock. Today her counseling appointment was scheduled for two p.m. Keeping to the speed limit, it took her about three hours and some odd minutes to get down to the Cities, so she had plenty of time to do a few more exercises, shower, and then pick up something to eat on the way. She did another set of bicep curls, then put those dumbbells away and moved down the rack to heavier weights for doing shrugs. She picked up two sixty-pound weights, held them at her sides, and drew her shoulders up, until her neck and traps screamed for mercy. She imagined that they screamed anyway—that was how it felt. After four sets of shrugs and four rear delt lifts to finish off her shoulders, she called it quits for the day. Her body felt pleasantly fatigued. In just a couple hours, she would feel more energetic, even though some muscles might be a little sore later.

It had been eight days since she had gotten drunk, and she felt like it had taken half that time for the alcohol to get out of her system. After that little fiasco, she vowed to be more active and take better care of her body. For the last week she had driven into

Duluth in the early morning and come to this gym to lift weights, then driven down to her counseling appointments. If it wasn't a counseling day, she went hiking or chopped wood in the afternoons. She still didn't feel she was getting enough sleep, but at least today she felt somewhat rested.

Gathering up her towel and nearly empty bottle of water, she headed to the locker room. In thirty minutes, she was ready to head out. She stopped at a café just outside Duluth and got pancakes and mixed fruit. As she sat eating, she examined the display of wooden boards painted with country scenes in Grandma Moses style. What did they remind her of? She thought for a moment as she poured some maple syrup on a pancake. She remembered seeing something like this up north in Grand Marais over Labor Day when she and Jaylynn had been together. She remembered the odd little café and how upset she had been that day about the relationship her mother and her mentor, Mac, appeared to be having. It seemed like so long ago, and yet, it was a mere three and a half months back.

She pushed the plate away when she finished eating, crossed her arms, and waited to catch the waitress's eye to get her bill. It was going on four months. So in a little over three months, so much had changed. She had no idea what to expect of the future—or if Jaylynn would even want to work things out with her. That filled her with fear and anxiety. She had gone over and over all that had happened in the last couple of months, and despite turning the scenes every which way, she could not figure out a way to change what had occurred.

The waitress left the ticket face down on the table, and Dez checked it, then threw a ten on the table and left. In the truck, she slipped Shawn Colvin music into the CD player and settled back for an easy drive to St. Paul. One thing she liked about driving was that she was able to think of positive, happy things most of the time. Maybe it was because she was partly occupied with having to attend to the road and partly focused on the CD's she played. She was just glad that bizarre movie projector in her head had gone on hiatus, and she didn't have to deal with its terrors.

The closer she drew to St. Paul, the tenser she got, though. Every time she went to see Marie it was always like this. This would be her fifth appointment, and by the time she was in the waiting room, she felt the same heavy dread she had each of the previous visits. She knew that once she was settled in the low brown chair for a few minutes, it would ease, but for now, she was on edge.

And for this session, being on edge was where she stayed. In the previous four sessions, Marie had been warm and supportive. Today, however, the therapist was just a little bit different, and Dez felt like she was being scrutinized much more closely than before. After a series of pointed questions, the tall cop finally lost her patience. "What the hell do you want from me, huh?"

"I want you to talk to me, Dez. I want you to tell me what happened on that night in June last year. I want details."

With exasperation, she asked, "What more do you need to know? We went on a call. This nut case had shot someone in the restaurant. We gave chase, and as we exited the building, Ryan was shot. He went down, but said he was okay. I went after the suspect, collared him, and brought him back. Ryan was dead." She paused, giving Marie a scowl. "That's it. What else can I say that you don't already know from the reports?"

Marie gave a half-smile. "Once more with feeling, Dez. The reports don't tell me your feelings."

"What's the point? None of my feelings will change the fact that Ryan is dead."

"But you are haunted by it."

Dez glared at her. "Well, I wouldn't go *that* far, but it's not a pleasant memory."

"How often do you see it in your head—in your waking life and in nightmares?"

The tall cop looked away.

"Listen to me, Dez. When a person is exposed to trauma like this—especially when it touched on someone for whom you cared very much—you tend to experience symptoms of post-traumatic stress disorder."

"What? I don't have that. That's crazy—it's like a—geez! Like a mental disease."

"Do you think you're crazy?"

"No."

"But you have all the symptoms—the dreams, sleep difficulties, anxiety, hyper-vigilance. I'm trying to get you to understand that you do have PTSD. *Many* cops and firefighters and paramedics experience it in response to catastrophes."

Dez's eyes narrowed and she leaned forward in the chair, ready to flee the room. "You're saying I'm crazy? Mentally ill?"

"Not exactly."

"What do you mean, 'Not exactly'? You think I'm crazy?"

"Do you think *I'm* crazy? After all, I have PTSD."

"What?" Dez was totally confused. Her legs suddenly felt weak, and she let herself lean back in the chair. "What are you talking about?"

Marie got up from her chair and walked over to a shelf. "I've been meaning to give this to you." She picked up a book and brought it with her back to her seat. She held it in her lap and met Dez's eyes. "You need to read a little bit about PTSD and deadly force encounters to take in some of the concepts. I'll be doing some workshops for your department throughout the year, too, so you'll be a step ahead of some of the others." She handed the book to the tall cop.

Dez didn't look at the book. She just set it on top of her coat next to the chair. "Now just wait a minute. Let's get back to the PTSD business. You're saying I have that?"

"Yes."

She crossed her arms. "How the hell can you know that?"

Marie looked at her, pursed her lips, and then looked up at the ceiling. She cleared her throat. "Okay, I'll make you a deal. Answer me one question, as honestly and fully as you can, Dez, and then I will tell you how I know that."

"Fine. What's the question?"

Marie met her gaze, and in a slow, measured voice said, "How did it *feel* to come back to that restaurant and find your best friend lying dead in the dark in a puddle of blood?"

The shock of the question, phrased so cruelly, hit Dez in the chest, sucking all the wind out of her. She couldn't have gotten up to leave if she had wanted to. She choked in some air and closed her eyes. And that little projector began to run inside her head. She saw the still figure, felt her dizziness and nausea, compounded by the aura of fuzzy darkness all around her. Lights flashed. She heard muffled sounds.

"Dez?"

She opened her eyes and realized she wanted to go across the table and choke the life out of Marie. She couldn't move. She could hardly breathe. Instead, she spoke in a soft voice. "It felt unreal."

"Unreal in what way?"

"Like it wasn't really happening. Like it was a bad dream. I didn't believe it—didn't believe them."

"Who?"

"The other cops and paramedics."

"Close your eyes, Dez, and talk me through what's happening in your head. How do you feel? What do you see and hear? What pictures are you seeing?"

Dez choked back tears. "Please don't make me do that."

"I can't make you do anything...but if you can, please, will you try?"

She closed her eyes. The projector was still running, and over the pounding of her heart, she tried to explain what she saw and felt. It was all a jumble and didn't seem to make any sense to her, but she tried to recount it as best she could. After a while, she became too distraught to go on and just kept her eyes closed while she cried.

She sat for several minutes with her face in her hands until she felt something touch her thighs. Looking down, she saw that Marie had put a box of tissues in her lap, and then the curly-haired woman went over to the kitchen area. Dez heard the microwave running and a minute later a *ding.* She pulled some Kleenex out of the box and wiped her eyes, then blew her nose. Keeping a couple tissues in her hand, she set the box back on the table.

Marie moved around in the galley kitchen, shutting a drawer and rustling paper, and then came over carrying two mugs, one of Minnie Mouse, and the other a plain white mug. She set both mugs down on the coffee table.

"I made you some peppermint tea."

As soon as the therapist said that, the mint aroma reached the tall cop. "Thank you." She picked up the white mug and blew on the surface of the warm liquid. She took a sip and felt a pang because the tea was sweet which made her think of Jaylynn.

Marie settled in across from her with one foot tucked behind the other knee. "Have you shared any of this with anyone?" When Dez gave her a quizzical look, the therapist said, "A friend? Your mother? A work buddy?"

Dez shook her head and sighed. "No. Raina Goldman knows a little about it. But no one else."

"Why not?"

In a voice full of disbelief, the tall cop said, "Geez, I'm not gonna go around talking about this to anybody."

"Why?" Marie said. "You deserve support and understanding just as much as the next person."

Dez shook her head slowly and narrowed her eyes. She set the tea mug on the table and sat back. "It's *crazy,* Marie. I'm not telling people. I...just can't!" She looked down at her hands in her lap, then shrugged.

"What about your partner, Jaylynn Savage?"

Dez started again, then looked away toward the gloomy skies out the window. "What about her?"

"Why don't you get together with her, talk to her about what you are going through?"

The tall cop's voice was quiet and weary. "She won't want to know."

"How do you *know* that? Why couldn't you share your feelings with someone who has been your work partner for the better
part of a year?"

Dez took a deep breath. "She's been more than my work
partner." Marie didn't seem too surprised, and she thought that
the therapist must know what everyone else did. "Look, she got
involved with me because she thought I was a strong person.
That's what she liked best about me, I think. I can't go breaking
down and whining, acting like some sort of weakling."

"Why?"

Dez rose and went to the window, letting the feeling of bleak-
ness roll over her. It had been nearly two weeks since she had last
seen Jaylynn, far too long since they had talked. She missed her
terribly, felt a lonely ache for her that nothing—not sleep, not
alcohol, not sheer will power—could assuage. Yet she knew that
to spend any significant time with the rookie *would* result in her
breaking down, totally losing it. Jaylynn brought out everything
weak in her, made her feel vulnerable in ways she couldn't
explain, much less understand.

Leaning with one hand on the molding around the window
frame, she said, "I just can't. I need to work this out, get my shit
together. Gotta do it by myself."

Marie sat in her chair, switching to tuck the other leg under
the opposite thigh. She smiled a little smile and shook her head.
"Desiree Reilly, you haven't got a clue!" When the tall woman
turned and faced her, a frown on her face, Marie broke into a wide
grin. "You, girl, need one great big giant lesson in intimacy. I
think I've been too easy on you lately. Get over here and sit
down."

With a flat, impassive look on her face, Dez slowly moved
over to the chair in which she had been sitting, and folded herself
down into it.

Marie squinted up her eyes, and grinned again.
"Hmm...where should I begin here? Let's see..." She looked up
to the ceiling as Dez watched. "Intimacy and trust—those are two
key elements here. It's interesting to see that over these few
appointments, you have opened up enough to me to show me
important and intimate details of your life. From these sessions I
already know you very well—probably better than your mother
does at the moment."

Dez nodded. "That's definitely a no-brainer."

"You hide behind those steely blue eyes. You think no one
knows or understands. You feel far too alone—more alone than

any human being should feel. And yet, affection and compassion and friendship are yours for the asking. And I *think* you know that. So tell me, why would you deny yourself the good things you deserve?"

"I don't know." She felt her face begin to flush, and then, with dread, it seemed that she might start crying again.

"How old do you feel? How old are you, Dez, right now, this very moment?"

The tall cop closed her eyes, and what came to mind was a pair of brand spanking new tan and white saddle shoes with brilliant white laces. She could see them from above, as though she were looking down at the legs of a ten-year-old. "Ten," she said, opening her eyes. She continued to look down into her lap, not daring to meet the therapist's eyes.

"If you are ten right now, how do you feel?" In almost a whisper, Marie said, "Your father is still alive, right?"

Tears welled up in confused blue eyes, and the t-shirt clad chest constricted so tightly that Dez couldn't breathe. A sharp gasp emerged from her, and the only thing that kept her in the chair was the certain knowledge that if she rose, she might fall over into a faint. She raised her eyes to meet Marie's, then looked away as she felt the first of a stream of hot tears running down her face. Crossing her arms over her chest, she fought to gain control, knowing that it was a losing battle. Still, she thought she ought to fight it.

Marie did not speak, and Dez would not look at her. She closed her eyes and thought of her father, the dark-haired, laughing dynamo who used to grab her by her wrists and swing her around the room until she was dizzy and shrieking with happiness. She could almost see his face clearly, drink in his love, imagine the smell of his aftershave.

It hurt too much. *Really*, she thought, *this is just too much to bear.* She closed her eyes and the first thing that came to her mind was a bar: a solid metal bar at eye level, parallel to the ground, with large weights on either end. In her mind's eye, she ducked her head underneath with her knees bent beneath her, grasped the metal rod on either side of her upper arms, and settled the bar across her shoulders. She imagined straightening up, stepping back out of the rack, and doing a deep squat, then rising swiftly. Air rushed out of her mouth, and she felt a surge of power throughout her body, even though she knew, simultaneously, that she sat in a deep brown chair, low to the ground, in a multicolored room overflowing with toys and papers and other stuff.

"Dez."

She opened her eyes and met the dark brown eyes across from her.

"Where did you go? Tell me about what just happened."

She didn't want to go back there, back to the saddle shoes, to the wool jumper and knee socks, back to the time before her father died when she still felt him, knew him, loved him. She shook her head, not trusting her voice.

Marie nodded. "Okay. I want you to think about this—maybe even write things down, too. The feelings you just had, the memories you just experienced, they are one of the keys to your pain. The unhappiness, the fear, the worry, the sadness—all of that—has to do with very old grief. You need to get it out, examine it, *feel* it—"

"I can't!" The two words exploded from the tall woman like a gunshot.

"Because it hurts too much?"

Dez nodded mutely.

"I will help you."

Chapter
Twenty-Two

Dez finished off a bowl of canned peaches. She had rinsed the heavy syrup from them, but they still tasted overly sweet. She'd eaten a bowl of oatmeal and her vitamins and decided that after she got the cabin straightened around, she would go on a very long hike.

Twenty minutes later the dishes were done, the kitchen floor was swept, and she had changed into hiking boots with gaiters, heavy jeans, a t-shirt, and a thick, long-sleeved wool sweater. In a dark green daypack she also carried a Gore-Tex coat rolled around a pair of heavy-duty mittens. When she hiked, she was usually more than warm enough so long as the temperature was above twenty degrees, but if something happened and she had to slow down, she might get chilled and need the coat. So far, even with all the walking she had done in the past two weeks, she'd never needed to take the coat or gloves out.

The daypack also contained a flashlight, matches in a water-proof container, her fully charged cell phone, a turkey and mayo sandwich, a bag of shelled peanuts, one Hershey's chocolate bar, and two peeled oranges in a small plastic bag. A quart of water was tucked into the mesh pocket on the left, and her gun and some spare bullets were in the right pocket. She was ready for anything.

She tossed the pack into her truck and gave Dewey a wave as she drove past his place. He waved back. If she didn't return by dark, he knew well enough to come looking for her. She figured on coming back to the cabin by mid-afternoon.

Up the road she went. Patches of snow that had been there only a few days ago had melted, and the ground was dry and fro-zen. With the leaves off the deciduous trees, the woods had dried up considerably. She might run into some muddy stretches, but for the most part, she expected the trail to be accessible.

It was only a few miles to an entrance for the Superior Hiking Trails. She parked the Ford in one of the many gravel lots hollowed out next to Highway 61. There were no other cars in the small lot, so she thought she would have a quiet and uneventful trek through the woods by herself—just how she liked it. She got out her daypack, locked up the truck, zipped the keys into the small pocket in the front of the backpack, then strapped it on. She breathed out, and it was so cold, she could see her breath. *Better get moving. It's damn chilly out here!* She walked along the side of the road for about a hundred yards, then when she came upon the wide path, turned uphill and strode off into the trees.

The incline was steep and would be for almost a mile, so she set a steady pace. She hadn't gone far before she was toasty warm. Her heavy hiking boots didn't dig much into the partially frozen trail, but she still had good traction.

December 16th...her thirtieth birthday. It had been several years since she had been alone—totally alone—on her birthday. She hadn't had a party for a while either. Most of the time she worked, and usually her work buddies gave her a bad time. Crystal and Cowboy could be counted on to give her gag gifts, and Luella usually cooked her something special, whatever Dez's heart desired. When she got back to the cabin, she thought she had better call Luella or she knew her landlady would be upset with her. It had been two weeks since she'd left the note for Luella, and it was time to touch base.

She thought about calling Jaylynn, too. She didn't think she was ready. *I am not going to call her and blubber on the phone.* And blubber was what she was afraid she would likely do. She had grown more accustomed to the constant ache behind her breastbone, and there was no way she wanted that to blossom into something more painful than it already was. *No, I'm not ready yet. And besides, it would be kind of tacky to call her on my birthday anyway—like I was expecting some response from her just because of that.*

She reached the top of the long hill, and ahead of her was an enormous expanse of woods, sloping upwards in a gradual ascent. She stood and surveyed the beauty ahead of her, half of it dead and half still alive. The birch and poplar had lost their leaves. Their light colored trunks and branches stood in stark contrast to the leafless gray-brown oaks and the dark evergreens, which dropped their needles steadily throughout the year. She took a deep breath and smelled sharp, pungent resin. The wind whistled through the trees, and she heard the far-off cry of a hawk, then saw the dark outline of the bird swooping low far ahead at the tree line. She was totally alone, with only nature around her. Her throat constricted, and the tears welled up in her eyes.

She took another step forward and went on, tears streaming down her face.

****

Jaylynn awoke from a nightmare, her heart racing. She was wrapped in the blankets and sheets, and for once she wasn't cold at all. She sat up, tossed the covers off, and waited for her heart to return to its regular pace. She recalled quite clearly the giant monsters that had been chasing her, and she wondered, for maybe the millionth time, how she was ever going to get rid of the alien dreams. When she slept with someone—slept with Dez, that is—they weren't so bad.

But it had been exactly sixteen days since she had last seen Dez. She continued to try to get some sort of information out of people at work, but so far, no one knew anything except that the tall cop was on admin leave and she'd been sent to the shrink. There was a great deal of speculation, but no facts to back anything up. The sergeants and the lieutenant were close-mouthed, too, so nobody who had the actual facts would tell her anything.

It was driving her crazy.

Every day she called the cell phone and the apartment, hoping that she might catch the tall woman. She cursed the fact that Dez did not have an answering machine. She had finally mailed a card. That had been four days ago, and still, no word.

The chilly morning air cooled her skin, and she shivered. Her hand ached, and the cast on her wrist felt itchy. She hated the damn thing, wanted to saw it off herself and throw it out the window. She counted down the number of days until the doctor would cut it off permanently and she could get back to normal.

Pulling the covers up, she curled into a fetal position, and for the first time, she began to consider what would happen if she had driven away the woman she loved. Lately she had not been able to stop thinking about it, instead berating herself over and over. Now that she was less angry at Dez, she thought about the scene at the hospital. The look that Dez had had on her face when she turned and left—she couldn't get it out of her head. Pain. That was what Jaylynn had seen. Stark, unmitigated pain. Now that she let herself realize the way the harsh words had affected the tall woman, she wished she could call them back, but it was too late. Dez had sped out of the room before she could gather her thoughts. *Who am I trying to kid? I was too indignant to even realize it at the time.*

She looked at her bedside clock. 10:20 a.m. *Time to get up and move around.* In less than two hours, at 12:15, she was due at the doctor's to have her wrist checked and a new cast applied. The thought of another cast made her want to throw something. Then before she went in to work at the main station, she had a final follow-up session with the students at Como High School to quiz them on holds and releases. It wasn't any fun to teach self-defense without her partner. For one thing, she had to work extra hard to explain things since she didn't have an experienced person to illustrate it, and with her bad hand, there were many things she couldn't do herself. Each time she showed up at the school, the pack of twelve and thirteen-year-olds were disappointed that the taciturn cop with the abs of steel did not accompany her. She had told them over two weeks ago that Dez had taken a vacation. Since this was the last day teaching self-defense, she knew they would all be dissatisfied that they never got to say goodbye to the tall cop.

She rolled out of bed and gathered clothes to wear for the day. She needed to go down to the kitchen and get a plastic bag to put around the cast so she could shower. *God, what a pain! I am just sick of this.*

Her clean uniforms were at work, so all she needed to do was find something suitable to wear to and from the station. It took her several minutes to find a clean t-shirt. She hadn't done any laundry since—*well, since when? How long had it been?* She couldn't remember when. Dez had taken to doing loads of wash down in the basement quite some time back, and Jaylynn had relinquished the task without a second thought, content to do all the folding and putting away when clean clothes magically reappeared.

Her eyes filled with tears, and wearing only her sleeping shorts and a flannel pajama shirt, she settled back against the edge of the bed. She was tired. She was sick and tired of waiting, of not knowing. She was tired of being alone, and she was tired of her heart hurting like this. She was also mad that she had had to buy her plane ticket to Seattle to go be with her family for the Christmas holiday. She had wanted the tall woman to accompany her, but she and Dez had never talked about that, and now it was too late. She'd had to book the flight 14 days in advance or she would have ended up paying an exorbitant amount.

After a minute, she rose and blotted her tears on her sleeve, then gathered up her clothes and hauled them with her to the

bathroom where she got ready to take a shower and try to wash
away her sadness.

Chapter
Twenty-Three

Dez and Dewey picked up a piece of 4 x 8 drywall and set it on an inch-tall board that ran along the base of the wall in Cabin H. Water damage had ruined the wall outside the bathroom, and she had taken great enjoyment in using a sledgehammer and pry bar to pull down the old wall. Now they were hanging the new piece of sheetrock and getting ready to mud and sand the entire wall. She liked how Dewey had named the cabins alphabetically. *No hokey names for him. The Dreamwater Special. Kingfisher's Haven. Sweet Hibiscus. Nothing like that would do.* Labeled A, B, C, D, and so on, they were easy to remember as they were in the order of appearance in relation to his cabin.

She had been working with Dewey whenever she wasn't venturing down to St. Paul for her therapy appointments. She didn't miss any of her possessions, and she usually didn't even bother to go by her apartment. So far, the only thing she missed was Jaylynn. Well, she missed Luella a little, too, but she was used to going a couple weeks at a time and not seeing her landlady. Jaylynn was another story. The day before she had finally broken down and sent a postcard from the tiny little post office in Lutsen. On it, she scrawled, "Thinking of you—truly. People always say that on postcards, but I really mean it. Love, Dez."

Dez thought about her ex-partner a lot and was sorry about how things had ended. She wanted to contact her, but she didn't yet feel ready. Besides, she was still afraid Jaylynn would turn away from her and send her off like that terrible day in the hospital. She broke out in a light sweat just thinking of it.

In the quiet of Cabin H, Dewey and Dez screwed the sheetrock into the wall studs, then stood back to admire their handiwork.

"Works for me," he said, brushing the dust off his hands. She nodded. "You know, kiddo, you could practically do this for a living. You're good at it."

She hated it when people complimented her, mostly because it made her blush, which she was doing right now.

"I know you don't like praise, Dez, but I just gotta say that it's been great having your help. We've gotten more done than I expected to do in two or three seasons. It gives me a real jump on things for next year. Once you go back to work, why don't you just keep that key to G until next spring? Then you can come up here all winter whenever you damn well please."

"Really? You sure?"

"Absolutely. You can come and go as you please. Anyway, I'll always know it's you with that big red truck. And when you're gone for a while, just turn the heat down to about 55, and nothing will freeze."

"Thanks, Dewey. You've been great."

He looked at his watch. "It's nine already. You gotta run?"

"In a bit. I can help you mud this."

"Nah...forget about it. You've done a shitload of work here, Dez. I should probably be paying you."

She smiled. "I've enjoyed keeping busy, Dewey. It's been fun to work with you."

"You got a sickness, girl."

She reached over and took a swipe at his chin whiskers. "And you have an awful lot of dust in your beard, Mr. Bunyan."

"It'll all come out," he growled. "Go on now and get where you're going." He turned back to the wall, then picked up a mudding knife. She hustled out into the cold, and as soon as she left his company, she felt the sinking sensation of grief hit her again. Despite the fact that she was starting to think she was getting good at letting her psychological bones be picked, she did not look forward to it.

She unlocked the door to Cabin G and hastened into the warmth. Even with her long-sleeved shirt on, just the short walk from H to G had given her goose bumps. It was cozy in her cottage though, and she marveled at how lucky she was that Dewey was so generous. This was the best cottage of the ten. It had a huge living room with a fireplace, a 15 x 20 foot bedroom with a deck outside it, a fully appointed kitchen, and a modern bathroom with a full tub and shower. He had done a nice job insulating and decorating it, and the rugs on the floor were thick and warm. She liked the golds and reds and dark blues of the furniture and the paintings of Lake Superior scenes on the walls.

She had made herself comfortable in Cabin G. The fridge was stocked, she had a stack of paperbacks to read, and her clothes were all unpacked in the dresser drawers. She could even see herself living here comfortably on a permanent basis—after all, her St. Paul apartment was much smaller.

She undressed, got in the shower, and spent time thinking about what she would do next. Yes, she was cleared regarding the incident with Bucky Reginald, but there was still an "informal memorandum" in her file about the rest of the event, and that memorandum would never be removed. If she had it to go back and do all over again, she would probably do the same thing under the same circumstances. That giant behemoth of a man might have killed Jaylynn, and it was all worth it to make sure that didn't happen. She reasoned that the price she paid was not too high. She didn't care if they gave her five reprimands or threw her off the force. The world would be a much worse place without Jaylynn.

She turned off the water and stepped out of the tub, hastening to get dressed. She spent a few minutes reading another chapter of the book Marie had given her. She was starting to understand the terrible effects of PTSD, and she found a curious comfort in reading the harrowing stories about other officers who had developed the same response she had. She finished a chapter and put the book, face down, on the end table next to the couch, then got up to ready herself for departure.

After a quick meal of cold chicken breast and toast, she packed a few things into the truck and selected a CD to listen to on the long drive down to St. Paul for her appointment with Marie. She stepped up to get in the truck, stopped mid-step, went back to the cabin to grab a water bottle from the refrigerator, and then returned to the truck to leave for her appointment.

****

Whenever Dez sat in Marie's waiting room, she was always relieved that no one else was ever there. People emerged from the office, sometimes teary-eyed, sometimes laughing, but she didn't have to wait with anyone else staring at her. It gave her time to do the breathing exercises Marie had taught her—and to talk to herself about not stressing out over everything. Marie had made it clear that it would take some time before she could work her way out of the "Disaster Prevention Syndrome" that she seemed to have going on in her head much of the time. She thought about how odd it was that the disasters she worried about were never about her, but always about someone else, most specifically Jay-lynn.

She thought about Jaylynn again for what she thought might be the hundredth time this day. She was glad in many ways that the rookie hadn't figured out how to track her down, but some days she wished she had. She missed her terribly, so much so that she found herself again marveling that she was used to that aching pain behind her breastbone.

Dez jumped when the door to Marie's office popped open. She'd made it a habit not to look up at the departing client, but when no one came out, she looked out of the corner of her eye, and there stood Marie, a smile on her face.

"C'mon in, Dez. How are you feeling today?"

"Not bad." She rose and followed Marie in.

"I suppose you still haven't taken up coffee?"

Dez shook her head. "Nope." She shrugged off her coat, and sat in a chair as she set her jacket on the floor next to her.

"I'm hooked on it and can't seem to quit. I get headaches if I don't have a couple cups a day."

"Tastes like battery acid."

Marie laughed. "You've drunk battery acid and lived to tell the tale, then?"

"Seems like it. Lately, anyway."

"How are you sleeping?"

Dez looked away, over toward the window. "Okay, I guess."

"Same dreams?"

Pausing, Dez pursed her lips, then met the therapist's eyes. "I think I liked it better when I didn't remember them."

"If you remember them, then you can deal with them."

"I suppose."

"Has anything changed in the two days since I last saw you?"

Dez took a moment to consider. She didn't seem to be wak-ing up crying quite so much. But she was struck more often lately with an aching longing, a deep yearning. "I'm lonely."

Marie nodded. "I see." She took a slurp of her coffee, then tucked a leg under her. "What have you decided to do about that?"

Dez looked at her, surprised. "What do you mean?"

"Companionship, Dez. What are you going to do to seek some?"

"Ah...well...nothing."

Marie chuckled.

Dez frowned. She hated it when Marie laughed that way. After this many sessions she now knew it meant that she had totally missed the boat about something so patently obvious that when they'd talked more, she would end up feeling like an idiot. In a cross voice, she asked, "Why don't you just save us both half an hour and tell me why that's so funny."

Marie's face became serious. "Somewhere along the way somebody taught you—or you just decided—to do *everything* on your own, all alone. It doesn't have to be that way. There is nothing wrong with reaching out to others for support, sharing your feelings with friends, and just spending time with people you enjoy. Companionship is a good thing."

"I'm doing fine right now."

"I'm not calling you a liar, but hey, you're *not* doing just fine." She set her coffee cup back down on the table and leaned forward, her elbows on her knees. "Look, Dez, part of the process of healing from post-traumatic stress is telling the story, but another big part is reconnecting with community. You have friends on the force, right?"

She thought of Crystal and Cowboy and Jaylynn. "Yes."

"And you have friends outside the department, too."

"Mm hmm."

"And you have a lover."

It was a statement, not a question. Dez felt her face flame red. "Wh-what do you mean by that?" She rose from the chair, stepped over her coat, and headed for the window, her heart beating furiously.

"I have the report from your police superiors, remember?"

Dez turned around and stalked back over to her chair. "Shows what *they* know. We've not had any contact since—well, not for a while."

"Not since she was injured, right?"

Dez nodded, feeling miserable through and through. She had thought this conversation was going to lead toward her feeling a little bit dense, and instead it had taken a turn right into something more painful than she wanted to consider. And across from her sat Marie, the world's greatest psychological archeologist, armed today with a shovel and pickaxe that obviously weren't going to go away. It was a losing battle. She caved and spilled her guts.

She lowered herself into the soft brown chair and told the other woman about how she had met Jaylynn and hadn't wanted to get involved with her because she'd been burned before by another cop. But little by little, she had grown to depend on the younger woman, to need her. "It's a terrible thing, too."

"What is? I don't know what you mean."

"Need. It's a terrible thing. I don't want to have it. I am trying not to."

Exasperated, Marie said, "Wait a minute. We all *need* others.
It's perfectly normal."

"Not like this." Dez spoke in a solemn tone. "It's—it's
like...well, shit! It's like terrifying."

Marie nodded slowly and looked up at the ceiling for a
minute, a pose Dez was also used to. She waited, full of apprehension, hoping that what was to come next would be a useful
observation. A few seconds went by before Marie met her eyes
again. "This is going to sound crazy to you, I think. I'm telling it
to you anyway, even if you can't believe it yet. Maybe we ought to
write it down." She smiled. "Dez, you deserve love. You deserve
to *be* loved. And I hope you will believe that you can survive the
terror of it. You have survived the *deaths* of others who were vital
and important to you. There is no reason why you can't survive
the love of a real living person."

In a gruff voice, Dez asked, "How do you know she loves me?
That's not in the report!"

Marie smiled. "No, that's not. But how do *you* know if she
loves you—or *not?*" Dez was at a loss for words. She looked
down at her hands, both of which were gripped in fists. "It's time
to take some chances, check things out. You need to find out who
your real friends are. Meet with Officer Savage. Meet with your
landlady. Meet with family members. Start talking about what
you've been going through. And I would like to see you decide to
join a PTSD group—all law enforcement type attendees, of
course." Dez drew in a deep breath, and she must have looked
alarmed because Marie said, "You don't have to do it *all* today.
Take one baby step, then come back and talk about it. Then take
another step on another day. But a lot of baby steps will add up
over time. Even if you have some failures, you are sure to have
some successes, too."

Dez narrowed her eyes and scowled. *How could Marie know
that for sure?* With her luck, she'd go talk to any one of those people, share her real, true feelings, then find herself rejected. She
crossed her arms and blurted out, "What if I refuse?"

Marie bit back a smile. "You can do anything you want. You
should know that by now, Dez. But whether you choose to seek
out connections or not, I do have one piece of news for you. After
another couple of sessions, I am certifying you ready for duty
again."

Dez knew her mouth dropped open in shock, so she shut it
quickly and looked down. "But it's been less than four weeks. I

thought I was considered nuts and dangerous?"

Marie laughed out loud at that, and to her chagrin, Dez found herself smiling.

The therapist set her sloshing coffee cup on the table in front of her. "You've never been nuts. You needed to understand what was happening to you—that was all. Remember: PTSD is a normal neurological response to an abnormal event. Once you fully understood that your brain was looping through the unresolved losses of Ryan and your dad, you have been able to begin to examine those losses and start dealing with the grief. You're doing very well, Dez, and you're nearly ready to go back to work."

"I can't believe they'd let me back on patrol."

"Well," Marie hesitated, "actually, you'll need to transition back to that. I think you'll be on desk duty for a little while at first."

Dez sighed and rolled her eyes, but she uncrossed her arms. She realized that she would be happy to go back to work—even on light duty—and that surprised her. "When?"

"I'd like to see you at least a couple more times, talk about some of the workplace issues, but then you'll be ready, so how about after New Year's?"

Dez gulped and nodded. "Okay."

"In the meantime, how about trying the other thing I suggested?" When Dez didn't answer, she went on. "Making connections, I mean. Sharing just a little with people you know and care about. Trying to—"

"Yeah, yeah, I get your meaning, Marie." She knew she sounded cranky and abrupt, but she didn't care.

"I'll see you again the day after Christmas. Try one connection, why don't you?"

Dez slowly shook her head in disbelief. This woman was as bad as Jaylynn—absolutely unrelenting. She couldn't even believe it, but she found herself assenting.

Fifteen minutes later, she was sitting three houses down from the house on Como Boulevard. Off to her left, patches of ice on Como Lake sparkled despite the newly fallen snow clumped up here and there. It wouldn't be long before the entire lake was iced over. A movement caught her eye and she saw a woman down the slope. She was bundled up in wind pants, a heavy coat, and an Elmer Fudd-type earflap cap, and she pushed a bright yellow stroller along the walking path. As Dez watched their progress, a five-foot-long icicle fell from the tree right across the street from her and broke into a multitude of pieces on the hard ground.

She sat in the truck for several more minutes gazing out at the brightness of the winter wonderland glistening around her before she gathered up her courage and pulled the truck forward to come to rest in front of Jaylynn's house. She put it in park, but left it running, the heater on low. She got out and moved swiftly up the walk to ring the bell. She waited for what felt like an eternity, then decided no one was home. She turned to leave and had taken only one step when the door flew open. Startled, she spun around to see Tim through the screen. His red hair was tousled as though he had just awakened. He stood shivering in baggy gray sweat bottoms and a white t-shirt. With arms crossed, she could see the goose bumps on his forearms.

"What do *you* want?"

"I was looking for-for Jaylynn," she stammered.

"She's not home," he said in an angry voice.

"Can you tell me when she'll be back?"

"No."

An uneasy feeling began to flood through Dez. "What do you mean, 'No'? Will she be back after work or what?"

"She's not at work. She's gone."

Dez felt a stab of alarm. "Gone? What do you mean?"

"I mean she's out of town."

Dez didn't understand his anger. In a polite voice she said, "Did I wake you up? I'm sorry if I did."

"You've got more than that to be sorry about."

He glared out at her, and she found her own anger and pride rising to the surface. "What's *that* supposed to mean?"

Running a hand through his shiny red hair, he spat out his answer. "Why should I tell *you* a damn thing? First you break her heart, then what? You showing up now to rub it in?"

She felt like she'd been hit upside the head and wasn't seeing or hearing clearly. "What? What do you mean?"

"Right. Go ahead and play dumb. You've been using her all along, haven't you?" More emphatically he said, "I told her I'd like to kick your ass—and I would—but I'm not a violent man."

Dez was shook up, but she had the presence of mind to stand there and ask more questions. "What in the hell are you talking about, Tim? Really...tell me. I don't understand."

"Love 'em and leave 'em—is that how you operate?"

"Tim, you *know* me. That's not...I don't...Tim, this doesn't make any sense!"

"Well, why don't you explain how you could walk out on her—just disappear off the face of the Earth? You've broken her heart—that's what you've done. And dammit! That's more than you deserve to know." He started to close the inner door.

"*No!* Tim, wait!" She rushed the stairs, grabbed the screen handle, and wrenched the flimsy door open. His face looked out at her, alarmed. "Please. Just tell me. Did she go to her parents' in Seattle or what?"

He leaned back, his eyes wide. After a moment's pause, he nodded, then looked away, his knuckles white on the edge of the interior door. When he looked back, he studied her face for a moment. "She's a good person, Dez, one of the best and brightest I'll ever know. You better not hurt her any more."

With a growing lump in her throat, Dez nodded, then choked out a reply. "I know."

"She flies in on Christmas night. You can see her then."

"You'll tell her I came by?"

His eyes narrowed, and he took five full seconds to study her. "What I *should* do is take all your shit from her room and throw it out on the lawn—and don't think that hasn't occurred to me!" Then he sighed. "I'll tell her though. She's a big girl. She can decide what she wants for herself."

"What time does she get in?'

He rolled his eyes and gave a big sigh. "Couple minutes after ten. I still can't believe I'm telling you all this." He crossed his arms, shivering in his thin t-shirt, then reached out to shut the door. She heard a soft click and let the screen door close. Back down the stairs she went to her truck, shaken and trembling. She was glad she had left the truck's heater on. It soothed her frazzled nerves as she sat there for a few moments until she calmed down. *So much for my first attempt at making "connections." Next time I'll pick someone more benign—maybe someone at a fast food window or the drugstore counter...or the psych ward.*

She smiled grimly. *I made it through my first negative connection and lived to tell the tale. It's a baby step all right I am sure Marie will be quite entertained.* She pulled away from the curb and headed down the road toward her apartment, trying to avoid the rising panic. Did Jaylynn want to see her or not? *I broke her heart? What about mine? She's the one who sent me away!*

Pulling into the garage behind the house, she locked up and made her way into her apartment. It smelled funny—stale and musty. She hadn't spent the night there for so long, and since the heat was down to 60, it was chilly. She went to the thermostat and cranked the heat to 70, then went in to run a bath. Some time spent in a hot, steamy Jacuzzi would do her good.

Chapter
Twenty-Four

The Sunday before Christmas, at a quarter after nine, Dez was on the way over to the other side of the lake. She looked through the windshield at a dull and wintry day, the sky a gunmetal gray. Heavy, ominous clouds crouched overhead, threatening to disgorge tons of snow at any moment. Despite the weather, she was happy to be heading over to see her two favorite 70-something-year-olds. When the phone rang at nine at her apartment the night before, she almost hadn't answered it. But she was glad she had picked up when she heard Luella's voice in the receiver.

"Dez! I am so glad to reach you. Where have you *been*?"

She didn't say anything right away. "Well, I've kind of been around, Luella."

"Jaylynn keeps telling me to get an answering machine, and I guess you should, too. I've called and called, hoping to catch you."

"Things are starting to settle down now."

"That's good. I've missed you."

"How's Van?"

"Oh, *much* better. Cranky some days, but improving."

"I am very glad to hear that. I'd like to come visit—soon, okay?"

"Yes, but Dez honey, I'm calling to ask a favor. It's just fine if it doesn't work out. This is late notice, I know."

Luella wanted Dez to drive her and Vanita to church the next day at ten a.m. Dez had heard her say something about ducks, but she figured she had misunderstood. She learned that, except for doctor appointments, Vanita hadn't been out of the house since her heart attack, and Luella said her sister was very much missing attending worship services. Dez agreed to drive them, though she hadn't much felt like going to church when they talked. She hadn't been to a Baptist service with Luella for quite some time, though, and today she found, to her surprise, that she did't think she would mind going after all.

She pulled into the driveway at Vanita's house. The curtains in the front window slid open, and then Luella's smiling figure stood looking out the window and waving. Dez couldn't help but smile back. It had been far too long since she had seen Luella.

She got out of the truck, yawning as her landlady disappeared from the window. The tall cop hadn't slept well the night before, which was nothing new. Strolling around the side of the house, she went toward the back door where Luella was waiting, leaning out as she held onto the door handle. Dez took the stairs two at a time and stood looking down at Luella, who, even though she stood one step higher than Dez, was still half a head shorter than her tenant.

"Hey honey, I am *so* glad to see you." Luella grabbed an arm and pulled the tall woman into the house. They stood in the alcove right outside the kitchen and hugged. "I've missed you."

Why does Luella seem shorter? And smaller? Dez stepped back, a frown on her face. "You've lost weight," she said in an accusing voice.

The older woman grinned and nodded, then took the big woman's hand and pulled her into the kitchen. "Thought you'd be pleased about that, Miss Granola Queen. I went on the same daily diet that the doctor put Vanita on. Didn't seem fair that I was still eating pastries and fried chicken and pie when she was on a low-fat, low-cal sort of deal."

She shut the kitchen door behind them. Dez took a deep breath and filled her lungs with the smell of cinnamon and coffee and something else, something indefinable that spoke of comfort and peace and Luella. She looked down into the dark brown eyes, saw a question on her landlady's face, and looked away, instead gesturing toward the living room. "Where's Vanita?"

"She fell asleep in the living room. We don't have to leave for another few minutes, so I thought I'd let her sleep."

Just then they heard a spirited, "Hey!" As they moved toward the living room, Vanita called out, "Y'all better not be in there talking about me. I may be old, but I've got good ears."

Vanita, too, had dropped weight, especially in her face, but otherwise she looked like the same feisty old cuss she'd always been—only smaller. She sat burrowed in the easy chair with a multicolored afghan draped over her lap and legs.

"Hey, Van, how's tricks?" Dez leaned down and placed a kiss

on the old woman's forehead.

"Still alive and kickin', even though I'm bionic now with this pacemaker."

Dez smiled. "This is unusual. You're both in slacks." Dez rarely remembered seeing either of them wear slacks, and certainly not both of them at once. Luella wore pale purple knit pants, large tan Hush Puppy shoes, and a pink and purple flowered sweater over an off-white blouse with a huge collar. What she could see of Vanita sticking out from under the afghan showed black slacks and the same kind of shoes.

"Today we're dressed for warmth, not with our usual elegance and beauty." Luella grinned, her white teeth sparkling in the early morning light.

"What's the plan, then?" Dez said.

Luella reached down and peeled the afghan off Vanita's lap and tossed it on the nearby couch. "We'd like to take Vanita's car because it'd be easier to get her in and out of. You want to go pull it out of the garage? I'll get my big sister ready to go. Keys are on the table in the front hall."

Dez nodded with relief. The thought of trying to pack either of them into her Ford truck had already crossed her mind, and it hadn't been a pleasant prospect. She went out, moved the truck to one side of the driveway, and opened up the little one car garage. She wondered how Vanita had ever parked the huge sea green Chrysler. The opening to the garage was, at most, six inches wider than the car, and the garage itself was so short that the front bumper touched the back wall, leaving perhaps a foot of room at the front of the garage. Inside, she calculated that there was— maybe—two feet of room on either side of the oversized automobile.

She squeezed around to the driver's side and opened the heavy door, then paused. There was no way she could squeeze in. To top it off, Vanita the Midget had obviously been the last person to drive the Chrysler because the seat was up as close to the dash as it would go. *Too bad it's not a convertible*, she thought. *At least I could have gotten in by leaping.*

She pushed the door open until it was pressed against the garage wall, then leaned in and rolled down the window using the old-fashioned metal crank. With the window down, she was able to get a leg in, jackknife over the door, and worm her way backwards into the car. On hands and knees, with her right side wedged up against the steering wheel, she felt under the seat until she found the lever to slide the seat back. Bracing her right foot on the floor, she pulled the lever and the entire front seat jerked back a good foot. She exhaled, got her legs out in front of her, and shut the door, relieved of the claustrophobia she had felt. Taking the keys from her coat pocket, she settled in behind the wheel and started up the car. In the rearview mirror, a giant cloud of exhaust puffed from the back of the car. It smelled pungent, like road construction, and she had a hunch it was time for some maintenance on the clunky tank. As she rolled up the window, she wondered how old it was—certainly late Sixties. It didn't have fins though, so that was one thing in its favor.

Keeping an eye in the side mirror, she backed out with barely three inches to spare on the sides, and rolled into the street and all the way out to the sidewalk leading up to the front door. She let the big green monstrosity idle and went into the house to help the two women.

Despite being two years older, Vanita had always been a couple inches shorter than Luella. Now she seemed to be half a foot shorter. She moved with effort, as though she didn't quite trust her legs to hold her up. Luella, solid and sturdy, helped her sister into a gigantic, puffy tan coat. Dez stood to the side, waiting and wondering how Vanita would ever make it up all the stairs into the church. She didn't recall ever seeing a side door—though there was a back door—but if they entered through the back, that just meant they'd have to go up the stairs on the inside of the church. If worse came to worst, she thought she might be able to carry Vanita. The old woman looked like she weighed all of about 100 pounds now.

With an arm firmly gripped by Luella and Dez, Vanita descended the six front stairs, and got settled into the front seat of the car. Dez jogged back to the house. At the top of the stairs sat Vanita's purse with two fluffy blankets folded next to it. She tucked the blankets under one arm and grabbed the handle to the large purse. Her finger gave a little twinge of stiffness, but it didn't hurt despite the fact that the purse was heavy. She returned to the smoking green car as Luella climbed into the back seat and accepted the blankets Dez handed her.

Vanita exhaled and smiled, looking around the car. "Lots of leg room up here, Lu. Hope you fit in the back okay."

"I'm not prone to grumble," her sister responded.

"Oh yeah, right. You haven't stopped grumbling since you moved in. Not enough spices. Furniture in the way. Storage not convenient. The sheets not percale..."

Dez hoped that Vanita's purse would fit in the back. It was the size of a small suitcase and she was sure it weighed more than a fifteen pound dumbbell. She started to hand it to Luella, but

Vanita shook her head. "Oh no. Gimme that. I got my box of tissues and Bible in there."

That explains some of the weight, thought Dez as she handed
it over. "Watch your fingers," she said, then closed both of the
heavy-duty doors. *Good God, they made these cars solid. The
four doors probably weigh as much as the entire bed of my pickup.*

She got in, saw that the two ladies had buckled up, and put on
the driver's old-fashioned lap belt. She pulled away from the curb,
got to the corner, and started to turn right.

"No, no, no, Desiree. Left." From the back seat, a wizened
old hand pointed to the left, touching Dez's right shoulder.

"But Christ's Cornerstone is that way—"

Simultaneously, Vanita and Luella said, "We're not going
there today."

Luella leaned forward in the back seat and poked Dez in the
right shoulder. "Go left. It's the duck service at the Lutheran
church north of here."

The tall woman didn't understand, but she did as she was
told. It occurred to her that perhaps they'd selected a different
church with no stairs that was more easily accessible. She drove
the route and listened to them dispute whose house was more con-
veniently outfitted for cooking, storage, and entertaining. She fiddled with the heater controls, pointed the vents toward Vanita,
and the old car heated up to a toasty warmth which both the other
occupants commented felt good. She herself was roasting in the
heat, but she knew both of them needed to keep warm. As she
drove, a wave of fatigue washed over her, and she suddenly wished
she didn't have to sit on a hard wooden pew for an hour surrounded by people she didn't know.

She continued along a snowy street bordered by occasional
piles of shoveled snow that had melted considerably. She slowed
the car to a halt at a stop sign as a gray Camry slowed across the
intersection. Her heart skipped a beat and she held her breath,
but when the other car proceeded through the intersection, she
saw that an elderly, gray-haired man was driving. She set her jaw
grimly. Every little gray car she saw caused her to jump like that,
but it was never Jaylynn's car. She wanted to kick herself for even
looking, but she couldn't help herself.

She drove the rest of the way in silence. They arrived at the
church and pulled into the back parking lot as Luella exclaimed,
"This is great! We're here good and early and can get one of the
best parking places. Toward the back of the lot is where the
church secretary said the reception isn't as good."

Vanita nodded and pointed. "Over there, Dez, next to the

building."

The tall woman slowed the car. "Why don't I let you out right here by the door? Less distance to walk then."

"Oh no. We're not getting out. This is the duck service."

Luella pounded on the back of the seat, pointing frantically, her hand stabbing just past Dez's ear. "Quick! Over there before that other car gets the spot!"

Dez hit the gas and steered over into the parking place they were both pointing at. *God save me from wacky old ladies. That'll be my prayer for the day.*

She threw the car into park and shut off the ignition. "There. You two happy now?" She reached for the door handle. As she opened it, a gust of cold air entered the car and both women hollered at the same time for her to shut the door.

Vanita said, "Lulu. Our chauffeur doesn't seem to have a clue. Did you explain what in tarnation is going on here?"

"Guess not. I thought she understood. Dez, it's the duck service, a great new invention. Turn the car back on. You'll see what I mean."

Dez didn't ask questions, just did what they asked.

From the back seat, Luella went on. "Vanita heard about it on the radio and called to find out more, and it sounds like a good deal. We sit here in the comfort of our car and listen on the radio to the service going on inside. They come out and give us communion and everything."

Dez cleared her throat. In a low, tired voice she asked, "And where exactly do the ducks fit in?"

There was a moment of silence, then the two sisters burst into cackles. Every time one of them tried to speak, they dissolved into more laughter. Dez turned to the small woman sitting next to her and waited as Vanita fished a tissue out of her purse and blew her nose. A compact car pulled up beside them, and through the passenger window Dez could see a harried looking woman in the driver's seat, two toddlers in car seats in the back, and a kid about five years old, still in Batman pajamas, in the front seat. He unbuckled his seatbelt and picked something up from the floor that Dez couldn't see until he put the bucket in his lap. *Legos.* He fiddled with a crosspiece of the red, white and yellow creation, then held it in one hand and moved it around as though it were a little plane soaring in the air.

Luella let out a last chuckle. "There's no ducks, Dez. It's Drive Up Church—D, U, C. I am sorry I didn't explain it better. It's already 9:35. You can turn on the radio to 88.8 AM. The organist should have begun at half past nine."

Sure enough, 88.8 came in loud and clear with the screeching tones of the organ wheezing out "Angels We Have Heard on High."

Vanita giggled. "What will they think of next? Isn't this wonderful? Wish they'd had this when my little demons were small. Would've saved on a lot of threats and spankings."

Dez watched through Vanita's side window as a mini-van pulled up on the passenger side of the car. She couldn't see into the back seats because the windows were dark, but the man and woman in the front seat seemed to get situated, then started drinking coffee from black and silver insulated mugs and reading the newspaper. The van's side door slid open and two children dressed in snowsuits tumbled out, slammed the door shut, and ran over to the swing set inside the fenced-in area next to the church's side door. She watched as they climbed onto the hard black plastic seats and started to swing. Puffs of frozen breath emerged from their mouths into the wintry air.

On the other side of the Chrysler, Batman Boy with the Lego airship pointed and said something to his mother, then listened and nodded. Dez couldn't hear a word that was exchanged but she imagined that his mother was reminding him that if he had gotten ready when she told him to, he could have dressed warmly so that he, too, might be out swinging and playing with those other kids. Looking like he might cry, the boy shrugged his shoulders and looked down at the Lego bucket in his lap.

They sat in the car for several minutes while the two women read from their Bibles and occasionally made some comment to one another.

Movement behind the swing set caught Dez's eye. She saw the church door open, and a white robed acolyte came out, pushing a cart full of books. He stopped at each car and handed out hymnals and programs for the day's service. By the time he made it to their car, he was shivering in the cold. Dez accepted three hymnals and programs and thanked him, then rolled the window up quickly. "Are you two warm enough?" she asked. She passed them programs and books.

"Toasty," Vanita said as she buried her nose in the program.

Luella said, "We have these extra blankets if we need them."

Vanita took off her glasses and squinted at them. "My, my, these bifocals of mine may need a tune-up."

From the back seat Luella said, "Could be that those old eyes of yours are what needs a tune-up."

Just then, the organ music coming through the radio faded to a quiet whine, and Dez heard someone clear his throat. A pleasant, bass voice spoke over the soft tones of the organ. "Good morning to all of you on the Sunday before the birth of our Lord Jesus Christ. We welcome all of you here for our fourth monthly Drive Up Church service. God's blessings to each of you, and may the grace of our Lord God rain down upon you all. We have plenty of room inside the church should any of you drive up participants decide to join us. The day is cool, but the church is warm. The rest rooms are available, too. Just come in the rear of the church behind the kids' play area. Otherwise, today's worship will consist of a standard service without any unusual bells and whistles. The first hymn will be number 176 in the red hymnal. A couple of housekeeping items to share with our drive up guests. First, we have two assistant pastors today to come out with communion, but due to a lack of acolytes, we will not bring any wine or grape juice. Secondly, at the sharing of the peace, please feel free to honk, but if you could limit your sharing to one brief honking of the horn, it would be appreciated by our neighbors around us. Thank you for attending today, and we'll get started in a minute or two."

Dez turned and looked over her shoulder at Luella to find her friend laughing silently. In a dry voice, she said, "This is the craziest set-up I've ever seen. You two been here before?"

Through giggles Luella said, "Nope. But so far, it's great." She went off into a peal of laughter, joined by Vanita.

The service began, and the three women followed along. Dez sang the hymns quietly, amused to hear Vanita's warbly old lady voice in contrast to her landlady's strong bellow. She thought that the noise coming from their car must sound pretty bad, but when she looked surreptitiously around at the occupants of other cars, everyone else was singing without reserve.

In a little while, when it was time for the sharing of the peace, she waited for the minister's cue, then honked her horn, one short blast, with the rest of the DUC attendees. The people in the mini van next to them smiled and waved out their window, and she waved back. The honking had awakened the two children in the back seat of the car on the other side of them, and she could hear their wails over the organ music. Vanita reached over and turned up the radio.

When the time for communion drew near, she told her friends that she was skipping communion. "This is too odd, ladies. I feel like we're at the A&W Drive-In."

"Your choice, hon," Luella said. She reached up and patted Dez on the shoulder. "Rest assured that they won't be bringing us any ketchup and mustard to go with the wafers." Luella laughed, a hearty bleat which her sister joined.

Vanita said, "And they don't roller skate out, either."

Dez shook her head and listened to them laugh some more. She wished she could find as much humor in this as they were, but she was tired and glum, and the world around them was cloudy and cold. The communion song began.

> *O God, the Rock of Ages,*
> *Who evermore hast been,*
> *What time the tempest rages,*
> *Our dwelling place serene...*

She listened to the clear soprano voice, joined by a huskier alto and a quiet piano. The church door opened, and two ministers bustled out and began to make their rounds as the duet sang on.

> *Our years are like the shadows on sunny hills that lie,*
> *Or grasses in the meadows that blossom but to die,*
> *A sleep, a dream, a story, by strangers quickly told,*
> *An unremaining glory of things that soon are old.*

Suddenly, she was filled with longing and an ache that pressed down on her chest so hard that she wasn't sure she could breathe. She squeezed her eyes shut and willed herself not to cry. *Too late.*

"I'll be back," she mumbled. "I need some fresh air."

She bolted from the car, slamming shut the big heavy door in time to see two pairs of surprised eyes peering up at her, then she took the shortest route past the rest of the parking lot attendees. She wasn't sure what it was about music that tapped the depths of her despair, but if anything made her feel vulnerable, it was a melancholy song. She strode quickly along the sidewalk to the front of the gigantic brick church, taking in deep breaths of the frozen air. *Talk to myself, that's what Marie says. Talk myself down off this ledge.* She paced the length of the block to the corner, then turned and stalked back toward the other corner. *I'm lonely. I miss her. I miss my old life. I miss Ryan. I miss feeling like a normal human being. I feel—that's it!—I feel. And I don't want to feel. It's easier to stay in control if I don't have to feel, dammit!*

Tears sprang to her eyes again. Marie had told her that because she had suppressed her emotions for so long, it would take some time to get used to how strong those feelings could be. And now that she had actually begun to feel them again, it was just as Marie had said. *How embarrassing.*

She heard Marie's voice in her head: *"You wouldn't say 'how embarrassing' to someone else who came to you for comfort, Dez. Why wouldn't you comfort yourself the way you'd comfort a friend or one of Ryan's children?"*

She reached the corner and turned again. The light breeze cut through her jacket, and she dug her hands into her slacks pockets. She slowed to a stroll, her head down, as she shivered, then stopped. *I can't live like this anymore.*

It was too hard to hide her feelings and too late to be embarrassed that she had them. Marie had told her that was what made people human—all those intense feelings.

It occurred to her that one major thing she liked about Jaylynn was how alive she was. She took on life with zest, whether she was investigating a crime, talking on the phone, eating something tasty, making love, or crying at a sad movie. *Why didn't Jay ever seem embarrassed by her emotions? How had she learned to let it all hang out like that?*

Dez didn't know the answers to those questions. She thought she would like to ask, but she didn't know how to go about it. *Yeah, right, just call up and say, Hey! Merry Christmas. I know I've been MIA for weeks now, but how 'bout we get together and chat? Yeah, right.*

She hunched down further into her jacket collar and turned back before she reached the corner. Now she strode quickly toward the parking lot and the warmth of the Chrysler. The heater was on full blast, and for once she was glad it felt like a sauna.

"Good timing," Vanita said. "He just finished the benediction, they collected the hymnals, and now we can process out the lot and go directly to Perkins."

Surprised, Dez asked, "Perkins?"

"My treat," the older woman said.

"But what about your diet—"

Luella spoke up from the back seat. "We'll both eat sensibly, Miss Worry Wart. Do you want to go or not? You in a big hurry to get somewhere?"

"N-no," stammered Dez. "In fact, I'm pretty hungry myself." She backed out of her space and fell in line behind the mini van.

From the back seat a quiet voice spoke up. "What do you think of giving Jaylynn a buzz—see if she could join us?"

Dez was glad she was driving so she didn't have to look at her landlady. Her stomach dropped somewhere she figured in the vicinity of the car's undercarriage. "I don't think she's back from Seattle yet," she said calmly.

She heard a high-pitched beep and glanced over her shoulder to see Luella grinning and holding a compact cell phone to her ear.

"Luella! You've gone modern."

"Come on, squirt. I worked for the phone company for 39 years. It's not like I'm unaware of the latest technology."

"But she bought it for *me*," Vanita said. "Always good to have a cell phone at your fingertips when you're in the tub or on the pot or rooting around in the basement."

"Like *you* do a lot of rooting around in the basement," Luella retorted.

In a prim voice, Vanita said, "Well, whenever *you* do, I've got the phone for if you fall over in a dead faint and don't answer my calls."

"Hush, it's ringing."

Dez wanted to tell her that she wouldn't reach Jaylynn, but she figured her landlady would figure it out soon enough. She continued down the street driving toward the Perkins. From the back seat she heard Luella say, "Yes, hello. This is Luella. Jay, give me a call at Vanita's when you get time. Bye." The phone made a beep noise, then Dez heard a snap as Luella closed the phone up and put it back in her purse. "You sure she's in Seattle?"

Dez thought for a moment. *Would Tim lie to me?* She didn't think so. He had been reluctant to talk to her, but she did think he had been telling the truth. "She's due back on Christmas Day, I think."

"So you've talked to her?"

"No. Not for a while."

Both women made little tsk-ing noises but stayed silent.

****

Dez helped Vanita out of the car and walked slowly toward the restaurant as she held on to the arms of both of the older women.

Vanita pointed up with her free hand. "Ever notice how Perkins has the biggest flag on the planet?"

"No joke," her sister said. "That thing'd cover a football field, don't you think?"

Dez looked up at the red, white, and blue cloth whipping overhead. It made a snapping noise in the wind, and it occurred to her they were right. She didn't think she had ever seen such a big flag.

"It looks ridiculous," Vanita said. "I'm going to tell the manager that."

Dez squeezed her eyes shut and hoped that Vanita would forget all about that lame-brained idea. They made it safely to the door, and she held it open for both of them. The after-church rush had begun, but they arrived in time to get a table in the back. Dez took charge of hanging up the coats and jackets, and when she returned to the table, the two sisters sat on one side of the booth, viewing the giant menus and licking their lips. She slid in across from them and folded her menu out onto the table.

Her landlady lowered the big plastic menu. "Long as we got you as a captive audience, we need to chat, Desiree. About little Miss Jaylynn and you."

Before Dez could recoil in shock, a harried looking waitress in a cotton candy colored uniform appeared at the tall woman's left. "Mornin'. What'll you have to drink?"

In unison from behind their menus, the sisters said, "Coffee. Black. And lots of it."

"And for you?" the waitress said to Dez. "Something hot? Something cold?"

Dez's mind went blank. She looked up and tried to focus on the pink-clad brunette who stood on her left with pencil and pad ready, but her mind was still on Luella's proclamation.

Luella lowered her menu. "Hey there, Miss Water Buffalo. Surely you're going to get *something* to wet your whistle?"

Water buffalo. Water. That would do. "Yes. Water," she croaked out. "A tall glass of ice water."

The waitress nodded and whirled off, and Dez turned back to her two friends.

"What are you two getting?" Vanita asked from behind her plastic menu. "I suppose you'll get eggs and bacon and sausage and taties and the works, huh?"

She said it with such longing in her voice that Dez almost felt bad. "You know what, Van? I think I'll get whatever you get. How's that for camaraderie?"

"Hmph," the old lady said. "Might maybe just get dry toast." Her eyes twinkled and she held back a smile.

Dez shrugged. "Guess I could get seven or eight pieces then. And I'm sure we can have jelly, right?"

"That's right," Luella said as she folded her menu shut and put it on the table. "Jelly's fine. But she's jerking your chain, Dez." She elbowed Vanita gently. "You're going for something more substantial than that, big sister. I know you far too well."

"Plain waffles, then. That's what I'll have. With jam. Sound okay to you, Desiree?"

Dez nodded and gave that order when the waitress came back. They all handed in their absurdly enormous menus, and she took a big drink of her ice water. When she looked up, she found two observant pairs of eyes across the table waiting patiently.

Her landlady smiled sweetly, and the younger woman knew she was in for it. There was some sort of plot going on here, and she felt like a fool for not picking up on it sooner. Luella started out. "Ordinarily, Dez, you know I don't like to nose into your business."

Vanita gestured toward her sister with her thumb. "Maybe *she* doesn't like to get in your business, but ever since my brush with death, it doesn't bother me so much." Irritated, Luella elbowed her. "You keep your elbows to yourself, young lady!"

"I want to go about this my own way."

"I've got some say in it, too, you know."

"At least let me give her some background, Vanita!"

"All right. Go ahead and hog the stage."

Dez settled back in her seat on her side of the booth and crossed her arms over her chest. She didn't know why it was so funny when the two of them got indignant with one another, but it never failed to crack her up. She was pretty sure they didn't have a very good plan for whatever they were going to discuss, so if she could just relax, it would likely turn out to be amusing.

"Vanita and I are trying to make a decision. We have two houses, but we don't need two houses anymore. Since she's so old and decrepit now, we need to consolidate." She jerked in her seat. "Ouch! You with the sharp elbows! Cut it out." She scooted over in the booth a little and directed a fake angry look at her sister.

Vanita returned a smug look. "Stick to the facts. I may be old, but I am *not* decrepit. I'll be up and running before too long."

Luella rolled her eyes and turned back to the cross-armed woman in front of her. "One day we'll decide we want to live in her place. The next day we think we should take mine. But after all the arguing and discussing and weighing and planning, it all comes down to what you and Jaylynn decide."

Dez looked from one to the other. "What do you mean?" She sat forward and put her elbows on the table, a puzzled look on her face.

Luella cleared her throat. "Well, if the two of you want to live together, then I think you should take Vanita's house and my big sister will move in with me. Otherwise, if you two are history, then you can stay right where you are, and Jaylynn could have the main floor of my place. I'll move over to Van's then. So start thinking about whether you're interested and which choice it'd be if you are."

Dez's gaze ping-ponged back and forth between the two women. They both sported happy, innocent faces, but beneath she could see there was something more. *Maybe their plan was better thought out than I had realized.* "Let me get this straight—no matter what, you two clowns are moving in together?"

They nodded, their brown faces shining in the midday light slanting into the window.

"And you want to sell one of the houses—to me or Jaylynn?"

Vanita said, "Or rent—or lease—just let you live there if you don't buy. We haven't really thought that out."

Well, I'll be damned. These two are playing matchmaker. That's what this is all about. She was surprised to come to that conclusion. "Have you talked to Jaylynn?"

At the same time, both women piped up with the answer. Luella said, "Sort of," while Vanita said, "Not exactly."

"Well, which is it?"

The sisters' heads swiveled toward one another. Up to this point they had done a credible job of looking casual and innocuous, but now they appeared positively mischievous.

The pink-clad waitress chose that moment to appear with their plates. She smacked the food onto the table in front of each woman and asked what else she could get for them. By the time she had left, both of the sisters were focused fully on their breakfasts.

"Doesn't this look great?" Vanita asked. "How delicious—my first meal out after all these weeks."

"Oh, yes," Luella said. "Scrumptious."

Dez picked up her fork and speared her waffle, then stabbed at it with her knife. She reached one long arm across the table to the rack holding three kinds of syrup and snagged the maple syrup, which she systematically poured all over the waffles on her plate.

"Hey," Vanita said. "Thought you were having jam with me."

"Yeah, well, that was before the two of you decided to gang up on me. Now I need all the fortification I can get." She took a big bite of the hot waffle. *Not as good as the ones Luella makes, but still, it feels good to eat.*

****

Dez perched on a stepstool near the back door in Vanita's

kitchen watching as Luella seared a beef roast. Vanita had run out
of energy and was crashed in the living room on the couch, covered with a couple afghan quilts. She had fallen asleep within
minutes of arriving back home.

Luella poked an enormous two-pronged fork into the roast
and turned it over. The oil in the pan popped and spattered, so
the older woman turned the burner down. Over her shoulder she
said, "You'll have to give me some low-fat cooking ideas, Dez. I
think there are a lot of my standard dishes that my big sister can't
eat anymore."

"I have a couple cookbooks you should look at." Dez pulled
her feet up on the bottom step of the stool. She put her elbows on
her knees and her chin in her hands. "Can she eat that kind of
beef? Seems it would be sort of high fat."

Luella leaned the fork on the spoon rest and wiped her hands
on the hot pink apron she wore. "She can have a small portion—
about three or four bites. That's it."

"It's not like she's burning mongo calories."

"True. I'm not giving her much meat, other than fish and
chicken. It's not that good for her, but it's not a problem for you
and me. You're staying for an early dinner, aren't you?"

She looked so hopeful that Dez nodded. She had nowhere
else to go anyway. Besides, brunch had been good, but a couple of
waffles and ice water weren't going to hold her through the afternoon.

"Good. And if I don't miss my guess, you're going to want a
snack here before too long."

Dez grinned. The older woman sure had her number.

"I've got some tuna salad and Christmas cookies—plus a variety of veggies and fruit, if you'd like that instead. When you get
hungry, let me know. Meantime, what have you got to say about
the Jaylynn proposition?"

Dez's hands went a little cold, and she found herself swallowing. She watched as Luella pulled open a cupboard door and bent
down to pick baking potatoes out of a brown paper sack. She
smacked the cupboard shut and moved to the sink to run water
and scrub the spuds.

The tall cop looked around the kitchen, then out the large
window above the sink where Luella was silhouetted. The silver-
haired woman methodically scrubbed the potatoes, humming quietly under her breath. One thing Dez had always liked about her
landlady was that Luella knew how to pose a question, then wait
for an answer. Sometimes she might have to wait for hours—or
days—but she never pressured her young tenant. She also listened

closely without seeming to form judgments or jump to conclusions.

Dez figured it was time to take another baby step, and who better to do it with than someone who had been a trustworthy friend for almost a decade? She didn't know how to begin though. She sat, chin in hands, and watched as Luella speared all sides of the potatoes and the ends, then shuffled across the linoleum floor to put them in the oven. When she opened the stove door, a wave of warmth wafted over, and Dez's hands didn't feel quite so cold.

"I'm afraid." Her voice was soft, almost reluctant. Again, she felt embarrassed, but with her heart beating fast, she went on. "I'm too afraid to lose her."

Luella glanced over her shoulder, nodding, then flipped the sizzling roast on end. "What's that all about?"

Dez let out a long sigh. "Oh, Lu, you're going to think I'm such a big chickenshit." She heard a deep chuckle and watched as her friend opened another cupboard and pulled out a roasting pan.

"Some days you are a little shit, but I wouldn't *ever* describe you as a chickenshit."

"I'm going to counseling."

Luella put the roasting pan on the counter and turned to give her a level gaze. "So? I think it takes a braver person to do that than to sit around ignoring problems."

"And I've got some doozies." Dez let out a snort and rolled her eyes.

Luella smiled, her brown eyes twinkling and warm. "You've got nothing worse than most, honey, and a little better than some. You just think it's all bad because you're not used to dealing with this sort of thing, and besides, it sure seems a lot of stuff snuck up on you all at once."

"That's one way of looking at it."

The silver-haired woman set the roasting pan on a cold stove burner and used the silver fork and a knife to spear the roast and get it into the pan. She smacked the lid on and put the covered pan into the oven next to the baking potatoes. When she stood up and turned around, she had a thoughtful look on her face. "Are you afraid that Jaylynn is going to leave you? Because I don't see that happening. I don't think you understand how she feels about you."

"I'm a little afraid of that, but, well—I'm more concerned about something happening to her."

Luella leaned back against the counter, her hands up on the edge. "Like what?"

"Fire. Gunshots. Abduction and torture. Stuff like beatings, car crashes, you know—something horrible. Geez, she's like...like a disaster waiting to happen all the time. She jumps into stuff. No, actually, it's like she's jumping off *cliffs* all the time."

"Ah, I see," Luella nodded deeply, "unlike you, yourself, who has never gotten into all sorts of potentially violent and dangerous situations."

"That's different."

"You girls are both smart, both resourceful, and both good cops. Don't underestimate her. Sure, something could happen, Dez, but you can't plan your life around what *might* happen. You have to enjoy each day, enjoy the good things all around you. And I know it sounds odd, but you have to put what might or could or will happen right on out of your head. It flies in the face of logic because you and I both know that all of us are going to die." She gave a toss of her head toward the door to the living room. "Case in point. Van could go any time, and I know it."

When Luella didn't say anything more, Dez cocked her head to the side, feeling perplexed. "How do you deal with that?"

Luella didn't answer at first. She took a deep breath and gazed out the window. It had grown dimmer outside so that less light was cast into the kitchen. When Dez focused on the tree in the yard, she could see flakes of white floating past the dark trunk of the big oak. She glanced back at Luella.

Luella shifted from one foot to another, then put both hands into her apron pockets. "Worry is a funny thing, kiddo. It can just about take over your life. But really, you can't control anybody or anything. Sure, you can cut your odds by being careful, using good sense, all that sort of thing. But you can't plan for everything that could possibly go wrong, and if you try to, well, what kind of life would that be? You'd have to sit at home, doing nothing, going nowhere, and even then things could go wrong. Look at my husband and boys, supposedly safe at home, asleep in their beds. Just some bad wiring, and poof!" She threw her hands up in the air. "They're gone."

"How..." The words stuck in Dez's throat, and she closed her mouth and looked away.

"How did I live to tell the tale?"

Dez nodded.

"You have to believe in something bigger than you. Some people would say God. Or a Higher Power. You know, something or somebody or some spirit that rules the Universe. People often say that God works in mysterious ways. He or She—or Whatever—*does* do that. And you have to believe that when something awful happens to take away someone you love, someone else will come along to help you with the hurt. People will show you love and caring, sometimes in ways you don't recognize. You're never really all alone. God will send someone for you to share with." She shifted against the counter, then took her hands out of her pockets and put them on the surface behind her. "I tell you, that's how I got through that awful time when my family died. Back then, we didn't truck much with psychiatrists or folks like that, but I spent a goodly amount of time with my pastor, crying and talking and praying. And you won't believe how many people came out of the woodwork—people I never knew or never paid much attention to."

Dez still didn't understand how Luella ever got through the death of her entire family, so she put forth the question she had always wanted to ask. "How come you never remarried?"

"I focused on my career. Even with the little bit of insurance I was left with, it wasn't enough to get by on forever. I used it to buy the house over on Como, then I got me a job. It took me a few years to regain my balance, you know. That kind of loss knocks the pins out from under a gal. I dated some very nice men in my thirties and early forties, and then it didn't seem so important. I didn't mind being alone. And finally I met George, and he stayed with me for a few years."

Dez looked startled. She'd never heard of any such person. "George? What happened to him?"

"He died. He was a lot older than me. If he were still alive, he'd be damn near ninety. He just passed on in his sleep at the nursing home. He lived with me for about seven years until he had a stroke. Then he stayed at a nursing home for—let's see, must have been about two-and-a-half years. He was recovering, starting to get his speech back and trying to relearn to walk when he had another massive stroke. He died before I could get there from work, so it was quite a blow. He was a quiet man. Very caring. He kept me company in ways that just made me feel loved and good. I still miss him."

"But God didn't send you someone new to replace him."

"Oh, but He did!"

Dez frowned and waited.

"George died, and three months later you showed up."

"Me?" The word tumbled out of her mouth like an explosive.

"Sure. Kind of like Jaylynn appeared out of nowhere for you a while after Ryan died. Or like Ryan came into your path after that rotten woman jilted you."

Dez stared at her open-mouthed. She had never ever thought of it that way, and she wasn't sure she believed it, even though her

mind raced to make connections. Her father died; Mac came into
her life. Her mother deserted her emotionally; various coaches
came into view. She even thought of her favorite bike, stolen
when she was eleven; she learned to skateboard that summer.
Maybe it wasn't so much that something or someone was sent to a
person, but that one adapted and learned to live with the changed
circumstances. In a quiet voice, the tall woman said, "I don't
think I could live through losing Jaylynn."

"So you're willing to run away from her and never have her at
all, never enjoy the years and years that you may have in front of
you?" Luella pushed away from the counter and moved toward
her, her slippers scuffing across the floor. She reached out long,
soft fingers and tipped Dez's chin up.

She felt hot tears well up. "It's not that easy, Luella."

"I know. You can't hold onto someone so tight that you
choke the life out of them. She has to find her own way, do her
own thing." She smiled a little bit. "You have to be willing to let
go. Let go at any given time. And know that you will be fine.
Alone or paired with someone else—either way, you're still all
together and all there. Sure, it'll hurt to lose her—or your mother
or brother. Or me. You'll cry. Your heart will hurt. But you'll go
on. You're a strong person, Desiree Reilly, and you deserve to
love and be loved. But you have to make a choice to take the
chance." She leaned into the bigger woman, and Dez wrapped her
arms around the solid middle, pressing her face into soft cloth that
smelled of oil and pepper. Over her head, she heard Luella's voice
go on. "I could lose Van any day, any night. I know that. She
knows that. But I push it out of my mind. Concentrate on enjoying her—whenever she isn't irking me, that is."

Dez felt the torso she was hugging contract as the older
woman giggled. There was nothing the younger woman could say.
Her throat constricted, and the tears flowed freely, though she
tried to turn off the waterworks.

Luella leaned away and reached a hand up to stroke the
braided dark hair. With a smile on her face, she said, "I'll tell you
one thing, though. You White people need to learn how to grieve!
I've never been to such somber funerals in all my born days as
when my White friends and neighbors have died. Black folk, *they*
know how to kick up a fuss when a loved one dies." She arched an
eyebrow. "You went to Mrs. Sutter's funeral—I believe you know
what I mean."

She looked at Dez knowingly as the tall woman nodded. A
smile broke through the tears. *What a wild funeral that had been.*
Mrs. Sutter, a retired teacher, had lived next door and had been ill

for many months before she finally died. Dez went to Christ's Cornerstone Baptist Church with Luella to pay her respects to the old lady who had traded rose and peony-growing tips with her over the back fence for several years. What she found was a church full of former students and members of the local community—mostly Black, but a few White and Asian. There was a full choir, four ministers, an honor guard, and pallbearers dressed in matching suits. Mrs. Sutter's fifty-something-year-old daughter had completely lost herself in her grief. Before the service, when it came time to close the casket, the daughter had thrown herself half over the shiny wooden coffin and let out a keening sound Dez associated with a wounded animal. As if on cue, the music director had struck a chord on the piano, and the choir launched into a rollicking spiritual while the Sutter family surrounded the grieving daughter and drew her away to a seat in the pews where they all wept and wailed together through the song. As the service went on, there was singing and testifying, wailing and crying, the likes of which Dez had never seen or heard before or since.

Luella was right: Black people knew how to grieve out loud.

But that wasn't Dez's way.

She felt Luella studying her face as the older woman stroked her hair. Dez hated being looked at when she cried. She felt so—words failed her for a moment—so defenseless. And weak. Yet at the same time, she trusted Luella, trusted her like no one from her past—other than perhaps her mother before her father had died. A remembrance of falling off her bike in the driveway washed into her memory. Fighting back tears, she had limped up the walk and into the house, her scraped and bleeding leg burning as though on fire. Her mother came out of the kitchen and squatted down, and she stepped in between the V of her mother's legs and leaned into comforting arms. Upon contact, the hurt abated. Even though she burst into tears then, it had less to do with the pain and more to do with the relief she felt at not bearing her suffering alone.

It occurred to her that the same thing had just happened with Luella. Maybe Marie was right. Maybe she *was* expending too much energy keeping her feelings in check. *Maybe I ought to share my feelings more with others...*but the thought of it made her feel terribly vulnerable. *Practice*, Marie had said. *All you need is practice.*

Her stomach growled. Luella cupped her face in her two soft hands. "You, my dear, are in serious need of a snack. I could hear that from here."

Dez nodded.

Luella pulled a tissue out of her apron pocket and handed it to her, then turned and went to the refrigerator. "Tuna salad okay?"

Dez finished wiping her eyes. "Onions?"

"Nope. Made it like you like it, with celery."

Chapter
Twenty-Five

Jaylynn let out a tired sigh. She wished she had slept better, but she was still running on a dearth of sleep even though she had flown into Sea-Tac three days earlier. The two-hour time change seemed to have thrown her off more than usual. And now she was trying to gut out the long afternoon of shopping with her mother and two little sisters, otherwise known as squirrelly Erin and indecisive Amanda. She and her mother had decided to drive to Target and each take one child for a while, then trade off. Jaylynn and each of her sisters always went in together on a present for the other sister. That way, she could pay the lion's share of the cost, while the girls contributed the few dollars they had. Her two little sisters were blabbermouths, but this year they were both intent on keeping secrets, something that, in past Christmases, had not worked out at all. Jaylynn thought that this might be the first year her younger sisters actually kept quiet.

Right now she stood holding items they had picked out for their parents. She shifted from one foot to the other in the middle of what she called "The Pink Aisle" while Amanda rooted through Barbie dolls and accessories. Everything around them was hot pink and rose-colored, peachy or Pepto-Bismol pink. And the row was absurdly long and packed full of gaudy boxes and packages. At eleven, Amanda was nearing the age where the impossibly endowed dolls would soon lose their appeal, but she was still just young enough to want clothes and shoes and bikes and little cars and houses for her doll horde at home. She had spent the better part of ten minutes fingering everything, despite the fact that Jaylynn had reminded her twice that Erin despised Barbie dolls.

"Look at this, Lynnie!" Amanda said with a sparkle in her

eye. She pointed to a package containing a pair of hot pink Barbie walkie-talkies. "Erin would love these! That's it! This is the perfect present."

Her face was so full of glee that Jaylynn almost didn't have the heart to discourage her, but she reminded her once again that Erin didn't like Barbie gear, much less the color pink. "We have to buy her something she would want, hon." Amanda's face fell and she frowned. "Look, kiddo, I think you're on to something. How about we go to the walkie-talkie department and look there?"

Amanda paused a moment, thinking. Reluctantly, she said, "Okay, where is it?"

"C'mon. We'll check electronics."

In short time, they found a kit that held walkie-talkies as well as a compass and a spy-glass. Amanda's eyes brightened. "She'll like this gray color, I think, don't you?"

Jaylynn nodded. She had already been through this same kind of scene with Erin, who had wanted to buy her sister a karaoke machine because *she* wanted one. Erin could carry a tune—somewhat—but Amanda couldn't. She steered her nine-year-old sister to the art supply department. The passion of Amanda's life—besides Barbie dolls—was drawing. She was quite good at sketching little outfits for paper dolls, and sometimes Jaylynn wondered if Amanda might grow up to be a clothes designer or graphic artist.

So she had talked Erin into getting their sister some high quality colored pencils and paper and a lap easel. They smuggled it out to the trunk of the car before coming back to the store to shop more.

Now that Amanda had made her selection for her younger sister, she and Jaylynn went to the checkout area, with the younger girl's head swiveling all around to keep an eye out for Erin. They made it safely through without being seen, and the walkie-talkies were small enough for Jaylynn to carry in a shopping bag.

Amanda looked up at her. "You're sure she won't be able to tell, right?"

Jaylynn smiled and shook her head. "No, punkin, she'll never know what we've got here. And we'll wrap it right up when we get home. How 'bout we disguise it when we wrap it, so when we put it under the tree, she'll never have a clue?"

"Yeah! Good idea."

They stood near the front, waiting, until their mother, Janet Lindstrom, headed their way. From the distance, her mother gave a toss of her head, so Jaylynn leaned down and said, "Amanda, let's go check out the purses."

"Oh, okay."

She steered the younger girl over through the watch department and to the bags, and they spent a few minutes looking at handbags and purses until Janet and Erin appeared, each carrying a shopping bag.

"My turn," her mother said. "Why don't you go hang out in the snack bar, and I'll take these two off to look for one final present." She met her daughter's eyes over the top of the littler girls' heads and winked.

"I can take this stuff out to the car."

"Good idea."

Next thing she knew, she was loaded down with three bags, which she hauled out to the parking lot and stowed in the trunk. Shivering, she hustled back into the store, avoiding a big sloppy puddle of water in front of the curb. She went to the snack area and bought a Coke, then sat down at the blood-red colored table to wait.

This was not how she had imagined spending her Christmas. After the great time she had had in St. Paul at Thanksgiving with Dez and Luella's clan, she hadn't even been sure if she would return to Seattle to spend the holiday with her family. All along she had assumed that Dez would come with her. And now she had to face the fact that here it was, two days before Christmas, and she was alone. She had already spent time working out elaborate scenes in her mind which entailed the tall woman flying in, unexpectedly, just in time, but she hadn't heard a peep from her. She was unwilling to admit that she was going to spend Christmas without Dez, but a part of her was practical. It had already hurt her heart enough not to be able to reach the tall cop on her birthday, and now she didn't even want to consider how awful she would feel—alone with only her family—on Christmas morning. A wave of sadness and fatigue washed over her, threatening to overwhelm her right in public. She looked around the snack bar, glad that she didn't recognize a single soul, then leaned on the table, head in hands, and closed her eyes to wait for the gleeful shoppers to join her.

****

Later that day, after the girls left for a Christmas party with their neighborhood Brownie friends, Jaylynn sought her mother out. Janet had already wrested most of the details—a few at a time—out of her daughter, but now her daughter was ready to confide her feelings. And confide she did—mostly focusing on how angry she was at the tall cop. Her step-dad wisely gave the family room a wide berth while she stormed and raged, venting her feelings. Her mom listened sympathetically. Once she got the angry words out, Jaylynn sat on the sofa and burst into tears.

In the rocking chair across the room, next to the warm fireplace, Janet took a sip from her cup of tea and smiled to herself. She set the teacup down on the side table, remembering being 25 and in love. Her daughter had been appropriately named: "Jay" after her mercurial father and "Lynn" after her father's sister, who was a wise and loving woman with much patience. Most of the time they called her Lynnie, a holdover to the time when her father, Jay, had been alive, and everyone got confused as to which Jay was being referenced. Jaylynn had many of her Aunt Lynn's good qualities, and she was also a great deal like her father had been: optimistic, lively, energetic, and with passionate emotions. Being with him had been like living through periodic lightning and thunderstorms punctuated by long periods of pleasant weather.

"Why are you laughing at me, Mom?"

She looked over at her daughter's miserable face and bit back her smile. "I'm not laughing at you—just thinking how very much you've turned out like your father."

"Hmph. He spent a lot of time crying?"

"No, but when he loved someone, he loved with all his heart. He fought for what he loved—he was a lover *and* a fighter. You're like that, too." She didn't know how to comfort her daughter, so she chose to ask a question. "What do you think is going to happen, Lynnie?"

Jaylynn kicked her tennis shoes off and angled herself into the back corner of the sofa. Janet watched as her daughter flexed her casted hand, winced, then cradled her wounded arm over her sweatshirted chest. "If I could just *talk* to her—well, I think we could straighten things out. But she doesn't answer the damn phone, and her cell phone and pager don't seem to be on. I don't know where the hell she is!"

Janet nodded as she rocked and watched the torrent of emotions on her daughter's face. "What happens if, for some reason, she withdraws from you permanently?"

She felt bad to see the fresh spate of tears well up in her daughter's eyes. Rising, Janet grabbed a box of tissues from the coffee table and held it out to Jaylynn, then sat down next to her, one hand patting and rubbing her daughter's leg.

Jaylynn wiped her eyes and blew her nose. "I don't want that. She *can't* do that. She promised me before that she would never cut me out of her life again."

"People don't always keep their promises—"

"No, Mom. Dez isn't like that. She keeps her promises." She hesitated, then took another tissue. Her next words came out slowly, as though she didn't want to say them. "I'm worried something is wrong—really wrong."

"Like she might do harm to herself?"

Tears spilled over again, and the young woman seemed to sink into an even smaller, tighter ball in the corner of the couch. She choked out her next words. "Her job is at risk, she thinks I'm gonna get killed on the job, and I sent her away."

"I don't think you're giving Dez enough credit, Lynnie." She thought about what she knew of the taciturn woman she had met the previous April and then again four months before. "Let's see. Her partner was shot on duty, and she's lived through that. She met *you* when Sara was attacked, and she lived through that."

Jaylynn smirked and smacked her mother's arm with the back of her hand. "Very funny."

With an innocent look on her face, Janet said, "I'm just detailing facts."

"Yeah, right."

"Let's see...you and she walked in on that robbery, she got shot, and you killed the man."

"Don't even remind me of that."

"Since then, my dear child, you've been hurt on the job, what? Three times?"

"No, just twice."

Counting off on her fingers, Janet said, "If I remember correctly, we have your wrist, your collarbone, and the trip to the hospital after the fire."

Jaylynn let out a little sputter. "You can't count minor smoke inhalation!"

"Sure I can. As your mother, I'm counting scraped knees, small bruises, and black eyes, too. Mothers count everything."

Jaylynn got a grouchy look on her face and let out a snort, but didn't say anything.

"And I expect lovers do the same." When her daughter didn't say anything, Janet went on. "Honey, Dez has had a real hard year—actually, more than a year. Sometimes love is not enough to help a person through something like that. After everything that has happened to her—to you—I don't blame her for going away to regroup. I think you need to be patient. I think you need to have faith. I know I haven't seen the two of you together since last summer, but there's one thing I do know." She reached over to smooth a shock of blonde hair out of her daughter's eyes. "She's crazy about you. I would be very, very surprised if she didn't come back. I can't even imagine it. I think you're just going to have to be patient, Miss Snappy Turtle."

Jaylynn found herself smiling at the old endearment. Miss Snappy Turtle and Miss Careless Kitty Cat—titles her mother used to give her when she was cranky or when she lost or broke something.

Janet reached over and put an arm around her daughter's shoulders. With a sigh, Jaylynn let herself relax against her mother, glad that she had talked things over with her.

After a moment, the older woman groaned. "The Brownie lunch must be over."

The younger woman looked at her watch. 1:30. "How do you know that?

"They're out front, I'm sure of it. Can't you hear Erin?"

Jaylynn concentrated for a moment, and then she heard what her mother's ears had already picked up—off-key singing—something about God wrestling merry gentlemen.

Janet rose and stretched a hand out to her daughter. "Well, you're the big sister. Are you ready for yet another round of Monopoly? Or would you rather take them to the movies where at least they'll be quiet for two hours?"

"I think we ought to spike their Kool-Aid with sleeping draught." She put an arm around her mother's waist.

"Now, now dear, they just have a lot of energy—and not even as much as you used to."

"Sure, that's what *you* say."

"Tsk-tsk-tsk...everything your mother says is gospel truth."

The two women passed through the kitchen and dining room, out to the foyer and to the front door to look out the window at two scrawny blondes in light brown dresses playing in the front yard. As she listened to Erin's plaintive warble, Jaylynn could only hope that her mother was a true oracle, in the same vein as those old time prophets in the Bible.

Chapter
Twenty-Six

Dez shifted the pile of mail from one hand to the other so she could unlock the door to her apartment. She tucked her keys into her coat pocket, flicked on the kitchen light, and picked up two shopping bags, one of which was bursting with tubes of wrapping paper. Passing through the small kitchen, she dropped the pile of mail on the table, then kept moving into the bigger room beyond where she set the bag on her bed.

After adjusting the thermostat, she headed back outside to her truck, and hauled in two more bags filled with groceries. Locking the kitchen door behind her, she took off her coat, and spent a few minutes putting food away in the cupboards and refrigerator. There was a fine layer of dust on the counter and table, so she got out a washrag and ran it over the various surfaces, making a mental note to dust the furniture in the other room in the morning.

Once the kitchen was tidied up, she moved into the other room, turned on the light over her roll top desk, and sat in her desk chair. She shuffled envelopes and bank statements aside and pulled out her bank savings book, opened it, and checked the balance.

More than enough. She shut the small book and left it on the desk surface, then sat back in the chair. It was the night before Christmas Eve, and she had several things to get ready before tomorrow. She checked her watch. It was already ten p.m., but she had plenty of time ahead of her.

She spent the next half-hour wrapping presents. After a while, she got thirsty and went to the kitchen for water. It was then that she glanced at the mail on the table and saw the over-sized envelope with her mother's writing on it. The card was thick and the paper a rich off-white color. She riffled through the pile of circulars, ads, and bills, and pulled out all the cards. She took them to her desk where she slit them open with a letter opener, then sat down to look at them. She remembered she hadn't gotten anything to drink and went back to the kitchen for ice water, then returned and resumed her examination of the Christmas cards.

The first was from Crystal and Shayna and contained a note inviting her to drop by any time Christmas day. The second was from her dentist's office, wishing her well, and urging her to brush regularly, especially through the sugary holiday season. She tossed it into the wastebasket.

The third was from Cowboy. His note read: "Haven't seen you around lately, Half Pint. Hope you have a good Christmas. Let's get together when you get things squared away. C." *That was nice of him to send me a card.* She hadn't expected it.

She straightened up in the chair when she saw the writing on the next envelope. She pulled the card out in haste to find it was not a Christmas card, but a regular note card. The picture on the outside was of a shimmery lake, evergreen trees on one side, and birds flying in the sky beneath fluffy clouds. Inside, it read:

> Dear Dez,
> I've been missing you terribly.
> Please let me know you are all right.
> Love,
> Jaylynn

She sat back in the chair, still holding the card. There was no date on it, but the envelope was postmarked eight days earlier from St. Paul. *She must have mailed this before she left for Seattle.* Dez brought the card up to her face and breathed in. There it was—the faintest whiff of something distinctive, a scent of Jaylynn. She inhaled again, but it was gone. Maybe it had been her imagination.

She laid the card on her desk and picked up the final envelope. As she tugged the thick packet out, she wondered why her mother had sent her something. Usually Colette Reilly called her daughter sometime on Christmas morning and wished her a brief "Merry Christmas," and that was it. She turned over the packet and for a moment sat stunned when the impact of the contents fully hit her.

Two shiny blue swans floating on water were embossed on the top part of the creamy bond paper. Below, in dark blue script, she read, *Colette Marie Lavelle Reilly and Xavier Aloysius Mac-*

Arthur request the honor of your presence at their wedding on the Fourteenth of February, 2002...

She got no further. *My mother marrying Mac? Marrying? Like a wedding and everything?* A full minute, maybe more, passed as she tried to get accustomed to the idea. At the end of the summer, she and Jaylynn had talked about Mac and her mother's relationship. At that time, Jaylynn had assured the disbelieving cop that they were a couple. As evidence, she had spoken of body language and small gestures she had noticed when Colette and Mac visited Dez at the hospital after she had taken a bullet in the vest. Dez hadn't been entirely convinced then, but now... *Damn! Jaylynn was right. I think I owe her bet money!*

The longer she thought about it and the more the surprise wore off, the better she felt about this news. Why shouldn't her mother and her mentor be happy? Who was she to say that they shouldn't marry?

She opened the card and a piece of translucent tissue paper fell out along with maps to the church site and to the reception hall. Shaking her head, she found herself wondering why wedding invitations always carried that stupid piece of flimsy tissue. *Jaylynn would probably know. Or maybe Emily Post or Miss Manners could shed light on that.* She had no clue. She crumpled it up and tossed it into the trash, then separated another envelope from the packet. This pre-stamped envelope was addressed to her mother and contained a gold *RSVP* card. On impulse, Dez picked up a pen, wrote her name on the guest line and scrawled a "2" where it asked for the number of guests. She licked the flap and sealed the envelope, then rose and grabbed her coat. Without giving it another thought, she clattered down the stairs to the outer door, strode to her truck, and got in, tossing the card on the seat beside her.

The truck engine roared to life. On the way to her mother's house, she had time to think about writing a "2" on the response card. She hoped Jaylynn would go with her. The wedding was seven weeks away, and surely that was enough time to work things out with the younger woman. She hoped so.

When she arrived at the three-story house, she found it dark. Houses on either side had Christmas lights blinking, but her mother had never been much for the multicolored lights, so the house was unadorned. Dez wheeled over to the curb and got out, leaving the truck running. She moved up the walkway, watching her step along the cement, which was eerily illuminated by the neighbors' white, yellow, green, and red blinking lights. The mailbox was at the foot of the stairs. She opened it, tossed in the card, shut the mailbox door quietly, and walked back to her truck feeling a sense of peace.

As she drove the three miles back to her house, she realized that she had one more shopping foray to make in the morning. She didn't relish the thought of going out to the store on the morning of Christmas Eve, but she figured if she went early enough, it might not be so bad.

She returned home, finished up her wrapping and labeling, and then sat down on the couch with her guitar. She held it gently, then stroked the strings with her thumb. Cocking her head to the side, she plucked the low E string, which she decided was a little flat. She twisted the tuning peg until she got the tone just so, then moved on to the next strings. Finally, she strummed it again, adjusted the high E, and was satisfied.

The last few days she had missed her guitar. She hadn't played it much in the last two months, but she had brought it back from the cabin with her. When she had felt her lowest, there was no way she could play it, but lately, it hadn't been so mournful. She still had a song in her head, a melody she'd been working on every so often for nearly as long as she had known Jaylynn. Lately, while out hiking or driving in the car, words and phrases had come to mind, and now she thought she had the beginning of the lyrics to go with the melody and guitar parts. She picked out the opening melody, then hit a G chord and riffed through all the chords. She loved the sound of C and F major chords, but she wasn't sure they fit in the scheme of the song. She started over again, playing the opening melody, and then settled into the first verse.

What are we gonna do
Is it all worth losing if we see it through
You look to me and I don't have a clue
If I could tear away, I'd run.
Lately, looking into your eyes
I'm finally starting to realize
All I really am is terrified
If I could give you up, I'd run

She kept playing, but she stopped singing. A little smile played at the corners of her mouth. *Ha. If I could give her up—yeah, right. I might have run away for a while, but I know I can't give her up. I hope I can make it right—make her understand...* That familiar ache behind her breastbone spread, and for a moment she felt she might cry. But she didn't. She sang the second verse and the bridge instead.

> *Fire's burning inside me now*
> *My heart is screaming without a sound*
> *Your love has brought me down to my knees*
> *There's no way to run.*
> *Lately looking into your eyes*
> *I'm finally starting to realize*
> *All I really am is terrified*
> *If I could let you go, I'd run*
>
> *Don't let them get inside*
> *They'll only leave you cold*
> *Never trust too far*
> *Never give your soul*
> *I learned long ago*
> *It's dangerous to feel*
> *Always hide your heart*
> *Love is never real*
> *Love is never real*

She thought that Marie would be proud of her for admitting those feelings. After the many disappointments in her life, Ryan being killed, the untrue lovers, the death of her father, her mother's failing her—well, she didn't even like to think about any of it. But she *was* thinking about it now, and in ways she had never done before. For once in her life, she was starting to think that maybe there was hope after all. It had been a long time since she had felt that way.

She picked an arpeggio and decided it didn't make for a good bridge back to the end verses. She backed up and sang the bridge one more time, then strummed into the next part.

> *Tear down all the walls I've built so high*
> *Hold me close until you make me cry*
> *If I could only make you mine tonight*
> *Think I'd leave my world behind*
>
> *Make me think it's gonna be all right*
> *Keep me safe so there's no need to hide*
> *I see myself almost taking flight*
> *If I can trust myself I'll run*
> *Straight into your arms*
> *Straight into your arms*

She liked it. The song expressed her feelings, though she didn't think the song was anything too striking. Someday, maybe she'd even sing the song for Jaylynn. She hoped she would get the opportunity.

Chapter
Twenty-Seven

Dez rose late the next morning after a night of tossing and turning. It always seemed that the first few hours she tried to sleep were hellish, but after a while, she was so exhausted that she would finally drop off into a deep sleep punctuated by nightmares. The dreams she remembered were variations on the same thing: she found someone she loved—usually Ryan or Jaylynn—lying dead, and there was nothing she could do to revive them. With reluctance, she decided that at some point, she was going to need to discuss the dreams, in detail, with Marie.

Dressed only in briefs and a tight t-shirt, she headed across the room to the bathroom and looked out the window. Fluffy flakes of snow drifted from the heavens to land in a still world. Dez could see no evidence of any wind at all, and the neighborhood was quiet, as though everyone in it were still asleep. The trees were coated with a blanket of white stuff. She estimated that six or seven inches had fallen overnight. *Gonna be a lot of fun shopping today,* she thought. But she only had one store to go to and a quick stop at the bank. Even though the streets had not been plowed yet, she knew she could get around with the truck in four-wheel drive.

She turned on the water in the tub and slipped out of her t-shirt and briefs. She checked the water temperature, and stepped in to take a shower. She let the warm water run over her for a long while. She was surprised that she wasn't more fatigued, but she felt alive and awake this morning. So alive, in fact, that she decided to eat breakfast, run her two errands, then go to the station to work out in the gym. *One thing nice about being a police officer—the workplace is never closed, no matter what.*

In less than an hour, dressed in sweats, workout clothes, and a heavy coat and boots, she was out the door, a gym bag in hand. She descended the stairs, pausing at the bottom to look toward Luella's place. Nobody home. Dez knew her landlady was spending most of her time at Vanita's. Still, she wished she were there right now.

The visits to the department store and the bank took about an hour. She left her purchase in the truck, locked up, and went into the station. As she expected, eleven a.m. on Christmas Eve was not a busy time. One lone dispatcher sat in her office, drinking coffee and looking cranky. Dez passed by, with little more than a glance and headed for the stairs. She was two steps down when she heard footfalls behind her.

"Reilly! That you?"

She stopped and turned, one hand on the banister. "Yes, sir." She felt her face begin to flush, but she stood her ground.

Commander Paar, dressed in civvies, strode toward her, a half-smile on his face. He had obviously gotten a hair cut recently. His silvering hair was cut close to his head, and the little bit of sideburns were trimmed and shaped. As he reached her, he held out a hand. "How you doing, Reilly?"

"Fine, sir. Much better." She clasped his warm hand, then let it go. He was a trim, compact man. Standing two stairs down put him only half a head taller than she. She shifted on the second stair and leaned a hip into the banister.

"I hear you're back in business here pretty quick." She nodded, waiting. "I'm glad. You know, Reilly, I knew your father pretty well. He was a good cop. So are you. He'd be proud of you."

She felt a big lump in her throat and didn't think she could speak, but when she did, it sounded normal to her ears. "Thanks. That means a lot."

The commander smiled and gestured toward her gym bag. "You here to work out?"

"Yes, sir."

"That's great. I'm always happy to see my officers staying in shape. Some of your peers don't take it seriously enough." He looked at his gold watch. "Geez! Already after eleven. I better get on the stick. I hope you have a real nice holiday, Reilly." He reached out again and took her right hand, then smacked her right shoulder with his other hand. "Glad you're doing so well."

"Thanks. You have a nice Christmas, too, sir."

With a final smile, the commander went off down the hall toward his office, and Dez descended the stairs slowly. She hoped no one was in the gym, though that meant she wouldn't have a spotter. She didn't intend to do anything heavy anyway. Though she had been lifting heavy at the gym in Duluth, today she just wanted to do a light bench routine and work her shoulders.

Turning the corner into the gym, she was happy to see her wish granted. The place was empty. The basement room smelled like pine, and looking around, she could see the janitorial crew had given it a good cleaning. The dust that usually gathered along the edges of the room had been swept away, and the cement floor looked freshly washed.

She went to the one lone piece of cardio equipment, a Stairmaster, and dropped her bag, then slipped off her coat and hung it from one of the hooks in the nearby power rack. After kicking off her boots, she rooted around in the gym bag and pulled out Adidas shoes. She laced up and tied the shoes, all the while looking around the room. A lot of the weights and equipment in the room had been purchased over the years by the officers, but much of it had been donated by Ryan. He'd been a bodybuilder and won a number of local competitions. Since he had died, she had never had as good a workout partner as he had been. Though she enjoyed working out with Jaylynn and Crystal, with Ryan it had been like magic. He had been much stronger in the upper body, but her legs were nearly as strong. He challenged her, pushed her, and egged her on in ways no one else could. And he knew just how far to provoke her, too, in such a way that they often ended up laughing as they competed for reps. Working out with him had spurred her on to lift more weight than she ever imagined would be possible.

She got up on the Stairmaster and spent ten minutes warming up, then stepped off to stretch her legs. In the weeks since she was put on leave, she had slimmed down a few pounds, and though she still felt a little awkward, she could tell her body was settling back into a comfortable zone. It was quite a difference to look at the bodybuilding pictures from last August where every muscle, every sinew was apparent. Now she thought she looked blocky. Big. Clunky.

She did some arm stretches and neck rolls, then loaded the bar with 45's on each side and settled on the bench on her back, ready to do a slow, steady warm-up at 135 pounds. The weight felt good, and the muscles in her chest and shoulders felt strong. As she added more plates, her spirits rose as they usually did when she lifted.

After an hour of bench presses, incline press, dumbbell shoulder presses, and lateral lifts for her deltoids, she called it quits. Her chest and shoulders were pleasantly fatigued. She gathered up her stuff and headed to the locker room to get cleaned up.

She emerged half an hour later in jeans, boots, and a black sweatshirt over a flannel shirt. She thought she might be a little over-warm, but she only had a short distance to go back to her place. She headed home and carried her purchase into the apartment.

Dez spent the early afternoon doing laundry, wrapping the last present, eating two small meals, listening to holiday music on the radio, and making out Christmas cards that she knew would be late. She actually felt at peace, though her thoughts went often to Jaylynn, and she knew how much she missed her.

At three p.m., she put away the tape and scissors and leftover cards. *Well, that's that. Everything I needed to do is done. Time to take some more baby steps.* With her heart racing, she picked up the phone and dialed the first of two phone numbers that she knew by heart but had been avoiding calling. Julie answered on the second ring, sounding rushed. "Merry Christmas, Mrs. Michaelson."

"Dez? Oh, it is *so* good to hear your voice! How are you? Where are you? What are you doing—"

"Whoa. Slow down." In the background she could hear excited voices, and Julie paused a moment and told them to calm down.

"Dez, as you can tell, the kids are asking if you are coming over."

"That's exactly why I was calling. You got some time in the next day or so?"

"We've got time right now—or else any time tomorrow. And you could come tonight for supper at seven if you like. It'll be a crowd, though, with family..."

"If you have a little time this afternoon, I would love to drop over for a bit now—that is, if you don't mind."

"We've just been getting things ready around the house. C'mon over."

Dez agreed and hung up, then picked the phone back up and sat holding the receiver in her hand. *Okay, you can do this. Just a small step. Things went fine with Julie, so if this doesn't go right, well, then one out of two isn't bad.* She punched in the numbers and waited through four rings. Just when she thought no one would answer, a woman's voice answered the phone.

Dez swallowed. "Hello?"

"Yes, hello?"

"Is Colette there?"

"Sure, just a minute."

There was a pause, and Dez had time to wonder whose voice that had been before her mother got on the line.

"Hi, Mom. Merry Christmas."

"Desiree! How are you?"

"Good. I'm good."

"I got your reply. Thank you. Mac and I are both very pleased that you are coming. I'll have a little shower type party in late January, if you want to come."

Dez smiled. "Actually, that's sort of why I was calling. I have a gift to give you, but you know me—I hate those shower things. I was wondering if I could drop it by?"

"Today?"

Dez's heart sank. It didn't sound like her mother would want her to stop off with the present today. She took a deep breath, steeling herself for disappointment, and in a flat voice said, "No, that's okay. I'm sure you're busy—"

"No! We're not! We're just sitting around drinking eggnog and waiting for the ham to bake. Please come whenever you want. You can stay for dinner."

A warm feeling started at the base of her spine and spread upward, and she found herself grinning in relief. "What time are you eating?"

"Oh, around six-ish."

"I'm stopping by to see Ryan's kids, then I'll come over, all right?"

"Yes, that would be wonderful. See you in a bit."

After they hung up, Dez continued sitting at her desk feeling dazed. She was two for two for the day—three for three if she counted the commander—and she could hardly believe it. After a few moments, she drew in a deep breath and stood. It was already half past two. Time to get rolling.

****

At five-thirty, Dez got in her truck, feeling pleased that the visit with Jill and Jeremy had gone so well. She rolled down the Ford window and waved toward the house, where the boy and girl stood in the front window, smiling and waving back. Jeremy had liked the Pokémon cards and the snowshoes. He had wanted to put them on and run right out into the falling snow, no coat, no hat. Julie had restrained him, and Dez promised to take him out when she had her snowshoes with her. Jill's eyes had shone when she opened *The Illustrated Wizard of Oz* book. Dez knew it was her favorite movie, and she thought Jill would like reading the book. She had also purchased a gift certificate for four horseback riding lessons for her. As far as Dez could tell, both kids were thrilled with the gifts, but neither had wanted her to leave. Jeremy had almost started crying, so she had made yet another promise: to come back and play after their Christmas vacation when she had more time.

Now she pulled away from their house, chuckling over the gifts they had given her. Six-year-old Jeremy had made a jewelry box out of tongue depressors and popsicle sticks which was held together by at least half a bottle of glue. He had used felt markers to stain the sticks various bright colors, and he was clearly very proud of his creation. Upon opening the present, Dez and Julie had met one another's eyes and shared the same look that said, *We know we can't laugh, but this is pretty damn funny.* He had obviously gone to a lot of work, and Dez told him so. He turned pink with happiness.

Jill made her a little book about four by six inches square. The cover was pale blue and showed a picture of two police officers, one with long black hair and the other with a scrubby blond flat-top. There were pictures drawn throughout the twenty or so pages of two kids and a mom and dad and the same black haired tall person that Dez knew was herself. The drawings were detailed, containing houses and cars, street signs, horses, and dogs in the backgrounds. Considering Jill was only eight years old, Dez thought the pictures were very well done, and she praised Jill so much that the little girl got embarrassed and hid her face.

She turned at the corner and didn't look back at the house. She had to admit that it was still—even after eighteen months— hard to spend time there. The ghost of Ryan lived on, and she expected that at any moment, he would come walking out of the den, a mischievous look on his face, and invite her to come out to the garage to work on some project with him. Tears sprang to her eyes. She didn't think she would ever stop missing him, ever stop feeling the loss.

She turned off Lexington Parkway onto Laurel Avenue and headed toward her mother's house. Parked cars buried in snow lined both sides of the street. The streets were thick with snow, and if the plows didn't come soon, this latest snowfall was going to get packed down into ruts that would make life difficult for everyone, not to mention for any emergency vehicles that might need to get through. She reached the house, but there were no parking spots anywhere nearby. Frustrated, she went up to the corner and turned around, then circled back to the previous block where she had seen some space.

The tall woman opened the cab door and took a dark gray bag and a pair of tennis shoes from behind her seat, then slogged through the snow, glad she was wearing Sorel boots. As she drew closer to the house, she thought that maybe she had bitten off more than she could chew. She hated not knowing what to expect. Like a good soldier, she marched forward until she reached the brightly lit house. With the porch illuminated, she could see there was a cheery wreath with a big red bow on it hanging on the front door, something that hadn't been apparent when she had dropped off the RSVP card the night before. She mounted the stairs, but before she could knock, it opened and Mac stood there smiling.

Mac and her father had always borne a resemblance to one another, though Michael Reilly had been much taller. Both men had had black hair, blue eyes, and the pale complexions for which the Irish are often noted. Sometimes when she used to think of her father, she confused his face with Mac's. But Mac was old enough now that his face was distinct from her father's. His hair was silver—going white in some places. Wrinkles surrounded his bright blue eyes. He was a little stockier than when she had last seen him. She stepped toward the doorway, and he clapped an arm on her shoulder and drew her into the toasty house, patting her on the back.

"Dez, it's great to see you. Merry Christmas." His voice was cordial and warm. He took the bag from her hand and set it on a table inside the door, allowing her to slip her coat off. She smiled at him and looked from the foyer out into the living room. Colette Reilly had risen and was moving across the room toward them, her face aglow.

The tall woman hung her coat on the hooks next to the door and stepped out of her boots. By then her mother arrived, and, surprising her daughter completely, wrapped her in a brief but fierce hug. "I am so glad you're here."

"Me, too." Dez looked over her shoulder into the living room where her brother Patrick sat—next to a beautiful brunette woman. Patrick met her eyes, his face a passive mask. *Ah, so that's how it is. He's still mad at me from the past. Well, if I can let go of our differences, then he can, too.* Suddenly she felt a little mischievous. *I'll show him how dumb that is.* She grinned and shifted her glance to the woman seated next to him. She didn't even have time to wonder who the woman was before Colette said, "Come in and meet Monique."

Dez slipped on her tennis shoes and bent to tie them, then stood and moved into the living room. Patrick and Monique got up off the couch, and the five adults stood in a circle around the coffee table. Patrick shifted toward the short brunette and took her hand. Dez looked from one to the other, and before her mother said a word, she knew this young woman was likely to be her sister-in-law sometime in the near future. She wondered if she'd like her.

Colette sidled next to the young woman, one arm circling her waist. "Dez, this is my soon-to-be daughter-in-law, Monique Mellingham. Monique, meet Patrick's sister, Desiree."

Dez found herself smiling, in fact, nearly laughing. She stepped forward until she felt the edge of the coffee table against her shins, and reached out her hand. Patrick had to let go of his fiancée so that she could reach over and shake hands with the tall cop. "I am very glad to meet you, Monique. Welcome to the family." She released the woman's hand and looked up to find her brother peering at her suspiciously. She glanced back at the tiny woman at Patrick's side. She wore black stretch pants, pink slippers, and a red sweater covered with green Christmas trees decorated with shiny silver ornaments.

"Thank you. I am glad to finally meet you, Dez. I've heard—well, a little about you."

"Don't believe most of it, Monique, especially if it came from my dear sweet brother." She looked over at Patrick who gazed back at her, confusion on his face.

"Gosh," Monique said, "you Reillys are tall people. I had no idea my sister-in-law would *tower* over me like Patrick does."

She said it in such a droll tone that Dez laughed out loud. It reminded her of the sort of observation Jaylynn would make. "My little brother had a heck of a time catching up to me, but once he did, he got me by a good four inches." In a conspiratorial voice, she said, "I think I can still pin him though."

Patrick's mouth dropped open. "Wha—wha—I don't *think* so!"

Dez laughed and glanced over her shoulder, finding a wing back chair. She moved over and lowered herself into it, letting out a sigh. Her mother did the same, settling into the matching wing back.

Mac interrupted. "Dez, you want something to drink?"

"Sure. What've you got?"

Mac listed out several selections, and she settled on a glass of red wine.

Patrick sat back down on to the couch, pulling Monique down next to him. "I didn't think you drank."

Really, this was quite fun. Her brother was off balance. His fiancée seemed very nice. Mac was happy, and her mother was beaming. She decided she was actually enjoying herself after all.

"I don't—not much anyway. But a glass of wine now and then is kind of nice."

"My sentiments exactly," Monique said. She pulled her slippered feet up under her and curled into a comfortable lean against Patrick.

Dez watched as her brother got a goofy, love-struck look on his face, and it made her happy. She knew just how he felt. "How did you two meet?"

Patrick looked uncomfortable as his fiancée poured out the tale of them meeting at work. She talked about how she had pursued her shy guy, causing the dark-haired man to blush a little. Dez looked at her brother. At his next birthday, he would turn twenty-six. His face was clear and unlined, his hair as black as hers. When she looked into his blue eyes, she saw a mirror of her own. She wondered if their nearly seven years of separation had changed him much. She hoped not. Other than being obstinate and opinionated—common Reilly traits—he had always been good-hearted. They had been close as children. Was it possible that they could rebuild their torn relationship and be close again as adults? She thought the answer was yes. She had nothing to lose by trying.

Colette served dinner a short while later, and Dez enjoyed the food. The ham was sweet and moist, and the baked potatoes and asparagus were cooked perfectly. She also enjoyed the conversation. Mac asked a lot of questions about the job, and she summoned up her courage to admit that she was on leave and dealing with what she called the "emotional fallout" of having two partners injured in a row. Mac seemed to already know some of this and didn't ask prying questions, for which she was grateful.

He nodded politely and said, "You're smart to do that, Dez. Some cops never do, and they become insufferable to work with." Then he changed the subject and asked about various officers they both knew. Soon Monique chimed in with a question about all the articles in the paper about racial profiling, and Mac, Monique, and Dez carried on a spirited conversation. Dez was aware that her mother and brother were watching, surprised, as all of this unfolded, but she was on a roll and feeling good. She wasn't going to do her hermit crab routine, no matter how much they might expect it.

After supper, Dez rose and began to clear the table. Her mother picked up a plate and stacked it on top of another. "You don't have to do this, Desiree."

"It's okay, Mom. I really don't mind. That lazy oaf brother

of mine can help me. You did all the prep work, so we can clean up, just like the old days." She smiled at Patrick.

Patrick sighed. "All right. I'll help."

"You better not wash. You never get all the crud off. I'll wash. You can wipe the dishes."

Exasperated, he said, "Dez! I haven't spent any time with you in seven years! How the hell do you know that I don't wash dishes well?"

She grinned. "Okay, fine. Go ahead. You can wash."

She picked up two glasses and a plate, leaving him to let that sink in. Behind her she heard him say, "Well, I'll be damned. She always hated washing..."

"I think you've been had, honey," Monique said.

Dez laughed out loud on the way into the kitchen. Really, things were going to be all right. She just knew it.

****

They were all sitting around the living room, still talking, and it was nearing ten p.m. when Dez finally said that she thought she better head home. She stood up and stretched, then caught sight of the dark gray bag on the table in the foyer. "Oh, shoot! I forgot all about the present."

She strode out and picked up the bag, then brought it to her mother. Mac stood up from his chair and came to stand behind the wing back chair Colette was curled up in.

Dez felt awkward for the first time since she had initially stepped foot in the door. She backed up and sat on the edge of her chair, her elbows on her knees and one fist tucked tightly into her other hand under her chin. She watched as her mother pulled the box out of the bag and removed the wrapping paper with gentle hands. She pulled the two halves of the box apart and sat staring at the crystal in her hands.

"Oh, Dez...where did you...how did you know?"

Tear-filled blue eyes met her own, and Dez knew she had guessed correctly. "I saw the swans embossed on your invitation, and I remembered seeing something like that at the crystal store— so I went back and got it for you."

"It's beautiful." She pulled the crystal swans out carefully and rose.

By then Monique was up and checking it out. "Wow. This *is* really cool, Dez. I love crystal."

"I'll remember that." She smiled at the younger woman as her brother leaned over their mother to look more closely at the swans.

"Geez, Dez," he said. "Must've cost you an arm and a leg."

"Nah, just a toe or two." She stood up and watched as her mother crossed the room and moved a candleholder aside and placed the figurine on the mantel.

Then Colette turned and gave her daughter a big hug. "I don't know what to say."

Dez felt the lump forming in her throat. In a gruff voice, she said, "That's okay. I just wanted to give you something special— something to let you know that I'm really happy for you two."

Her mother gave her a final squeeze, and then Mac hugged her, too. When she glanced over at Patrick, he sat on the couch with Monique next to him, and she thought he looked pleased.

"Well, folks, guess I'd better go now." She walked the few steps to the foyer and put on her boots and coat. There were hugs all around, even from Patrick, and when she started to shake Monique's hand, the small woman wrapped strong arms around her waist. Dez patted her on the back awkwardly.

"I am so glad to meet you finally, Dez, and I expect to have lots of fun times with you."

The tall woman suppressed laughter. "I can see the whole family is going to have fun times with you, Monique."

She wished them all good night and Merry Christmas, then tucked her shoes under one arm and paused on the front porch to zip up her coat. The tennis shoes, warm in her bare hands, grew cold quickly. It was windy, and the cold air chilled her hands. *Should've brought my gloves. I bet it's less than ten degrees.* Reaching the end of the walk, she looked back. Her mother stood in the doorway. The silver-haired woman gave a little wave, then closed the door, and Dez turned onto the sidewalk and trudged down to her truck. Despite the cold, she felt warm inside. As far as she was concerned, this was far more than a baby step. The events of the day could be classified, easily, as great big, giant steps.

She climbed into her truck and drove off, looking forward to the passing of the next 24 hours until she could address her next great big, giant step.

Chapter
Twenty-Eight

It had taken some doing, but Dez convinced Tim to allow her to meet Jaylynn's plane on Christmas night. When she had called over to the house, she wanted to talk to Sara, thinking the rookie's best friend might be more receptive to helping her, but she was dismayed to learn that Sara and Bill were celebrating Christmas at Bill's folks' house in Michigan. So she was stuck with having to persuade the red-haired man.

"I don't know," he had said. "I just don't know what she'd want."

She gripped the phone in her hand and spoke with as much calmness as she could muster. "C'mon, Tim. I'm asking you to trust my judgment, to just trust me."

"I'll go out there with you then, Dez. She expects me."

Dez shut her eyes tight and shook her head, glad he couldn't see her expression. "I need some time alone with her. Just give me a chance, Tim. Please." She was not used to pleading, and she wasn't willing to humiliate herself completely by begging outright.

"What if she doesn't want to talk to you?"

Dez sighed. "I'll put her in a cab and pay for it to deliver her right to your house—no questions asked, no strings attached."

After pondering a moment, Tim told her the exact time and flight Jaylynn was due to arrive on. Then she had to hold on for another two minutes while he went on and on about how she should be extra cautious of Jaylynn's feelings. She assured him she would be a perfect gentlewoman.

And now, here she was at the Minneapolis airport, pacing nervously on the gray carpet. The place was a madhouse with people crammed in all the waiting areas, little kids running down

the concourses, and harried adults carrying bulky bags and dragging suitcases behind. Every gate at the Northwest hub seemed to
be standing-room-only. That was okay with Dez. She didn't want
to sit anyway.

She looked at her watch. 9:45. According to the arrival
board, touchdown was due, on time, at 10:02. She stepped aside
as a heavyset woman, followed by a horde of kids, pushed past
with a cart that was loaded down with two oversized suitcases and
a pile of kids' pink and blue and yellow backpacks. She closed her
eyes, wishing she had earphones or earplugs. The din was giving
her a headache.

****

The plane began its descent, and Jaylynn could feel the
change in pressure as her ears popped. She sat next to the window, gazing down at the lights in the speckled landscape below.
The specks were mostly buildings, all of which were surrounded
by glaring white snow and ice, which reflected quite a lot of light
back up even in the late evening.

For once she was glad to be small and slender. The man in
the middle seat was tall—over six-six—and broad-shouldered,
causing the plump woman on the aisle seat much discomfort. She
thought that Dez would have hated this flight. Jaylynn was able
to lean against the wall of the plane and still be somewhat comfortable.

She picked up the adventure paperback in her lap, stuck a
bookmark in it, and tucked it into the bag under her seat, then
turned back to the scene below. She could see the twisty path of
the Mississippi and Minnesota rivers, as well as the dark outline of
skyscrapers and city buildings in the distance. She was back to
her home away from home, and all she felt was a gnawing ache.

Her sisters, especially Erin, had been mad at her for not
bringing Dez along. It was all she could do to hold it together
every time Erin or Amanda mentioned the tall woman who they
called "Our Hero." How could she explain to them what was
going on when she didn't even know herself? It has been twenty-
three days, and never a word from her ex-FTO. She had hoped—
even prayed—that Dez would call her at her parents' house.
Every time the phone rang, her heart skipped a beat, and she
found herself waiting, breathless. But it was never Dez. And for
all the times that she had tried to call the apartment, the phone
had continued to go unanswered.

What if it's over for good? It was hard for her to believe that could be true—she didn't want to believe it. *But what if that's the case?* Sara had told her once that she was self-sufficient and she'd be just fine on her own, but now she wasn't so sure. What a wreck she'd been for weeks now, irritable, lonely, crying at the drop of a hat. *Some self-sufficient person I turned out to be.*

Her eyes filled with tears, and she was glad to be looking away from the other passengers and out the little porthole into the snowy night. *I shouldn't have been so harsh with her.* She'd told herself that a hundred times. *I should never have lost my temper. It's all my fault.* She gritted her teeth and frowned. *But dammit! She did ask for it.* Jaylynn closed her eyes and drew a long, deep breath. The swing from one set of emotions to another was draining. She wished she could stick with one feeling—anger or grief or just general sadness—but instead, she felt like she was continually ping-ponging back and forth. She let out a deep sigh and opened her eyes.

Watching as the lights on the ground grew closer, after a time she could make out roads and see the headlights of cars and trucks so small that they looked like miniature toys. The plane banked slightly and flew over a narrow river, which was so crusted over with ice that from above, it looked like aluminum foil. She took a deep breath. Though she couldn't see it, she knew the airport was now close. This was the part that always bothered her the most. Hadn't she read somewhere that eighty percent of all crashes take place at landing or take-off? Or maybe it was ninety percent. Her heart beat faster in her chest as she watched the ground grow closer. The pitch of the engines whined higher and louder as she clutched the arm of the seat with her one good hand, her cast pressed against her chest. Suddenly she felt the thump of the landing gear hitting the tarmac and the squealing shriek of the engines. The plane's rapid deceleration pushed her back against her seat.

She was home.

****

Dez was overly warm, but with the pack of people at the gate, there was nowhere to put her coat. She was sorry she had worn a long-sleeved flannel shirt over her t-shirt and under her down coat, but it was, after all, only three degrees outside. With the wind-chill, she figured it was closer to ten or fifteen below zero. The truck had never warmed up during the ride from St. Paul to the airport, so she had been glad for the extra layer. Until now.

She checked her watch again. 10:05. For the last six minutes, the sign up by the Northwest counter had been flashing ARRIVED over and over next to the display that read *Flight 796-Seattle*. Still no plane at Gate 62 though.

Her hands felt cold and stiff. And moist. Everywhere else on her body she was roasting, but her hands were frozen blocks. She paced out along the concourse all the way down to gate 58 and back. Some of the crowd thinned when flights from Philadelphia and Houston had come in a bit ago, so there were a few less people to dodge.

A flash of white in the darkness outside caught her eye, and she turned to see the red-nosed plane meandering toward gate 62. Threading her way through people and chairs and haphazardly placed baggage, she went to the window where she watched the airport personnel get ready to bring the plane in.

She shut her eyes. *Okay, this is it. I can do this. I'm gonna be okay.* She started to count the small windows on the side of the plane. Under the bright artificial lights shining outside in the night, each window was dark as a chip of obsidian, and she couldn't see in. She wondered if they could see her, and she backed away abruptly, feeling vulnerable.

Oh boy. She ran a cold, nervous hand through her dark hair, then tucked her hands into her jeans pockets, hoping she could warm them up.

****

The plane jolted to a halt, and everyone around Jaylynn leapt to their feet. She didn't know why they bothered. She figured the aisle was all of a foot wide. *Well, maybe two feet.* It wasn't like anyone could stroll on up and out. Nobody was going anywhere until the people ahead of them moved along. She was in the middle of the plane, so she knew there were nearly a hundred people to disembark before she should even bother to get up.

The hulk of a man in the middle seat next to her had risen, and now he stood, bent over, not able to stand at his full height due to the low ceiling above the seats. She sighed and looked back out the window to watch the baggage handlers maneuver a flatbed truck toward the plane.

It was ten more minutes before enough of the people ahead of her cleared out. She picked up the canvas bag from under her seat, stood, and reached into the overhead compartment to grab her down coat. *God, I hope it's not too cold. I should have checked the weather before I left.*

She dragged along behind the rest of the passengers, pausing, shuffling, pausing again as though she were in a chain gang. Stepping out of the plane, she felt a shock of cold air from the cracks between the fuselage and the boot attached to the walkway that led into the airport. After the fifty-degree weather in Seattle, she had a hunch Minnesota was going to come as a shock to her system. If she saw a wide spot in the walkway, she thought she might want to stop and pull her coat on.

Shivering, she hustled after the hulking man ahead of her. The further she moved up the walkway, the more warmth she felt wafting her way. *Ooh, that's much better.* Her coat stayed over her casted arm, the canvas bag in the other hand.

As she passed through the doorway, her eyes swept the busy waiting area, searching for a shock of red hair. She saw two red-headed women seated and reading, but no thin, red-haired man. Following the crowd, she continued forward, allowing her eyes to sweep left to right. She caught sight of a figure out across the concourse leaning against a white supporting post, and her eyes jerked back.

Jaylynn stepped next to a railing out of the flow of passengers. She didn't feel the traveling bag she was holding when it hit the ground and bumped against her leg. *Dez. It's Dez.* When she realized her legs were shaking, Jaylynn reached out and grasped the metal railing. Her coat slipped off her arm. She met the tall woman's gaze, but then her own eyes filled with tears, and she couldn't see anything clearly any more.

Dez stepped away from the post she was leaning against, her heart pounding. She saw the small blonde stumble out of line and lean into the side railing. It was now or never.

She strode across the concourse, squeezed her way through the passengers flowing toward her, and came to stand before the smaller woman. "Jaylynn?"

The shorter woman tipped her head back and looked at her. A tear ran down one cheek, then the other.

Dez bent slightly, reached over and grasped a shoulder. "Are you all right?"

Jaylynn shook her head and squinted her eyes shut, then blotted her face with one quick swipe of her sleeve. She bent over to grab her coat and pick up the bag at her feet, but Dez beat her to the bag. The tall woman took her arm and guided her away from the flow of traffic, off to the side of the concourse. Worried, she looked down to search out the hazel eyes.

Jaylynn angled her head upwards, seeming to have recovered somewhat. In a quiet, plaintive voice, she asked, "Where have you been?" Dez shrugged. With a face full of pain, she said,

"You just left me, Dez."

Dez felt her face begin to flush. "I didn't have a choice."

The hazel eyes studied her, eyes full of misery and starting to brim with tears again. "I missed you terribly." With a whimper, she let the coat fall to the ground between them and leaned into the big woman, her face pressed into the flannel shirt and her arms inside Dez's coat and tight around her waist.

The tall woman dropped the canvas bag and wrapped her arms around her. She leaned back against the wall, her heart still beating fast, but steady. The relief she felt swept over her like a wall of warm water. She let herself believe that maybe the hard part was over.

The small body in her arms trembled, and Dez realized she was still crying. "Ah, c'mon Jay. It's okay. Everything's gonna be all right." Jay nodded her head against the broad chest and snuggled closer. "I'm sorry it took me so long...but—but then you were gone."

Jaylynn leaned back and looked up at her. "Why didn't you call and let me know you were okay?"

Dez glanced away. She couldn't explain it at the moment. Not here, not now, not in the middle of a busy thoroughfare. People passing by were already giving them curious stares, and she felt self-conscious. "Let's get your baggage and go home." She bent and picked up the canvas bag as Jaylynn retrieved her coat from the floor. "I hope you don't have a camera or anything breakable in here."

"Why?"

"It's been dropped pretty hard twice now."

"I don't care." The rookie wormed her good arm under Dez's down coat and hooked her hand under the big woman's belt next to the flannel shirt. The taller woman threw an arm across Jaylynn's shoulders and they started on the long walk toward the main terminal.

Jaylynn shivered and moved closer. "Oh, Dez, you do not know how much I've missed your warmth."

For the first time, Dez got choked up and didn't know how to respond. She'd missed so much more than just her partner's warmth.

****

The ride home from the airport was subdued, and yet Dez felt light-hearted. Jaylynn huddled right next to her, buckled into the middle of the truck seat. She had continued to cry periodically all the time they were waiting for the luggage, but she hadn't let loose of Dez, not even when her two suitcases finally came down the chute. She was composed now, but quiet.

"I'm real sorry it's so cold, Jay."

"Ha. Like you could do anything about it. At least you came out and warmed up the truck for a while."

"For all the good it did."

Keeping her eyes on the road, Dez reached behind her seat and rooted around until she found the old blue blanket she liked to keep in the truck in case of emergencies. She pulled it out from under the suitcases that sat on it, dragged it over the seat, and with one hand, unfolded it. "Maybe this will help a little." Her gloved hand tucked it over Jaylynn's chilled legs.

The smaller woman shivered next to her. "I don't know how my body could become completely de-acclimated to the cold in a mere six days."

Dez reached over and clicked the heat control up to the last notch. The air that blasted out was tepid. "It's not that. It's unusually cold. Hell, it's so damn cold it can't even figure out how to snow right now." She looked at Jaylynn out of the corner of her eye. "Don't worry. If you want, I'll get out the hot water bottle and the heating pad and crank the thermostat up to eighty— whatever you want."

"Where are we going?"

"Where do you want to go?"

"Florida? Texas?"

Dez chuckled. "I've got a better idea. We can be at a nice warm house in—oh, say, ten or twelve more minutes. Or we can turn around, go back to the airport, and wait for a Florida flight in that nice drafty place with all those hacking, wheezing, cranky people. You pick."

"Hmmm. Hard choice. You paint such a nice picture of my options. Okay, I'll stay. My place, or yours?"

Dez shrugged. "Guess that's up to you."

"Me? Why me?"

Dez wasn't sure how to explain. She felt she had made a terrible mistake by staying away so long. There were so many things she realized now that she hadn't understood earlier. To top it off, she felt stupid for being dense and fearful. Instead of opening that Pandora's box, she took another tack. "You're the weary traveler. I'm well rested and flexible right now. You choose, and I'll do whatever you want."

"Anything?"

Hearing the playful tone, she shot a glance over at her companion, then back to the road, and then down at her companion again. "Yeah. Anything."

"Okay, stop at the house so I can just run in and get a few things. Then let's stop at the mini-mart for a frozen pizza and go to your place."

"Actually, I have frozen pizzas in my freezer. And tater tots and some lasagna Luella made recently. Oh, and ice cream."

"You're kidding! Miss Health Food Nut has gone *insane.*"

Dez turned off the freeway and headed down Lexington toward Jaylynn's house. "In case you haven't noticed, I've tanked up considerably."

"No," she said in mock horror. "It can't be! Oh my God, I'm in love with a great, big, giant fat woman."

Dez gave a snort of laughter at the delivery, but then her breath caught when she fully realized what Jaylynn had just said. Feeling a solid lump in her throat, she turned off Lexington and headed to Como Boulevard, then pulled up in front of the house.

"I'll only be a minute." Jaylynn wrenched open the door, leapt out and slammed the truck door, then took off at a run for the house. Dez glanced over her shoulder at the suitcases behind her and sighed. Leaving the truck running, she got out, grabbed the suitcases, and hauled them up to the door. Just as she got to the bottom step, the front door burst open again, and Tim and an apologetic Jaylynn took them from her. The rookie disappeared inside the house.

"You want to come in?" the red-haired man asked as he paused, half in the house and half out. He sounded a lot friendlier than he had the previous three times she had seen or spoken to him.

"Nah. I left the truck running." She gestured with her thumb. "I'll just go make sure it stays warm in there."

He smiled, showing straight white teeth. "Okay, you do that. Wouldn't want the Little Princess to get a cold tush from here to your house."

She grinned. "That's right. See ya, Tim." She headed to the truck where she waited another ten minutes. By the time Jaylynn finally emerged, it was almost warm in the truck. The smaller woman held the handles of two duffel bags in her good hand and a large-sized grocery bag cradled in her bad arm. Dez was out of the truck in an instant, took the bags from Jaylynn, and helped her into the truck.

In short order, the big Ford covered the distance from the Como house to Luella's duplex. The stucco house was dark. Dez parked in the back and grabbed up the two duffel bags. Jaylynn again held the paper bag with her casted arm, and used her good arm for balance on the icy path. They both moved swiftly in the cold night air to the back of the house. Dez fumbled with the keys, so Jaylynn pulled them out of her loaded down hands and found the right key, inserted it, and pushed the door open. She stepped in and stood looking around. "Gosh," she said, sniffing. "Sure can tell Luella isn't here. This place even smells unoccupied."

The porch was chilly and the stairs dark. Dez leaned toward the wall and with an elbow, flipped the light switch on, illuminating the creamy yellow walls and casting warm light on the wooden steps. Jaylynn shut the door and turned the deadbolt, then followed Dez up the stairs to negotiate the apartment door. When they got into the tiny kitchen, the rookie set her paper bag down on a chair as Dez walked through the room to the larger living room/bedroom area and set the duffels on the bed.

Jaylynn followed her and stood shivering in the middle of the room with her hands in her coat pockets. "What happened to all the aforementioned heat?"

Dez grinned. She moved back past the smaller woman and turned the thermostat up to 78, then wheeled around to face the shorter woman. "It'll be warm in a jiffy. These baseboard heaters really crank it out." She shrugged off her jacket and hung it over the desk chair. "You can keep your coat on for a couple minutes if you like. Are you hungry?"

"Always."

At least some things never change. "Like starved?"

"I'm more starved for you than for food."

Dez felt a lump rise in her throat again, and she stood awkwardly. Before she had a chance to respond, Jaylynn's head was against her chest and her arms around her waist. She put her arms as far around the rookie as the coat would allow. It was hard to swallow, but she forced herself to choke out a few words. "This coat of yours is huge, isn't it?"

Jaylynn sighed. "How can you not be totally frozen?"

Shrugging, Dez said, "Just lucky, I guess." She bent her face close to the short, blonde hair and inhaled. Jaylynn almost always smelled good, and now was no exception. In a quiet voice, she asked, "You want pizza?"

Hazel eyes rose to meet hers. "Is this what it's come to? Romance through food?" She laughed, the sound of it light and musical. "No, I do not want pizza—not right this moment." She stepped back and grabbed the long arm, letting her hand slide down to the tall woman's wrist, then pulled her toward the bed.

She dumped the two duffels off the spread and to the carpet below. "I want to crawl right in here, right now, and get completely warmed up. If you know what I mean."

"That big ol' coat is sure gonna be fun."

"You can wear it then. I'm ditching it." She shed the coat and tossed it toward the couch, then slipped her tennis shoes off, pulled back the covers, and hopped up on the bed. Dez bent and untied her shoes, then kicked them off and under the bed. She unbuttoned her jeans and stepped out of them, tossing them toward the couch. Jaylynn lay under the sheet and blankets shaking with the cold. "I'm telling you, Dez, you need flannel sheets."

The tall woman slipped under the covers and the two women moved toward one another. "I'm the closest thing to flannel that you're ever going to get on any bed I sleep in. Way too hot."

Jaylynn snuggled up close. She worked her casted arm under the pillow beneath the bigger woman and moved her other hand down to stroke the warm leg next to her. "Oh! Your skin is better than flannel any day!"

In a husky voice, Dez replied, "At your service, Miss Ice Cube."

Jaylynn smoothed a dark curl off the pale forehead before her. "Oh, you think you're pretty cute, don't you?" Dez blushed and shook her head. "Believe me, you are—especially when you blush."

"I am not blushing," she said in a low, indignant voice.

"That's what they *all* say."

"All who?"

"All you big tough macho cops."

It occurred to Dez that if Jaylynn had been around her any of the last few weeks, she wouldn't be able to say such a thing. *I know for a fact that I'm in no way tough. Not anymore anyway.* "We need to talk, Jay."

"No more fluffy, mushy topics, huh? Time to jump right into the heavy duty stuff?" Jaylynn moved back a bit and busied herself rearranging the pillow her head rested on. "About what?"

"About us." The smaller woman shifted over on to her back, looking up at the ceiling. Dez frowned. She studied the face before her, and suddenly she realized that the rookie was scared of something. "What's the matter?" She came up on her elbow, on her side, and put her head in her right hand. She took a deep breath and waited for Jaylynn to answer.

"Nothing. I'm just—well, I'm...I'm waiting."

"For what?"

Fearful eyes turned toward her. "To find out what you have

intended for us."

"I think that's a decision for both of us to make."

Jaylynn sat up. She leaned forward to sit Indian-style and put her elbows on her thighs. "You mean like the decision you made to leave without telling me?" She didn't look toward Dez, instead pulling the covers up over her lap and shivering. "Do you remember you made me a promise earlier this year? You said you would *never* turn away from me. You promised, Dez."

Dez remembered that earlier, at the airport, she had thought the hard part was over, but it occurred to her now that perhaps she had been wrong. She wasn't sure what to say. All she really wanted to do was take this woman into her arms, tell her that she loved her, and hold her so tight neither of them would ever want to let go. Why couldn't she make herself do that? But she couldn't—not quite yet.

Dez chose her words carefully. "I had to go—to pull myself together, Jay. I was—it was like..." She struggled to find the right words. "I was self-destructing. I couldn't go on like that." She paused and thought for a moment. "I had to go away and figure out how to deal with my fears, how to allow you to be yourself—to accept your choices—without me interfering."

Jaylynn squirmed a little, making a quarter-turn in the bed until she was facing Dez and still sitting cross-legged. She rearranged the blankets over her and hunkered down. "You never interfered."

Dez let out a big gust of air. "I did more than interfere—I was ready to run your life."

"What in the *world* are you talking about?"

"This is why we need to talk. I have some things to tell you." She sighed. "That morning in the hospital—the day after the Bucky beat-down—I delivered a sort of ultimatum. And you did, too."

Jaylynn looked puzzled. "I remember our argument. I remember your ultimatum—but mine?"

Dez took a deep breath. "You told me to get lost if I couldn't live with your choices."

"That wasn't an ultimatum. I was just mad. Geez!" She sputtered for a moment. "That's not what I meant, Dez. Where in the world did you ever get that cracked idea?"

"From you."

"I *never* said that!"

Dez smiled and looked at the indignant woman. She was so openly emotional. A person could read almost every thought on her face. "Jay, I think you said I could get the hell out until I could learn to live with your choices. Something like that any-way...so I did."

"I didn't mean it that way—*not* as an ultimatum."

"Sure sounded like it."

"I was angry." For emphasis she reached out and poked the blankets over the taller woman's hip with her index finger.

"You were also right. At the time, all I could think of was that you were in danger. Every day, you could have been killed. Every time you went on patrol without me, I lived in fear. I imag-ined every horrible thing that could occur—and I knew I wouldn't be there, wouldn't be able to protect you. I couldn't take it. I needed help, but I couldn't admit it."

"So you just disappeared?"

She gazed up at the worried hazel eyes. "Yeah. I wasn't going to beg. And you're more stubborn than me—you weren't going to quit. I could see that." She reached into the layers of blankets and sheets and found Jaylynn's good hand, enclosing it into her own. "I contemplated what it would be like to go away forever. I don't think I would have come back. I don't think I could have." She looked away, feeling a tightness in her chest.

Jaylynn gripped her fingers hard, as though she expected the big warm hand to be pulled away at any moment. "What's changed then?"

"Nothing. And everything." She felt the rookie's eyes upon her, and she was glad that it was night so that the dim light in the room didn't illuminate her face much. She knew she was turning red, tearing up, and it was all she could do to stay there and not get up and move around to dispel her unease. "The department made me see a shrink. After the beat-down, that is. You weren't the only one delivering ultimatums. My job was toast if I didn't go." Jaylynn waited, and though Dez felt her gaze, she couldn't meet her eyes. In a matter-of-fact voice, she said, "So I went. Luckily, they didn't send me to Raisa Goldman." She gave a little smile. "Never liked her a bit."

Jaylynn shook her head slowly. "Dr. G is a-okay. You two just clash, that's all."

Dez nodded. "I have new respect for Lt. Malcolm. He sent me to somebody else—not the regular department headshrinker—a psychiatrist named Marie Montague."

The heaters in the room were working overtime. Dez was suddenly warm and sweating. She slid the blankets and sheet down until only her legs were covered. "She's a specialist in post-traumatic stress disorder."

Jaylynn gripped her hand more tightly, so the tall cop raised

her eyes and looked up at her. Jaylynn had a funny look on her
face. "You're diagnosed with PTSD?"

"Yes."

Jaylynn's mouth dropped open. "Why didn't you tell me?"

"What the hell did I know? I didn't know what was wrong.
And I was...I was..." She had no moisture in her mouth, but she
choked it out, "I was afraid."

Jaylynn shook her head, closed her eyes for a second. Then
she took the flat of her hand and smacked her palm against her
forehead. "Am I dumb or what? I've got a major in psych, and
did I notice? No!"

"It's not like you're a shrink, Jay."

"No, but I've spent hours and hours—days and days on end—
with you. Why didn't *I* figure this out?"

"It couldn't have anything to do with the fact that I hide
things well?"

"No. Yeah...well, you do hide things—but still, now that you
say that, it makes sense. Your sleeplessness, the crankiness, your
over-protectiveness. Oh, brother! I feel like a total dummy."

Now it was Dez's turn to shake her head. She smiled and let
go of the shivering woman's hand. She shifted over onto her back,
sliding up towards the headboard and adjusting the pillows behind
her. She reached out a hand to the huddling woman. "Jay, please.
Come here."

She launched herself forward, clonking Dez on the kneecap
with her cast.

"Whoa!" Dez let out a startled laugh, then got the smaller
woman settled against her. "I hope you get that damn thing off
pretty soon."

"Tomorrow. And I can't wait."

On her side, Jaylynn's right shoulder nestled between the V of
the tall woman's legs with the white-blonde head resting on her
abdomen. Dez pulled the covers up and stroked the back of Jaylynn's neck, which caused the smaller woman to shiver. She
reached around her to pull the covers up higher and tuck them in
until the rookie was totally swathed in blankets, only her head
showing.

Jaylynn sighed. "You're not the only one who's been afraid,
Dez. After a while, I started wondering if you were ever coming
back."

Dez nodded. "I didn't realize that's how you'd feel. I wasn't
thinking very clearly at the time." She thought about all the
nights alone when she *had* considered not returning. But that was
a temporary fantasy, a way to avoid the reality of her pain and

grief. Once she got to the point where she learned how to unlock and release some of the trauma, she realized where she belonged—and with whom. Then the idea of leaving for good left her mind as easily as a tiny leaf falling from a tree and being carried away on the breeze. She cleared her throat, and in a soft voice said, "Jay, I can't promise you that I won't run away again." Closing her eyes and leaning back against the headboard, she took a deep breath. "I should have never made a promise like that 'cause I couldn't keep it. I can make you a different promise...that I'll always come back...eventually."

She felt the smaller woman's hand tighten on her knee, and she thought that Jaylynn was crying again. She stroked the soft blonde hair. "Hey, I know I've got some more work to do, and I know for sure that I can't promise I'm always going to be reasonable when it comes to your safety, but I'm willing to try."

They lay quietly for a while, and Dez actually began to feel sleepy. And relieved. It was as though the world had been tilted off its axis ever since the beat-down—no, actually, ever since Ryan had died the year before. But now the world was righting itself, spinning in balance, and things were making sense again. She took a deep breath and felt her body relax even more. She closed her eyes.

"I passed probation."

Dez's eyes popped open. "You did?"

"Lt. Malcolm and the sergeants signed off on it just before I left for vacation. I'm off work until New Year's Day, so they told me there was no use in holding off."

"You're kidding?"

Jaylynn's head came up off the bigger woman's abdomen, and in an indignant voice, she said, "You don't have to sound so shocked! I'm a perfectly acceptable cop."

Dez began to laugh. "I meant about the time off—not about passing probation. Hell, I knew within a few weeks that you'd be a good cop. I just didn't count on you turning into Calamity Jay and getting hurt all the time."

Jaylynn was now on her knees between the V of Dez's legs. She grabbed a fistful of the front of flannel shirt. "You take that back! I don't get hurt all the time...just *some* of the time."

Dez smiled as she reached over and caught hold of her partner at the waist and squeezed. Jaylynn let out a shriek, but she couldn't prevent the stronger woman from tickling her. Instead, she collapsed on the broad chest, heaving with laughter. Dez wrapped her arms around her and pulled her tight. "One more thing," she whispered into one pink ear, and the rookie slowed her thrashing around and waited, her breath coming fast. "I love you. I want to be with you for the rest of our very long lives."

Jaylynn pulled back until they could look into one another's eyes. Grinning, she said, "Oh Dez! I have *always* felt the same way, from the moment I first met you—I just knew."

Dez nodded. "I want us to live together, in sickness and in health. I want to hold you every night and love you, just you alone. I want to have your babies—"

"What!" Jaylynn tipped her head back and squinted toward the steely blue eyes. "You? Pregnant? I don't *think* so!"

"You know what I mean. If we decide to have kids, then we could adopt. Or I *would* carry the bambino, for you—for us." She gave her partner a wide smile. "But I'd be more than happy to bow to you if you should decide you'd rather."

Jaylynn leaned into her partner and kissed her. The kiss was long and sweet, and gradually it became more passionate. She broke it off and met Dez's eyes. "Hold that thought. We have one problem."

"We do?"

"Yes. You're not going to believe this." She shook her head. "I'll tell you I'm plenty warm now, but if I don't eat something soon, I truly *will* faint from hunger."

Dez let out a snort of laughter. "So much for romance. God help me if your blood sugar should drop." She sat up, and slid out from under Jaylynn. Sitting on the edge of the bed, she asked, "Do you want me to bring you a spoon and the container so that you can immediately mainline ice cream? Or would you find it possible to wait until a pizza heats up?"

"Yes."

Dez arched one eyebrow. "To which?"

"To both."

"Figures." She stood, dressed only in her socks, briefs, and flannel shirt, and moved across the room.

Jaylynn let out a whistle, and the tall woman cast a glance behind just before she disappeared around the corner into the kitchen.

Jaylynn smiled. She settled back into the bed, pulled the covers up, and reveled in the warmth. She felt drunk. Drunk with happiness. Perhaps it *was* her blood sugar, but her whole body was buzzing. And growling. The tight rumbling in her stomach almost hurt, and she grimaced a little, feeling the pain.

Dez returned to the room. Crossing over the shaft of light from the kitchen, for a moment she was illuminated and backlit with golden light. Jaylynn admired the long, muscular legs, the broad shoulders, the milky white skin, and then she was being handed a small Neapolitan ice cream cup with a wooden spoon attached to the top. "Oooh. Ick!"

"What! You don't like this kind?"

"No, not that. I'm not eating it with a wooden spoon. Gross."

"It's wrapped in plastic."

"So what. It's porous. Who knows where that wooden spoon has been?"

Dez rolled her eyes and went back to the kitchen, returning with a teaspoon. "Here ya go, you whiner."

"Thank you," Jaylynn said with dignity, as she exchanged the wood spoon for the metal one.

"At least with that spoon," Dez called back over her shoulder, "you know where it's been—sitting in my dusty silverware drawer for years."

"Still probably lots cleaner than that porous wood stick." Holding the frozen plastic container, Jaylynn shivered. She pulled back the cardboard top and plunged in, making short work of the few ounces of pink, white, and brown ice cream. "Hey!"

"Hey, what?" Dez poked her head around the doorway.

"I'm done."

"And?"

She held out the empty plastic cup.

"What am I—maid for the day?"

Jaylynn grinned and nodded. "I would put it on your bedside table, but you don't have one. I didn't think you'd appreciate it if I tossed it over on the couch."

"Right." Dez took it from her and started back toward the kitchen.

"It's very cute of you to make pizza for me in your underwear."

As she turned the corner the big woman said, "It's so damn hot in here now that I ought to be doing it in the nude."

Jaylynn smiled and started to laugh. "I'd like that," she choked out.

****

Jaylynn was warm and secure. She lay on her side, her body swathed in soft blankets and tucked up against a torso radiating heat. She opened her eyes and shifted onto her back. A dim beam of light poured in through the small, porthole-like window above Dez's bed. Turning her head to the left, she looked at her partner's slumbering face. The sleeping woman lay on her side, facing her, with dark hair starting to come out of its raggedy French braid. Jaylynn wondered what time it was. She couldn't see the VCR clock, and there was no clock near the bed. When Dez awakened by an alarm, she used her wristwatch. Jaylynn thought her own watch was in her coat pocket, and Dez's was now hung around the curlicue of wood on the headboard, which Jaylynn couldn't reach without waking her.

Her stomach didn't feel empty and it was still fully dark out, so she didn't think more than a couple hours had passed since she had fallen asleep. She didn't usually awaken in the night, except if she had a nightmare, but right now, she definitely felt she had no nightmares in store for the near future. Content, she turned onto her other side, facing Dez, and let herself just laze in the warmth.

It had been a wonderful evening full of joy for the small woman. Eating, talking, holding Dez tightly—it was like a dream. She didn't actually remember falling to sleep, and she was a little embarrassed about that. She had wanted to make love, but some-where along the way, her fatigue caught up with her. *I think I can make up for that tomorrow.* She smiled to herself and let herself feel contentment for the first time in—well, she couldn't figure out exactly how long. She realized that she had been tremendously edgy during the past weeks without Dez. She hadn't thought that another person could have that kind of effect on her. *I'm self-assured...independent...happy-go-lucky...right? Ha. That's what I* thought *anyway. So much for that noise. Who am I trying to fool?* She simply did not want to imagine her life without this wonderful woman beside her. And it wasn't like she could even begin to explain why. She could only say that with Dez, she felt at home.

She studied the pale face beside her. Even in sleep, Dez had a tendency to frown. The big woman shifted and emitted a soft groan, the scowl on her face deepening. Jaylynn watched as the sleeping woman brought her fists up to her chest. From the relaxed, slumbering state of a moment ago, Dez went tense. Jay-lynn opened her eyes wide, watching the scowl change to a gri-mace. She thought she could almost hear the grinding of teeth, and she shifted back a few inches when the tall cop's knees came up and she curled into a fetal position on her side, her fists partly blocking the view of her face.

"Unnhhh...no...nuh...nuh...no!"

Jaylynn pulled a hand out of the blankets and started to reach out. Something stopped her. Fascinated, she watched the full transformation from placid face to savage contortions. The body next to her began to tremble, and Dez's breath came fast. Her head shook back and forth. "No, no...stop! Not you. No," she wailed. "No!"

Jaylynn couldn't take it anymore. She could almost feel the pain radiating from Dez. As she reached out, though, blue eyes snapped open. One single tear rolled from the corner of Dez's eye and dropped onto the pillow. She stared, and Jaylynn didn't think she was seeing anything.

"Dez? Dez, it's just a dream...just a bad dream, sweetie." She scooted closer and pulled the stiff body to her. She could feel the big fists pressed into her chest. "It's okay. You're safe."

A hoarse whisper replied, "No, it's not okay. He's dead. He's dead...and it's my fault."

Jaylynn wrapped her arms tightly around her. "No, it's *not*. It's not your fault. Shh, it's okay."

"No, it's not," was the strangled reply. "It'll never be okay."

"Oh, Dez. Shh." She reached up and smoothed the dark hair out of the colorless face and was surprised when her hand came away damp with tears. She had never seen Dez cry—get choked up, maybe—but never had the big woman wept in front of her. "Oh, sweetie..."

Dez's hands came up in front of her head, the big palms and fingers completely covering her face. She shook. But she didn't turn away. Jaylynn's heart went out to her, but she knew there wasn't anything she could do but hold the tall woman and let her cry. Making soothing noises, she held her shaking partner, patting and stroking her until she stilled. Through it all, Dez kept her hands in front of her face, and when her tears abated, she turned away toward the pillow and started to roll over.

"Ah-ah-ah—no, you don't." Jaylynn touched her hand to Dez's face. "Don't turn away from me. Please. You've seen me cry a million times, and I bet this won't be the last time I'll see you cry."

"It's not the same."

Jaylynn smiled and shook her head slightly. "Pain is pain. Comfort is comfort. It's all the same."

"It's more embarrassing for me."

"Oh yeah? And why is that?" She tucked her head into the hollow under Dez's chin and wriggled her way into her embrace, one knee between the long legs and the other pressed up against the warmer woman's thigh.

"I don't know. It's just that way."

"You don't have to be embarrassed with me, Miss Macho Cop. And I don't want to be embarrassed with you, either. You're the one person I want to share all my feelings with, no holds barred."

Dez didn't say anything for a moment. "It's still embarrassing."

"Like you think I'll laugh at you or something?" When Dez didn't answer, she went on, "Why would I laugh at you when I go around emoting all the time? If anyone should be embarrassed, wouldn't it be me?" Dez made a "hmph" sound and tightened her grip. "What was the dream about?"

The tall cop took a deep, ragged breath. She definitely did not want to revisit that dreamscape, but it was the same thing repeatedly, and Marie *had* said that she should talk about it. She cleared her throat and took another shallow breath. "It's the same thing, over and over. I see the scene, the restaurant where Ryan was...was shot. It was out on the terrace—this little lanai to the side of the place..."

She remembered it all in a herky-jerky series of action frames, almost like a flawed amateur movie. One minute they were strolling up to the dilapidated steakhouse in living Technicolor, ready to bounce a drunk about whom the owner had called in a complaint. In the next moment, as they entered the restaurant, a shot rang out. There was a scream, the din of shouting, glass breaking. Dez felt the cold metal of the gun in her hand. Looking back, she didn't even remember unholstering it. She and Ryan entered the main dining area, he low and she high. A white-shirted man dove across a table from a booth along the side wall, landed on the floor, and was up on his feet running toward a door near the back of the restaurant.

"Stop! Police!" Ryan's voice was loud and authoritative.

The man smacked through the emergency exit and fell into the night. All around, the patrons were pointing, shouting, "Get him!"

Both officers hastily threaded their way across the room past a dozen tables, most of which displayed half-eaten meals. Click. The feel of crunching glass under her feet. Click. The smell of burnt powder from the gunshot. Click. The white face of a male in a bloody business suit clutching his bleeding upper arm.

Ryan hit the door first and blasted through. Loud reports...bang...then a pause...three quick reports...pain in her knee...shooting stars...gasping for breath...Ryan down.

She rolled and came to a squat a few feet from her seated partner, her gun in hand.

"Oh shit!" he said.

"You hit?"

"Yeah, but I'm fine," he panted. "Just a leg wound. Get the sonuvabitch! Get him!"

She looked down at the rip in the knee of her pants, but knew she wasn't shot. One last look at his blue eyes and she was on her feet. Encouraging her, he pointed. "Get that asshole! I'll call in." He reached for his shoulder mic and turned his face to talk into it. She heard him call the code, then, in slow motion, she rose.

She saw the man's back as he ran away. Dressed in tan slacks and a white shirt, he'd be easy to see in the night. He must have been quite drunk because he ran with difficulty. She could have shot him then. Later, she wished she had. Instead, she sprinted after him as he staggered around the side of the restaurant, and out of sight. She overtook him easily. Tackled him from behind. Bashed his head against the sidewalk. With effort, she cuffed the panting man and flipped him over. He stared up at her, a dazed look on his face. He was an ordinary looking White man with thinning brown hair and crooked front teeth. She pushed the button on her shoulder mic and, gasping for air, called in. She could hear sirens and see the flashing lights already behind her.

She jerked him to his feet, saying nothing further. He didn't speak either as he wheezed, staggering in front of her. It seemed to take forever. She pushed him down an uneven walkway, squinting toward the flashing lights. He fell. She helped him up. Coughing, he slipped and fell again. She dragged him to his feet, and around the corner they went, to the vacant lanai. Earlier, it would have held a crowd of happy diners, but it was late, and the gnats were so thick that the restaurant had closed the section, moved the tables off to the side, and turned off all the lights. Now the area was lined with people standing silently.

Two police cars, an ambulance. Lights flashing everywhere. Dez could see something dark, maybe wine, pooled in the middle of the lanai's smooth cement. They must have done a poor job sweeping and tidying up. Two figures were on their knees, probably cleaning.

Flashing lights—neon red and blue and white—swirled all around her. She heard shouting, the sound of the dispatcher on the radio. The dark-clad figures in front of her came into focus, their navy blue uniforms looking black in the night.

Ryan? Cold fear ran through her veins.

She pushed past the gunman and dragged him forward, the metal of the handcuffs cold against her hands.

"DRT," said a deep voice.

"I know," the other paramedic responded.

Dez let go of the suspect and fell to her knees above the figure lying so still on the ground. In a low, menacing voice, she said, "He's not Dead Right There, you sonuvabitch! He's not DRT. Help him." She touched his face. It was clammy—cool with sweat, she thought. She met the eyes of the medic, then grabbed his shirt front. "He's not dead—he's not! He can't be! He needs to get to the hospital!"

"He bled out...there's nothing we could do, Officer—"

She struck him a weak, glancing slap to the side of the jaw. Click. The paramedic's shocked face. Click. Dead blue eyes looking up and past her. Click. Flashing lights and noise. Click. A swirl of stars and lights in the dark night. She heard her name called out...

Next thing she knew, the gunman was on the ground and she was kicking him as hard as she could with her steel-toed service boots. Her chest hurt and her breath came in short gasps. She felt only blind rage, ready to kill this man who had shot her partner.

Many strong arms grabbed her, pulled her away, away from the lanai and around the corner of the restaurant.

She looked up but there was no moon, no light from street lamps. Only the neon lights cast any illumination, but they made her sick to her stomach. She smelled something dank and sour, like poison gas, and it stung her eyes. Scalding hot tears ran down her face. She reached up to wipe them away and was shocked to see, in the flashing lights, that there was blood all over her hands. She bent forward, held upright by several hands, and screamed out the sound of a wounded animal...

Her body shook with sobs, but she was safe, safe in Jaylynn's arms. "It was my fault...I—dammit—I shouldn't have left him."

"How could you know, Dez? And even if you had, what could you have done?"

She choked the words out. "I could have—slowed the blood flow—helped him—helped somehow until—'til the medics arrived."

Jaylynn shook her head. In a quiet voice she said, "I read the report one day when I was working downtown, Dez. His femoral artery was severed. Nobody—except *maybe* a doctor with the right equipment—could have done anything, and only if they were on the spot in the first minute or so."

A fresh wave of tears hit Dez, and it was all she could do not to leap up out of the bed and run out into the street. She was conscious of Jaylynn's cast against her shoulder and of a soft hand stroking her back. She tried to concentrate on that while breathing deeply. After a moment, she said, "I should have been there, Jay. He died alone. All alone. And I wasn't there."

Another tear traveled down her face. She felt it on her cheek, and then Jaylynn reached up and wiped it away. Dez was abashed about the weakness she was displaying, but another part of her didn't care, instead feeling intense relief.

"And that's why you went nuts at the Bucky beat-down, huh?"

Dez nodded. "I guess. I hardly remember what happened, to tell you the truth."

"You and me both." Jaylynn let out a sigh. "Crystal still thinks you hate her."

"Whoa! Total switch in topics."

"Well, that just popped into my head. I've talked to her a lot these past few weeks, and ever since my injury, she's been awful hard on herself. She wouldn't tell me what happened between the two of you, said it was something she had to settle with you."

The big woman nodded, realizing that there were more people than just Jaylynn to make peace with. "I should have called her before now. I was really ticked at her that night, but I got over it."

"Why were you so mad at her?"

Dez wiped her eyes on the hem of the sheet and let it drop. "I sorta put her in charge of keeping you safe. I trusted her. And then you got clobbered by some dumb asshole. I was furious with her." She paused when Jaylynn lifted her head and shifted over to sit, legs out, next to her. "I know, I know. I'm about to get a lecture about this, right?" In the moonlight she could see Jaylynn sporting a crooked smile.

"Damn right. Nothing that happened was Crystal's responsibility. It was that idiot's fault. She did everything by the book. The only thing she could have done differently was to shoot the guy, but that wasn't a good idea either. Dez, you should call Crystal."

"Oh, I will."

"No, I mean now."

"Jay! It's the middle of the night. And on Christmas to boot."

Jaylynn frowned. "Oh yeah. Well then, tomorrow. Tomorrow you should call. And by the way, speaking of the phone, why in the *hell* don't you have an answering machine?"

"Waste of money. Nobody ever calls." She turned over on her side, and Jaylynn snuggled in next to her.

"I have a hunch that I have called—oh, maybe *three hundred times* in the last few weeks. So don't give me crap about nobody ever calling."

Dez didn't answer. She found herself marveling about what had just happened. Ryan had died a year ago last June—eighteen months back—and until lately, she had never told the story in full, emotions included, not even to the homicide investigators. And in the last two weeks she had told it twice. For a year and a half she had kept it at bay, and now, well, now she could hardly keep it out of her waking thoughts or her dreams. She felt awful, like her eyes were swollen shut and her throat and breathing passages burned to a crisp, but at the same time, a sense of relief flowed through her. *What had Marie said?* "Trauma is too heavy a load to carry alone." She said it out loud, and Jaylynn responded. "What?"

"Marie keeps saying stuff like that—you know, that trauma shouldn't be kept inside."

"Marie, the psychiatrist?"

Dez nodded. "Yeah. She's pretty smart."

Jaylynn giggled.

"What? What's so funny?" The tall cop's tone was no nonsense.

"You are. I never ever thought I'd hear you admit that some *shrink* was okay, that's all."

"She might be the only one."

Jaylynn laughed, the sound warm and rich and delighted. Dez loved to hear her laugh. Just the thought of the younger woman's laughter, of her energy and sense of humor, made her smile. She was glad Jaylynn wasn't looking at her face in the cool moonlight. She didn't feel quite ready to express every feeling she had, especially the ones that felt so totally mushy and melodramatic. She let out a sigh, and instead said, "I hope you know what you've gotten yourself into."

"With you? Or with therapy?"

"With me, of course. I'm not quite sure, but I think I have nightmares more than once a night."

"How come you never told me before?"

"Lucky for me, you usually sleep like the dead."

"Oh, no, I don't! I have my own bad dreams, you know."

"Yeah, yeah. You don't usually wake up though. All I gotta do is nudge you, maybe wrap an arm around you, and you settle right down."

"You must be exaggerating."

"Nope."

"If you were shaking and crying out like you did tonight, I

would for sure have known something was wrong. I know I would have woke up!"

"Yeah, maybe. Listen here, wild thing—" That comment, made in a mocking tone, warranted her a poke in the ribs. "Hey! Cut it out. You never woke up because until the last month, I've had insomnia so bad I just about went crazy. I've spent more hours lying here watching you sleep than I care to count."

"Why didn't you wake me up, you fool?"

Now it was Dez's turn to laugh out loud. "And do what? Play cribbage? Go out for a two a.m. run? You have *no* concept of how crabby you get when deprived of sleep."

"I do not!"

Dez kept laughing. "Hunger, lack of sleep, and mean people—not necessarily in that order—are the three things that irk you the most. And don't try to deny it. I've known you long enough to be able to put forth three or four *hundred* examples. Don't even get me started."

"Okay, maybe—"

"No 'maybe' about it. It's true." She reached an arm back and behind her to snag her wristwatch from the headboard. "Unbelievable. It's only three a.m. What time did we fall asleep?"

In a grouchy voice, Jaylynn said, "I don't know...maybe one thirty or so."

"Whew, pretty early for us."

Jaylynn yawned and nodded slowly, her face pressed next to Dez's bare collarbone. "Feels like I haven't slept for days."

"Tell me about it."

The rookie's breath evened out, and Dez lay holding the sleeping woman for quite some time. *Marie was right. Companionship was a good thing. And love was even better.*

Chapter
Twenty-Nine

The tall cop awakened shortly before ten a.m. and grinned when she found Jaylynn sleeping deeply next to her. Despite Dez turning over and rearranging covers, her slumbering partner didn't move. She extricated herself from the smaller woman's grip, eased out of bed, and went into the bathroom to take a shower. When she came out some time later, the rookie hadn't stirred and was still curled up on her side, facing the wall, holding her left arm protectively to her chest. Dez slipped on jeans, a long-sleeved red t-shirt, and tennis shoes, and went into the kitchen to brew some tea and make breakfast. The smell of food would wake the rookie up in a good mood if nothing else would.

Dez mixed up pancake batter from scratch, plugged in a griddle, and switched on the oven to its warm setting. She waited for the griddle to heat up, and stood with her back to the counter, her arms crossed over her chest. With everything that happened the night before, she hadn't had the chance to give Jaylynn the strange Christmas present she had to offer her. She peeked around the corner. Jaylynn slept on. She stepped into the room, to the entertainment center, and hunted through her CD's until she found the one she was looking for. She opened the plastic case and popped out the disk, leaving the case on the shelf. In the kitchen she put the disk in a small CD player and turned the volume to low.

The griddle was good and hot now, so she smeared some butter on it and dripped four circles of batter from a handled mug. They sizzled and spread. Within seconds, bubbles formed in the batter. Dez could smell the cinnamon and her stomach rumbled.

She sat down at the kitchen table to wait. In the background, an acoustic guitar played softly, and then the husky voice sang. She hummed along to the medium beat.

I've been waiting so long...longing for you
Getting harder and harder to hold on
Come and give me your love
Come and take mine...come and take mine

Late at night, early in the morning
Late at night, early in the morning

She got up to turn the pancakes over. They had cooked to a deep, rich golden brown. She took a plate down from a cupboard, and when the other side had cooked, she flipped them onto the plate and stuck it in the oven. After buttering the griddle again, she poured four more circles of batter and then opened the refrigerator to get more eggs. She decided that if she was going to eat a high sugar and high fat meal, she may as well have some protein—scrambled eggs—to go with it.

A movement in the doorway caught her eye, and she turned to see Jaylynn barefoot and wrapped in a comforter. In the background, the music played.

Parallel line...I'm waiting for you
Take me higher and higher and I just hold on
The look in your eyes
It's all right...
It's all right...

"Do you know how many times I played this CD, Dez?" The taller woman shook her head. Jaylynn stood barefoot, and they both listened for a moment. "I grew to love and hate *Hydraulic Woman.*"

"Why?" Dez frowned as she listened to the song fade out.

Late at night, early in the morning
Late at night, early in the morning...

Jaylynn moved into the kitchen and pulled a chair out, then sat down wearily. "Her voice is a little like yours, and some of the songs made me think of you."

Dez checked the pancakes to find they weren't quite ready to turn over, then leaned against the counter by the sink. "I know what you mean—the songs reminded me of you, too." She stepped over to the table, punched the button and turned off the CD player, then looked over at the rookie, sitting swathed in the thick quilt. She couldn't help it—she found herself grinning.

"What?" Jaylynn asked, a scowl on her face.

"You just look so damn cute."

Jaylynn blushed. "I don't feel so damn cute. I feel like I need a shower and about 45 pancakes."

"Not in that order, though, right?"

The rookie shrugged. "Doesn't matter." She looked over miserably. "All I know is that if you don't have a bread bag that I can put this blasted cast in to shower, then I don't know what to do. I can't *wait* to get it off."

Dez rooted around in one of her kitchen drawers, then looked in a cupboard. "Nope, sorry. Don't have one. I've got zip-lock bags and plastic wrap, but no bread bags." She picked up the spatula and flipped the pancakes over. They sizzled and popped when the wet side hit the hot grill. Still holding the spatula, she shifted until her hip leaned against the counter. She noted that Jaylynn had a sour look on her face, so Dez took two steps over close to her. "Didn't you sleep well?"

"Yes. No. Hell, I don't know. What time is it anyway?"

Looking at her watch, the tall woman ran the fingers of her other hand through the short-cropped blonde hair below her. "It's ten-forty."

"Well, then, I guess I slept fine."

"You gauge it by the clock?"

"I got enough hours, so I must be okay."

"But aren't you still on West Coast time?"

A look of comprehension passed over the rookie's face. "Yeah, that's it. I feel like it's two hours earlier—or at least my body thinks that. No wonder I'm so tired."

"You could go back to bed if you like."

She yawned. "No, I better not. It'll probably take me two hours to get ready, and I have a one o'clock doctor's appointment to get this thing sawed off."

With a grin, Dez said, "Too bad we don't have the Aikuchi All-Purpose Kitchen Knife here. I'm sure we could take care of it and save money on doctor's fees all at once."

"Don't think I haven't already thought of that." She turned in her chair and put her elbows on the table, chin in hand. Yawning again, she looked around the kitchen. "The pancakes smell good. What else have you got that's good for me to munch on?"

Dez didn't answer. Instead, she bent and placed a soft kiss on the back of the smaller woman's neck, which caused them both to shiver. She set the spatula on the table and wrapped her arms around Jaylynn from behind, her hands coming to rest on the smaller woman's chest. Jaylynn sighed and squeezed the red-clad forearms. "Dez?"

"Yeah," she said softly into the pink ear.

"I love you."

"Right back atcha, pardner." Dez straightened and picked up the spatula. "You ready for the first round of vittles?"

"I thought you'd never ask."

The tall woman dished up all four pancakes and delivered them to the table along with a container of maple syrup. "Eggs coming up." She cracked four into a bowl and used a fork to whip them up with a little milk, salt, and pepper, then poured them onto the griddle and chased them around with the fork. When they were cooked nice and dry, just how she liked them, she swiped Jaylynn's plate out from under her and spooned half the scrambled eggs onto the plate, then returned it to the table. "*Violá*. Instant eggs."

"Thank you. I was hungry." She yawned once again.

"Cut that out! You're making *me* feel tired." She returned to the griddle and turned it off, then picked up an oven mitt. She flicked the oven switch to off and opened the door to remove the warming plate from inside. Once she had scooped the last of the eggs onto the hot plate next to the pancakes, she sat across from Jaylynn to eat, remembering just as she was seated that she didn't have anything to drink. "Want some milk? Or juice or something?"

"Milk would be good."

Dez rose and poured them two glasses. "You know what you need?"

"Besides a shower, a healed arm, and some energy?"

"Yeah."

"What?"

The tall woman grabbed a napkin out of the holder on the table and wiped some syrup off her chin. "You need a good Christmas present to cheer you up."

Jaylynn set her fork down with an alarmed look on her face. "I have a birthday present for you, Miss Disappearing Act, but I don't actually have a Christmas present. Not yet anyway."

"Don't worry about it. You can call the birthday gift a combination present, okay? I don't mind. I didn't expect any present at all."

Jaylynn pushed her plate away, leaving half a pancake and a couple bites of eggs.

Dez reached across the table and cupped the smaller woman's forehead in a big hand.

Jaylynn scowled. "What?"

"Just wondered if you had a fever. You usually scarf up all your food and half of mine."

"Oh, I just got full, that's all." Actually, it had suddenly occurred to her that when she'd purchased Dez's birthday present a few days before Thanksgiving, she had been full of hopes and expectations. But later, she hadn't ended up buying a Christmas present for her, because—she now realized—she had lost faith to a certain degree. She hated to admit it, but she had plunged into so much doubt that she got to the point where she didn't believe Dez would come back. That bothered her. Dez believed in her enough to get her a Christmas gift, but she herself hadn't felt the same way. In fact, she realized she had been so angry at her partner that, at one point, she had thought about taking the birthday gift back, though she knew she couldn't because it was personalized. The entire train of thought made her feel small and petty.

She looked up into bright blue eyes, eyes full of concern, and she couldn't help it. The tears came. She closed her eyes and looked down at the awkward cast in her lap as the tears leaked out. A warm hand grasped her cool fingers, and she opened her eyes to find Dez squatting next to her chair, a concerned look on her face. "What's the matter, Jay?"

The smaller woman couldn't speak, but she allowed Dez to pull her up out of the chair and lead her into the other room to the couch. The big woman sat and tugged Jaylynn down into her lap, enfolding her in a warm embrace.

"I must just be tired still, that's all."

"Umm hmm, right. I'm sure that's all."

The sardonic tone of Dez's voice caused her to turn her head and lean back so that she could get a good view of her face. "What's that supposed to mean?"

"You never cry for no reason. Something's hurting you, and you're not telling me what it is. And that's okay. You can tell me if and when you want to."

Jaylynn reached a hand up and stroked along the side of the pale face above her, letting her hand trail from face to neck to the middle of the wide chest where she brought her hand to rest. "When did you get so smart?"

"Must be all the therapy."

This brought a smile from the smaller woman. "If that's it, then I guess I need to meet this shrink."

"You will." Dez touched three fingers to Jaylynn's cheek and wiped away the tears, then kissed cool lips. "You taste like syrup." She tightened her hold on the figure swaddled in the comforter.

"Guess that's better than the dragon breath I had when I first woke up."

"Let's see. I believe we were talking about Christmas and holiday presents when you launched into the tears. I take it that some infidel has informed you that there is no Santa."

Jaylynn laughed out loud, not expecting the joke from Dez. The tall cop was like that, usually so serious, and then just when least expected, making some sort of deadpan comment that cracked her up. She got up and tossed the quilt on the couch beside Dez. Wearing only a t-shirt and underwear, she hurried across the room and went to the grocery bag by the doorway. She rooted around in it until she found and pulled out a small box wrapped in shiny blue and silver paper. She spun and started back toward the couch, but Dez pointed. "Will you get that envelope over there on my desk?"

The rookie reversed course, picked up a thick envelope, and came back to the couch. She handed both items to the tall woman, shivered, and grabbed the quilt. After she wrapped herself in the comforter, she let herself be pulled down again into Dez's lap. She shivered.

"Good grief, Jay! It's ninety degrees in here. How can you be cold?"

She shook her head. "I hope you don't mind having this conversation for the next, oh, say, eighty years. I don't think we are ever going to have complementary thermostats."

Dez smiled. "No kidding. I think your comfort range is all of about five degrees one way or another. Maybe you should put on some weight. That would keep you warm. Sure works for me."

Jaylynn rolled her eyes. Before Dez could say anything more, she pointed to the package in her hand. "Open that."

Curious, Dez shifted her arm so that she could unwrap the shiny paper. She took the lid off a small white box and found a velvet covered gray box inside of that. She turned the white box over and let the one inside fall out into her hand. Stroking the soft velvet with the side of her thumb, she wondered if this was what she thought it was. Sure enough, she found a silvery-colored ring made of white gold nestled inside. The ring, partly buried in satin, glinted in the light and took her breath away. It looked like a simple wedding band, except that there was a pattern circling the band. She pulled the ring from its satin bed and squinted at it closely to see that the pattern was actually made up of the letters *JD* all the way around the ring. The script blended together, and it wasn't until she examined it closely that she recognized the two letters.

She raised her eyes to meet Jaylynn's and could see that the younger woman was uncertain, fearful again. Holding the ring between her thumb and forefinger, Dez said one simple word. "Wow." She looked back at the shiny silver and noticed the inside was also engraved. Peering closer, she read the script there: *You are the Love of my Dreams—Forever—Jaylynn.*

Dez opened her mouth, but nothing came out. She raised her left hand and slipped the band onto the ring finger. It was snug over her knuckle, but fit just fine once she slid it down. She looked into the anxious hazel eyes, and once again wondered why Jaylynn was so nervous. "This is perfect. I love it, Jay. It's...it's beautiful. Thank you."

Jaylynn relaxed against her. "That's a relief. I was afraid it was—well, I don't know. You don't wear any jewelry that I've ever seen. I wasn't sure you would like it."

"I more than like it. But I have to admit, it's so much more personal than what I have for you." She hesitated, as though she had more to say, then shrugged and picked up the envelope from the couch beside her and handed it over. "Here, open this."

Jaylynn got a finger under the flap and tore the back open. She slid a sheaf of papers out and something fell onto the quilt. She looked up at the bright blue eyes above her, then picked up a gold key. "What is this to?"

Dez gave her a crooked half-smile but didn't respond.

The rookie unfolded the papers and looked at them. "But this is Vanita's address...oh my! They talked to you, too. Dez! You bought Vanita's house?"

"Not yet. If we do it, you have to fill out that sheaf of paperwork."

"We? You mean us—together?"

"That's what I was hoping."

"But I don't have any down payment money. Well, I have a little, but not much, and then I'd be broke..."

"That's no problem. I have enough to pay for about a third of the house, and then we'd finance the rest."

Jaylynn stared down at the shiny key in her hand. "Dez...that's not fair. I wouldn't be doing my part."

"Sure you would. You could do all the yard work, massage my aching muscles morning, noon, and night, and—you know—wait on me hand and foot."

When Jaylynn realized her partner was kidding, she poked her in the ribs. "Very funny."

"Jay, I want it to be 'share and share alike.' I want you to have everything of mine and vice versa."

"You just want to get a hold of my Aikuchi kitchen knife."

Dez laughed out loud and pulled the smaller woman tight against her. "I've been waiting all my life for you, and now I want us to share everything."

"I think I have more debts than you do."

Dez shrugged. "So what. Little by little, we can pay them off together. Please say yes. Vanita's house is a good one, and if, after a few years, you decide you don't like it, we can trade up."

"Oh, I *love* her house. The woodwork is great, and it's a nice, cozy solid place. It's a wonderful house."

"We'll have to tear down that horrendous garage, though, and build a new one this summer. But that won't be too hard. I can get someone to pour the concrete, and I can easily frame it and roof it. Crystal and I built Luella's garage a few years back. It's easy."

Jaylynn laid her head against Dez's chest and let the feeling of contentment roll through her like a wave. "I shouldn't have doubted you."

"What? You don't think I can build a simple garage?"

"No, that's not what I meant. I mean that by Christmas Eve, I just sort of lost faith in you." She felt terrible to admit it, but she forged on. "When I hadn't heard from you for so long, I felt awful, and then I got mad, and then I didn't think I could ever forgive you, and by the time I flew home, I felt so godforsaken because I was starting to try to figure out how I could live without you." She looked down at her lap. "But you never gave up on me."

"Jay, look at me." With one big hand, she turned the smaller woman's face so that their eyes met. "I not only gave up on you, I gave up on me, too. I walked out of the hospital a wreck that day, shattered into pieces that I still haven't gotten all put back together. We've both had our crises of faith, and I'm sure we'll have more in the future. I didn't know how you'd react last night, either. Do you realize that? I was afraid, too. But that's past. Let's not waste another minute of time feeling bad about what has happened. Let's just move on, okay?"

Jaylynn nodded. She took a deep breath. "All right. I'd like that. More than that, I'd like to move on to a shower, and I bet you'd like to finish your breakfast. After that maybe you'd better take me back to the house. I have a stash of bread bags there."

"Luella probably has one, but hey, I have another idea. How about I run you a bath? You can keep your arm out, and you could relax in the Jacuzzi. I'll even wash this rat's nest for you."

"Wh-wh-what?" She was so taken aback she sputtered. She reached up and ran her good hand through her short-cropped hair. "What's wrong with my hair?"

"Not a thing...if you don't count the 22 different varieties of cowlicks."

"Very funny." Despite the mock glare she was giving Dez, Jaylynn was relieved. "Okay. I have no desire to go outside anyway. A bath would be fine—if you'll help me, that is."

"Nothing I like more than helping you undress." She gave the smaller woman a wicked smile and was rewarded with a kiss.

Chapter
Thirty

Jaylynn sat in the center of the bench seat in Dez's truck waiting for her partner to hurry up and fill the gas tank so that they could turn the engine back on and get the heat going. The winter weather had warmed up considerably since the day before, but it was still only ten degrees outside, and the dark clouds above promised more snow soon. As far as the rookie was concerned, it was positively bone chilling when the wind blew. She stretched her sore arm out in front of her and flexed her hand, then shivered. The protective splint she now wore was lightweight with Velcro straps, giving her some extra needed support and a reminder not to do anything too sudden. Getting the cast off had been such a relief, but her sore arm was colder than the other one. *I hope I never ever get hurt again. It's been awful.*

She was still full from the eggs and pancakes Dez had made earlier. If she were slightly warmer, she could say she felt just fine. As it was, she thought that she still felt pretty decent—in fact, emotionally she had never been better.

The door to the mini-mart opened and one tall, long-legged woman ambled out. In the hiking boots she wore, Dez stood close to 6'2". Jaylynn watched her partner stride toward her, the bright blues eyes looking all around and taking in everything. When they came to rest on Jaylynn, neither woman could help but smile. Dez quickened her pace. Reaching the truck, she opened the door and swung up into the cab, bringing in a gust of cold air. Jaylynn gazed up at her, smiling and happy, waiting for her to shut the door.

"What?" She turned the key in the ignition, and the heater kicked on.

The smaller woman sighed. "Nothing. I'm just happy."

Dez's right hand dropped to the rookie's thigh, and she gave it a gentle squeeze. "I'm glad. I'm happy, too." She pulled forward and out of the lot.

"I don't know how you can go without gloves. Brrrr. I'm freezing even with 'em on."

"It's just easier to drive. I like being able to get a good grip on the wheel." She raised her left wrist and checked her watch. "It's easier to get to my watch, too."

"You going to be late?"

"Nope. My appointment is at 2:30, and we should be right on time."

"You positive you want me to come with you?"

"Yeah, sure—that is, if you don't get too bored sitting in the waiting room for an hour." She changed lanes to steer around a line of cars trying to make righthand turns.

"No, I don't mind at all. I've got a book to read. And besides, I would really like to meet this miracle worker who has you all excited about counseling."

"Whoa, whoa, whoa! Let's not go *that* far." Dez chuckled as she turned onto the interstate and headed downtown. "I still don't enjoy it—not one bit."

Jaylynn made a fist around the splint with her left hand and opened her fingers again. Her whole arm felt weak, and she couldn't hold a fist for more than a second before the muscles in her forearm screamed in pain. The doctor had said it would take several weeks of exercises to get it back to anywhere near its former strength and coordination. She wasn't looking forward to that.

"What's the matter?" Dez asked as she exited the freeway. "Your hand isn't hurting, is it?"

"Not really. It just feels weak."

"I've got a gripper thing—a hand exerciser—that you should borrow. It helped a lot when my arm was healing. One day I could hardly grip a thing, and it seemed like just a while after, it felt back to normal." She pulled up next to a brick building and turned off the truck, then put her hands on the steering wheel and took a deep breath. "Well, here we are."

Jaylynn picked up her book from the seat beside her and tucked it under her right arm. She examined the profile of the woman sitting next to her who was gripping the wheel so hard that the veins in her hands stood out. She leaned into the solid frame and stroked the thigh nearest to her. "Dez?"

She took another deep breath. "I hate this."

Jaylynn started to smile, but bit back the grin. "It won't be too bad. Come on. Let's go before I freeze to death."

Dez groaned. "I don't want to. You don't know what it's like."

She reached across the bigger woman and grabbed the door handle. "Oh, yes, I do." She leaned into her companion playfully. "Are you going to make me eject you? Or are you going willingly?"

"Like a good prisoner, of course." Dez sighed and shifted over. Jaylynn prodded her in the butt as the tall cop slid off the seat. "Hey! Enough of the pushy stuff."

Giggling, Jaylynn scooted under the steering wheel, swung her legs around to the side of the seat, and prepared to hop down from the tall truck. Dez stepped forward and grabbed her on either side of her hipbones and set her down on the icy street. She ended up standing inches from the tall woman, a wide grin on her face, so Dez took the opportunity to lean down and plant a kiss on the smiling lips. She raised her hands up to cradle Jaylynn's face, then broke off the kiss, glancing to either side of the deserted street.

"Don't worry, Dez. Nobody's looking." Jaylynn gazed up at her with an amused look on her face. "Ooh, don't take your hands away. They're so nice and warm." She took a deep breath, and the air that came out when she exhaled formed a visible puff of vapor.

Dez gave her a gloomy look. "Nice job trying to distract me." She dropped her hands to Jaylynn's shoulders and pulled her to the side, then shut the truck door. Gazing back at the shorter woman, she said, "Guess we better go in, huh?"

"Look at the bright side—when we're done here, we get to go eat goodies at Luella's." Jaylynn hooked her gloved hand around Dez's arm, and walked next to the taller woman, off the street, and onto an even icier sidewalk. They walked carefully toward the front door of the building and into the warmth of the foyer. "I never even knew this place was here. It's kind of nice what they can do with old warehouses these days."

Dez didn't answer. She took off toward a door near the elevator and held it open so that her partner could pass through and start up the stairs. By the time they reached the top, Jaylynn was peeling gloves and jacket and talking about being overly warm. Dez laughed to herself, which calmed her nerves. She couldn't help but think, *Some things never change. She's right, too—I hope I don't mind having this same conversation about the temperature for about the next 80 years.*

Once they reached the blue door of Marie Montague's office,

though, she was nervous again. She put her coat on the hook inside the door and sat in a soft chair in the waiting room. Jaylynn hung up her down coat and sank into the chair next to her, steadying her book in her lap with her good hand. Taking a deep breath, Dez leaned forward and put her elbows on her knees, letting her hands relax, palms down. She closed her eyes and let air in and out just as Marie had taught her, concentrating on relaxing all the muscles in her chest. After a moment, she felt a warm hand on her back and peeped at the woman sitting close to her. "What I wouldn't give for a backrub right now."

"Lie down on the floor," Jaylynn said, amusement in her voice. "I'd be happy to oblige."

Dez let out a snort. "Yeah, right." She looked at her watch. "She'll be opening the door any—" The wooden door popped open, and Dez was on her feet before the figure appeared before them.

"Well hello, Dez!"

The tall woman cleared her throat. "Hi, Marie. I have someone here I'd like you to meet." The rookie rose, extending her hand as Dez went on. "This is my, uh, partner, Jaylynn Savage."

The two women shook hands, both smiling broadly. "So nice to meet you, Jaylynn."

"Me, too. I've heard good things about you."

Marie released Jaylynn's hand and looked up at Dez with a mischievous smile on her face. "You've heard good things, huh? Why, Dez, I'm surprised at you!"

In a gruff voice, the tall cop answered, "What was I supposed to tell her? That you're really a merciless psychic digger who's excavated all my secrets?"

Marie nodded. "Yup. Something like that." She stepped backward into the doorway. "Come on then. I've got to get my pickaxe out, so we can get started. Make yourself comfortable, Jaylynn, and I'll have her back to you in short order."

Dez followed the therapist into the office feeling rather pleased with herself. *That went well. I didn't fall over into a dead faint or anything.* She settled herself into one of the low chairs and held back a smile that was threatening to erupt.

Marie sat down in a chair facing her and tucked her right foot under her left thigh. "Looks like you took a baby step after all, huh?"

Dez nodded, and now she couldn't hold back the grin. "I took way more than one."

"I see. Tell me about them."

They spent the next hour discussing and analyzing what had

happened with Jaylynn, as well as the visit with her mother and Mac, seeing her brother for the first time in years, and her feelings about her work. The hour flew by. When Marie announced that time was up, Dez was surprised. For once she hadn't watched the clock at all.

She rose and stood waiting uncertainly. "Marie, we're scheduled for a session on Thursday. What would you think if we skipped it?"

Marie got up, too, and looked at her thoughtfully. "I can't release you quite yet, Dez, though you can go back to work next week."

"Oh, I know that. I don't mean skipping out forever. It's just that I want to drive up north with Jay, and I'd like to go tomorrow and stay through the New Year's weekend. I don't want to leave tomorrow and have to get up the next day and drive here for the appointment and then back—"

Marie interrupted. "Oh, well, then why don't we just stay with the day after New Year's and call it good?"

"Yes. That's exactly what I had in mind. Thanks. I really appreciate it." On impulse she stretched her right hand out over the narrow coffee table, and the therapist accepted it with a warm smile on her face. "I also appreciate all you've done for me, Marie. I know I I well, I haven't been an easy person to work with."

Marie released her hand and turned toward the door. "Nonsense," she called out over her shoulder, "you've been a peach." Dez let out a laugh as the therapist opened the door. Marie stood aside as Dez passed through into the waiting room, still smiling. "I'll see you next week, kiddo."

The tall woman grinned again. "Okay, thanks." The door shut and she turned to see Jaylynn gazing up at her with an odd look on her face. "What?"

The rookie closed her book and stood, reaching for her coat. "Considering how much you were fighting coming here, I guess I'm surprised to see you so jolly."

Dez slipped on her coat and helped Jaylynn wrestle hers on over her splint. They went off down the hallway, passing multicolored office doors as they made their way to the stairwell. For the first time since she had been seeing Marie, Dez felt like she had made real progress, that perhaps she was emerging from the sadness and depression that had gripped her like a vise for so long. "I don't know exactly why, Jay. The session just went well." They entered the stairwell and started down. On the landing at the very bottom, the tall woman stopped and turned. Jaylynn was still two

steps up, holding the book against her unzipped coat with her
splinted hand and the banister railing in the other hand. Dez
reached inside the open down coat and encircled Jaylynn at the
hips, pulling her up into the air against her.

"Whoa! Dez, put me down! Be careful. My cell phone's in
my coat pocket!" She whacked the bigger woman on the back, but
was careful not to use her sore left arm. Dez gave her a wicked
grin and spun around causing Jaylynn to let out a laughing shriek.

In a low voice next to Jaylynn's ear, Dez said, "I think the
session went well because you were there. That's what I think."

"So you're rewarding me by—oooh—making me lose my
lunch?"

Dez set her back on the steps, but she didn't let go. She
looked up at the shorter woman who was now about six inches
taller standing on the second stair. "You haven't even had lunch
yet. I can't believe you aren't hungry. We ate quite a while ago."

"Truth told, I *am* hungry now."

"I figured as much." Dez put one foot up on the first stair
and pressed her hands to Jaylynn's sides under the fluffy coat.
Her hands weren't big enough to span all the way around the
smaller woman's waist, but she could get a solid grip. She looked
at the hazel eyes in front of her, conscious of the smell of shampoo
and cinnamon and something else that was just Jaylynn. A lump
rose in her throat, and in the eyes before her, she saw only love
and acceptance. Like a galvanized jolt, the realization hit her that
this one small person loomed larger in her life than anyone had in
a very long time—perhaps ever. In wonder, she said, "I love you,
Jaylynn. I can't help but keep saying it." She shook her head
slowly. "How embarrassing."

Jaylynn let out a throaty laugh, a laugh of pleasure. "It's not
embarrassing, you fool. I love you, too, and I want to tell the
world." Dez felt the shift as the smaller woman leaned off-bal-
ance to relax forward into an embrace, trusting that her sturdy
partner wouldn't let her fall. Soft lips pressed down against Dez's
mouth, and she closed her eyes to let the kiss flow through her like
an electrical current she could feel from her fingers to her toes.
When Jaylynn broke off the kiss, they were both breathless.

The hazel eyes, so close to her, shone with flecks of gold and
green and brown. She loved how the warm eyes seemed to change
color depending upon the lighting. Before she could tell her that,
Jaylynn whispered, "You are so beautiful, Dez. So incredibly
beautiful." Dez looked away to the side and brought her other
foot up onto the first stair to steady her partner into a more
upright position. Jaylynn reached up with her right hand and

touched the averted chin. "You hear me? You're beautiful. Don't even try to argue with me."

Dez blushed. She felt the flush rise up her face, to her ears, up into the roots of her hair. She imagined her face was as crimson as blood. Very slowly, she stepped back off the stair, allowing Jaylynn to get her balance, then watched as the hazel-eyed woman went down the last two steps. Reaching for the doorknob, she said, "My grandmother used to say—when I was a teenager—that I would grow into a handsome woman. That's the word she used—handsome. I was about five-nine at the time. She was appalled at how tall I was." She hesitated. "No one has ever thought of me as beautiful."

A hand on her arm stopped her from stepping through the doorway. "Ever since the first moment I laid eyes on you, I've thought you were, Dez. And I'll never stop thinking of you as anything less than beautiful through and through."

Dez smiled. "Guess you need glasses more than I thought you did." She quickly exited the stairwell, followed by one indignant blonde wielding a paperback book as a battering weapon.

Chapter
Thirty-One

Once again, Dez was driving the dark highway from St. Paul toward Duluth, only this time she wasn't alone. A sleeping figure with hair shining silver-white in the moonlight lay next to her on the bench seat of the truck. A mushy pillow pressed against the tall woman's right thigh, and Jaylynn lay on her side, tucked up next to her partner with a blanket over her. Every so often, Dez liked to reach out and put her forearm across Jaylynn's shoulder and feel the solidness of the young woman. She let her hand brush lightly over the cap of short hair as she let out a sigh of comfort. It was just after nine p.m., and the sun had set long ago. If not for her headlights, it would be pitch black on the highway. Streetlamps were few and far between, so she kept a vigilant lookout for deer.

The radio played 70's tunes softly in the background, and she thought about how well the day had gone. First, waking up next to Jaylynn had been a joy, and then their breakfast and gift exchange had gone fine, even with the one bout of tears. She figured they were even, after the crying jag she had had in the middle of the night.

It was also a relief that Jaylynn had gotten her cast off. Dez knew it had been making her miserable, and she was glad to see her practicing her grip and getting accustomed to having full use of the hand again, even if it wasn't strong yet. The counseling session had gone well, something for which she was quite thankful, and she had enjoyed eating lunch with Luella and Vanita and exchanging gifts. She'd added Jaylynn's name to both her gifts to the sisters—a chair heating pad for Vanita, and for Luella, a low-fat cookbook filled with funny sayings and jokes as well as recipes. Vanita had knitted both of them scarves, royal blue and black for Dez, and gold and bright orange for Jaylynn. Luella gave them each a certificate for the Dinner of Their Dreams. She'd made a little menu that each of them could fill in with all their favorite dishes, and she said she was ready to start preparing sumptuous banquets whenever either of them said the word.

After spending the afternoon at Vanita's house, they went to Jaylynn's so she could pack. That took so long that Dez used the phone to call over to Crystal and Shayna's place. She apologized for her neglect of them and ended up having a good conversation with both Shayna and Crystal on the line. They agreed that, after the first of the year, they would all meet up and have a dinner and a night on the town.

When Jaylynn finally appeared with a suitcase and duffel bag packed, Dez carried them out to the truck. They stopped by the apartment to pick up her guitar and a few other things, which took only ten minutes, but then they had to stop for a snack. Dez shook her head. It was a major undertaking just to get out of town. They didn't get on the road until almost seven p.m. She rolled her eyes a little and smiled to herself. Obviously, traveling alone was much quicker—but then again, traveling with someone else was a lot more fun. She watched the mile signs go by and knew that it wouldn't be much longer before they reached Duluth.

So much had happened in the last two days. It hadn't even been quite 24 hours since she had picked up Jaylynn at the airport. Realizing that caused her to shake her head in amazement and glance down at the tousled head resting against her leg. Since the rookie had arrived home, they had held each other, cried on one another's shoulders, and been in almost constant physical contact every chance they got, but they hadn't made love yet. They also hadn't explored all the topics that needed discussion. Even though she harbored a few misgivings, she was praying that everything would work out fine.

A glow ahead caused the sky in the distance to look brighter, and she knew they were nearing the city. They would pass through Duluth and continue north to Dewey's cabin, but at this rate, it would be well over two hours before they arrived. The truck made its way up the long, gradual hill and burst over the rise. She took the slow curve of the road cautiously and looked out upon the dark expanse off to her right, which was Lake Superior. In the darkness, she only knew the lake was there. She could not actually see it at all, sort of like the worry about the unknown that lurked in the back of her mind. She made her way through a series of tunnels and underpasses, and in a few minutes, they were outside the city limits again and steering north.

She wished she could trust the comfort and happiness she was feeling, but she could not—would not. Every time she slipped into the kind of reverie she had just been experiencing, frightening thoughts interfered. She put a hand protectively on Jaylynn's shoulder, and the younger woman stirred, then settled back into sleep. Luella had been right. There was no reason not to plunge in, but then again, the risks were great. It would be a lot easier not to take the road she and Jaylynn were on. *I'm not going to think that way. I won't...I can't. I will not go back to that terrible loneliness.* But she couldn't stop worrying. What if something happened to Jaylynn? What if she, herself, blew it and ruined things between them? So many things could go wrong, and a long string of awful possibilities began to parade through her head. She didn't know how to make the fears stop, and try as hard as she might, a part of her wanted to curl up inside and block out all the love and affection Jaylynn so cheerfully bestowed upon her. She didn't know exactly how to get around that obstacle, and she feared it would rise up and follow her, needle her, and worry her when she least expected it. *God, if you really are there, please help me out here. Give me a sign...* And before the thought was even complete, a deer ran out in front of the truck.

The buck paused for a split second, scared eyes seeming to meet Dez's, and then he leapt out of the way, even as Dez swerved and hit the brakes.

She skidded out of the lane and onto the shoulder of the road, her heart beating like a bass drum. The violent braking and abrupt stop tossed Jaylynn forward, though the seatbelt around her middle held her. She awoke and cried out, then struggled up and looked around, bleary-eyed. "Wh-what's happening?"

"Almost hit a deer." Dez steered the truck further off the roadway and idled on the side of the road. She had gripped the wheel so tightly that the ring on her left hand had dug into the soft flesh on the underside of her finger. It took a moment for the pain from that to abate. Jaylynn stared out the window, her eyes searching the highway, and for a few seconds, neither of them spoke.

Dez swallowed with difficulty. "Damn, that was close. Keep an eye out. Where there's one, there's usually more." She took her foot off the brake and pressed lightly on the accelerator, but before she could go more than a few feet, she saw movement in the rear view mirror and ahead of her.

"Look, Dez. It's a mother deer and two babies." She pointed out the window with excitement.

Heart still beating loud in her chest, she nodded. Once the three deer crossed the road, she navigated the truck forward, half on the shoulder of the road. Looking to the right, she could see the reflection of more eyes among the trees. "Geez, it's a whole herd."

Jaylynn nestled closer and tightened up her seatbelt. She leaned into the bigger woman. "Good driving, partner. If I was at the wheel, I bet I might've hit one of them."

A snort of laughter came out of Dez. "I bet you would, too. How many car accidents have you had now anyway?"

Jaylynn looked up at her, and what she said next came out sharply. "I'll have you know I've never had an accident, not one! Not even a ticket!"

"Hey, hey! Okay. I stand corrected."

"I have perfectly good reflexes, Miss Mario Andretti. I got rated higher than 95% of the officers at pursuit training."

Dez had been gradually accelerating, and now she was up to 50 miles per hour. She took her eyes off the road for a split second to look Jaylynn in the eye, then returned to scanning the highway. "Yeah, what about that little accident you had at the speedway?"

"You can't count that! We were *supposed* to learn how to crack up the cars."

Jaylynn's voice was filled with so much indignation that Dez was having a hard time holding back laughter. "I think you're supposed to learn how to *avoid* cracking up the cars."

The rookie crossed her arms in front of her and stared forward. After a moment, she said in a quiet voice, "You need to understand that I've never done one damn risky thing in my life, Dez. I was never a foolhardy child. I have always been responsible and organized and...and...well, downright boring."

"You've never been boring."

"Don't patronize me."

The words had come out sharply again, so Dez chose her next words with care. "I have known you less than a year and a half, Jay, but I can honestly say I have never found you boring. Responsible, yes. Organized, mostly. But never boring." Jaylynn didn't respond right away. Dez reached a series of curves in the road and slowed down to 40. Ahead of her, she saw two bright pinpricks of light that grew larger as they neared. The other driver turned down his bright lights at the same time Dez did, and when the sedan passed them, she flipped the brights back on. She took that moment to glance at her traveling companion and saw that she was fuming. She reached down and placed her hand lightly on the rookie's taut thigh muscle and gave a little pat.

"Don't try to butter me up, Dez."

The big woman didn't move her hand. "I'm not trying to butter you up."

"Yeah, you're trying to humor me."

"No, I'm not. I'm reaching out to you because I want to understand why you're upset."

It all came out in a torrent. "You don't think I'm good enough to be a cop, to take care of myself on the job. You think I'm weak. You do, don't you?" The rookie looked up, accusingly, but she didn't wait for an answer. "Just because I don't have the experience *you* have doesn't mean I'm a mediocre officer."

It occurred to Dez that this was a continuation of the ultimatum conversation in the hospital, and she wasn't quite sure how to resolve it. "Jay, I think what we need to do is separate out your skills and abilities from my fears—and from your fears, too." She didn't go on, though Jaylynn seemed to be waiting for more.

"What's that supposed to mean?"

"You have excellent skills. You're great with people. You make good judgments—most of the time anyway. We all make mistakes here and there. You adapt well and you work hard to follow the rules and do the right thing. You were an excellent recruit, and with few exceptions, your rookie year has been exemplary. The captain and all three lieutenants in our precinct have been very impressed with you."

"But *you*, what about your opinion?"

The tone of misery in her voice clued Dez in. This wasn't about what the brass thought or what her partner's test scores were. This was something else entirely. She took a deep breath. "I love you, Jay. I don't want you to get hurt again. Ever. I don't want to lose you. I *never* want to come in from the field to learn that you have been harmed in any way. I don't want to be awakened in the middle of the night the way Julie was, with the lieutenant and the chaplain on our doorstep." Her voice broke and she took a moment to recover. "I want to trust your actions and judgments, and believe me, when I was there on patrol with you, I almost always did. The mistakes you made were normal rookie mistakes, all minor. But then, well, when we were separated, things started happening, and I was plain scared. My fear has little to do with you or your abilities. Don't you see? It's *my* fear, *my* pain."

Jaylynn uncrossed her arms and rested her splinted left hand on top of Dez's. In a soft voice, she asked, "What makes you think I'm not afraid? It could just as easily be you killed in the line of duty."

"Nah. Think about it. I've already been shot once—and by

the way, don't ever forget that you're the one who saved my ass."
Jaylynn didn't say anything, so she went on. "I know you have
very good instincts. I have them, too. The odds of me being shot
again are slim. I've got the odds in my favor."

"Maybe." Jaylynn's voice was skeptical.

"Look, I was wrong at the hospital for telling you to quit the
force. That was fear talking. And I was so afraid that I used a
really unfair argument—that you are small and not as strong as
me. You are smaller, and I am stronger, but hell, you can outrun
and outlift pretty much every other woman in the department, not
counting Crystal. You make Pilcher look like a toad."

Jaylynn let out a laugh at that. "She couldn't run more than a
block if you paid her extra."

"And we won't even talk about Cal Braswell."

"For sure."

"Look, my love, Luella told me the other day that I needed to
work at letting go of all this worry and fear and enjoy what I have,
even if it doesn't last forever. That's a novel concept for me, but
I'm trying. You've gotta help me, though. You're way better at it
than I am."

Jaylynn nodded thoughtfully. "I'll try, but I'm really not all
that great at it either—obviously—since I'm haranguing you here
like some sort of bitchy shrew. I'm really sorry, Dez."

"I'd rather have you tell me your feelings. I guess I'd rather
get it out on the table and talk about it."

"Ah, I see. Well, you'd better be prepared to reciprocate,
Miss Reticent. The road has to go both ways."

"Yeah, yeah. I think Marie has dug around enough that I'm
actually getting used to it."

"And a fine, fine woman *she* turned out to be." Jaylynn
grinned and squeezed the big hand in her lap. "By the way, when
the heck are we going to get there? We must be in Canada by
now."

"Maybe another forty-five minutes."

"Seems like we've been on the road for hours."

"We *have* been on the road for hours."

"Oh, okay." She grinned mischievously. "Forty-five minutes,
you think? That's just enough time for another nap."

"Oh, yeah, go ahead and desert me in my hour of need."

Jaylynn was already nestling down next to her. "I know
you'll be fine, sweetie. Look at what a good job you did with that
herd of deer."

"Yeah, sure. You want the blanket?"

"Heck no. I don't really need it. You're better than a blanket any day."

Dez put her hand on the rookie's shoulder and Jaylynn shifted a bit so she could pull the warm hand to her chest. Dez cradled her protectively, her fingers laced with the smaller woman's. It wasn't very long before her companion fell asleep, and the tall cop was left to her own musings again. She decided that the next time she wanted a message from God, she ought to make sure she wasn't in a moving vehicle.

****

They arrived at Dewey's place shortly after midnight. Dez drove slowly past her friend's cabin and down the long gravel drive to the parking spot in front of Cabin G. "We're here, sleepy-head." She shook Jaylynn's shoulder only to hear the smaller woman groan.

"I was just having a really good dream," Jaylynn said in a sleepy voice.

Dez pulled into the slot and put the truck in park. She opened the door as she said, "Just get out, stagger in, and get in bed."

Jaylynn sat up, shivering, and rubbed her eyes. She yawned. "Geez, it's freezing." She watched as Dez slid out her side of the truck and opened the door to the rear of the cab. She grabbed some of the bags while Jaylynn scooted over and followed her out the driver's side. "Brrr." The rookie reached over the back of the seat, fumbled around until she found her gold and orange scarf, and wrapped it around her neck. "I swear to God, it's colder here than down in the Cities."

"Could be." Dez shifted the bags around and fumbled with the keys, finally asking, "Jay, will you take the keys out of my hand and open the door?"

Yawning again, the younger woman grabbed the keys. She pointed at the cabin. "Right here? We go in here?"

"Yup." Dez followed her up to the wooden door and waited while Jaylynn inserted the key and got the door open. "Light switch just inside the door to the left."

Jaylynn wasn't prepared for what she saw when she flipped the light switch. Several lights in the huge living room were connected to that switch, and when they popped on, they cast light into the kitchen as well as the living room. Her eyes took in a stone fireplace, thick colorful rugs on wooden floors, paintings of Lake Superior scenes on every wall, and a couch and three easy chairs all upholstered in golds and reds and dark blues. Dez bumped her from behind, and she stepped out of the foyer and into the doorway of the half-lit kitchen. The tall cop carted the bags into the living room and through a doorway off to the side.

Jaylynn reached out to the kitchen wall and felt along it until she found the switch to turn on. *Wow. This is really nice.* The stove and fridge were both off-white, the cupboards made of shiny pine, and the walls painted a high-gloss shade of ivory. On the little bit of wall space not covered by cupboards or blocked by appliances, colorful forest scenes were hung in wooden frames. The vinyl floor was a shiny green and white with gold speckled highlights throughout. She stepped over to the counter next to the oven and touched the dark green Formica. It was smooth and cool, and everything was clean.

She heard Dez open the front door and go out for the last load, so she went to the foyer to look through the small window and wait for her to reappear. When the tall cop came back, loaded down with a duffel, her guitar case, and two grocery bags, Jaylynn opened the door for her, then closed it tight and turned the deadbolt. "This place is really something, Dez."

"Dewey has done a nice job with this little resort of his." She put the two grocery bags down on the kitchen counter.

"I'll say. Must cost you a fortune to stay here."

"Nope. I've done a lot of work for him, so it doesn't cost a thing. C'mon, I'll show you the rest of the place." As she passed through the living room and into the doorway to the left, she paused and turned the thermostat up. "The heat here works pretty fast. Should be nice and warm in short order." As Jaylynn followed her, she looked over by the wall on the other side of the kitchen wall, which she hadn't been able to see from the foyer. There stood Dez's acoustic guitar stand. Now that she thought about it, she hadn't noticed it at the apartment. Next to it was an easy chair and a small bookshelf piled full of paperbacks. A stack of newspapers nearly a foot high was heaped to the side of the chair.

Dez disappeared into the dark room and turned on the bedroom light. She tossed the duffel bag on the king-sized bed. Jaylynn followed her in, feeling the thick wall-to-wall carpeting under her feet. She looked around in wonder. The room was wallpapered in a forest green and off-white swirl pattern. She had thought the living room was large, but she saw that the bedroom was, too. In the center of the 15 x 20 foot space sat a huge king-size bed with a massive wooden headboard and a multicolored quilt on it. On either side sat bedside tables, and each had a clock/radio on it. Directly across from the foot of the bed, on the opposite wall, was an entertainment center on which a large TV and VCR sat. Through the glass doors in the lower half of the stand, Jaylynn saw a row of videos. On the other wall to the right of the bed, a glass door was covered with mint green colored floor-length drapes. She strode over, slid the curtain to the side, and peeked out.

"It's a really nice deck, Jay. There's a gas barbecue grill out there and lots of lawn chairs, but they're in the storage shed right now for the winter. There are still two Adirondack chairs though, since they're made of wood and weather the storms."

Jaylynn couldn't see any of this very well. The moon was behind the clouds, and all she could make out were lines and shadows. She let the drapes drop and turned around. On the wall opposite from where she stood were two doors. She could tell one led to the bathroom because she could see the sink in there. The rookie moved over toward the other open door.

Dez said, "That's a cool storage closet." She angled past Jaylynn and stepped inside to pull the string for the overhead light. "You can hang clothes and keep shoes on this side." She gestured to the maple cubbyholes and the long rod half-filled with hangers and hanging clothing. "On the other side here, we can keep staples—you know, canned goods, the vacuum cleaner, detergent, TP, cleaning supplies."

Jaylynn nodded as she looked around the 6 x 10 foot closet. She leaned into Dez, happy suddenly to be able to feel some heated air circulating her way. Her good hand found its way into Dez's, and she smiled when she felt the warm palm against her cooler fingers. Dez reached up and pulled the light switch off, but not before the rookie noticed that there were a lot of familiar-looking clothes hanging up, along with a backpack, one of Dez's weapons, and two boxes of ammunition. She followed the tall woman out of the closet and poked her head into the bathroom. The light switch was right where she thought it would be—just inside the door. Letting go of Dez's hand, she stepped onto a plush mint green area rug and looked around. This room was painted a glossy tan and trimmed with a white and green tree border around the top of the walls. The full-size tub and shower took up the majority of the cozy little room, and suddenly, a hot bath sounded inviting. Some of the towels sitting on a white wicker shelf to the left of the sink were maroon and some were blue, and neither quite matched the color scheme. On the counter sat cologne, lotions, and various toiletry items.

As she turned to leave the room, Jaylynn frowned. Everywhere she looked, Dez's stuff was hanging up or set carefully or organized and ready to use. When she thought of the condition of the apartment at Luella's, it occurred to her that the place had looked pretty bare. "Dez, it looks like you've totally moved in here."

The tall woman shrugged. "I guess I practically have, little by little."

Jaylynn unzipped her coat and removed her orange and gold scarf. "Well, we had better get some things squared around. Once we get a little bit unpacked, I think I want to crash. How 'bout you?"

Dez nodded. "You hungry at all?"

The rookie shook her head. "Just tired." She didn't understand why she felt so deflated, but she had lost energy as she had looked around the cabin. Something was bothering her, but she wasn't sure what. She slipped her coat off and tucked her scarf into the sleeve.

"There's a front closet, Jay. Here let me take that." Dez took the brown coat and left the room. Jaylynn wandered along behind her. Next to the front door there was, indeed, a wide closet with bi-fold doors. On the floor sat a jumble of cross-country skis, bags, and boxes. Several coats—some Dez's, some not—hung in the closet. "Every time someone leaves something here, Dewey just co-opts it for the cabin. There's about 10 extra coats here and a bucket of mittens."

"What's in there?" Jaylynn pointed to a door next to the closet.

Dez turned the knob and swung the door open so she could see the sink and toilet. "It's a guest bathroom." She shut the door and turned around, then leaned back against it.

Jaylynn tipped her head back and looked up at the tall woman. "Dez?" The tall woman bit her lip and looked her in the eye. "What's wrong, Dez?"

An emotion passed over the taller woman's features, but Jaylynn couldn't identify it before she squelched it and assumed a more passive look. Dez arched an eyebrow. "Why?"

"I don't know. It's just...hmmm." Jaylynn took a step forward and leaned into her companion. Long arms encircled her and pulled her close, and her arms found their way around the small of the bigger woman's back. She could feel Dez's chin resting on the top of her head, and with her right ear pressed against the flannel of Dez's shirt, she heard a slow, steady heartbeat. In contrast, her own heart beat a rapid thump-thump, and without warning, a flush of warmth engulfed her. No longer tired, she pulled Dez to an upright position, turned her around, and guided her toward the bedroom.

"What about the unpacking?"

Jaylynn laughed. "I don't give a damn about the unpacking." As she passed into the room, she gave the light switch a swipe with her good hand, and the room went dim, with only the light from the living room shining in.

Dez stopped at the foot of the bed, her back to the younger woman, and kicked her shoes off, which Jaylynn also did. Then the rookie pushed her toward the bed. Dez put a jean-covered knee on the quilt and crawled toward the top of the bed, but before she could get turned around, Jaylynn was beside her, pressing against her until she shifted onto her side, then to her back. The smaller woman hovered above, her fingers tangled in the dark French braid. She smoothed a tendril of dark hair to one side to expose the smooth creamy skin of the pale neck below, then kissed her behind her ear. The effect upon Dez was electric. Her body went taut and the rookie could feel the response. Jaylynn's lips sought out the other woman's mouth, and an urgent hunger over-took her kisses. She unbuttoned the flannel shirt, reached inside the material to find warm skin, then sighed. She closed her eyes and reveled in the sensation of the toasty smooth skin under her fingers. Reaching down to fumble with the button on Dez's jeans, she became aware that something had changed. One minute Dez was awash with passion, and now the long body had stiffened.

"Wait. Wait, Jay."

"Isn't it terrible? I just want to devour you—touch every part of you. I feel absolutely greedy." Dez didn't reply, so the rookie took a deep breath and scooted up. She let her body slide to the side, her left elbow digging into the quilt next to the dark-haired woman, and her right leg still across the jean-clad legs. "What's the matter?" She tried to look into her partner's eyes. In the dim light, she saw that Dez's eyes were shut tight. With alarm, she asked again, "Dez, what's the matter—what's wrong?"

The tall woman put her left arm over her face, and her voice, when it came, was husky. "I don't know. I'm just..." She took a deep breath. "I'm afraid."

Jaylynn felt the energy that had been building, the excitement that she had been feeling, rush out of her. In its place, a whirl-wind of doubts came into her mind. She pushed those fears aside and as calmly as possible, asked, "Why? Why are you afraid?"

There was a break of time before Dez's next words came out, this time in a whisper. "I...I don't know how to explain it."

Jaylynn waited, but Dez didn't move and she didn't say any more. Another wave of fear, this one coupled with fatigue, washed over her. She rolled away and swung her feet off the bed and onto the floor. For a few moments, with all that blood pumping through her body, she had been quite warm, but now she shivered. She unbuttoned her shirt, unhooked the clasps of her bra, and shed both. *We were fine on the way up here. We've been communicating well until now. What is this all about?* She racked her brain to try to understand, but no bright ideas floated up. Unbuttoning her pants, she thought about all that had happened to them. It hadn't even been two full days yet since she'd flown home. Of course they had things to talk about, things to consider, but she had hoped they could get to them leisurely over the next few days.

She stepped out of her pants and slipped her socks off, then pulled the covers back on the edge of the bed. "Shove over, you big galoot," she said in a falsely hearty voice. "Better yet, why don't you get out of those clothes and get in here and warm me up?"

As Jaylynn squirmed in, Dez rolled the other direction, across the expanse of the king-sized bed. When her feet hit the floor, she sat on the edge of the bed, her back to the rookie. Jaylynn didn't know what to do. *Do I go to her? Talk to her? Yell? Cry? What is the right response here?* Because she didn't know the answers to the questions running through her head, she decided just to wait.

After a moment, the tall cop stood and slipped out of her clothes, leaving on only her briefs. She stood a moment, as if uncertain, and then Jaylynn watched as she went toward the living room and disappeared around the corner. For a moment, Jaylynn was alarmed. Before she could consider the reasons why Dez would leave the room, the lights went out, plunging the whole place into complete darkness, except for the red displays on the clock/radios on either side of the bed. The faint red glow gave only just enough light for her to see the tall form that ambled back into the room and around the other side of the bed. Dez pulled the covers back and joined her under the cool covers. As her partner scooted over, Jaylynn moved toward her until they were both in the middle of the bed, right next to one another. The smaller woman turned onto her side and pressed the front of her thighs against the side of Dez's legs, which, she was surprised to feel, were chilled. She snuggled up against the bigger woman, both of them shivering, until gradually, they warmed to one another.

I don't know what's wrong, and I don't know what to do. She let herself agonize for a few moments, worrying that she had said or done something to upset or offend Dez, but then she pushed

those thoughts out of her mind. Whatever was wrong with her
taciturn partner probably didn't have as much to do with her as it
did with all that had happened in the last few weeks. Something
was definitely bothering her, but until the tall cop chose to share
that with her, she would just have to wait. She bit her tongue and
forced herself not to ask any more questions. Weariness overtook
her, and she fell asleep.

****

Dez lay in the darkened room, wide awake. She had noted
the exact moment when Jaylynn's breath had gone from its regular
waking tempo to slow and measured. Glancing at the clock, she
saw that it had been almost an hour ago.

*What a disaster I made of this evening. Everything was going
perfectly.* If she could have smacked herself without waking Jaylynn, she would have. Instead, she lay very still, listening to the
younger woman's soft breathing as she upbraided herself for what
she thought of as stupidity. *Afraid? I'm afraid? What the hell am
I so damn scared of? That's ridiculous.*

But she could not escape it. She *was* afraid. She felt shaky
inside, short of breath. It had been coming over her in waves since
shortly after she and Jaylynn had tumbled into bed. *And what
must Jaylynn think of me? Does she think I'm nuts, or what? If I
were her, I would.*

She threaded her fingers together, feeling the solidity of the
metal band around her ring finger. For several minutes she toyed
with the ring, twisting it first one way, then the other, feeling the
engraved pattern all around it.

She turned over on her side facing Jaylynn's back, and the
warm figure next to her squirmed and adjusted until her back and
legs were tucked against the front of Dez's body. She put her arm
across the smaller woman's hip, and Jaylynn settled down again.

*I need her so much...I love her so much that it's scaring me to
death. What if I lose her? What if she leaves me? What if she
gets hurt or dies on duty? Oh God, how can I deal with this?* She
wanted to cry. She wanted to scream. She wanted to get up, pack
her things, and run away.

She didn't move. She lay next to the slumbering woman, her
heart beating fast, while a rampage of horrible visions of death
and dismemberment played in her mind. Not only could she feel
her heart pounding, she could hear it, too, the thud beating in her
ears, a steady drumbeat that she couldn't make stop. She no
longer needed to sleep and dream to be confronted with these

fears; she could lie there wide awake and visualize all the scenes of everything she was afraid of in vivid Technicolor. Her skin went cold, her flesh crawled, and despite feeling chilled, she was sweating. She thought she now understood what a waking nightmare was, and if she had had any idea whatsoever that she would feel this way, she would perhaps have brought it up with Marie earlier in the day.

Despite the fears coursing through her mind, she was so fatigued that after more time passed, she felt herself drift off to sleep. With a start, she jerked awake, afraid of what she might experience if she did allow herself to lose consciousness. She was about ready to rise and creep out to the living room when Jaylynn turned over. In a sleepy voice, she said, "Okay. We're to the point now where you have two choices—either you lie still and sleep peacefully, or else you tell me what the *hell* is wrong."

Dez's breath came out in a rush, and her heart was beating so violently that she couldn't speak.

Jaylynn went on, her voice grumpy. "I'm happy I got a good fifteen minutes of sleep, but since then, you've been twitching and flipping around like a beached fish. Just tell me, Dez. Whatever it is won't kill you."

Dez gulped and for a moment wasn't able to breathe. When she finally opened her mouth to speak, her words came out in a quiet whisper. "What will I do if you leave me?"

Jaylynn answered promptly. "I'm not leaving you."

"But how do you know that? How can you be sure?"

Jaylynn shifted up toward the head of the bed, punched at the pillow, and wriggled until she got comfortable. "I don't know how I know, but I do." She reached out and put her hand on a tight shoulder to pull her closer, and Dez let herself be reeled in.

"It's embarrassing to admit, but I'm still afraid."

Jaylynn let out a sigh. "Look, I'll sign anything you want—in blood, too. I'm not going anywhere, Dez. I love you."

Dez wrapped the smaller woman in her arms and pressed her face into the short hair, which smelled faintly of strawberries. In a muffled voice she asked, "How do you know your feelings won't change?"

"They will."

The warmth Dez was feeling went away suddenly, replaced with a cold chill. She was so afraid she was going to start trembling that she could not utter a word.

"Look, Miss Worrywart, both of us are going to grow and change and feel more and more deeply about each other. I'm looking forward to that, to finding out all the rest of your quirks and oddities." She stroked the bigger woman's back, letting her palm run down to the slim hip and along Dez's thigh, then back up. In a soft voice, with her mouth near the tall cop's ear, she said, "I don't know how to make you understand how I feel—except by making love with you."

Dez shivered, but this time it wasn't from cold. Her heart beat a little faster, and she swallowed. "So that's what you're telling me at those times, huh?"

"Yes." She giggled. "I'm not *just* getting my jollies. It means so much more." She pressed her lips into the soft neck in front of her. Her next words came out in a whisper. "Can I kiss you?"

Dez didn't answer, but her lips found Jaylynn's and made contact. The kiss was sweet, and Dez could tell the smaller woman was holding back the insistence she had shown earlier. She rolled the rookie over onto her back and deepened the kiss. When she pulled away, they were both breathless. She wished she could see Jaylynn's face better, but there was only the faintest of light in the room. She considered getting up and switching on a light, but before she could even move, Jaylynn spoke up.

"I'm afraid."

Now it was Dez's turn to be confused. "What?"

"I'm afraid you're squishing me!" She let out a shriek and jabbed her fingers into Dez's sides, tickling her as furiously as she could and knowing that she'd be overcome by her stronger partner in seconds. Laughing, Dez used her strong arms to push up and scramble away until she was kneeling halfway down the bed and fending her off.

With mock seriousness, she asked, "I tell you the secrets of my heart and soul, and you tickle me?"

"You got that right." The rookie shifted up onto her knees and used her hands and body to push against the bigger woman, but Dez held her off until she steadied the two of them by putting her arms around Jaylynn's waist. Knee to knee, balancing on the soft mattress, they both breathed deeply, still laughing. Tentatively, Jaylynn reached up with her good hand and touched the tall woman's breast. "Is this okay? Can I touch you?"

But the nervousness arose again, and Dez felt her heart beating painfully. She couldn't control the wave of panic. Now she was glad that it was dark so that Jaylynn couldn't see the flush of embarrassment that she felt spread from her breastbone, up her face, all the way up to the roots of her hair. Closing her eyes, she stopped breathing, and tried to force all thought out of her mind.

"Dez?"

"Hmm?"

Taking hold of one of the tall woman's hands, Jaylynn sat back from her kneeling position onto her heels, leaving Dez towering over her on her knees. "Why don't you lie down, and I'll just rub your back?"

Without a word, she leaned forward, sliding around Jaylynn, and sank down onto the bed face-first. She took a pillow and wadded it up inside the circle of her arms and pressed her forehead into it.

Jaylynn pulled the covers up over her shoulders, and settled herself along the left side of Dez's long form, her right leg over the back of the big woman's left thigh. Supporting her upper body with her left elbow, she stroked Dez's bare back with her right hand. "I still remember way back at the end of last winter when I came over to your apartment and made the moves on you. I didn't understand then what I know now—and what I learned over Labor Day weekend. You close up like a hermit crab, Dez, anytime you are worried or afraid." She scooted up closer to work the muscles in the tense neck below her, using her fingers to dig in a little bit every so often. "You don't have to be that way with me. I'll tell you how I feel, and you tell me what your feelings are. It's pretty simple. I guess I don't expect you to trust me one hundred percent immediately, but maybe over time?"

Dez turned her head to the side and her voice came out in a raspy whisper. "It's not that I don't trust you." Jaylynn waited for something further. "I don't trust the world. It's a pretty damn awful place."

The smaller woman stopped rubbing the muscles in her upper back and nestled in with her arm around Dez's ribcage. "That's why we're supposed to be a refuge for one another."

Dez let out a big sigh and shifted so that she was facing her partner. "That's how it's supposed to work, huh?"

"Yup."

"What if I'm no good at it?"

Jaylynn let out a giggle and pressed firmly against the side of the warm waist that was snug against her. "Then I'll just do the tickle torture on you every chance I get until you learn."

"I see. Well, all I have to say is that I'm glad Marie's my shrink and not you. She practices a hands off policy when I get like this."

A deep throaty hum came from Jaylynn, and she said, "I could never keep my hands off you, Desiree Reilly."

Dez shook her head. "I keep wondering if you're nuts or what." She started to go on, then paused a moment. "And I keep wondering when all of this is going to end, because believe me when I say, nobody feels this way about me. It's never happened."

Jaylynn's right hand came up and found the tall cop's face. She cupped the overly warm cheek in her hand, and said, "You were due." Dez smiled. "And maybe I was due, too. Did you ever consider that?" She snuggled closer to the smooth body next to her, and let her hand stroke down the neck, along her companion's shoulder, and down her arm, but made no move to do anything more than stroke the satiny hip and thigh near her. She lay quietly, waiting.

"Would you stay with me, Jay, if we could never make love again?"

Without hesitation, she said, "Yes."

"Why?"

"Because I love *you*—not just your body, but all of you. I like being with you. I like your sense of humor. I love the way you think, the things you know, the stuff you tell me. I need to talk to you, to have you listen to me. I crave that. I need it like, well, like—air. I almost went crazy these last few weeks without you."

Dez gathered her tighter into her arms and pulled her close. "You would've gotten over it. Really. You're very resilient." She brushed the blonde hair out of Jaylynn's eyes, stroking her cheek and the side of her neck softly.

"I wouldn't ever have gotten over it. Don't ever say that again. Maybe the hole in my heart would have healed, but the scar would be there always, a little ache that would never totally go away."

Dez nodded. She knew—with a sudden poignancy—what Jaylynn was saying. There were people in her life whom she had loved so deeply that when they left or died, they, too, left a terrible scar. And maybe it was the fear of further scarring that was making her so afraid tonight. At the same time, as they lay there, some little part of her heart was also filling up, expanding, as though to say, *Yeah, I'm battered and scarred, but I'm a long way from quitting*. Tears sprang to her eyes, and she felt a sense of gratefulness wash over her that just a few minutes earlier, she would never have guessed she would feel. She tipped her face against the smaller woman's shoulder and choked out, "I just love you so much, Jay. I can't help but worry."

"It's okay. I understand. I worry about you, too." They lay there for several moments, wrapped in a tight embrace and then Jaylynn sighed. "Shall we try to get some sleep?"

Dez responded by leaning closer to her partner and seeking out her lips. She willed herself to relax, to let any bad thoughts out of her mind. "No," she murmured into the small ear below her. "Not quite yet. I'd like to...to make love with you." Her legs shivered with weakness, and very quickly all thoughts, good and bad, fled from her mind and were replaced by the pleasure of communicating the love she felt through touch.

****

Later, well after three in the morning, Dez was leaning against the headboard, pillows behind her. Jaylynn sprawled on her side between the V of the big woman's legs with her head on the reclining woman's abdomen. Dez had pulled the covers up around the rookie's neck, but she herself was, as usual, overly warm. In a while she planned to get up and turn the heater down.

As she stroked the white-blonde head resting below her rib cage, she took a deep breath and let it out slowly. Her body was finally relaxed enough to sleep, but her mind wasn't quite there yet. She was still puzzling over too many things.

"Dez?"

"Hmm?" She had thought Jaylynn had fallen asleep.

"How come you were never afraid when we made love before?"

"Who said I wasn't afraid?"

"You never seemed afraid—well, except for our very first night, I mean. But that was different."

Dez looked across the dark room and out into the living room. A shaft of light from the moon must have been shining in because there was an odd silver tone out there. "Maybe back then I was better at denial. I didn't let myself think about things that I'm worrying about now."

"Why is it that I'm not the one worrying that you will leave me?"

"Because I'm more reliable?" She let out a hearty laugh that she squelched when she felt a sharp pinch on her hipbone. "Hey, just kidding."

"Yeah, I know—but I was serious. How does either of us know that the other won't leave?"

"I guess we don't."

Jaylynn started to push up off her elbow, but it was her left arm, and her weak wrist was at an odd angle that made it hurt. She turned her forearm over, palm up, and pressed, while scooting upward. She hefted herself up and over one of Dez's thighs and arranged herself along the bigger woman's right side. Pulling the covers up over herself, she snuggled in close. "I won't leave you,

Dez. I can't promise anything more than that, but I want to be with you. I love being with you. I'm yours as long as you want me."

"Oh, Jay, I'll always want you." She snaked a long arm around the rookie's neck and turned slightly so that they settled into a comfortable embrace with the tousled blonde head under her chin.

They were still lying that way four hours later when Dez awakened again. She looked out into the living room where shafts of sunlight slanted into the room, then glanced over at the clock on her side of the bed. She closed her eyes and slipped back to sleep.

Chapter
Thirty-Two

Dez drove the big Ford, and Jaylynn rode in the center seat leaning her head against her partner's shoulder. She held the big woman's hand tightly, even though her arm and left wrist were bothering her. The doctor had told her to be careful with it, or she could easily be reinjured. She was not sure what she had done to it the night before, but it felt slightly strained, so she decided to make a point to protect it a little more today.

On the seat next to her was a black backpack filled with mittens, sweatshirts, and an extra layer of dry long underwear; and behind the driver's seat was another backpack that Dez had packed with snacks and supplies. A bright blue, Gore-Tex anorak with a hood lay over the back of the seat, too, so she figured that wherever they went to hike, she would be warm. She was wearing padded hiking boots, gaiters from knee to ankle, and several layers of clothes. They'd only been in the truck a few minutes, but already, she was a little too warm and reached over to turn down the heat.

"What?" Dez asked. "The Frozen Princess is turning the heat down? Unbelievable!"

"Thick socks, long underwear, and lined hiking pants will do that to a person. For once, I'm actually too warm."

"Don't worry. We're almost there." She went another quarter mile and then turned into a graveled lot next to Highway 61. As usual, there were no other cars in the small area. She drove in, backed up and turned, parking the truck facing out toward the road. "Okay, here we are. Ready?"

Jaylynn was pulling her second mitten on over her stiff hand. She nodded. "Yup. Let's do it."

Dez picked up the daypack from behind her seat and waited

until Jaylynn slid out behind her before locking up the truck. "Hey, did you want to take anything out of that other backpack?" She gestured toward the front seat.

"Nah. If I get wet, I can come back and change, right?" Dez nodded. "Then there's no need to haul it around. And I can take turns carrying that pack if you like."

Dez zipped the truck keys into the pocket in front of the backpack, then adjusted the straps. "If I get fatigued, I'll be sure to take you up on that."

Jaylynn grinned. She knew full well that her hiking partner would never admit to getting tired. "Suit yourself. Just wanted you to know I would do my part." She breathed out to check if she could see her breath, but it really wasn't that cold. There were heaps of snow alongside the road and melting patches of ice here and there in the parking lot, but she didn't think it was any colder than thirty degrees, and there was almost no wind. "Weren't we lucky to get such a nice day?" Dez nodded. "Is it going to be slick and slushy where we're headed?"

"No. Not too much. This trail is somewhat protected from the wind and snow—lot of big evergreens on it. But there are some sloppy spots and some ice ridges. We'll get around 'em. Don't worry."

"I'm holding you to it. Better not be any avalanches."

Dez just smiled and didn't answer. She turned and walked through the lot and along the edge of the road pavement until she came to the wide path which turned uphill and led off into the trees. "Jay, have you ever been here before?"

"No, I haven't. Hope we don't get lost. Are we wandering, or do you know really where we're going?"

Dez let out a snort of laughter. "Yeah, I know this whole area better than the back of your hand."

"My hand's been in a cast. Sure you haven't forgotten?"

"Nope." The rookie fell in behind the taller woman to begin the hike up the steep incline. They quickly fell into a steady pace. Dez had walked up this hill so many times in the last couple weeks that she did feel she knew it well. She smelled the pungent evergreen and behind that, the mustier smell of mulch and evaporating water. It was cool and shaded under the trees, and as long as they stayed under the cover of the branches, the ground was frozen solid and easy to tread. She was so focused on the scenery, and upon the feeling of being alive that coursed through her body, that she didn't notice the first time Jaylynn cleared her throat. The second time, she checked her stride, then paused and turned. The smaller woman was straggling along behind.

"Ahem. Is there any reason why we're practically running up this hill?"

Dez grinned. "It's not even been a mile."

Jaylynn caught up to her companion and reached out her mitten to touch the front of Dez's lightweight jacket. In an accusing voice, she said, "You told me we were going out for a hike in a beautiful forest."

"We are. But don't you want to get your heart rate up? Burn a little extra fat?"

"Are you calling me fat?"

Dez snickered. "Not you, honey. Me!"

"You can lose weight any old time, but how am I supposed to see this beautiful forest if I'm practically running—and uphill, at that?" Dez swept her into her arms, pulling her tight to her chest. "Hey, no fair! I can't even get my arms around you with this fat pack."

In a gruff voice, the tall woman said, "I'll have you know that *fat* pack mostly contains stuff for you."

"*I* didn't bring two quarts of water—or the Glock."

"Always handy to have a weapon, you know."

"Yeah, just in case we wanted to target shoot or deer hunt."

Dez snickered, and then bent slightly and lifted Jaylynn off her feet.

"Whoa! Put me down! You're getting to be as bad as Cowboy."

Laughing, the big cop set her back on the dirt path, then leaned over and planted a brief kiss on her lips. When she pulled back, she was still smiling. "Okay, cut out the whining, and I'll slow down and stroll with you. It's a bit too narrow here, but when we get to the top of this long hill, it's not so steep, and the path—well, the meadow—is wider and more open.

They toiled up the hill, and just when Jaylynn said she thought her thighs were going to burn up, they reached the crest. Dez slipped the backpack off, set it at her feet, then reached back to take her partner's hand and pull her up onto the ridge. They stood there, arms around one another, looking out over the woods ahead of them. The evergreen trees stood in stark contrast to the leaf-less birch, aspen, and poplar. Icicles had formed on some of the tree branches, but at the moment they were frozen solid and twinkling in the sunlight. Patches of snow and some deep drifts made the field look like a picture from a Christmas card. The greens and grays, silvers, tans, whites, and browns were a combination of colors pleasing to the eye.

"It really is beautiful," Jaylynn said. "And I'll bet it's just gorgeous when all this is in bloom."

Dez nodded as she felt a lump grow in her throat. Every other time she had been here, by the time she had hiked to this point in the trail, she had been crying with pain and loneliness. Now, tears welled up in her eyes, but not tears of anguish or sadness. A light wind blew against her face, and she felt an expanding feeling in her chest, almost as if she were filling up with some invisible magic air. *Hope*. The one word came to mind. She felt a sense of possibility and hope. When she turned and looked down, she found the younger woman examining her with a funny look on her face. "What?" she choked out.

"What does this place mean to you?"

Dez bent and opened the "fat" backpack and removed one of the quart bottles of water. She uncapped it and took a long pull from it, then offered it to Jaylynn who shook her head. She took another drink, then wiped her mouth on the back of her mitten. The rookie was waiting patiently for an answer to her question, so Dez squatted down, and while she returned the bottle to the backpack, she said, "I've walked this trail and that other one down there," she pointed, "almost every day that I have been here at Dewey's cabins. I've spent a lot of time thinking—and crying— and wondering about my life." She stood and Jaylynn watched her, an open look on her face. "I guess I wasn't sure how I would feel up here because it has been such a place of sorrow. But it doesn't feel that way today."

Jaylynn nodded as though she understood completely. "It's light and...and cheery. Sort of a bright spot in the middle of the forest. It seems like a place of hope, Dez."

The tall woman thought it was funny that Jaylynn would use the word hope, but she didn't say anything, instead, nodding. "It's been a good place for me to hike and get my priorities straight."

"How many miles can you travel on this path?"

"I don't know. I've walked five or six different trails, but I always hook up with this one path that will eventually lead back down to the string of parking lots below. If you want to walk for forty minutes, there's one way to go. If you want to hike for three or four hours or anything in between, there's another way. Depends on what you want."

"We won't get lost, right?"

"No, I can promise you that."

"Then let's just go. Take me wherever you want. Show me everything."

Dez scuffed the heel of her boot against a rock in the path

until it came up, leaving a walnut-sized hole. "We could be out here quite a while..."

"I don't care one bit. That's why you're carrying that fat pack full of food."

The tall woman grinned. "So I am. Well, then, let's get going, little lady. We've got miles to go before we sleep."

****

Late in the afternoon, just before dusk, they returned from their long hike. At the cabins, Dez pulled into a parking space next to Dewey's truck. "I want you to come in and meet my friend, Jay. Okay?"

The smaller woman stifled a yawn. "All right." She'd only been in the warmth of the truck for a few minutes, but already she was sleepy. She followed Dez out the driver's side and shut the door behind her. The wind was starting to pick up, and she hastened to catch up with her long-legged partner.

Before they even reached the front door, the big burly man had it open. "Desiree! It's been days. How the heck are you?"

Jaylynn watched as Dez broke out in a grin. "I'm good."

"Get in here, the both of you." He threw the door wide, ushered them in, and slammed the heavy wood door shut. They stood inside, taking off coats and scarves and mittens. "I think you ought to stay for supper—that is, if you didn't already have plans?" The two women looked at one another and shrugged. "I've got about three gallons of beef stew going."

Dez raised an eyebrow. "Gallons?"

"Yeah. I like to make big batches, freeze 'em, and eat 'em later. Saves me a lot of time. Go ahead, have a seat and warm up by the fire."

"Dewey, I'd like you to meet my partner, Jaylynn Savage."

Jaylynn smiled and said, "It's good to finally meet you, Dewey."

The big man stuck out his warm hand. He leaned in close and said, "I was wondering when she was going to get around to that minor detail of introducing us. She's got her own sense of timing." He released her hand. "Nice to meet you, too, Jaylynn. How long you two been riding together?"

There was a moment's hesitation before Dez cut in. "Actually, Jay and I are partners, Dewey—as in she's like...well, my spouse."

"Oh." Dewey stood for a moment with his mouth open and a puzzled look on his face. Five seconds passed, and then he said,

"Girls, it's hell getting old. I just had a very, very old memory hit me upside the head." He looked at Dez and then the rookie. "Have a seat. I think I have to explain this one."

Dez's heart was pounding. She wasn't sure what was coming next, but in the nearly four weeks she had been staying at the cabin, she hadn't ever seen her burly friend look so stunned. With a queasy feeling in her stomach, she followed her partner into the sitting area, passed by the recliner and rocking chair, and lowered herself onto the loveseat right next to Jaylynn.

"I'm going to give this stew a quick stir." He moved over to the galley kitchen and picked up a long metal spoon, pulled the cover off a huge silver pot, and gave the steamy contents a vigorous blending. He banged the spoon against the edge of the pot, replaced the lid, and tossed the spoon in the sink. Wiping his hands on a towel, he came over to the rocking chair and sat, still holding the towel in one hand while pulling at his beard with the other. He shook his head back and forth slightly, then met Dez's eyes. "How long have you two been together?"

Dez glanced at Jaylynn and didn't know what to say. She was relieved when the rookie spoke up. "Depends on what you mean by together, Dewey. I guess you'd have to say that our relationship is only a couple months old, but we've known each other over a year."

The big man smiled and looked up at the ceiling as though he was recalling something pleasant. He rocked slowly backward and forward. "Let me see if I can remember all of the details of this. Dez, do you remember that Frogtown TV store robbery that went bad and the owner got shot? Back when you and my son were both in junior high?"

"Yeah, why?" The tall cop's voice was gruff and guarded.

"Remember Lance Varona?" Dez nodded. "He and your dad had a bet. Your dad said that you and he had discussed it, and you both thought the store owner set up the robbery. Lance bet your dad it was random. Come to find out, you and your dad were right." To Jaylynn, he said, "The stupid store owner hired some thugs to come in and fake a robbery so he could write off money he'd gambled away. There's such honor among thieves that they held him up for real when he wasn't expecting it, took his money, and shot him for good measure. He didn't die, though, and when the moron came to in the hospital, he named names and told all. The day the news broke, Lance, Dez's dad, me, and three or four other cops were sitting in Uncle Al's Coffeeshop over in Frogtown, and your dad was so proud because he said he hadn't really figured that out. You did, Dez. You'd predicted it."

Dez frowned. At a total loss, she cleared her throat. "And?"

Dewey let out a big sigh. "Dez, he was just so proud of you. So tickled by your smarts. All us guys bragged about our kids all the time, and he talked about you and Patrick a lot. He really teased the hell outta old Varona. Lance's kids were in trouble all the time, and if you remember Varona at all, he was a know-it-all who just thought he was right about everything. Overly critical, too. So we all gave him a bad time that day, but then we got to talking about our kids, and after a while, your dad confided that you were having some trouble at school. You were a big, tall girl, real athletic. He was proud of that, but I guess you'd been getting some flak from classmates about not being feminine enough." Dez narrowed her eyes, preferring not to think back to those teen-age times. "Good old Varona, that big mouth ass, he pipes up and says, 'Well, Reilly, what if she turns out to be queer?'" Dewey let out a huff of air and shook his head slowly. "Now, if I'd been your dad, I'd've decked him. Instead, Michael just sat back, crossed his arms, and said, 'She might well be, Varona, but I don't care. It doesn't matter one bit. She's the best daughter I could ever hope for, and that's all that matters.' Something like that anyway."

Dez leaned back against the loveseat, her fists clenched in her lap. She fought back the rising tide of tears that threatened to burst forth. Fortunately, Dewey went on, allowing her to maintain her composure.

"When you just now told me about you and Jaylynn here, that whole scene—the smell of coffee, the cigarette smoke, the warm sun shining in the dirty window—it all came back to me like it just happened. Gee, I haven't thought of that for, what? Fifteen years?"

"Seventeen."

"Hmm?" He looked over at Dez, eyebrows raised.

"Seventeen years. Dad died a little over seventeen years ago." She thought her voice was calm and controlled, but Jaylynn looked up at her with concern etched all over her face, so she wasn't sure. The smaller woman laid her hand on Dez's left thigh, gave it a squeeze, and left it there.

Dewey shook his head. "It's hard to believe that sometimes, kiddo. Sometimes it seems like just yesterday."

"Why are you telling us this, Dewey?"

He grinned. "Well, hon, I guess I owe him some money. When the rest of those yahoos left, I bet him ten bucks you'd grow up, get married—probably to some varsity boys basketball star—and have a whole houseful of really tall kids. *He* said he thought you'd grow up and be a cop and that you'd never get married." He pulled at his beard and grinned. "Well, your dad was right a lot more than he was ever wrong."

Jaylynn spoke up, her voice warm and amused. "I do play a little basketball, Dewey, but any children we have who get my DNA are seriously unlikely to be hoop stars."

Dewey met Jaylynn's eyes and chuckled, then looked at Dez. "I know I keep saying this to you, Dez, but your dad would be real proud of you—and probably happy for you now, too."

Though her chest was burning, and she was fighting back tears, Dez choked out the next words. "I'm not so sure of that."

"I am. You knew him as a child knows a parent, but I knew him as an adult, and I knew him pretty damn well, Desiree." He leaned forward and popped up out of the rocking chair, hitching up his jeans as he went. "I don't know about you two, but I think it's time for some supper. We've got some stew, some brown bread, some wheat bread, and beer or milk or orange juice. Which do you prefer?"

****

It wasn't until later, in bed, that Jaylynn brought up the subject of Dewey and the bet. She had watched her partner carefully for the last couple of hours. Though Dez started out being quiet at dinner, she gradually became more animated. By the time they had departed into the cool evening air two hours later, she seemed her normal self. They'd jumped in the truck for the short, chilly ride back to their cabin, and without a single word, they hung up their coats and headed straight into the darkened bedroom, with Jaylynn in the lead.

Before the shorter woman could get to the bedside lamp, Dez wrapped her arms around her from behind and whispered in her ear. "Hey."

The soft breath made her shiver. "Hey, yourself." She put her hands on top of the arms encircling her waist and looked back over her shoulder.

"I'm not feeling particularly scared right now. Wanna have a roll in the hay?"

Jaylynn giggled. She turned in Dez's arms and hugged the bigger woman, pressing her face into the front of her shirt. In a muffled voice, she answered, "I thought you'd never ask."

This time when they made love, she thought Dez was fearless.

****

Jaylynn had drifted off to sleep, but after a short while, she awakened, feeling strong arms holding her tightly. She turned her head, saw that Dez was awake, and snuggled against the crook of the shoulder beneath her. In a whisper, she said, "You okay?"

"Mm hmm." Dez's response was languid, almost dreamy.

"That was quite the story Dewey told, wasn't it?"

Dez didn't speak. She nodded and looked up at the ceiling.

"Your father must have been pretty close to him."

Dez swallowed and cleared her throat. "Yup, they rode together a lot on swing shifts."

Jaylynn nestled in close, lying alongside the taller cop's body. She had one arm over Dez's ribs and her head on a firm shoulder tucked under Dez's chin. "I know you didn't want to take the ten bucks from Dewey—"

"It wasn't necessary."

"I know, but he tucked it into the pocket of my jacket as we left."

"What? Geez, that nut."

"When you were putting your coat on, he said to tell you he always pays his debts."

Dez didn't speak for a moment, then she choked out, "I only wish he could have paid the debt to the person he owed it to."

"Me, too."

****

They spent the next four days exploring the forest and each other, taking their afternoon meals in little cafés in the string of towns along the highway near Lake Superior. On the fourth day, New Year's Eve, they awoke to three inches of snow and decided not to do any hiking. Instead, they put the truck in four-wheel drive and headed north to the town of Grand Marais to have brunch at Gwen's Goodies, a place they had eaten lunch at the previous Labor Day weekend. Mostly, the two women talked—about the past and about their future.

After brunch, they returned to the cozy cabin and lounged in the living room on the couch with Dez sitting up and Jaylynn lying on her back with her head in the tall cop's lap. Both of them were over-full from pancakes and sausage, so they stayed on the couch, sitting silently, for a while.

Jaylynn was feeling drowsy and not really thinking at all when Dez asked, "Jay, where do you want to be when you're, oh, say, about sixty?"

Taking a deep breath and yawning, she replied, "Can't we

stay right here...forever?"

"Yeah, right." Dez grinned. "Afraid not. Sorry. Tomorrow's our last day. What was your second choice?"

The rookie looked up into deep blue eyes. "I really don't know. I haven't imagined that far into the future. Have you?"

"Some. I'm already halfway there, you know."

Jaylynn chuckled and shook her head. "You've got a lot of years ahead of you until then. Why don't you narrow it down? What do you imagine for yourself over the next couple two or three years?"

With a frown on her face, Dez put the flat of her hand on Jaylynn's solar plexus, just below her breastbone. The smaller woman reached up with both hands and covered the large hand, hugging it tightly to her. "I think I've been living my life around my work. I can't remember when things were normal—though I know the line of demarcation was when Ryan was killed. But since then, I don't know, Jay. I haven't really felt I had a future to look forward to. Well, until lately. Between you and Marie, it's like the world is sort of coming back into focus after being really fuzzy for a while." Jaylynn didn't say anything, but just squeezed the hand she held. "I think I'd like my life back, please, and way before I turn sixty. What about you?"

"It seems like most of my main attention right now is getting a career in order."

Dez nodded. "You're past probation now. You can bid around to different sectors, take on various special assignments, whatever."

Jaylynn had a thoughtful look on her face. "I honestly don't know what I want to do. Are you going back on patrol?"

"Sooner or later. It's either that or join the circus."

The reclining woman burst out laughing. "Trapeze Artist or the Strong Woman? Or maybe a combo of both?" Dez pressed her fingers into the abdominal muscles under her hand. "Hey, hey! None of that now. Be serious."

"As serious as you're being?" She rolled her eyes and sighed. "Okay. Maybe I'll take the sergeant's exam."

"You'd pass, no problem."

"Maybe. Maybe not. There's more to it than just the paper exam."

"Yeah, but sweetie, they love you down there. You're a cop's cop. You've got the brass in your pocket."

"After the last few weeks, I wouldn't go that far."

Jaylynn sighed. "Dez, you just don't ever give yourself enough credit. Guys at all levels are in awe of you."

The tall cop shook her head and gave her a funny look. "Where do you get these ideas?"

"I've just spent weeks hanging out at the main stationhouse. I'm young, have an innocent face, and I have great hearing. I've heard Commander Paar's comments as well as a whole bunch of off-the-record comments by lieutenants and captains, not to mention the rank-and-file. Trust me. You are very much respected."

Dez gave a little snort and shook her head slowly from side to side. "Wait 'til they get a load of this condition I have. I won't be so respected then."

Jaylynn sat up and turned around to face her. "I got news for you, pal, you aren't the only one with PTSD."

"What?"

"I understand that you are going to be inducted into an exclusive little club when you go back. There's several guys who have had the same experiences as you." Dez frowned at her, the scowl on her face deepening as though she didn't believe the rookie. "Listen, sweetie, I'm *not* making this up. I heard Commander Paar tell Lt. Graul that he expected him to come talk to you."

"Graul? Why?"

"Graul was involved in some sort of critical incident twenty years ago, when he worked for another city. I guess he shot a teenager. The kid didn't die, but Graul has had the same symptoms you did." Dez's face was a mix of surprise and hope. Jaylynn got up on her knees and scooted along the couch until she could climb up onto Dez's lap. Strong arms went around her, and she reached up to stroke the pale cheeks with both of her hands. "You aren't alone, Dez. I'm pretty sure that everything is going to work out just fine."

"Think so, huh?" She eyed her partner as the hazel eyes moved closer. Soft, warm lips covered her own. She tightened her hold, gathering in the smaller woman as close as she could. She leaned to her right, and Jaylynn slipped to the side, on her back and lying across Dez's lap, cradled in her arms. Dez pulled away from the kiss, her heart racing. She looked shyly into the hazel eyes below her, then shifted out from under the warm body, leaving Jaylynn lying on the couch, her head against the pillow next to the arm of the sofa. As she lowered herself onto her partner, she asked, "I'm not squashing you, am I?"

Jaylynn grinned. "Not a bit. I love the feel of you on me." She tucked her fingers inside the waistband at the back of Dez's jeans. "Besides, I don't know how you did it, but you've sure lost weight. I don't know why you're worried about your weight, you crazy woman." She poked under Dez's ribs, and the big woman flinched. She moved her hands up, and massaged the muscles in her shoulders.

"It was all the walking...and pining over you."

"Pining? You pined?"

Dez settled her elbows in against the rough cloth of the couch, on either side of the soft neck below her, and looked across the room. "Yeah. You could say that." She looked back down and pressed her face against her lover's cheek.

Into her ear, Jaylynn said, "You're so funny, Dez. I ate *way* more than usual. How could you eat less?"

"Hmm. I've just spent the last four weeks thinking and crying and remembering and letting Marie the Archeologist excavate all my best kept secrets." She sighed. "I didn't have the energy to eat."

The rookie ran her hands down the big cop's back to the firm waist and then to the tight buns, which she grabbed and squeezed.

"Hey! That's not the kind of touching I had in mind, you little tease." When Jaylynn snickered, Dez found her lips and kissed the giggle away. The smaller woman responded to her kiss immediately, and slowly the passion between them escalated until Dez came up for air. "Whew. Is the heater in here malfunctioning? Seems a little warm."

The rookie took a deep breath. "No, it's perfect. I feel very toasty and comfortable. But if you want to cool down, you can take off any clothes you want, you know." With a sly grin on her face, she said, "I'll even help." She scooted herself up a little, and unbuttoned the top of Dez's flannel shirt, but she couldn't get to the lower buttons because Dez was lying on them. "Here. Help me out a little..." Reaching past the bigger woman's head and to the middle of her back, she grabbed the bottom of the shirt and tugged it up over the dark head.

Suddenly Dez was all tangled up in her shirt. "Wait a second." Her voice came out muffled as she managed to get one arm out and then her head. "Geez. They always make this look so easy on TV." She let the shirt slip down her arm, and now her skin was warm against Jaylynn's sweatshirt. In a breathless voice, she asked, "What about your top?"

"Hmmm...we'll get to me in a moment." Jaylynn ran her hands up the broad back and down the sides of her ribcage. "You're definitely thinner. I can feel your ribs again." She reached around and unsnapped the clasps on Dez's bra. "Oooh, you have such nice skin—so incredibly soft." With her arms, the tall cop pushed herself up off the sofa enough to let the bra slip down, and she dropped it out of the way and onto the floor.

Before Dez could settle back down, Jaylynn reached up and put her hands on the wide shoulders, then let her hands caress down the collarbones to the chest and then to the breasts. Dez trembled, and Jaylynn whispered, "I thought you were too warm."

"I'm not shivering from cold." She closed her eyes and exhaled a long breath as Jaylynn stroked the front of her. In a raspy voice, she said, "Oh, wow." Every nerve ending tingled, as though a current of electricity had been turned on. She trembled again and swallowed. "That feels really good, Jay." Breathing fast, she lowered her upper body and tucked her face in next to the right side of the warmer woman's neck. She leaned a little to the side, shifting a bit, and her hand found its way under Jaylynn's thick sweatshirt. She untucked the t-shirt underneath.

"Ooh, you're letting the cold air in—ooh—! Whoa. Whoa! That feels good." Jaylynn turned a little, and they ended up lying on their sides, with the rookie pressed against the back of the couch and Dez teetering on the outside. With her free left hand, Jaylynn stroked her partner's pale skin with a gentle, emotion-filled touch. She trailed small nips down the long neck, then found Dez's sweet mouth and kissed her lips and face, which ratcheted up the intensity even more.

When they broke off, Dez opened her eyes and looked into the face so close to hers. "I missed you so much, Jay. I—I just...I don't know how to explain it."

"Me, too."

Dez closed her eyes. In a slow, quiet voice, she said. "I'm so sorry I hurt you."

"I hurt you, too, you know. I didn't mean to either."

Dez whispered. "I know. I know you didn't." In the small pink ear, she whispered, "Jay, I will never ever leave you—never for good, anyway. I love you. I just want to be with you now and forever. Okay?"

Jaylynn answered by kissing her once more, then she said, "Don't worry. I'm not going anywhere. I'm stuck like glue."

Dez laughed quietly. "That's lucky because my ass is hanging off the sofa and without that little bit of glue, I'd be on the floor."

Jaylynn giggled and tucked her head under Dez's chin. She tightened her grip. "For all the things I want to do to you, I think we require a little more space."

"I agree."

"Shall we retire to a little larger playground?"

Dez nodded. "Good idea. Don't let go too fast, though, or you'll be picking me up off the floor."

****

Jaylynn lay on her side, swaddled in blankets, and pressed up against her sleeping partner. They had made love three times over a period of a couple of hours, and she was now pleasantly fatigued. It was mid-afternoon, and she knew she would soon be hungry, but until then, she lazed next to the slumbering woman, reveling in the warmth. Before Dez fell asleep, Jaylynn had said, "You know, for someone who just a few days ago was nervous about letting her guard down, you sure have been a wild woman today."

Dez laughed and pulled her closer. "It's 'cause you're irresistible, hon."

"Yeah, right."

"It's true. I'll be lucky if I can keep you to myself. I'll be fighting off packs of love-struck people—both men and women."

"Oh, brother! I don't think so!"

Jaylynn thought that was an odd thing for Dez to have said, but as she thought about it now, she realized that she thought the very same thing about her partner. Didn't everyone want to touch her? To kiss her? To pull her to themselves and hug her tight? How was it that nobody else had come along and been swept off their feet by the blue-eyed beauty? *There must be a God, and he—or she—is definitely looking out for me.*

If someone had asked her, "Why Dez?" she didn't think she could answer. She didn't know exactly why. It was everything all rolled together. Her touch, her smell, her stubbornness, her sincerity, her sense of humor. When she fixed those piercing blue eyes on a person, Jaylynn felt they could see right through. She liked the fact that there was a defensive fortress around her taciturn partner, but that the tall cop had let her find the few chinks in the armor so that she had free access to come and go as she pleased. She thought there was a strange balance between the two of them. On the one hand, she felt safe with Dez, as though her partner was a refuge of warmth and safety. At the same time, she also felt that she protected and defended the bigger, stronger woman, who was, in many ways, so very vulnerable. The more she thought about it, the more it seemed an odd juxtaposition.

Dez stirred and turned over. Jaylynn lifted her head and slid her arm up, bent it at the elbow, and rested her head in her hand. Her wrist felt very tight, but it didn't hurt and she was grateful for that. As she peered over in the dim light, Dez's eyes looked gray. They stared blankly up at the ceiling, and Jaylynn knew she wasn't fully awake yet. The tall woman cleared her throat and blinked, then turned her head to look at Jaylynn. "I had the oddest dream."

"About?"

She didn't say anything for a few moments. Then in a soft voice, she recounted the dream. "I was in the cockpit of some sort of small plane, going very fast, and I crashed into water. I went down, way down—way to the bottom of the ocean where the aircraft broke open, and I swam out and up. At first I was panicked, and then I found I could breathe under the water. So that was weird. When I broke the surface, I was treading water looking around, and you were on the beach screaming to me and holding a baby. So I swam toward you, but it was really hard. The waves were choppy, and the wind was blasting, and both of us struggled like crazy. But you hung in there, standing in this hurricane of weather, until I dragged myself out of the ocean onto this windy, sandy beach. And then, the baby—and Jay, this was a tiny little baby—this little black-haired baby smiled up at me and said, 'Good swimming. Way to go.' She reached up for me. I took her into my arms, and then the rain started pouring down, so we went into this big beach house where it was warm and cozy and...well, I guess that's all I remember." She turned on her side and slid the pillow under her head. Her braid was starting to come undone, and there were tendrils of hair around her face. She brushed a few strands up off her forehead. "What the hell do you think that was all about?"

"Beats me."

"But it's so clear. I don't usually remember dreams like that...unless you count my horrible nightmares."

"What does Marie know about dreams?"

"I don't know. I've only talked about nightmares."

"Ask her, why don't you?"

Dez nodded and then yawned. "Wonder what that baby was all about? I've never given kids a whole lot of thought."

"Babies in dreams can mean a lot of different things, if I remember correctly from my class on Jungian psychology. New life, growth, something being born."

"Guess that makes sense." Dez yawned again.

She reached out her hand and threaded her fingers through Dez's. "You have really good hands, woman."

Dez smiled. "Yours aren't half bad either."

"Are we going to lie around all day? Or how 'bout we get up and go get something to eat?"

The tall cop lifted her head and looked over Jaylynn's shoulder at the bedside clock. "Oh wow! We've gone without food for, what? Three and a half hours? Quick! Better hurry."

Jaylynn shook her head and rolled her eyes, then she pounced. Dez wasn't ready and made an *oomph* sound when the smaller woman dove on her. They wrestled, giggling and laughing, for a few moments, then settled down, wrapped in one another's arms. Jaylynn lay against her lover's chest, her breath coming fast. Suddenly, she heard a gurgling sound and lifted her head up in surprise. "Hey! That's you!"

"Yeah, so I got hungry before you for a change. Is it a crime?"

Jaylynn grinned. "No, but it's a first." She sat up, pushed the sheet away, and clambered out of bed. "Let's get a move on. We could go get a really good dinner somewhere, and then later, we can usher in the new year."

Dez raised an eyebrow? "At a restaurant?"

"No, you fool. Right here, in bed—with lots of snacks to fortify us."

"I see. Well, your wish is my command."

"My wish is that you get outta bed and get dressed. We're burning daylight."

****

"Dez," Jaylynn whined, "how can it be Tuesday already?"

"Comes right after Monday, I guess." She opened the refrigerator door and started pulling items out either to throw in the garbage or stack into a box.

Jaylynn sat at the dinette table and looked around the cabin's tidy kitchen. "I don't want to head home."

"I don't either, but I'd like to get out of here by noon. I figure this New Year's Day traffic is going to be pretty treacherous. Let's get home while it's still light."

"I can see now why you moved all your stuff up here."

Dez paused and turned around. "I didn't move everything here."

"Well, close."

"No, not close."

"Look around, Miss Obviously Blind As A Bat. I hope we can get all this into the truck."

The tall cop straightened up and looked around the kitchen. She had to admit that she already had two boxes packed in here, and sitting in the living room there was a three-foot-high stack of boxes, bedding and towels, her guitar, a box of CD's, about twenty books, and an assortment of other things. On the bed were five duffel bags—though two of them were Jaylynn's—and a couple of other smaller kit bags. She frowned. *How did I get so much stuff up here?*

Jaylynn watched her tall partner and wondered what was going on behind the troubled blue eyes. She wondered if she should ask—then worried that if she did, Dez might close off from her like she so often had in the past. Before she could say a word, the tall cop spoke up.

"I think you might be right," she said thoughtfully. "I had a lot more stuff here than I realized."

"How did you manage that?"

Dez shrugged. "Seemed like every few times I went down to the Cities, I grabbed some more stuff."

"I can't believe how unlucky I was that for all the times I called your apartment, you never happened to be there."

The tall cop shut the fridge door and turned around, her pale face turning pink. "Ah, well, actually, I just never answered the phone."

Jaylynn gaped at her. That had never occurred to her. "You mean to tell me you could have answered the phone, but you didn't?" Dez gave an embarrassed half-smile and a slight nod. "I can't even begin to tell you how mad that makes me." Jaylynn's face turned red, and Dez was taken aback by her vehemence. "You just disappeared, and dammit, Dez! Not hearing from you, not knowing if you were okay, was really maddening."

Dez's face started to flush, too, and what she really wanted to do was flee the room. Instead, she took a deep breath and stayed rooted where she was. "I'm sorry about that—but hey, at least I did send you a postcard."

Jaylynn stared at her for a moment. "I never got a postcard."

The big woman shrugged. "Well, I sent one."

"When?"

"Geez, I don't know. A couple weeks ago, I guess."

"When we get back to St. Paul, I'd better check through my mail."

"What, you don't believe me?"

Jaylynn's face had returned to its normal color. "No, that's not it. I guess I just tapped into a little bit of the anger I felt at you. Ooh! I went back and forth between being so mad at you and then just hurting and then missing you." She looked up silently into Dez's face, her hazel eyes a little troubled, but then she took a deep breath. "Sure is lucky I love you, you big lug. 'Cause if I didn't love you so much, I'd get up and smack you."

"Oh, you would not. You're all bluster and bravado, Jay."

She stepped over and grabbed the ribbed collar of the rookie's sweatshirt as the smaller woman rose. With mock roughness she pulled the other woman to her. "Go ahead. Smack away." Bending her head and looking her partner in the eye, she grinned slyly, then leaned in, hands on either side of Jaylynn's face, and put a firm kiss on the pink lips.

Jaylynn wrapped her arms around the tall woman's waist and kissed her back. When she pulled away, she looked up into eyes that looked dark blue in the dim light. "You're incorrigible, Desiree Reilly, and I can't help it—I'm still crazy about you."

"Let's just keep it that way, shall we?" She dropped her hands to the narrow shoulders below her. "I guess you're right that it'll be a bit of a stretch to get all this crap in the back and in the Xtra cab. I'll take the first load out."

"I still don't want to go."

"Me neither, but we have to go to work tomorrow."

"Don't even bring that up!"

"Let's just get this stuff loaded up and go home, Jay."

Jaylynn smiled and took her hand. "The house or the apartment?"

Dez shrugged. "Doesn't matter. Anywhere you are is home."

Chapter
Thirty-Three

Dez took down another banker's box, and pulled the lid off. She checked her list. *Box 1148—Case No. 004-01: Jenkins Homicide—02/14/98.* She upended the box and dumped the contents on the table. *Must've been a* really *bad Valentine's Day.*

She found two clothing items wrapped in plastic, three large manila envelopes, and one small white envelope, which felt like it contained jewelry. She turned that over and saw that someone had written *004-01—02/14/98—Victim's Necklace.* Most of the boxes here belonged to cases that had not yet been solved, and for most of them, what she was finding could easily be filed in much smaller boxes.

She looked around the large, dimly lit Evidence Room. In the three days she had been working in it, she had managed to reorganize the open, metal shelves so that everything was stored in numerical order, by box number, but every shelf was crammed full, and there were boxes stacked all over the floor. It looked worse than it had when she had first started, but she knew everyone would have to put up with a little disorder until she got things better organized. Already she had found sixteen articles that others had neglected to return to their proper boxes. The previous Tour II Evidence Room attendant, who had recently retired from his day shift, likely meant to re-file those pieces of evidence, but over time they had, instead, wound up stuck between the wall and a shelf, or on the floor behind everything. She knew for a fact that the absence of one of the items she had found, a switchblade, had caused the prosecutors to hold off from charging a gang member with a stabbing six months earlier. Lt. Finn was quite happy when Dez went to see her discreetly to explain her discovery. The dark-haired cop remembered what happened in the stabbing case because the crime had occurred in her sector, though it hadn't been her call. She didn't know about the other fifteen articles, but she had made a list and would notify the detectives on those cases just in case.

Once she re-filed all the "lost" items and got things in numeric order, she found that several boxes on her manifest were not there. That could mean that the case was solved and the contents relegated to the Closed Case storage—or someone had not properly checked out the evidence. *Not good. I sure hope I can track those down.* Five boxes on her list were highlighted, and she decided to track them down later.

Now she was going through each box, starting with the ones from the last couple years, to find out if the contents could be fit into smaller storage boxes. Everything from the Jenkins murder fit neatly into a carton one-third the size of the big brown banker's box. She relabeled the smaller carton and carefully blacked out the data on the side of the original box so that she could use it again.

She put the lid on the smaller box and placed it on the upper shelf, then yawned. Glancing at her watch, she found it was only noon. Working the day shift had been a real change. She wasn't at all adjusted to rising in the early morning and coming to the station, then leaving, like normal people, at five p.m.

She lowered to one knee and bent over another box, then heard a rustle at the front window. With a sigh, she rose from bended knee and set the black marker aside. *What do they want now? This organizing would go a hell of a lot faster if people would just stop dropping by to chat.* She wiped off her dusty hands on her blue duty pants and went around the tall shelf toward the window. The hazel eyes that met her gaze made her smile and blush. She leaned her elbows on the counter and slouched over it, holding the rookie's gaze. "What's up?"

Jaylynn sighed. "I'm bored. I'm hungry. What are you doing?"

Dez looked at her watch. "In about fifteen minutes, my relief will come, and I can get some lunch with you. Okay?"

"Sounds good. In the meantime, can I come in and take a look at the crime scene stuff from the Tivoli murder?"

"Sure. I know exactly where it all is, too." She pushed away from the counter and went to the locked door to open it so Jaylynn could enter. "You gotta sign in and follow all the regs, you know. No special treatment."

"Oh, yeah. I know." Jaylynn picked up a pen off the counter and started filling in the sheet Dez placed in front of her. "I haven't ever looked at the evidence. I've read the files and records, so I know everything that's in there, but I'm curious."

Dez nodded, then led her to the far side of the dusty room, stepping over and around boxes until she stopped in front of a stack of boxes that looked new. "Here we go. We've got four boxes, total. What do you want to start with?" She picked up the first one and set it on a waist-high side counter, then put the other three next to it all in a row.

Jaylynn flipped the lid off the first one, got on tiptoes, and looked in. She then pulled the tops off the other three, too.

The dark-haired cop stood to the side smirking. "You want a boost or a little ladder?"

Jaylynn gave her a mock glare. "I'm not too proud to accept some help. Sure. Where's the stepstool?"

Dez eyes searched the messy floor until they came to light on a stool with two steps. She made her way across the room and brought it back.

The rookie scooted it in front of the box and stepped up on the first stair. "Okay, looks like this has the contents of the snack shack." She pulled out plastic bags and manila envelopes, opened the clasps and looked in the envelopes, and read the titles on the sides in an absent-minded mumble that she didn't expect Dez to answer. The tall woman went back to where she'd left off in consolidating items.

"Ooh, yuck! Dez, look at this." The rookie held up a big zip-lock bag filled with several smaller plastic bags containing bright yellow packages of Peanut M&M's.

The big cop set down the box she was carrying. "What about it?"

"There's dried blood all over these M&M's. Blech!"

"Yeah, Jay. It's evidence. They collect it however they find it." She bent and picked up a different box and set it on the middle shelf.

Jaylynn put that zip-lock back in the box, put the lid on, and moved to the second container. "Hmm, what have we here? Oh, this stuff is from the station wagon."

Dez turned and looked at her, but Jaylynn wasn't paying attention to her at all. She just kept talking out loud. "Here's a worn out old blanket, a pair of sunglasses, a denim shoulder bag full of girlie junk..." She rooted through the bag. "Strawberry flavored lipstick, garish eye makeup, eyeliner, two mirrors—oh look, a Hello Kitty wallet. My little sister loves Hello Kitty." She opened the snap on the wallet and found two crumpled dollar bills and some coins in the change purse. There were five school pictures slid into the plastic holders, four girls and one boy. All appeared to be junior high aged. She pulled each picture out, one at a time, and checked the backs. Not a single one had a last name on it, though three of them did have first names: Courtney, Britany, Jim. She fished through everything in the wallet and the bag, but nothing gave a clue as to the identity of the dead girl. She replaced the shoulder bag and picked up a sealed plastic package. With a frown on her face, she turned to Dez. "Hey, you. I still want to know how come you never ever called me the whole time you pulled your disappearing act."

Dez sighed. She put a lid on the box she had just rearranged and slid it out of the way with her foot. "I didn't have a phone at the cabin."

"What about your cell phone? I called it after about a week, and it always said it was out of service."

She shrugged. "I mostly kept it off, and then, after a while, the battery died."

"How hard would it have been for you to buy some phone cards like these?" Jaylynn held up the package she had just found. "Listen here, Miss Uncommunicative, these babies are only $22.99 for 5 cards and you get 100 minutes on each. Pretty good deal, too." She cocked her head to the side. "Hmm, wait a minute..." She examined the package, turning it over, then peeled some of the plastic away from the hard red cardboard backing.

"Whoa." Dez strode quickly across the room and stretched her arm out to take the package. "You don't want to open that, Jay. It's evidence."

The rookie pulled back. "I'm not opening it. It's already *been* opened."

"What?" Dez leaned down and peered at the red package Jaylynn was picking at.

"See, someone peeled open the end, took a card out, then this gooey stuff on the plastic sort of reattached itself so it doesn't look open. There's only four cards in here and the plastic instruction card." She slid one out the side. The remaining cards rattled against the hard plastic. She took all of them out, too.

In a dry voice, Dez said, "No matter how much you want me to keep in touch, you can't give me that, Jaylynn."

The rookie giggled. "Don't be silly." She turned the cards over and studied the tiny lettering and numbers on the back of each. "Check this out. There are only four cards in here and this fifth card is just some sort of informational instructions. I'll bet the detectives looked at this, saw it contained five credit card sized cards, and didn't realize it had ever been opened. What if the fifth card was used by Tivoli?" She looked up, excitement etched all over her face. "Dez! What if we could find something out from the phone records?"

Dez nodded, surprised. "That's a really good idea."

The rookie flipped through the cards in her hands. "The cards are numbered in order. All four of them are 398-045—and then there's a third set of numbers that are consecutive—0642, 0643, 0644, and, oh, this one's out of order, 0641. So that means the fifth card should either be 0640 or else 0645."

"Is there a number to call for information?" Jaylynn nodded. "Looks like you have a clue to follow up on."

"I'll be back." Jaylynn sped over to the closed door, wrenched it open, and fled down the hallway without even shutting the door.

"Hey!" Dez called out. "Wait a minute. I thought we were...having lunch." It was too late. She was long gone. Dez looked at her watch. She doubted that Jaylynn would be back any time soon, so when her relief came, she would go up and check on her, then go to lunch by herself if she had to.

****

Jaylynn emerged from Lt. Finn's office, her excitement evident to everyone in the squad room. She hustled over to Tsorro's desk. The lieutenant followed close behind, speaking very calmly. "It might not be anything, Savage. Don't get your hopes up."

"I've got a feeling about this, Boss." She plopped down into the desk chair and grabbed the phone to punch in the numbers for the phone card provider. Once she connected, she was put on hold. She grinned up at Lt. Finn. "I'm on terminal hold."

"Just get whatever information you can, and then come see me. Where are they located?"

The rookie checked the number on the card. "I can't tell. It's an 800 number. I'll find out."

"We may have to send a court order to them. I don't suppose we'd be lucky enough to have the company here in Minnesota."

Jaylynn shrugged. "The cards are sponsored by one of our own local department stores, but who knows."

Lt. Finn brushed her dark hair off her forehead and looked out the window. She turned on her heel abruptly. "Let me know what you find out," she called over her shoulder as she headed back to her office.

It took Jaylynn twenty minutes and gradually more complicated explanations to four different people, but eventually she spoke to someone in charge. When Dez came by, she was in the middle of a heated conversation and didn't even notice the dark-haired cop wandering past. She told her story yet again, and the manager agreed to send her the records if she would fax him the request, signed by her commanding officer. He also said it would take at least a day to research the information, but that he would do all he could to cooperate. Since today was Friday, he told her he would try to have it to her by Monday afternoon. Lastly, he informed her that they could not keep records of where calls came *from*, only where they went *to*.

She tossed the phone back on the cradle and nearly ran into the lieutenant's office. "They're sending us the info! All you need to do is write a formal request and then fax it to them at this number." She thrust the piece of paper at Lt. Finn, a grin splitting her face.

Finn looked up her and couldn't help but smile. "You know, Savage, if this leads nowhere, you will have wasted an awful lot of energy."

"I've got a hunch. It just *has* to lead somewhere."

"Go out and write up a letter for my signature, and let's get it out of here."

"You've got it, Boss!"

The lieutenant was shaking her head when the rookie left the office, but the older officer couldn't help but smile at all the youthful exuberance to which she had just been treated.

****

Dez sat in the break room, holding the last of her chicken sandwich, when Jaylynn came skidding into the quiet room. "It could be something, Dez! They're sending us phone records."

The veteran cop nodded as she watched the rookie whip open the refrigerator door and root around inside until she found her lunch bag. Dez swallowed the last bite of the sandwich. "I haven't seen Tsorro and Parkins lately. Do they know about this?"

"I called Tsorro to tell him what's happening. Can't tell Parkins until he comes back from vacation." She closed the refrigerator door with a smack.

"What happens if it's nothing?"

Jaylynn set her bag on the table and pulled out a chair. "Well, at least we're trying. If this isn't it, that's the way it goes." She sat in the hard metal chair and scooted up close to the table. "Sorry I left you in the lurch."

"It's okay. I understand." Dez smiled and crumpled up the

paper bag on the table and tossed it at the garbage can in the corner. She missed.

Jaylynn swallowed in a hurry. "Oh my! The great Desiree Reilly has missed the game-winning shot."

Dez rose and picked up the brown bag and dropped it in the can. "Nobody ever said I was perfect."

"Close enough for me." She beamed up at her, then took a big bite out of her sandwich. With her mouth full, she said, "What do you want to do tonight?"

"Nothing in particular. You got something in mind?"

"Maybe catch a movie?"

Dez sat back in her chair, nodding. "Don't you think it's kind of weird to switch to day shift?" Jaylynn nodded as her partner continued. "I'm so used to being home in the middle of the day. I know it hasn't even been a week, but I just can't get used to having evenings free."

The rookie swallowed. "I feel like I have hours more time. I was getting used to going to bed so late, and then it seemed like I needed ten or twelve hours of sleep to compensate. Lately, eight or nine hours have been plenty."

Dez checked a smile. She still didn't get eight hours of uninterrupted sleep, but it was getting better. She looked at her watch and started to speak, but two other cops came into the break room just then.

"Hey, Reilly," said an older officer named Leonard. "How's it going in the Evidence Room? You got some of that crap organized that was laying all over?"

Before she could answer, the cop she thought of as Pretty Boy Barstow piped up. In a mocking voice, he said, "Sure doesn't look like it. It's messier now than it was when Floyd ran it." He moved to the refrigerator and pulled out a 20-ounce bottle of Mountain Dew.

Dez ignored him and directed her answer to Leonard. "I am systematically working through it. Gonna take me a few more days."

Barstow slid past Jaylynn's chair and seated himself at the other table, with Leonard joining him. After taking a big swig of soda, Barstow wiped his mouth on the back of his sleeve and said, "You *still* got a few more days left in there? I hear the guys are hoping you'll get back on patrol pretty soon. Got any idea when that'll be?"

Dez considered that Barstow was actually being halfway decent, so she responded. "I can't be sure, but I think it'll be pretty soon." She glanced across the table at Jaylynn, and was surprised to see the look on the younger woman's face. The rookie was glaring at Barstow as though she was barely able to keep herself from flying out of her chair and choking him. Tense and red-faced, she looked away from the handsome Barstow and met Dez's eyes. Dez recoiled in surprise. *Geez. She's really doing a slow burn. Wonder what that's all about.* She gave a slight wink to Jaylynn and, looking to the side, jerked her head slightly. Both of them rose.

"See ya, guys," the big cop said as she and the rookie pushed their chairs back under the table.

"Yeah, yeah." Barstow set his soda pop bottle down hard. "Hey, didn't mean to run you girls out." He chuckled.

By then, the two women were at the door. Dez raised a hand into a wave without looking back. "No problem. Break's over anyway."

When they got out in the hall, Jaylynn erupted into a noisy whisper. "Who the *hell* does he think he is?"

"He's just being himself, a total ass. He can't help it."

"Just because he's good looking does not give him the right to make fun of you."

They reached the Evidence Room, and the tall cop unlocked the door. The officer relieving her slid off the stool at the window. "That was quick," he said. "Not anywhere close to 45 minutes."

"Yeah," Dez said. "I can finish my break sitting in here just as easily as in the crowded break room, Monteith."

"So, you don't need me any longer?"

"Nah. Not until 3:45. See you then."

"Okay, Reilly."

"Thanks, Monteith," she called after him, but he was already gone. Dez shut the door behind Jaylynn who was still visibly upset. "Jay, this place is a major gossip and rumor mill, just like any big organization. They all know why I'm on desk duty. No use in getting upset when someone says something about it."

"But he had no call to make fun of the work you are doing in here."

"Well, he's right...as far as *he* can see. It does look pretty disorganized right now, but by tomorrow it'll look much better. Listen, I can take a little ribbing. I can deal with jerks like Barstow— been doing that for a lot of years. You don't need to worry about it, or...or, well protect me or anything like that."

Jaylynn walked slowly over to the step stool and sat on the second stair, one foot on the floor, the other on the first step. "Partners are supposed to look out for one another."

"Yes, that's true." She resisted the urge to go over and wrap her arms around the very upset young woman. "But this is one incident where I really am fine and don't need any looking out for."

The rookie took a deep breath, then groused a little more. "Why are people so small-minded and stupid? Dammit, it makes me mad."

"It's the shape of the world we live in. Don't waste energy on people like him. And don't worry, I'll let you know when I need protecting. Now, are you going to finish going through those boxes for the Tivoli case?"

Jaylynn shook herself out of her thoughts, literally, and took another deep breath. "Okay. I did leave off in the middle, didn't I?"

"Yup." She watched as Jaylynn got into the third box and started to root around. "Jay?" With a frown on her face, the rookie turned and looked over at the tall cop. "You remember that I leave at a quarter to four to go see Marie?" When the rookie nodded in a distracted manner, Dez said, "I'll be back a few minutes after five to pick you up." Jaylynn nodded and turned back to the boxes, and Dez started back at the organizational task before her.

****

It was midway through the session with Marie, and Dez was feeling pretty good about how easy it had been to talk about things. Mostly, they had focused on the reunion with Jaylynn and on how going back to work was feeling. But then Marie asked about her mother, and Dez felt herself sink into the chair. Despite the fact that she had managed to make it through the Christmas celebration with her family, she found that her mother was still a sore subject. "What do you want to know?"

"I was just wondering what precipitated the distance between you and your mother? What happened to cause that?"

Dez looked away, toward the window. Outside it was cloudy and still cold—typical January weather. She looked back at the curly-haired therapist. Try as hard as she might, she couldn't force herself to answer the question. She looked down at her hands in her lap as the silence in the room stretched on.

Marie put her clipboard on the coffee table. "Dez, do you see those photos over on the wall there?" She pointed toward the wall over the worktable where five framed 8 x10" black and white photos hung.

Dez squinted at the picture in the center of a thin, young

woman with curly black hair who wore Army fatigues and a baseball type Army cap. "Is that you in the middle, Marie?"

"Yes."

Grateful for the change of topic, the tall woman rose and
stood before the gallery of photographs. All five people in the pictures wore Army uniforms. On the far left a chunky White guy
stood, profile to the camera, wearing an apron over his uniform.
Smiling mischievously, he held a cigarette in one hand and an
enormous slotted spoon in the other. The second picture, right
next to the one of Marie, showed the upper half of a woman opposite in coloring from Marie. She had light-colored hair, light
eyes—Dez assumed blue—and a serious look on her face. To the
right of Marie's photo was a head-to-toe shot of a scrawny-looking
black man. He stood at attention, arms tight to his sides, and
chest pushed out, but the official looking pose could not disguise a
look of roguish playfulness. Dez imagined that the moment the
shutter clicked, he collapsed into fits of laughter. The last picture
was a side shot of a woman who obviously didn't want her picture
taken. As she backed away, she held up a hand, trying to ward off
the photographer, but to no avail. The camera caught her in a
wince-like grin, protesting. Dez turned to look at Marie and
waited.

Marie cleared her throat. "I know that in a way this is sort of
corny, but I think of that as my Guardian Angel wall. Remember
me telling you about my nursing friends from the Da Nang hospital during the war? Those photos are all I have left of them—of
Mark Dieter, Sandy Flynn, DeShawn Johnson, and Deb Maris."

Dez was struck mute. She had no idea what to say and just
stood there feeling stupid and not quite trusting her feet to walk
the three strides back to her chair.

"I tell you this, Dez, because you, too, might need a wall like
mine, if not in reality, then in your head."

"I-I just...I don't know what you mean." The tall woman
hazarded one step forward and then two more, and quickly lowered herself into the chair, her heart beating fast.

"Well, they were, literally, my comrades in arms. And you
lost your comrade, too. But then nobody understood. You had
nowhere to turn to deal with it. Earlier in your life, you lost your
father, also a sort of comrade to you. Again, no one understood,
and from what you have told me about your youth, you went
underground emotionally. All of your life, it seems, you have had
no way to commemorate your losses for yourself—or to share your
sorrow with others.

"I still don't understand."

"With all of that in mind—especially the loss of your father—I asked you what precipitated the break between your mother and you."

Dez's eyes filled with tears. "If you already knew that my father's death caused the break, why do you need to ask?"

Marie smiled. "Details. I don't know the details. What happened after your father died? What do you recall?"

Dez took a deep breath, swallowed, and tried to compose herself. What did she remember from the days after the shock of her handsome, dark-haired father's death? She closed her eyes. "My mother crying. Sleeping and crying nonstop for days. Patrick and I, hungry, and both of us trying not to cry, trying not to upset our mom." She thought of her brother's pale and pinched face, how he disappeared into their mother's room several times each day, how he tried to bring her snacks, water, anything. She herself had, at first, felt desolate and grief-stricken, but then she recalled a rage surfacing that she'd quickly squelched.

"What else?"

Dez's eyes popped open, and she felt a rush of anger race through her. "She drank. She started drinking herself to sleep and waking up in the mornings with a hangover, then drinking some more."

"Does she still do that?"

Dez shook her head. "It seemed like it lasted forever, but I guess it really didn't. At the beginning of my freshman year in high school, she went back to school—to medical school—to become an ophthalmologist. So she must have quit drinking before that." She looked down at her hands and tightened them into fists, feeling the muscles in her forearms flex.

"Then what happened?"

Dez leaned forward a little and looked down at the floor. "Shoot, I don't know. Time passed. Patrick and I learned to take care of ourselves and each other a little bit, and then by the time he was in ninth grade, he didn't need me anymore. Actually, he always seemed able to relate to my mother a lot better than I could."

"Why do you think that was?"

Dez shook her head slowly as she shrugged. "She didn't have the time, really. She spent most of her waking hours studying and trying to keep up the house."

"But not you kids?"

"Yeah, us, too."

"Not really, though, right? She didn't understand your loss any better than she understood hers."

"No," Dez said in a mournful voice, "she must not have."

"And how did you feel about that?"

Dez wanted to get up and move, to wrench open the door and leave. *I haven't felt this way for several sessions—why now? I thought I was almost done with this awfulness.* She took a deep breath, held it for a moment, then exhaled and brought herself back to the question. "How did I feel about that? Lost. I felt lost." The next words came out hesitantly. "Alone. Very much alone...and unloved. And deserted. I felt completely deserted and like I no longer mattered to anyone at all."

The curly-haired woman nodded. She picked up her coffee mug and took a sip, then looked up at the ceiling.

Uh-oh. Dez took a deep breath and prepared for the next questions, which she had a hunch would be tough ones.

Marie kicked her foot out from under her thigh and resettled herself in her chair. "And you have never entirely gotten over that feeling of desertion and aloneness, have you?" Dez shook her head, unable to say anything. "And you have never forgiven your mother." Marie said it as a statement, not a question. "Hmm, how did you go on? Who did you rely on?"

Dez looked at her, feeling a little surprised. "I don't know. A coach here, a teacher there. Later on, Luella. My mother was there; she just wasn't *there*, if you know what I mean. Now it seems as though she has a sense of that, and it's seems possible that she wants to relate better to me, but neither one of us knows how to talk about it. Besides, I don't need her now anyway." The tall cop heard a little chuckle come from the therapist. She scowled. "Why is that so funny?"

"It's that rugged individualist in you coming out again. You always want to do it all yourself." She smiled at the younger woman. "And yet, Dez, when you successfully connect with others—in your family, at your work, in your personal life—you are a much happier person. So, I would suggest to you that you *do* need your mother. We know you can't go back and rewrite the past. You can't escape the fact that, in her grief, she abandoned you; and really, she did a dreadful thing in not knowing how to help you work through the loss of your father. But what about Ryan? She had a chance to redeem herself when he died. What happened?"

Closing her eyes, Dez summoned up the scene at the hospital, pacing in the waiting room seconds after the paramedics had taken her partner's lifeless body in through the sliding glass doors. Using lights and siren, she had actually beaten the ambulance to the emergency room entrance and met them at the doorway as they rushed him in. When the medics disappeared into the ER, she had had two minutes, tops, before a whole raft of other cops descended upon the place. But in those two minutes, she remembered feeling the same despair and desolation she had felt when she discovered her father was dead. Even so, she had harbored the tiniest flame of hope that the paramedics had been wrong at the scene. Ryan wasn't dead. He hadn't bled out. The physicians would perform a miracle. Instead, a doctor emerged from the ER shaking his head. But by then, Cowboy was there, red-faced and crying. Julie came through the doors with the lieutenant and a chaplain and needed only one look at everyone to collapse into a chair sobbing. Even Crystal broke down. Their tears stopped Dez in her tracks. Every cop around her was crying, it seemed, every one of them unavailable and lost in their own grief.

She turned away from them all.

And then, some time later, her mother and Mac had materialized before her, had tried to reach out. She stared at them, stone-faced, and told them to go away, that she needed to be left alone. As soon as Colette Reilly left, Dez felt herself crumple inside. Once again, her mother had failed her. This time was just as unforgivable.

"Dez?" Opening her eyes, Dez blinked back the tears that had been seeping out. "Can you tell me a little of what happened between you and your mother when Ryan died?"

"She showed up. I pushed her away. She left. She never came back." The tall cop crossed her arms and pushed down the pain that was rising in her chest.

"I see." Marie sat for a few seconds nodding and thinking to herself.

Dez glanced at the clock and was relieved to see that the torture she was feeling would soon be over. She actually let out a sigh of relief.

"You know you've got resources and you're much stronger now, right?" The warm brown eyes met Dez's and held. "You're not alone, and you aren't thirteen anymore."

"Yeah, I know that."

"But it still hurts, doesn't it?"

Receiving a nod from her client, Marie said, "That's enough for today. Let's talk some more about it next time, okay?"

In a wry voice, Dez said, "Well, that's something to look forward to." She rose, grabbing two tissues from the box on the coffee table on the way up to her feet. She wiped her eyes and blew her nose, then placed the tissue in the wastebasket by the door as she said goodbye to Marie.

****

Jaylynn sat at Tsorro's desk, putting the finishing touches on her database update, when someone crept up behind her and startled her.

"Scared the hell out of you, didn't I?" the Italian man chortled.

She should have known it was Tsorro from the aftershave smell. "There's no hell left to scare out, you rude dude." She tried to hold back a smile, but didn't quite succeed.

He grinned back at her, then looked at his watch. "It's five after five, sweet pea. Time for you to toddle on home, right?"

"Yes, I will relinquish your desk, Tsorro."

"I don't need the damn desk, little *orsetta*. I'm going home pretty quick, too." He walked toward the coat rack with her. "I just have phone calls to make, then I'm out of here. I'll be glad when Parkins gets back from vacation. It's no fun without him to rib."

"Don't worry. You can always pick on me while he's gone."

"Yeah, right. Good idea. Well, I have a couple of calls to make, and I'll see you in the morning, doll."

"'Night, Tsorro." She smiled. He seemed to have a limitless supply of pet names for her, some of which were in Italian. She wasn't even sure what some of them meant. For all she knew, he could be calling her terrible names. But knowing him as long as she had now, she thought that each Italian comment he made was a special term of endearment. She shook her head as she watched him wander into the lieutenant's office, all the while adjusting his jacket. She got up and pulled her coat off the rack and around her shoulders. As she slipped her gloves on, she walked toward the lieutenant's office, stuck her head in, and said goodbye to Finn and Tsorro. As soon as she'd wrapped Vanita's wool scarf around her neck and zipped up her coat, she headed for the front door.

Bursting into the cold winter air sometimes took her breath away, but today it actually seemed slightly warmer—if fifteen degrees could be described as warm. There was no wind, so that made it seem less bone chilling. She still shivered a little as she descended the stairs, scanning the parking lot in search of Dez. She waited a minute, watching for her partner to roll into the lot. *Nope. No big red truck. Guess I'll go back in and watch from the window.* Before she could turn around, someone smelling of cheap men's cologne hooked her arm and pulled her down the last two stairs and into the parking lot.

"Hey! What—" She lost her footing on a patch of ice, and as

her feet slipped from under her, her right arm was yanked up so that she did not fall. She fought to regain her balance and tried to pull away from her assailant. He wrenched at her arm again as he thrust her forward, and her head jerked back. Her footing slipped again, but not before she got a glimpse of a very red-faced, angry looking Dwayne Neilsen. She got her feet back under her and tried to pull away, but he had a firm grip on her arm and shoulder and propelled her off to the side of the lot between a dirty, black conversion van and an old, green Impala. "Take your slimy hands off me, Neilsen!" she shouted as loud as she could, then drew back her foot and kicked him in the shins.

He snarled, sounding very much like a wild dog. "You stupid bitches cost me my job!" Before she could even respond, he shouted, "You got everything the goddamn easy way because you're a fuckin' woman!" He tightened his grip on the front of her coat and smacked her back against something cold and metal. "They handed it to you because of that. You and her, that bitch!" He shoved her against the side of the dirty van again and got in her face, kicking at her, pressing against her, screaming at her with his mouth so close that she could feel spit hit her face.

She tried to knee him, but that only enraged him more, and she could not get away.

****

Dez drove up Wabasha Street in a funk. The session with Marie had drained her of energy, and she felt as though she needed about ten hours sleep. She knew Jaylynn wanted to see a movie, though, and she wondered if she would be able to perk up enough to go along with the plan. The rookie was probably going to be pretty wired. After all, she had to wait a couple of days to find out if the phone card clue would pan out. Knowing Jaylynn, Dez figured she would be on energy overload and have enough vigor for the both of them. *Good, then she can make supper tonight.*

The last of the daylight was quickly disappearing. Thick, ominous clouds overhead didn't help the illumination, either. The whole day had been dreary. Peering over the steering wheel and up through the windshield, she stole a quick glance at the skies. She could tell they were in for more snow any time.

She pulled into the police station lot and looked at the clock display on the dashboard. 5:13. The five o'clock shift had peeled out since she left, and half the lot was already empty. There were no blonde-haired women in sight, so she pulled into a space facing the building to wait. The door to the station opened, and at the same moment, a muffled sound came to her ears. She heard it over the hum of the heater. It was not repeated, but the hair on her arms stood on end and she shivered, though not from cold. Without knowing why, she opened the truck door, swung her legs out to the side, and listened. While keeping her eye on the opening precinct door and the figure that stepped out, she reached back, turned off the ignition, and tucked the keys in her jacket pocket. Her heart beat fast for no reason that she could have explained.

She slid out of the warm truck. At the same moment, she saw that it was Detective Tsorro leaving the building. The muffled sound came again. This time she located it: to her right and along the parking lot fence. With a growing sense of urgency, she moved toward the spot where she thought the sound had come from. At the same time, Tsorro's head came up. He picked up his pace, descending the stairs.

The Italian cop reached the back of a dirty, black van one step before Dez did, but they both saw the same thing simultaneously. In one voice, they let out an identical roar. *"No!"*

Neilsen stood over Jaylynn, his right fist raised in the air and his left hand gripping her coat at the collar. His head whipped their way. His fist wavered. Blood was smeared on the rookie's face, but she was far from down and out. She kicked and struggled, pushed and squirmed.

Tsorro edged Dez out by a step and reached Neilsen first. He grabbed the bigger man by the arm and pushed him. Neilsen lurched to the side and lost his grip on Jaylynn, and when he did that, the rookie wrested away from his grasp. He pitched to the side and banged against the Chevy Impala.

By then, Dez had scrambled up on the trunk of the Impala. She launched herself past Tsorro's right shoulder to tackle the already stumbling Neilsen and knock him to the ground between the two vehicles. On her knees, she straddled one of his legs, grabbed his coat front, and tried to hold him down. There was nowhere for him to go. He tried to roll to one side, but the van's tire was there. He struck out at her, catching her in the eye, and she let out a shriek of pain. Her fist flew through the air and landed a glancing blow to his jaw, and then she saw a black wingtip shoe in the right corner of her peripheral vision. As if in slow motion, the point of the shoe traveled past her face to the side of Neilsen's head.

The big man let out a yowl, and for a moment, Dez saw not Neilsen, but the face of the big man, Bucky, from the Forest Street attack the month before. A strange gray haze surrounded her, and she couldn't see out of either eye very well. *Wait a minute! Stop! I can't lose track here.* She shook her head vigorously and loosened her grip on the man below her.

"I'll blow your head off!" Tsorro yelled. Dez saw the gun in Tsorro's hand, and so did Neilsen. He stopped struggling and held his hands, palms up and open, on either side of his head.

Dez's vision cleared in her right eye, though she couldn't see at all through the other. Then someone was pulling at her collar, and she let herself be dragged up and away, all the while watching as Tsorro yelled and kicked and stomped Jaylynn's attacker repeatedly. Bent half over, Dez staggered backwards, but she smacked a palm against the muddy van and regained her balance. She leaned forward, put hands on her knees, and tried to catch her breath. Jaylynn reached out to touch her face, but she shrugged her off and kept her eye on the two men. "I'm fine," she wheezed. "It's okay, Jay."

The rookie's voice came out sounding strangled. "But yo' bweeding—"

Dez swept her coat sleeve across her brow. "I'll be fine." She tossed a quick glance toward her partner. "What about you?"

Jaylynn wiped at her face with her scarf. "By dose hurts like hell. T'ink he bwoke it."

Dez squinted toward the two men. Her eye throbbed, but when she saw Neilsen roll into a ball and cover his face and head with his arms, she jumped forward. "Tsorro! Tsorro! That's enough." She grabbed him by the arm and pulled him away, out of the small space between the car and van.

Gasping for breath, he pointed the weapon, his right arm down and straight out, and stood staring at the man on the ground. "Who does this...this *malfattore* think he is? I spit on you, *anima dannata*!" He made good with his promise and let loose some saliva. "How dare you hit a woman, and a good, kind woman at that? You are scum." He sprang forward, letting loose a string of Italian invective, and gave Neilsen another final kick in the side before backing away for good.

By then two cops in full uniform were striding up. "What's going on?" one asked.

"Patterson," Dez said with relief. "This...this *jerk* attacked Savage." Neilsen rose, on shaky legs, panting and coughing. His lip and chin were bleeding. His face was mottled with rapidly rising red marks, and from the way he held his midsection, Dez could tell he was hurt. "If Tsorro and I hadn't come along when we did..."

Tsorro lowered his gun hand and held his left forefinger in the air. He turned and pointed dramatically at the coughing man. "This asshole needs to be arrested. If you don't do it, I will. Aggravated assault is a good charge for starters."

Patterson gaped at Dez, then at Tsorro, and moved toward Neilsen to cuff him. He and his partner, Bentley, hauled the big ex-cop toward the station house.

Jaylynn sat down suddenly against the bumper of the dark green Impala. "By dose won't stob bweeding."

Tsorro holstered his weapon and pulled a clean handkerchief out of his pocket. "Here, babycakes," he said in a concerned voice. "Take this." He leaned over her, put his arm around her shoulders, and dabbed at the blood on her face.

Dez stood and watched through one eye, as her stomach spun and heaved. She put her right hand to her brow, and when she drew it away, bright red blood stained her hand. For a moment, she was afraid she might faint. Tsorro, still comforting Jaylynn, stood and turned her way. Dez reached out and steadied herself against him. The shoulder pad under his coat felt thick, but substantial.

Tsorro looked at her, a scowl on his face. "Jesus Christ, Reilly! You both look like hell. C'mon. We're going inside to call the paramedics."

****

Before she knew what was happening, Jaylynn found herself seated next to Dez in the break room, a bag of ice on her face. Six uniformed cops crowded into the room along with Tsorro, one of the dispatchers, and Lt. Finn.

"What in the world happened here?" the lieutenant asked, concern etched on her face. She made her way through the crowd of men and leaned down to look, first, at the rookie's face and then Dez's. "You both better keep the ice on."

Jaylynn let Tsorro and Dez do the honors of describing what had happened. Her mind was in a whirl. She had always thought Neilsen behaved badly and that he was selfish and arrogant, but she hadn't actually expected anything more from him than intimidation and threats. *They fired him? He said we cost him his job. What was that all about?* She moved the ice bag away from her nose. Two more officers crowded into the small room, and she was feeling claustrophobic and dizzy. "Was Neilsen fired?" Everyone was talking at once, and her question was lost in the din. "Hey!" she yelled out. The noise dropped off and quizzical faces turned to look at her. Her head was pounding, but she choked the words out. "Whad habbened wid Neilsen?"

A crew-cut, thick-necked officer named Bob Finch answered. "I heard he got canned."

Another cop nodded. "Lost his appeal hearing."

All eyes moved to the lieutenant for confirmation. She made a fist and turned her hand over to rap against the table with her wedding ring. "You are both correct. Dwayne Neilsen did not pass probation." She paused as though considering her next words. "Obviously, the decision not to allow him to join the force permanently was a good one."

Jaylynn's eyes slid to the right to check on Dez. The tall cop had an ice bag over her left eye, and she looked unusually pale.

A commotion occurred at the doorway, and the blue-shirted crew of officers stepped aside to allow two EMT's into the room. The medics put their big orange bags on the break table as Finn waved all the cops back. "Okay, everybody. Out. Give these guys room to work." The dispatcher and pack of curious cops backed up, one by one, and exited the room, followed by the lieutenant.

A brown-haired EMT squatted down in front of Jaylynn. "Hey, my name's Chuck, and I'm going to take a look at you. Are you hurt anywhere besides your nose?"

"I don't.. I don't t'ink so."

"So," he looked at the nametag on her uniform as he stood, "Officer Savage, can you sit up straight—no, don't tip your head back too much. There. Just sit back and let me check you over."

Jaylynn's nose throbbed, and her neck canted at an uncomfortable angle as the medic examined her. He shone a light in her eyes, then pressed along the base of her skull, up the sides of her head, to the top. "You got this from a blow to the face?"

"Uh huh."

He pressed the bridge of her nose and her cheekbones lightly. Though he was gentle, the pressure brought tears to her eyes. "Guess that hurts?"

"Yeah."

"You're going to have a lot of bruising and swelling, Officer. I don't think it's broken, though. You should be checked over by your doctor to be sure. He or she may wish to do an x-ray. But you'll be okay for now. Apply ice on and off for the next several hours."

The other medic spoke up. "Take a look at this, Chuck. What do you suggest?"

The medic turned and stood with his back to Jaylynn, so she couldn't see. She scooted her chair back and stood, moving over next to the break room counter and behind Dez. *Gosh, she sure has been quiet.* Suddenly, a shiver ran through her as she listened to the two men muttering back and forth. "What's the trouble there?" She put a hand on Dez's shoulder, and found the muscles there tense. *Oh, my, she's in pain.*

Chuck stepped back. "Excuse me, ma'am, let me get around here." He angled himself between the rookie and the back of the chair and shone a skinny penlight down into the injured officer's eyes. He snapped off the light, looked up at his colleague, and asked, "What do you think? Butterfly? Stitches?"

"Good question," the other EMT replied.

Chuck clicked off his penlight. When he stepped aside, Jaylynn leaned over Dez's shoulder and peered around into her face. What she saw stopped her short. The big cop's left eye was swollen shut. Above it, along her eyebrow, the skin was split and gaped open, oozing red. Chuck shifted away, fished around in his bag and pulled something out. As he opened a small package, he turned and bumped into the rookie. With irritation in his voice, he said, "Excuse me, Officer. I need room to work here."

Just then, Lt. Finn returned to the room. "How's everyone doing?" She smoothed her dark hair out of her face and looked expectantly at the medics.

Chuck answered. "I don't think Officer Savage needs to go to the hospital, but her nose is going to be pretty sore for a while."

The other EMT added, "Officer Reilly here needs stitches, and I'd like a doctor to take a look at this wound."

Finn's face took on a surprised look at the same time that Dez said, "Hey, wait a minute." Her voice was slow and slurred. "Don't I get a vote in this?"

The lieutenant moved around the table. She reached out an arm and patted the injured cop's shoulder. "No, in this case, I'm afraid not." She turned toward the EMT's. "Guys, if it's all the same to you, I officially request that you take both of these officers to be checked over by the hospital medical personnel. It's basically a work comp injury, so the department would prefer that they be fully examined."

As she rose, holding the ice to her forehead, the tall cop said, "I'm *not* getting on a gurney."

Finn chuckled. "Never would have suggested it."

Dez didn't say anything further, but she allowed the medics to help her put her jacket on, and then she started toward the door. She stepped out in the hall and stopped. "Jaylynn? You coming?"

The rookie had stood, but a bout of dizziness overtook her. She took a deep breath and closed her eyes, opening them when she felt a hand on her elbow. Chuck was hunched over, squinting into her face, a look of concern in his eyes. "Officer Savage, looks like you may need some help here."

She closed her eyes again and nodded. The throbbing pain in her head was killing her.

****

The ride to the hospital was uneventful, and when they arrived at the emergency room entrance, the EMT's helped both women in. Tsorro and Lt. Finn were on their way, too, but hadn't yet parked and come in.

Nothing had changed since the last time Jaylynn had been there. The same brightly lit, spacious waiting room was filled with the same uncomfortable vinyl chairs. It didn't look like a very busy night, but that wouldn't have mattered. There was an unwritten, unspoken rule that when cops were brought into the ER, they were bumped to the head of the line. Neither officer even had to check in. A nurse took one look at the blood on Jaylynn's coat and uniform shirt and immediately beckoned them to follow through the sliding door to the inner sanctum.

They were taken to examining tables next to each other, but the nurse pulled the curtain between Jaylynn's nose hurt too much for her to protest. The perky nurse helped her get her coat off and efficiently removed the young woman's uniform top and t-shirt, then had her slip out of her shoes and slacks. She checked her patient over, making clucking noises and saying, "There's the beginning of a bruise...and another one...and another." She pointed to one above the rookie's right breast. "Does that one hurt?"

Jaylynn looked down with effort and shook her head. She wasn't feeling any serious pain except in her sinuses, so she was surprised to discover how many bruises she had and how many strange places they were located. She racked her brain to try to figure out how she could have gotten one on the back of her neck. She didn't remember bumping her head against anything. The nurse suggested it could have been from Neilsen's grip, and Jaylynn thought that might be true.

The nurse handed Jaylynn her ice bag. "Here you go, dear," she said, as she adjusted the examining table so that the head was raised up. "Why don't you just lie back and rest for a minute until the doctor comes in?" She pulled a sheet up over her, then saw her shiver. "You cold? Let me get you a blanket, too." She disappeared through the curtain and reappeared moments later to smooth a blanket over the trembling figure. "That better?"

The young woman nodded and closed her eyes. The melting ice made her nose feel much better. With her eyes shut, she strained to hear what was going on next to her. She could hear the murmur of a deep voice, but that was all. Then she must have dozed for a moment, because she started awake when she felt a pressure on her knee through the blanket.

A young Chinese woman in a white coat stood before her. "Hi. I'm Doctor Chang. How are you holding up?"

Jaylynn let out a breath of air. "Just got quite the headache."

"I would imagine so." The doctor was gentle with her probing, and in just a couple minutes, she came up with exactly the same comments that the paramedic had. "It's not broken, but you are badly bruised. Ice on and off for the next few hours, twenty minutes on, half an hour or so off. Take Ibuprofen. In fact, I think I will have the nurse give you some right now to start off with."

"Thank you, Doctor."

"No problem. You're good to go, Officer."

"Really?"

"Yes. Just try to keep your head elevated on a pillow tonight when you sleep, and you'll be fine. You can also put ice on your brow and cheeks to help keep the swelling down. As for all the body bruising, I want you to ice any area that feels tender or sore, especially around your thighs and pelvis. No hot baths for a day or so, all right?"

"Okay, thanks. How's my partner doing over there?"

"Not sure. Let me get the nurse to help you dress, and I'll go check."

She disappeared through the curtain at the foot of the bed, and within seconds, the pleasant nurse was back and bustling around to help her get dressed again. The nurse kept up a steady stream of chatter, but right in the middle of a sentence, Dr. Chang poked her head in through the curtain and interrupted. "Officer, I'm going to release you, and you can step through here to see your partner. I'm off duty now, too, so I just wanted to wish you good luck."

Jaylynn thanked her, and then the nurse handed over a small Dixie cup full of water and a large white pill. "800 milligrams of Ibuprofen," she said. "Doctor's orders." She took the empty cup from the rookie when she was done, and held out her down coat. Jaylynn took them and thanked her, then followed her through the white curtain to the next cubicle. Dez lay flat on the table, balancing an ice bag on her forehead with both hands. With pants, shoes, and socks off, her long legs were crossed at the ankle, and a thin sheet covered her from mid-calf to waist. She still wore her white tank top undershirt. Somehow a smear of blood had gotten on the ribbing at the top of the shirt, leaving a stain that was bright red in the middle and turning dark brown around the outside. When she heard the rookie's voice, she reached out with her left hand. "Jay?" She didn't lift the ice bag from her head, instead waiting for her to take her hand. She felt the cool fingers close over hers, and then she could feel Jaylynn standing as close as the bed would allow. "Are you okay?"

"As the EMT's said, my nose is not broken. What's your prognosis?"

Dez took a deep breath. "Well, as far as I can tell, this guy on duty, Shelton, is a greenhorn. He's not sure if anything is wrong, but he sounds worried. His bedside manner leaves a shit-load to be desired. I said I—"

The curtain whipped aside just then. "Oh. Hi." The lanky young doctor hesitated, then stood awkwardly opposite Jaylynn and cleared his throat. He held a clipboard in his pink-colored hands. An unruly cowlick in the front of his dark hair made him seem about twelve years old, though he was likely in his late twenties. "Ah, Officer Reilly, I've, um, called the supervising doctor." His voice was deep, and he looked troubled. He glanced up when Dez shifted the ice bag up further on her forehead, and he seemed taken aback that she was blinking at him with her good eye.

"You called the supervisor?" she said.

"Yes."

"Where is he—or she—at?"

"He's doing rounds and won't be done for—" he looked at his watch, "twenty more minutes or so. But you aren't in any danger, so don't worry about that. The butterfly bandage will hold the brow wound for now until we decide if we want to suture it closed."

Jaylynn asked, "Is Doctor Colette Reilly on duty tonight?"

He frowned, looking puzzled. "Dr. Reilly? No, she's never on duty at night. She works over in the clinic."

Nodding, Jaylynn said. "Let's call her and get her down here."

Shelton looked alarmed. "Oh, no. We can't do that."

She gave him a little half-smile. "Sure we can. This is her daughter."

"Well," he said, "doctors are supposed to be objective, so if they're related, that might not be a very good idea. And besides, what if Dr. Reilly has surgery to perform in the morning? We aren't supposed to disturb the surgeons unless the supervising physician orders it."

"So you won't call her?" Jaylynn asked in a controlled voice.

"It wouldn't be appropriate. I wouldn't be allowed to. I—"

Dez squeezed the younger woman's hand and spoke up. "Forget it, Jay. It'll be all right."

Jaylynn gave her a withering look. "How do you know that? Your mother is an expert. We should get her in here."

Before Dez could respond, Dr. Shelton said, "I'll go see if I can hurry things up." He swept out of the area, leaving a swirl of curtain behind him.

In a quiet voice, Jaylynn said, "Maybe *he* won't call, but we can." She fumbled around in the oversized pocket of her coat and pulled out her cell phone. "That is, if Neilsen didn't bust the damn thing." She pressed the *On* button, and the phone lit up with a dial tone. "What's your mother's number?"

The tall cop recited it from memory, and Jaylynn pushed the corresponding keys, then pressed the phone into her partner's hand. Dez set the ice bag back over her brow, being very careful not to touch the sore eye, and listened to the phone ring. It was picked up on the fourth ring. "Mom?"

"Dez?"

"Yeah."

"What's the matter?" Her mother's voice was sharp.

"Now how do you know something's wrong?"

"I don't know. I can just tell."

"I think I need your help. I'm down here at your delightful hospital with an eye injury." She heard her mother's intake of breath. "I don't know if it's anything or not, but neither do these ER docs. Could you—"

"I'll be right there." Dez heard a click on the line and then dead silence. Blindly, she handed the phone up and away until she felt Jaylynn take it. "She didn't give me a chance to say much before she hung up, but I guess she's coming down here."

"Good," Jaylynn said in a worried voice. "At least *she* knows what she's doing." She held Dez's hand tightly.

The injured cop smiled. "I don't suppose it would look too good if my mother arrived and found you curled up here next to me, huh?" Jaylynn let out a snort of laughter. "Believe me, Jay, I wouldn't mind it. To be honest, this is scaring the crap outta me."

"Why?"

"Either this doctor is a total amateur or else something is seriously wrong. I can't see out of my eye at all. It doesn't help that it's practically swollen shut, but even when I open my eyelid a little, I don't see anything—just a glob of black with a little gray around the edges." She felt a soft stroke on her arm, and she opened her good eye to find Jaylynn leaning over her, tears in her eyes. "Damn, Jay, you've got quite the couple of shiners starting there." She reached up and touched the rookie's cheek lightly with just her index finger. "I hope your eyes don't turn as black as they look like they will."

"Me, too. At least my nose stopped bleeding."

"Well, don't start crying, 'cause if you sniff, it's gonna hurt."

"True."

"We are pressing charges against Neilsen, you know."

"No doubt about that. He's going to jail. I might have been easy on him in the past, Dez, but not anymore. He's going to pay."

"Oh yeah, and if I end up with a peg leg, an eye patch, and toting a parrot on my shoulder, I'm gonna sue him in civil court, too."

Jaylynn started to giggle. "A parrot? Where did that come from?"

Their conversation was interrupted by a noise outside the curtain, and then a woman's voice called out, "Where's Doctor Lefsky?"

The deep voice of the lanky Doctor Shelton answered, "On rounds. He should be down any minute—"

The curtain whipped open, and Colette Reilly entered. Her normally pale face was red and her eyes fiery. She carried a black bag in one hand and was followed by a crew, all of whom crowded around the foot of the examining table. Jaylynn recognized Mac MacArthur, Lt. Finn, and Tsorro. A woman the rookie didn't recognize held the hand of a dark-haired man. She did a double take when the tall man looked at her, his blue eyes sharp and steely. She stared in wonder, realizing that this was surely Patrick, Dez's brother. They looked enough alike to be twins. Dr. Shelton crowded in behind Dez's mother and gaped over her shoulder.

Dez lifted the ice bag away from her forehead. In a tired voice, she asked, "Geez, Mom, what'd you do, call in the cavalry? Hey, people, what are you all doing here?"

Colette took the ice bag from her hands and set it aside. "We were at dinner, so they came with me."

Mac said, "It's handy to have a retired cop along, Dez. We broke every speeding record getting down here."

"Yeah, you must have. What's it been—four minutes?"

"Maybe less," Mac said. "Luckily, nobody stopped us."

Colette leaned down, one hand on her daughter's forehead.

"Settle back, and let me see." She clicked on a slim penlight, then got out a magnifying scope, which also had a light on it. She examined the injured eye, asked questions, and checked the brow wound. "How did this happen?"

"A guy hit me."

. "With what—a board with a nail in it?"

Jaylynn said, "No, he wears a big signet ring on his right forefinger."

Dez's mother nodded her head slowly. "Ah—that's consistent with this injury." The curtain behind her flapped open again, and someone else crowded in. She looked around in irritation.

"Colette!"

"Oh, good. It's you, Brad. I could use your help." She set the penlight and scope on the edge of the examining table along Dez's thigh. Absentmindedly, she took hold of her patient's hand and patted Dez's hip with her other hand. "Desiree, this is my colleague, Bradley Lefsky. Brad, this is my daughter. Age 30, in good health, with what looks like a traumatic hyphema to the left eye. Dez, hyphema is simply a bruise to the eyeball." She looked around at all the people, suddenly aware of how crowded it was. "All of you—out. We need room to work now. Should only be a few minutes and we'll come report to you." Everyone, including Dr. Shelton, moved to file out. "Wait, Officer, you stay. And Shelton, where do you think you're going?"

"Uh, you said, everybody out."

In an exasperated voice, she said, "You're not *everybody*. You're the physician on duty. Get over here so you can observe and learn a thing or two. But first, give Dr. Lefsky the rundown on the patient's vitals." Shelton, red-faced and stammering, flipped through the pages on the clipboard and spoke to Lefsky on the side. Meanwhile, Colette's eyes came to rest on the rookie, and the irritation in her voice dissipated when she spoke. "I'm sorry, I've forgotten your first name."

"Jaylynn."

"That's right. You look too worried, Jaylynn. Don't be. My daughter's eye is injured, but she won't lose her sight. Pull that damn curtain open, Shelton, and get Jaylynn a chair. The poor woman looks like she's about to fall over." With concern on her face, she turned to look down at the patient below her. "Shelton," she called out over her shoulder as the resident slid a chair up behind the rookie. "Get on the horn and get the best surgeon on duty. This cut needs stitches, not just a butterfly bandage. My daughter is *not* going to look like a prizefighter. And while you're at it, get the x-ray tech. We need to rule out any occipital fracture or crack. Okay, Brad, what do you think?" The two doctors poked and prodded, shone lights in her eyes, and Dez listened as they discussed the injury in that strange, acronym-filled language that only other medical personnel understand.

Despite the pain in her eye and forehead, Dez felt a strange bubble of happiness floating up through her, beginning somewhere in the vicinity of her solar plexus and traveling up to her heart and into her throat. Her eyes filled with tears, but at the same time, she couldn't hold back a grin. Her mother probably thought it was because she was relieved to hear that her eye was just badly bruised, but that wasn't it. For the first time in many years, she realized how much she loved her mother.

****

It was after nine p.m. before the two cops finally made it back to the parking lot at the police station to pick up the truck. Despite feeling exhausted, Jaylynn decided she should drive them to Luella's place because Dez's left eye sported a large gauze bandage, which threw off her depth perception. Her mother and Dr. Lefsky had initially been concerned that her eye had sustained serious injury. After what seemed like hours of examination, they had determined there was no structural damage, and she hadn't fractured any bones in her face, but the blow had caused some bleeding in the anterior chamber of the eye. She would have to keep it covered for a few days until the blood reabsorbed and until what amounted to an internal bruise healed. She had been given medication to reduce any possibility of increased pressure in her eye.

Colette Reilly had been concerned, too, that her daughter might have suffered a concussion, but after further examination, she decided Dez was a little woozy because she was in a lot of pain from the trauma to both the exterior and interior of the eye. The cut was deep and in a line just beneath her eyebrow, so the surgeon on duty placed eleven stitches with very fine needle and thread, then dressed it and sent them on their way.

Now she sat, a passenger in her own truck, feeling grumpy, and her head pounding. She was also hungry. "Jaylynn, I swear to God you've become a trouble magnet."

"What?" The rookie glanced over and back to the road, looking alarmed.

Dez shook her head. "We're like the walking wounded. Look at us."

They shared an amused examination, and then Jaylynn

focused on driving again, saying, "You look worse than me."

"Hah. Your whole face is going to be black 'n' blue—in fact, it's already turning blue under your eyes and around your nose."

"And *you're* not going to have a huge shiner?"

"Like I said, we look like hell." Dez was glad to see the alleyway to the garage.

Jaylynn pulled the truck in, waited for the garage door to open, then gunned it up the little hill and inside. "Think we can make it into the apartment without getting attacked, falling, or having a piano drop on our heads?"

Dez took a deep breath. "I don't know. I'm just glad that Luella's not home."

But she was wrong. They approached the back of the house to find light shining from all the windows on the main floor, and when they entered, the door to Luella's place popped open.

"Girls, girls! Hey, it's great to...see...goodness! What happened?" She looked from one to the other. "You look like you fell into a pit with a bear!"

"It was something like that," Dez said.

Jaylynn sighed. "Hi Luella. You're a sight for sore eyes—or in Dez's case, sore eye, singular."

"Very funny," Dez grumbled. "What are you doing here, Lu?"

"Vanita and I started movin' in. Her granddaughter brought us over earlier today and a load of our stuff, too. Figured we might as well start getting settled in since you two are going to want to get into the other house and make changes."

"We haven't even signed the papers, Luella," Jaylynn protested.

The older woman smiled and shrugged. "It doesn't matter. It'll all go through. Worse case scenario would be a contract-for-deed. Either way, it's a happening thing."

The door behind Luella opened wider, and Vanita appeared. "Jiminy Cricket—I go off to the bathroom, and all the fun happens. What's going on here?" She squinted into the bright hallway and surveyed the two tired looking women. "Geez! How bad does the other guy look?"

Jaylynn shook her head. "Courtesy of one very angry Anthony S. Tsorro, the other guy has some serious dents upside his head. I also wouldn't be surprised if his ribs are broken."

Luella gestured at them, beckoning them in. "Why don't you two get in here and tell us all about it. I'll make you some tea. You hungry? I've got left over chicken pot pie."

"You *are* a guardian angel," Jaylynn said. "This is one time

I'm not going to be shy. Yes, I am starved beyond belief. Feed me. I would gladly pay you on Tuesday for a chicken pot pie today."

If she could have rolled her eyes, Dez would have. Instead she smiled and relaxed. Her eye throbbed and her head hurt a little, though the painkiller they'd given her at the hospital had numbed things; but she knew they would be all right. In more ways than one.

Chapter
Thirty-Four

Dez slept restlessly, waking every half-hour or so with a throbbing in her eye and a headache that wouldn't quit. She wanted to sleep on her side, but she was afraid she might dislodge the bandage on her eye, so she tried to stay on her back, which, after a few hours, wasn't that comfortable. Each time she drifted off to sleep, she was eventually jerked awake by bad dreams filled with fire, blood, and blades. She awoke sweating from one nightmare where she and Jaylynn had been chased by a wraith-like man with a knife. He kept drawing closer and closer, his breath on her neck and a maniacal laugh tickling her ear. No matter how fast she ran, she couldn't elude him.

Sometime after five a.m. she lay awake, a pulse beating in her eye and forehead. Jaylynn slept quietly next to her on her side, her blonde hair tousled. Dez thought about getting up to take a painkiller, but before she could make a move, Jaylynn cried out, "No! No, please...no!"

Dez rolled up on her side and reached for the smaller woman's shoulder. "Jay," she said quietly.

The sleeping woman tensed up, her legs thrashing. "No, don't!" She shook her head from side to side, burrowing into the covers and moaning "No" over and over.

"Jay! Wake up. It's a bad dream." The rookie kicked out, her instep nailing Dez in the kneecap. "Ouch!"

"No, no, don't lemme fall...no."

The dark-haired cop scooted over on the bed and pressed against the smaller woman. "Hey, hey, wake up, sweetie. Wake up."

Panting and whimpering, she came to, her eyes focusing slowly in the dim light of the room. She groaned and swallowed with difficulty. Her voice was raspy when she spoke. "Oh, God...what a nightmare."

"Yeah, seems like it. C'mere." She pulled the smaller woman into her arms, and Jaylynn snuggled in, shivering. Dez sat up a bit and with one long arm, grabbed the rumpled quilt and tugged it up and over them. "What was that all about?"

In a flat voice, she answered, "Same dream as always. Same scary shit."

"Not a replay of Neilsen's attack?"

"No." Jaylynn shifted so that her head was against her partner's shoulder and she was lying pressed up against the right side of the tall woman's body. She put her leg over Dez's right thigh and held on tight. "I've been having these same dreams ever since I was a kid. It's like these horrible, giant, alien monsters are chasing me and getting closer and closer, and trying to rip me to pieces and devour me."

"Sounds a little familiar. I was just having a similar dream— only my monsters are more human sized."

"This one was a double whammy because I climbed up and up in this building, trying to get away, and finally I was on the roof, running fast as I could. I looked over the side and the whole thing was going up in flames. I had to choose—jump into the smoke below or stay and burn to death, and all the while, I could hear the monsters' footsteps and this deep growling. So I jumped, but then one of the aliens was waiting below with the same old blood and guts all over his teeth and jaws. As soon as I jumped, I just knew he'd be there. He's *always* there, and I couldn't figure out why I was so stupid that I had jumped again. I'm falling and falling, and it scares me shitless, but there isn't anything I can do."

"You've had this dream since you were a kid?"

"Something similar."

"Did something happen in your childhood to provoke this?"

"I watched Sigourney Weaver in *Alien* in grade school. Apparently, that was all it took. My parents were pretty mad that I'd done that, because I've been having nightmares for years."

"Hmm." Dez lay on her back, thinking of her own bad dreams as she stroked Jaylynn's back through the sleep shirt the smaller woman wore. "I didn't used to have trouble sleeping at all—not until Ryan died. I'd pay a lot of money to sleep the way I used to."

"You and me both. Guess I'll have to go back to my old fantasy and utilize it." She lifted her head a little and tried to look into Dez's eyes in the shadowy light. There was enough illumination for her to see the thoughtful look on the taller woman's face.

"Hey, how's your eye feeling?"

"I think it's better than the way your face looks. You've got the beginnings of two of the biggest shiners I've ever seen." She lifted a hand to touch the side of Jaylynn's face and caress her cheek tenderly. "What fantasy?"

"What?"

"The fantasy you use."

"Oh, you mean for bad dreams?" Dez nodded, and Jaylynn let her head drop back down against the cotton sleep shirt that the reclining woman wore. "It's sort of embarrassing to admit."

"Good," Dez mumbled. "It's your turn to embarrass yourself, anyway."

Jaylynn giggled. "It's just that it's sort of juvenile. When I was having these dreams as a kid, my Auntie Lynn came to visit. She's a psychotherapist, you know, and she taught me some guided visualization stuff to think of before I fell asleep and to try to incorporate into my dreams if I could."

"What kind of visualization stuff?"

"That's kind of the embarrassing part. I would visualize a hero, someone to protect me, and then if the monsters showed up, all I had to do is call for help and ask my hero to come."

"So you imagined what—Ghostbusters?"

"No. I imagined you."

"Huh?" She tipped her head to the side and tried to see Jaylynn's face, but the other woman was pressed too closely against her chest for her to examine her expression.

The rookie went on, her voice slow and thoughtful. "I didn't know if I ever wanted to admit this to you because it sounds so bizarre. But you've already got a good idea of all my strange quirks, so you may as well know one more. The hero I created had long black hair and looked and felt and sounded just like you do. I let her save me practically every night. I got so used to seeing my hero that I almost enjoyed the bad dreams. I loved it when this tall, strong woman showed up. She was really fierce and absolutely fearless."

Dez let out a snort of laughter. "Well, it wasn't me, then. I might have a little fierceness in me, but no way am I absolutely fearless."

"Hey, Miss Prince Valiant, you are one of the bravest people I know."

"Yeah, right."

Jaylynn pulled away and sat up. "I'm not kidding, Dez. To have gone through all you have experienced—well, that's taken some real courage. You face your fears. None of us are *really* fearless, except maybe in fantasy, but you don't let that stop you."

Dez wasn't so sure about that. She'd felt like a great big chicken lately, and one of the major strong emotions she had been dealing with felt like plain old fear. "I wouldn't put it that way, Jay. I'm not fearless. Besides, you didn't even know me when you did this visualization stuff."

Jaylynn swung her leg over the bigger woman and straddled her hips, then lowered her upper body. With her elbows on either side of Dez's head, she shifted until she was comfortable, her face close to her partner's. "The moment I saw you, for the very first time, in Sara's room, I was electrified. I knew it was you, my dream hero. I can't explain it. I can't prove it. But I believed it then, and I still believe it now."

Dez peered up at her through her one good eye. She lifted her hands, put them on Jaylynn's ribcage and slid them down to her hips, then worked her hands up under the t-shirt, feeling the warm skin at her partner's waist. "If I'm such a great hero, how come you're still having the bad dreams?"

Jaylynn shivered. "I don't know." Her head dropped into the hollow at the right side of Dez's neck, and she held on tight. "I guess I haven't been doing a very good job visualizing in my dreams since you're right here in my waking life."

****

They had fallen asleep again, and when Jaylynn woke up later in the morning, the sun was shining in through the small window over the bed. She heard a clunking noise from somewhere downstairs, and then the distant sound of water running, so she knew either Luella or Vanita—or both—were up and about. She extricated herself from Dez's embrace and tiptoed over to use the bathroom, then washed her hands and face, and stood looking at herself in the mirror. A dark purple bruise the size of a dime adorned her right cheekbone, and above that, she saw two pale plum-colored circlets under her eyes. Both eyes were pink and bloodshot, and as she surveyed the state of her face, she had to admit that she looked awful. Puffy, swollen skin around her eyes and brows and an especially pale face contributed to making her look tired and wrung out. *Oh well. I don't feel so bad, though I do look terrible. It's not as wretched as it appears, though.*

She still had a bit of a headache, but it wasn't the pulsating, painful kind. With a little food and liquid, she figured she'd be ready to roll by noon. She stepped into the living room area and looked across the space to the bed on the far wall where Dez lay

sleeping on her back, her face turned away from the light coming
in the little window. It wasn't like Dez to sleep longer than Jaylynn did, but she figured there was some heavy duty healing going
on, and she wouldn't begrudge her any rest.

She stood in front of the couch and rooted around in a pile of
clean laundry until she came up with one of Dez's sweatshirts and
a pair of dark blue sweatpants, which bagged on her when she
slipped them over her bare legs. She pulled the white drawstring
tight and looped it into a snug bow, then found some thick socks.
After tugging the sweatshirt on over her sleep shirt, she paused a
moment to examine the tall woman as she lay sleeping so peacefully. She didn't show any signs of waking, so Jaylynn crept from
the room, through the kitchen, and to the back door to head down
the stairs.

Later in the day, they were supposed to stop by Colette
Reilly's house so that she could re-check Dez's eye. Jaylynn didn't
think the tall cop needed another exam, but she did think that a
certain mother and daughter needed a good excuse to be in one
another's company. In the hospital, the night before, she had
observed the desperation Dez's mother had been trying to conceal
when she first arrived. It wasn't until Colette and Dr. Lefsky had
ascertained that the eye injury was only mildly serious that the
older woman had relaxed. Jaylynn didn't think that if she were a
doctor she would ever want to examine her own wounded child,
but Colette Reilly had done an admirable job, remaining calm and
focused. Only the closest observer would have detected the slight
tremble of her hand or the almost imperceptible crack in her professional demeanor.

But watching Dez the night before was even more revealing.
The big woman drank up her mother's attention as though it were
water at an oasis in the Sahara. At one point, Jaylynn could have
sworn that her partner teared up and was going to cry—and not
from pain either.

And then after they'd finished the exams, the x-rays, and the
stitching, the tall woman had received nothing short of a hero's
welcome in the waiting room when they went to leave. Lt. Finn,
Tsorro, and Mac had been speaking to one another over in the corner, and Patrick and Monique stood, arms around each other,
looking out the window into the parking lot. When the sliding
glass door from the ER bay opened, and mother and daughter
emerged with Jaylynn in tow, Dez was hugged by everyone, even
Tsorro. Jaylynn watched. Despite the fact that her head was
pounding and her eyes watered, it was clear that the Reilly clan
loved their black sheep daughter. How Dez could think any differ-

ently was a real mystery to the rookie.

She made it to the bottom of the cold stairwell and tapped on Luella's back door. When she heard a voice call out, "Come in," she turned the knob and stepped in to the fragrant aroma of cocoa. "In here," she heard Luella say.

Standing in the kitchen doorway, Jaylynn smiled. The two women sat at the little kitchen table in the corner, drinking from steaming hot mugs. "Hey, Luella, Van, how are you both this morning?"

Vanita grinned at her, and raised her cup. "Great. Want to try some low-fat cocoa coffee?"

Before she could answer, Luella gestured toward the third chair at the dinette table and rose. "Grab a chair and I'll whip you up some of this good stuff and some oatmeal, too, if you'd like."

"You don't have to go to any trouble."

"No trouble at all. I made enough for an army, hoping you two would come down." Jaylynn moved toward the chair, and Luella gave her a gentle swat on the butt as she went by. "Where's the other fugitive from the chain gang?"

The rookie settled into the chair, her elbows on the table and hands folded in front of her. "Believe it or not, she's still sleeping."

Vanita reached over and patted her hands. "You look like hell, girl, and don't let anyone tell you any different. You definitely need some coffee."

At that moment, an oversized tankard of chocolate-smelling coffee was placed in front of her, and Jaylynn picked it up, took a sip, and smiled with delight. "This is low fat?"

"Yup. Pretty good flavor, huh?" Luella set a bowl of oatmeal in front of her, too, with a spoon, a dish of brown sugar, and a tiny plastic container of raisins. "It's high in sugar, but not much fat at all."

Jaylynn grinned. "I do believe I'll be drinking a lot of this from now on." She took another sip. "Yum. It's great."

Luella lowered herself into her chair. "Got it from that low-fat recipe book Dez gave me for Christmas. I've found a couple of good recipes in that. You like raisins in your oatmeal?"

"You bet."

"I can also make you some toast or—"

"No thanks, Luella, this is all right for the moment. I don't even know how much I'll be able to eat. Let's wait and see." She picked up her spoon and scooped some brown sugar onto the oatmeal, then mixed it all together and took a bite.

Vanita took a slurp of her coffee cocoa. "I sure hope you don't work today."

Jaylynn swallowed. "No, thank goodness. I might've had to call in sick. I feel like a truck hit me."

"It's a shame that man is such an ass," Vanita said. "I can't believe he'd beat up on two women."

"Well, Van, if you'd seen him when they hauled him away, I think you'd have to admit that he regretted it. With the pounding Dez and Tsorro gave him, he was looking more than a little rough around the edges." She took another bite of the oatmeal. "Mmm, this is so good. Thank you."

The silver-haired woman beamed at her. "You're welcome, Jay."

They talked for a little while longer, and then Luella cleared away the dishes and asked for a favor.

"Sure, what can I help with?"

"Normally I'd have Dez do this, but you're just as strong. How's your head feeling?

"Pretty good for the moment."

"Would you feel up to helping us rearrange some furniture?"

"Absolutely. What needs moving?

Fifteen minutes later, when Dez tapped on the back door and poked her head in, the three women were busy in the living room. Vanita stood by giving instructions as Luella and Jaylynn moved two couches and five chairs—two of them recliners—around the room, trying to make them all fit in a sensible way. The tall woman stood in the doorway and watched for a few moments before Jaylynn looked up from behind a wingback chair and caught sight of her. "Hey, you."

"Hey, yourself."

Luella strode across the room and put her arm around the tall woman's waist. She looked up at the bandaged eye. "How's that eye feeling this morning?"

"Besides the little man pounding mercilessly on the backside of it, just fine."

"We need to get you some ice, girl."

Dez inhaled. "I think what I really need is some of that cocoa smelling stuff."

Luella grinned. "I take it you wouldn't want the coffee I've been mixing in it."

"Ahhh...no."

"I can offer you some oatmeal, too."

Dez nodded and followed her wearily into the kitchen with Vanita and Jaylynn on her heels. Suddenly the kitchen was overflowing with people, and Dez felt claustrophobic.

"Sit down, Dez," Luella said. "Van, sit yourself down over there. You, too, Jaylynn. Give me some room to work here."

The wounded woman settled herself at the table in the corner of the kitchen and closed her unbandaged eye as the staccato pounding in her temple continued. She opened her good eye, startled, when she felt a cool hand on her forehead. Jaylynn said, "You know, I think you have a fever. Feel her forehead, Luella."

Next thing Dez knew, the three women were fussing over her, agreeing that she did, indeed, have a fever. Luella disappeared from the room for a moment, then came back and handed Jaylynn a cell phone. "Here. Give Colette a call, Jay, and get us some free advice."

"I'm fine," the tall cop said in an obstinate voice.

"Yeah, yeah," her landlady said. "If you're so fine, then why are you in such pain?"

"It'll pass."

"Listen, you stubborn ox. If you can reduce the pain, then you'll heal quicker than sitting here tense as all get-out. Tell her your mom's number."

Wearily, Dez recited the numbers, and Jaylynn was soon talking with Colette Reilly. In the meantime, Luella dished up a small bowl of oatmeal and set it before her. Dez picked it up, cradled it in her hand, and spooned up small bites. Before she had eaten half of it, she put it down and closed her good eye. *Why is this pounding so much?*

Luella set a steaming cup of hot cocoa in front of her and stood next to her, one soft hand on the back of her neck. "Why don't you try to get some of that down, kiddo? Take in some calories. You need 'em."

Jaylynn said goodbye to Dez's mother and flipped the phone shut. "She says that we should meet her down at her clinic, and she'll take a look. She said it could be a lot of things—infection, complications, or something like that."

Vanita rose. "Well, I'll go get my purse and coat, and we can all ride over in the Chrysler."

Jaylynn followed her. "I'll go change into something a little more presentable."

"Good idea," Luella said. She turned, went to the stove, and turned off a burner. She picked up the pan there, scooped the oatmeal into a plastic container, and put the pan in the sink, turning on the water and letting it run while she put the oatmeal into the refrigerator. "Can you finish that cocoa or oatmeal, Dez?" When the tall woman murmured, "No," Luella cleared the dish and cup from the table and set it into the sink with the other mugs. She ran water over her hands and dried them on a kitchen towel hanging from the fridge door.

In short order, Jaylynn was behind the wheel of the big green Chrysler, seated next to Vanita, with Dez and her landlady sitting in the back seat. The trip down to the clinic was uneventful, with everyone trying to keep their voices low so as not to make Dez's headache any worse than it already was.

Dressed in casual slacks and sweater and wearing a white lab coat, Colette Reilly was already at the clinic when they arrived. Since the eye clinic was closed on Saturdays and Sundays, she had waited in the entryway to let them in. She greeted them warmly, took hold of Dez's arm, and led the whole crew into the dimly lit examining room, pulling up chairs by the doorway for the older ladies. "Dez, go sit in the examining chair there. Jaylynn, you'll have to stand, if you don't mind. I don't have another chair."

"No problem, Dr. Reilly."

Colette focused steely blue eyes on her. "Call me Colette, why don't you—or else Mom. No need for formalities, is there?"

Dez opened her good eye enough to see Jaylynn blushing, then caught Luella looking at her with concern on her face. She closed her eye again. She felt her mother's competent hands removing the bandage over her left eye. Though she knew both her eyes were open, she couldn't see anything out of her left eye but gray fuzz surrounded by white light. For a moment, it hit her that she might lose the sight in that eye, and the thought frightened her. "Mom?"

"Mm hmm?" Colette had an ophthalmoscope in her hand and shone it first into one eye, then into the other.

"Am I going to lose my sight, and you're just not admitting it to me?"

The light went off and she felt her mother's hand on her forehead. "No, I seriously doubt that anything like that will happen. Here, open up." Dez opened her mouth, and a thermometer slid under her tongue, and she sat, patiently, waiting for more information. Her mother rolled the slit lamp up close to the examining chair and adjusted it up to her tall daughter's height. When the thermometer beeped, Dez pulled it out and handed it to her mother who looked at it and said, "101.1. You've definitely got something going on. I'm going to take a look at each of your eyes, and then we'll take that other bandage off your eyebrow and see what's happening with those stitches." She moved the slit lamp frame in close and instructed Dez to put her chin on the rest. "Jaylynn?"

"Yes, ma'am?"

Colette laughed and turned in her seat. "Will you hit the lights, Ms. Savage?"

"Uh, yes. Sure." The lights went off, leaving only one dim side light.

Dez's mother spun around and moved close to the slit lamp. "Just a reminder: no need to be so formal."

"Yeah, yeah. Okay."

The tall cop thought Jaylynn sounded a little nervous, and she hadn't heard a peep from the old ladies, so without moving her head, she asked, "Van...Lu...you guys sleeping over there?"

"No," they said in unison. Then Vanita went on. "We're just so glad to hear that you won't be a cyclops."

"Vanita!" Luella said, her voice sharp.

Dez chuckled, and her mother said, "Keep still, Desiree. I'm almost done. Look up...down...left...now right. Blink...blink again." She shifted the light from the right eye over to the left eye and quickly went through the same routine, then shut off the machine. "Lights, Jaylynn." When they came on, she stood, moved the slit lamp out of the way, and came over to stand at the tall woman's side. "Okay, first thing that you need to know is that your eye already looks a little better than it did last night. It's healing. Eyes heal surprisingly quickly."

"But I still can't see."

"True, but it takes a while for the blood and fluid to dissipate. Be patient. Another 72—maybe even 48—hours and you'll be amazed at the difference. Now, let's look at the stitches. Tip your head back against the seat now and try to relax. I'm going to remove the bandage from the sutured area." With skillful hands, she worked the tape up off Dez's brow and peeled it and the gauze away. "Hmmm..."

"Hmmm? What does 'hmmm' mean?"

"How is your head feeling now?"

"Still pounding—but not quite so bad. Why?" Dez felt her mother's fingers probing. "Ouch! That's really sensitive there."

"I'm not surprised. I think you are starting to have a bit of an infection here, and that's part of the reason why your head hurts. I am going to give you something for the pain and inflammation, and then I want you to put a small bag of crushed ice on this—gently—for ten to fifteen minutes every two hours for the rest of today."

"And you're sure I'm not going blind?"

"Yes," she said in an annoyed voice. "I would not lie to you about that, Dez. You can sit up now." She turned around to the counter next to her and wrote on a pad of paper, then took a key out of her pocket and unlocked a cabinet over the counter and picked through it until she found two bottles. She slid open a drawer under the counter and removed two small envelopes, then smacked the drawer shut. As she counted out pills, she said, "I'm going to give you enough meds to get you through today and tomorrow, and then on Monday, I will have Dr. Lefsky call your pharmacy with the antibiotic and a pain medication for you."

Dez started to frown, but it hurt her eye. "Why wait until Monday?"

"I don't think it's appropriate for me, as your mother, to prescribe for you. I'll confer with Brad, and I know he will agree with my findings and course of treatment. The medical review board wouldn't have any problems under these circumstances. In the meantime, you can get started on these meds." She ran some water in the small sink, filled a Dixie cup, and turned around to hand it to Dez along with two capsules.

"Are we done then?"

"No, let me get a bandage back on the suture and a protective covering over your eye."

"Oh, geez, Mom. Do I have to have a big patch there? I feel like a pirate."

"Yes. You need to protect it for the next couple days. And you need to rest. Once your vision starts to clear, you'll be able to remove it and get up and around a bit more."

Luella piped up from the corner. "Colette, just who do you think is going to force her to rest? She hasn't rested a day in her adult life."

The doctor smiled and, leaving her hand on Dez's shoulder, she turned to face the three waiting women. "I'm banking on Jaylynn. You two sit on her, and Jaylynn can handcuff her if necessary." She turned back to find the tall woman blushing and staring daggers at her with her one good eye. "What? Now you *listen*, daughter of mine, your eye is a delicate instrument, and the cut in your brow is still very tender, not to mention mildly infected. You need to lie low around the house until Monday. If you feel better Monday, then you can go to work, but if your headache persists, you can't. I expect the truth from you about your medical condition, too, understand?"

Dez nodded slowly as she shifted forward in the seat and prepared to rise. "Yes, Mother."

Colette patted her on the back. "Good answer. Jaylynn, I expect you to rat her out if she doesn't take care of herself in the manner her doctor has ordered."

"You've got it."

Vanita and Luella got to their feet, and Luella said, "It's near lunch time. How about we all go over to my house—" Vanita cleared her throat and elbowed her sister. "Okay, I mean *our* house. We've got some good sandwich makings and fruit, not to mention coffeecake. Well? What do you all think?" She met Colette's eyes and smiled.

"That would be very nice, Luella. I'd like that. Give me a few minutes to make notes and close up shop, and I'll be right over."

****

Later that night, when Dez looked back on the events of the day, she felt a sense of satisfaction. For one thing, although the pain meds made her feel tired, the headache was gradually diminishing, and it was such a relief that she felt almost punch drunk. As the five of them had sat around the dining room table earlier, she'd been giddy with relief and fatigue—and something else she couldn't quite explain, but it felt like something lost long ago had been regained. Once her mother took off her doctor's hat—and her mother's hat as well—she had told stories and made a lot of jokes. She and Jaylynn seemed to have conversed amicably, and Vanita kept everyone hopping with her observations. The food, what little she ate, was excellent, and before she knew it, it was nearly two in the afternoon, and she could barely stay awake. She took a deep breath and tried to shake herself out of her torpor when her landlady said, "Dez, you don't look very lively."

"I'm beat." She closed her eyes and sighed.

Luella said, "Time for you to take a nap then. Go on now. Get up." Dez rose without complaint and let her landlady take her hand and pull her through the living room and down the hall.

Colette called out, "Time for a little ice, too."

"I'll get that." Jaylynn disappeared into the kitchen to pound ice cubes into bits with Luella's meat tenderizing hammer as the silver-haired landlady led her partner to the second bedroom, which now was Vanita's, and made her lie down with an afghan throw draped over her. Then a cool ice bag was brought in to soothe her forehead, and that was all she remembered. She slept so soundly, and dreamlessly, that she wasn't even aware of the ice bag being removed, and she didn't hear anything that was said, though Jaylynn informed her later that she and Colette and the two sisters had had a rollicking good time laughing and talking out in the living room.

She didn't awaken until after five p.m. when she felt a hand on her forehead, and her mother leaned over, said a few quiet words, and kissed her cheek. She wasn't even fully conscious, and then Colette was gone, leaving the faintest trace of her perfume in her wake. Dez felt drugged, and in reality, she was. She took a deep breath and slipped back to sleep and didn't awaken for another hour.

Chapter
Thirty-Five

By Sunday night, both Dez and Jaylynn were feeling much better. Dez's headache was gone. The wound in her brow seemed to be knitting back together, and the pink puffiness was dissipating. Even more encouraging was that the vision in her left eye had come back—not one hundred percent clear, but close. She went to sleep Sunday night without the awkward eye bandage, and as far as Jaylynn could tell, her partner had slept well, not waking her once during the night.

Of the two, Jaylynn looked far worse. The bruise on her cheek had spread out, dark purple and blue and green, and the left side of her face still looked swollen. But it was her eyes that were the real standouts. The blotchy black-and-blue moons under her eyes had also spread. Vanita laughed with her all weekend as the younger woman helped the two older women with organizing and unpacking. At one point she asked Jaylynn how it felt to look like an albino raccoon.

After a full night of restful sleep, the rookie rose early Monday morning, even before Dez awakened, and got ready for work. She was filled with a sense of anticipation and excitement. When she emerged from the bathroom after having showered, the tall cop was sitting on the edge of the bed yawning and looking bleary-eyed. The rookie ran her hands through her damp blonde hair, smoothing it back, and then, wrapped only in a towel, strode over to the bed and stepped between Dez's knees. The sleepy woman's arms went around her waist, and Jaylynn leaned into her. "How you feeling, Dez?"

"Mmm...not bad." She tightened her grip around Jaylynn's waist, and then suddenly picked her up off the floor and levered her back onto the bed, turning as she did so that they ended up lying on their sides, facing one another.

Jaylynn chuckled. "How did I know you were going to do that?"

"Ya got me."

"No, you've got *me*."

Dez slid her hand under the maroon towel and let it rest on the smaller woman's hip, her thumb caressing the soft skin. In a husky voice, she said, "I think we've got each other."

"Well, you got that right." Jaylynn reached up and cupped both sides of the pale face before her. With her fingertips, she lightly stroked the high cheekbones. She looked into bright blue eyes that were so near she could see three different shades of blue all woven together in the right iris. The left eye was still blood-shot and the iris was partly obscured by a dark fluid that shifted slightly as Dez tipped her head. It looked entirely different than it had 48 hours earlier though. "Your eye looks so much better, sweetie. It's improved immensely."

"Mmm hmm. It has. And I know I'm healing, because my eyebrow is starting to itch like crazy."

"Let me see." She lifted her hand and reached up to touch Dez's forehead. The bandage had been removed, leaving a tiny strip of stickiness from the adhesive that stuck to her finger. "They did a *very* good job on the stitches. I don't think you'll even be able to see that scar."

The tall cop nodded, gathered the smaller woman into her arms and pulled her close, tucking her face into the warm spot between Jaylynn's neck and shoulder. "Would you stay with me if I was horribly scarred or disfigured?"

"You *are* scarred, my dear." When Dez pulled back and looked at her with alarm on her face, Jaylynn went on. "Just because the scars are internal, doesn't mean they aren't there. And yes, I would stay with you. Always. I have to admit I do love how you look, but if something happened to change that, you're still the same person inside, and I love that person."

Dez pulled herself up a little more, leaned her head on her elbow, and rested on her side, her face only a few inches above her partner's. "Well, I suppose we're going to get old and decrepit eventually, so we aren't always going to be *this* beautiful."

Jaylynn laughed out loud. "I've looked in the mirror more than once this morning. Vanita isn't that far off with the albino raccoon thing."

"Yeah, yeah. You look a little worse for wear, but your general beauty still shines through." She bent her head down, closed her eyes, and placed a soft kiss on the red lips below hers.

When they parted and opened their eyes, Jaylynn shivered. "I hope you always have this effect on me."

"And what effect is that?"

"You know, careening back and forth between feeling safe, comfortable, and loved, and then feeling like I want to ravish you for hours at a time." She wiggled one arm under her partner's torso and brought her hands up under Dez's t-shirt to stroke her back.

"I see I have failed in my quest. You're supposed to feel all of that at once."

Jaylynn smiled. "I do. In varying degrees." She caught her breath as two warm hands shifted from her lower back up to the sensitive skin on her sides and at her ribs. She took a sharp intake of air as the towel fell open and she felt cool air on her chest and stomach. As she wrapped herself around her bigger partner, she trembled again, this time more from arousal than the chilly air.

"Are you cold?"

She shook her head. Breathlessly, she said, "Not really." She swallowed as she gripped her partner's shoulder tightly. "More like excited—now there's a good E word for you."

Dez laughed. "How did that E business get started anyway?"

Jaylynn shrugged. "I'm not sure..." She looked up at the ceiling, her forehead furrowed. "I can't quite recall." She looked back at the blue eyes and smiled. "We could go on to another letter. How about 'S'?" Dez waited. "Don't you want to know all the words I had in mind?"

"I know you're going to tell me." The tall cop moved from her side and eased her torso over on top of the smaller woman, covering Jaylynn's shivering body with her warmth, her elbows on the quilt below, on either side of her partner's neck.

The rookie inhaled and closed her eyes. In a whisper, she said, "Sexy. There's your 'S' word for the day. I find you incredibly sexy." Dez grinned and a blush began at her neck and rose, coloring her face so that when Jaylynn opened her eyes, she found the other woman's face nearly scarlet. "What? You don't believe me?"

Dez lowered her face into the crook of her partner's neck so that when she answered, her voice came out muffled. "If you say so."

"You doubt my opinion?" She tightened her arms around the broad back, then pushed the shirt up until she was touching bare skin. "Oh, Dez, you've got such good hands. And you're a great kisser. And you're so responsive. And—"

"Shhh." Dez lifted her head and put a finger lightly over Jaylynn's lips. "I can't take that much information. Here's an 'S' word for you: shy."

Jaylynn giggled. "Yeah, I know. I'll try to feed it to you in small doses."

"Jay?"

"Yes?"

"What time do you have to be to work?"

Jaylynn's head jerked up and looked over toward the clock display on the VCR. "Geez, in about half an hour!"

As Dez rolled away, she sat up and scooted off the bed. The tall woman said, "If you want to eat anything before you go, then we had better stop shirking—now there's a good 'S' word. Shirk." She smiled, her face warm and open.

Jaylynn rose, grabbed the towel, and took it over to the laundry basket. "Guess I'd better get a move on. What time do you go in?" She moved back over to the couch, picked up a duffel bag there and rooted through it until she found a pair of clean jeans.

"No later than ten. Don't forget I leave at three p.m. to go see Marie, and I won't go back to work. I'll see you back here when you're off duty." She sat back against the edge of the bed and crossed her arms over her chest.

"I have the nine to five shift, and then I'll head back here. Hey!" She stopped stock still, one leg in a pair of jeans and one leg out.

"What?"

"That guy's supposed to call!" She looked at Dez, the excitement in her face bringing extra color to her cheeks and making the black eyes slightly less noticeable.

"What guy?"

"The phone card guy." She stuck her foot in the other pant leg and hastened to get them pulled up, zipped and snapped. As she hustled to finish dressing, she reminded Dez about the Tivoli lead. "I can't believe I forgot about that the entire weekend! What a space cadet I've been."

"It's probably for the best, since you had to wait for so long."

"Yeah, maybe. What have we got to eat?"

"Not a whole hell of a lot." The tall woman strode over into the kitchen and opened the fridge. "Milk, eggs, frozen chicken breasts, leftover lasagna, some yogurt." She turned back to Jaylynn as she shut the door. "Tell you what, go downstairs and eat with Luella." She leaned back against the counter, lifting one bare foot and pressing the sole against the cupboard behind her.

"We've been mooching off her all weekend, though."

"Yeah, and I'll go grocery shopping for her and spend about a hundred bucks on good stuff for her and Vanita. And for us. I'll be more organized now that I feel better, okay?"

"Are they up?" Jaylynn ran her hands through her still-damp hair.

Dez laughed. "Are you kidding? Luella's up before it's light. Listen..." They both paused for a moment, and far off, the sound of a thump came their way, and then the distant drone of a voice. "See? They've probably been up for three hours, and nothing would please them more than to see your lovely face."

"Yeah, right—lovely. Okay. I'll be up in a bit to say good-bye."

"I'm going to go hop in the shower." Jaylynn went to her and encircled the taller woman's waist, letting herself lean into a tight embrace. She felt Dez's warm face against the side of her damp head, and then quiet words whispered into her ear. "I love you. Forever and always."

Jaylynn trembled once more. "I'm thinking of that 'S' word again. Ooh, and a new one, too, because you're making me *shiver.*"

"That's just 'cause your hair is wet."

Jaylynn leaned back, an amused look on her face. "Oh, that's all it is, huh?" She grinned and squinched up her face. "You totally underestimate yourself, Miss Bashful." Stepping back, she said, "I'll be back up in a flash."

"Okay. I'll be cleaned up by then."

****

Jaylynn was excited to be going back in to work. As she drove the couple of miles from Luella and Dez's duplex to the main stationhouse, she reflected on how quickly the last few days had flown by. Since Christmas, the time had whirled past—and yet, she didn't feel fatigued in any way. Even the wounds Neilsen had inflicted seemed inconsequential, and instead, she was filled with a sense of hope and excited expectation. *I've got no idea whatsoever of what the future holds, but I'm healthy, I've got a good job, and—hey!—I've got Dez! I am pretty sure I can handle anything.* Grinning, she turned into the parking lot.

The brisk wind she stepped into as she got out of the car found its way down the collar of her coat. She had thought her hair was dry, but clearly it wasn't, since her scalp tingled with the chill. She took off at a fast clip for the front door and, with relief, burst into the warmth of the station. She turned left and headed to the squad room. When she turned the corner and headed toward the coat rack, the first person she ran into was Parkins. He was hanging up his overcoat, and upon seeing her, said, "Savage, hey. How are you?" He frowned. "What the hell happened to your face?"

She grinned at him as she unzipped her coat. "Looks pretty bad, doesn't it? I can only hope that Neilsen looks half as bad." She hung up the brown jacket. "I'm sure glad you're back, Parkins. Got some promising news."

"Forget that and tell me what happened to you."

They walked over to the coffee machine, and he poured them each a mug full of the acrid brew while Jaylynn began to detail the events of the previous Friday. She went on to say, "I'm still not sure why Neilsen didn't pass probation, but I guess he had a meeting or a hearing or something on Friday, and he was mad as hell when he came out of that, and that's why he decided to knock me around a little bit." She heard a voice over her shoulder and turned. "Hi, Tsorro." The Italian cop and another investigator, a gray-haired man named Marquette, joined them by the coffee machine.

Tsorro grinned. "Hey there, doll. Looks like you could've used a little makeup. You know, I think my wife calls the stuff foundation."

Jaylynn rolled her eyes. "I think not. And good morning to you, too."

Marquette said, "I heard you asking about Neilsen's hearing. I've got a little background. Didn't you guys hear about his little stunt before Christmas?"

The rookie looked up at Tsorro, who was shaking his head. Parkins said, "I've been on a much needed vacation these last two weeks. I haven't heard a thing."

Marquette brushed his gray hair out of his eyes and grinned, his teeth gleaming in the morning light. "He roughed up a couple of young pups at the Gas-N-Go over near Highway 36. Apparently they had made some sort of disparaging remark—like calling him a 'pig' or something like that. The kind of thing we're supposed to ignore."

Parkins nodded as he slipped off his ill-fitting suit coat and slung it over his forearm. "What do you mean, he roughed 'em up?"

"I'm not sure of all the details, but one of them had a bloody nose, and they both said they were victims of brutality. After taking witness statements, the brass couldn't support Neilsen's actions at all. Oh, and one more thing..." Marquette looked over his shoulder, and then back at them. "One of the young kids he hassled is dating the daughter of Lt. Commander Fullmer."

Jaylynn shook her head. "Oh boy, that was dumb. But it sure sounds like a typical Neilsen move. Where was his FTO?"

"Alvarez had gone into the bathroom at the Gas-N-Go, and by the time he came out, Neilsen had one of them handcuffed to the gas pump and was threatening the other with his weapon. Really makes us look stupid when some punk rookie screws up like that."

"I'll say," Tsorro agreed. "I'm glad they canned him. I would have been glad to blow his head off after I caught him doing what he did to this sweet kid." He gestured toward Jaylynn. "How is Reilly holding up?"

Parkins rubbed his hand over his balding head and looked back and forth between the two of them. "Geez, I go on vacation, and things fall apart. Now what the hell happened to Reilly?"

Someone from the corridor called out Marquette's name, and he glanced at his watch, then excused himself, saying he had a meeting he was late for. He dashed from the room, leaving the two men standing around the coffee machine with Jaylynn. She and Tsorro took turns describing more of the events of Friday night, and the rookie gave them both an update on the condition of Dez's eye.

"Wow," Parkins said. "Sounds like I missed quite a bit of action. What's happened on our cases?"

Jaylynn broke out in a grin. "We've got a lead on the Tivoli case!" She told him all about the phone cards and that she expected to get information sometime during the day.

Parkins clapped her on the back gently and congratulated her. "Now if only there is something useful in the phone records."

Tsorro nodded. "We can always hope, but don't get your hopes up too high."

****

The detectives went out on a call regarding another crime, and the day dragged by for the rookie. She updated her database, took a few phone calls, and helped a new Criminal Intelligence technician set up a database for a string of residential burglaries that had yet to be solved. Her lunch break overlapped with Dez's by fifteen minutes, so they spent a little time in the break room talking, but she was eager to get back to the phones.

The rookie was alone in the squad room just after three p.m. when the phone call from the manager at the phone card company finally came to tell her the fax was on the way. She hung up, leapt from her chair, and went to stand across the room by the fax machine. She flexed her bad hand, squeezing and opening her fist, waiting, as her heart beat quickly. *Please let this be the lead that cracks this. Please.* A good two minutes passed, and then the fax machine clunked on. The thin paper slowly emerged from the machine, and once it rolled out, she grabbed up the page and stared at it.

October 11, one nine-minute call to a 312 area code. Every day from October 14th through October 27, calls to the same number: 717-555-0123, all of which lasted four to seven minutes.

She practically ran over to Tsorro's desk and dug through the upper right-hand drawer until she found a small book with an area code directory, but it was only for Minnesota. She tossed it back in the drawer and slammed it shut, then went to a computer and began a search. Two minutes later she knew that 312 was in Chicago and 717 was in Pennsylvania.

At this point, she got up and went to Lt. Finn's office. The brunette officer was hunched over a report on her desk. She gave Jaylynn a distracted look when she burst into the office.

"I've got the phone numbers, Boss!"

"For the Tivoli murders?"

"Yup."

"Local?"

"No. One call to Chicago and sixteen to Pennsylvania."

The lieutenant set her pen down on the desk, crossed her arms, and leaned back in her chair. "What do you think your next step is?"

Jaylynn raised her eyebrows. "Go down to telecommunications and have them do a phone company search?"

Finn smiled. "Very good. Then what?"

"Come back and tell you what I've found?"

Finn nodded. "If it's anything useful, call Zorro and Tonto and get them back in here."

"You've got it." Without another word, she spun around and took off at a fast pace down the hall. It took the better part of fifteen minutes for the tech to get her the information she needed, but when he did, she thanked him and sped back to Investigations. The 312 number belonged to Raymond D. Archamble at a residence in Illinois. The 717 number went to *Easy As 1-2-3 Game Enterprises*, a business in Pennsylvania. She headed back to the computer and spent the next half-hour researching. At the end of that time, she sat back in her chair, puzzled. Raymond Archamble was deceased and, according to Ancestry.com, had been dead since 1991. Still, his phone was in service. The other number was for a business that had been incorporated in 1999, and according to records registered with the State of Pennsylvania, they ran toy and marketing campaigns for fast food chains.

On a whim, she dialed the number for the business. When she connected, she was treated to a twenty-second serenade of peppy electronic music, and then a pre-recorded voice came on. At this point, Jaylynn looked down at her watch and began timing the call. The tape gave a one-minute introduction to the wonders of the burgers, chicken, and fish sandwiches at a nationwide fast food restaurant. Then the electronic music resumed, and an excited male voice came on the line to announce the beginning of the game. He gave the option of answering questions about Poké-mon, Mickey Mouse, Lara Croft, or The Rock. After a moment's hesitation, Jaylynn pressed two on the touch tone phone to select Mickey Mouse, assuming that she might know more about that cartoon character than the others. As she listened to the questions, the irritating electronic music kept bubbling and popping in the background. She feared it was going to give her a headache.

By the time she had correctly answered five questions, she estimated that a total of five minutes had passed. She missed the sixth question. *Who knew the two buttons on Mickey's shorts were yellow and not gold? Geez.* The music ground to a halt and emitted a raspberry sound.

"We're sorry you missed that one, but you can carry five points over to your next game. Please enter your phone number, area code first, and tomorrow you will be eligible to try again. And here's a list of prizes..."

She listened a bit longer to learn that 20 accumulated points would get her a free burger. 35 accumulated points resulted in a hand puppet, and 50 points yielded a stuffed animal. She debated whether to enter a phone number but decided against it. When she hung up the phone, she'd been on the line a little over seven minutes.

She made a few notes on the printout, and rose, moving thoughtfully into Lt. Finn's office. Finn looked up when she entered the room. "No go, huh, Savage?"

"Actually, I don't know yet." The rookie sat down in the visitor's chair and relayed what she had learned thus far. "I'd like to call this company and see if I can find out what kind of records they keep. Maybe we could cross-reference the phone calls that came in at those times on those days in October. And maybe who-ever used the phone card after the murders knows something. In fact, maybe the murderer used it." She paused. "Though why the killer would call this kid's promo line is beyond me."

The lieutenant nodded. "Good point, Savage. Could be that someone just found the card. What do you think we should do about the other number for the private home? That call occurred before the murder, right?"

"Yes. I didn't call that number. I am afraid that if it belongs to the killers, they would get a heads up, and I didn't want that. If it's a witness, I think he—or she—needs to be interviewed."

"Very good rationale. I'm glad you didn't rush headlong into it."

Jaylynn grinned. "Believe me, Boss, I wanted to. So what do we do in a case like this where the person—or people—are outside our jurisdiction?"

"Tsorro and Parkins call out there and talk to some of their contacts. After we brief them, their local cops go out to the address and determine what the appropriate thing to do is. Why don't you call the guys and find out when they plan to come in from the field? Meanwhile, call this fast food promo company and get whatever information you can, then get all the data together and we can share it with the detectives."

"Roger." Jaylynn rose from her chair and hustled into the squad room.

Chapter
Thirty-Six

Dez sat in Marie's waiting room. She had spent the morning sorting and organizing more of the Evidence inventory, and things were shaping up. If she had time before she was reassigned, she intended to go through all of the Property items. Since Floyd had retired, no one had gotten together all the stolen and lost and found items to auction them off. Usually that was done every 90 days or so, and they were long overdue to do that. She wasn't sure whether she would have time, though, as she didn't know when she might go back on patrol.

The door opened and the curly-haired therapist stood smiling in the doorway. As Dez rose and came toward her, Marie tilted her head to the side and got a quizzical look on her face. "Dez, what happened to your eye?"

The tall cop paused in front of her. "It got bruised in a fight."

Squinting, Marie looked up into her tall client's face. "Hyphema?"

Dez was surprised that the therapist had popped up with that term, but then she remembered Marie had been a combat nurse and had likely seen eye injuries like this and other injuries that were much worse. "Yeah, now it's more like a hemorrhage, I guess. It started out as something called hyphema."

"Can you see?"

"Yes. Pretty well now. I couldn't for a couple days though."

"Looks painful. How are the stitches there on your brow doing?"

Dez shrugged. "Mostly they itch."

"Hmm. Must've hurt. Come in and tell me about it." She held the door wide, and they entered the room. Dez tossed her coat on the floor next to the chair and lowered herself into it.

"You want some tea today?"

Dez shook her head. "No, but thanks."

"Okay, then." Marie settled into her chair and brushed errant curls up off her forehead. "You want to talk about the fight?" Dez nodded and explained what had happened the previous Friday. The therapist listened intently, giving a little whistle partway through the story. "So you mean to tell me this big hulk was smacking Jaylynn around—little as she is?"

Dez paused and didn't answer right away. Marie had just asked the very question that haunted her. When she spoke next, she was looking out the window and purposely not meeting Marie's eyes. "Jaylynn is going to run into a lot of big jerks like that, and I'm not—well, I'm not all that sure she can handle them."

"I see." Marie nodded. "So this is still troubling you." She said it as a statement, not a question.

With a nod, the tall cop went on. "I've tried my best not to think of this all weekend. Bottom line is that I don't know what she would have done if Tsorro and I hadn't gotten there when we did."

"So tell me what happened to you when you did get there. Anything unusual?"

Dez closed her eyes. She remembered that just as Neilsen struck out at her, things went gray and hazy and she had gotten confused. "For a brief moment, Marie, I didn't see Neilsen. I saw that big oaf who attacked Jaylynn last month." She paused, frowned, then went on. "But it was sort of like I shook myself out of it. I told myself to concentrate, and my head cleared."

"Excellent! That's exactly the right thing to do. Did you read a little bit about that in the book I gave you?"

"Yes, but it's not like I thought of it during the heat of the fight."

"Just putting an idea into your head often makes it available to you later. What you're doing right now, Dez, is retraining your mind—in fact, re-tooling the neural pathways. Under extreme stress those pathways do strange things, and you have to work to correct that by preparing in advance. Sounds like that is just what you did. What else happened in the aftermath?"

She told the counselor about her mother's role, and Marie asked questions, and then Dez said, "I guess I ought to 'fess up about the bad dreams I'm still having." They spent most of the rest of the time discussing her nightmares and the odd dreams, and by the end of the hour, she was feeling relaxed, unlike so many other sessions. "You know what, Marie?"

The curly-haired woman raised her eyebrows. "Hmm?"

"I must be healing or improving or something because I actually don't mind talking to you so much anymore."

Marie laughed, her eyes merry. In a mock-serious voice, she asked, "Don't tell me you used to dread these visits? How could that be?"

"Seems like you were meaner at the beginning, but over time I've probably worn you down."

She was answered with another laugh. "Now there's a case of projection if I ever saw one." The curly-haired woman sat smiling at Dez and didn't say anything for a full ten seconds. The tall cop started to feel a little edgy, but then Marie cleared her throat. "You've been through a lot, Dez, but as near as I can tell, you have gone through a lot of the recovery process." She held her left hand up and pointed to her index finger with her right pointer finger. "First, you had to gain a sense of safety and security, but you couldn't do that on duty. Taking time off and getting away from everything was a good move on your part."

Dez gave her a little half-smile. "It's not like I had a choice about the time off."

"True, but you took the extra step of going out of town to get away to think. That was smart of you, even though you may not have realized it at the time." She held up a second finger on her left hand and pointed to it. "Secondly, you allowed yourself to remember the loss and mourn it—actually to mourn *them*. Ryan's death was a trigger to your father's death, and both of them have been very painful to you, though you have avoided examining that until recently. Third, when you were ready, you took steps to reestablish connections with people from both your past and present, and it looks like you've embarked once more on what I hope you will find to be a normal life for you. This is all good work—hard work—work that many, many people never have the resources or courage to take on." She dropped her hands into her lap. "I'm pleased with your progress, and I very much respect your work ethic. You're doing good, kid."

Dez felt her face flame red, but she met the therapist's eyes and gave her a nod, then looked at the clock. "Time for me to go, huh?"

"Um hmm. Also time for you to get back to your regular job, don't you think?"

****

When Jaylynn arrived back at Dez's apartment, her excitement level was high. She came in through the back door, hollered "Hi" to Luella, and raced up the stairs. "Dez!" she said breathlessly. "You'll never guess what!"

Dez turned from the stove, where she stood cooking stir-fry vegetables. She raised an eyebrow and waited as Jaylynn shucked her coat and tossed it over a kitchen chair. The smaller woman was pink with exertion and excitement, and Dez grinned with pleasure to see her smiling face.

"We ID'd the girl!" She strode the three steps across the small kitchen floor and wrapped her arms around her partner's waist.

"No kidding?" Dez set the wooden spoon down on the edge of the fry pan and encircled the rookie in a big hug.

Jaylynn tipped her head back. "She's definitely Tivoli's daughter. Anna Maria Archamble. Her mother, Lena Frances Archamble, died last August. It was a drug overdose. So Anna went to live with her grandmother in Chicago. In September, Tivoli found out the girl's mother was dead, and he went to see this maternal grandmother. That's when he found out that his daughter, age 13, was pregnant. She wouldn't give up the baby's father, though. Anna stayed with grandma for a few more weeks, and then she was acting out so much that Mrs. Archamble put her on the bus to St. Paul. That was October 11th. Two days later, she and her dad were both dead."

Dez brought her hands up and cupped the back of Jaylynn's shoulders. "And you found this out how?" She dropped her hands and reached over to pick up the wooden spoon to stir the Chinese vegetables.

Jaylynn crossed her arms, unconsciously cradling her still-sore wrist. She leaned against the edge of the counter. "The phone card company gave us the lead. Anna called her grandmother on the evening of October 11th to tell her she'd arrived safely. We got hold of the Chicago police, and they went right out and talked to Mrs. Millicent Archamble and discovered all of this for us. We just got the information at the end of the day. That chicken looks good." She reached over to a dish sitting on the counter and snagged a chunk to pop in her mouth. "Mmm, it is good. Tasty spices." She turned and went over to the small kitchen table and sat in a chair. "At least now the girl's people know she died. And I'm glad *I* didn't have to tell a little old lady that her granddaughter and her son-*not*-in-law—they never got married—are dead." She put her elbows on the table and her chin in her hands. "The only bad thing is that we're still no closer to a motive for the murder. The Chicago guys are going to do some investigating for us, so maybe they'll turn something up."

Dez took the lid off a pot that emitted a puff of steam, then stirred it.

Jaylynn breathed in the cooking smells. "What's that?"

"Spicy brown rice."

"Hey, I have to tell you, it's nice to come home from work to a home-cooked meal." She gave the tall woman a smirk. "Want to be my wife on a permanent basis?" Dez gave her a look out of the corner of her eye, all the while smiling, as the rookie rose and took a deep breath. "I'm going to go put on some loose sweats. Be right back."

While Jaylynn was in the other room changing, Dez set the table. She had some news of her own to share.

In short order, the two women sat down to stir-fried chicken and veggies, rice, and big glasses of milk. Jaylynn dug into hers with gusto. "Mmm, this is so good. The broccoli is just right. I hate it when it gets all soggy or oily." She shoveled in another bite with obvious glee.

"We'll be eating like this a lot for a while."

"Oh?"

"Yeah, I'm going to take off these extra few pounds. I need to get back to my regular workouts and be a little more cautious about what I eat. Bacon, French toast, and fried eggs on toast are now *verboten*."

"I suppose ice cream is outlawed, too."

"And chips. You can eat 'em if you like, but I won't. I think my metabolism is slowing down." She speared a piece of steaming chicken and held up the fork. "People say when you turn thirty, that happens."

"Yeah, 'cause you are oh-so-old." Her eyes shone mischievously.

"Easy for you to say, Miss Spring Chicken."

Jaylynn sputtered and nearly coughed up her food. She shook her head and swallowed. "Geez, you should warn a girl before you poke fun at her when her mouth is full."

Dez popped the chunk of chicken into her mouth, chewed it up, and swallowed. "Okay, let's be serious now. It's lucky I got the Evidence Room pretty well squared around today. I'm going back on patrol very soon."

"You are? That's great!" She reached across the table, put her left hand over Dez's and squeezed, then let go. She looked down at the table and frowned, then put her fork down. When her head came back up and her eyes met those of her partner, they looked troubled.

"What's the matter?"

"We're never going to see each other, sweetie. I'll be on days, you'll be on evenings."

A wisp of a smile crossed Dez's face. "I'll bid off swing shift."

"You will?"

"Yup. Won't be quite as exciting as swing shift, but what the hey? Let's see where you get assigned. If you end up on Tour II, then I'll just stay where I am, but if you get on days, I've got the seniority to switch."

"You know I can't go on Dog Watch."

Dez chuckled. "Jaylynn functioning after midnight? I don't think so. But I don't think you'll have to worry about it too much. There are a lot of openings right now, and the brand new rookies are going to get stuck with the least desirable ones, including Dog Watch."

They continued to talk about their jobs and then, once they had finished dinner, they cleared the table. Jaylynn washed the dishes and handed them to Dez to dry, as they kept up a steady conversation. The tall woman dried the last item, the frying pan, and put it away in the lower cupboard. She draped the damp dish-towel over the back of a chair and then turned to face the smaller woman. "So, when do you think we should move over to the new place?"

Jaylynn's face lit up. "Oh, I can't wait. It's going to be so great to have our own house." She came to stand in front of her tall partner and gazed up at her wearing a grin. Reaching around Dez to grab the towel, she wiped her hands dry and said, "If we move the weekend before the first of February, Luella can get someone else in here—if she hurries, that is."

Dez put her hands on top of her partner's shoulders and mas-saged the back of her neck with strong fingers. She glanced off to the side. "I'm really going to miss this place." Jaylynn tipped her head back, and Dez paused. She looked down into the hazel eyes below her. "But I know I'll like the new place, too. It's just that...well, I've been here practically a third of my life. I'll miss it."

Jaylynn smiled. "So you want to hang on to it as a retreat place for when we have big fights?"

The tall woman looked surprised, then alarmed. "Hell, no. If you get abusive, you can just sleep on the porch."

Jaylynn's mouth dropped open, and then a screech of laughter erupted from her. She tossed the damp towel up into Dez's face, startling her, then ducked around the tall woman, and ran shrieking into the other room. Dez followed, laughing to herself, and cornered the giggling rookie next to the bed. Jaylynn tried to duck again under a long arm, but her partner was ready for that and grabbed her around the waist instead. They piled back onto the warm comforter on the bed, with Jaylynn laughing and hollering out, "Stop, stop! You can't make me sleep on the porch. You can't! Just try to make me."

Dez put her hand gently over the shrieking woman's mouth. "*Sashiya*—now there's an 'S' word for you. *Sashiya.*"

Jaylynn paused, then grabbed Dez's wrist and moved the big hand away from her mouth. Breathlessly, she asked, "What does that mean?"

"It's Taiwanese slang for 'you are so loud I want to die.'" She broke out in a wide grin, barely suppressing a laugh. "And believe me, it's the truth."

The rookie let out another shriek of laughter. "You better get used to it, or *you* can sleep on the porch!"

She wriggled to the side, attempting to get free, but Dez encircled her tightly and threw a leg over the squirming woman below. In her ear, the tall cop whispered, "I know two sure-fire ways to quiet you down." The woman in her arms stilled a moment, looking off to the side, waiting. "Feed ya...or...kiss ya. Guess which one I'm gonna do?"

Jaylynn turned her face back toward her, unable to hold back her grin. "I just love you, Dez. You make me laugh." She put her hand behind the dark head and pulled it down for a kiss. When they came up for air, she said, "All I know is that we definitely do need a bigger house. It's too easy for you to catch me in this tiny place."

"Works for me." Dez leaned down again and covered warm lips with her own, forgetting all else.

****

Jaylynn was thrilled when *Easy As 1-2-3 Game Enterprises*, the business in Pennsylvania, called at ten past nine the next morning. She had just finished building a database for the second of two murders, both over ten years old, which investigators were re-analyzing for leads. When she picked up the phone, she didn't expect it to be the game company. She took down the phone number they gave her and sat looking at it.

A St. Paul number. 651-555-9482. She rose, intending to head down to telecommunications, but stopped with a niggling thought in the back of her mind. She pulled up her Tivoli database on the computer and sorted the record electronically, then scanned the phone numbers in numeric order. The bottom of her stomach dropped out, and she gasped out loud.

She pushed away from the desk until the rolling chair bumped against the wall two feet behind her. Mouth open, she turned and ran the ten steps to Lt. Finn's office. "Boss! Boss! You won't believe this!"

The lieutenant gave her a curious look. "Whoa. Hold your horses. Sit down, Savage, and tell me what you've got."

Jaylynn stepped around the visitor's chair and plunked down into it. "It's the Vangs. The calls are coming from the Vang household!"

"All of them? The calls to the game number, you mean?"

The rookie nodded. "The game company allows you to carry over points from one game to another, but you only get to play once a day. Someone in the Vang house played every day until the phone card ran out."

"Refresh my memory on the Vangs."

Jaylynn explained that Sai Vang had been one of the boys at the scene who had come upon the bodies with his cousin and a friend. Her brow furrowed. "I just can't believe they would lie to us. I really thought the Vang kid—in fact, all three of those kids—were straight shooters."

"Might be nothing, Savage. He may have found the card later. Could be a coincidence that doesn't help us at all."

Jaylynn gave a deep sigh. "I was really hoping this lead would crack it wide open."

Lt. Finn nodded. "I know you were. You've worked hard on the case, and it's been a good one to learn on. We try our best to get an arrest in every murder, every assault, every robbery, but some of the leads just don't pan out. Still, take this to the end of it. Get hold of Tsorro and Parkins. You can make another trip over to see these kids this afternoon once school lets out. This time, I suggest that you round up all three boys and talk to them together."

"You think we need to bring them down here or go to them?"

Finn paused for a moment, thinking, then said, "I suppose it would be better to just go see them. It's likely to turn out to be a dead end, and if so, I hate to drag three families down here and intimidate them any more than they already have been. Maybe you could convene at one family's house and meet with them all at once."

"Okay, sounds good." Jaylynn rose. "I'll touch base with the detectives, then I have work and home phone numbers for all the parents. I'll go schedule appointments."

The lieutenant returned to her paperwork, and the rookie headed back into the squad room feeling deflated. No sooner did she sit down than the phone rang. It was the physical therapy office, rescheduling her afternoon appointment because the therapist was out ill. She hung up the phone. *That was lucky. I totally forgot about PT and would have missed the appointment anyway.* She flexed her stiff hand. She knew she was close to getting it back to normal, but it still wasn't very strong. Rising, she let out another sigh and walked to the coat rack where she fumbled around in her coat pocket until she found the hand gripper that Dez had lent her. *Long as I'm going to be on the phone for a while, may as well work my hand with this.*

She organized the database papers, found the phone numbers for the Lee parents and for both sets of Vang parents, then got to work calling to make arrangements.

****

Both Tsorro and Parkins were grim when they picked up Jaylynn at 3:45. Nobody had much hope that this final lead would take them anywhere. Jaylynn thought they were all trying to be realistic.

"If things don't work out," Tsorro said, "don't feel too bad, Savage. At least you ID'd the girl, and that was a major step."

Since the two Vang families lived in the same complex, she had made arrangements for the Lee family to travel the two blocks to meet in the party room at the Vang's apartment building. When the officers arrived, the three youths were waiting nervously for them along with five adults and four other small children. The little ones sat in the corner of the room with coloring books, crayons, and sketchpads. When the three cops entered the room, the kids were talking and laughing, but Sai Vang's mother, Mrs. Her, said something in Hmong, and all seven kids sat still in their respective places and fell silent.

Standing in the middle of the room, Parkins took the lead, reintroducing his partner, Jaylynn, and himself. None of them had met Pao Lee's father or Xiong Vang's parents, but Mrs. Her and Mrs. Lee were familiar faces. Jaylynn sat down in an overstuffed chair large enough for two people, and Parkins sat in the matching one across from the three couches which, from Jaylynn's perspective, formed an upside down U. Tsorro stayed on his feet, working a toothpick between his lips with his teeth.

Sai Vang, his cousin Xiong Vang, and the other boy, Pao Lee, sat in a row on the middle of the three couches. All of the boys looked very serious. Pao looked scared. Their parents sat on the sofas on either side while the other four children remained quiet behind Jaylynn, in the corner to the right of the party room door. Sai squinted in the young officer's direction and pointed toward her, then toward his face. She smiled. He had noticed her black eyes. She whispered, "Tell ya later," and he nodded.

Tsorro cleared his throat and began. "Some evidence has come to light, boys, so we need to know every single piece of the story about the night of October 13th. There is one thing you are all leaving out. Now, Pao..." Pao, the smallest of the three boys, flinched. He looked up, wide-eyed, at Tsorro. "Tell me, Pao, were you three boys together every minute? Or did you separate at some point?"

"Together."

"You never split up? You saw every single thing each one of you did?" Pao nodded solemnly as did the other two boys. "One of you found something on the ground, something you took with you."

Sai frowned, then shook his head. He looked at Pao and Xiong, and all three boys shook their heads. Sai said, "We took nothing. There was nothing to take."

Mrs. Her spoke up. "Are you saying the boys stole from the snack shack?"

Tsorro shook his head as he met her eyes. "No, ma'am. We do not believe that." He redirected his gaze to the center couch. "Boys, one of you picked something up or took it out of the station wagon. You will not get in trouble if you tell us about it, but we need to know. Xiong, did either of your buddies pick up something?"

"No, sir. I never saw any such thing."

Tsorro took a deep breath. He pulled something out of his breast pocket, then squatted down in front of the boys. He held up a red plastic card. "Does this look familiar?"

In concert, three dark-haired heads leaned forward, squinting, then shook side to side like a trio of bobblehead dolls. Jaylynn watched their faces, particularly Sai's, and she decided that if he was lying, he ought to go into time-share sales or become a politician. She'd never seen anyone that young lie so convincingly. She stood, circled around behind the chair she had vacated, and leaned her elbows on its padded top. Tsorro stood up from his squatting position, too. He looked behind him and saw the open chair and settled into it, the red card still in his hand.

Parkins let out a sigh. He scooted forward and perched on

the edge of his chair, his beefy stomach hanging over his belt. "Sai, are you sure there isn't anything you're not telling us about?"

The boy was starting to get defensive now. "No, sir. There isn't. I don't know what you're talking about."

"All right then." The heavy-set man ran his hand back through his thinning hair, then scratched his bald spot. "Let me give you a little information. Every day from the day after the killings and for about two weeks after, someone called using a phone card that belonged to the man who died." He pointed at Tsorro who held the red card up in front of him.

Pao's father spoke up in broken English. "We not understand how this means for us...for our kids."

Parkins let out a gust of air again and looked down. Jaylynn could see he was trying to decide how much information to let out. When he looked up, it was Sai Vang he pinned with his gaze. "Someone has been making phone calls using this phone card, and all the calls have come from your house, Sai."

There was a collective gasp from all the adults in the room, and everyone turned to look at Sai. His eyes were wide, and his mouth dropped open. "But...but...I...I didn't do it!"

Again, Jaylynn believed the boy. She watched as his face darkened and his eyes filled with tears. She rested her left wrist against her abdomen and rubbed it as her mind cast about for possible scenarios. She glanced over at the righthand corner of the room to see Sai's little sister, Sue, lying on the floor half-asleep. Two other small boys lay on their stomachs, whispering quietly, and coloring in open books. Against the wall, knees up to his chest, sat Sai's little brother, Tong. With arms crossed, he was clutching a book to his chest, and he looked terrified.

Click. She remembered her last visit at Sai Vang's apartment, and it all fell into place. Jaylynn didn't ask for permission, didn't say another word. She caught Parkins' eye from across the room, and when she was sure he saw her, she gave a toss of her head and walked slowly toward the little boy, Tong. She sat down, cross-legged, in front of him. "Tong, how are you doing today?" She adjusted the cloth on the legs of her blue uniform and leaned her elbows on her knees. "Let's take a look at your drawings, okay?" The small boy stared down at the carpet. She could see a fast pulse in a vein in his neck. "Don't worry, Tong. No one is going to hurt you." She reached out and patted his knee. "Your mom is here. Your brother is here. The police are here. No one will ever hurt you."

By now, the adults were on their feet, and all three of the big-

ger boys were on their knees peeking around the chairs that Parkins and Tsorro had been sitting in.

"You have some drawings to show us, don't you, Tong? You
know who the bad man is, and you want to tell us some things
now, don't you?"

From across the room, Sai said, "My brother doesn't talk
much, lady."

Jaylynn looked up and over at Mrs. Her. "How long has he
been silent?"

The thin woman hesitated. "He's never been much of a
talker. He hasn't said anything much for a very long time. He
only seems to talk when he cries out in the night from bad
dreams." She put her hand over her mouth for a moment, then
with tears in her eyes, she said, "The school counselor has been
worried about him. I...I haven't...known what to do."

Tong looked up at his mother, his eyes full of misery, and Jaylynn watched as tears gathered in his eyes, then streaked down his
cheeks. His little sister, Sue, sat up and yawned. She studied all
the people in the room and frowned, a puzzled look on her elfin
face. She looked over her shoulder at her brother, and then let out
a sigh. "Tong, Tong, Tong," she said, in a musical voice. She
crawled over to his side and huddled next to him, seeking out his
hand which he let her enfold in her little mitt. "It's okay, Tong,"
she said. "Everything be ohh-kay."

The rookie asked, "Tong, can you help the police? They want
to catch the bad man. If you can tell us what you know, we can go
put him in jail where he can never hurt anyone again." For the
first time, the boy met her eyes. He gave her a slow nod. It broke
her heart to see the pain and fear in this eight-year-old's eyes, but
she shoved her own feelings down. She could cry for this poor
child later. For now, she needed to be strong for him. She whispered, "Show me, Tong. Please."

He uncrossed his arms and hesitantly offered her the drawing
book. She scooted back a couple inches and set it facing him, so
that she was looking at it upside down, then opened the cover. It
was the same artist's book she had looked at in the previous visit,
only now it was nearly full, and there were multiple pictures on
every page. She leafed forward a few sheets. The scenes were
similar, some more detailed than others. She turned more pages
until she found the drawing she remembered seeing before. In it,
there was a long line of evergreens in the background. A tank-like
car, with smoke coming out of an extra-long tailpipe, sat next to a
boxy house. There was a dark figure with a gun. Drops of blood
dripped from the muzzle of the weapon. She tapped the picture

and looked up at Tong. He nodded slowly.

A shadow fell over her shoulder, and without looking up, she knew the detectives were standing over her. A glance down at wingtip shoes next to her confirmed that Tsorro was on her right and Parkins' oxfords were on her left. There was a silence in the room as everyone waited, seeming spellbound. Jaylynn picked up the book, turned it around, and leafed through it. By now Tsorro was squatting next to her, and Parkins was down on one knee. In a quiet voice, the Italian said, "We ought to have the agency shrink take a look at these and talk to this boy."

Jaylynn continued to examine the drawings quickly. They were violent sketches full of burning houses, crashing planes, guns, and clearly rendered figures bleeding from holes in their chests and heads. In almost every picture, the car was large, out of proportion for the rest of the picture, and dark gray. In several portrayals, the man who was in the car or getting out of the car had yellow hair, a brown jacket, and very red lips. His gun usually had blood dripping from it. Jaylynn looked closely at the car. She turned the pad of paper toward Tong and pointed to a box on the back of the vehicle. "What is this, Tong?" Her fingernail touched a rectangle with three letters that looked like "@qq."

Tong picked up a red crayon from the floor and took the drawing book from her. He set it on the floor and shifted around until he sat cross-legged. With deliberate speed, he wrote a capital letter: E, then two more letters, G and G.

The rookie cocked her head to the side. "Egg?" When he nodded, she said, "Egg. What does that mean?" He pointed to the back of the car with the tip of the red crayon and looked up at her. She tried to figure out what he meant. "Egg—car...egg—groceries? Farmer?"

He shook his head with vigor and gave her a frustrated look, then began to write with the blood-red crayon. "L-I-S-E-N   P-L-A..."

Before he could get any further, she blurted out, "License plate!" He stopped and nodded, and for the first time, there was something of a smile on his face. "So this is part of the bad man's license plate number?"

Gravely, he nodded.

She glanced up at Parkins, for the first time feeling uncertain. As though reading her mind, Parkins muttered, "Don't look at me. You're doing fine. Stay with it."

"Is there more to the license plate than E-G-G?" Tong nodded and wrote three numbers down.

"That's very good that you remember that. Very smart of

you! Now are you sure these are correct?" He nodded once again, his dark brown eyes meeting hers.

The two little boys, Pao's brothers, were watching everything silently, and Sue sat leaning against the wall, right next to her brother. The little girl looked like she was getting restless, and despite the fact that everyone was very quiet right now, Jaylynn worried that something would happen to wreck the mood or make the frightened boy crawl back into his shell. The thing that was bothering her the most had to do with how Tong had seen anything at all. Where was he at the time of the murders? She purposely made her voice soft and low. "How did you get to the snack shack, Tong? You were there, right?"

The dark-haired boy gave a deep nod, looking up at her mournfully. His mother let out a wheezing sound, and behind her Jaylynn could hear rustling sounds, but no one spoke. Tong dropped the red crayon and picked up a blue one. He drew two circles next to one another, then bisected the circles with lines.

Jaylynn wondered at first if he was drawing glasses, but then it hit her. *No, those are spokes.* Before he went any further, she said, "Your bike? You rode over on your bike?" He looked up over her shoulder, and then his face crumpled into tears. "Your mom didn't know you went out, right?" He shook his head. "Don't worry." She reached over and put her hands on his knees. "Nobody's mad at you. It's not your fault that you saw that, Tong. It's not your fault."

She felt someone brush past her, and the perilously thin Mrs. Her squeezed in between Sue and Tong, muttering in another tongue, speaking words Jaylynn didn't know the meaning of, but which were very clearly soothing to her son. Now he began to cry in earnest. Mrs. Her leaned back against the wall and took the sobbing boy into her arms. He slid down between her legs and leaned sideways against her chest. It brought tears to the rookie's eyes, but she forced them back.

Still speaking Hmong, the black-haired woman said a few sentences in a firm voice and gave a toss of her head. The Hmong adults in the room rose, as did the two little boys. Xiong, Sai, and Pao got to their feet reluctantly as Mrs. Her reached next to her and patted Sue, saying something in a quiet voice. Although Jaylynn couldn't understand the language, she instantly knew that Mrs. Her had said something along the lines of, "You, too. Go with the others." In a few seconds, everyone had cleared out of the room except mother, weeping son, and the three cops.

Jaylynn wasn't sure what direction the interview was going next, but she sat cross-legged, waiting. Neither Parkins nor

Tsorro said anything as they stood overhead, and as the silence lengthened, she wondered what she should do. She met Mrs. Her's eyes. "Your son has been very brave. He's been holding this in for so long. He will need help to deal with this."

Mrs. Her gave one nod, then smoothed the hair back off her small boy's forehead. "Tong. It is time now to speak. In English—in Hmong—I do not care. Now is the time. Be brave, as the lady says. Be brave like your grandfather was. Sit up now."

Tong shifted his legs over his mother's and nestled back against her. He ran the sleeve of his sweatshirt across his face, wiping away some of the tears, took a deep breath, and said his first words in almost three months. "Mama was in the bathtub." His voice was raspy and much lower than Jaylynn expected. She waited until he went on. "I took my bike for a ride. To buy candy."

****

The ride back to the station was tense. Jaylynn and the two detectives were wired beyond belief. They had a description of the man, details about the crime, and a possible license plate number.

"What happens next?" Jaylynn asked.

Tsorro let out a sigh. "We go work on what we have learned, and we get one of the department's shrinks to start working with the boy."

"I feel so sorry for that little guy," Jaylynn said. "Think we should call the Victim/Witness people over at the prosecutor's office?"

"Yeah, doll. That's a good idea."

"This isn't possible," Parkins said. He shook his head and cleared his throat repeatedly as he steered through a yellow light. "I can't believe an eight-year-old boy might be the key to this whole sordid mess."

Tsorro agreed. "Thank God the murderer didn't see him, or we would've had three vics."

"You know," Jaylynn said, "he's actually a very smart kid. He had the presence of mind to duck under the snack shack and hide. It must have scared him half to death. For our sake and his, I only pray the information pays off." She was hoping with all her heart that the license number was correct and that they could quickly capture the killer. If she were an eight-year-old, she knew she would be terrified that the bad man would come for her. That thought bothered her, but most of all, she couldn't stop thinking about the little boy who, because of the fear and trauma, hadn't spoken for three months. She wondered if he would have ever gotten psychological help and, at some point in the future, come forward. *What if witnessing the murders and being scared half to death had twisted him in some weird way?* She had no way of knowing, but she thought that she would try to keep in touch with Mrs. Her. She couldn't help but feel both concern and curiosity.

They arrived back at the station shortly after 5:30 and caught up with Lt. Finn to update her. Though shift was over for all three cops, they immediately headed to the computer to run their checks. Parkins ran down to telecommunications and pulled some information, while Jaylynn and Tsorro checked other databases. Ten minutes later the three cops sat in wobbly desk chairs, deflated. There was no such current license plate number—not with EGG at the beginning or at the end. With EGG as the preceding block of figures, the number *had* been in existence, but it had been seventeen years since it was last used.

The rookie scowled. "How can this be? Is it possible the plate could have been used illegally?"

Parkins looked off in the distance as he shook his head. "Highly doubtful. Expired plates back then were usually turned in to the DMV. Besides, they looked totally different. Surely in seventeen years, some astute cop would have picked up on it not being kosher."

Jaylynn put her head in her hands. She wanted to scream. "Dammit! This is just too frustrating."

"Tell me about it," Parkins said. "It's the way a lot of investigations go."

She shook her head. "What do we do next?"

Tsorro stood. "We get the psychologist's take on this in a day or so. We talk with Tong some more and go over the evidence again—and again and again." He pulled at the cuff of his long-sleeved shirt and tipped his neck first to one side, then the other. "The other thing we should do is double-check surrounding states. Might not have been a Minnesota vehicle. And if Wisconsin, Illinois, Iowa, and the Dakotas don't turn up anything, we'll try every state in the union and follow up every vehicle until we've eliminated them all."

Jaylynn's eyes lit up. "That's a thought. What if it's someone from Chicago? What if it's *not* Stephen who was the intended victim, but Anna?" She took a deep breath and held it as she looked down at the desk and let the implications of that run through her mind.

Parkins gave a nod. "That is always a possibility. Maybe we ought to get more information from Illinois about the girl. All

we've got so far is cursory. I'll go get in touch with my contact."
He picked up the phone on his desk. "Don't fret too much now,
Savage. This case isn't dead yet."

Chapter
Thirty-Seven

The dark-haired cop was working Tour II, but it was a late start—from ten a.m. to six p.m. It was after four already and the first half of the shift had been uneventful. She had always known that calls picked up considerably after two o'clock, when the schools let out. In keeping with that pattern, she was on her way to the Target store on University to check out a retail fraud complaint. Store officials were holding a male juvenile. She couldn't believe how much shoplifting was done most afternoons. In fact, she wondered if the majority of all retail thefts didn't happen before dinner every school day.

As she traveled the last mile to the store, she reflected upon how well things had been going. She was acquainted with most of the officers on her shift, but didn't know any of them particularly well. A lot of them were older and family men. There were only two women, both of whom were pleasant and collegial toward her. All in all, she felt welcomed and had already been called as backup a number of times without any unexpected incidents.

Now she pulled up to the Target store and parked around the side and out of sight, then hustled through the cold January air to the automatic front door. She knew her way around the store, and headed back to the manager's office where she found a 13-year-old boy seated in a red plastic chair and trying very hard not to cry. Within sixty seconds she had his story and had decided he was probably a halfway decent kid who had made a really bad decision. Another kid at school had threatened harm and had ordered him to steal music for him or be beaten up, so this boy had come to the store to take Tool's new CD. As he waited for his parents to show, the teenager was totally cooperative. He admitted to the crime, and Dez felt sympathy for him.

As she took down the kid's name and parents' information, the store's Loss Prevention Officer, Joyce Gray, shook her head. She was staring into a huge bank of 10-inch TV sets that showed mostly eagle-eye views of various departments. With a sigh, Joyce said, "Good God, we're getting hammered today."

Dez paused in her writing. "What do you mean?"

"Look at these guys." The blonde-haired store detective pointed to one of the TV displays. There in all the splendor of black-and-white technology, Dez watched as a kid in "phat" trousers and a baggy jacket shoved a stack of at least three CD's, plastic theft holder and all, down the front of his pants. The other kid, dressed similarly and wearing a Twins baseball cap, walked behind a shelf with a stack of CD's in his hand and came out seconds later empty handed.

Dez shook her head. "Yeah, this must get old." She turned her face into her shoulder mic and quickly informed Dispatch there was a retail theft in progress and asked them to send another unit. She turned back to the kid. "You're going to have to sit here and wait until I come back." Solemnly the youth nodded. "If you leave this office, we'll track you down, you know." With a mournful look on his face, the boy nodded again, and his eyes filled with tears.

Joyce leapt up from her chair. "Oh, hey! Officer, they're heading for the exit." She pointed at one of the TV's in the middle of the twelve sets that allowed the store official and Dez to watch the guys on the cameras as they worked their way to the front of the store. As they watched, the tall cop relayed information to Dispatch so that the backup car would have full descriptions of the two males. She mentally crossed her fingers and hoped that Pace and Rinaldi would arrive in time and be waiting outside when the two teenagers exited the store.

Dez strode quickly from the security office, down the long aisleway, and toward the red-framed sliding doors. Joyce Gray followed her part of the way, but looked back to the office and made the decision to keep an eye on the kid she already had. When Dez glanced over her shoulder, she saw the blonde-haired detective disappear through the office doorway far away at the end of the hall.

When the tall cop passed through the sliding doors into the cold winter air, Pace and Rinaldi were standing in the chill air on either side of a white Ford Explorer parked in the Handicapped slot closest to the front door. With the front windows rolled down and the back doors open, the cops stood talking to the occupants. As Dez approached, they pulled the kids out of the back and pat-

ted them down, finding seven unwrapped CD's between the two.
Pace was shaking his head as she joined them. Without warning,
the kid in the baseball cap stepped to the side and took off across
the parking lot.

"I'll get him," Dez said.

Her long legs tore up the turf. Despite his panic, the boy's
baggy pants slowed him down, and before he reached the far corner of the lot by the Blockbuster store, she had clapped a big hand
on his shoulder and jerked him back. He stumbled and nearly fell,
but she held him up, grabbed his arm and twisted it behind him,
then slapped on cuffs. She turned him around and pushed him
back the way they had come. "It's a shame you're not only a thief,
but also stupid. Where'd you think you'd go, little man? You've
got three friends back there just waiting to give you up."

"They wouldn't," he panted.

She smiled. "Yeah, I'll just bet." As she walked the teenager
across the lot, the chilly wind nipped at her nose. She took a deep
breath of air and felt her heart rate return to normal, then looked
up at the thick clouds and smelled dampness in the air. *More
snow is on the way.* The air smelled so fresh, and for just a
moment, there was no sound of traffic coming from the street, and
all she could hear were footsteps and the beating of her own heart,
slow and steady.

In the distance, she saw Rinaldi cuffing the other kid as the
blond-haired Pace stood at the driver's window writing something.
*Oh, that's rich. He's giving the driver a ticket for parking in the
handicapped spot. That's great.* A bubble of merriment rose up in
her, and she wanted to laugh out loud, but knew that it wasn't
appropriate. *Ryan would have loved giving a ticket like that.
That is so* totally *Ryan! Wait'll I tell Jaylynn this one. She's
gonna howl.* She and the sullen boy reached the Explorer, and she
handed him over to Rinaldi. When Pace closed his ticket book, he
came around the other side of the white Ford and took hold of one
kid's arm while his partner escorted the other. He jerked his head
toward the store. "You've got another one locked down?" When
Dez nodded, Pace said, "Okay, we'll take these two. Good job,
Reilly."

"My pleasure," she answered with a grin. "Throw the book at
'em." She watched as her two brothers in blue stuffed the kids in
the back of their cruiser and then got in the front. As Pace stuck
his leg in the vehicle and slid into the front seat, she was struck by
how much the blond-haired officer looked like Ryan from behind.
And then as she turned away, in the back of her mind, she heard
Ryan's voice: "Yeah, good job, kiddo. You've still got wheels,

even at your advanced, decrepit age."

It was exactly the tone he would have taken, the words he would have used, and she could almost see that mischievous smirk of his and those baby blues winking at her. She took a deep breath, and for the first time in a year and a half, her memory of her old partner wasn't crushingly painful. Instead, she felt a strange surge of bittersweet happiness when the tears rushed to her eyes. Happiness that she had known him. Happiness that he had been in her life. Sadness that he was forever gone.

She paused a moment to compose herself, still thinking about her old partner, then nodded a bit to herself. *I'm back in business, Ryan. Yup...back in business.* With that thought in her mind, she squared her shoulders, took a deep breath, and headed back toward the entrance of the store.

****

The next couple of days moved quickly for the rookie. She went to physical therapy and learned some exercises and stretches to use on her hand, and she found out that in a few days her hand would be strong enough to allow her to return to patrol. In the meantime, she and Dez worked over at Vanita's house—soon to be their house. Vanita's clan had finished helping her move all her things over to Luella's, and now only a few garage sale items remained. They would pack them up and store them at the duplex until spring when Luella planned to have a big sale.

Jaylynn loved Vanita's house. The kitchen was roomy, with new appliances, and the living room, spacious. The carpeting had been replaced just five years earlier, and the bathrooms on both floors had been modernized. Vanita told them that the reigning color schemes had once been olive green and gold, but she had remodeled in 1990. The interior of the house was now off-white and warm peach colors, contrasting delightfully with all the gorgeous oak woodwork and trim. With the exception of the downstairs bedroom needing a coat of paint, the main floor was in excellent shape. The upstairs was a different story. All three bedrooms and the hallway and stairwell needed painting, and the woodwork would require some scrubbing with a good dose of Murphy's Oil Soap. Other than those cosmetic changes, though, the house was solid and clean.

After work, the two women put on their painting clothes and headed over to the house in the truck. Snow swirled in the air and blew across the roadway. Jaylynn could see very clearly how breezy it was. The bare branches of the maple trees along the route bent and swayed in the wind. She tumbled out of the truck and slogged up the front walk through the light, fluffy snow, climbed the stairs, and for the first time, inserted her key in the lock to let them in. "Brrrr, it's nippy in here."

"Actually, it's plenty warm enough to paint."

"Maybe for the *paint*, but I'd like just a little more heat, Dez."

The tall cop slipped off her boots in the hallway and set them on a piece of thick carpeting under the coat rack. She opened a paper bag she was carrying and took out two pairs of old tennis shoes, handing one pair to Jaylynn and then putting hers on. When they were tied, she went to the thermostat and turned it up. "It'll be plenty warm in here soon enough."

They headed upstairs. Jaylynn went first into the front bedroom that they had just painted the night before. She turned on the overhead light, then clicked on the two work lights which cast a strong halogen glow. "Wow! Dez, this looks great." She looked back at the taller woman who stood leaning against the doorframe, her hands in her jeans pockets. "What do you think, sweetie? Should this be our room? It's the closest to the bathroom, and I like it best, I think." It was also the largest of the three rooms and contained a small walk-in closet as well as a set of cupboards and drawers built in behind the door.

Dez surveyed the ceiling, then met Jaylynn's eyes. "Yeah. I was thinking that, too."

"Excellent. We can put the bed here...and our dressers there." She pointed to various spots in the room, talking out loud as she made suggestions, then looked over at the tall woman, her eyes shining. "What's your opinion?"

Dez took her hands out of her pockets and moved across the room to put her arms around the rookie. "Works for me, Jay. When we get tired of one arrangement, we'll just move things around. The room is plenty big enough for that."

Jaylynn gave the tall woman a squeeze. "Well, let's get cracking. We ought to be able to get at least one of those other rooms finished in an hour or two tonight." She turned out the work lights and dragged the stand into the other room and turned it on there. Dez spent a couple minutes shaking up the paint can. Then they set to work opening cans, selecting brushes and rollers, and setting out newspaper and drop-cloths. Jaylynn poured a splash of paint into an empty plastic butter tub and dunked her paintbrush in. She set the container down and flexed her left hand.

Dez finished arranging the ladder and turned toward her. She frowned. "Is your hand hurting you?"

"Mmm, well, no. It's just really stiff."

"Should you be painting then?"

"Oh, sure. My right hand is fine. I just don't think I'll hold on to the paint tub too much. I'll set it down and dip from it."

Dez looked skeptical. "There's really no hurry to get things done, you know. Take it easy on yourself, and let's just do whatever we can before February rolls around. Then we'll have lots of time to keep making improvements once we move in." She picked up the can of paint, poured a big glop of it into the rolling pan, set down the drippy can, then gently dunked the roller and made sure she evenly distributed paint on the roller sleeve. She'd already rolled the ceiling the night before, so they only had to coat and trim the four walls. She started in the corner opposite from Jaylynn and rolled the first strip. The latex went on smoothly and adhered well. The walls in the upstairs hadn't been painted many times, so they held the paint effectively, unlike a living room in a house she remembered working on when she was part of the paint crew in college. There had been so many layers of paint—some water-based, some oil—that the only way to get the coat to adhere was to rough up every inch of the walls with sandpaper. It took hours. She was happy that Vanita's house wasn't that way. Using the ladder, she got up close to the edge of the ceiling and wall and rolled horizontally as close to the white ceiling as she could, knowing that would give Jaylynn less to have to trim.

She got down off the ladder, reloaded the roller, screwed an extender on the other end, and started spreading it on the wall again. The paint was going on nearly orange, but Jaylynn had assured her it would be a deep tan color when dried. She had tried to hold out for a bright blue, but Jaylynn had rolled her eyes and told her the room would feel and look arctic. Dez wasn't so sure about that. She had gotten her way in the room next door, though, which would soon be a bright blue den. But since this particular room was going to be the guest quarters, she accepted Jaylynn's reasoning.

"Dez?" Without a pause in her rolling, the tall cop waited for the rookie to go on. She had that tone in her voice that meant she was going to ask some tricky question. "Under what circumstances would you have quit the force and moved up to Dewey's?"

She stepped back and set the roller down in the paint tray. She thought about the question and about some of what had happened since she was suspended on the second of December. She brought a big hand up to her long hair, which was tied back in a ponytail, and smoothed back a few stray strands. "I'm not sure I know how to answer that."

Jaylynn paused from her kneeling position where she was working along the floorboards. "Why?"

"Too many 'ifs.' I can't say anything for sure, but I don't suppose I would have done that." She loaded the roller with paint and touched it to the wall. "Maybe if I had lost my job."

"Did you really think you'd be let go?"

"I didn't know. I don't know if they would have fired me, though I thought they might at first. But before too long, it seemed to me that it was sort of up to me whether I went back or not. I felt like I had to swallow my pride with the counseling and all."

"Did you feel that way about coming to get me at the airport?"

"What?" The tall woman stopped rolling and looked over her shoulder. "No. Why in the hell would you think that?"

"Just wondered." She had a sheepish look on her face when she turned back to the trimming.

Dez put the roller head back down into the paint tray and stood, one hand on her hip, the other holding on to the long extending handle. "You, my love, were the main reason I was drawn back here. I'll admit I was very afraid I would lose you, but more of me was hopeful that you'd wait and we'd work things out."

"Oh, I would have waited, that's for sure." Jaylynn looked up and grinned.

The tall cop's eyes narrowed. "Thought you said at Christmas time you gave up on me."

The rookie rose and looked at her right hand, which was now stained with orangey-colored paint. The brush was overfull, so she went to the corner where Dez hadn't yet rolled and brushed there. She turned to face her partner who still stood in the same position. "I didn't know what to expect. I didn't know where you were. I had some moments of real weakness and doubt, but I can tell you for a fact that I really believed that if I could see you and talk to you, we could make things right."

Dez gave a nod, and neither woman spoke again. After a few seconds she picked up the roller again, and finished the wall she had been working on, then stood back to look for lines or globs in the paint. "How does that look?"

Jaylynn leaned down to set her paintbrush across the lip of the little container and surveyed the wall while stretching her arms and shoulders. She swiveled the work lights a few inches on their stand and examined the wall more closely. She came to stand next to Dez, put her arm around the tall woman's hip, and hooked a thumb through the belt loop of her jeans. "Looks great. Isn't this going to be a pretty color?"

Dez let out a snort. "Not the way it looks right now. I feel like I'm standing inside Cinderella's pumpkin coach."

"Guess you'll just have to trust me, huh?" She leaned into the tall woman as Dez put an arm across her shoulders. "I hope we always like to work together on projects."

"Why wouldn't we?"

"No reason. Isn't it great to see something like this all come together and look so nice?"

"Yes, it sure is." She leaned down and set the extension handle on the paint tray, careful not to jar the roller end or spill any paint, then took Jaylynn into her arms and kissed her. In a husky voice, she said, "Too bad we haven't got a stick of furniture in here."

"You mean like a bed?"

"Yeah, that would be nice."

In a mock serious tone, Jaylynn said, "Listen, you hedonist, get back to work. No excuses. As soon as you're done with your chores, then—and only then—can you sluff off and start making the fancy moves on me."

"Promise?"

Her gaze was met by twinkling hazel eyes. "Of course. But if you want to get any quality time in our nice warm bed, then you'd better get on the stick, missy. We haven't got all night."

****

Thursday was a day Jaylynn figured she would always remember. It was the day the Tivoli case, at long last, came together. It had taken 72 hours, but the Chicago detectives finally called with a ton of information, and between their data and the facts gleaned from further interviews with Tong Vang, the picture was coming into focus.

The rookie found it interesting that Tong had been interviewed every day of the week by a high-level department investigator and a psychiatrist named Marie Montague. When she'd told Dez, the tall cop hadn't seemed surprised. She had said that Marie didn't work solely with adults, but also dealt with young children who had been exposed to trauma and destruction. Somehow it warmed the rookie's heart to think that the therapist capable of reaching and soothing Dez might be the one to do the same for Tong. A part of her wondered if perhaps she might not like a similar sort of job.

But she put that out of her head as she worked on cataloguing the information that Chicago had provided. Their prime suspect was Tom Flanders, a 33-year-old married man, father of two, who drove a silver 1992 Buick with a license plate number beginning with EGG. He also happened to be the Youth Lay Pastor at the church where Anna Maria Archamble and her mother had attended until Lena Archamble's drug overdose in August. The Chicago cops had Flanders under surveillance until further instructions came their way. What they had found out from Anna's friends gave them plenty of clues about the young girl's attachment to the older man, whom she had apparently trusted. Even before her mother died, Anna had spent considerable time at the nearby church, and her closest girlfriend, age 13, had actually been aware that Anna was pregnant.

Jaylynn shook her head and felt the same anger surface that she had felt so many times concerning this murder case. *How could a man in his thirties—older than me—do such a thing to that tiny little girl? First he gets her pregnant, then he kills her to cover that up?*

Just then Tsorro and Parkins came striding into the squad room. "Well, sweetie pie," the Italian said, "have we got news for you." He rubbed his palms together, looking positively merry.

The rookie pushed her paperwork aside. "What? What's up?"

Parkins tossed a file folder on his messy desk, slipped off his suit coat, draped it over his filing cabinet, and lowered himself into the straight-backed visitor's chair next to her desk. Tsorro came over and leaned against the edge of the desk behind Parkins. "Well, doll, Tong really gave it up."

"Yeah," Parkins said. He had a half-smile on his face, a sort of satisfied look that Jaylynn didn't recall ever seeing before. "With the help of the shrink, he was able to reconstruct what he heard and saw, and we've got motive and a positive ID."

"You're kidding!" Jaylynn said with excitement. "He picked the guy out of a photo spread?"

Parkins nodded. "And we went out of our way to be sure we're covered. Two prosecutors were there as well as a Public Defender, and we showed him 15 photos total. No sweat. He nailed him in seconds."

"So we really do have the right guy then." It wasn't a question from the rookie; it was a statement of disbelief.

Tsorro said, "If there is anything to be said in his favor, it might be that he probably didn't come planning to kill either one of them. From what Tong heard, he brought the gun because he thought that Tivoli was an ex-con who might hurt him."

"Here's what we think happened, Savage." Parkins stood and spun the chair around so that the back of it was in front of him. He sat down and settled his forearms on the chair back. "Flanders drives up after dark. He parks off to the side of the snack shack about the same moment that the Vang boy rides up on the path behind the shack. He never saw the boy, otherwise we all know what could have happened. Flanders had probably waited there until there was a lull in the action and no customers were around. He gets out of the car, leaving it running, and slips around to the screen door. He goes in. The kid, back behind the shack, heard one voice say, 'Hey, who the hell are you? Get out!' or something like that. Tivoli is a head taller than Flanders and outweighs him by fifty, sixty pounds. Flanders gets out the gun and tells Tivoli to get on his knees."

Jaylynn's thoughts flew to the young girl. "Where was Anna?"

Tsorro nodded. "In a second."

Parkins continued. "Tivoli knelt. Flanders held the gun to his head and told Tivoli he wasn't afraid of him. He demanded to know where the girl was. From the way Tivoli fell and the fact that he was shot in the right side of the head, Flanders had to be standing with his back to the window of the snack shack. Anna Maria was sitting below the counter there, shielded partly from view by all those empty candy boxes. From what Tong heard, we think the girl got up to run, and Flanders pulled the trigger. She could have jostled him. He could have just been trigger-happy. But then he turned around and shot at her, hitting her in the back as she went through the screen door. At this point, Tong ducked under the snack shack in the shadows, behind the big tire. Little Anna fell down the stairs and tried to get away. Flanders followed her and finished her off not ten feet from Tong." Parkins stopped and cleared his throat. "Lucky for us, Tong saw his face very clearly as Flanders knelt down. In fact, Tong has been terrified that he was observed. He doesn't fully understand that Flanders was in a shaft of lamplight, but that he, himself, was concealed under the snack shack."

Tsorro said, "We think that when the gun went off, Tong was already off his bike and getting ready to walk around to the front window to buy candy. As soon as he heard the shot, he dropped down and scooted behind the tire and beneath the undercarriage of the trailer. Just in time, too. It must have all happened so fast. We are so damn lucky that Flanders never noticed him, or he might have gotten away with murder."

Parkins let out a sigh. "It was so useless and stupid. This Flanders guy just killed two people and likely screwed up one eight-year-old boy for life."

Jaylynn nodded slowly. "Hmm. So how did Tong get the phone card?"

Parkins frowned. "He's a little fuzzy about the phone card. He had some trouble putting things in sequence. The shrink said he is still so focused on the sight of the gun at the girl's head, but as they talk more, he may remember things better. The only thing Tsorro and I can figure is that Anna had dropped it earlier. When Tong first arrived, he saw it on the ground and picked it up. Could be that the few seconds in picking up and examining the card were just enough of a delay to keep him from being shot, too."

The rookie shook her head. She looked up at Tsorro, then Parkins. "What happens now? Do you guys go to Illinois and arrest him?"

Tsorro stood and tilted his head to one side. "Chicago has already done that, I think." He cocked his head to the other side, stretching his neck. "Soon as they compare the fingerprints, we'll know for sure. We'll get him extradited soon. Take some DNA samples to link him to Anna for good measure. We'll nail him for murder, crim sex assault, and anything else we can throw at him. By the way, Tonto, show her the guy's photo."

Parkins spun around and picked up the file folder he had come in with. He opened it and pulled out an enlarged photo and handed it to her. She looked down at the Illinois Department of Motor Vehicles color photo in amazement, first noting that Flanders weighed 140 and was five feet, seven inches tall. But what she was struck most by was that the man was as beautiful as Kevin. He had soft blond hair, blue eyes, and a beguiling smile. It was one of the nicest DMV photos she had ever seen. Somehow she always expected murderers to be ugly, unkempt, and scary-looking. This guy looked like a choirboy, and he certainly did not appear much older than 25. Glancing up at the investigators, she let the photo drop to the desk. "This just makes me feel sick."

"Tell me about it, babycakes." Tsorro looked at his watch. "On that note, I'm knocking off a little early today. Soon as the lieutenant gets back from wherever the hell she is, we can update her and get the hell out of here for the night."

"Yeah. Me, too," Parkins said. "We've put in plenty of extra hours on this one the last week or so. You want to go a bit early, Savage? I'm sure the lieutenant wouldn't mind."

She shook her head. "No, I'll finish up a few things here.

Tomorrow is my last day anyway, guys..."

Tsorro looked outraged. "You're leaving us again?"

The rookie grinned. "I'm pretty well healed up, so I'm going back on patrol on Monday."

"Oh, no! This is ridiculous. A little slip of a thing like you! For Christ's sake, Savage, you've got a good head on your shoulders. Stick around here and work with us."

"Afraid it doesn't work that way, guys. I have to have more than a good head on my shoulders to warrant a promotion to detective."

Tsorro adjusted the cuff of his jacket. "Well, that's senseless. We need you here."

"Yeah," Parkins said, grinning. "It's all about us, you know."

Jaylynn heard the sound of footsteps clicking on the floor, and the two cops turned and watched as Lt. Finn entered the area. As she headed for her office, Finn saw they were all looking her way, and she hesitated.

"Over here, Loot," Tsorro said in a raised voice. She came their way, looking classy in a blue skirt, white blouse, and jacket.

"Good news?"

Parkins said, "The best. We put down the Tivoli case, mostly compliments of Savage here."

Lt. Finn gave them a big smile. "Oh, wow. That certainly is good news. Congratulations. So the phone card lead ended up paying off after all. Good work, Savage, and you two, as well. You've all worked very well as a team."

Tsorro cleared his throat. "That's true, we've been a super team, and we'd like to have a word with you about that. Savage needs to stay on here. She tells us you're sending her back to patrol."

"Actually, I'm not doing any such thing. To be precise, she belongs to the Western Precinct and we've just had her on loan. They have reclaimed her now that she's no longer on desk duty for medical leave."

Parkins chuckled. "You're making her sound like a library book, Boss."

Everybody laughed, and Jaylynn said, "Guys, don't worry about me. I'm looking forward to getting up and around again. I like this job a lot, but really, I very much enjoy patrol."

"But it's *dangerous*," Tsorro said in disbelief, "and you're just a tiny thing."

She felt the blood rush to her face, but before she could say anything, she met Denise Finn's eyes, and then the lieutenant was speaking. "Tsorro, Savage is one capable officer, and she belongs to the Western Precinct. If she wants to come back here, she can apply for jobs as they open, but hey, I can't kidnap her." She let out a trill of laughter. "You're just mad because you're losing a fine assistant, and now you have to do your paperwork yourself."

Tsorro looked like a big dog getting his hackles up. "This girl's got a fine mind. She could do our jobs. The brass is wasting a resource."

"No." The lieutenant reached a hand out and put it on Tsorro's forearm. "Savage's skills and talents have been duly noted, and I'm not going to forget. In the meantime, I've requisitioned for a new position, a Criminal Intelligence Technician, who can work with you guys and also with the Arson and Vice investigators."

Parkins' mouth dropped open. "You're kidding? Really? We're actually going to add staff, not cut?"

"That's right," she said. "Savage, you are welcome to apply, but it isn't an officer position. It's a very important civilian job, though."

From her seat at the desk, Jaylynn nodded. "Thanks, Boss. I'll think about it." She had settled back in her chair and calmed down in the wake of Tsorro's sexist comments, and now she knew it wasn't worth the challenge to him. He had his own agenda, and it wasn't just about her, but also about needing help. She met the lieutenant's eyes and could tell just by the look on her superior's face that the lieutenant shared her amusement at this situation. *When I started here, they were keeping track of things on three-by-five cards. Now they're scrambling to get a CIT because they liked the computer work I did.* Her superior smiled at Jaylynn and turned away, and all of a sudden the rookie wondered how much of this Lt. Finn had orchestrated. *Well, no matter. All I know is that you* can *teach an old dog new tricks—or at least make him want to use the new tricks. And hey, it's always nice to be appreciated.*

Tsorro followed Finn toward her office, still arguing, and Parkins dropped back into his desk chair. After a moment, he rose again. "Will I see you tomorrow, Savage?"

"Oh, sure."

"Okay, then I'll save my goodbyes. Have a good night, kiddo."

"Thanks. You, too." As he left, she checked her watch. 4:30. She still had some time left to kill. She put her elbow on the desk and her chin in her right palm and sat thinking. *What an anticlimactic resolution to the Tivoli case.* She was thankful that it was actually coming to a close, but it troubled her that even though the killer had been caught, it didn't change anything. A man who had been trying to put his life in order after engaging in criminal activity and who had finally attempted to do right by his 13-year-old daughter was now senselessly dead. He had seemed ordinary enough to Jaylynn, and now he was dead along with his little girl. Nothing could right that wrong. The sense of justice she had expected to feel in catching the murderer wasn't there. Now some woman and two children were likely finding out that their husband and father was a murderer, and unless the wheels of justice derailed badly, Tom Flanders was going to jail for a very long time. Everybody involved in the case, right down to an eight-year-old witness, was scarred by the actions of one desperate, amoral man.

Despite the fact that Zorro and Tonto so generously praised her and asked for her to join them, she didn't think she would want to work in Homicide for any great length of time. In fact, perhaps she had had enough of it with just this one case she had worked intensively and the few others she had touched on when needed. It was something to think about and puzzle over. She turned back to her desktop and lost herself in paperwork.

The next time she looked up at the clock on the wall she was surprised to see it was eight minutes after six. *I'd better call Dez and let her know I'm going to be late.* Before she could reach for the telephone, a movement by the lieutenant's office caught her eye, and she swiveled in her chair to see two lieutenants—Finn and Malcolm—standing outside the Lieutenants' office. Another man in street clothes whom she didn't know stood speaking to them. She had begun to turn away when she overheard Finn say, "She's still here. I'll get her."

The rookie's head jerked back up, her heart pounding. She watched as Lt. Finn strode toward her with an odd look on her face, then called out, "Savage, we need to see you for a moment."

The bottom fell out of her stomach, and she thought she was going to be sick. *Oh, my God. Dez? Oh, my God.* She rose, mechanically, her legs wobbly beneath her, and forced herself to take one step forward, then another.

As she reached Lt. Finn, the older woman turned and walked alongside her, back to the doorway where the two men stood. "Looks like we're all going to be here a bit late tonight, Savage."

Now Jaylynn was shaking. Lt. Malcolm extended his hand and said something to her, but the blood was rushing in her head, and she couldn't do anything more than shake his hand, feeling fear and something cold and liquid-like running through her limbs. Then he introduced her to the other man, but she hardly heard his name. He, too, reached out and shook her hand.

"Graul is working in the Lieutenants' office now," Finn said, "so let's go over to the conference room."

Jaylynn took a deep breath and her head cleared a little. *This can't be about Dez.* She looked at Malcolm and then Finn, and even a quick examination revealed that neither was upset or even nervous. *Uh oh, I think I just overreacted.* A grim smile crossed her face, and the relief that blossomed through her body made her feel tingly and overly warm and damp. She knew she was blushing with embarrassment and that she only had a few steps to compose herself. Taking another deep breath, she tensed her shoulders and arms, making fists, and then blew out the extra air she had been holding in. Then they were all passing into the small room to the side of the squad room, and she grabbed a chair and plunked down into it.

Puzzled, she looked up at Finn as the dark-eyed officer seated herself. "Is this about the Tivoli case?"

"No," Lt. Malcolm said before Finn could answer. Still standing, he removed his overcoat and slung it over the back of his chair. "This is about the Savage case." He had a half-smile on his face as he seated himself at the head of the table with Finn and Jaylynn to his left and the other man across from the rookie on his right. "Sergeant Vail here helps run the Police Training Academy. You remember Sergeant Slade?"

"Oh, sure. He was my favorite instructor when I went through the Academy."

"Vail is newly assigned to the Academy, and he and Slade are revamping the curriculum and reorganizing to prepare for one of the biggest classes of new cadets we've ever recruited. We also have a record number of women. That's where you come in." He smiled at her. "I was just going to discuss this with Lt. Finn and Sergeant Vail, but as long as you're here, we may as well talk about it with you present. We've hatched up a plan, and Commander Paar is in favor of it—if you are, that is."

Now Jaylynn was out-and-out curious. She looked at Malcolm and then across at Vail. Like Slade, Vail was fairly young. She put him at around thirty. He had a head of thick dark brown hair—almost black—and his eyes were dark and soulful. A very handsome man, but he seemed unaware of it, almost shy. His forearms rested on the table, his fingers interlaced with one another, and she could see the wide gold band he wore on his left hand. She met his eyes, and he smiled hesitantly. She got the distinct feeling that she would like him.

Finn said, "It's kind of funny to talk about this today, Savage, especially after what Tsorro and Parkins were saying earlier. I already had a bit of information about this, but I couldn't say anything at the time." The rookie sensed the excitement the other three officers were feeling, and a nervous thrill ran through her. Finn went on. "We've got a proposal for you. You can think it over for a few days if you like. I've written a favorable report— well, actually, a glowing report—about the work you have done here in Investigations."

"And I concur regarding the work you've done on Patrol," Malcolm said. "We think your talents can be used in a couple areas, and here's what we've come up with."

****

Jaylynn's head truly felt like it was swimming as she drove home at a quarter to seven. Between the Tivoli case and the job arrangements, her mind was full. The momentary panic she had felt when she saw the lieutenants and the sergeant also surfaced, and she thought for a moment about how frightened she had been. *Is that what Dez has been going through? Geez! If that's the kind of fear I have to look forward to, well, then I'm not looking forward to it at all.*

Before she left the station, she had made a quick call to the apartment to let Dez know she was running late, and the tall cop asked her to stop on the way home and buy milk, so she steered into the mini-mart and, as if in a daze, meandered back to the dairy case and picked up a gallon of milk. She was nearly to the counter when she looked down and saw the red cap on the milk, then tilted the plastic jug so that she could see the label: Homogenized Whole Milk. *Oops. Can't have that. Dez's diet would go all to hell.* She reversed course, grabbed a green-topped skim milk, and headed back to the checkout stand. As she waited for the man in front of her to purchase cigarettes, she thought about the job offer. She couldn't wait to discuss it with Dez.

Quickly, she drove home, parked, and dashed up to the apartment. She set the jug of milk on the counter and tugged off her coat as she cut through the kitchen to the front room. Dez sat on the couch with the new Melissa Etheridge CD playing softly in the background and the libretto in her hands. She looked up and smiled. "Hey, you."

Jaylynn kicked off her shoes and started to unbutton her blue uniform shirt. "You're never going to believe this. We solved the Tivoli case and the Chicago police are going to pick up the guy— well, by now they have probably arrested him. And another thing..."

Dez tipped her head to the side a little and waited.

"...Finn and Malcolm called me in today and offered me a new job."

The tall cop's eyebrows went up, as did her heart rate. *New job?* She took a deep breath and waited.

Jaylynn stepped out of her slacks and grabbed a duffel bag up off the floor that she rooted around in until she found a clean t-shirt. She pulled it over her head. "They've got a whole new class of rookies, a really big class, coming through, and they need train-ers. Sgt. Slade—he was my teacher at the Academy—suggested that it might be helpful to have a woman trainer. They asked a couple other cops, but no one wanted to do that on a part-time basis. So the new sergeant working with Slade—his name's Vail—came over to the main station with Malcolm and Finn, and they asked me." She strode over to the bathroom door, reached around to the other side of it, and snagged a pair of sweatpants from the hook on the back.

In a low voice, Dez asked, "What'll you do with the other part of your time?"

The rookie smiled broadly, then stepped into the sweat bot-toms. "Downtown beat patrol, mostly in the skyways. Doesn't that sound great? I'll be out of the cold."

A snort of laughter burst from the tall cop, and then she was laughing out loud in relief. It was just like Jaylynn to be excited about a warm assignment. She hoped the rookie would take the job, even though she, herself, would go crazy with boredom if she were expected to wander the skyways in downtown St. Paul. The rookie, on the other hand, would get to know all of the restaurant, store, and business owners and be a positive presence. It would likely be an excellent post for her. "You'll be very good at the training piece, and I think the skyway beat patrol could be fun for you. Congratulations on that, and it's great you solved the case."

"I didn't do it alone."

"No, but you *did* find the one true lead. That was nice work, and we should whoop it up. Let's go out for a big dinner and cel-ebrate the solving of the case and the new job."

Jaylynn sputtered and gave a half-laugh. "I haven't even accepted the offer yet. I wanted to talk to you first. What if I decide against it?"

Dez shrugged. "It's nice to have options. And besides, I just feel like celebrating. That and this." She picked up a packet of papers that was sitting on the couch next to her.

Jaylynn moved over to the couch, and knelt on the cushion

right next to Dez, then curled up against her. The tall cop set the papers and libretto down on the couch, put an arm around the other woman, and pulled her close. She pressed her face into the short hair and inhaled the soft fragrance of strawberries.

Jaylynn tilted her head up and looked into the bright blue eyes above her. "What have you got there in that stack of papers?'

"Credit approvals and approved loan paperwork. Looks like we're pretty well set for the house loan."

"And did you have any doubts?"

Dez shrugged. "You never know. When Crystal and Shayna went for a simple car loan one time, they ran them through the wringer. And when Julie and Ryan bought their house, he ended up with someone else's credit problems on his report. Took him weeks to get it straightened out."

"But ours turned out fine?"

"Yup."

"Well, that's good to hear." She reached up a hand and smoothed a stray lock of hair off the tall woman's forehead.

"What do you think? Want to go get something to eat? I meant to cook something, but I just got carried away listening to this new CD."

Jaylynn smiled. "That would be nice. You mean like at the Cutting Board?"

"Nuh uh. I mean let's go someplace nice. You know, dress up."

"I just got changed."

Dez laughed. "It's not irreversible. Put on some nice duds, and we'll go get any kind of food you like a lot."

"Like Italian?"

"Sure. If that's what you want."

"But what about your diet? Pasta equals lots of carbs."

Dez blushed and frowned. She started to speak, but Jaylynn interrupted. "Dez! I'm teasing. Don't take things so seriously. I'm just kidding you."

"But I like Italian food."

"What'll you have: three olives and an ice water?" Jaylynn laughed.

Dez elbowed her gently in the side. "You've got a cruel streak, you know that?" But she said it with a trace of a smile on her face.

"Okay. I'll go." Jaylynn gave her a squeeze around her middle.

"Which olive and ice water joint do you want to visit?"

"Definitely Pazzaluna. Kevin and Tim have been raving

about it ever since—well, for ages. But I have to go over to the old place and get some clothes out of the closet. I don't have anything nice enough at your place."

"Wait a second, Jay. I hear that Pazzaluna is hard to get into. I think we'd better call and get a reservation."

"I know *just* who to call to get in at the last minute." She rose and grabbed up the phone.

Dez picked up the sheaf of papers and slipped them into the manila envelope in which they had arrived, then put the libretto back in the CD's jewel case. By then an animated Jaylynn was talking to Kevin, and it certainly sounded like he was going to get them in.

She hung up the phone and turned to Dez, triumphant. "No sweat. 7:30." She looked at her watch. "Whoa! Doesn't give us a lot of time. I'll have to hurry and run over to the house to get decent clothes."

"What? You don't want to go in those old gold sweats?"

"Not really." She whisked around the room, putting on shoes, gathering things up, and then went into the kitchen to grab her coat. Dez followed her and stood leaning against the cabinet nearest the living room door. Jaylynn zipped up her coat and said, "You go ahead and get beautified, all right? Then I'll come back and pick you up."

The tall cop shook her head slowly. "No, you take longer than me. Just go and get ready. I'll pick you up about 7:20." She smiled, then tilted her head to the side. "Meanwhile, I'll just put away this rapidly warming milk."

Jaylynn stared blankly for a second, then got an amused look on her face. "Oops. I was in such a hurry to tell you all the news."

Dez grabbed the milk jug and opened the refrigerator to put it in. "You're nuts, you know, Jay? I never know what to expect from you."

Sheepishly, Jaylynn said, "Keeps life interesting, don't you think?"

****

Jaylynn dressed carefully in an outfit she hadn't worn since she became a police officer. A black toreador style jacket that accentuated her slim waist topped black tapered pants and a lime green silk blouse. In a pair of black leather zip-up boots with two-inch heels, she thought she looked tall. She came down the stairs and peeped out the window just as Dez drove up in her red truck.

She grabbed her coat and pulled it on, picked up a pair of mittens, and tore out the door and down the walk. When she got to the truck and opened the door, she was surprised to see the tall cop dressed all in white. Standing on her tiptoes, she looked in the open door of the passenger side. "Wow! Get out and let me get a look at that suit."

"No way," Dez said, as she tried unsuccessfully to keep from blushing.

"Oh, come on. I've never seen you in such finery."

"You can see at the restaurant." The dark-haired cop was embarrassed, but grinning.

"All right, be that way." She crawled up into the cab and slammed the door. "Great jacket though. And how the heck can you sit there in that suit without a coat on? Aren't you freezing?"

Dez shook her head and pulled away from the curb. "I've got an overcoat behind the seat if I need it. Heck, we're just going from the truck to the restaurant and back. I'm not going to get cold." She glanced to the side at Jaylynn and smiled at her.

"I'm in black. You're in white. Sure hope no one confuses us with the salt and pepper shakers."

The dark-haired cop grinned. "Not with that neon green on."

As she drove, it occurred to Dez that she was feeling nervous. She hadn't ever dressed up and gone out to a fancy place with Jaylynn. She was glad her stomach was empty because it was churning. She didn't want to blow this. She wanted it to be a perfect night for her partner.

"Whatcha got for tunes in this heap?" Jaylynn asked.

Dez flipped open the armrest. "By the time you pick something out, we'll be there."

"I bet not." Jaylynn extracted a CD case and pulled out a disc, then slid it into the player and advanced the tracks. After a second, the sounds of an accordion filled the truck cab. "This is one of my favorites ever."

"Mine, too." Dez thought about how k.d. lang's song "Constant Craving" reflected the reality of her life. It had only been the last few weeks that she realized she even had cravings. *Thank God for Marie. I don't know what I would have done without her.* When she thought of all she had learned in the last couple of months, it almost made her head spin. But at least it wasn't spinning as badly as it had in the wake of Ryan's death. So many bad things had happened in the last year and a half—so much confusion. From such violent and painful events came the dawning of the knowledge that she wanted to live, to be happy, that she wanted to feel again. And that it was okay to admit not just those desires, but also that she was in love and that she felt tremendously vulnerable, that she hurt at times, and that she did indeed cry. And even though she had no idea how exactly to proceed, she knew she wanted to keep sharing those things with Jaylynn.

They pulled into the restaurant parking ramp as the song ended. "Guess you were right," Dez said. *About more than one thing,* she added to herself. They got out of the truck, and when she came around the back of the vehicle, Jaylynn looked her up and down and whistled. Dez blushed, but she was pleased that her partner thought she looked good.

They cut across the darkened street, walking under a decorative lamppost that illuminated the corner in a strange orangey hue. A trifle ill at ease, she followed Jaylynn into the restaurant. She looked down at the marble-chip floors and painted tiles, and then around at shiny wood and tall, antique columns and thought the place was quite beautiful. The first face she saw was Kevin's, and he was grinning with glee.

"Yo, girls. I have *just* the spot for you." He waited for them to check Jaylynn's coat and then led them past several occupied tables and over to a corner booth that was a bit out of the way and more private than some of the tables. In a stage whisper, the handsome blond man said, "I arranged for our best waiter to cover you guys. You'll like him, and you'll get the absolute best of everything.

"All right, that's great, Kevin," Jaylynn said. "Thanks a million." He reached down to squeeze her shoulder and then strode off toward the front.

For no good reason at all, Dez found herself at a loss for words, but Jaylynn didn't seem to notice. As usual she more than held up her end of the conversation, telling Dez all the details of what had happened on the Tivoli case. When the exceedingly polite waiter came over, they ordered soda as their beverage and Focaccia Contadina for an appetizer.

"Hey, Dez, guess what I found when I got over to Tim's tonight? I should've brought it with me."

She shrugged. "What?"

"A nearly shredded postcard delivered in one of those clear plastic containers that the Post Office uses when they screw up."

Dez looked at her blankly with no clue as to what she was talking about.

"The entire upper half of the card was ripped up, but two words at the bottom were clear: Love, Dez."

A wisp of a smile started on the tall woman's face. "I told you I sent you a card."

"I believed you! But isn't it funny that out of the zillions and billions of cards and letters, they picked *yours* to be the one to mangle?" She shook her head. "I'm telling you, I could've really used that card back then."

Dez raised an eyebrow. "But now, it's pretty useless, huh?"

"Well, we sure won't be saving it for the Tretter Gay/Lesbian Archives at the U of M." She giggled and started to say something else, but just then, the waiter arrived carrying a platter of four tasty-looking pieces of Tuscan flatbread with white bean puree, chunks of roasted garlic, warm goat cheese, and olive oil. Jaylynn took one look at the plate with all the food displayed so elegantly, and said, "Yum! Two for each of us."

"No, three for you and one for me."

Jaylynn gave her a stern look. "I thought you said you were going to splurge tonight."

"What? I can't fill up on appetizers. I wouldn't be able to eat whatever decadent main course you make me order."

"Okay, so no argument then, because I'll be thrilled to eat all three." She proceeded to smear cheese, oil, and bean puree on the bread and then groaned with delight as she savored the first bite. "Oh...isn't this luscious?"

Dez laughed out loud. "You enjoy food more than anyone I've ever known."

"Isn't it great?"

In a flash, Dez was filled with a sense of peace and well-being unlike anything she'd felt for a long time. She actually felt like getting up and doing a few jumping jacks or a jig. Instead, she stretched her legs out under the table, nudging Jaylynn in the process. "Whoops. Sorry." She smiled and Jaylynn beamed back as she took another bite of the tasty morsel.

"I've never been here before," Jaylynn said, "but Tim's right I can tell already this is going to be a fabulous night."

"And I'll bet the food will be good, too."

"Why, I do believe you have a sense of humor after all, Miss Big Shot Cop."

"Thank you," Dez said smugly. "Contrary to popular belief, I'm not *always* grim and unforgiving."

Jaylynn looked thoughtful. "No, you're not. I think your real nature is to be mischievous and kind."

Dez shifted in her seat and thought about that. "Ryan and I used to play a lot of practical jokes, but you're right, not the mean kind. Like, one of the best ones ever was how every night for a week we took Sergeant Andres' keys out of his jacket pocket and moved his car from wherever he'd parked on one side of the lot to the other. I usually kept a lookout, and Ryan moved it. Pretty soon everyone knew but Andres, and you never saw anyone so befuddled in your life!"

Jaylynn picked up another piece of flatbread and began to decorate it. "You miss him terribly, don't you?"

Dez looked away. "Yeah. I think about him a lot."

"Sometimes I can tell. You get this wistful look in your eye."

The tall woman turned back to her partner. "How do you know I'm not thinking about you then?" It popped out before Dez could even think about it, and she held her breath.

Jaylynn gave a short bark of laughter. "Desiree Reilly, you're getting positively *flirty*!"

Dez felt the flush start at her neck and wash up her face, but she smiled back at the rookie as the waiter appeared to take their order. They ordered Rigatoni for Jaylynn and Manicotti con Ricotta with extra meatballs for Dez.

"You're actually having that with meatballs?" Jaylynn asked.

"Big night. Gotta celebrate."

There was a moment's pause at the table as the two women waited for the appetizer dishes to be cleared, and then they were alone again. They looked at one another shyly, neither fidgeting, neither moving.

In a quiet and low voice, Dez said, "I've never liked going to places like this. In the past, when I've imagined getting all dressed up and going out to a fancy place, I thought this would be hard. I haven't asked anyone else out—to do something like this—ever before. I was always too...you know...too nervous. But now that we're here, and it's you and me, it's not so hard after all."

"Why? Why would you be nervous? You look wonderful, Dez. You seem totally at ease." Jaylynn couldn't help but smile at the other woman who looked so beautiful in the flickering candlelight, the lines in her face magically gone, the usual tension around her eyes softened.

"We'll see how at ease I stay when these plates of *red* sauce show up."

Jaylynn looked down at the stark white suit her partner was wearing. "Just try not to get too close to me. I've been known to be messy."

Dez rolled her eyes. "Believe me, I've already thought of that." She met the rookie's eyes, and they both laughed, but then the laughter trailed off and Dez suddenly felt breathless. She cleared her throat and looked away, and when she looked back, she said, "I brought you a present."

"You did?" Jaylynn asked, voice full of excitement. "Where is it?"

Dez patted her suit jacket pocket. The tiny box there contained a ring exactly like the one she was currently wearing. She blushed some more. "Should I give it to you a little later?"

"What? Are you kidding?" Dez shrugged and grinned sheepishly. "Desiree Marie Reilly! You can't just say something like that and expect me to sit here for the next hour or so wondering." She put her hand out. "Give it up."

Rolling her eyes and shaking her head, Dez pulled the small white box from her pocket. She set it in the center of the table, next to the shiny glass vase which contained a single red rose. Jaylynn reached out for the box, then met Dez's eyes. "Is this what I think it is?"

Dez nodded. Suddenly she was nervous, so she crossed her arms in front of her and leaned forward until her elbows were on the edge of the table. She watched as Jaylynn opened the tiny box and poured out the fuzzy velvet gray box inside. It landed on the table with a quiet thud, and a quick hand darted out and wrenched open the two sides.

"Oh, wow!" The look on Jaylynn's face made Dez smile. She was so obviously delighted. "Dez, it's gold."

"Yup."

With thumb and forefinger, she removed the ring from the box. Circling the simple wedding band was the same exact *JD* pattern that Jaylynn had designed for the ring she gave to Dez at Christmas. She reached over and grabbed Dez's left hand, pulling it toward her and holding her ring next to the big hand she gripped. "Hey! They're exactly the same—except mine's gold and yours is white gold."

Dez nodded. "You look best in those warmer colors, Jay— you know, gold and tans and oranges and all. They look horrible on me, but I thought this would look nicest on you."

Jaylynn slipped it over her left ring finger and held her hand up to the light. "How did you get this to be the exact correct size? And how did you duplicate the pattern so perfectly from your ring?"

"Call me devious. For sizing, I stole your high school ring out of your little jewelry box on your dresser, and I went to the same jeweler you did. They do keep records, you know."

"You are *such* a sneak." Her smile was wide, and she kept looking down at the ring as if in amazement.

"I found it funny that your ring is just the perfect size to fit right inside mine. That's how much smaller your hands are from mine."

"You calling me wimpy again?"

Dez shook her head. "Of course not. Nope. No way. Wouldn't ever. I learned my lesson on that one." She lowered her head and said, "Aren't you going to check the inscription?"

"Oh. My goodness, I never thought of that." In haste, Jaylynn wrenched the ring off her finger and squinted at it, twisting and turning it every which way in the dim light. "Dang it, I can't quite see it. They engrave this stuff so small."

"Guess there's one advantage to having big hands," Dez said. "The lettering on my ring is about twice as wide."

Exasperated, Jaylynn looked up at her. "I need much better light. It's too damn dark in here. Tell me. What does it say?" She slipped the ring on again and looked across the table expectantly.

Dez moved the bud vase to the left of the table and reached out, taking Jaylynn's hands into her own. "You are my light. Love Forever, Dez."

"Oh..." It came out as a sigh, and Jaylynn's warm hands squeezed Dez's tightly. "I can't believe how incredible you are." She smiled and looked across the table, her face shining. She whispered, "Dez?"

"What?"

"How am I gonna make it through this meal?"

With a puzzled look on her face, Dez asked, "What do you mean?"

"I have this overwhelming need to touch you," she looked down, "and I mean more than your hands." She looked around at all the other diners in the room and then felt two warm legs press up against either side of her calf.

"Best I could do on short notice," Dez said conspiratorially.

"Uh oh." She released her hands and sat back.

"What?" Dez asked, alarmed.

"Now it's worse."

Dez moved her legs away and tried to stifle a grin. "Don't make me laugh." She took a sip of her ice water and said, "Weren't you the one who once said food was as good as making love?"

In mock horror, Jaylynn said, "No! I would *never*—I'm sure I said *almost* as good."

Dez smiled. Without a thought as to what others might think, she reached across the table and put her hand over Jaylynn's again. She leaned forward, and in a soft voice said, "I love you very much."

"Likewise, pardner."

She squeezed the smaller woman's hand, then let go, but she hooked one long leg around Jaylynn's calf and smirked.

Jaylynn shook her head slowly from side to side. "You're not going to make this easy on me tonight, are you?"

"Nope." Dez crossed her arms over her white jacket. *In fact, tonight may be the night that I sing that song I wrote for you.* She sat smiling to herself as Jaylynn launched into a question about where they might want to go on their first big vacation, and once again she was hit with the realization that everything was going to be all right.

Chapter
Thirty-Eight

The second of February dawned cold and clear, with the smell of burning firewood wafting through the neighborhood. The tall cop dressed in sweat pants over running tights, thick socks, running shoes, and an insulated but breathable skintight shirt under a zip-up jacket with a tall collar. She wore a Thinsulate hat that pulled down over her ears and tied under her chin, and she had on lightweight Gortex gloves. Right now, it felt a little chilly, but once she got moving, she knew she'd be fine—perhaps even overly warm.

According to the thermometer outside Luella's back door, it was 24 degrees out, but there was no wind, so Dez expected a pleasant run. She walked alongside the duplex and out to the sidewalk, then turned left and headed for the lake. At seven-thirty on a wintry Saturday morning, it was still halfway dark, with the last vestiges of night beginning to lift. The streets and walkways were deserted. She could only hope that the park personnel had done their jobs and cleared the running path around Como Lake. Otherwise, she'd have to run in the street, and with all the patches of ice, that didn't look too promising.

She quickened her pace to a very fast walk and let the kinks in her legs work themselves out. Stretching her shoulders and arms and rolling her head a little, she felt her muscles start to warm up. When she reached the arch a few moments later, she was pleased to see that the paths were clear and well-lit, with the electric lights still shining silvery beams all around the lake. She walked a little further until she was ready to pick up to a slow jog.

It hadn't snowed for three days, but there was a thick layer of the white stuff over the top of the ice-covered lake. Some brave soul had stomped down the embankment to the edge and then walked across the ice all the way to the other side of the frozen water. His or her boot prints pointed toward the Pavilion on the far side. It had been well below freezing for several weeks, but still, Dez didn't think she'd take that kind of a chance out on the ice.

She continued forward, extending her stride now that she felt she could trust the surface of the footpath. Looking off to her left and across to the other side of the lake, the tall, white columns on the front of the Pavilion stood, sparkling as the early morning sun rose. The green tiled roof looked almost black. She chugged along toward it and started around the turn. Now, beyond the parking lot, she could see the wood frame over the fountain. The wooden cover for the fountain had been painted green, but it looked out of place, like a giant mottled toad plopped down next to the stately building, which was all closed up for the winter. As she ran past it, she thought about the Tivoli murder and how senseless it had been.

She put that thought out of her mind, and now, up on her right, she could see the house where Tim and Sara and Jaylynn lived. *Not for long,* she thought. Just a few hours and she and the rookie would be unpacking at their new house. They hadn't actually had the closing on the property yet, but the two sisters were insisting that they move in and start getting settled. They had the rest of the month before the new tenant, a greenhorn police recruit, moved into the apartment above Luella on the first of March. She was glad Jaylynn had found a nice female cadet, and the new rookie, Meghan Petersen, was thrilled with Dez's place.

She felt a pang of sadness. As much as she looked forward to the new adventure of moving into a house with the love of her life, still, she felt a sense of grief. She had been pushing it into the background and telling herself for days to stop feeling it, but it hadn't worked. The same sad feelings crept up on her when she least expected, and here they were again. She slowed her pace and let herself feel.

Fear. It was fear again. What if something happened to Luella—or to Vanita—and she wasn't there? What about her calm, orderly life? Would she and Jaylynn drive each other crazy? What if she wasn't meant to live with someone else? What if it ruined things between the two of them? How could she be sure this was the right move? Once the new cadet moved into the apartment above Luella, Dez knew she couldn't move back. What would happen if something went wrong?

She slowed to a walk, panting less from fatigue and more from the stress of asking herself these questions. Her breath came out of her mouth in puffs of white mist. She fell into a quick walking pace, and then—pop—the electric lights around the lake all went out at once. She surveyed the sky and saw a weak sun trying to peek through the clouds.

All right, let's be logical here. She went through her questions in her head again and reasoned with herself, walking at least a third of the way around the lake before she suddenly heard Luella's voice in her head. "Dez, honey, you have to believe in something bigger than you, something or somebody who rules the Universe. Things have a way of working out if you just trust that. Just trust in the Universe or God or whoever. That's all you have to do. Focus on trust."

That sounded just like something Luella would say. She took a deep breath and leaned forward to start jogging again before she got too cold. But she couldn't prevent tears from springing to her eyes. Luella was old. She wasn't going to last forever. *What would I do without her?*

And then another voice came into her head, that of Marie Montague. In an amused tone, the therapist said, "You never totally lose anyone you love, Dez. They are always there in your head—in memories that you can draw upon."

The tall cop frowned. She didn't remember ever hearing Marie say that to her, and yet, it was exactly like something Marie would say. A startled laugh emerged from her, and she found herself thinking that Marie and Luella's voices *were* there, in her head, in her memories, in her heart. Just like her father's sometimes was—and Ryan's. Not just people who were alive, but also the voices of the dead. In fact, more and more, lately, she had found herself carrying on little conversations in her head with Jaylynn, and later, when she broached the subjects with the rookie, much of what Jaylynn actually did say ran along the lines of what she had imagined in her musings.

She picked up the pace. *Okay, now I guess I'm losing it. This is way too weird.* But the more she thought about it, the more it made sense. She could integrate a lot of people's viewpoints and ideas, even their voices. *What was so wrong with that?* She continued to think about it all as she reached the arch and completed her second lap around the lake. She wondered for a moment if she should head home, but she decided to take one more lap. Lengthening her stride, she asked herself the key question: *do I want to move over to the new place with Jaylynn?* She picked up the pace, pumping hard with her arms.

Is it a good idea, and do I really want to do that?

And without a doubt, the answer resounding in her head,

with each pound of a footstep, was: "Yes, yes, yes." After leaving her parent's home, she had lived in three different dorm rooms and then in the apartment above Luella. Getting ready to move to those four places had been a little exciting, but nothing like how she felt now. She thought about Vanita's house, about having three bedrooms upstairs and one downstairs, a big kitchen, a roomy living room and dining room, a full basement where she could set up a workshop, and a nice yard where she and Jaylynn could grow plants and flowers. Sure, they'd have to rebuild that dinky garage, but that would be fun. She and Jaylynn could cook and eat and entertain and sleep together every day, every night, all the time. There would be room to grow, to laugh, to love, to wrestle, to grow old.

When she thought of it that way, the sadness she was feeling squeezed over into a corner of her heart. It was still there, but it was only a piece of all the feelings she had. She could still acknowledge that sometimes to gain something, she had to lose something, but what she was losing wasn't as terrible as she had worried. *I'll still see Luella as much as I can. I'll definitely be over there periodically helping with the yard and other things. And now Jaylynn can help, too. She's good at painting, and hey, she can help me with the shingle job on Lu's front porch. I'll miss my old apartment—especially the whirlpool bath—but maybe we can install one at the new house.*

The longer she thought about it, the more she became certain that there was no reason all of this would not work out just fine. In fact, she started to question why she had been worried. She reached the arch and turned right, heading at a slow jog down Como Avenue toward her landlady's place. By the time she was a block away, she had slowed to a walk. All around her, the neighborhood was waking up. A newspaper boy rode along on a wobbly bike and threw the *Pioneer Press* toward houses, more often than not missing the porches. A woman dressed in a bulky jacket over a skirt, hose, and heels came out of the house across from Luella's carrying a silver insulated coffee mug. The brown-haired woman gave a little wave, and Dez waved back, then she turned up the walk to her landlady's place. Obviously, everyone was up. There were lights shining in every window, up and down. When Dez opened the back door, she could hear the trill of a whistle and smell something cinnamon-flavored. She kicked off her running shoes, removed her hat, and headed up the stairs.

****

Jaylynn woke slowly, light filtering into her consciousness ever so gradually, until she became aware of a shaft of bright light shining through the porthole of a window over Dez's bed. The air was cold on her face and neck and she snuggled deeper in the blankets and quilts, then reached out to find the space next to her empty. She opened her eyes and surveyed the room. No Dez. She wasn't in the bathroom, and she didn't hear the tall woman in the kitchen either. *Wonder where she is? Maybe downstairs with Luella and Vanita.*

Jaylynn turned over on her side and looked at all the boxes stacked up in the middle of the room. It was hard to believe that this bare apartment had yielded so many packing cartons. They sat stacked four boxes high and three or four deep. Of course the books and videos and CD's had taken up a lot of space, and who knew that Dez had packed away so many things under the eaves in the deep closets there. Some of those items were not easily boxed up—a backpack frame, a tent and poles, other camping gear, two toolboxes, a ladder, and various odds and ends. She was surprised to discover that Dez owned three times more things than she herself did. *Where did she keep all that stuff? She's just better at organizing than I am, that's all.*

With a groan, she sat up and slid out of bed. Barefoot, she hustled over to the thermostat and turned it way up, then went in to use the bathroom. When she emerged, hugging her flannel top, she scooted past the boxes, took a few running steps, and leapt back on the bed, grateful that it was still warm. She curled up under the blankets on Dez's side of the bed, and once she got settled, looked toward the entertainment center to check the time, but the VCR player was packed and the stand was bare. She had no idea what time it was, but she could hear someone bustling around downstairs, and she smelled something sweet and breakfast-like, so she figured it couldn't be too late. Besides, they had planned to start loading around ten a.m., and surely Dez would have awakened her if it was getting close to that time.

She took a deep breath and exhaled in a rush. *Today is the day.* She had thought that it would never come, and now that it was finally here, she decided she was a little bit nervous. She wasn't sure what that was all about. Picking up her pillow, she stacked it on Dez's and got comfortable with her back against it and the covers pulled up to her neck. She was glad that they had invited Sara, Bill, Crystal, and Shayna to come help them pack up the truck and then unpack at the new house. She hadn't seen Sara, except in passing, for days and days, and she realized she missed her best friend. She hadn't talked to Tim for three weeks either, though she had recently seen Kevin at his restaurant. It would be fun to have a few friends helping with the move. There was more to carry than either she or Dez had anticipated.

She rubbed her hands together and felt the metal on her finger press into her palm. Pulling her hand out from under the covers, she examined the band she wore on her left ring finger. She wasn't used to wearing rings, but this one she had grown accustomed to quickly. Every time she looked at it, she felt a shiver of happiness. She liked to slide it off and look at the engraved inscription on the inside: *You are my Light – Love Forever, Dez.*

She smiled. *I love this ring.*

Her thoughts shifted to how life was going with her tall partner, and she considered how things had been the last couple of weeks. Settling in to work at the Police Academy had been much easier than she'd expected. Until mid-March when this class completed their training, she was assigned there full-time, and she came home each day physically and mentally fatigued from all the exercises and activity. She was thankful that the work assignment and the painting over at the new house had only overlapped by one day. It hadn't been until the last two days that she had gotten over feeling stiff and sore. She ran and lifted weights and did calisthenics with the recruits, and she didn't think it would be very inspiring if she complained or showed fatigue.

She was tired each night by ten, but Dez wasn't always home by then. The dark-haired cop was working mostly Tour II days, but sometimes they had her on Tour III swing shift or late-starts that took her until after midnight or as late as two a.m. They both agreed they didn't like having such divergent hours, but it was only a matter of time before Dez was transferring away from the Western Precinct so she could assume a day shift. Jaylynn had worried about that, but Dez said she was fine with it, that she was ready for a change. In the meantime, they were getting by and trying to adjust to odd hours.

She yawned and rolled over on her stomach, burying her head in the pillow. She wanted to go back to sleep, but she knew she should get up and get going. She started to shift onto her side when, without warning, she was clutched from behind and felt arms slip around her. A startled yelp came out of her mouth, but at the same time, the grip was familiar. The sound of the breath by her ear, the smell and the presence were all welcome. "How in the hell did you sneak up on me like that?" She managed to twist around so that she was looking up at the energized figure who had piled on and was now smiling down at her. Dez's face was pink from exertion, and though her clothes felt cold, she herself was emanating heat like a furnace.

"You've gotta be half-deaf. I strolled up here noisy as you please." She shifted to the middle of the bed and turned on her side, up on one elbow. With her free hand, she unzipped her jacket and wrestled her arm from the sleeve, but before she could get the other arm out, Jaylynn reached over, grabbed her and pulled her tight. Dez shifted so that she was lying half over the prone woman, and then Jaylynn kissed her.

"Brr. Your face is cold, Dez."

"Mmm, and yours is warm for a change."

"In contrast to yours, I'm a heating pad."

"Believe me when I tell you I'm plenty warm." She wriggled her other arm out of the jacket, leaving the skintight, insulated shirt.

"You're also damp."

"Yeah, this shirt wicks away the sweat."

"Where've you been?"

"I took a little run around the lake. I needed some exercise."

"Why didn't you wake me up to go?"

Dez laughed. "I think you've had enough exercise lately. Besides, me coming in late last night woke you up. I thought you might need the sleep. I got up and made all sorts of noise, and you didn't budge."

Jaylynn didn't know how that could be. She always thought she slept moderately lightly. Noises in the night often woke her up, but if she felt safe and comfortable, even the TV didn't cause her to stir. "What time is it?"

"About a quarter after eight."

"That's all?"

"Yup." She slid a hand under the covers and found a warm patch of skin at the rookie's midsection. "This feels nice."

Jaylynn shivered. "What a switch. You're usually the warm one. You have to be freezing."

"Actually, I'm not. My skin feels chilled, but my muscles are stoked and burning. I feel fine."

"Yeah, right. Take those clothes off and get in here with me."

Dez raised an eyebrow. "That sounds suggestive." Jaylynn didn't answer. Instead, she unzipped the insulated shirt and pulled it down and off the tall cop's shoulders. Pushing the bigger woman off to the side, she tugged at the waistband of the sweat pants. They slipped down with no problems, but the running tights were another matter. They clung to the damp skin.

"Good grief, Dez. You're soaked."

"I told you, these tights wick away the sweat. My skin's not so damp—just the clothes." She shifted a long leg off the side of the bed, then swung her other leg over and stood to peel the tights off. Briefs, socks, and bra landed on the floor on top of the tights, and then the tall woman was sliding under the covers next to the flannel-clad furnace. She shivered.

On their sides, they lay nose to nose, giggling, as Jaylynn's warm hands stroked the chilled skin next to her. The smaller woman, still in her pajamas, closed her eyes and breathed in, feeling rapidly warming hands caressing her shoulders, her back, and her breasts.

"You feel very good right now, Jay—real toasty."

She let out a sigh. "Thought you didn't like flannel."

Dez let out a throaty chuckle. "I wasn't talking about your pajamas." She worked her hands up under the cloth and kneaded the muscles in the smaller woman's upper back, then pulled a hand out and unbuttoned the front of the sleep shirt and swept it back so that her lips could have free rein in the crook of her partner's neck.

A door slammed downstairs, and Jaylynn opened her eyes. "Umm..."

Dez's head came up and their eyes met. In a breathless voice, she said, "We've got plenty of time. I told our helpers to come at ten, and Luella doesn't expect us down there until then."

"Mmm-kay." The rookie closed her eyes and forgot all about any noises downstairs, focusing instead on her partner's smooth skin—skin that had somehow heated up to the burning point. So intent was she on kissing the tall cop that she hardly shifted when long arms slipped off her flannel bottoms, but then she realized she was grateful to feel skin on skin, warm legs wrapped around hers, hands pressing against the front of her, and the steadily increasing heat at her center. They made love slowly, deliberately, without speaking a word, each sensing what the other needed, and when their passion was spent, they lay wrapped tightly together, whispering words of love and pleasure.

When she caught her breath, a quiet laugh escaped from Jaylynn. "Now *that* was a real nice wake up. You ought to go running in the wee small hours of the morning more often."

"It wasn't quite that early." The tall cop shifted onto her side, lying pressed up against her partner, then settled with her dark head on Jaylynn's shoulder. She placed her hand, palm down, on the warm chest and let out a sigh. "I love making love with you, Jay. You're just so...so...I mean, we're just in sync."

"Yeah, that's a good way of putting it. We fit together. It's comfortable, and at the same time, it's terrifically exciting." Her hazel eyes looked down into the bright blue eyes gazing up at her. "I hope it's always this way—that you don't get tired of me."

A big grin broke out on Dez's face. "I'm not gonna get tired of you, sport. It just isn't gonna happen." They both jumped when a door slammed below them.

"Geez, what's with Luella today? She trying to send us a message?"

"Could be." Dez pushed herself up to a sitting position and tossed the blankets off, then flexed the muscles of her broad shoulders and back. "Well, what do you think? Should we get up and get going?"

"I suppose. I have no idea what time it is. I totally lose track of everything when we make love." Her face turned a little pink at that admission.

Dez leaned down and gave her a soft kiss on the lips, then crawled over her and strode across the floor to the bathroom. She picked up her watch off the counter and called out, "Hey, we've still got fifty minutes."

Jaylynn got out of bed and followed her. "Brrr, it's cold outside the blankets. Want to jump in the shower?"

"I've got a better idea." The tall cop reached down and turned the water on in the tub. "Let's run a bath and sit in the Jacuzzi." Jaylynn frowned. With a hopeful look on her face, Dez said, "C'mon, Jay. It's the last time we'll ever get to use it."

Thirty minutes later, Jaylynn wasn't exactly sure how she could be expected to carry boxes up and down stairs and haul furniture into their new house. Her legs were warm and relaxed, not so much from the second round of lovemaking, but from the hot, frothy water. She also wasn't sure why she and Dez hadn't used the Jacuzzi more often. It was wonderfully relaxing. "Oh, Dez, you're going to have to carry me out of here."

"Dream on, baby," she said with a wicked smile as she rose up from the steaming bubbles. Water sluiced off her unnaturally pink skin, and she stood above Jaylynn looking like a muscular goddess.

"Whew. You have any idea how beautiful you are?"

The tall woman turned even redder as she grabbed a towel and rubbed it over her upper body, then lifted one foot out of the water and dried off her leg. She stepped out of the tub and onto the maroon rug, then dried off the other leg. When she was satisfied that she was sufficiently swabbed off, she wrapped the towel around her middle, under her arms, and tucked the end off to secure it. She picked up her hairbrush from the counter and ran it through her hair, then, in a few deft motions, she worked her long tresses into a French braid. Once finished, she turned back toward the tub. "C'mon, you little hedonist." She reached down and took a hand and hauled her up to her feet. "Here's a towel."

Jaylynn trembled for a moment, but she took the folded dark blue towel, and once she got to work drying off, she warmed in the misty air. Dez reached out and wrapped an arm around her as she stepped out of the tub, and they embraced for a moment on the soft rug.

"I'm always going to remember this morning, Dez. It's a nice way to say goodbye to this place."

Dez looked away, out toward the living room. "It's been a good home for me."

"Will you miss it awfully?"

Her voice sounded so wistful that Dez turned back and looked into the worried hazel eyes. A little smile crept to the corners of her mouth. "I'll think of this place fondly, but you were right the other day."

Jaylynn frowned. "About what?"

"That you need more room to run. It's way too easy for me to catch you in this apartment. You deserve a little more room in our new place."

Jaylynn put her arms up on the tall woman's shoulders causing her own towel to fall to the floor. With one hand on either side of Dez's head, she said, "And we need a porch for you to sleep on when you're mad."

The tall woman let out a guffaw. "Nice try, sweetie. You're stuck with me, mad, sad or glad."

Jaylynn felt herself falling into those bright blue eyes above her, but then the front door below them slammed shut, and she shook herself from her reverie. "That's our signal to get rolling, I guess. How much time before ten?"

Dez picked up her wristwatch from the counter beside the sink. "Eleven minutes. Get a move on."

By the time they got downstairs, it was a few minutes past ten. Jaylynn had taken the time to dry her hair, but Dez's was still damp in the back. She didn't care. She figured it would keep her cool. They weren't going right outside anyway. Luella had made coffee cake the day before, and the tall cop knew she and Jaylynn would want to visit for a while and take a few minutes to eat before they started hauling things around.

Leaving the apartment door open, they moved out onto the landing, Dez in the lead and reaching back to hold Jaylynn's hand. She ducked around the eave and descended the stairs, rounded the newel post, and tapped on Luella's door. As they waited to hear one of the ladies call out, she looked down at Jaylynn and found her smiling up at her. The shorter woman's eyes communicated a very clear *I love you*, so the tall cop smiled and nodded. "Me, too." They stood grinning at one another like fools, when the door opened.

"It's about time," Luella said, a big smile gracing her lovely face.

"'Morning, Luella," Jaylynn said.

"Good morning. I'm so glad to see you two are finally up and about."

She stepped back to let them in, and for a brief moment, Dez had an inkling that something was up. She passed down the hall, still holding Jaylynn's hand, and heard the door shut quietly behind them. By the time the thought registered that neither Luella nor Vanita had ever slammed a door in their lives, she was through the doorway to the living room and stopped short. Jaylynn bumped into her, then pushed around as a roar of laughter rolled over them.

Dez stood with her mouth open, just about as stunned as she had been the last time people had surprised her. The first thing she thought to say was, "How in the hell did you all keep so quiet?"

More laughter from everyone. Crystal called out, "Everyone wanted to help you two sleepyheads move."

"Wouldn't miss it for the world," Mac said.

Dez gazed around the room, a giant lump forming in her throat. Crystal and Shayna, Bill and Sara she had expected. But not her mother and Mac, Patrick, Monique, Julie, and Ryan's two little ones, Jeremy and Jill. Vanita sat in one of the three recliners with Tim on one arm and Kevin on the other. Mitch Oster and his new wife, Donna, sat in the other two recliners, with Cowboy towering over the two of them. Everyone was dressed in jeans and sweatshirts, and most of them had steaming mugs of coffee or chocolate.

Jeremy wormed his way through the living room and ran past the length of the back of the sofa before throwing his six-year-old self at her legs. She let go of Jaylynn's hand and picked him up, feeling the solidness of his little boy body. He was getting bigger, but she could still hike him up on her hip and hold him comfortably. He patted two little hands on either side of her face. "We're gonna help you move your stuff, Dez, and then guess what—we're having a big party!"

"Oh, we are, huh?" Her voice came out sounding fine, but she was choked up. She felt another small hand find hers, and Jill looked up, her sweet face shy and serious.

"We're not too little to help, are we, Dez?"

"No, Jill. Not at all. You're going to be a big help." For just a moment, surrounded by all this love and affection and the wealth of expectations around her, she could almost feel Ryan in the room. A brief dagger of sadness cut through the bittersweet pleasure she was feeling, but then it crossed her mind that Ryan would be very happy for her today, and she put that thought aside.

"Breakfast first," Luella called out from the dining room where she had been hovering.

Dez strode forward, Jeremy on her hip and Jill walking hand in hand. She glanced over her right shoulder to see Jaylynn's face shining, then met her mother's smiling eyes across the room. She turned back to the dining room table to see the spread of not just coffee cake, but three warming skillets filled with scrambled eggs, sausage, and pancakes. The table was loaded down with toast, preserves, and fruit.

"Eat before it gets any colder," Luella said. Jeremy squirmed to be let down, and Jill let go of the tall cop's hand. There was an orderly rush forward, and both Dez and Jaylynn stepped to the side, next to the built-in buffet. Jeremy and Jill went first in line, followed by Patrick and Monique. All around her, the adults were talking and laughing. Colette made her way to her daughter and gave Jaylynn a hug, then Dez. Julie grabbed the front of the big woman's sweatshirt and kissed her on the cheek. Everyone was talking and laughing, and the noise level was considerable.

Dez looked over at her partner. When there was a lull in the hugging, she tilted her head down and said, "I still don't know how they stayed so quiet that we didn't know they were here."

In a whisper, Jaylynn said, "I just hope they thought we were asleep." She gave Dez a knowing smile, and the two of them started laughing, then tried to stifle it.

Vanita shuffled across the hardwood floor and came to stand in front of them. "You two better get some food in you before the rest of these gluttons hog it all up."

Dez reached out and put her hand on Vanita's shoulder, then pulled her close, hugging her gently. "Thanks, Van. You're the best." She released her and if she hadn't known better, she would have sworn there were tears in the older woman's eyes.

Vanita drew herself up tall. "Hate to tell you, but you can't give me much credit. That wacky sister of mine is responsible for this little shindig."

Luella, who was helping Jeremy with his plate as he carefully balanced an overly full glass of juice, looked over and smiled. She guided the boy to the table in the kitchen where his sister was already camped out, then she came back to the dining room and put one arm around Dez's waist and one around Jaylynn's. "Well, girls, have at it, why don't you? I've got plenty more in the oven if we run out."

"Thanks, Luella. This is just great." Dez planted a kiss on the cocoa brown cheek below her and squeezed her tight. Quietly, in the silver-haired woman's ear, she said, "I love you, Luella."

In response, her landlady gave her a squeeze around the middle. Dez stepped forward and snagged a heavy-duty paper plate. She grabbed up a silver fork and speared a Little Smokey sausage, then looked back over her shoulder as she popped the whole thing in her mouth. She was grinning as she chewed, then she shouted out, "You all better eat up. You're gonna need the energy. We've got a *lot* more stuff than any of you realize." And suddenly Cowboy was in her face, making fun of her and pointing across the room at Crystal.

Dez knew it wouldn't last forever, but right at that moment, she felt a thrum of elation—almost like an electrical current—run through her body, and she knew she was nearly as happy as she could ever remember being. There were people missing, so the circle wasn't quite complete, but still, it was quite the circle. She looked to her right and met Jaylynn's eyes, smiling with glee. It occurred to her that a whole new life was beginning, and at long last, she was anxious to get on with it.

Also from
Quest Books

Gun Shy

While on patrol, Minnesota police officer Dez Reilly saves two women from a brutal attack. One of them, Jaylynn Savage, is immediately attracted to the taciturn cop—so much so that she joins the St. Paul Police Academy. As fate would have it, Dez is eventually assigned as Jaylynn's Field Training Officer. Having been burned in the past by getting romantically involved with another cop, Dez has a steadfast rule she has abided by for nine years: Cops are off limits. But as Jaylynn and Dez get to know one another, a strong friendship forms. Will Dez break her cardinal rule and take a chance on love with Jaylynn, or will she remain forever gun shy? *Gun Shy* is an exciting glimpse into the day-to-day work world of police officers as Jaylynn learns the ins and outs of the job and Dez learns the ins and outs of her own heart.

Second Edition
ISBN: 1-930928-43-2
Available at booksellers everywhere.

Another Lori L. Lake title
available from
Yellow Rose Books

Ricochet In Time

Hatred is ugly and does bad things to good people, even in the land of "Minnesota Nice" where no one wants to believe discrimination exists. Danielle "Dani" Corbett knows firsthand what hatred can cost. After they suffer a vicious and intentional attack, Dani's girlfriend, Meg O'Donnell, is dead. Dani is left emotionally scarred, and her injuries prevent her from fleeing on her motorcycle. But as one door has closed for her, another opens when she is befriended by Grace Beaumont, a young woman who works as a physical therapist at the hospital. With Grace's friendship and the help of Grace's aunts, Estelline and Ruth, Dani gets through the ordeal of bringing Meg's killer to justice.

Filled with memorable characters, *Ricochet In Time* is the story of one lonely woman's fight for justice—and her struggle to resolve the troubles of her past and find a place in a world where she belongs.

ISBN: 1-930928-64-5
Available at booksellers everywhere.

Different Dress

Different Dress is the story of three women on a cross-country musical road tour. Jaime Esperanza is a gaffer/electrician and roadie. The headliner, Lacey Leigh Jaxon, is a fast-living prima donna with intimacy problems. She's had a brief relationship with Jaime, then dumped her for the new guy (who lasted all of about two weeks). Lacey still comes back to Jaime in between conquests, and Jaime hasn't yet gotten her entirely out of her heart.

After Lacey Leigh steamrolls yet another opening act, a folksinger from Minnesota named Kip Galvin, who wrote one of Lacey's biggest songs, is brought on board for the summer tour. Kip has true talent, she loves people and they respond, and she has a pleasant stage presence. A friendship springs up between Jaime and Kip—but what about Lacey Leigh?

It's a honky-tonk, bluesy, pop, country EXPLOSION of emotion as these three women duke it out. Who will win Jaime's heart and soul?

Jumping Over My Head

Something a little different from novelist Lori L. Lake. Here is a book of short stories written about ordinary people with uncommon—and also universal—problems.

A mother and daughter having an age-old fight. Small children bullied on the playground taking back their power. A father trying to understand his lesbian daughter's retreat from him. A frightened woman attempting to deal with an abusive partner. An athlete who misses her chance—or does she? An elderly couple stalked by an old woman. These stories and more are told in Jumping Over My Head & Other Stories.

The collection has been described as a series of mini-novels, with each story being odd and quirky, as though slightly off-kilter at the beginning and regaining stability by the end.

Other titles from
Quest Books

Vendetta
By Talaran
ISBN 1-930928-56-4

Blue Holes to Terror
By Trish Kocialski
ISBN 1-930928-61-0

Staying in the Game
By Nann Dunne
ISBN 1-930928-60-2

Murder Mystery Series: Book One
By Anne Azel
ISBN 1-930928-72-6

High Intensity
By Belle Reilly
ISBN 1-930928-33-5

Shield of Justice
By Radclyffe
ISBN 1-930928-41-6

Available at www.rapbooks.biz
and booksellers everywhere.

Lori L. Lake lives in the Twin Cities area with her partner of two decades. She writes on the weekends and doesn't always sleep soundly what with all the oddball characters parading through her head. In "real life," Lori works as a supervisor in a government office. In her off hours, she is a writer, editor, and book reviewer. She enjoys singing, playing guitar and banjo, weightlifting, the movies, reading, her nieces, nephews, and godchildren, and thinking about the wonders of the outdoors from the comfort of her writing den.

Ricochet in Time and *Gun Shy* were her first published novels. Her fourth novel, *Different Dress* will be published by Renaissance Alliance Publishing in 2003, as well as a book of short stories, *Jumping Over My Head.* She is at work on her fifth and sixth novels, a post-apocalyptic action/adventure tentatively entitled *Isolation 2020,* and *Missing Link,* which is a coming out story about an 18-year-old high school basketball player.

Lori very much likes to hear from her readers. You may write her at Lori@LoriLLake.com. Further information about her can be found at her website: http://www.LoriLLake.com.

Printed in the United States
6072